Amansun
the Dragon Prince

Book 1
The Beginning

Vincent Robinson

Tampa, Florida

This book is a work of fiction. The names, characters and events in this book are the products of the author's imagination or are used fictitiously. Any similarity to real persons living or dead is coincidental and not intended by the author.

The views and opinions expressed in this book are solely those of the author and do not reflect the views or opinions of Gatekeeper Press. Gatekeeper Press is not to be held responsible for and expressly disclaims responsibility of the content herein.

Amansun the Dragon Prince: Book 1 The Beginning

Published by Gatekeeper Press
7853 Gunn Hwy, Suite 209
Tampa, FL 33626
www.GatekeeperPress.com

Copyright © 2023 by Vincent Robinson All rights reserved. Neither this book, nor any parts within it may be sold or reproduced in any form or by any electronic or mechanical means, including information storage and retrieval systems, without permission in writing from the author. The only exception is by a reviewer, who may quote short excerpts in a review.

Library of Congress Control Number: 2022948679

ISBN (hardcover): 9781662929779
ISBN (paperback): 9781662929786
eISBN: 9781662929793

To the love of my life and amazing wife Ji as well as our two amazing daughters, Kristy and Alyssa, and their beautiful families. Thanks for all of your support, advice, and encouragement.

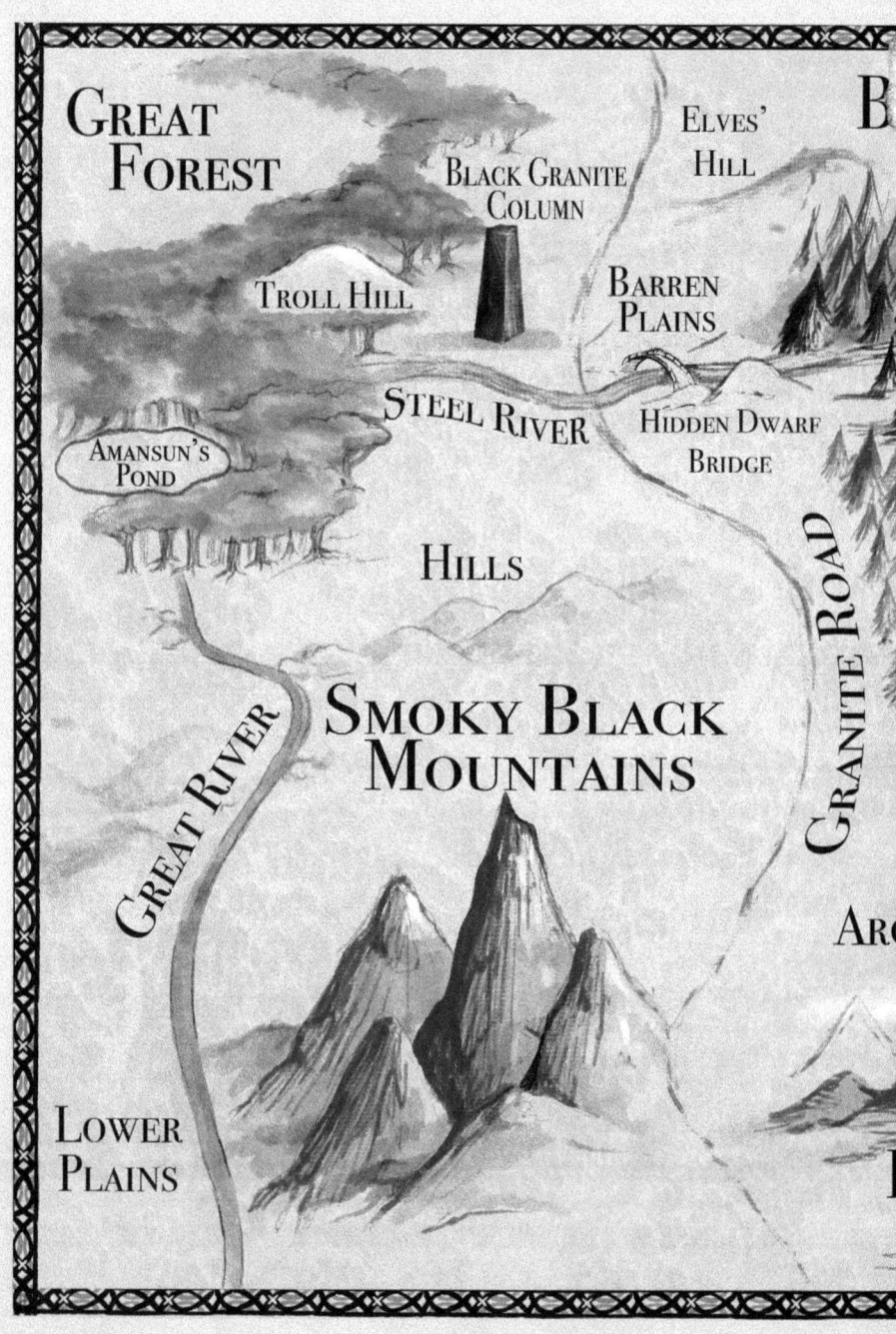

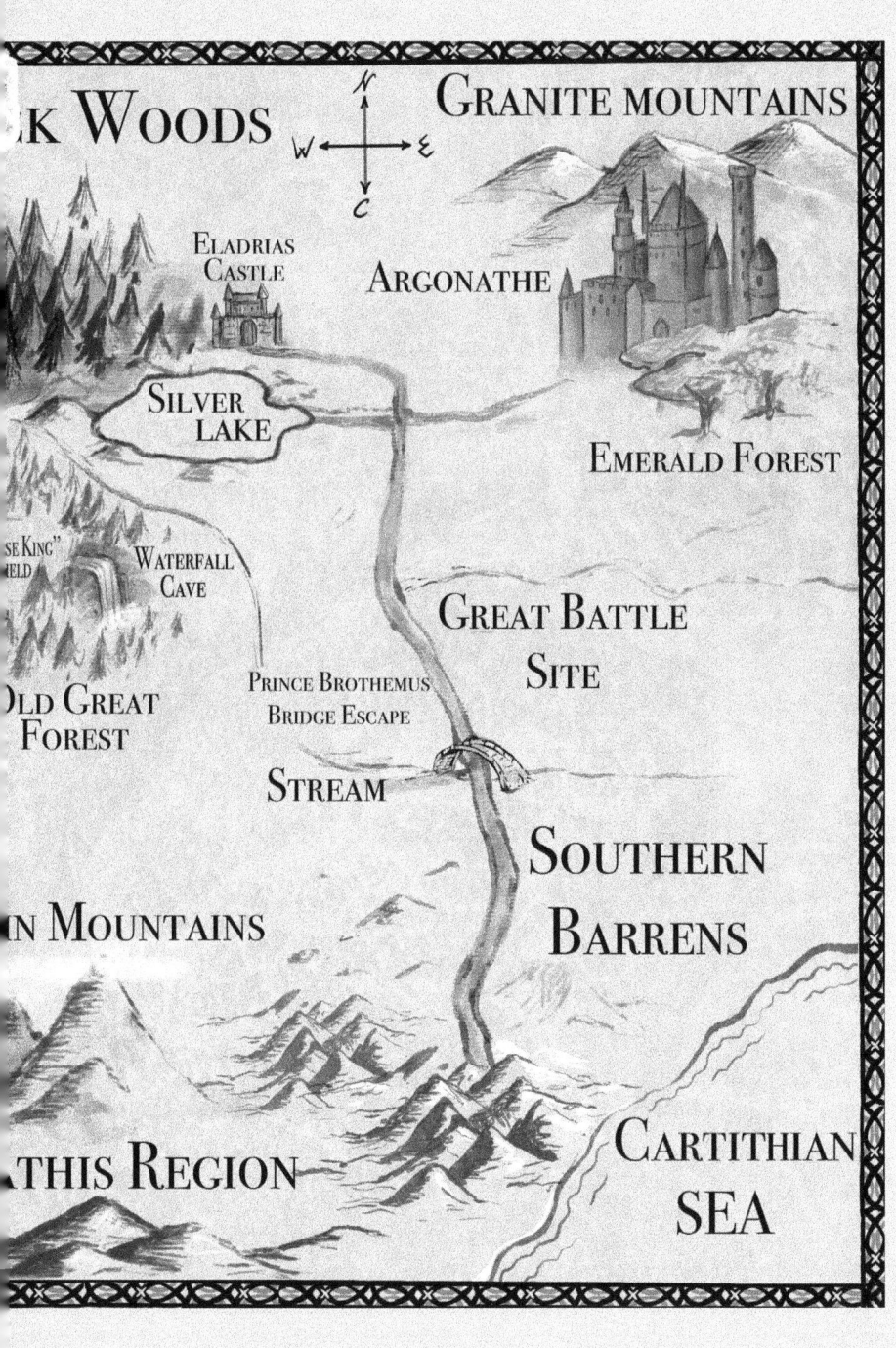

CHAPTER 1

Long ago in a far-away land there lived a colony of dragons whose home was amidst the steep and jagged cliffs of the Smoky Black Mountains. These mountains could be seen from far away, and few if any ever traveled near, because of the reputation of the dragons that lived there as being ruthless killers who would sweep down out of the sky and burn alive or carry off any unfortunate travelers who happened to get caught out in the open. The lands leading up to the base of the mountains were black and barren from years of being scorched by the young dragons who spent their days learning how to ambush prey, breathing searing hot dragon's breath onto the few bushes and shrubs that clung to life in this hostile land, and scouting for the occasional rabbit, wolf or wild boar that was foolish enough to be following the rutted, worn cobblestone road that slowly meandered from the woods up north down through the lower plains leading down to the great river.

The colony was made up of many families of dragons, ranging from the smaller brown and black variety normally found in the low lying hills and plains of the west up to the mighty copper and bronze colored dragons who came from far up north back when the lands were younger. Finally there were three families of large and rare golden-skinned dragons who originated from the oldest line of dragons from the distant east, and from whom all other dragon lines had come. This large gathering of dragons had taken over these lands many decades past, when the area had been a thriving trading outpost for the wild men of this part of the world. The combination of flat, fertile plains and valley floor coupled with the mighty river that flowed from north to south had made this a flourishing town once upon a time, until the dragons learned of the plentiful food to be had along with the welcoming collection of caves and nesting sites scattered throughout the mountain range just above the town's edges.

When the great beasts had started arriving in the area, there had been many great battles, and many legions of soldiers from far-away lands were sent in to dispatch the monstrous invaders in the hopes the trading outpost could be saved. All the brave souls that were sent here eventually met their end, either defending the last remnants of the town and the surrounding farmlands or while helplessly trying to escape back to the woods of the north or along the river heading south. Over time the farmlands were laid to waste, the livestock were scattered far and wide across the plains, the animals all eventually made their way into the caves of the dragons as food, and the building sites and homes of the men smoldered and decayed into a mere shadow of what once was.

Over time the dragons were bothered less and less, as the great caravans of men trying to move their trade up and down the old roads along the mountain range stopped coming. Even when protected by large garrisons of heavily armored soldiers, these trade caravans were no match for the now densely populated dragon colony, and word soon spread that only fools and death seekers would be foolish enough to venture into these parts. Along the old road that passed through the valley there could be found bent iron wagon wheels, blackened suits of armor, and weapons of every shape, size and style left lying on the earth where their keepers had fallen in battle. Anything of value had long been collected and taken back to the various caves and tunnels of the dragons in the mountains, as they were fond of anything shiny and colorful such as the decorated swords and sheaths of the soldiers and the chests of gold and silver coin, along with other precious items like jeweled cups and plates, bronze-plated armor pieces, and brightly decorated shields painted with depictions of the lands they were carried in from.

With no one left to fight, the dragons soon settled into a peaceful, lethargic lifestyle, largely made up of sleeping for long lengths of time disturbed only occasionally by hunting raids into the surrounding lands in search of livestock and other prey to feed the colony as needed. The eldest of the dragons gathered on occasion to discuss colony matters while the young were left to play, hunt, and develop their own skills to become proper dragon warriors. This is how the years passed for a very long spell, and this part of the land became a quiet and somewhat peaceful area once again. The individual families of dragons became more and more suspicious of each other over time, since they had no outside matters of consequence to deal with. Each pair of adult dragons watched over their broods and encouraged them to be aggressive and competitive in nature, so that they could establish themselves within the colony. Apart from size and genealogy, the most important traits for these youngsters now became their ability to fly, hunt, scorch and provide food to the colony, and there were fierce competitions held each year so that the youngsters had an opportunity to show their worth. These competitions and skills helped to determine a family's rank within the colony's hierarchy, and every set of adults wished to be considered as one of the reigning families.

Of the three golden-hued dragon families, one was made up of a male and female, Scythe and Wraith, along with their three young offspring—two males, Amansun and Darken, and a female named Flame. Amansun was the eldest male and quite large compared to the other young dragons of the colony, and yet slighter in stature than his younger brother Darken, who was immense for his age and stronger and more powerful than even some of the adult males in the colony. Flame, their sister, was not quite two-thirds the size of her two older brothers, yet she was lean and fierce and had long, razor-sharp claws that even her brothers avoided with care when she was in one of her foul moods. Together the three of them would have made a truly terrifying sight if hunting in a pack, but this seldom was the case as Amansun, the eldest, had taken to wandering off alone, normally preferring to stay away from the colony, the burnt-out surroundings, and the other young dragons that made up the colony's young.

Like most of the other young dragons in the colony, Flame and Darken would fly off every morning to play games with the others. The young dragons would practice hunting small animals, burning trees to the ground, flying around the tops of the mountain tips, and gliding over the low fields and plains that lay at the foot of the mountain range, hoping to catch unwary travelers coming up and down the old dirt and cobblestone road that headed northeast away from the Smoky Black Mountain ranges toward the lands where men still lived in great numbers. The skies would have appeared to any who would have been there to see them to be full of the mighty beasts, as there were as many as twenty of the young dragons in flight at any given time. Their large wings cast shadows on the valley floor as they slowly glided over the now deserted fields and town remnants, in search of any living creature that had the misfortune to be out during the daylight without the cover of darkness to hide in.

Unlike his brother and sister, Amansun kept to himself and would quietly fly off north towards the deep green woods that lay some distance from the colony's home every morning. Flame and Darken didn't understand why their brother chose to go off alone each day, but being among the favorites of the colony's young, they didn't care as long as he did not get in their way or cause them any embarrassment. If he chose to be an outsider, that was just fine, as long as his actions didn't negatively impact their own reputations. Darken, being the largest of the colony's young males, was seen as the leader by most of the others, and this was just fine by him. It was nice not having his older brother around to get in his way, since some of the others may have regarded Amansun as a leader as well, based on his age and maturity. With Amansun out of the picture, Darken was clearly the leader of the group, and he was free to do as he pleased with no challengers to bother him.

For many years Amansun was able to soar off on his own to his favorite spot. He would lie out in the sun in an open field of green grass, just at the edge of a brilliantly blue stream teaming with trout, bass and other fish that grew old and large out of sight and away from any fisherman, as none would ever travel this close to the dragons' lands. The stream was one of many that splintered off from the main river that entered into the great forest from the east, wound its way in a westward direction, then slowly dipped back south, eventually bursting out from the forest back into daylight as it headed down along the old road in a bending, twisting fashion in the direction of the Smoky Black Mountains and Amansun's home.

Amansun had many friends at the clearing, as over time the animals of the field and forest came to know him as a gentle and harmless creature, even if he was a large young dragon who by appearance looked to be quite dangerous and alarming. At first the clearing would be empty without so much as a cricket chirping when Amansun made his first visits. Over time, some of the smaller creatures like the field mice would cautiously come out to get a drink from the stream where the edge of the land dipped low, venturing out onto a beach made up of small green and gray pebbles the size of peas. This was the easiest spot for the mice to get at the cool, fresh water without the risk of falling in, as sometimes happened when they would try to stretch their furry necks out from atop the larger rocks on the steeper parts of the stream's edge.

Once the squirrels noticed that the dragon was not presenting a danger to the small mice, they too decided to risk short trips to the water's edge for an afternoon drink. Seeing the squirrels come to no harm, the rabbits, possums and foxes decided they too should be safe, and they all ventured out into the dragon's view as they each in turn made their quick visits to the water's edge. It was in this fashion, from smallest to largest, that all of the animals of the forest grew accustomed to the dragon's presence, and eventually even the bears, deer and elk made their way out to drink when they wanted. Over time it became clear that the only creatures that had to fear the dragon were the unusually large fish that gathered in great schools in the depths of the stream, where the currents ran slower and a pool formed around a half-circle of half-sunken giant boulders. Here the water was so pure and crystal clear the dragon could easily spot the largest of the fish, as they floated in place as if they were caught in ice. Amansun would patiently stare into the stream, waiting for one of the larger fish to appear, and then he would suddenly and with surprising speed and accuracy plunge his head into the frigid water and pluck out the fish of his choosing. Once settled back into the plush grass bedding of the field, Amansun would slowly enjoy his fresh caught meal and then drift off into careless slumber, with his underbelly facing up at the blue sky to allow the warmth of the sun's rays to gently ease him into sleep. Sometimes when Amansun wasn't particularly hungry he would share his catch with some of his friends, like the fox family, the badgers, and even the raccoons, although they were usually trying to steal away part of his catch every chance they could anyway.

Being a dragon, Amansun was naturally very intelligent, and he was able to speak with many of the smart animals that came to pass their time playing and relaxing at this secret clearing. Some days there would be deer, foxes, beavers, bears, rabbits, squirrels, skunks, and even an occasional wolf. The animals would spend their time talking with Amansun and telling him stories and tales from their lives. All who came to this magical spot felt safe, prey and predator alike treated each other as friends, and no one was made to feel alone or outcast. Because Amansun was able to speak with these creatures and develop friendships with each of them, he did not feel right even thinking about eating them on occasion. He knew that he would have to eat whatever was presented at his family's cave to avoid uncomfortable discussions and explanations, but here at the clearing Amansun stuck with fish and that put everybody at ease.

Sharing Amansun's love for fish was his greatest friend, a wise old owl named Barnby. Barnby was over one hundred years old and he had taught himself over time to speak many of the languages of the various creatures of the forest and meadow. Barnby had inadvertently become so familiar with the many field mice and smaller rodents that called this clearing home that he had reached a point where he too could no longer consider eating his "friends." Because of this unusual group of relationships that Barnby had made, he now was strictly a fish eater, though he preyed on the smaller fish that swam close to the surface of the water, unlike Amansun who enjoyed snatching up the five-foot monsters that lurked in the depths of the pool. Amansun and Barnby spent many days chatting together, speaking of their own lives, discussing the workings of nature, weather, history and even some of the old-world magic that Amansun was almost entirely unaware of. Being a dragon meant that you had very few enemies or creatures you had to fear, so Amansun had never had to bother much with legends of fairies, wizards, witches and the like. He did believe that some of the old stories must have had truth in them, but he had never encountered one of these spellbinders or magic workers so he didn't give them much thought.

In this environment, young Amansun learned the importance of treating others with care and respect, and he valued the friendships he made. He truly enjoyed his time with the other, smaller creatures of the forest, and he wondered how it was that the other young dragons of his colony could hunt down and kill these same animals with no regret or remorse. Even his brother and sister, Darken and Flame, had become well-known for their special skill and ability to track and hunt these same animals he called friends. Even when the other dragons of his colony were not hungry, they would relish in the hunt and take great satisfaction in roasting whatever poor creatures they happened to stumble across into piles of ash and bone. Amansun often wondered to himself why he was so different from his siblings and the other young dragons from his home. He would have liked to fit in more, but something just never felt right. It was as if he knew what he was supposed to do and how he was supposed to behave, but he just couldn't get past the fact that he had felt very uncomfortable when he had gone on hunts in the past and reluctantly killed a few animals.

This is how the three young dragons of Scythe and Wraith passed their time as they grew older and slowly became young adults in the colony. Darken and Flame ignored their older brother but kept his secret travels to themselves, as they were having too much fun and were afraid if they told their parents about Amansun's strange behavior they might be stuck watching him and having to take him wherever they went. If Amansun wanted to be an outcast, then that was his choosing, and they were just fine leaving him be.

Everybody was happy with this arrangement and it seemed like everything would be just fine, Darken and Flame spending their time with the other young dragons and Amansun heading up north each day and relaxing at his secret spot. But all of that would change one day. The events of that day that would change the life of Amansun and all that he had come to know as his life there in the Smoky Black Mountains.

CHAPTER 2

As many of the colony's young dragons were now turning into young adults, the elders of the colony held a meeting to arrange a special hunting party so that they could watch their young hunters in action as they chased down their prey. This was a tradition of the colony and every three years a similar hunt was organized. The only thing that changed each time was the location of the hunt. Over the years the dragons had pretty much eaten up and burnt down everything within a reasonable flight's distance from their mountain. The hunts were now being held at the borders of their lands and this usually meant a long half-day's flight each way there and back. This year would be no exception, and the elders had all agreed that they would have to select a new hunting spot even further away than any they had previously chosen. Scythe and Wraith, being one of the only three gold-skinned dragon couples in the colony, were already counted among the nobles and therefore were members of the elders group deciding upon the hunt's location.

One of the elder bronze dragons spoke up and recommended that the colony fly out west well past the Great River and far beyond the valley that marked their territory. He spoke of large herds of cattle that had lived there in the past and suggested that some of the survivors may have raised young and repopulated the fields there.

The wisest of the copper dragons had a feeling that they would have better luck if they circled around the mountains towards the south and followed the river until they reached the outskirts of an area where men were known to travel from time to time. If they were lucky enough to catch a caravan of travelers on the road, they would have plenty of horsemeat to go around and maybe even some new treasure to collect.

Greyden, one of the eldest among the group, told the others of a forest clearing he had seen long ago while flying up north. He said that the trees were very old and large and that it was likely there would be many animals there, since he did not believe any hunters or trappers dared to travel within a day's flight of the foot of the mountains. The roads that wound past that area were old and worn and had not seen travelers for years, perhaps longer. Greyden mentioned that he had often thought this would be a great spot for one of their hunts but that he had wanted to save it until the time was right. The field he spoke of was well-protected by the forest itself and could only be seen when you were directly above it in flight. There were no trails or roads in or out and he felt that the animals that lived in that part of the forest were sure to feel safe by now and would likely not expect an attack from the dragons until it was too late.

After much bickering over whose idea made the most sense, and some rather hostile taunts back and forth, the elders decided that the spot up north in the forest sounded perfect for the hunt, and agreed to take the young dragons to this spot the very next day. They would all meet at the peak of their mountain home, a large crater of cinder and ash that was large enough for the whole colony to gather, and had been used for generations as the colony's meeting place. They would meet shortly after day break and send out the young hunters first to lead the pack while they flew above to observe the hunt and see which dragons were the most skilled in the group.

Late in the afternoon, Amansun left the clearing in the forest and flew back towards his mountain home, soaring high above the lazy river and fields that covered most of the ground between his secret spot and the edge of his colony's territory. As usual, he met Darken and Flame atop one of the low-lying hills several miles from home, so that the three of them could arrive at their cave at the same time as they had done for so many years now. In this way, they had managed to make their parents believe that they had been spending their time together all these years. The three said little as they flew south towards the base of the mountains, until they started beating their long, powerful wings faster and harder to gain height as they started the climb up towards the craggy cliffs that marked the entrance to their family's cave. Like their parents, the three young dragons had golden-hued skin and looked very majestic as they glided high in the air with the now darkening sky catching the final rays of sun. Though smaller than his younger brother Darken, Amansun in particular looked very proud and noble. The way he carried himself, the beating of his wings, the way his long tail gracefully arched out behind him in flight; all of these traits gave him an aura of royalty. Darken and Flame flew just as fast, looked every bit as muscular, and had most of the same look as Amansun, and yet there was a difference to the three that could be seen even at a distance to any who observed them in flight. Where Darken and Flame appeared powerful and threatening, Amansun gave the impression of grace, balance and control in his fluid movements.

As the final flashes of the sun setting in the distant west reflected off the trio's bodies as they flew the final distance to their cliffside home, Amansun's skin shone brilliantly and radiantly with a flash of pure gold, nearly blinding to any who may have been caught staring directly at him when the suns' rays bounced off his glistening hide. As each dragon touched down on the craggy step that marked the entrance to their home, they stepped quickly in turn and shuffled into the large cavern, each heading for their own private room. Amansun, as was his custom, beat his wings and hovered in flight just outside the cave while his brother and sister lighted down on the step and proceeded in. The sound of his massive wings beating the air at the mouth of the cave gave notice to all nearby that a large dragon was in the area and Scythe and Wraith, already deep in one of the cave's chambers, heard the approach of their eldest. They could tell each of their young from the distinct sound the beating of their wings made, like the voice of a child to a mother, and they moved off to the dining chamber, anxious to announce the news of the elders meeting and the upcoming hunt the new day would bring.

That night as the family gathered for dinner in the largest chamber of their cave, everything seemed normal until Wraith discussed the next day's planned hunt. Darken and Flame could not contain their excitement as they squealed and hissed their approval. Amansun, unlike his brother and sister, was quiet and distant. This odd behavior surprised Wraith and he questioned his eldest why he didn't share the same excitement as his brother and sister. Amansun, not wishing to upset the other members of his family, blurted out that he was just not feeling well and stated he did not know if he would be up to the challenge on such short notice. He wasn't really lying, as the mere thought of watching all of the helpless animals being scorched alive was making him feel ill. Wraith growled out his displeasure at Amansun's comment and shot an evil glance over at Scythe, who also seemed puzzled by her eldest's response. Amansun pretended not to notice the glances his elders were sharing because of his comments, and he instead pretended to be very interested in the large boar that had been placed atop the still-glowing embers of the family's roasting pit, where most of their meals were set before being set ablaze by a single blast from his mother's nostrils. Dragons liked their meat well-cooked, so everything had the same blackened, sooty appearance no matter what type of meal was being served. Regardless of this fact, Amansun busied himself staring down at the boar, carcass, as if he were trying to determine what type of animal they were about to consume.

Wraith went on to discuss the next morning's gathering at the old crater. He told his three youngsters that this hunt was very important and that their performance would not only help them show their proper place in the colony's standing, but also that a poor performance by any dragon would cause his family great shame and dishonor. Wraith and Scythe both stared menacingly at Amansun as they discussed the hunt, and he was quite aware that they meant for him to understand in no uncertain terms that they expected his best performance.

Amansun was already lost in his own thoughts, trying to think of a way out of the following day's hunt as his father went into more detail about the next day's events. How could he bring himself to hunt down and kill the same types of animals that he had learned to call his friends over these past few years at his secret hiding spot? He imagined the animals of the clearing where he spent his time daily and shuddered at the thought of how they would feel if their home was the place being burned down and destroyed. He imagined the look of fear in the eyes of the animals as they scattered about, frantically trying to escape the shooting flames coming from every direction. He pictured the larger beasts like the bears and elk running to the safety of the forest only to discover that other dragons were already circling in the air above, lighting the trees ablaze in a large circle around the entire clearing, effectively creating a large "circle of death." Worse yet, Amansun now imagined the sight of the dragons of his colony carrying away the charred and smoldering bodies of the larger animals that would be shared back at the large crater atop their mountain home as a feast for the hunting party.

Just as things seemed like they couldn't get any worse, Amansun's attention was suddenly drawn back into his family's conversation when he heard his bother Darken ask his father, "Where will this hunt be taking place? There are few animals left to track down that we have not already searched out and killed."

A shudder of fear and dread went up Amansun's back as he heard his father say, "We will be flying far off north to an old and seldom visited section of the Great Forest." He explained to them what Greyden had said.

Now truly feeling ill rather than just pretending, Amansun announced that he was going to go to bed early to get rest before the long day ahead of them. Wraith called out to his eldest as he departed, "Make sure you get right to sleep, as I want all three of you to make a good showing at the hunt tomorrow. It's been three years since the last hunt and it's time for you to show us how much your hunting skills have improved."

Amansun, with a dry mouth and barely able to speak, managed to get out, "I will, and good night to all of you." He continued along the dark tunnel lost in thought. Back in the dining chamber, Darken and Flame made snide remarks to one another, sharing their opinions of how they imagined their brother would perform. "I'm not sure he will be even able to make the flight there and back," Flame whispered to her brother, to which Darken breathed back, "Even if he does manage to get there, it's likely he won't be able to catch a thing." He chuckled.

As the embers from the family's main eating chamber slowly died away into a soft amber glow, Amansun still lay wide awake in his own room. He could clearly hear the loud snoring of his parents in the back depths of the cave and his brother and sister had fallen asleep some time ago. Amansun was left alone in the darkness of his cavern to fret over his situation. He quietly wept, something very few, if any, other dragons would do, and eventually drifted into a light and restless sleep full of disturbing dreams and images.

* * *

In the light of the new day Amansun circled high overhead, just out of the view of the elders, as he watched the hunting party of young dragons speeding towards his very own special secret spot, with nostrils blazing great plumes of fire and claws outstretched as they reached for the animals fleeing the clearing in a wild panic. The trees all around the field blazed in brilliant shades of orange and red; and everywhere, the thick black and gray plumes of smoke and falling ash obscured the paths that led back into the forest and away from this killing field. Amansun's eyes filled with tears as one animal after another was carried off into the heights to be torn apart or dropped down into the inferno below, while the roars of approval from the elders above rang in his ears relentlessly. Off to his right he noticed a very large owl, frantically beating its wings as fast as possible as it tried to elude a young dragon that was closing in on him from above. One moment the owl was clearly visible and in an instant it disappeared into a puff of white and gray smoke, as the dragon that had been chasing the owl belched out a fiery blast of flame from its nostrils as it closed the distance between the two. Further below in the clearing Amansun saw Gruawth the bear, one of his best and largest friends, standing high on his rear legs snarling in defiance at the dragons circling above him. In an instant his brother Darken had swooped down, grasped the bear in his claws firmly, and flew upwards with a look of pure ferocity in his eyes, laughing out loud as the mighty bear hung limp in his claws, dying. Amansun's eyes filled with tears as he wondered to himself how this could be possible and why he hadn't been able to do something to save his friends. In just a few short moments the entire field he had once called his secret spot had become a black, sooty pit, and every creature he had come to know and care for had perished in the most cruel and painful ways imaginable. All around him the great forest was ablaze, and even the stream itself seemed to be hissing and steaming from the relentless attack of the colony's youngsters.

Amansun jerked up from his nightmare in a cold and panicked sweat. Around him were only darkness and the soft murmurs of his family asleep in the other chambers of the great cave. "It was only a dream!" he said to himself quietly as he wiped the tears away from his eyes. "I still have time to do something."

Amansun did not know what exact part of the Great Forest Greyden had planned on taking the hunting party to, but he knew his father had clearly mentioned the direction of north, a clearing with a stream, and lots of animals, and that was too close as far as he was concerned. As far as he could tell, they must have been talking about his special place. He clearly had to fly off into the night well before daybreak to warn the creatures of the clearing that the raiding party was heading in their direction and that they should all make for the middle of the forest and remain out of sight for some time to come. This was the only solution he could think of, and he tried not to think of what would happen if he were not able to fly there and back again before the rest of his family woke up the next morning.

As visions from Amansun's nightmare raced through his mind, he quietly and stealthily made his way down the cave's twisting, turning tunnels out to the great ledge that marked the entrance to his family's home. Amansun knew that he had to at least try to save his friends, and a middle of the night journey was his only chance. Stubbing his right toe on a large rock as he made his way down the path, Amansun fought back the urge to call out in pain, knowing if he woke his family his rescue attempt would be over before it started. Amansun gingerly moved his sore foot along, being ever so careful not to stub the same toe, as he knew he would not be able to control his voice should he be unlucky enough to hit the same spot again.

Upon reaching the ledge, Amansun took in a deep breath of cool night air and stared out across the jagged mountainside, searching for any signs of movement. From years of experience, he could tell that the night was still young and that he still had time to fly to the clearing and back by sunrise if he flew with all his might and did not stay long. Far in the distance Amansun could see the reflection of moonlight on the Great River as it flowed to the west. The river was too far off to be heard, but even at this distance it could be seen weaving along the valley floor like an enormous snake swaying from side to side.

Knowing that the caves of other dragon families of the colony were nearby tucked into the ledges of the great mountainside, Amansun decided he would have to step off the ledge and allow himself to fall towards the valley floor before opening his wings, or the sudden whoosh of wind would alert others that someone was taking flight outside in the dark. Stepping gently to the edge, Amansun edged closer and closer until at last he could feel the edge of rock. Still moving carefully, remembering the sting and pain in his right foot, Amansun edged closer and closer to the cliff's edge. With great care Amansun brought his entire bulk to the ledge and with one concerted effort he leaned out over the ledge and allowed himself to fall.

Plummeting to the valley floor below, Amansun stared intensely into the darkness, trying to guess when he was getting close to the bottom. If he guessed wrong, not only would he die suddenly, but also he would have passed in vain as his friends to the north would still likely be hunted in the morning. After passing the last of the ledges of the cliff's face where he knew cave entrances were located, he decided it would be safe to start flying. With a final glance at the cliffs now falling beside him, he gently spread his mighty wings apart and outward, and immediately started a graceful glide out and across the barren plains. Drifting silently along and catching a draft of wind, Amansun slowly started his way towards the Great Forest to the north. He knew that in order to get there and back before sunrise, he would have to push himself and fly faster than he had ever flown before. Years of flying back and forth to his hiding spot had given him great wing strength and stamina, and he pulled hard on his muscles as he propelled himself along. Few, if any, of the other young dragons would have been capable of making this flight in the time he had available.

CHAPTER 3

As the first rays of sunlight began to hit the entrance of Wraith's home, he hurriedly sped from room to room waking his three young dragons. His heart was racing and he was eager to have the rest of the colony elders see his brood in action at the great hunt. Scythe was also up and had made her way to the great dining chamber to gather a quick meal for the others.

Wraith came to Darken's cave first and woke him with little trouble, as he was anxious to prove himself the top dragon in the colony. He sprung to his feet and started preparing for their morning. Likewise, when Wraith reached Flame's cave, she was already grooming herself in dragon fashion, having already heard the commotion in her brother Darken's room. Lastly, Wraith reached the rear of the cave where his eldest slept. At first there was no sound and Wraith had to shuffle all the way into the dimly lit chamber. Wraith peered into the darkness and saw the outline of Amansun still lying on the floor in apparent slumber. "Wake up, you sleepy oaf!" he said. "This is a very special day for this family and we are not going to arrive late at the gathering because you are still sleepy, even though you were the first among us to retire for the evening last night."

Lying in his chamber exhausted, still out of breath from his daring nighttime adventure, Amansun answered, "I'll be right out." Indeed, Amansun had just managed to fly back to their cave, silently shift his bulky body to the rear of the space, and get into a prone position only moments before his father had started to stir. Exhausted, thirsty and hungry, Amansun knew this would be a long, tiring day with no rest to be had.

Stepping out onto their cave's entrance one at a time, the family of dragons started off with gently beating wings as they headed west to catch the rising morning wind drafts, then let the rising currents drift them back up and north then finally east as they slowly spiraled up towards the top of the Smoky Black Mountains. As they drifted higher and higher, they saw groups of other dragons also heading to the gathering place, and the skies seemed to be filled with dragons, young and old, large and small. Gliding into the black and gray ash-filled crater, Wraith touched down gently followed by each member of his brood in the spot that was saved for them.

As soon as Wraith and his family had settled down, they noticed other dragons glancing in their direction with scorn and heard murmurs of disapproval. Wraith noticed a group of elder dragons making their way towards him and his clutch. Upon making their way to Wraith's location, the group demanded that Wraith and Scythe follow them to the center of the crater, where the other elders had gathered into a large circle and were speaking in loud, harsh tones. Scythe told their brood to stay put while they went to see what all the fuss was about.

Darken and Flame stood in their spots, looking around at the other dragons that were obviously upset with their family for some unknown reason. Neither had any idea what had happened, and they were still anxious for the great hunt to begin once the entire colony had arrived. Only Amansun felt and looked nervous, though he was careful not to gaze in the direction of his brother and sister and had certainly avoided making any eye contact with his obviously upset father.

Feeling more alone and different from the others than ever, Amansun ran the previous evening's events through his head repeatedly, trying to determine what he may have possibly done wrong that could have brought on this obviously threatening situation. Finding the courage to glance off in the direction of the now completely circled group of elders, he struggled to glean any piece of information from those around him and the group meeting off in the distance. Was it possible that someone had seen him leaving or returning from his journey? Or perhaps he had not calculated right while falling from the cliff, and the sound of his opening wings may have alerted one of their neighbors to his flight? Amansun nervously thought over the possibilities and continued to ignore his brother and sister as they glanced around the crater now nearly filled with dragons.

The answer to the family's predicament, and ultimately his own, was suddenly made clear to him when one of his elder brother's friends called over to the three siblings from nearby. Thrax, one of the eldest of the younger dragons, and a good friend and hunting partner of Darken, whispered over to them that a large black eagle, one of the last of its kind in the area, had flown into the gathering a short time earlier and had caused quite a stir amongst the elders who had been gathered in the center of the crater upon his arrival. No one was quite sure what he had shared with the group, but it was obvious that something very wrong was afoot.

Looking directly ahead at the large circle of elders now gathered in the center of the crater, Amansun suddenly saw his mother and father glance back at the three of them then turn back towards the group with heads hanging low, swinging from side to side. Wraith, one of the largest and mightiest beasts in the colony, known for his impressive, threatening posture, now appeared much smaller as his shoulders drooped and his great wings closed together and folded behind him in a clear sign of despair.

Darken, Flame and Amansun huddled closer with trepidation as they saw their parents break away from the group of elders and slowly start plodding in their direction, in a sign of humility uncommon for the pair. Upon getting within earshot of the youngsters, Scythe called out they were to all return back to their cave and await further notice from the elders. Wraith, without even so much as a glance at his young, spread his wings and started flying out of the gathering area in the direction of the caves.

Darken and Flame questioned their mother as to what had occurred at the gathering and Scythe mumbled almost inaudibly that something unexpected had been announced by the elders, and that the great hunt had been cancelled and replaced with an emergency colony meeting of a serious nature. "I will wait for more news from the elders before I tell you the rest of what we were told at the gathering," she managed to get out before turning to head off in the direction of her mate. "Perhaps you should ask Amansun what it could be about?" she suggested as she walked off in an almost dreamlike state.

Darken and Flame immediately surrounded their brother, pushing and shoving him, all the while demanding to be told what this was all about. Still unsure what may have been found out about the previous night's events, Amansun decided his best play was to plead ignorance and go along as if he too were in the dark, and he turned quickly away and sped off in the direction of the family's cave. Darken and Flame were relentless as they pestered him on the flight back to their cave, but Amansun remained silent and refused to make so much as a grunt during the entire flight. Upon reaching the cave's ledge, Amansun landed immediately, uncharacteristically for him, and shuffled off to his chamber as quickly as his feet would carry him. In the distance he could hear his parents' raised voices as they argued back and forth over what was to come and what they would likely need to do to make amends to the colony. It was obvious that the colony elders must know something, but what could it be? Amansun was still very puzzled by what had happened this morning and what was yet to come.

After what seemed like an eternity to the waiting dragons, the sound of large wings beating outside of their cave entrance announced that news had finally arrived. While Darken, Flame and Amansun waited in the main dining chamber, Wraith and Scythe made their way to the entrance of their cave where two elders were waiting. After a few moments of quiet discussion and condolences from the elders, the two large dragons took flight and Wraith and Scythe made their way back to the dining chamber.

Wraith walked into the cavernous chamber where his brood was waiting around the embers of the fire, followed by his wife. Visibly shaken as he gathered his thoughts together, Scythe took her position at his side. "I have some strange and terrible news to share with you Darken and Flame", he stated. "There is no need to worry about telling your brother Amansun about what the commotion was about, because he *is* the commotion."

Stunned, the two younger siblings looked at their older brother and waited for an explanation. "I'm not sure I understand what this is about," said Amansun feebly.

"Liar,", roared Wraith. "You have betrayed your family, your colony and yourself with your actions." He shook violently with rage. He then went on to explain how the large black eagle known as Carack had witnessed Amansun warn all the creatures of the forest about the next day's hunt. Next he discussed what the two visiting elders who had just departed from their ledge had shared. The colony had decided that Amansun had to be punished for his betrayal. He would have to compete a task to prove that he could again be trusted and considered one of the colony's own.

It was at this moment that Scythe, Amansun's mother who had been quiet up until this point, wept and blurted out that she would share what the great task given to Amansun to prove his loyalty would be. Struggling to hold back her tears, with her voice trembling in sadness and despair, Scythe announced that Amansun had been judged to be "too gentle" to be one of the colony. His unusual actions and friendship with the forest animals showed that he was very unlike his friends and family, along with the other dragons of the colony. If Amansun was to prove he was worthy of being a member of the Smoky Black Mountains clan, he would have to show that he could be ruthless and warrior-like as well. Amansun would be banned from the colony and would have to travel alone to the far east, to the land of men up past the Emerald Forest, beyond the Granite Mountains where the Steel River emptied itself into the great-mirrored Silver

Lake, where a great castle was said to stand. There, Amansun would have to kill the daughter of the king and return with her body to prove to all that he was not a weak oddity of the colony.

Carack the eagle was quite put out that his favorite hunting grounds had now been ruined, possibly forever, so he had been anxious to get revenge on this absurd dragon who seemed to act like no other he had ever heard of. He had been only too happy to share the news of the now rebuilt castle in the far east, and had mentioned to the dragon elders that a mighty king held court there and that he was rumored to have an incredibly beautiful daughter whom he prized beyond all else. One of Carack's distant relatives, whom he saw only on rare occasions, had given him this news only a few short months ago.

Being cold and calculating, and not wanting Amansun to have an easy time of making amends to the colony, several of the eldest members had quickly decided that a great task was in order. The capture and killing of a beautiful princess from afar was just the sort of thing that the dragons of old would have decided upon. Besides, the elders guessed that this new castle would be protected by a significant number of knights and soldiers, so it was quite likely that Amansun would likely be killed in this quest. This seemed like an acceptable fate for one who had caused such a disruption to the colony and its plans. Surely none would miss Amansun if he were never to return, and many of the lesser elders, especially those from the ranks of the brown and copper dragon families, saw this as a great opportunity to diminish the rank of Wraith, whom many had come to feel was becoming too much of a leader in the colony.

Amansun's throat was suddenly very dry, and he had a strange feeling in the pit of his stomach as the words he had just heard sank in. Travel far off on his own? Kill a beautiful princess? Wage a battle against an entire fortress of soldiers alone? Was this real? Could this be really happening to him? Wasn't there some other simpler, less frightening alternative?

As Amansun's eyes drifted from one family member to the next, he began to realize the harsh reality of the moment. Darken and Flame both had blank looks on their faces as each of them imagined their brother trying to set out on this journey all alone. Scythe was staring at the ground beneath her feet, slowly shaking her head from side to side, and breathing deeply and with an occasional sigh of despair. Wraith was the only member staring directly back at Amansun as his eyes moved from one face to the next. His eyes stared into Amansun's intensely, and with a hatred that clearly showed the anger, resentment and rage that glowed within. Wraith was literally fuming at his eldest's actions that had so embarrassed their family as long trails of black and gray smoke drifted from the ends of his long snout, curling up into the highest reaches of the chamber, then drifting in all directions along the ceiling of the great cave as it sought an escape from the confines of the dragons' retreat.

Not wanting to make this uncomfortable moment last any longer, Amansun slowly turned away from his family and unsteadily shuffled off in the direction of his own chamber. Completely lost in deep, unconscious thought, Amansun bumped and plodded off into the darkness, hitting nearly every stone, outcropping of rock, and knob in the tunnel leading to his room. Even when his head struck a particularly low hanging overhang solidly as he rounded the bend to his room, Amansun hardly took notice, as he was already imagining the battle at hand outside the walls of the great castle as knights rode out on horseback to challenge him and scores of archers fired huge bows, sending iron-tipped arrows at him as he hovered outside the castle walls.

Back in the dining chamber, Wraith was in no mood for idle conversation or questions from his two youngsters. With a deep guttural growl that Darken and Flame both recognized all too well as a "let's get out of here quick" sound, Wraith announced that there would be no more discussion this evening and that they should retreat off to bed and quickly.

Flame and Darken both took the warning seriously and with great haste made their way out of the dining chamber. Flame was ahead of her brother Darken and she scurried along the corridor in rapid fashion, disappearing around the bend without so much as a word to her brother, as she did not want to risk upsetting her father any further. Seeing that his sister had already retreated out of sight, Darken suddenly stopped midway down the corridor and, with great care, settled himself along the corridor's edge, craning his neck back towards the direction he had just left in the hopes he might glean some more information from his parents, who he guessed would continue speaking once everyone was out of earshot.

As dragons are very large creatures and do not normally hunch up along cave walls for any amount of time, Darken soon began to feel the discomfort his awkward stance was causing. Each moment he spent in that crouched, hunched-over position, trying to remain as still and quiet as possible, further added to his discomfort, and soon his legs started to tingle with numbness. As the tingling in his legs started to slowly turn into a burning sensation, Darken started to wonder if this had really been such a great idea. After all, wasn't his father angered enough over the actions of his brother Amansun? Did he really want to risk the explosion that was surely to happen if Wraith happened to catch him hiding here in the hall trying to be a sneak? What was likely to be his punishment if he too happened to get caught?

All of these questions and doubts were pouring through Darken's mind as he watched his muscles twitching uncontrollably. Now racked with considerable pain as the result of his awkward stance, Darken considered just abandoning his plan and retreating back to his chamber. As he began to try and move his now immobile limbs, numb from the pain of remaining still these past moments, he attempted to stretch out one leg slowly. As he struggled to move without making any sound, he suddenly became aware of soft whispers coming down the corridor. While Darken had been fighting his own battle of trying to remain calm and quiet while his body quaked in pain, his parents had begun to whisper to each other far off in the dining chamber. He cocked his head out even further into the hall and pointed one ear in the direction of the dining hall.

At first all Darken could make out was soft mumbling with no real words. Over time, though, as his breathing slowed and his ears adjusted to the low pitch of the voices from the other room, he was able to pick up on certain words and phrases. It was still too quiet to understand and hear everything being said, but he was now able to get an idea of the conversation that was taking place.

"Never should have gotten involved with a wizard. That's what I said from the beginning," he thought he heard his father say.

"It was the only choice we had available to raise our own," the soft voice of his mother answered.

"Always knew nothing good could have come from this," Wraith grunted in answer.

"Too late now to change things," Scythe responded.

"Well, it is likely out of our hands now anyway," he heard his father say quietly.

Suddenly the voices from the corridor grew quiet once again. Darken thought he could hear the sounds of movement coming slowly in his direction, but he still could see nothing. With a great amount of effort, and quite a bit of pain to match, Darken forced his still frozen limbs into action, and he turned the great bulk of his body around and slowly moved off towards his bedroom chamber. Just behind him he could clearly hear his parents also making their way down the corridor to their chamber and he sped up his pace, not wanting to have to explain why he was still out in the middle of their great cave. As Darken quickly settled into a resting position in the center of his cavern, his mind raced with curious thoughts about what his parents could have possibly been talking about. What wizard were they mentioning? How did this have anything to do with Amansun? Darken wanted to share what he heard with Flame, but he dared not risk going to her room this night. Instead, he slowly moved his arms and legs around, trying to get the blood flowing again to the parts of his body that had been most affected by his crouched position, and he slowly drifted off to sleep.

CHAPTER 4

The new day came just as they always had and Amansun sleepily opened his eyes in his room. As he glanced around calmly, his eyes searched for something, as he had the feeling that something was lost or missing. Suddenly like a great slap to his face, his eyes opened wide with the realization that his dreams had only been the start of his problems. He now began to rewind the actions and events of the previous day and he was painfully aware that he had not dreamt the entire thing. He had been seen at the Great Forest and the entire colony, including his parents, were aware of what he had done. He thought once again about the punishment that had been handed down and he wondered how long it would be before he would be forced to start on his journey.

Two chambers over from Amansun's, Darken and Flame were hunched over together, whispering back and forth about their bother's predicament. Darken had shared the little bits of information he had overheard the night before and Flame was trying to make some sense of it all. No one in the colony had seen any wizards in quite some time now, and while everyone knew they existed, the young dragons of the colony spoke of them as if they were merely myths or legends. Flame was quite convinced that her brother was making the whole thing up or that even more likely, he had dreamed the entire event during the night. This upset Darken immensely, but nothing he did or said was able to make Flame think otherwise. Neither had ventured off to their gathering chambers, as they did not want to be the first to see their father this morning, not knowing what state of mind he might be in.

Out on the ledge at the entrance to their cave, Wraith and Scythe were speaking with Graudling, the eldest of the colony's dragons and their current leader. Graudling was informing Wraith and Scythe of the rules of Amansun's banishment, along with the expected start of the journey as the colonies elders had set it down the evening before.

Amansun was to leave on his journey at once and would not be welcomed back into the colony until he returned with the princess, dead or alive. It was made very clear that if no princess were recovered then Amansun would never be allowed to return to the colony's home under penalty of death. As he turned to step out over the ledge and fly off, Graudling cautioned one last time, "By the setting of the sun this very evening, Amansun must leave our mountains, or you and all of your family will be in great peril." With a short step out and over the ledge, Graudling fell into the void and then with a loud *whoosh* his wings filled, spread effortlessly out into a fan, and he glided out across the valley. Two massive dragons, Graudling's personal guards, one from each side of the mountain near the entrance to Wraith's cave, dropped into the sky and settled into flight just behind him. Wraith and Scythe had not even noticed their presence but knew they had to be nearby, as the elder never went anywhere without them and they without him.

Wraith bellowed out to his youngsters once he and Scythe had reached their dining hall, and all three jumped up and scrambled to the sound of his voice. Once gathered together, Amansun, Darken and Flame were advised as to the counsels' decision. Darken and Flame looked at their brother with mixed feelings,—relief that they were not the ones being forced to leave, and guilt that they somehow could have prevented this from occurring if they had never allowed their brother to go off on his own all these years now. Each was grateful that Amansun had chosen not to share the truth that he had been going off on his own all this time. Darken had always resented his older brother for choosing not to spend his time with them, but he also had felt there was something different about his brother, something that pulled him in a different direction and made him act the way he did. Either way, Amansun had caused the entire family and their reputation great harm; so as far as he was concerned, the sooner Amansun left, the better.

Flame felt closer to Amansun than Darken had, and she had always appreciated the way he tried to look over her and take care of her. Amansun had always waited during meals for Flame to take her portion before taking his, unlike her bother Darken who grabbed for his share with no concern for the others. Flame would miss her brother, and she genuinely felt sympathy for his plight. She leaned over towards Amansun and softly offered words of encouragement, adding that he would surely be successful in this task and be back with the family in hardly any time at all.

Wraith, still outraged and bewildered by Amansun's actions, was quite distant and emotionally unaffected. He stated matter-of-factly, "You can rest here today as long as you need, but plan on flying off on your quest well before the setting of the sun this evening. I will not allow you to jeopardize the safety of the rest of the family because of your ridiculous actions."

Scythe approached Amansun and told him to follow her off to her chamber so she could speak with him privately. They walked off together down the corridor, leaving Darken and Flame alone in the dining hall once again to continue their discussion on what they thought was to become of their older brother. Normally they would have flown off by now to spend the day with their friends, but neither one felt too comfortable about venturing out this soon after all the excitement of the previous day. They were actually quite concerned as to how the other dragons would treat them in light of their brother's actions. "Best we stay in our own cave safe and sound until tomorrow after he leaves," Darken suggested.

"I was thinking the same thing myself just now," Flame replied. "No sense heading out into a fight with the others, as they are sure to be on their guard until they know Amansun is gone and off on his way."

Scythe and Amansun had moved down the corridor of their cavernous home until they reached the room that Wraith and Scythe had chosen for themselves. This room tucked well into the recesses of the mountainside and provided a quiet resting spot, along with the benefit of being much more private when they had something special to discuss. In this room it was possible to carry on a conversation without having to whisper. There was a slight bend in the entrance as you passed into the chamber and this prevented noise from escaping out into the cave's corridor.

Scythe saw the agony and shock in Amansun's face, and she knew he must be terrified at the thought of going off alone. She wanted to tell him everything, to explain why he had acted the way he had, but this was not to be. The conditions set by the old wizard had been quite clear with regards to these matters, and even after all these years she and Wraith did not dare break the rules they had agreed to at the risk of losing everything. Dragons are large, clever and powerful creatures, it is true, but they are still no match for a wizard as old as the Great Master, and they knew it.

Amansun looked into his mother's eyes with shame as he choked out an apology. "I am so sorry for the harm I've brought to our family," he said. "If only there was some way to go back a day, I would change everything to take back what has happened."

"The time for looking back has passed now, my son," Scythe said softly. "We must plan for the future now, and you in particular need to focus on everything that is likely to come across your path as you make this dangerous journey alone. I cannot see into the future like the great seers of old, but I do worry that you may encounter more than just men and beasts as you make your way north and then east in search of this great castle and princess who is said to live there."

After a long pause Scythe went on. "You will undoubtedly pass through, over, or near the Great Old Forest that sits to the far east of us at some point during your journey, my son." She spoke in so soft a voice that Amansun could barely hear her, and he leaned in to hear her better. "I know you will likely come across great trolls, ogres, warriors and knights during your adventure, Amansun, but what troubles me most is the Great Old Forest. There is legend of a very cruel and evil sorceress who has resided there all these past millennia, and it is said that the trees, creatures, and even the land itself there bows to her spell and command. It is best that you avoid this area at all costs, as tales say that even the great Dragon Lords of old were no match for the magic and power of this sorceress."

Amansun thanked his mother for her counsel and then resigned himself to the fact that he would have to get ready for his journey. He had already embarrassed his family and put them in harm's way, so the last thing he wanted to do was risk any further harm. "I will take a short rest and then set out shortly, Mother," he choked out as his mouth struggled to speak. "I do not know what fate befalls me, but I will not put you and the rest of the family in further jeopardy, so I will leave well before the time that was allotted."

* * *

Well before the setting of the sun, Amansun awoke in his room. He was now twice as tired as prior to settling down to rest. It seemed that every muscle in his body was wracked with pain, and he struggled for every breath he took as he made his way along the corridor in the direction of the family dining chamber. Once there he found Scythe, Darken and Flame all gathered together in a somber mood. They had prepared a small meal, apparently as a going-away gesture, and it was set out in the spot where Amansun normally sat when they gathered for meals as a family. Wraith was nowhere to be seen, as he had no desire to see his foolhardy son off. He was actually sitting on one of the great ledges a few hundred feet above the ledge of the family's cave, close enough to be sure that Amansun would be leaving on time, yet far enough away so as to not be seen, so that he would not have to make any last awkward gestures as his son departed.

The four dragons said very little as Amansun ate his meal. He may as well have been already gone because he felt completely alone and miserable. After forcing down a few bits of roasted mountain goat, he pushed his serving towards his brother Darken, who even in this sad and awkward moment was only too willing to snatch the remains up and make quick work of it. Darken polished off every bit of the meal in quick fashion and then, only after having eaten every last bite, he sheepishly glanced up at the three other dragons, just now realizing that perhaps a little more empathy may have been called for.

Amansun and the others plodded along the remaining section of corridor leading out of their cave. Not being able to hug his mother goodbye, something no dragon could do because of their large wings and clumsy forearms, Amansun instead rubbed his neck against his mother's as is customary among dragons. Flame too rubbed necks with her brother as he moved past her side. Darken made somewhat of a grunt as his brother passed, and the two lifted their heads up at each other in a mutual nod of acknowledgment.

With a final word of farewell, Amansun stepped out onto the ledge that marked the start of his journey, adjusted his shoulders and wings, and with one graceful step forward fell off the ledge downwards as he had done so many times before. With a flutter of wind and a burst of sound as his wings filled, Amansun was off on his way and he arched his back towards the right, dropping his right wing under his chest as he slowly veered off and steered himself into a northerly direction. Not wanting the others to see that he was now crying, he flew off without so much as a glance back. If he had looked back, he would have seen the shape of a very large golden dragon falling from the heights above the ledge he had just stepped off from, his father now slowly gliding and making his way back to his home, satisfied that his son had left within the guidelines set. Wraith was actually quite relieved to see Amansun's silhouette growing smaller and smaller as he disappeared off into the distance. After a few moments he was little more than a speck in the sky, and Wraith realized that for the first time in many years the stress of raising this oddity was likely behind him.

Amansun's vision had been blurred with the flood of tears that relentlessly poured from his eyes. The blast of wind now rushing over his face as he glided ever further from his home soon dried his eyes, though, and with the clearing of his eyes came a clarity of thought as to his own plight at this exact moment in time. While saying his last goodbyes, and during the previous evening's restless night, spent mostly feeling sorry for himself and trying to come to grips that this banishment was actually really happening to him, the young dragon had not given much thought to his actual journey or how it would play out. Floating several hundred feet above the ground now, catching air currents and drifting in a northerly direction, Amansun suddenly realized that he had no clear idea of what he was doing, where he was headed, or how he was to get there. Secretly, he had foolishly imagined that at the last moment the colony would change their mind and allow him to stay.

Amansun's mind raced through the endless possibilities that now faced him. Where should he fly? Where would he sleep? How long would this task take, and would he ever really return? The grandness and uncertainty of what now faced him suddenly sent him into a panic, and the large beast decided that he had best land somewhere and give himself time to develop a plan. Any plan. Surely anything was better than just blindly flying off into the great unknown without so much as an inkling of what he was to do.

Off in the hills ahead was the spot where he and his brother and sister regularly met up each day before flying home as a group. This seemed like as good a spot as any to spend some time thinking, so he flew off in that direction as he noticed the now sinking sun and realized that darkness was just a short time away. He took some comfort in knowing that this hill was well-known to him and that he was sure no harm could possibly come to him this close to home. He was still within the realm of the dragon colony and there were very few, if any, that would ever dare come this close to the dragons' mountain territory.

Amansun's thoughts drifted in and out as he covered the remaining distance to the hillside. Normally he only spent a short time waiting here on the hill for Darken and Flame to join him, but this time he would be bedding down for the night. These hills were close enough to have felt the breath of flame from many of the colony's young, yet far enough away so that many of the plants and trees had once again started to grow back and provide some color to the mostly desolate surroundings. Amansun circled the hillside once before selecting a spot that appeared to be greener than the rest. He knew this meant that much of the old grass had now grown in, and that this spot would likely provide the most comfortable spot to rest his immense body for the night.

As Amansun slowly shifted his weight and searched for just the right spot to lay down, he glanced at the river that flowed down from the great forest. He knew that with just a little effort, and a short flight to the river and back, he could have enjoyed one of the large fish that swam there. He really had no appetite to speak of, though, and wanted nothing more than to settle into a deep sleep so he could pretend that this entire day had been nothing more than a bad dream. He was to have this same thought and desire many times in the days ahead. Amansun adjusted himself a few more times, shifting his leg one way, his wings back another, and so on until at last he felt he was in just the right position. As he gently closed his eyes to rest, he twitched just a hair, realized that a large rock was right under the crook of his back, and started the whole process all over again, with some groaning and mumbling to himself the entire time.

In the valley just below the hills Amansun slept in, the various smaller creatures that still remained in this area began their evening routine of foraging for food. Even the animals that normally could be found moving about during the day in most areas of the world had become accustomed to using the cover of darkness when searching out food or making their trips to the river's edge for a drink. Over the years, the animals that had chosen to journey out in the light of day had eventually been picked off one by one by the dragon colony's youngsters as they practiced their hunting skills in this area. Now these same creatures did most everything at night and spent their days sleeping in their burrows, nests and thickets, out of sight of any predators that might be circling up above, hiding in the rays of the sun.

A lone young wolf that had ventured down from the edges of the forest perched atop one of the large boulders that sat in the clearing below the hills. With his neck craning upward and his long nose pointed up at the heavens, he howled out into the quiet night with his lonely song beckoning his brothers to come and join him. Some of the animals in the nearby area froze momentarily, looked up into the skies and searching for large shadows or dark silhouettes, and then went back to their foraging and chattering amongst themselves when they saw no immediate danger. Only Amansun, who had actually been enjoying his first few peaceful moments of sleep, was really bothered by the constant howls off in the distance. He opened one weary eye just enough to survey his surroundings and make sure he was still alone and safe where he lay. The loneliness of the wolf's calls made him feel even more alone as he lay there on the bare earth. He shut his eyes once again and forced himself to fall asleep, as he knew he had another long and uncertain day ahead of him. As he lay there, shivering with the coolness of the evening air, he made a note to himself that from now on he would be sure to make a pile of glowing rocks near his bedding at night to keep him warm. Dragons do not normally lie out in the open, preferring the safety and seclusion of a nice cave or the dark chambers of an old abandoned castle, and were therefore not accustomed to being out in the cool air overnight.

Eventually the lone wolf moved off in the direction of the great forest and the sounds of the night faded away. The few animals that had stayed out into the deep of night glanced back and forth at each other with curious looks as they listened to a strange rumbling coming from away and above them. Up near the top of the hill, Amansun, now sound asleep once again, was twitching as he slept, snoring loudly as thin wisps of smoke gently drifted out of his nostrils up into the cloudless night sky.

CHAPTER 5

Daybreak brought a fine day to the valley and the rising sun shone brilliantly as it slowly crept up behind the great Smoky Black Mountains range, now far south from where Amansun lay. As he opened his eyes and raised himself up into a sitting position, he glanced to the left and to the right, taking in the view of the Great Plains below him. He had woken as if from a dream and at first was startled to find himself out on this hill, by himself, sitting in the coolness of the morning. It only took a moment for the reality of the day to hit him and once again Amansun was all too aware of where he was, what had happened, and what was to come. Though dragons can go for weeks, even months without eating if they choose, Amansun felt that a meal would perhaps brighten his day. After surveying the skies and seeing nothing of concern, he walked over to a ledge and stepped off, spreading his wings as he started a slow glide down towards the river.

Amansun circled the river, squinting his eyes tightly as he searched the river's depths, looking for a good-sized fish for his meal. After spotting a sizable fish he tucked his wings forward and under his chest, now falling into a steep dive as he approached the water's surface. With a sudden lunge into the water with his sharp clawed feet, he grasped the enormous fish and beat his wings upward as he headed in the direction of the hills he had just come from. Amansun liked the feel of the hill he had slept on. This was still familiar territory to him and that put his mind at ease. Once comfortably seated back at his bed site, a short blast of flame was all that was needed, and Amansun had his first meal as a solitary dragon set and ready.

The fresh catch felt good going down and after finishing his meal, Amansun once again shifted his focus on what his next move should be. As he was already halfway to his secret spot that had caused all of his problems, he thought it might be nice to pay a short visit there now. He would be sure to keep an eye out for Carack while there, as he felt he might want to show the great eagle exactly what he thought of him.

Amansun was in no particular hurry to get anywhere, as he knew that with each passing mile he flew, the further he was from his old life and the closer he was getting to the unexplored. He took his time flying north, following the river as he had done so many times before. It didn't take long even at this leisurely pace before the edges of the woods came into view. As he drew closer to the forest, Amansun changed the angle of his large wings and sped up the pace of his thrusts, as he wanted to gain altitude to make it easier to see his special clearing. Even though he had been here many, many times, it was still easy to miss the small patch of clearing amongst so many trees and the seemingly endless expanse of deep green treetops. As the valley floor behind him faded away, he swept effortlessly over the trees now a few hundred feet below. Soon he was scanning the changes of elevation in the treetops as they rose and fell with the hills and gorges far below the forest canopy. Amansun was intimately familiar with these subtle changes in the rolling landscape below. In no time at all he found himself circling above his field and with the greatest of ease he gently touched down, only a few paces from the edge of the stream.

It was common for the animals to be in hiding when he used to arrive in the past, as they wanted to be sure it was "their" dragon that was standing in their field. He waited silently for a few moments, curious to see if any of his usual friends and acquaintances would come out to greet him. It soon became apparent that the field was deserted. He wasn't surprised, as it had only been a few days ago that he had been here in this very spot, urging them all to flee for their lives into the depths of the forest to escape the hunting party that was to come in the morning. Amansun paced over to the stream's edge and drank deeply of the icy cold water. He could still see the same schools of fish swimming down in the depths of the pool, but he had just eaten and was in no mood to eat again now that he was feeling alone and empty again. He had hoped that coming to the field would cheer him up, but now he realized that seeing his resting spot deserted and empty like this just made him feel all the worse. He was happy in knowing that the field and all the animals that once lived here were safe, but this didn't stop him from feeling sorry for himself and the predicament he was in.

Amansun settled down under the eaves of the trees with the lower half of his large body stretching out into the sun. In this way he was able to feel cool and comfortable, with his eyes out of the bright sun, and yet he felt warm and cozy at the same time as the sun's rays beat down on his feet and lower limbs. Old habits die hard and soon Amansun was sound asleep, temporarily removed from the anxiety of his real life. He dozed far into the afternoon and had the last peaceful nap he would have for quite some time. As he lay there, resting at peace, some of the smaller animals that had decided to return to the field, having seen no real danger over the past few days, ventured out into the open. Most of the larger animals were still in hiding, scattered over miles and miles of the dense forest. These were some of the smallest creatures such as the field mice, some rabbits, and an old badger who lived alone and, being somewhat of a stubborn recluse, had decided he would stick around and take his chances with the supposed dragon hunting party. As Amansun snored and shifted this way and that, the animals went about their daily routines of searching out food, grooming themselves in the sunlight, and getting long drafts of water from the stream's edge.

At midday Amansun awoke from his restful slumber, stared ahead into the forest, and imagined that his old friend, Barnby the owl, was staring back at him. He was sure he was dreaming, the first pleasant dream he had had in some time, until the large owl took flight from the tree branch he had been perching on and flew to within a few feet of where Amansun lay. As the owl settled down just a step away from the dragon's nose still settled on the ground, he cooed out a welcome. While Barnby and the other animals hadn't seen any proof of a hunting party of dragons, he felt quite certain that the dragon had indeed told them the truth and had managed somehow to stop the raid from occurring.

Amansun, thrilled to see his great friend here so unexpectedly, jumped up and began recounting the entire story of what had transpired since his late night visit up through the events of this very morning. "Sounds like you've gotten yourself into quite a pickle," Barnby muttered.

"You have no idea," Amansun countered. "This is just the first day of my banishment and this was the only place I could think of coming. From here on out it will be uncharted territory for me, with no friends, companions or help to speak of."

The large owl studied the face of the dragon for a good deal of time, obviously going over everything he had heard these past few minutes. "Well, there is no need to worry over the large loud-mouthed eagle, at any rate," Barnby stated. "He appears to have left the area, as none of us have seen him in two days now, and that is quite unusual to say the least. I know you have already had one nap today, but humor me with another, since you will be needing your rest in the days ahead anyway. I will fly off to visit with one of my relatives that lives east of here and see what I can learn about this fortress of men you are in search of." Without so much as a "goodbye" or "nice to see you again," the owl flew off into the forest and was immediately swallowed up by its immensity.

Normally the sight of an immense dragon would send animals running in a panic, but these animals were very familiar with Amansun so paid him no mind. All except for the old badger, that is. Digger the badger was always known for being quiet and distant, and while Amansun remembered seeing him on occasion in the past, the old grump had never said so much as a word to him, or any of the other animals in the field as far as Amansun could tell. Digger sat there for quite a while; keeping his distance yet staring the large dragon down as if the two were locked into a staring contest of sorts.

Amansun, having no one else in particular to talk to, as the rabbits and field mice were busy scurrying about for nasturtium seeds and other food, motioned for the badger to move closer.

If truth were told, Digger the badger had never really come to terms with being so close to the large beast. In the back of his mind he had imagined that the dragon was just getting the animals to let down their defenses so that one day, when he was particularly hungry, he could just fly in and help himself to a large feast of unsuspecting animals. Still, for all the times the young dragon had stopped in, he had never seen any signs of aggression, and he had certainly never seen anyone come to harm aside from the fish from the stream which just happened to be one of the old badger's favorite meals himself. In time Digger gave in to his curiosity and waddled over to within a few short yards of the beast.

"Amansun's my name," the dragon spoke out as gently as he could.

"Yes, I know who you are", the badger replied. "We have seen you here many times over the past year or two. Most call me Digger, though that's not my real name."

"Well, what is your name?"

"Does it really matter?" Secretly Digger wanted to tell the dragon his name, partly because no one in the field even knew it, but his apprehension of the dragon was still great, so he thought best to keep at least a few secrets to himself. "What brings you back to our simple field once again, dragon? None of us expected to see you around these parts again. At least not for some time to come."

"I have been sent away on a special mission," Amansun replied. "I have a task I must do, and it involves traveling far up to the northeast lands, so I chose to pass through here on my way."

"Well, can't say I'm glad to see you one way or another," Digger replied. "You gave everyone here quite a scare a few days ago and most everyone has cleared out by now. Not sure how many will plan on coming back, if any." The badger snorted. "I wasn't too partial to most of them anyhows."

" Well, it's nice to make your acquaintance all the same," Amansun said as he bowed his head in a gesture of welcome. Digger bowed his head low in return, and that is how the conversation between the two began.

Now Digger may have looked like a recluse these past few years, and he may have even acted like one too; but make no mistake, Digger was a talker! Amansun and the badger were soon locked into a deep, detailed and lengthy conversation. At first, they talked of simple things. The weather. The meadow. The stream. Safe, simple, easy topics that required very little thought or participation. Soon, however, Digger began delving into deeper topics requiring much greater focus and attention. Science. Magic. Life's quest!

Amansun was greatly interested as Digger proceeded to tell him things about creatures of the forest, good and evil. He shared things he had heard over the years about magic places in the forest, of unusual beasts and monsters that were rarely seen but all too real just the same. Amansun had many questions; but as it turns out, Digger knew a great many things in general, but very little in actual detail. Digger could speak of trolls that lived in the hidden caves of the forest, but not where these caves were, what the trolls did, or even when they had last been seen.

The conversation between these two unusual acquaintances went on and on and for the most part Amansun was pleased and genuinely interested in what the badger had to say. Eventually, though, the badger started talking about badgers in general and about himself in particular. As a matter of fact, when the subject came to Digger, he seemed content to ramble on and on and on. It didn't take long for Amansun to realize that the other animals of the field didn't see Digger as a grumpy old recluse, they just avoided speaking with him, as apparently anyone foolish enough to start a conversation with this badger soon found himself in a one-way dialogue with no apparent end or escape in sight.

The hours ticked by as Digger went on to explain how he came to live in the forest, who his parents were, why badgers were such noble beasts, and on, and on, and on. Even though Amansun had slept most of the day away already, he soon felt the weight of his eyelids as he struggled to keep his eyes open and focus on what the badger was so eagerly chatting about. Not wishing to appear to be rude, he struggled as long as he could to keep awake. Eventually, though, his eyes began to win the battle. His lids drooped and sagged lower and lower as he continued to fight to stay awake by staring directly at the badger's face. Soon the dragon was just focused on the badger's mouth, opening and closing at a speed to be appreciated. Amansun wasn't even hearing the words coming out of the badger's mouth by now; he just saw the animal's small mouth flapping on endlessly as he succumbed to sleep and once again drifted off. Digger seemed to pay no mind to the dragon's slumbering. He was so happy to finally have a captive listener that he continued to drone on long after the dragon had passed out. Sometime after drifting off to sleep, Amansun thought that he heard voices from a distance, and as he reluctantly opened one eye, he saw that the badger was still speaking on endlessly. He closed his eye once again, snorted out a small blast of smoke, and fell into a deep but restless slumber.

Amansun knew somehow that he was fast asleep and dreaming, and yet he wasn't capable of waking himself up. He had drifted into an old yet familiar dream that he had seemed to repeat over the years in his unconscious mind. The dream was much clearer this time around, though, and the visions seemed much cleaner and crisper now. In this dream he was inside the walls of a great castle, with immense rooms filled with tapestries, great wooden tables and chairs, brightly colored rugs and runners, and suits of finely polished armor lined up as far as the eye could see, winding down the corridor of a great hall. He seemed to be effortlessly drifting along these corridors and in front of him and behind him walked an armed troop of soldiers. Each carried a large black shield and on the front of each the same crest appeared: a radiant sun with flames reaching out in all directions in the background, with a large white lion standing on its hind legs, front legs raised into the air as if in a striking pose, and a golden mane of hair flowing down the great beast's back and head. On each of the soldier's chestplates, a similar but smaller crest was painted, and each soldier had a long broadsword hanging from their belt. In their hands each held a large lance, pointing directly up into the air, and they stepped in perfect precision as they moved along the corridor.

Eventually the group marched into a massive chamber with 50-foot ceilings, painted with incredibly striking scenes of great battles of old, complete with flying dragons, gleaming swords, and hordes of brave soldiers charging across the battlefield. In the great chamber there were scores of soldiers, knights and other people wearing brightly colored robes and sashes all lined up, facing towards the front of the great room, where a set of polished stone stairs led up to a massive platform with two ornately carved chairs of royal oak wood. On the first chair sat a great king with long brown hair, a majestic beard, and a crown glittering of gold and precious gems, and a radiant white suit of armor with the same designs as the soldiers Amansun had marched in with. Seated to his left was a beautiful woman dressed in a flowing silver and white gown. She too had an ornate crown on her head and together the two of them sat facing the hundreds of guests gathered in the room.

Amansun watched the king rise to his feet as the crowd below cheered with thunderous applause. He could almost hear the words the king was reciting to the audience, but they made no sense to him no matter how he struggled to hear. As the crowd raised their voices in a single cheer once again, shaking their swords and lances in the air, he was suddenly startled by a sound very close by. As the dragon lifted his head and shoulders up off the ground he saw two things at once. First, the sight of the old badger, now lying fast asleep just a few yards away where he must have eventually talked himself into sleep; and second, his good friend Barnby, now standing just a few feet away. Amansun noticed that it was now pitch black and the coolness of the night air told him that he had managed to sleep well into the night, although this had not been a restful sleep by any means.

"You were really twitching and jerking in your sleep, old friend," Barnby told the dragon. "It took me three of four calls to finally rouse you."

"Just having a nightmare of sorts," Amansun replied. "I've had this dream before but it never felt as real as this night. I'm glad you happened to wake me when you did, my friend." Amansun described his dream to Barnby then said, "What news have you for me?"

Barnby informed Amansun that he had spent most of the night flying across the forest in search of his cousin Barthus. Barthus lived further east and Barnby had hoped he would be able to share better information about the castle. "But he had little he could tell me, I am afraid, old friend," Barnby went on to say. "He claims the castle is many days' flight even from where he lives, out across the Great Plains and east of the ancient Black Woods. There may be some old relatives of mine along the way, but none who live that far off. The legends from the Black Woods go back as far as time, and none of my family who has ventured that way has ever returned."

"Thanks for at least trying to help out," Amansun offered. "You have done more than expected and I truly never imagined to see you here in the meadow to begin with. At least I know I have a friend somewhere, and that is a very comforting thought indeed. I should have expected that the castle would be a good distance off. It would not be much of a quest, I suppose, if my goal was in easy sight, now would it?"

"So what is your next step, then?" Barnby questioned. "Will you be heading off in the morning or do you plan on staying and resting in our meadow for a time?"

"I will be off mid-morning, I imagine," Amansun offered. "I am, after all, on a mission, and it will be challenging enough as it is without lengthy pit stops along the way to slow me down. It's not likely I will be successful in my quest anyway, but I would at least like to make an honest attempt."

"Then mid-morning it is," Barnby exclaimed in an excited tone. "I have often dreamed of traveling afar and what an experience this will be after all. Who ever heard of an owl with a great dragon for a companion, do you suppose? I will just need to eat something before we head out."

"You are truly a loyal and brave friend," Amansun said hesitatingly. "Yet I must go off on my own, I am sad to say. I plan on flying at great haste, and while your heart is certainly in for the trip, I am afraid that your short little wings will be no match for mine as I push on. Besides, little friend, this meadow is your home and there will be many dangers along the way. I risked all to save your life once already, and I certainly don't want that to go for naught. I could never forgive myself if some harm came to you as a result of my journey."

"If that is your decision, then I suppose I will have to respect it," the owl muttered. "I can't say I can argue your logic, as it would likely take many beats of my little wings to match one of yours. I am sure you would be miles ahead of me in no time and then I would be lost and on my own besides. At least I have more help to offer you before you go off on your own. My cousin has sent off one of his sons to fly ahead, spreading the news of your journey. Our family will send out scouts as far as the east edge of the Great Forest, all the while gathering what information they can about the castle you are searching for. When you have flown past the last trees marking the forest's boundary, look ahead for a large column of rock made entirely from black granite. It will be hard to miss as the column stands very high, or so I am told, and it should be easy for a dragon to spot even from a distance. It is there that I had planned on taking you myself. A member of our family will be waiting for you there, with whatever news they have managed to gather along the way."

"I am entirely in your debt, Master Barnby," Amansun offered as he lowered his body towards the owl, nodding his head in thanks. "At least I now have a plan and that is much more than I had upon arriving not that long ago." Barnby said his goodnights for the evening and flew off into the night, promising to return in the morning to see his friend off. Amansun lowered himself back into a prone position and quickly shut his eyes, hoping to give the impression that he was still deep in sleep. It had just occurred to him that the badger could wake up at any moment, and then he would be stuck listening to more badger facts well into the light of the new day.

CHAPTER 6

When Amansun awoke he found that many of the creatures of the meadow were once again going about their business, paying him no mind. Digger was nowhere to be seen so he imagined the badger had finally crawled off to his hole. Barnby had returned as promised and he was happily munching on a freshly caught silver trout. "Breakfast is served!" the owl hooted with pride, upon noticing that the dragon was awake. "A parting gift for my best friend the world traveler."

Amansun glanced down near his feet and saw a trout lying there. It was nowhere near big enough to be considered more than a morsel, but not wanting to make light of his friend's gesture, he made a great showing of enjoying the meal, taking care not to gulp the fish down with one quick bite. After licking his talons clean, being sure to appear very satisfied, Amansun thanked Barnby profusely for the meal and announced that he would be departing after a nice sip from the stream. Within minutes, the two friends were exchanging words of goodbye and good luck and the young dragon was off on the next leg of his journey.

The forest was really quite beautiful, Amansun thought as his mighty wings slowly beat up and down in rhythmic motion. He had never flown over so much of it, and only now did he realize the vastness of its size along with the myriad shades of greens, yellows, browns and blacks that made up the colorful patches of land below him. He was in no particular hurry so he decided that he would continue to fly at a somewhat leisurely pace. He thought about Barnby's relatives, flying off ahead of him, trying to pass on information as they went, and realized that if he reached the great granite column too soon, he would likely be stuck there waiting for the last flyer to arrive. Not wishing to be out in the open in this unknown Great Plain, he decided it would be best not to arrive too soon.

The slowness of his flight gave Amansun time to enjoy the views all around him, and yet it also gave him time to think about all that had happened these past few days. Worse yet, it gave him time to worry over what was still waiting for him up ahead. Amansun tried to clear his mind of these distractions but this proved to be futile. No sooner had he stopped fretting over the perils of the journey ahead than he found himself struggling over what the details of his dream had meant. Was he being led to his own slaughter in front of the great king seated high on the stone platform? Was he somehow seeing into the future and witnessing his own demise? Had the soldiers captured him so easily and handily that the great hall in his dream was still filled to capacity with chanting legions of the king? All these questions poured through Amansun's troubled mind and he soon took no joy in the sights and sounds that he was witnessing for the first time. The brilliant shades of green from the treetops and the silvery flashes sparkling far below, when the trees would part just enough to allow the sun's rays to catch the mostly hidden river underneath, soon became little more than a dull blur. Amansun was lost deep in thought now, and it was merely the repetitive beating of his powerful muscles and great wings that kept him in flight. In this trancelike state, Amansun managed to cover the bulk of what remained of the Great Forest before the sun gently lowered itself back behind him in the west.

Amansun suddenly became aware that the land ahead of him was shrouded in darkness. The thought that it would soon be dark and that he was in entirely unknown lands made him feel quite uncomfortable indeed. It was too dark to now see how much of the Great Forest lie ahead but he was sure he must have covered most of what remained by now between his starting point at the grassy meadow, and where the edge of the woods lay. He changed his flight pattern from a direct eastern path and began slowly circling the woods below, peering beneath him for a suitable spot to bed down for the night. Amansun knew there would be no friendly faces joining him this evening, but he wanted to at least find a spot that did not appear to be threatening.

After three or four large, arching spirals, Amansun spotted a large hill that rose up and out of the dense forest, like an island floating out in a great sea of green. The hill had somewhat of a flat top on one side of it where the trees were less dense because of a large grouping of boulders that bunched together, not allowing the mighty pines and spruces room to grow. In the center of the boulders there was a small field, smaller than the meadow Amansun had just left, yet more than large enough for him to land and settle down for the night.

As Amansun settled down in the clearing he took notice of the area to be sure there were no obvious signs of danger nearby. The field was quite flat, and the grass that grew there was tightly tamped down as if it had been trod on for years. There were the usual signs of small animal trails marching to and fro but nothing seemed amiss, so he decided the spot would be acceptable and he began arranging himself as best he could to get into a comfortable position. There seemed to be one area where the boulders parted more than anywhere else, so Amansun decided it would be best if he lay facing that direction. Remembering his promise to himself from two nights before, he remembered this time to push a few mid-sized boulders into a pile beside him, and with a few short blasts of fire he soon had a nice glowing pile of red-hot rocks to keep him cozy through the night.

There are few creatures in the world that would confront a dragon even if that dragon happened to be caught unawares and sound asleep. Great stone trolls, on the other hand, are not only incredibly strong and enormous, but they are also not the brightest creatures that ever walked on the face of the earth. The hill that Amansun had selected to bed down at for the night just happened to be the home of one such stone troll. Gargaroth the troll had lived in his hillside home for at least a hundred years by the time Amansun happened to stop by. He chose the spot because it was a short walk from the great river that flowed just to the south, and he liked the fact that the hill rose above the rest of the forest so he could enjoy the cool northerly breezes that blew down during the winter. He also liked being able to see out over the forest for miles. He had spent months digging a web of tunnels under the hillside, and he was able to pop out from three sides of the hill by raising various immense boulders that he had positioned strategically in the event he ever had to deal with unwanted intruders. Stone giants are very reclusive and they almost always live alone. Should one of his fellow kind ever happen to show up, it would not be because they wanted to stop by for a friendly visit. Being rather dimwitted and lazy, they often wandered the wilds looking for a nice "home" they could steal away from another.

Amansun had never traveled abroad before, as the dragons of his colony had been content to stay hidden in their mountain retreat. If he had, or had he been taught as to what signs to watch for when out in the wilds, he would have known that hills with piles of boulders such as this one were in fact perfect locations to find the occasional stone troll or perhaps one of the smaller varieties such as a cave troll, woods troll, or the smallest in the group, the bridge troll which could usually be found living under old manmade bridges in the wilder parts of the land. The second giveaway was of course the flat trampled grassy field located in the center of the boulders. Trolls have enormous feet, as everyone knows, and they are also incredibly heavy, being hard as stone, hence the name stone troll. Years of walking over and over the grassy field had all but crushed the life out of the grass in the area. Even the most simple-minded creatures of the forest knew better than to venture into this field, as they knew all too well that there was obviously a stone troll living here or nearby.

Completely unknown to the young dragon, he was now being carefully eyed by Gargaroth, who was using his limited reasoning abilities to try and think of what his chances might be in catching this winged beast unawares in his sleep, which is of course the way most trolls go after their prey. While the dragon seemed quite large, and his fiery breath had made quite an impression on the large troll, Gargaroth couldn't help but to imagine what a feast he would have if he were to kill this beast and set him over the now red-hot boulders just at his side. Gargaroth's mouth watered at the thought, and he muttered to himself as trolls are known to do, since they have no one else to speak with on most occasions. "Ye'll have meat to feast on fer days to be sure," he gleefully announced to himself. "Can't begins to 'member the las' time I was in fer that much food at one time!" Gargaroth gently lowered the boulder he had been peering from and he quietly shuffled beneath the surface of the grassy field as he happily made his way to another boulder on the far side, smiling from ear to ear with his silly grin. He knew he would have a better vantage point from the next spot, as he should be able to look directly at the dragon's face as he lay on the ground resting. Even though Gargaroth was not wise, he had lived long enough and been foiled enough times trying to catch animals, beasts and men unawares to realize that he had to be stealthy and sure before springing the trap. Only when he was sure the dragon was sound asleep would he make his move.

Gargaroth took a deep breath and with arms as thick as the nearby trees, he ever so gently lifted the next boulder, knowing exactly where he would be facing. The enormous boulder lifted so slowly it was almost impossible to notice, aside from the few small insects that happened to be walking across it at the exact moment the troll began lifting. They suddenly found themselves walking directly under the large stone rather than walking onto and over it. The parade of ants took no real notice of the change in their path, and they just proceeded forward while their brothers and sisters continued marching up and over the boulder that just happened to be floating in mid-air for now.

Peering ahead into the distance, Gargaroth was thrilled to see that not only was the dragon's head resting exactly where he had hoped, giving him a clear view from where he was now standing, but the dragon also appeared to be sound asleep. The troll had to momentarily set the boulder back down into its normal resting place, as he was so pleased with himself that he could hardly hold back his laughter. "Yer goin' ta be eatin' meat fer weeks, ye lucky sod!" he snorted. "Thinks I'll be startin' wit' one of dem legs to be sure." Gargaroth gave himself a few moments to celebrate his good fortune before gently raising the boulder up again to proceed with his ambush.

Now, while it is true that Amansun could be accused of being naive in not knowing how to select a better, safer place to spend a night, he was after all to be given some credit, as this was his first time journeying about on his own. While he had not recognized the obvious signs pointing out the danger of a troll in this hillside spot, he was after all still wise, and wary enough to keep his wits about him while sleeping in an unknown field far from home. He had not slept well the previous night, having been troubled by dreams of castles and knights, along with being bored by the mutterings of Digger the badger. Yet even with that, he had rested more than he would have thought, and he had just now been idly resting, eyes closed, as he thought over the details of his plans for the next day. Unbeknownst to the troll now lurking in his tunnel just below, dragons not only have amazing vision, but also incredible hearing. What Gargaroth did not yet realize was that the large dragon resting above him had heard every whisper he had made, every step he had taken as he traveled far below the surface of the field, and even the whisper of the boulder's rise and fall as the troll raised and lowered the great stone from its resting place.

Having been so pleased with himself, Gargaroth—still distracted with his delight in the thought of his soon-to-be feast—made the great mistake of not checking to take one last glance to be sure the mighty dragon resting above was still fast asleep. If he had gently lifted the boulder from which he was now safely hiding under, he would likely have had a chance to quickly drop said boulder and scurry deep into the tunnels of his hillside home upon realizing that the dragon was no longer where he thought. Alas for Gargaroth, he had done none of these things.

Amansun, deep in thought but still wary of this field, had noticed strange scents and sounds from the moment the troll had begun moving about. While he was unsure exactly what foe was stalking him, he knew he was in harm's way, so he had kept his eyes shut tight and concentrated, focusing all of his attention to his hearing. He heard the unmistakable sounds of a large animal moving below the spot where he lay, and he had been able to determine the exact spot from which this beast would likely appear based on the gently moving rock he had observed not thirty paces in front of him now. Guessing that he was about to be ambushed, he decided to take the upper hand of surprise, and he had ever so quietly moved to within a few feet of the menacing boulder.

Gargaroth's last thoughts surely were a combination of joy at the feast he was about to enjoy, mixed with the terror and surprise he certainly had to have experienced as he raised his trap-door boulder a few feet into the air, only to see the massive head of his adversary just a few feet away, mouth open, followed by the blinding fireball that raced at him before his slow-witted mind had even a second to react. In an instant, the stone troll had been engulfed in flames and the smell of roast flesh filled the air, even as the troll's now dead body fell down and into his secret hiding place and the boulder, once hovering a few feet in the air, now fell once more into place, securely enclosing the troll into his self-dug burial chamber.

Confident that the large troll below had been killed, Amansun walked back over to the middle of the field once more. He was aware that trolls generally lived alone in the wild, but he thought it wise to remain at least half-awake for the remainder of the evening just in case there might be another out there wanting to exact revenge for his killing the first. With both ears on alert, and one eye open, Amansun drifted in and out of a very light, unsettling sleep.

Amansun found himself running down a large set of stone stairs that spiraled around again and again as he made his way down floor after floor of a great tower. Mounted on these curved walls were large portraits of men and women, some shown wearing brightly colored robes and gowns, others portrayed in full battle armor. He thought the walls to be quite high as when he passed each painting, he found himself looking up at the figures rather than towering over them. Occasionally there would be cross-shaped windows designed into the perfectly cut stone, looking out over the lands outside. He wanted to see what the countryside looked like outside of the stone walls, but he was not tall enough to see. Upon reaching the last of the stairs, he found himself in the middle of a great chamber once again. Beautiful tapestries hung from the walls, and there were stone statues of wonderfully carved creatures throughout. Amansun didn't feel particularly frightened, even though he once again realized in his state of semi-consciousness that he must be dreaming once again. A sudden snap behind him startled him out of his dream and he whirled his head around, expecting to see another troll charging him, or perhaps even the first troll from earlier in the night, this time disfigured and with his face black with ash from the burns he must have received from the dragon's hot breath.

Amansun's first thought was to unleash an enormous blast of flame in the direction from which the sound had come. Seeing nothing in his path, he scanned slowly back and forth from the left and to the right, upwards and downwards. His eyes finally narrowed on a simple round stone, no bigger than a frog, laying about twenty paces from where he had been resting. Amansun had not noticed this stone before and he was quite sure that it had just arrived in that spot. Amansun looked around once again, and not seeing anyone or anything about, he decided to call out into the darkness. "I know someone is there, so show yourself," he stated defiantly, adding as an afterthought, "I mean you no harm as long as you are here on peaceful terms."

"I mean you no harm either!" the voice said as it traveled across the space of the field. "We have seen what you have done, and I have been asked to determine if you be friend or foe. We don't see many of your kind in these parts, at least not have not for quite some time anyway, and we are wondering what your intentions here might be."

Dragons, as you may have heard, are very intelligent beasts and very curious besides. It is in their nature to carry on long and interesting conversations with their enemies, even if they mean to kill them in the end, much like the cat plays with the caught mouse for amusement. Knowing this, the originator of the voice had correctly guessed that he would be in no immediate danger if he did not appear to be an immediate threat.

"My intentions are entirely my own," Amansun replied wisely. He guessed that he had the upper hand now, as he was sure he was the larger and more powerful of the two locked into this unexpected conversation. Firstly, he could tell by the strength and tone of the stranger's voice that his stature had to be several times less than his own. Secondly, he surmised that if the stranger felt confident in his ability to beat the dragon in a fair battle, surely he would have charged out at once and challenged him to battle from the start.

"You are indeed as wise as you are large and majestic, Sir Dragon," the voice from the shadows replied. "I had guessed that you would be clever enough to realize that I was no real threat to you and had hoped we could enter into a peaceful conversation under a temporary treaty of peace if that suits your mood."

"Your request is a fair one," Amansun countered, "and I will agree not to dispatch you as long as you abide by the treaty of peace. Be warned, however, that I am weary and in no mood for trickery."

"Then we are agreed," the voice came back. "I will make my way into the light of the moon now, as I have had your word that no harm shall come to me, so that we may look upon each other and join in conversation."

"Agreed," Amansun responded, now quite curious as to who and what this stranger might be. "Do come out and let's have a look at you now. You have clearly had the advantage as I sit here in plain view for you to observe from a distance."

At first there was a moment of great silence, followed by the sounds of clicking on rock. The clicking faded away and became a gentle thud as the stranger obviously had entered into the packed earth of the edge of the field still just out of sight. From the rhythmic sound of the steps approaching, Amansun guessed that it was actually two strangers approaching, as there were clearly two sets of feet approaching. The young dragon, still wary from the foiled attack by the troll just a few hours earlier, suddenly felt some hesitation as to whom these individuals might be. Surmising that even two great-armed warriors would be no match for his strength and size, he calmed himself once again and peered ahead into the darkness.

As the silhouette started to show against the backdrop of the boulders, Amansun could clearly make out the shape of a man's head and a set of massive, powerful shoulders just under it. *It is a man just as I had suspected*, the dragon thought to himself. As he continued to watch the stranger's approach, he wondered to himself what strange type of boots this man must be wearing that would sound so much like the noise a mountain goat makes as it walks across a field of grass.

Grasped tightly in the strangers' left hand was a large wooden shield, roughly hewn, with no markings to speak of. In his right hand was a long spear, also carved of wood. As the stranger moved further into the field, the light of the moon started to reflect further down his body, allowing Amansun to see more and more of his guest. Amansun suddenly pulled his head back in surprise as the full outline of his visitor came into view. Standing naught but twenty paces directly in front of him now stood a centaur, neither man nor beast. From the waist up the guest had a very muscled man's physique with bulging arms, a puffed chest covered with hair, and a handsome face with wavy brown hair falling down his back and over the sides of his face. He had large ears shaped like an elk, which twitched back and forth as he approached closer. From the waist down the creature had the body of a horse, only taller and more muscular. His cloven feet, all four of them, were the last thing to come into plain view, and these clearly explained why Amansun had thought there were two guests approaching rather than just the one.

"Greetings to you, Sir Dragon," the centaur beamed. "I have been sent by my people to learn what I can regarding your visit here and to what your plans might be for the future. We have lived for generations now in great peril of the large stone troll that we have witnessed you destroy this very night. As he was our enemy, we are in hopes that you may be one we can count as friend?"

"I am just passing by on a quest of sorts," Amansun said. "I happened upon this hill purely by coincidence and mean to make no claim to it. I shall be off in the first light of the new day. I mean no harm to you or any others that call this place home, and only killed the troll as it became aware to me that he had intentions that were not in my best interests, based on his stealthy and cowardly behavior."

"Well, then, let me say that my people and I shall look on you as a short-term guest but friend for life, and advise you that we are indebted to you for ridding us of this miserable monster that has taken entirely too many of our kind over the years. I am called Arxes in our native tongue and I would ask that you honor us by allowing us to provide you with some type of gift of thanks to show our appreciation."

Amansun advised Arxes that there was nothing he needed at this time, other than to be assured that no one else was likely to try and attack him during the rest of his short visit. With a good-natured laugh, Arxes assured the dragon that he would come to no harm, as even now a group of his own family had set up a circle of defense around the top of the hillside. "Please let us repay you in some small manner," Arxes begged.

Amansun thought long and hard, and suddenly a thought popped into his head, and without even meaning to he offered aloud, "Well, I am quite parched to tell you the truth, friend. I have not drunk since early this morning, and I had no time to look for the river in my hurry to seek bedding for the night."

"If that is the best we can do, then consider it done, great Dragon!" Arxes replied. "I will send word to my brothers to bring a great vat of cool water at once." Amansun watched as the centaur quickly disappeared out of view, and then he heard voices chattering back and forth. A moment later Arxes returned with an eager grin on his face and announced that the water was on the way. "We shall deliver your water and then leave you to rest for what is left of this night," Arxes said. "You will need your rest for the journey tomorrow, but sleep well knowing that our scouts will be keeping watch over you until you awaken in the new day. Perhaps in the morning, after some thought, there may be some other help we can offer."

Amansun drank deeply when his water appeared a short time later, and then he bedded down for the night. From all the things he had ever heard said about centaurs, he knew that they were extremely honest and trustworthy, so he felt no concerns in allowing himself to fall into a shallow sleep.

CHAPTER 7

Amansun felt as though he had just closed his eyes for a moment, but when he happened to open them briefly, while tossing in his sleep, he noticed that the sun had already risen and it was well into the early morning. Every hour that had passed since he had left his home seemed like it was filled with adventure, and if not for the strange surroundings his eyes opened to, he would have thought that he had dreamt the whole thing. As he rose from the flat grassy ground underneath him, his mind went over the events of the previous evening. There had been the troll, the centaur, a large vat of water (which was still resting just a few feet from where he now stood), and of course another strange dream. It was starting to become difficult to tell what reality was and what was a dream.

Looking around the field, Amansun noticed that he was not able to see much because of the large circle of boulders the troll had fit into place to create his home. There were also large trees growing from just beyond the circle of stone, so Amansun made his way to the open space.

Amansun strode through the opening and was quite surprised by what he saw. At first his eyes stared straight out towards the horizon, and he was able to see far off into the distance towards the east. The hill he had chosen to land on was high above the forest below, and the endless sea of green spread out before him. He could see that the tree line ended just a few miles up ahead, so he had been correct in guessing that he had almost made it to the edge of the forest the evening before. Even though the view from this hilltop was quite spectacular, it was what Amansun saw next that really surprised him. The green patch of grass that marked the trail out of the circle of boulders slowly swirled in a downward direction and switched back and forth upon it like a giant serpent snaking its way down the hill. There were spots where the path widened out quite a bit and in these larger areas there were a great number of centaurs, young and old, large and small, all rising now to look up in his direction and cheer together. Many of the adults carried spears and shields in their arms like the ones he had seen the night before, and they shook these violently as they chanted in unison a word which in the centaurs' language stood for "great winged warrior." Amansun guessed there must be at least two hundred of the creatures spread out below him on the hillside and path leading down. Just last night he had seen his first centaur, and now here were hundreds more all cheering for him. It was truly a great feeling and the moment brought quite a bit of joy to his otherwise lonely and sad journey.

Amansun brought his attention to a group of three large centaurs now making their way up the hill from the highest point of the path. In the center of the group he saw Arxes, beaming with a broad smile as he trotted up towards the dragon. The centaur to his left resembled Arxes a great deal and was of the same height and stature. The centaur on his right, though large as well, appeared to be much older than the other two, and while he kept pace with the others, it was apparent that he was one of the elders of the group.

Upon reaching the dragon, Arxes introduced his companions to Amansun. The centaur on his left was Arxes' younger brother, Artec, and the elder to his right was Altus. "Do all centaurs' names start with 'A'?" Amansun asked.

The three centaurs laughed aloud, shaking their heads and nodding in agreement as Arxes replied, "Only in our tribe it would seem," as they continued to laugh.

"It must seem very confusing to you, Master Dragon," Altus went on to say, "but we have very few visitors in these parts, and over the centuries we have grown fond of the sound that letter makes."

Amansun spoke with the centaurs for a good amount of time. They told him of their tribe, their lives, and some of their history, and of course they kept thanking him over and over again for killing the stone troll. Amansun tried to assure them that he had been thanked quite enough now, but they seemed to not understand that he was actually starting to get tired of hearing their thanks repeatedly. In the end, he decided the only way to get out of this was to announce that he did have to move on to begin his adventure once more, which was of course quite true. Who knew what this new day would bring or where he would be when the day ended. After his close call the night before, Amansun thought it a good idea to settle on a resting place earlier in the day so that he could check things out a bit more carefully this time.

"It was certainly nice meeting you all," Amansun began. "I must really be on my way now, as I have places to go and things to do." He quickly stood up and bowed low to his three visitors.

"Isn't there anything at all that we can do to repay your kindness?" Altus inquired. By now the entire tribe of centaurs was again on their feet, chanting and making quite a racket that must have been heard for miles in all directions.

"Well, I am headed out east for now, and I was told to meet some friends at a great column of stone in the plains ahead. Would any of you happen to know of the place? It would be a great service to me if you could give me some direction as to where to head off to next."

"It has been many years since we have ventured into the plains," Altus the elder explained. "There are many dangers out in the open and we learned long ago that our kind are most safe when we remain under the cover of this great forest. Even with stone trolls and other creatures roaming in these woods, we are still better off not venturing out into those empty fields and grassy plains, where we have nowhere to hide if enemies approach. There is a great tower of rock many days' walk from here, just northeast of our home. You should have no trouble finding it if you fly to the edge of the forest and then head up north. With your mighty wings you should be able to make the journey in a short time. Our elders told us of the great Sky Rock long ago, though none of us has been there in recent memory. The rock you speak of is well into the plains, and we would not have any reason to go anywhere near it, as the forest provides us with everything we need."

"Well, I think I should be going now. Thank you for your kindness," Amansun said as he prepared to fly off.

"Thanks to you for your friendship," the centaurs responded.

"Our ancestors came from the Ancient Black Woods long ago, where you are now headed," Altus stated. "While all we have now are myths and legends of that land, I can tell you it is likely our relatives still live in those woods. Should you encounter any centaurs while you are there, be sure to tell them that you are a friend of the Anthroughs clan. He was our great ancestor who led our people across the wasteland all those years ago. His name may still be known where you now go. You would do well to keep your eyes and ears sharp while traveling in those lands also, for there are many creatures, good and evil, that still dwell in those dark places."

With a last nod of farewell, Amansun beat his mighty wings and slowly lifted into the air. As he glanced back he saw his new friends beating their chests and raising their shields and spears into the air as they all chanted "Great Warrior" again and again. Amansun did two full circles around the hill then he headed off in an easterly direction with his sights on the edge of the forest.

Amansun had not expected to make any new friends during his journey, so this was a very pleasant surprise. His only friends in the past had been the animals of the clearing, so he felt much better now realizing that not all of his journey would be filled with fear and depression. Perhaps there would be others along the way that would welcome him as a friend…if they could get past the fact that he was a terrifying dragon, that is.

Amansun quickly found himself in the same predicament as before. While he had a general idea of where he was heading, and he was still hoping against hope that relatives of his friend Barnby would be waiting for him at the tower of rock, he realized that he had no idea where he would be headed next or what other encounters awaited him. He knew he had always been independent at heart, but he was quite surprised at how brave he had been up to this point. What seemed even stranger than anything now, however, was that even though he was flying further and further from his home, he was actually feeling more and more excited as the miles passed underneath him. He was actually starting to enjoy the thought of journeying to places he had never seen or been to. Perhaps he was an adventurer at heart after all.

Amansun had left the troll's hilltop later in the morning than he had planned on, with all the goodbyes and farewells. By the time he reached the edge of the forest it was approaching midday. The great tower of rock was nowhere to be seen at this point, but he did recall that Altus had mentioned it would be several hours north of where he was. From the high altitude he was now traveling at, he could clearly see the mighty Steel River flowing across the land until it disappeared into the forest he had just left. He spotted a nice clearing about two miles from the edge of the forest where he knew he could not be ambushed, and decided to land there for a drink and a short rest.

As Amansun flew toward the clearing in the distance, he took notice of the land just outside of the woods. While he had heard several mentions that it was a barren plain, he could see now that the ground had small rolling hills in places and long flat spells with little to no vegetation. Compared to the Great Forest he had just left, the plain was quite flat, but only by comparison. He spotted several animal tracks as he flew lower and lower to the ground, indicating that there were at least some animals in the area. Far off in the distance, Amansun could make out what appeared to be a green tinge on the horizon, and he guessed this to be the leading edge of the Great Old Forest. It was obviously a great distance away, and further off still he could make out what appeared to be a mighty mountain range far higher than any he had ever seen himself. The tops of these mountains disappeared into the clouds and Amansun thought to himself how exciting it would be to go there one day for a visit.

As was his practice, Amansun circled the area he had chosen several times prior to landing. Once certain that there was no apparent danger in the area, he touched down a few dozen feet from the river's edge. With a few quick steps he was soon getting his fill of the cool and fast running water. There was a good-sized hill covered with boulders and short trees on the far side of the river, but Amansun had decided it would be best to avoid that side after his encounter with the stone troll. The centaurs had warned him that there were still some dangerous creatures living in the flat plains, and he imagined the hill to be a perfect hiding spot for whatever may be laying in hiding, waiting to spring a trap on an unsuspecting victim.

As Amansun drank from the river he kept one wary eye on the far bank, but he never noticed anything more than a few rabbits and squirrels that scurried to and from the water's edge to the bushes growing at the foot of the hill. The water at this spot was flowing very quickly and was murkier than he was used to, so he couldn't really see if there were any fish to be had. Fortunately, he had eaten not long ago, so he was not really hungry anyway.

After an uneventful rest Amansun once again took flight and continued heading north towards his destination. The land below him changed little as he flew ever north, although he did notice that the plain was becoming greener with large amounts of grassy fields, higher rolling hills, and taller trees than he had first seen when he had flown out of the forest. Off in the distance he could see taller sets of hills laying out in the farther reaches of the great plain, and he wondered to himself if each of these might be protected by their own hill trolls.

After what seemed to be a short flight, Amansun noticed a large, narrow tower just off in the distance. This pillar was a good distance more inward from the forest which he had been paralleling this past hour or so. He changed his course slightly, veering in towards the center of the plain, and began adding altitude as he grew closer, as he wanted to approach this giant pillar of rock from a great height, just in case some great winged serpent might be calling this tower home. It was not unheard of to have a single isolated dragon living in places such as this, as some of his kind preferred living in solitude, and he was not looking for a fight. He had enough troubles of his own to contend with already without doing battle with some unknown adversary just trying to protect its piece of territory.

As Amansun continued to soar higher and higher, he suddenly noticed two things. First, there appeared to be a second river, or more of a stream perhaps, that went from north to south along the flat parts of the plain near the pillar of stone. This stream seemed to be dead calm as there was no sign of movement below. Second, he noticed that in the not-too-distant foreground there appeared to be large beasts moving along this still stream. Puzzled by this unexpected sight, Amansun spun off towards the east and began a large and slow arching bank to see what type of beasts he was approaching. As Amansun grew nearer he noticed that what had appeared to be a stream from up high was in fact a paved road, obviously laid with the same black granite as the tower of rock he had been approaching, as it shown dead black from above and had given him the impression of water. He then noticed that what he had first mistaken for large beasts was in fact a caravan of wagons, moving in single file, protected by a large number of soldiers on horseback at the front, middle and rear.

Amansun was flying quite high at this time and the sun above hid his silhouette. His father Wraith had taught all three of his young that it was always best to approach in this manner to avoid detection when out hunting, and Amansun had inadvertently followed his father's advice way out here on his own. Even though he felt an odd yearning to get closer to the men traveling below, he knew it would be best to press on to the tower of granite now just a short distance in front of him. For one, he did not wish to panic the men in the caravan who had apparently taken no notice of him up to this point, and for another, he did not want to attract any attention to his task at hand. Amansun had no idea who these travelers were, where they were from, or where they might be headed. The last thing he wanted was for word to get out that a large dragon had been seen flying in this area. He was still trying to figure out how he was going to accomplish his task, and having a castle full of soldiers waiting for his arrival was the last thing he wanted.

Amansun continued flying ever higher as he pressed on towards the towering pillar of black rock. He craned his neck to the left and looked back at the caravan that was still moving along the black road, still oblivious to his presence. Now that he was even closer than before, his sharp eyes could make out that at the very rear of the procession there was a large troop of smaller soldiers marching in unison, carrying great double-edged axes that shone brightly in the sun. This was a band of two hundred or so black dwarves from down south, though he did not know this at the time. They had come up as part of the caravan to mine obsidian and the black granite that was abundant in this area. Though Amansun didn't see the contents of the last twenty wagons in line, the men and dwarves of the south had filled them to the brim with the dark precious stone.

Having finally reached the tower, Amansun observed that the top of this unusual rock formation was nearly six hundred feet across. The valley floor was well below, so anyone standing on the top of this jagged tower would be able to see for miles in every direction. As he circled the tower once to get a better feel for the place, he noticed that the tower of rock was indeed very steep, jagged, and appeared to be impossible to climb. This seemed to be the safest possible place to rest that he had seen since leaving his own cave behind. If truth were told, he had not rested well since the night before his colony had discovered his secret, so he was excited to think about the rest he would get this evening.

The top of the great rock had scrub bushes growing upon it, along with a few taller trees that added just a bit of cover to the western side of the formation. Other than that, the surface was relatively flat, and it had the appearance of a level field. On the northernmost part of the field there was a circle of rough-cut stones that had been evenly placed at intervals of ten feet. These appeared to have been chiseled into narrow, rectangular blocks each about twelve feet high, and they had odd symbols etched into them.

Amansun made his way over to the westernmost part of the tower where the largest trees grew, and stared back across the plain at the enormous forest he had left only a few hours earlier. He had hoped to find Barnby's relatives waiting here as was planned, and was in fact surprised to see that the trees were deserted at this time. The trees made up a great screen that he could hide behind so that anyone who may have been looking out towards the plain from any part of the forest would not be able to see that a dragon was now resting on its summit. While Amansun had imagined that he was traveling dreadfully slow, he had in fact outflown the continuously changing relay of Barnby's messengers by at least a half a day.

Realizing that there would be no better place than this to rest, Amansun decided to lie down and close his eyes for the time being. As he lay there, sun beating down on his thick hide, he thought of the travelers who had made up the caravan passing by, and he wondered who they might be and where they could possibly be headed. Even though he guessed they must have been going in the wrong direction, he couldn't help but ask himself if these men might be the very soldiers who lived in the castle he was now searching for. He lifted his mighty head up and, looking out over the ledge of the tower, he could see the caravan slowly growing smaller and smaller as it faded into the horizon, moving ever south. He gently lowered his head once more, shut his eyes, and drifted off to sleep.

Amansun felt the soft, polished river rocks beneath his feet as he approached the outer stone wall of a mighty fortress. The first wall appeared to be painted a dull gray and it circled left and right away from the main roadway that he was now walking along. The walls appeared to be at least thirty feet tall and there were large turrets built into the top at intervals of three hundred feet. At these turrets, large white banners waved in the breeze and the image of a standing lion could barely be seen as the ripples in the fabric swayed to and fro. An enormous wooden gate nearly forty feet wide and as tall as the fortress walls stood some distance ahead of him, and he could see guards posted at either side, heavily armed, stopping all who approached the entrance to this outer point protecting the city that was visible just inside the ring of stone. As he looked left and right he noticed that armored soldiers flanked him on each side, and with a turn of his head he saw that there were another twenty armed men to his rear. He appeared to be marching along in unison with this group of warriors, although he felt out of place and realized that they were there to make sure he was not able to change his direction of travel, nor change the pace of his march, which appeared to be a brisk walk now. There were numerous men and women along the roadway on either side and they moved quickly out of reach as he approached. He couldn't help but notice that all eyes were upon him, and he heard whispers and murmurs coming from most of their mouths as he slowly marched past each group of them.

Looking up and beyond the approaching wall ahead, Amansun could see a great city of stone shining brilliant white, complete with towers, spires topped with great flags, windows cut into massive stone walls, and ornately carved pillars of stone. The city was made up of multiple levels, one on top of the other, stacked ever higher as the levels grew toward the center and topmost portion of the fortress.

Further above and beyond the fortress, he could see a mighty set of mountains that dwarfed the city of stone, reaching up into the heavens themselves. The distant snowcapped peaks grew whiter and whiter as they stretched up and into the fluffy white clouds above. The bases of the mountains shone brilliant green, and he could almost make out the detail of the massive tree line that separated the hills from the steeper parts of the mountain.

As Amansun allowed his head to lower once again down to the field he was now walking across, he heard the cheers and chanting of the large numbers of people he and the soldiers were passing as they made their way to the gate. Though the men and women along the road appeared to be very aware of his presence, they did not shrink in fear or run off, as he would have expected. Instead, most if not all of them dropped to their knees, lowering their heads and cheering one name repeatedly as they continued to march on.

Amansun half-expected to have been forced to stoop over and half-crawl under the gateway they were now about to pass through; and yet as they drew nearer, he realized he was now looking up at the highest points of the gate and still had at least twenty feet between his head and the bottom portion of the gateway. All along the top of this causeway there were archers bearing large oak bows, and they stood at attention as he and the large group of soldiers filed underneath.

Passing under the gateway, Amansun noticed that the stone roadway now split into two roads veering off at ninety-degree angles to his left and right. Being in the center of the group, he automatically adjusted his direction to the right roadway as the soldiers around him had already done so, leaving him little choice. Now inside the first wall, it became apparent that another equally high wall had been built just thirty feet inside the other, and he stepped along briskly as the road under his feet started to rise in elevation. Still more people lined the inside roadway, dressed in robes of various colors, wearing leather sandals and carrying bundles of fruits, vegetables and other items of trade. These people also chanted the same name repeatedly as they backed themselves closer to the walls now on either side of the road, making room for this large procession to pass by. Amansun was once again caught by surprise when he noticed that the children of the town squealed with delight as he and the soldiers marched by. He would have thought they would run off screaming at the sight of an enormous beast such as he was.

Amansun became aware that he had an itch at the top of his long snout and he shifted his right forearm in an attempt to swipe away whatever it was that was causing him this discomfort. The tickling sensation disappeared for a moment and then returned once again this time a little further off to the left side of his face. Now reaching across the length of his face, Amansun swatted at the annoying pest with his left forearm and then noticed that along with the tingling sensation he had felt, he was now aware of a soft, low voice calling his name aloud. As he gently lifted his eyelids, he was startled to see his good friend Barnby standing just in front of him. He shifted his enormous head upward and realized that he was not actually looking at his old friend the owl, but another owl with similar coloring and facial expressions. Clearly this was a relative of Barnby, and he now, still coming back from the depths of his slumber, just realized that his awaited messenger had arrived during his nap.

"Greetings, Sir Dragon," the owl offered, as he bowed low and lowered his right wing in a sign of courtesy. "I am Aranthus, son of Arthan, and fifth cousin to Barnby of the Western reaches. Begging your pardon, your greatness, but I thought it best to wake you from your repose, as the messengers that came before me assured me that ours was an urgent mission and that you were to be found and given what information we had to share in the timeliest means possible."

Amansun rose to his full height now and, looking down upon the large owl in front of him, he assured Aranthus that he had no need to apologize, as he was glad to have the company and was indeed very anxious to learn what the owls might have to share.

"I have information for you, it is true, Master Dragon," the owl said in a hushed voice while looking to the left and to the right suspiciously. "But we should leave this tower of rock at your earliest convenience and say no more until we do so."

"What have we to fear on this isolated tower of stone?' Amansun answered, now also moving his head from side to side, trying to determine what possible adversaries may have gone unnoticed upon his arrival.

"None that can be seen, to be sure," Aranthus went on to say. "But please take me at my word, for my people have lived long in these parts and there are unseen dangers that lurk in our very presence, perhaps even now. It is wise and prudent that we take flight soon, as the sun is near ready to set and neither of us should be lingering atop this haunted monolith once darkness creeps in."

Amansun was truly puzzled by his new visitor's obvious concern for their safety, though he guessed not what type of creature might approach a dragon. Seeing how fearful and alarmed the owl was, Amansun walked over to the ledge of the great pillar and glanced over to the owl, stating, "Lead where you may, for I have just rested and am anxious to learn what secrets you may have to tell, especially now."

Without any hesitation, Aranthus the owl quickly flew off in a northeasterly direction and called for the dragon to follow. Amansun stepped off the tower of rock and did his best to fly as slowly as he was able, in order to not pass by the owl who was clearly putting as much distance between himself and the stone tower as possible in short fashion.

CHAPTER 8

The sun had just started to fade as they flew on, and Amansun noticed the owl looking back nervously time and time again over his shoulder at the tower they had just left moments before. Amansun turned his head back himself, curious even more at what the owl had feared, and he thought he noticed a soft glowing light at the top of the tower. He shook his head and thought to himself that it must be a trick of light caused by the setting sun, and he once again turned his attention to flying behind the owl, now frantically beating his poor wings as fast as he was able.

As the two drifted with the currents of air guiding them north, Amansun noticed a large hilltop ahead and guessed this must be their destination. While the sun had gone down by now, there was still enough daylight to make out that the hill was the tallest of a cluster of them that rose out of the otherwise flat plain below. There were trees and bushes covering most of the ground near the lower hills, but the tall one they were heading for appeared to be mostly clear.

Aranthus looked back towards the large beast flying just behind him and called out that they would be landing at the peak of the hill as Amansun had guessed. The owl stopped beating his wings and settled into a slow glide as they approached the top of the hill. Amansun continued to beat his large wings rhythmically, though he slowed his pace and adjusted the angle of his wings to accommodate their decreasing speed. A moment later the two were at rest on top of the hilltop that, while smaller than the pillar they had just left, was quite flat and empty of any rocks, trees or brush of any kind.

Now seeming to be a bit more at ease, Aranthus edged closer to the large dragon and opened up in conversation. "I am sorry to have kept you waiting, kind Dragon. But we had to leave the tower of rock at once, make no mistake. There is great evil on that pillar of stone, and it is quite fortunate that I was able to reach you before cover of darkness had approached."

"What kind of beast is there that would have openly challenged a full-grown dragon such as myself?" Amansun questioned.

"The worst kind, Sir Dragon," the owl answered. "My kind have lived at the eastern edge of the great forest for generations untold, and while none of us have had the courage or foolhardiness to find out for ourselves, it is said that a group of ancient druids once lived upon the tower of stone. Legends say that each night, as the end of day draws to a close, their spirits rise from the very rocks sitting at the top of the pillar, and they hold their councils of enchantment from now until the end of all days. Many brave souls have found ways to the summit of the tower, and each has met an untimely death. Most jump to their deaths, as can be seen from the skeletons that litter the base of the tower. Others were rescued from the tower of stone at break of day, only to be found mad with insanity. There was a time when the men from the north tried to post lookouts upon the tower to watch for approaching enemies from the south, but they quickly gave up as their scouts died or went mad one at a time."

Glancing back at the tower of granite now some distance away, Amansun could now clearly see that there was a soft light illuminating the top. The greenish yellow vapor seemed to grow strong and then fade back and forth, and even from this great distance he could plainly feel uneasiness and sense a presence of evil. He now realized why he had neither seen nor heard any birds or other small creatures while taking refuge at its summit. Looking down upon the clearly exhausted owl standing near his feet, Amansun realized the risk and danger this owl had put himself in, having chosen to fly to the great tower of rock so close to sunset, and he felt a great deal of respect for the small creature.

"Clearly I am indebted to you, Master Aranthus," Amansun offered while bowing gracefully as a sign of respect. "I do not know what hold these ancient spirits may have had over a dragon such as myself, but I am sure it was best that I not linger there to find out. Either way, you showed great courage, and it is possible you may have saved my quest from ending in a most unpleasant and unexpected way."

"I consider it my privilege to have served you, Sir Dragon," Aranthus offered. "It is said that you are truly a noble dragon, and my cousin Barnby states you risked all to save him and his friends just a short time ago. Now that we have left that wretched and forsaken tower, we can discuss matters that pertain to your journey."

As Amansun sat with Aranthus on the hilltop, shrouded in darkness and privacy now, he learned that the goal of his quest did in fact exist, and that it was just a few days' journey from the point he was at now. Barnby's numerous relatives and connections had speedily gathered all the information they could for the dragon, and they had found that a large castle was at the easternmost part of the ancient Black Woods at the edge of the massive Silver Lake. The fortress had been there for centuries, and a mighty warrior king and his people presently inhabited it. It was thought that the king had a vast army of soldiers at his command, and many of the trade routes of old had opened once again, with travelers from the north and south making their way to the castle to do business and make trade with the people there. Aranthus went on to say that he had given instructions to his own relatives to fly on towards the forest on the other side of the barren plain to see what other help they could find. While there was no location determined for a future meeting, he felt it was highly likely that Amansun would find some of his people when he drew near the castle itself.

"This news is better than I could ever have expected," Amansun told the owl. "You and your family have given me great hope, and I now have a clearer sense of where I must go and what I may find when I get there. It would be foolish to continue my journey in darkness, so I will wait until the new day and then head out at first light."

Aranthus agreed with the dragon and added, "I am quite exhausted myself after today's events, good Dragon, and I will beg your forgiveness for not being better company, but I feel I shall fall over of weariness soon, even as I am speaking to you."

"Then rest, brave Aranthus," Amansun offered in reply. "Sleep in peace knowing you have me as your own personal sentry for the night. No harm shall come to you as I stand guard, and I have much to think over and plan out in my head, so it is best that I have no disturbances, which works out well for the both of us." With that, Aranthus bedded down for the night and Amansun sat at attention, lost in thought, yet occasionally glancing over at the eerie light glowing off in the distance.

The cool evening air caused even Amansun's thick armor-like hide to tingle as he sat there in darkness, listening to the heavy breathing of the owl now nestled beside him. He could have easily collected a few rocks from the hill they now rested on and set them aglow, but his desire to avoid any observation from the apparitions that were on the distant rock tower outweighed any thoughts of sitting beside some warm rocks. His mother Scythe had warned him that he might encounter supernatural and magical beings during his journey, and he now realized just how right she had been. The lair of the stone troll a few days before should have been easier for him to identify as an unsafe place to be, but the apparent safety of the granite tower had truly unsettled him. Amansun now realized that even when things looked quite harmless, he could never really be sure that he was out of harm's way. Amansun shivered once more as he sat there, this time from the thoughts of what might have happened had Aranthus not arrived in time to save him from his unknown plight, rather than the cold night air that seemed to sit on top of this barren hillside like a blanket of snow on a winter's day.

Amansun kept true to his word and stayed attentive throughout the night to ensure that no harm came to his new friend. While it is true that he never fell fast asleep, he did slip in and out of deep thought, and occasionally his mind wandered off to distant lands and times since forgotten.

All around him, Amansun heard the shouts and screams of panic as he saw many men—mostly soldiers covered in full battle gear, along with others who wore leather garments and tunics of heavy black material—running in every direction, as great bursts of flame and searing heat erupted around them. He was standing on a paved road of sorts, and the darkness of the sky above led him to believe it was nearly sunset. In the dimming light he could see rows of wagons pulled by enormous horses, larger than any he had seen before. Many of the horses were rearing up on their hind legs, trying to break free of the heavy harnesses that held them to these heavily laden wagons. Others managed to break out of the line of wagons nearly stacked end to end, and these he saw bursting out on either side of the road, dashing wildly, trying to escape the battle that seemed to be coming at them from every side. On one side of the road, he could make out the glimmer of water and the reflection of the bursts of light that seemed to come from everywhere. On the other he saw enormous trees bursting into flames and the shapes of men running into the thick brush.

Amansun could clearly see the silhouettes of great winged beasts flying low in the air all around him, and a large group of soldiers bearing large lances and broadswords, some with bows and arrows, set up a circle of defense all around the area where he now stood. A thick, smoky pungent smell of singed hair and burnt flesh hung heavy in the air, and as he looked ahead and behind him, he noticed the slumped and charred bodies of many men who had apparently already fallen in the first moments of this battle. While he felt terrified by all he saw around him, he could not seem to move, and he felt as though he was frozen in place. He could hear the frantic grunts of the men surrounding him as they did battle against these enormous, winged beasts that appeared to dart in and out of sight, as the air grew ever blacker and thick with a choking sooty smoke. Amansun's eyes burned in pain, and he wondered why it was that he was not in the air flying with the other beasts rather than standing on this road in obvious harm's way, surrounded by men all yelling in anger as they struggled to encourage each other to keep up the battle. He saw a number of men approaching on horseback from the front of the caravan and, as they drew nearer, he could see that one of the warriors was clad in an all-white suit of armor, sitting high in the saddle with a broadsword in one hand and an enormous shield in the other, held upwards as if trying to fend off some unseen creature just above his head. The men were all yelling and screaming at each other, but the man in white was staring directly in Amansun's direction, sword pointed at him and waving him on as if to say "come this way, come this way."

As the bright starlight of the evening began to fade with the first new light of the coming day, Amansun once again shifted his gaze to the tall stone pillar, miles off in the plain ahead. The greenish-yellow light flickered briefly from dim to bright a few more times, then with a sudden spark it vanished completely. Hearing a noise behind him, he turned to see that Aranthus had already woken up and he had also been gazing out into the distance. "That light doesn't show itself every evening," the owl said, "but it looks like we picked the right night not to get caught up there. Won't be long now before the sun lights up the plain and we can start thinking about breakfast."

Anxious to get on with his journey, Amansun declined the offer to stay for a meal. "I really should be getting on now," he added. "I will forever be indebted to you and your brave family, but I really want to move on now and see what lies ahead. I should be passing over the great river once again at some point, and I will take my meal then, as I have grown quite accustomed to fish over these past few years."

"Have a safe journey, then, Sir Dragon," Aranthus said. "I am sure there are some nice plump rabbits about at the lower portion of this hill, and I will need a nice meal before I make my way back to my own home back in the forest. Should you ever run across my cousin Barnby again, please be sure to let him know that we were able to pay back his favor after all." With that, the great owl turned and sprung lightly into the air, and with a quick flap of his wings he was once again airborne and heading off across the hillside. Amansun watched the owl as he gained elevation and then started a slow banking move back in his direction. Just as the owl passed overhead, Amansun heard his soft voice cutting through the air as he added, "Don't forget to look for our relatives when you get near the castle now. It is quite likely that some of them live near the great Silver Lake, as we have a long history of having great fisherman in the family." With a quick smile and a nod of the head, Aranthus drifted out over the bank of the hill and disappeared around the other side.

Moments after the owl had disappeared, Amansun realized that the two of them had never discussed which direction he should go next. He knew he had to cross the plain, obviously, and that Silver Lake and the castle itself were on the east end of the Black Woods, but he had never considered where he should go next from where he was currently standing.

As Amansun knew his goal lay to the east of where he stood, he decided there would be no harm in flying south until he reached the Silver River once again. Since the river traveled east to west, it would be smart to use it as his guide. Following the river would guarantee that he continued to go in the right direction, while also providing him with plenty of water to drink and fish to eat. Having no other plan to speak of, this made the most sense, and he felt quite happy with himself for thinking of this on his own.

The flight to the river took little time in Amansun's now rested condition, and as he grew closer he changed his course slightly so that he was once again heading east with the river just below him. With his eyes scanning in all directions for any signs of trouble, he now started his journey across the Great Plain in earnest. Far below him, he saw that the black road of granite crossed over a large bridge as it continued south. The caravan was nowhere to be seen so he guessed that the travelers must have sped on through the night without stopping. He squinted with his powerful eyes and saw the fresh wagon wheel tracks in the dirt along the side of the road where they had drifted from its course from time to time, and was certain that they were in fact now out of sight.

Amansun decided to lower his altitude for now, since the danger of being seen by the caravan had passed. By flying lower, Amansun had less difficulty battling the strong winds that were blowing quite fiercely north to south at the higher elevations. Even with his renewed strength and considerable stamina, he thought it would be wise to conserve as much energy as possible for any challenges that may still lie ahead on his journey. From what he had heard from the centaurs and owls, he was not likely to run into many adversaries as he passed across the Barren Plains.

Amansun had been flying easterly, following the great river for some time, when he realized just how large the plains truly were. While he could make out the edge of the Black Woods far off in the distance, he still appeared to be a long way off, and it became apparent that he would in fact most likely run out of daylight before he had reached the far side. While this concerned the dragon considerably, he came to the realization that finding a safe spot to sleep in the Black Woods would be no less of a challenge, so the point became moot. Whether he reached the woods or not, he would be taking his chances bedding down for the night once again, and he pondered what new types of challenges he would soon encounter.

The funny thing about getting lost in thought about what might happen to you in the future is that quite often it stops you from seeing the clear and present danger that may be facing you that exact moment. Amansun, without realizing it, had been slowly flying lower and lower to the river, as he focused more and more on thinking about where he would wind up at the end of the day. While he had left the granite road well behind him some time ago, he had not bothered to notice that there was another road, this one a simple track in the dirt and sand that made up the floor of the plain, that had meandered down from the north and was now parallel to the river as it headed east. This less traveled and less noticeable path had been lying right under his view the past several miles as it plodded along, waiting for a way to cross the river. Just ahead in the distance, two small hills, one on each side of the river, each covered with trees, distracted Amansun from realizing that another bridge lay just ahead. This was a large one, constructed of massive wooden beams, spanning the river at one of its narrower points where these two hills sat just apart from each other. The banks of the river were thick with pines and firs where the bridge had been constructed, and the combination of hills, trees and narrow river had prevented Amansun from noticing the manmade object until he was practically upon it.

Suddenly snapping out of his deep thoughts, Amansun happened to glance down, and he spotted the large wooden bridge spanning the river below. The bridge was over two hundred feet in length, was wide enough to have two carts pass over side by side, and stood just about the same height as the tress it had blended into. On each side of the bridge stood wooden towers that sat twenty feet above the road, and they appeared to have walkways leading up to what appeared to be doors. Tucked into the hillsides, Amansun thought he saw other carefully concealed wooden structures that appeared to be doors leading right into the very hills themselves. Amansun took all of this in with a glance, and at the same time the thought occurred to him that this bridge might not be just a deserted outpost.

At the same moment Amansun decided it might not have been such a good idea to be flying this low to the river, he heard the unmistakable sound of horns being blown in alarm, and several large, fast-moving darts went whizzing right across his chest and face. He quickly realized he was under attack and, as he shifted his wings to quickly bank left, he became aware of a multitude of armored dwarves racing on top of, along, and near the bridge, all scurrying to get to their weapon posts. Another volley of darts flew past him as he quickly beat his wings to get behind the low row of trees on the northern edge of the river, most passing clear of his body but one managing to just clip the leading edge of his right wing. He winced in pain as he deftly maneuvered behind the trees, swooped low to the ground, and disappeared around the backside of the hill. In the near distance he could hear more and more horns calling out in alarm.

Once he was hidden behind the rear of the northernmost hill, Amansun quickly climbed to an elevation of a few hundred feet to escape any more potential darts, and circled around and over the hills to see what his enemies were up to. He was happy to see that the rear of the hills had not been as protected as the fronts had been along the river, as the only movement he noticed on the back of the northern hill was a small group of dwarf archers shooting harmlessly in his direction, as he had climbed to a safe elevation. Glancing to his right, he could see a large wooden shaft tipped with a shiny silver tip, still protruding from his wing. Although it had hurt quite a bit when it had first pierced him, it no longer bothered him much and it had not affected his ability to fly.

Scanning the bridge fortress from a safe height while he slowly circled over the area, Amansun counted no less than sixty dwarf warriors, all positioned along various parts of the bridge and surrounding towers, while others still clambered out of the now open hillside doors. He could see far below him the same darts that had pierced his wing flying up at him and then dropping harmlessly down to the ground below. He cursed his foolishness for having not paid more attention to where he was flying. This was new territory for him, and this was a life and death quest. He promised himself that from now on he would stay more grounded in the present. As he circled high above, he thought about what his options were now. Clearly, he had been seen. That was obvious. The question now was what he should do about it. The dwarves hidden below appeared to be well-armed, judging by the bolt still protruding from his wing. And they had the advantage in numbers and location. He could easily wait for cover of darkness and burn the hills, but that still left their hiding places in the hillside. This could turn out to be a lengthy battle and one where he could potentially get hurt, affecting his ability to go on with his quest. A battle was out of the question. And besides, how could he blame these warriors for attacking him without provocation? He was a dragon, after all. Perhaps they thought he was flying in low to burn their precious bridge to the ground?

Amansun took all of this into consideration and finally decided that what he really needed was more time to think. Clearly something had to be done, and for now he thought it probably would be wise to at least land somewhere and remove the dart from his wing before it caused him any more harm. Amansun slowly drifted back north, not wanting the dwarves to know from which direction he had really come. He glided as much as possible to reduce the damage to his wing, and drifted behind a set of hills a few miles from where the ambush had occurred.

CHAPTER 9

Once back on land and with the dart safely removed from his wing, Amansun decided that his best move would be to linger in the area long enough to put some fear into the dwarves guarding the bridge. He was certain that they would try and send out messengers to alert others of the presence of a dragon in the area. If he prevented their scouts from leaving, at least for a short time, they would most likely hunker down into their present position and try to wait him out. Once he had convinced them they were not safe leaving the area, he would once again set off on his quest. By the time they realized it was safe to try again, he hopefully would have already reached the castle and finished his quest or died trying.

After a short rest, Amansun took to the air once again and surveyed the land near the bridge. He noticed a rather tall hill that sat just east of the hills where the ambush had taken place and decided it provided the best possible vantage point, as he would be able to see any scouts sent out in all directions but west. As the caravan he had seen the day before was traveling from north to south, he guessed that any scouts sent out would likely head in one of these two directions. After sweeping the hill from the air a few times and not seeing any potential danger, he settled down on the peak of the hill and started his vigil.

As Amansun fought back the urge to daydream, the hours ticked slowly by. It was mid-afternoon before the first scouts were sent out as he had guessed. Amansun waited until the dwarves had crossed enough ground that he would be out of range of the weapons that they had used earlier in the day. He knew the scouts would be armed with little more than knives and perhaps bows, as they would have to travel quickly across the open ground. Amansun thought of how much his brother and sister would have loved to be in his position right at this moment. They would have reveled in the excitement of the hunt, and their satisfaction at roasting these helpless dwarf scouts would have been immeasurable. Luckily for these dwarves, Amansun did not have a taste for revenge, or dwarf for that matter! As the scouts approached at a distance, he took to flight at a height he felt would be safe, gathering altitude as he prepared to dive at the first scout heading in a southern direction from up high.

Attacking from a high angle out of the west with the sun directly behind him, he was upon the scout before the dwarf even noticed he was in danger. Choosing to terrify the now panicked dwarf rather than kill him, Amansun shot a tremendous burst of flame just in front of him and blackened everything within one hundred feet. The dwarf, now lying in a ball on the ground, trying to cover himself as best he could, did not notice the large beast sweeping back into the air for a second dive. With a sudden leap to his feet and a mad dash as fast as his short legs would allow, the dwarf bolted in the direction from which he had come, dropping his weapons, pack, and anything else he could, to give himself the best chance at running as fast as possible back to his hills. Amansun took a slow pass overhead again and fanned the heels of the dwarf with enough flame and heat to let him know that he was running for his life. Off in the distance Amansun heard the horns being blown in alarm once again, and he circled back around towards the hills to see if the other scouts were running back to their camp. Sure enough, he spotted dwarves running back towards the hills where the bridge lay, coming back from the north and east as he had guessed. With impressive speed Amansun took turns terrorizing each scout, buzzing over their heads and sending them running as he sent torrents of flame at their heels as he had done with the first.

Once Amansun was sure all the scouts had been turned around, he headed back to his hiding spot on the hill to the east, being careful to fly at a high enough altitude so as not to be seen. After setting down once again, he settled in for another wait.

Amansun was pleased that he had guessed correctly regarding the scouts being sent out to warn others of his presence. He would have been happy to continue his journey once again, but he had the feeling the dwarves would make at least one more attempt under cover of darkness before giving up for a while. Amansun decided it would be best if he waited it out to just after sunset to do one more patrol before moving forward with his quest.

The hilltop Amansun had chosen to be his vantage point turned out to be a lucky choice after all. It was relatively steep, had no easy access to its top, and appeared to be as safe a spot as he was likely to find. The river was just a short distance south and easy to approach without being seen, so he decided he could swoop down after his second patrol, gather a drink for the evening, and then slumber lightly into the night before flying off east, as the new day broke unseen by any dwarves that might be on watch.

* * *

As the great beast rested on his new hill out of sight, the dwarves gathered themselves deep in their hillside and discussed strategy. Burgling, a scout who had managed to make it back to their camp after the dragon's first attack, described the immenseness of the dragon and the incredible power of his blast that he had felt firsthand. "I've never felt such heat in all my years," the dwarf muttered. "Even in the deepest mines down south I have never felt that kind of sheer heat."

"Quiet, you pitiful fool," snapped Balden, the captain in charge. "Better you died in the flame than made a coward of yerself, dropping yer weapons and supplies likes a child as you fled for yer life." Balden eyed the younger dwarf with disdain and muttered quietly to himself as he rubbed his large beard and chin, "I don't knows how youse three managed to git aways from that dragin, but mark my words, we're not through here yet."

"Seems to me our bes' bet would be ta try it agin after nightfall, cap'n", another dwarf added.

"Great suggestion," Balden chided with menace. "Did ye think of that all on yer own now? Course we'll try it agains tonight, pea-brain. What did yer expect were'n going to do, give up and hides under this dirt fer weeks?"

"I was just tryin' ta help", the young dwarf said out loud by accident.

"Well tanks fer nothin'!" Balden snorted as he turned and smacked the dwarf on the top of his head. "Leave the thinkin' to mes if'n you don't minds. That's why's they puts me in charge here, idn' it? And dat goes fer the rest of yous too!"

Balden paced to and fro in the low light of their cavern wrenching his hands, staring off into the distance but seeing nothing. With his body swaying slightly from left to right and back again like a pendulum, he muttered aloud, "We makes our move at secon' darks t'nites. Once tha shadows of firs' dark have faded in ta blackn's, we sends out scouts in every direction. Tha dragon can'ts be everywheres at once, cans he? One of ye pitiful fools is likes to 'scapes inta the darks, and thens yous be tankin yer cap'n once yous are mades into a hero fer g'tting' out and spreaden' word of the dragon."

Another young dwarf standing off to the side raised his hand upward timidly, looking carefully at Balden to get his attention. "Yes, Halfred, yous have sumting to add?" Balden asked in an inflamed tone.

"Don't ye thinks the dragin will bees outs dere just a-waitin' to picks us off'n in the night?" the young dwarf asked in a wavering voice.

"Yous bets he wills!" Balden shouted out with a laugh. "An' tanks fer volunteer'n ta bees the firs' one out!" This drew laughs and applause from all the dwarves huddled together.

"Grrreat!" Burgling muttered to Halfred as he walked close by the other young dwarf. "Looks likes it's the youngsters gettin' sent out on this death mission. Guess Balden was rights bout havin' wasted mees time runnin' backs to save my life earlier todays. The two a us shoulda be deads well befores morning."

"Well, at least thars some good news to celebrate," Halfred countered in a halfhearted laugh.

"And whats would that be?" Burgling asked.

"I run fasters than yous," Halferd said with a broad smile, laughing as he walked off towards the pantry for what he guessed would be his last meal.

"Har de har har," Burgling sniped back. "Let's jest sees who the faster runner is tanite!"

* * *

Amansun was lost in thought as usual, but this time he kept his promise to himself and stayed alert, still remembering his lesson from earlier in the afternoon. He had been careless and he now had a wound in his wing and a job to do before he could move on as a result of his daydreaming. He wanted to be sure that no scouts snuck off before nightfall, so he forced himself to stay focused on the hills in the distance. When he felt like he might slip off into sleep, he would get up and move about to get his blood flowing again.

After what seemed like an eternity to the dragon, the sun started setting in the west and the hills of the great plain started laying down long shadows. As the last remnants of light faded, Amansun took flight into the sky above the plains. He could clearly see the small details on the plains below, as a dragon's eyes are sharper than any other, even in low light. As he circled the hills that hid the bridge, he didn't see any activity. *Perhaps the dwarves had learned their lesson after one scare,* he thought to himself. *Not likely*, his inner self cautioned. These same dwarves had shown enough courage to attack a large dragon in broad daylight. They were not likely to give up sending out messengers after only one try.

Inside their hillside retreat, safe from the dragons' eyes, the majority of the dwarves had gathered together to toast their brothers who would soon be running for their lives. "Here's ta fast feets an' brave hearts to keep 'em runnin'," Balden roared as he addressed his troops. "It's likely that sum er all of yous may die tanite, but dats the price we pays to gets the word out that we has a dragin here after all dees years. Imagines how wurse it'd be if'n we don'ts get the word out an' a whole troop of yer brothers gets wiped out by tha' dragin 'fores they even sees they're in danger." All the dwarves gathered together in the dim light roared in agreement, and even Burgling and Halfred could not argue the logic of their less-than-liked captain.

"Good luck to one an' all," Halfred exclaimed as he raised his large stout to his lips and drank deeply.

Amansun continued to circle the hills well after all light had faded, and he was starting to question his plan when he noticed some activity on the land below. This time there were four separate groups of dwarves on the move, one going in each compass direction. Heading out east and west were individual dwarves moving quickly on their own. Going north he spotted two others fleeing together. He would have to intercept these two first, he determined, as there were hills in the not-too-distant vicinity. Lastly he spotted three scouts heading in a southerly direction. He guessed that this was likely where the dwarves came from, since the largest number of scouts had been sent in this direction.

Having had all day to think over his plan of action, Amansun was quite prepared for even this four-way attempt at escape. While circling the area early in the day, he had made note of every possible escape route, every hill or patch of trees, every ditch or low-lying bramble of thorn bushes, every place a dwarf might try to escape to or seek shelter during their flight. It was true that Amansun had avoided all the hunts and training these past few years that his brother and sister had participated in, but the truth was that none but a dragon was a better strategist or tactician when it came to planning out a battle (or defense from a battle, for that matter).

Under cover of darkness Amansun no longer had to worry about what angle to approach from or where he was in relation to his enemies. He could now see them as plain as day. While it is true that dwarves have excellent night vision, theirs pale by comparison to that of a dragon. As planned, Amansun approached the group heading north first and sent out a furnace blast to the left, right, and directly in front of their path. The dwarves threw themselves down in panic and watched in horror as the great dragon lit the entire path in front of them by setting ablaze trees, bushes, and an entire hillside a few hundred yards north from where they cowered one after the other. The entire northern area that had been pitch black just moments ago was now completely engulfed in flames and lit up as bright as a midsummer night's bonfire. With nowhere else to hide, the dwarves picked themselves up and ran back to their hillside as fast as their feet would allow.

Hidden atop the northernmost hill of the dwarf's encampment, behind the first line of trees that had been planted to help camouflage their bridge site, Balden the dwarf captain was fuming and swearing aloud to those gathered around him. "Curse and confound dis damn dragin," Balden spewed out. "Surely he has roasted Goren and Bulgurth by now. We can only hopes that while he feasts on thur poor charred bodies, our bothers escape in all other directions."

"You wants I sound the great Horn of Bergrath?" one of the dwarves questioned in panic.

"No, you fool, be still," Balden snapped. "If he hears the alarm go out now, he'll realize we has other scouts afoot!" The dwarves nearby all groaned in agreement at their leader's sound advice as they stood there frozen at the dark treeline, staring out across the plain, trying to make out the silhouette of the great winged beast against the now glowing hillsides in the distance.

As Balden and the other dwarves stared off north hoping to get a glimpse of the dragon, they were caught by surprise when far off to the east they saw another series of bursts of flames lighting up the dark night. "Can there be twos of tha great beasts?" another dwarf called out in panic.

"Of course not, yous fool," Balden growled in his usual threatening manner. "It's the same beast attacking from the east now. Hurry, sounds the horn while dere's still time. This dragin's very cunning and surely plans on fencing us in from all sides. I have misjudged his wit and tit's likely that young Halfred has joined his brothers in sacrifice by now. We can only pray for the others now."

As if on cue, Amansun lit up the hillside and areas surrounding the lone dwarf who had been rapidly fleeing in a westerly direction. All the other dwarves aside from Balden, their captain, wept aloud and cried in vain, shaking their raised fists into the cool night air. They shouted curses into the night and swore vengeance against the dragon, even though each and every one of them knew there was little to nothing they could hope to do now. "That would be young Burgling dis time," one of the dwarves muttered as he stared off blankly into space.

"Quickly, all of yous now, you fools," Balden shouted. "We must makes it backs into our hillside 'fore this dragin finishes off our friends headin' south. Surely he will bees on tops of us next or I'ms a fool."

As the dwarves scattered down the hillside towards the large doors that marked the entrances to their retreats on both sides of the river, the sound of the Great Horn of Bergrath continued to sound, and those dwarves that had not been on the same side of the river as their captain could only guess what may have been taking place on the other side. All they could see for certain is that their brothers on the north side of the river were running to their hill retreat, so they made haste to do the same. Even as they scrambled down the side of the two hills, they began to see the first bursts of flame coming from down south.

As Amansun finished lighting the hillsides and brush on fire around the southernmost band of dwarf scouts as planned, he once again flew higher to see what he had been able to accomplish. Flying low overhead, yet high enough to not be seen or heard, he could clearly make out the shapes of all seven scouts making their way back to their bridge site. Some were still running, some were crawling, and some were just walking up right like dead men waiting for the final blast to come and take them, yet all were making their way back to their camp. *Success*, he thought as he smiled to himself for the first time today. *Just like I planned. Now for a quick flight back to my hill, a drink of water to be refreshed, and then I can rest a few hours until daybreak and be off before they realize what's happened.*

Sitting deep in the bowels of the northern hill, Balden and the others kept quiet and listened patiently as they waited for the attack that they were sure was about to take place at any moment. "Perhaps the whole bridge and hillsides are already ablaze?" one of the dwarves whispered.

"Not likely," mumbled Balden. "But then agains, how can we tell from inside this hillside? It may be morning before we learns what happened outside and what's become of our scouts."

The other dwarves gathered around their captain and glanced nervously about, heads tilted one way or the other, trying their best to hear any sign of what might be happening above them in the open. "Did everyone makes it in safely?" Balden asked.

"All but Halford and Bairdrus," one of the older dwarfs replied. "They refused to comes in, as they insisted on staying at their post with the great crossbow on the North Tower. They're want'n another shot at the great beast."

"Very noble indeed," Balden answered with an almost soft tone. "And not unexpected eithers, considering Halford's brother is outs there in the burning plain somewheres." He shrugged his shoulders with a look of helplessness.

Well out of sight and hidden on the southern side of the river, Amansun now settled down for a much deserved drink of water. It had been years since he had done anything like this attack, and he had forgotten how exciting it could be, as well as how tiring one could become in such a short time. He had been flying to and fro across the hills and plain from north to south and east to west, and now he realized how happy he was that he had decided not to engage the dwarves in full battle. He was certain he would have come out the victor, but it would have been quite senseless to kill all these strangers merely because they had chosen to protect something that was clearly very valuable to them.

Amansun drank deeply from the cold river and felt refreshed once again, although he knew he would need a nice rest before he started off again in the early morning. Glancing up at the dark skies above, he realized he had been lucky there had been no moon this evening. Judging by the temperature of the evening air, he guessed it was still quite early and that he would have plenty of time to rest. After drinking his fill, Amansun flew off to his hiding spot on the eastern hill and settled down to continue his watch and perhaps get at least a few moments of sleep in between his vigil.

Back in the depths of the dwarves' northern chamber, Balden was still swaying from left to right as he started blankly into the darkness of the cavern. As he pulled gently on the long, coarse beard that grew from his chiseled chin and face with his short but muscular fingers in a downward motion, his lieutenant Kildren eyed him nervously. "It's not the missing scouts nor the dragin dat bothers you now, Captain, is it?" the lieutenant asked. "We've lost brothers in battle before, and I know ye don't fear the winged beast out there neither. Something out there has you spooked, don't it?"

"Keep it low, Kildren," Balden whispered as he motioned the lieutenant to follow him further into the recesses of the cave. Once the two dwarves had made their way out of earshot along the far wall of the chamber, Balden started up again. "Did you see it out there too? The greenish light floating off in the distance this evening during the attacks?"

"I thought I saw something, Captain, but I can't says what it mighta been. What with the dragon belching out flames and the horns blowing and the troops all scattering about, it was hard to keep an eye out."

"I saw it too," the captain whispered softly, seeming to be speaking to no one in particular, with a blank stare looking right through the lieutenant, hands ringing each other over and over once again, still swaying gently from side to side as if in a trance. "I saw it too."

"What were it then, Captain?" Kildren asked, now more fearful than ever and wondering what it could be that had set his captain into this unusually fearful demeanor. He had never known his captain to be afraid of anything or anyone through all their years of battle together.

Suddenly standing frozen still, and looking around the chamber very carefully to be sure no others were close by enough to hear, Balden looked deep into the lieutenant's eyes and whispered almost inaudibly, "I believe it were one of the keepers of the tower." He stated this quickly, as if saying it faster would somehow make it safer to be said. Once he had made this statement, he looked around nervously about the chamber and in front of him, behind him and even the ceiling above him with large seeking eyes. "It's said that the keepers of the tower aren't trapped atop that cursed pillar of granite as most say. Some of the old-timers says that back when they used to travel in these parts, decades ago, they would see the green flashes from the tower shoot off into the night sky in different directions. Only at the last moment before the break of the new day would they see the green flashes shoot back atop the mountain and then disappear from sight in a blinding flash. No one knows what they are or where they went."

Not sure if his captain was losing his mind or serious about the green watchers he was talking about, but feeling quite uneasy himself just the same, the lieutenant suggested that they keep this to themselves. "No sense upsetting the troops any more than they are already, with the dragon flying about and scouts to mourn."

"Right you are, lieutenant," Balden finally answered back. "I thoughts I seen the green light hovering over the battle this evening, almost like it was watching what was going on down here. That will be the last you will hear me speak of it, though, as you be right that it won't do no good to mention it to anyone." After asking the lieutenant to swear to never discuss the conversation they had just had with anyone else, ever, he snapped back into his usual self and barked out so that the others could hear, "Double up the guards on the doors for the night and wake me if you hear anything at all!" and he walked off to his personal chamber.

From Amansun's hilltop retreat, he could see some of the scouts as they grew closer and closer to the hills their fellows were hiding in. He imagined how surprised they must be to still be alive, and he thought the other dwarves would be equally puzzled when they learned that all seven scouts had returned alive and safe. Dragons are excellent hunters and ferocious beyond compare, so he laughed to himself imagining how puzzled the dwarves would be as they tried to understand what could have happened this night to prevent the scouts from being consumed by the dragon. As he sat alone on the hill, Amansun realized he was indeed very different from the other dragons of his colony, and even from his own family, as any other dragon would have surely destroyed the entire dwarf troop without mercy or compassion.

Amansun got into a comfortable resting position, half seated and half lying down, that allowed him a view to the dwarves' hillside encampment but still let him be somewhat comfortable. As the minutes and then hours ticked by, Amansun took turns keeping a wary eye out for more scout activity in between short catnaps. Eventually the catnaps won out as Amansun, not sensing any additional activity from the distant hills, allowed himself to slumber into a deeper, restful sleep. Unseen to the dragon, and the dwarves who were now hiding in their hillside fortresses or laying low in the trees near the bridge, a soft greenish-yellow ball of light floated high in the air above the battlefield for a few short moments, then retreated back in a northern direction as quickly and mysteriously as it had appeared.

CHAPTER 10

Amansun was seated at the edge of an immense wooden table that stretched out fifty feet in either direction. The tabletop was covered with vessels of food, from bowls of fruits and baked goods to large platters with various game beasts generously roasted and glazed with aromatic sauces and gravies. All around the great table were seated noble men in colorful robes and knights, all engaged in loud conversations with one another. At each guest's place setting were large goblets of ale, wine and cool stream water, which many were drinking in long, savored draughts.

Sitting across from the position where Amansun found himself was the great king and queen he had remembered from previous visions. They were also engaged in conversation with those nearest them, and everyone seemed to be laughing and enjoying the feast. After a few moments the king stood and motioned his hands to the gathered guests to settle down so he could make a speech. As the large group seated at the table realized the king meant to say something, they all quieted down until the room was quite silent and all that could be heard was the crackling of wood from the immense fireplaces that were off to the sides of the great room.

"This marks a very special time for our kingdom," the king began. "In just a few days' time, our army will march out to the far lands of the southwest to claim new lands in the unsettled territories and collect treasures to replenish our depleted vaults. We are unsure of what unknown perils and adversaries await us, but we know that we shall be victorious, as we have the greatest military force gathered together in this fortress and nothing or no one will stand in our way." The gathered guests quickly jumped to their feet and cheered their king's speech as they raised their ale mugs together to toast. As these large cups were knocked together, Amansun was showered with large drops of ale as they splashed out.

Amansun moved his head in the hopes of avoiding the flying ale droplets, but realized that no matter which direction he moved, the constant pelting would not stop. Soon he felt the cool drops hitting his entire body from head to feet, and he glanced out across the now fading table only to see that he was actually peering across a dark land shrouded in the mist of a shower that had blown in from the east as he had been carelessly drifting in and out of sleep. As he glanced out over the still dark plains from his hiding spot, he noticed that the gentle rain had put out most of the fires that he had started earlier this evening.

The dark sky was partially filled with pockets of low-lying clouds and sheets of rain, creating a perfect cover for Amansun's departure from the area. Most of the dwarves were still huddled together in their underground hillside retreats, waiting for enough time to pass to come out and survey what damages may have been caused by the rampaging dragon. As Amansun took to the air and started flying off in an easterly direction once again, none were there to take notice.

Only Halford and Bairdrus remained outside at the bridge, where they had hoped to have another chance to shoot down the great winged beast with their large crossbows. Each dwarf had taken up a spot on opposite sides of the wooden bridge, guessing that in this spread-out manner they would have the highest likelihood of getting off a shot, regardless of which direction the dragon approached from. As they called out to one another from each side of the wooden structure, they hoped to fill each other with the courage to face the dragon or at least make it through the night. They were both tremendously surprised when they noticed small figures stealthily approaching their locations from both sides of the river.

Halford wept openly and without shame when he saw that his brother and the others had somehow been spared. They gathered together in quiet celebration before making their way to the now locked wooden doors on the northern side of the river. As they banged on the barred doors without any answer from inside, they soon realized that the dwarves inside were too afraid to risk opening the doorway, so they quickly retreated back under the safety of the bridge and took shelter there, huddled together under the enormous beams of the lower section of the structure, as a soft gentle rain started to fall over the plain. Here they stayed hidden from view, and it was thus that Amansun easily departed without any detection.

While the gently falling rain did not affect Amansun's ability to fly, it did make it much more difficult to get a clear idea of what he was flying over or which direction he was going. Even though he had made the mistake of flying too low the previous day, this time Amansun intentionally chose to fly low over the river to ensure that he would not lose track of direction. This time he stayed alert and paid attention to what was coming in the distance ahead. As the late evening began to fade into the first hints of the light of a new day, Amansun slowly raised his altitude so that when the first rays of sun burst out over the far eastern mountains, he was already flying several hundred feet above the plains below.

Amansun was now well away from the spot where he had been ambushed just the day before. He had actually been quite happy to see the sun come up this morning, as he had been afraid that in the darkness of the night he would be pursued by the flickering green light he had now seen twice in the past day. As the immense plain below passed underneath the great dragon, he soon was able to see the details of the approaching forest that now lay just east of his present location. The incredible depth and thickness of the forest was very apparent, as the dark green hue he could see was much darker than any section of the newer forest he had spent time in behind him to the west. There were more patches of hills and bunches of trees on this side of the plain, and the temperature had dropped several degrees although it was still comfortable enough.

When Amansun reached a point that he felt was just a few miles from the leading edge of the now nearby forest, he started to slow his flight and earnestly began searching for another place to stop and rest.

It was now midday and he had covered the distance from last night's spot to where he was now much faster than he had expected. In truth, it was likely because he had been quite alarmed by the sight of the green light the night before, and he had flown at a substantially higher speed than what was normal for even him. As he started to circle the land below once again, he tried to pick out the best possible spot to set down. In just a few short days, he had learned that everything was not always as it seems, and even the most unlikely spot can turn into a trap if not scouted thoroughly. After narrowing down the choices to a flat bluff near the river and a hilltop with minimal tree cover, Amansun settled on the flat bluff, not knowing what could be potentially hidden under the trees, and he set down in the middle of it just a short distance from the river. Amansun stretched his wings out and surveyed the spot where the dart had hit him just the day before. While he could still feel some pain coming from the area, the dart had not caused any significant damage to his wing, and he was quite sure he would be just fine moving on in this condition.

Peering out over the few remaining miles of sandy plain that stretched to the edge of the Black Woods, Amansun could see that, like his own forest back home, this old forest had many changes of elevation. He could see the rise and fall of the great trees that made up the forest, and he could guess where the hills rose up high and where deep valleys lay as the trees sunk lower and lower into pools. Off in the distance, the mountains that Amansun had first seen two days before from the western side of the plain raised up even higher than he had expected, and the tops of their peaks disappeared into the clouds above. These were higher than any he had previously seen, and he suddenly was filled with an urge to abandon his quest and to just fly on east up to these towering heights to see what lay hidden at their tops under the cover of the wispy clouds. The thought went away as quickly as it had appeared when he realized that he would be all alone in that far-off land, and that the only family he had known was still waiting for him back in his own Smoky Black Mountains.

As Amansun looked out at the seemingly endless Black Woods, he was suddenly overcome by the size and depth of the forest. Looking up at the sun, he guessed he had just a few short hours of daylight left. The more he sat there and thought about it, the more uncomfortable the thought of flying into that dark, foreboding forest became. In the end, Amansun decided that his best move would be to settle down for the night on this relatively safe bluff for the night. He had already had two very unsettling nights in a row, and the thought of searching for a safe resting place while flying over this dark wood with little time to find a good spot was more than he was willing to face.

Just as Amansun was convincing himself that staying put on this bluff was the best decision, he began to have the unnerving feeling that someone or something may be watching him from the darkness of the woods ahead. He determined that it would be prudent to change his location after the sun went down. He realized, after all, that he was very likely in plain sight of anyone who happened to be tucked into the woods and looking out into the plain.

With this thought in mind, Amansun decided he would fly down to the river's edge for a drink and survey the land around his bluff. In this way he could secretly pick out an alternative spot to spend the night without being too obvious about it. He made no attempt to hide his current location and slowly beat his wings and rose up from his bluff retreat cautiously, being sure that anyone or anything watching would be absolutely sure of where he had taken flight from. Next Amansun made a very deliberate flight down to the river's edge, where he was able to once again drink all the water he cared for.

While this was the very same river he had been following for some time now, at this end of the plain the water was quite clear and easy to see into. Amansun had no trouble spotting some large fish lurking just under the water's surface, and while they were unlike the fish he was accustomed to eating, these were just as easy to catch, and the large fish he selected to eat actually had a very clean and fresh flavor, unlike many of the fish he had eaten earlier on this trip. Amansun guessed that the sandy plains that spilled into the great river as it ran from forest to forest likely clouded up the water and made it appear to be murky at the other end.

When Amansun had completed his meal and drank his fill, he once again took flight. This time, instead of taking a direct route to the bluff he had rested at earlier, he flew to a height of several hundred feet and carefully circled over the area once again, being sure to take note of every feature he could see. In this fashion, he was able to locate two other areas that looked like suitable sights to bed down in. Once this was accomplished, Amansun once again dropped down to a lower elevation and then made a direct approach back to the bluff. By this time, the sun was just starting to set off to the west, and the shadows from the surrounding trees started stretching out back in an easterly direction towards the Black Woods.

Amansun was careful to wait until the last traces of light had completely faded from the sky and darkness had settled in for the evening. Only then did he quietly and skillfully sneak off to the western edge of the bluff where he had been resting to take flight. Walking all the way over to the edge, he gracefully stepped from the bluff and spread his great wings out as he noiselessly glided off at a very low height, just high enough to avoid getting tangled into the few surrounding patches of trees. Once he had covered about a mile from the bluff's edge, he sped off in a northerly direction, still staying quite low, and then he doubled back to settle down on a low-lying hill with patches of trees he had noticed, north and slightly west of the bluff's location. Amansun quickly flew into the thickest patch of trees on the small hill and settled down, being careful to hide himself from view yet leaving himself a direct view of the edge of the woods, along with a sightline to the bluff he had spent the afternoon on. Not sure of the safety of his new hiding spot, Amansun was careful to stay at high alert, and he surveyed the area around him while listening carefully for any signs of movement or danger. While he was unsettled about his new location, he still felt much better than remaining out on the unprotected bluff he had selected for the afternoon, and felt sure this was a good decision and that he was finally starting to get the hang of this traveling thing down.

As the hours slowly ticked by without any sign of movement, Amansun started to think that maybe the events of the past two days had started to make him a bit paranoid. Glancing back and forth from the treeline of the woods to the bluff, he found himself fighting the urge to fall asleep. He had, after all, flown a great distance since his last stop, and this was after a very restless night with little to no sleep. As the familiar weight of his eyelids started to induce him towards slumbering, he started imagining things. With partially closed eyes Amansun struggled to look into the distance, now completely shrouded in second dark. He could almost make out slight traces of movement between the Black Woods treeline and the front of the leading edge of the bluff.

Struggling to lift his weary head, Amansun leaned forward and, straining both his eyes and ears, made a real effort to see if something was out there. The more Amansun stared into the pitch black, the more his eyes got accustomed to the lack of light. He was now able to discern various landmarks far off in the distance. A large rock here. A small tree there. Bushes lining a small path along one of the distant hills. All these types of things were now becoming easier to see. As his keen eyes' focus got narrower and more intense, he was suddenly surprised to see what he thought might be some type of movement out there on the plain. At first Amansun thought his eyes were playing tricks on him. There was just the slightest trace of movement far off in the distance. It wasn't really true movement at all, more like the faint rustle tall grass makes when it's gently blowing in a light spring breeze. He thought he detected traces of shadows and hints of something passing along from the woods to the base of the bluff he had been resting on earlier.

As Amansun continued to watch as intensely as he could, he saw these wisps of shadow, these traces of movement, make their way along the slowly rising bank of the flat bluff. Just when he thought he might be imagining everything he heard a small whistle. Not a loud, lingering sound but just a short fine-tuned note, like a small bird might make if trying to let its mate know that it is nearby but without attracting the attention of any nearby predators. While he couldn't be sure, he thought the sound came from the bluff he had been intently staring at all this time. Suddenly, all at once and without any warning, a brilliant burst of lights sprung up from all over the base, sides and top of the bluff he had left a few hours earlier.

After the shock and brilliance of the sudden light had worn off, Amansun focused on the bluff once more and clearly saw a large number of beings moving about, scurrying atop and all over the bluff and its gentle slopes. Everywhere Amansun looked he could see little bodies, thin yet tall, moving about with torches in their hands and spears and bows. These appeared to be wood elves, an entire colony from the looks of it. Amansun knew that wood elves were to be found in most forests, even back at home in small numbers, but he hadn't expected to see them on the edge of the woods nor here on the top of this bluff so far from the safety of their trees. These weren't the graceful and intelligent elves that were found further into the deep reaches of the old forests of the world, but an offshoot of them, bastardized by interbreeding with men. Numerous as ants and dangerous as any troop of armed dwarves, these wood elves were not to be taken lightly.

"Looks like a false sightin' as I'd suspected," an elf named Ilfden said to the others as he surveyed the entirety of the bluff from its highest point. "Never b'lieved a dragon would be here enyhows."

"Imma telling ye, the beast was a true dragin and make no mistake," Eorden quipped back sharply with resentment. "Me eyes don' lie and I thinks I know er dragin wen I sees one, ye see!"

"Well jus' the same, there bes no dragin here nor any types o' beast fer that matter, now is there?" Ilfden snorted as he continued to look about.

"Captain, captain!" another elf called out from the western side of the bluff, "Ye best look over here quick as can! There be tracks here the likes a which we ain' ever seen. Something very big an' heavy moved 'cross this top today, make no mistake. I thinks it were a dragin!"

Suddenly filled with new excitement and a bit of boastfulness, Eorden yelled back at the captain, "Looks like yer the one te be explaining how it is that a dragin, a full-sized true dragin, spent an entire afternoon jus' out of your section of the woods with ye takin no notice now, doesn't it?"

"That's enuf of that fer now, ye ole geet!" Ilfden called out as he hurriedly rushed over to see the tracks for himself. "Don't you suppose it be a good time ta kill these torches, nows as how we see there's a dragin on the loose?"

Suddenly all the torches that had been covering the bluff went out as one and silence fell. Amansun, caught off-guard once again, but not as blinded as before since his eyes had been shut to a narrow squint, waited a moment then stared out into the darkness as his eyes readjusted once more to the black void. Off in the distance he could see the shadows once more, moving faster than before, rushing back towards the woods. This time he thought he could hear small traces of whispers flowing across the breeze as the wood elves scurried back to the safety of their trees. From the soft sounds he was able to make out, he thought he could hear Eorden's voice heckling Ilfden still, and he chuckled to himself. "Captins never wrong, says he," he was whispering.

"It'll be yer tail in the fryin' pan if that dragin hears us, ye stupid geet," Ilfden whispered back.

Then all was quiet and the last of the shadows vanished into the dense trees. Amansun continued to stare off into the black of night, watching for any new signs of movement, and as the minutes ticked past his head slowly nodded gently at first and then fell with a thud to the soft ground below as he drifted off at last.

Amansun looked out from where he was standing and observed all the activity going on just below at the ground level of a mighty fortress. There, between two massive sets of stone walls, an army was getting packed up and ready for a trip. The walls were quite high and the stonework was very impressive, as each large block of stone was cut and perfectly fit in between the others that lay all round, above and below. A narrow cobblestone street lay between the two rows of walls and here Amansun saw a seemingly endless caravan of horses, carts and wagons of all shapes and sizes. Amongst the carts and wagons there was a great deal of bustling going on, as burly men with massive arms and legs were rolling barrels of water up onto carts while others were tying down loads of food, weapons, heavy kegs of ale and the like onto others. Many of the men were singing aloud as they went about their business, and Amansun thought he recognized the tune although the words were unfamiliar.

Some of the men in the street were seated atop magnificent saddled horses, and they slowly rode from one cart and wagon to the next, pointing at a loose rope here or a missed crate of cargo there, and he imagined these must be the captains in charge. One of the men on horseback, a handsome dark-haired fellow with broad shoulders and a black leather vest, was obviously making fun of one of the workers who appeared to be moving more slowly than all the others below. "Shall I tell the king that we should wait until after winter passes to go on our mission?" he called out.

The other men on horses laughed aloud, along with some of the workers loading the carts, and one of the other captains chimed in, saying, "Of course Bartle will be wanting to drag this on as long as he can, Hrothgar. You know how much he loves working hard like this!"

A roar went up from the men and the very unamused looking man now moving even more slowly shouted out, "'Tis fine by me if we skip this early start, as I was caught short on me beauty sleep this morning, as you know. A few days' sleep would fancy me jus' fine!"

Once again, a loud roar went up amongst the men gathered below, and Hrothgar bellowed out, "Me thinks a whole month of extra beauty sleep won't fix you none at all from what I can see, so press on with those kegs of ale or you'll be amongst the first complaining we didn't bring enough along on this trip."

Again the men roared in laughter and Bartle sheepishly whispered to those around him who could hear, "That captain's a smart one, he is, make no mistake, but he has my number to be sure," and a small snort of laughter rose from the small group still loading the kegs.

Amansun watched the men and captains below as they continued to kid with each other, as the wagons and carts were slowly filled and secured for what he guessed would be a very long journey. The noisy bumping, laughing and singing slowly faded into a soft whisper as he felt a cool breeze start to pick up.

When Amansun opened his eyes next, he was looking up at a dimly lit sky through the cover of firs, birches and pines. The smell of the trees was very familiar and it gave him a sudden feeling of peace, as he recognized the smells of his own field now so many miles behind him. He realized that the men from his dream did not really exist, and once again he imagined that the lack of rest and sleep these past few days was starting to make him quite mad indeed. He thought about his vision and the young captain, Hrothgar, who he suspected was a decent fellow and someone he would enjoy meeting in real life.

CHAPTER 11

Sitting up from his hidden hilltop position, Amansun scanned the distant bluff and forest's edge to see if there were any signs of the wood elves from the previous night. While there was no movement to be seen, he imagined it was very likely that there were numerous sentries on watch looking out at the plains even now as he sat there. Not knowing if he would be passing through this way again, Amansun decided it would be best to not give away the secret of his hiding spot, so instead of just flying off he decided he would slowly walk down to the northern side of this hilltop and then take flight from a spot where it would be difficult to be seen.

Being quite large and immensely heavy, dragons don't move particularly fast when they walk from place to place, so this was a slow and arduous task for Amansun. He really was in no particular hurry for the time being anyway, still dreading his trip into the Black Woods now just a short distance away, so he took his time heading down the side of the hill, being careful to stay under the cover of the trees as much as possible along the way.

The new day appeared to be quite pleasant from what he could see, and the cool breeze from the night before had given way to a very mild morning. Amansun could see various animal tracks as he made his way down the hill, and the trees were full of the sound of birds singing, but he saw nothing stirring larger than a field mouse as he made his way. He imagined that any animals in the area must have been terrified to see a dragon in their home, and he guessed they had all moved on as quickly as possible before this slumbering giant decided it was time for a meal.

Once he had reached the bottom of the hill, Amansun surveyed the land and decided this was as good a place as any to take flight. Beating his great wings, he slowly lifted off from the sandy floor of the plain and made off in a northerly direction, deciding he would prefer flying over the forest from a spot further away than where he had seen the wood elves enter the night before, as he did not care to have any pointy arrows flying up at him as he flew by.

Once Amansun had headed north for a few miles, he changed course and headed directly due east towards the Black Woods. In just a few short minutes he was leaving the comfort of the sandy plain behind and flying over the dark denseness of this old forest. Still wary of foes that may want to shoot him out of the sky, Amansun kept to a reasonable height above the trees' canopy. From this height the woods looked less foreboding than they had just the day before, and he soon realized that while much denser and darker than the forest he was accustomed to back west, these woods actually looked similar and the rise and fall of the treetops was just as predictable as the woods of home. He noticed that the trees here grew together very closely, leaving very little space for the rays from the sun to penetrate the depths of the wood. As he slowly flew mile after mile into the heart of the woods, he noticed he couldn't see anything below other than the constant blur of trees passing by. No warm inviting fields. No silvery patches of river. Just the endless patches of black, gray, brown and green that changed as he passed.

Looking ahead as he flew, Amansun could see that this wood went on as far as he could see and there appeared to be small mountain ridges as he passed along, as he found himself having to fly higher and higher the further east he flew. After a time he glanced back towards the plain he had slept on the night before and realized that not only had he come a great distance so as the plain was quite shrunken and nearly out of sight, he had also risen in altitude a good deal. Swinging his head forward, Amansun saw that the one constant that hadn't changed was the immense snow-covered mountains off in the distance. These still appeared to be far off and they had grown even larger and taller if that was possible. The Black Woods seemed to stretch out all the way to the base of the mountains until the color of the treeline changed and turned to a brilliant shade of forest green.

Seeing nowhere to set down for a break, Amansun decided his only course of action was to just keep flying. As the rhythmic beating of his wings and the soft whisper of the breeze lulled him into a dreamlike state, he pressed on unconsciously now, not really paying attention to much other than the gently rolling trees below and the shiny whitecapped mountains ahead. Up and down Amansun's massive wings beat again and again as his thoughts faded back and forth, like the waves surging then retreating endlessly on the shores of a distant land.

Amansun found himself standing perfectly still in the shadows of the woods, trembling as he stared out past the small meadow he was waiting in. He had been separated from the others who had joined him this day, and he was now left alone, looking ahead into the darkness of the thick patch of trees that the rest of the group had disappeared into. To his left were a group of saddled horses, huddled together and peering in the direction of the trees. He was leaning forward with his ears perked up, trying to detect any sound from the darkness ahead, and the horses beside him were nervously stomping at the ground and fidgeting about.

Out of the blackness he heard a snapping sound, as if something quite heavy had just stepped upon a twig and had it break under its weight. Suddenly the pack of horses reared up on their hind legs as one and charged off in the opposite direction from which they had all been staring. Amansun quickly glanced at the bolting horses heading one way, then glanced back into the darkness where the snapping sound had come from. Still standing perfectly still as if frozen in ice and unable to move, he now saw the outline of something quite large just ahead in the shadows. The unmistakable sound of a low guttural growl permeated the air and before he could react, he realized that an immense gray wolf had stepped out into the meadow not twenty paces from him. Before he could even think about turning to run or defend himself the beast was upon him, teeth gnashing together and claws tearing into his chest.

As Amansun struggled to push the wolf away, he heard bowstrings being released and then felt the hairy beast suddenly go limp. The entire weight of the animal fell atop him as he was crushed to the ground, and he felt the warm trickle of his own blood as it spilled across his limbs. As he lay there in shock and pain he started to drift in and out of consciousness, and he thought he heard a familiar voice calling out his name and telling him to lay still. Glancing up towards the sky, Amansun looked from beneath the enormity of the wolf and saw Hrothgar, the captain from his last vision, standing over him with bow drawn and an arrow ready to fly, aimed at the beast that now covered him. Again and again, he heard his name being called out, first quite loudly then getting softer and softer as his eyes slowly closed.

Suddenly glancing forward and realizing that he wasn't high enough to avoid hitting the next range just ahead of him, Amansun broke right with his wings by dipping his right shoulder down steeply, and he banked in a slow arch as he glided up and over the row of trees he had nearly flown into. He was beginning to get used to having these strange visions, but now they were not only starting to come more frequently but also in broad daylight when he wasn't even asleep!

Amansun puzzled over the meaning of these visions. He was starting to think that someone or something was trying to enchant him and possibly take over his mind. His mother had warned him that there were spirits, sorcerers and enchantresses out in the world, and that he was to stay alert for these magical beings at all times. He shook these thoughts off and focused on his flying once more, taking a moment to get his bearings straight now that he was out of his daydream. Amansun wasn't sure how far he had actually flown by now, but he could tell by the angle of the sun that he had been flying at least past mid-morning while being distracted with his visions and fantasies.

Up ahead he saw a clearing in the trees for the first time, as he rose over the ridge and started to glide down towards what appeared to be a sizeable valley. There was an open field at the center of this valley, and being the only clearing he had seen all day, he decided this might be his one and only opportunity to set down for a rest. Circling the field a few times, Amansun scanned for any hints of trouble. From this height there was nothing to be seen, so he slowly tightened the arc of his circles as he descended lower and lower until at last he was just a few feet above the tallest of the trees on the boundary of the field. With one last look around, and still seeing no signs of danger, Amansun gently beat his wings up and down as he lowered himself to the ground.

As the giant dragon set down on the field there was a sudden rush of small animals all scattering for the safety of the trees. These were mostly rabbits along with a family of field mice, a large skunk, and a pair of foxes that had been busy trying to stalk the aforementioned mice up to the point where the sky had darkened, and they had all froze when they saw a gigantic dragon heading in their direction. Not knowing quite what to do with the unexpected arrival of this great winged serpent, this last group of creatures had been paralyzed with fear, and they all stood as still as statues in a garden up until the last moment, when they realized that the beast was going to land right next to them and there was no apparent option other than running for their lives.

With two feet firmly planted on the ground, Amansun looked about at the field he now stood in. Aside from the scrambling of animals which he had expected, having been through this many times over the years, there appeared to be no direct threats to him, at least for the present time. Not seeing any water nearby, Amansun guessed that he had flown a bit too far north now and that the Silver River was likely due south of his present location. Being somewhat tired from his flight and in no mood to wait for an ambush from some unforeseen enemy, Amansun called out in the direction of the trees and asked if there were anyone there who would be willing to engage him in conversation. This was of course polite dragon speak for "I have some questions that need answering. Are there any among you brave enough to speak with me, or have you all scattered by now?"

To no surprise, there were a few moments of complete silence. Amansun sensed that there were still creatures in the area, but he was relatively certain none of them would be willing to give up their locations or actually speak to a dragon so unexpectedly. He looked off into all directions waiting for a reply and finally started walking off towards the southern side of the field, having given up that any would accept his offer.

As he slowly walked across the field, his acute hearing picked up a small, faint voice from behind him. As he turned and looked back, he swung his massive head from side to side, trying to determine where this voice had come from and more so who it belonged to.

He began to think that perhaps he had just been hearing things, or even more likely, maybe he had just drifted off into another of his curious visions. Just as Amansun turned to start walking across the field again, the same faint voice spoke out, but this time just a bit louder than before. "I am willing to speak with you, Sir Dragon," the voice went on to say. "Turn, and you and I shall have a chat."

Turning in place once again, Amansun spun around to see who was addressing him. "Show yourself, stranger," he called out to the voice. "You have nothing to fear from me if you mean me no harm and do not try any trickery upon me."

"I am right here, Sir Dragon, right in front of you even now," the voice went on to say.

Still not seeing anyone or anything in the direction from whence the voice was coming, the puzzled beast went on to say, "Be you a strange creature with magic powers? Surely you must be invisible, for even now in the clear light of day I see naught in front of me."

Now chuckling, the mystery voice stated, "I am not invisible, nor am I a magical being either, good dragon. If it pleases you, please look straight down below you at your feet, as I am not hiding from you and am in fact in plain sight even now." Lowering his head and staring nearly directly at his large, clawed feet, Amansun could now see that there was a field mouse bowing low just in front of him, right arm tucked to his chest as he lowered his head, nodded, then raised himself up again. "I am but a plain and simple field mouse, Sir Dragon," the mouse continued. "I am not worthy of conversing with one such as yourself, yet no others were willing or able to face you, so I am taking it upon myself to stand in where others would not."

"You are a very brave mouse indeed," Amansun stated, "and I would be happy to confer with you now, as I am not from this land and I am in need of some counsel and direction."

"I am happy to oblige, kind Dragon," the mouse went on to say. "It will be the highlight of my family's honor to serve one such as you, even if only in a small capacity such as giving directions to you on your journey."

"Well, before we exchange any further pleasantries and commence with proper introductions, Sir Mouse, let me first ask if you are aware of any adversaries in the immediate area I should consider dangerous at this juncture?"

"There are none here that you need fear, Sir Dragon. Except for old Milo the skunk, of course, but he has just run off anyway." He gave out a large laugh. "He is one of my dear friends, it is true, but even I fear him when he has eaten a bad patch of daffodils."

"Well, if that is the case, and I am in no immediate threat of harm, good mouse, then let me introduce myself. I am called Amansun and I have traveled many days on a quest that takes me through your fair woods." Amansun was truly impressed by the courage shown by this little mouse ,and he felt he would be in no danger offering his name to one with such valor.

Bowing low once again as before, the mouse, bending nearly over to the point where his nose was about to touch the ground, stated calmly but firmly, "I am Radibus, son of Radington, grandson of Barrington."

"I am pleased to meet you, Sir Radibus," Amansun offered. "I am just passing through your woods and have settled in your field for a short rest and to get my bearings. I am headed in an easterly direction and would welcome any advice you could give me on how to make for the large lake that I am told lies near this location."

"I am but a simple field mouse, I am afraid to say," Radibus replied. "I have lived in this beautiful field that we now stand in my entire life, as did my father, and his father, and his father's father and so on. We are not large or worldly creatures, so we keep to what we know and seldom travel more than half a day's journey from the safety of this spot."

As Radibus spoke, the long whiskers on the end of his nose twitched up and down as if they were dancing on the breeze. Amansun thought the small mouse quite charming, and he was amazed how fearless this small creature was. He thought back to his own field so far away now and realized that he had made the right decision rushing to warn his friends of the impending raid. Even though he was now on this impossible quest and barred from his own home, he knew he would not have been able to live knowing that his small friends had all perished because he had not risked warning them.

Amansun thanked the mouse for his trouble and did his best to make him feel as though he had been helpful in at least some small measure. "You have been very kind and welcoming all the same, Sir Radibus, and I thank you for taking the time to confer with me here in your lovely field. Once I have taken a short rest I will be on my way once again, and it is likely that there will be others who will be able to point me in the right direction."

"Of course, that's it!" the mouse exclaimed happily as he grinned from ear to ear and hopped about in place as he clapped his hands together. "Others can show you the way." He looked lost in thought. As Radibus stared off into the distance of the trees, as if searching for some unseen friends to emerge, he flicked his tail forward and caught it in his hands, which he had been rubbing together up until this point. Now slowly running his hands over and across the end of his flickering tail, the field mouse looked up at the dragon and stated, "I may not know what lies beyond the edges of my field, Sir Dragon, but I know who will. Indeed, this individual likely knows every inch of these immense woods from one end to the other."

"This is great news indeed," Amansun answered. "When will I be able to meet this individual, and do you think he will be willing to help me?"

Radibus continued to wring his tail in his hands now, a little firmer than before, now staring off again towards the ring of trees surrounding his field. "It is likely that they will be suspicious," he half-muttered to himself while his nose twitched and his tail flicked from side to side, trying to escape the clutches of his own hands. "Yes, this may prove to be tricky at first, but I think we can make this unusual meeting take place without too big of a commotion."

"You said 'they' just now, kind mouse," Amansun said, now growing a little more concerned and unsure of the actual merit of this unexpected meeting. Up to this point he had already been stalked, chased, shot at, and perhaps followed by some unknown magical creatures that glowed in the night. Meeting a group of unknown strangers in these odd Black Woods now seemed anything but exciting. "I don't want to put you to any bother," he continued. "I am just passing through and do not want to cause you any inconvenience after all the hospitality you have shown me, kind mouse."

"Nonsense, good dragon," the mouse replied. "Any friend of mine is a friend of my friends, and these creatures are among the most intelligent and honorable one could hope to meet. It is true, they will be quite startled to see one such as yourself sitting here in our small field, a very unlikely meeting to be sure, but that is not to say they will be entirely upset. It has been several generations in my family, I am certain, since one such as yourself has passed through this way. I am not sure exactly how they will react when they see you here, but we will worry about that when the time comes. For now we should see to it that you have the opportunity to rest, since that is the reason you settled into our field to begin with, is it not?"

"You are too kind," Amansun responded. "I would enjoy a bit of rest, it is true, although I am unsure how restful I will be in this unknown land, even if this clearing is quite lovely and seemingly welcoming."

"You have my word on my father's honor, Sir Dragon. No harm shall befall you while you rest in my field, of that you can be sure." And with that, Radibus gave a sharp whistle and almost immediately a troop of field mice, all of the same approximate color, build and look of Radibus, appeared in two well-spaced rows, all at attention, facing the dragon and his new friend.

"All present and accounted for," the mouse closest to Radibus shouted out as he snapped his heels together. "What does his Majesty bid?"

"Post your men at each quarter of the field, Captain Barding," Radibus announced in an unexpectedly clear and demanding tone while sheepishly smiling in Amansun's direction. "Make sure that no creature, large or small, makes it into the perimeter of our field without my knowledge. We have a guest who needs some rest, and it is your new task to assure that he is neither bothered nor threatened while he takes repose here in our field."

"It shall be as you command, your Majesty," the captain promptly stated. Just as quickly as they had originally appeared, the field mice now all scattered away in every direction, as silently as the mist that creeps in on a cool midwinter's eve. Amansun and Radibus were once again standing in the field completely alone as before, though the dragon eyed his new friend with a new look of wonder and puzzlement.

"Just a simple field mouse, are we?" Amansun said as he lightly smiled and chuckled.

"Well, it is true that I am but a field mouse, Sir Dragon," the mouse replied. "It is also true that I am the king of my field, but I thought it not much of a title to one such as yourself, who claims respect and fear from all he comes across based on your size and appearance alone."

"I am honored to meet you just the same, Your Highness," Amansun stated as he now bowed before the tiny mouse. "I thank you and your people for your offer to watch over me, and now feel that I will be able to shut my weary eyes for a bit, even though I am quite unfamiliar with my present surroundings. What of the meeting between your friends and myself that you mentioned earlier?"

"Best you just rest and relax for now, good dragon," Radibus answered. "It is still early in the day, and these travelers will not venture near my field until day's end, when the shadows start creeping."

"Then wake me when I am expected, your Majesty, for I am unaware of how many restful nights I will have in the days ahead, and I am only too happy to take advantage of this highly unexpected but fortuitous meeting today."

"Rest well and fear not, good Dragon, you are now in the care of the Radibus clan and no harm shall befall you while my troops stand guard," Radibus confidently affirmed.

Amansun made his way to a large patch of clover and wild grasses just at the edge of the field where he could lay half in shade and half in sun, as was his custom. Glancing about the field using his keen, piercing eyesight, even from here he could see tiny bodies standing at attention all around the perimeter of the field, staring in every possible direction. As he lay there and glanced up at the clouds slowly rolling by in the sky above, he felt a sense of ease and carelessness that he had not felt for some time, and he allowed himself to drift off to sleep.

CHAPTER 12

Amansun woke abruptly with that eerie feeling one has when they wake suddenly while away from home and realize they have no idea where they are. As he lifted his head and looked about, he saw a large field in front of and around him, surrounded by trees. His first thought was that he was back in his own field, and he glanced about for his old friend Barnby the owl. Instead of the familiar sounds of the cool running stream and the chatter of animals moving about, searching for tender pea shoots and nasturtium seeds, he saw the silhouette of a small rodent standing naught twenty paces from him, eyeing him carefully as he began to raise his immense body into a standing position.

"I thought it best not to wake you, Sir Dragon, as you were obviously in a deep sleep," Radibus stated. "You were tired indeed and at times your body twitched and tensed as one having an unpleasant dream."

Amansun continued to look over his surroundings, remembering all that had passed these past few days, along with his earlier conversation with the field mouse now walking over to where he was standing. "I don't think I have slumbered that deeply in many days, your Majesty," he said as he watched the mouse approach, having quickly remembered that he was in fact speaking to a king of sorts. The day had moved by quickly and the last rays of sun were leaving as the sun sank far off to the west. The evening air was just beginning to cool and Amansun felt a faint chill on his skin as he noticed that Radibus' sentries were still frozen in place. "It appears as though I have managed to sleep through the entire day, your Majesty," Amansun shared.

"It was a very peaceful and uneventful day all the same, Sir Dragon, so fear not as you missed nothing of importance, and you have proven to me what a true friendship we now have. Only one who completely trusts another would have slumbered so long and deeply as you have just done. The confidence and trust you have shown me and my clan are the greatest honor you could have given us."

"And you and your clan have proven yourselves to me as well. For I must admit I have not slept that soundly in many days, and no harm came upon me, as was promised. Even now I see that your troops are watching over me, though they must have stood silently at their posts this past half a day or more."

"It was our honor to do so, Sir Dragon," Radibus squeaked, overcome with pride. "Let it not be said that the smallest among the creatures of these woods cannot prove useful to even one as mighty as yourself."

"Truer words were never said," Amansun replied. "I am blessed to have found a friend such as yourself, and make no mistake, I will return the favor someday if ever the chance comes."

"We ask for no favors from you, good dragon, and you owe us no debt. Just know that we will always be here in this field ready and waiting to assist you as we can, if ever the need comes again in the future." Amansun looked down at the small mouse once more, even more amazed now by the humility and compassion shown by this king, and thought how awfully lucky he had been to choose this field of all places to land at this time in his journey. "Darkness approaches, Sir Dragon, and I have been thinking of how best to introduce you to the friends I mentioned earlier in the day. While it appears that you are truly a friend and one to be welcomed with open hands, your appearance is nevertheless quite fearsome, and I think it prudent that you stay somewhat out of view whilst I explain our situation to the travelers."

"Clearly I am trusting in your wisdom, your Majesty," Amansun replied candidly. "I know not who comes to this field and they be your friends alone, so I will take heed of your advice and follow your direction as best I can. Clearly it will be nigh impossible for me to disappear in this flat field, hidden from view."

The mouse rubbed his chin ever so gently as he took in the dragon's words. "I believe there is no need to hide you, Sir Dragon, as our guests may be startled when you do eventually emerge. My plan is to have you stand at one edge of the woods just under the shadows until I have had time to explain your presence and give our guests the opportunity to be made aware of your location."

"Then it shall be so," Amansun confidently replied. While he was unclear of how this evening would play out, he did still feel somewhat comfortable that his new mouse friend would not put him in harm's way if possible. Still, he would be very wary this night and fully intended on making his size and strength clearly known if the need arose.

"I think it best that you follow two of my men to the far side of the field now," Radibus announced. "The depth of second dark approaches and we can expect a visit anytime now. While I am the king of this field, it is true, there are others with greater domain in these woods than I, and they make it a rule to patrol all areas, near and far, to ensure that their people are safe and out of harm's way. There are many dangers in these old woods, make no mistake, and even a dragon is not the oddest thing that can be seen passing through from time to time."

Amansun saw two unusually large and somewhat round field mice marching in their direction. Once these mice had come within a few short paces of where Radibus and Amansun were now standing, they each bowed low in turn, announcing, "Harting and Feridus at your service, Sir Dragon. Please allow us to escort you to the far side of the woods where we shall take shelter away from prying eyes."

"Lead on, good sirs," Amansun replied. "Be sure to stay alert and ahead if you intend to lead, as I do not wish to step on either of you as we walk. I suspect my paces will be somewhat larger than yours." He smiled.

With a few nervous glances between the two mice, they both realized the truth in the dragon's comment and offered, "Perhaps it best that you do the leading, Sir Dragon. We'll stay behind and protect the rear, as it were." They chuckled.

Amansun started to pace across the field as slowly as he could possibly manage, and he had to do his best to not laugh out loud as he heard the two mice behind him, huffing and puffing as they did their best to run at full speed to not fall hopelessly behind the slowly moving dragon. Once he and his escorts had reached the far end of the field, they requested that Amansun move the bulk of his immense body up under the trees so as to blend in with the edge of the wood. By this time it was quite dark indeed, and it was very difficult for any of them to see completely across the length of the field with great clarity. Amansun, having eyes more finely tuned then even the great eagles of the far north, was still able to make out the silhouettes of Radibus and his band of soldiers as they stood nearer the far edge.

"Won't be long now," Harting the mouse commented aloud.

"They come pretty much at about the same time every evening, they do," answered Feridus.

"Perhaps we should stay still and quiet," Amansun suggested. The truth was, not only could he see the shapes of the field mice across the field, but also his keen hearing was able to pick up even the faintest whispers and conversation coming from that side. Amansun had begun to get the impression that perhaps Harting and Feridus weren't exactly Radibus's best soldiers and that these two were likely offered up to "escort" the dragon merely to get them out of the way from the action taking place at the other end of the field.

"Yes, yes, right you are, Master Dragon," Feridus chimed in.

"Not another peep from any of us, to be sure," Harting added, now trying to look very serious and alert as he caught himself nearly dozing off, now that his long day of standing watch was over.

The three of them had only been standing there in the darkness of the wood's edge for a short time when there appeared to be a disturbance at the other end. Amansun thought he heard new voices drifting out across the field; muffled and quite soft, yet different, he was quite sure, almost melodious in tone, and graceful even at this distance and at this muted volume. "So, the rumors are true then, good king," one soft voice was uttering.

"'Tis been many passings of the seasons since one of his kind passed across our skies, much less lighted down to speak with those who dwell in this wood," said another.

"Your scouts were correct indeed," Amansun heard Radibus's voice whisper. "Even now he stands just across the way."

"And how can we be sure that this is not an ambush or some sort of magical trickery?" the first voice replied once again.

"Clearly my men and I, along with our field and all who dwell here, would have surely been roasted by now if this dragon meant us any harm," Radibus's voice went on. "He is surely a clever and honorable dragon, or I have no sense of character at all."

"Well, let's bring him out and have a look at him, then, shall we?" a new third voice chimed in. "Certainly he is at least looking to seek our counsel, even if there are other ulterior motives behind this unusual beast's actions."

With that last comment there was a brief pause of silence, then Amansun clearly heard the voice of his new friend Radibus as he called out across the darkness, "Come out into the field, Sir Dragon. There is no one here who wishes you harm, and they are anxious to meet you."

"I will come into the field as you request, your Majesty," Amansun called over, "but perhaps your friends will meet me at the center of the field as well, as neither of us have had an opportunity to see the other as of yet?"

"This is a fair request and one that I would have asked myself if the tables had been turned, I am sure," the first voice spoke out. "Come and we shall see this majestic beast together with our own eyes, now that we have come this far."

As Amansun and his two escorts made their way towards the middle of the clearing, he looked out and saw not three but an entire troop of figures, twenty at the least, slowly emerging from the darkness of the trees at the opposite side. He could see that these strangers were quite tall, nearly six feet in height, and also quite thin from what he could gather. Their clothing matched the colors of the field and trees behind them so well that they almost appeared to be at one with their environment, as they gracefully covered the distance between where Amansun was and where they had left the trees.

As Amansun continued to make his way across the field, his eyes began to pick up subtle bits of detail from the approaching group. These were not men as he had first guessed, nor were they wood elves which had been his second guess, having encountered some of these just the evening before. No, he thought, these are real elves, descendants from the great elf tribes of the northeast. Each elf had a longbow hanging across his back along with a full quiver of arrows, and he was glad to see that none of them had their weapons drawn, which further put him at ease over this unexpected meeting.

When both parties had met at the approximate center of the field, they stopped marching and stared across the last forty paces between each other. "Sir Dragon," Radibus called over across the short distance. "It is my pleasure to introduce you to one of my greatest friends and allies here in the woods, Eoren, captain of the elves of the Black Woods, guardian of the western boundaries of this land."

Amansun looked over at the lead elf, dressed in green and brown garments from head to toe. The elf captain had brown boots on his feet with matching brown leggings, a green long-sleeved shirt with matching green gloves, a light coat that seemed to change from light brown to light green as the elf stood there in the faint breeze, and a green tufted hat. The only piece of clothing that did not blend in perfectly with the darkness of the wood and the night was a small brooch, which was fastened at the shoulder where it met the elf's chest. It appeared to be shiny, as if made from silver, and it looked to be a clasp of some type, most likely used to secure the elf's coat in place. "If this elf, and his troop joining him here in the field, is a friend of yours, your Majesty," he said, "then let me extend my friendship and greeting to them as I did to you not half a day earlier when we first did meet."

Amansun continued to look over the group standing before him. All were of approximately the same build and height and in fact most had very similar outfits on, though he observed some of them had opposite color patterns on their pants, shirts and gloves. All had the same color-changing coats on with the same silver clasps. The only real difference he could plainly see was that their hair, which flowed out from beneath their small hats and cascaded down their shoulders, varied from blonde to brown to black. Indeed, the color of their hair seemed to be the only real way to tell one from the other.

"My kinsfolk and I are pleased to meet you as well, Sir Dragon," Eoren answered back calmly. "It has been some time since one such as yourself has come this way, and it is truly a rarity that we find ourselves standing here now speaking with you in peace, as we have in the past encountered naught but fighting and battles of great endurance amongst your kind in the past."

"That may have been the case in past encounters, I would imagine," Amansun replied, "but I am merely passing through your lands and have no intention of harming any or being harmed myself, if that outcome is possible."

"Then truly this is a momentous occasion for all involved," Eoren exclaimed as he smiled broadly at the beast. "Let us each thank our mutual friend and ally, good King Radibus, who managed to arrange this meeting so that no unnecessary harm or misunderstanding could occur between our parties. We had been expecting the worst, truth be told, and expecting a battle at the least." He laughed aloud.

"This is a night for celebration, it be true," Radibus added as he smiled from ear to ear, looking at the elves to one side and the dragon on the other in turn. "Let us build a great bonfire in the center of our field so that we can all see each other more clearly, now that greetings have been extended." Radibus called out to his men and directed them to fetch what wood they could gather so that a large fire could be built.

"There is no need for your men to be troubled searching for firewood, your Majesty," Eoren announced "Let my elves do the gathering, as we are larger in force as well as size, no offense meant."

"Surely your men are as mountains compared to mine," the mouse king admitted, "but don't be so fast to judge the size of my army." With that, Radibus called out to his mice in the field, and in seconds there appeared a sizeable host of mice of every shape and size. For one moment it appeared as though the very ground itself was moving, such was the number of mice at Radibus's command.

"I am astounded by the size of your army, it is true, good king," Eoren said as he smiled at the leader of the field mice. "Yet you are not the only ally here that came ready for battle this night." With that, the elf lifted his right hand to his mouth and gave a swift series of whistles, using his fingers and tongue in a unique fashion. Suddenly the edge of the woods began to rustle as if a sudden gust of wind had suddenly sprung up from the calm evening. From every side of the field a large host of elves, all dressed in the same fashion, most with bows drawn and arrows at the ready, appeared in unison, all converging upon the center of the meadow. As the host of elves gathered around the group already standing at the center of the field, the size of Eoren's force was now plainly in sight. Not twenty or thirty nor even fifty, but two hundred elves had appeared within a moment's time.

The leader of the elves looked proudly upon the dragon, and with a warm smile stated, "We elves never take our foes for granted, Sir Dragon, nor do we show our true force lest we give too much advantage away at the start of a battle." With this, all the elves that had by now formed a large circle around the mouse king, Amansun, and the mouse army, all hung their longbows over their backs and smiled, seeing that no battle was needed.

Radibus, surprised and quite impressed by the size of the elf army gathered in his field, smiled at his friend Eoren and graciously countered, "Clearly your group is larger than mine, old friend. You may have the honor of retrieving the wood for our bonfire…just be sure not to step on any of my troops as you do it!" He laughed.

The captain of the elves spoke softly to those closest to him, and immediately a group of no less than fifty elves vanished into the woods without a sound. In no time at all the elves returned from the woods, each with an armful of tree branches and pieces of wood of various sizes, from a few inches to several feet. Some of the elves had broken into pairs and were now carrying logs of great size as a team. The elves arranged the wood into an impressive pile in the exact center of the field and then slowly retreated several paces. Amansun, wanting to be of some help, offered to light the bonfire with his breath, but the elf captain would have none of it. "You are the guest of honor at this gathering, Sir Dragon," Eoren stated. "Just relax and we shall tend to the fire."

Eoren lifted his arms in front of himself and with a gentle waving motion of his hands softly uttered, "Ilumeneth arboretum." Immediately a soft glow of red, yellow and orange sprung from the very center of the woodpile, and almost instantly the entire pile of wood and branches burst into flame. Within moments, the group gathered together in the field were seeing each other clearly for the first time. Elves, mice and Amansun himself all glowed in the warmth of the fire's radiance, and all present looked upon the immenseness of the winged serpent standing in their midst in awe.

"Very impressive," Amansun uttered aloud unintentionally. "I have heard of elf magic, it is true, but never have I met with your kind before, and that was the first time I have seen wood burst into flame as quickly as if ignited by dragon's breath."

"We still have some power over the elements, it is true," Eoren countered, "but I am afraid we have lost more than even I can remember over the centuries since our fathers first arrived on these shores."

Eoren next motioned for some of his men to step closer and remove their hats so they could be properly introduced to the dragon. As a group of four elves moved up from the edge of the circle, Eoren removed his own hat and then announced each as they stepped forward to bow to the dragon and mouse king in turn. "Eonus, my brother, our most able archer," Eoren announced as the first elf moved forward, his long brown hair pouring over his shoulders. "Hyaclis, our best scout, able to track a black wolf's path even in the darkest hours of second dark," he went on next. As the third elf approached and removed their hat, Amansun saw that the elf was in fact a woman of great beauty, with blonde hair braided like a golden bracelet and pure eyes of blue that pierced into him as she stared. "Aarowen, daughter of our king, wise beyond her years and able to see visions of the future unseen to all others." Lastly, the fourth elf appeared and it was once again another woman, this time with black hair as dark as the night itself. "Mythra, my cousin from the eastern woods, faster than any man I have and able to run for days with no rest if needs be."

"You are as I had imagined," Aarowen said softly, her eyes still focused on the dragon's, piercing right into his thoughts. "I had a vision some time ago in which I met one that looks just as you, although I only imagined it to be a dream since we never see your kind. It is likely years untold since our kinds have met in such fashion, if ever."

"It is true," Eonus spoke in turn. "Aarowen told our council of elders that a creature such as yourself came to her in a vision, but even the wisest of them never believed that it was more than the imagination of a young girl, even if she is the daughter of our king, Eorethroughs."

Amansun looked uncertainly at the elf king's young daughter and shifted uncomfortably, as his mind raced with notions and questions as to why his appearance may have been foretold by this maiden's visions. "Clearly your visions have a purpose greater than any of us can guess," the dragon spoke aloud as he glanced at the elves standing amongst him. "It may be more than chance that brought this group together here in this field in the midst of this great Black Woods, but I am sure only time will tell what that purpose may be."

The small group gathered together at the center of the field fell silent upon hearing Amansun's heavy words. "'Tis true that only time will tell what has brought a cast of individuals such as we together this night," King Radibus echoed in agreement. "Whatever secrets the future may hold, let us be thankful that for now we all face each other as friends, not foes, even if for only a single night."

"Well spoken, King Radibus," Eoren added. "But for now, I suggest we gather in a smaller number to discuss what little we can, based on our limited time spent together. I am sure we all have questions for each other, and it is best that these thoughts be kept to as small a group as possible. Besides, it would seem prudent that we organize our troops into a defensive posture now that we have lit up this field for all to see, friend and foe alike. I would gather it has been many years since any has seen this part of the forest lit up bright as day at second dark."

The mouse king, Amansun, and the four high ranking elves standing with Eoren all nodded in agreement with this wise and thoughtful suggestion. In the excitement of this strange meeting, they had never bothered to notice that the small field they now stood in was likely drawing much interest from those that lived in the woods, and it was impossible to know who or what might be lurking just outside the circle of light that now sent sparks soaring up into the air high above the tops of the trees, as the numerous branches and logs in the fire crackled and sputtered in the otherwise quiet evening.

Eonus and Hyaclis walked over to the elves standing closest to them and explained that they and the rest of the elves were to spread out into the woods and along the perimeter of the field to create two circles of defense, so that the council taking place in the center near the fire could continue without interruption or threat of attack. With lightning speed the words were passed from elf to elf and in no time at all the field was now empty of elves except for Eoren and his four leads.

Radibus, not wanting to be outdone, called his senior field mouse Captain Barding over and gave him instructions to send his troops out into the night as well. "Be sure to send out scouts well into the woods in all directions to make sure that none can see or hear what is being discussed this evening," he directed.

Soon the small group of seven were standing alone in the center of the field, just far enough away from the fire to not feel the great heat being fanned out in all directions, but close enough so that they could still look into each other's eyes. "I am quite certain that, like us, you are wise enough to not share intimate thoughts and details with complete strangers," Eoren stated while looking into the eyes of the large dragon just yards away from where he now stood. "Clearly none of us can be completely honest or straightforward with the other in a situation such as this, yet hopefully we can find a way to share some information that will be helpful and not harmful to the other, so that we can part company at the end of this magical night feeling good about the other's intentions."

"I agree that none of us present appear to be fools," Amansun remarked while smiling at the others, "and you are indeed accurate in that I am in no position, or state of mind, to tell you any more than the simplest of details at this juncture of our short-lived relationship. Still, I have been impressed beyond belief by the courage and hospitality shown to me by good King Radibus since our first meeting earlier this day, and your decision to send all your troops back out into the field and woods to defend our position certainly puts me more at ease. I am quite confident that had you meant me any harm this evening, you certainly would not have sent your archers away, leaving the rest of you quite unprotected against a creature of my size and abilities!"

"Then as it seems we are all in agreement that there can be at least some conversation shared between the three parties gathered here," Eonus offered, "is there anything you can or would be willing to say that might help us understand how it is that we are now standing here in this field, deep within our own forest home, speaking to one such as yourself? As my brother has stated, the daughter of our king, Aarowen, foretold of your coming, yet none of us knows or could guess how or why you are now here among us."

Amansun glanced at the elves gathered about him as well as the almost unseen mouse king, who even when standing at full height was just visible in the flickering light of the fire, and thought for a moment before answering the question. "Suffice it to say that I am here in this part of the land on personal matters of my own, and that my business lies east of where we are now gathered. It is purely by chance that I happened to touch down upon this field, and had it not been for the friendly greeting of good King Radibus here, I would have been well on my way before this chance encounter could have ever been realized."

"I agree that you believe your visit to be pure chance, good Dragon," Eoren softly added. "Yet it is clearly evident from the vision seen by our own good Aarowen that this chance encounter was not only meant to happen, but had to happen whether it was known to any of us or not." As the captain of the elf troop stared deeply into the intensely burning fire as if lost in his own thoughts, he suddenly turned his gaze to the elf king's daughter and whispered just loudly enough so that only those present could hear, "Tell us of this vision that you saw, Princess. Is there more to the vision that you can recall or share, now that your dream has come to pass?"

Aarowen stated, "This is clearly the dragon that came to me in my vision. I do not know why he is here, what he plans on doing, or why we have all been gathered together though."

"That's very encouraging," Mythra blurted out quite unintentionally, "but that doesn't seem to help any of us with understanding any better what this all means, now, does it?"

"That's no way to speak to our princess," Eonus snapped back while shooting a warning glance over at the visiting elf. "Keep in mind that you are a stranger in these lands, here as a guest, and we are not known for allowing our royalty to be insulted without repercussion!"

"I'm sure she meant no harm," Princess Aarowen chided. "I can understand that she and the rest of you as well were probably hoping for some type of explanation for what is going on."

The princess suddenly stood up straight, arched her shoulders as if stretching, raised her hands in front of her chest, the fingers from each hand stretched out and touching the fingers from the opposite hand as if forming a diamond, and began breathing deeply as if putting herself into a deep trance. She stood there for some time like that, her hands touching each other as she breathed more slowly and deeply each moment, appearing as if she was standing in the field completely alone without a care or concern, as the others watched silently, patiently, waiting to see where this was leading.

Aarowen suddenly opened both eyes, opened her arms up to her sides, and gazed up at the stars flickering brilliantly up in the heavens high above. As she lowered her gaze back to the individuals gathered about her, focusing last on the great dragon now intently gazing down upon her, she stated, "I cannot guess how this dragon fits into the vision I saw some time ago, but I do believe he is somehow involved with the return of a mighty king to the kingdom that lies east of us at the feet of the Granite Mountains. Though the vision is still quite vague to me now, I have seen the dragon, a mighty warrior king, and a castle of incredible beauty and grand scale all flashing in my thoughts, though the details are unclear to me, and I am not sure how these things relate to each other."

"Surely you can't be speaking of the castle that lies just east of our woods, Princess," Hyaclis mumbled, the first time he had felt obliged to say anything this evening. "The men of that castle already have their own king in place, as well as his queen and their royal family."

"You are correct, indeed, Hyaclis, as our elf chieftain in our area of these Great Woods meets with the king from time to time," Mythra added. "Though they are not close, they do maintain a relationship so that there is peace between our peoples."

Aarowen, still looking at the others as if still in a trance or off in a distance, whispered, "There is another even grander castle that lies further east of our woods. It sits right at the base of the Granite Mountains, hidden in the Emerald Forest, out of sight. It is there that the king will be returning, although I don't know how I know these things."

"But how does the appearance of this great dragon fit into the return of a king still unknown to us in a far-off castle that none of us have seen or ever traveled to?" Eoren asked. "Is there anything from your vision you have left out or perhaps failed to share up to this point?"

Aarowen slowly turned to face the elf captain, then said very softly, "There is another piece to the vision I have kept to myself until now, Captain Eoren. In my vision I also saw two mighty forces engaged in a massive battle in a strange land unknown to me. In this battle there are elves and men fighting side by side against a host of dwarves and dark creatures from the south. A young but brave and valiant knight who rides upon a white stallion leads the men and elves, and he is dressed in a fine suit of armor bearing the standard of a charging white lion upon a brilliant sun. They are facing an evil force bearing north from the Southern Lands and I fear their leader is the Dark Underlord himself." She now trembled with those last words.

Eoren suddenly moved forward towards the princess and softly whispered, "That's quite enough for now," as he carefully glanced over at the dragon that had obviously heard every word uttered. "We all agreed at the onset of this dialogue that we would only share what we feel we are comfortable sharing, and I believe we may have crossed over that line just now."

Amansun glanced down at the elf captain and offered, "No harm done, I am sure, good Captain. For one, I know nothing about a great warrior king. Second, I have never encountered or engaged with any men. Lastly, I am sure my kind are quite unwelcome amongst castles, kingdoms, or any other lands where men are present. Your princess's visions don't appear to have anything to do with me at all. I know no kings of men nor do I plan on engaging in any battles with an underlord whom I have never heard of before."

"That may be true, indeed," Eoren countered, "but it has been some time now since a truce has been in effect between the men who live east of our woods and our own colony that calls the western portion of the Old Great Forest and Black Woods our home. We have no intention of stirring up any ill-will towards our elf brethren, and while it has been decades upon decades since elves and men last fought, those wars were particularly bloody and vicious and neither side is anxious to see a feud develop once again. Besides, I don't recall you stating exactly what your business east of us was, and unless you are now willing to share that information with us, I think it best that we bring this evening's conversation to an end. We cannot be part of any type of actions that might be considered harmful to the men who live east of our colony, and I am quite certain that our bothers who live in the Eastern Woods, where Mythra comes from, would not want to be implicated in any kind of plot either."

"While I can understand your concern, good Captain," Amansun responded, "I am still not able to share my personal matters with you and your friends, so I would agree that it appears the time for conversing is ended and we best go about our separate ways whilst we still consider ourselves friends of a fashion."

Radibus, who had been quite excited by the day's events up until these past few moments, was quite upset and disturbed to see these new friends suddenly growing apart at an alarming rate, and decided it was time to jump in and stop the bleeding before there was any real damage done. "It has been quite an exciting and eventful day to be sure," the mouse king stated. "As we are well into the evening now, it would appear that all parties have said all they care to say at this time. As Amansun is our guest for the evening, I suggest we leave him to the field so he can rest and recuperate before he starts off once again on his journey in the morning."

"That sounds like a splendid idea indeed," Hyaclis offered. "I will join my men in the woods and ensure that the field is kept safe until Amansun departs at daybreak."

"I will also take up a position at the edge of the field myself, good Dragon," Eonus added. "Rest assured that nothing shall bother your rest while you remain here in King Radibus's home."

"I believe we will all say good night for now, Sir Dragon," Eoren and Eonus chimed in. "This was certainly an unexpected and unusual night to be sure, and one I am sure we will all remember for some time to come. Forgive us if we don't say goodbye in the morning, but some of us will be spending shifts on watch throughout the night so it is likely we may miss you when you depart."

"My thanks to all of you, then," Amansun replied. He thought about asking the elves for some direction on how to proceed to the lake and castle where he might be likely to find the princess he had been sent to claim, but decided it would be the wrong thing to do since the elf captain had already made it very clear that he did not want to create any incident against the men of the east that might be seen as harmful to them.

As the five elves made their way across the field, quickly blending into the shadows of the woods, King Radibus walked over to the dragon and offered his apologies that the evening had not gone quite as well as he had expected. "Things certainly started off well, one would have to say," he cheerfully remarked.

"I think the entire evening was actually quite a success, all things considered, your majesty," Amansun countered. "After all, none of us knew the other as of a few short hours ago, and you certainly can't expect perfect strangers to be sharing all their personal secrets and thoughts."

"True you are, Sir Dragon," the mouse uttered, "and yet I can't help but feel as though I may have let you down this evening. After all, you were hoping to get some directions to a lake, as I recall when we first met."

"That is quite true, good mouse. I was hopeful that your friends might be able to point me in the right direction of the lake, said to be somewhere east of here."

"Well, I can't say with any certainty," Radibus said while rubbing his chin once again while squinting into the now dying fire. "It would seem that the lake shouldn't be too hard to find, considering that the river runs from east to west just below our present location, and it would be my guess that the river must flow from that lake at some point, shouldn't it?"

"That would certainly seem to make sense, my friend," Amansun said while smiling at the small creature he had grown to enjoy so much. "I will scout for the river in the morning from up on high and follow it east as you suggest."

"Just be sure to stay clear of the center of the Black Woods as you fly, if you are able," the mouse suddenly offered in a very somber tone. "There are tales of a powerful enchantress living in the blackest center of those woods, and it is said that she can control any and all who cross too close to her domain, whether it be walking on the ground or flying up above."

"I will take heed of your words, good mouse. A thousand thanks once again for the hospitality and friendship you have shown me this past day and evening."

As Radibus slowly walked away there was just the faintest sound as of wings beating in the still blackness of the sky just above the field. Amansun peered deeply into the jet-black sky and, just as he noticed three black crows flying above the field, he heard the silent pluck of bows and then the hiss of arrows in flight. Before he and Radibus could make a sound or even exchange glances, three crows fell out of the sky, each pierced with a half a dozen arrows. "Well, I guess that proves the elves are still on watch, I would have to say," Radibus chuckled aloud.

"That appears to be true," Amansun agreed. "Good night."

Looking back at his new friend the dragon, Radibus added, "I can tell you are still a little uneasy about bedding down for the night. I tell you what I can do to put your mind at ease. I am going to send up two of my best men to stand guard and keep watch over you for the remainder of the night. They will be up shortly, and rest assured you will be in good hands."

"Thanks for understanding, King Radibus," Amansun said politely as he wished the king good night.

"Think nothing of it, Sir Dragon," the mouse king offered. "I will see you in the morning unless you decide to depart prior to first light."

With that, the mouse king walked out of view and Amansun lay there with both eyes open, carefully listening for any signs of danger in the air. After a few short moments he could make out the shape of two round field mice walking in his direction. As he lay there quietly chuckling to himself, the two mice approached, bowed low, and announced, "Harting and Feridus at your service, Sire!" and Amansun closed his eyes wincing at the pain of trying not to explode into laughter.

"I guess I will be able to rest easy after all, now that I know the two of you are on watch," Amansun managed to squeak out, "Good night and I will see you in the morning."

"Fear not, Sir Dragon," Feridus replied. "None shall disturb your slumber whilst we are here on watch!"

* * *

Back in the woods under the cover of darkness, Eoren turned to Aarowen, Eonus and Mythra. Hyaclis had already made his way deeper into the woods to check on his troops circling the area. "How is it possible that you kept the deepest and most concerning portions of your vision from us until just this evening, Princess?" he demanded. "Surely you realize that I never would have asked you to speak in front of that beast had I known you were going to discuss battles and even mention the Underlord, someone who even our Majesty is reluctant to speak of when seated at the Council of Elders?"

"I apologize, good Captain," Aarowen offered. "I meant no harm and it was as if I had no choice in the matter, besides. It was almost as if I was in a dream and the words just floated out of my mouth without my ability to react."

"It has been some time since anyone has mentioned the Dark Underlord to be sure, and this was certainly the last thing I had expected to hear this evening. It has been years since anyone has even mentioned his name aloud, as I recall, and it would seem wise that we keep this matter to ourselves from this point on."

"I don't think that will be possible, Eonus," Mythra said while shaking her head from side to side. "Your princess's vision now seems much more than a simple dream, and the mention of a large battle, with men and elves fighting side by side no less, tells me that this is information that I must take back and share with the elders from my tribe. Don't you remember the poem from our youth that our sitters use to sing?"

"I was thinking of the very thing myself," Eoren admitted. "I am sure we all heard that lullaby along with the other poems and chants of old all those years ago." He recited it out loud:

When Men and Elves Fight Side by Side in Distant Lands Once More
   Against the Dwarves and Cruel Beasts from the Southern Shore

  Then Look Upon the Mighty King of Men who Bravely Leads
  A Host of Armored Knights Upon their Swiftly Charging Steeds

And Thou the Sky Turns Dark as Night the Battle Will be Fought
A Dragon King Will Need to Lead or the Fight will be for Naught

The Dark Underlord Himself will Rise to Lead His Troops 'Tis Said
Without the Flame of Dragon's Breath Elves and Men Will be Dead

"I understand that you feel you must share what has been seen and discussed this evening with your own," Eoren spoke calmly to Mythra, "but do me this one favor, lest we start needless concern amongst our tribes. Return with us to our king once the beast has departed tomorrow and we shall let him decide how best to interpret these things we have seen and heard. Once he has spoken, then you will be free to return to your home and share what you feel you must."

Mythra nodded her head in agreement and stated, "We will return with you, and after receiving counsel from your king we will set out home to share this unwelcome information."

"Then it is agreed," Eonus spoke. "I am off to inspect our troops' positions and cover a watch myself on this very unusual night. It makes me quite uncomfortable when I hear mention of the Underlord, and I want to be awake and alert just in case there are other, less friendly, beasts roaming about tonight."

"Let's all meet up here at this large oak just before first light, then," Eoren suggested. "Once we see the dragon depart with our own eyes, we can make for home and request a meeting with the king."

"That's fine," agreed Eonus. "I will seek out Hyaclis whilst making my rounds and let him know of our plans."

With that, Eoren wandered off into the darkness of the woods to have a look at their defensive positions for himself. Aarowen and Mythra sat down at the foot of the oak tree, whispering in silence and speaking of the old lullaby and other tales they remembered from their early years.

CHAPTER 13

Amansun had less-than-restful sleep that night, although he did manage to nap here and there in between his lapses of wakefulness. While the evening proved to be uneventful, he was bothered by a soft strange rumbling noise that seemed to come and go throughout the night. It had taken him some time to realize that the soft rumbling was in fact coming from his two guardian mice that were snoring in off-key notes together. Harting's snore had a sort of thin raspy sound while Feridus's was more like a wheezing with the occasional odd snort thrown in for good measure. Both scouts appeared to be passed out for most of the night and their relentless snoring put Amansun more at ease, as the stillness of the evening air had been quite unbearable.

It had been quite hard for Amansun to believe that he was lying in this field surrounded by such a large number of elves, as try as he might, he had been unable to detect even the slightest noise coming from those hidden about in the woods just out of sight from the field. Amansun had a new respect for the stealthiness of these elves, and it made him realize that even when he felt he had been alone in the past during his time away from home, it may have been possible that others had been lingering nearby without him knowing. He made it a point to remember in the future to be as quiet as possible whenever traveling or speaking when he was in or nearby woods.

As the coolness of the night deepened, as is always bound to happen when the morning approaches, Amansun realized that first light would soon be approaching. He thought of the coming day and all the endless possibilities that lie before him. As he lay there in darkness, he thought about his discussion with Radibus earlier in the evening and went over his plan to fly along the route of the river, whether he could plainly see it or not, until he was able to get a glimpse of the Silver Lake that had to be lying ahead at some point.

The trick here, he realized, was to see the lake before he himself had been seen. From the limited information he had been able to gather, it appeared that the castle he was in search of was right on the eastern shore of the lake, and it was very likely that there would be scouts that would be able to see a large beast like himself approaching from quite a distance.

Amansun reasoned that he would have to have two separate flying tactics for the coming day. As it is very difficult to see what is approaching when one is flying quite low to the treetops, he would have to fly at quite a high altitude in order to spot the lake as he approached it. He also realized that in order to not be seen he would have to approach the lake from a very low altitude, preferably as close to the tops of the trees as possible, to not be seen. This meant he would have to alternate between flying very high and very low as best as he could manage until he spotted the lake from up high and then ducked down low to approach.

Amansun looked up into the stars and listened to the soft rumblings of Harting and Feridus as they continued to sleep through the night. When he suspected that first light was about to approach, he kindly let out a short but loud snort just loud enough to startle anything or anyone who may have been close by. He knew this was likely to startle the two sleeping mice into wakefulness and, in this way, they could be at attention when their relief came by at dawn. As expected, Harting and Feridus jumped with quite a start when they heard the dragon snort. They both leaped to their feet, now standing at attention, and began walking about to give the impression that they had everything under control. Amansun made a few rumbling noises and gave a good show of appearing to be waking from a long and restful slumber.

"Good morning, your Majesty," Harting called out.

"All's well and in hand," Feridus added, snapping to attention and beaming a wide smile to the great beast.

"Is it morning already?" Amansun groaned as if in amazement. "What a restful sleep I had last night. I must be sure to thank good King Radibus for providing me with such attentive and trustworthy scouts."

Harting and Feridus grinned from ear to ear and winked knowingly at each other as they accepted the praise of the dragon. "Think nothing of it," Feridus offered.

"Just doing our duty, Sir Dragon," added Harting as they both bowed low and backed away from the magnificent beast just yards away from where they now stood.

"Guess we'll be returning to the captain for a little rest and relief, then, if you won't be needing anything further, your Majesty?" Harting said sheepishly.

"I am wide awake and quite all right now," Amansun offered. "Off the two of you go and be sure to get some sleep now that the new day has finally arrived."

"Right you are, your Majesty," they both happily agreed as they retreated to find Captain Barding. "Best of luck to you on your journey, and be sure to come back for a nice relaxing visit anytime," Feridus called out as the two faded out of view.

Amansun stood up in the center of the field now as the sun's rays began to lighten the westernmost part of the field. As he peered off towards the woods, he could clearly see the elf archers still on watch, spaced evenly about every thirty paces or so. Most were still facing into the woods where danger would be more likely to come from, but a few had turned to look into the field and get a better glimpse of this enormous beast now standing in the well-lit field.

"I suppose you are ready to begin the next leg of your journey, then?" Radibus questioned.

"Indeed," Amansun agreed. "I have been quite an inconvenience since we met yesterday, I am sure. Best I be on my way so you and your troops can get some very well-deserved rest as well."

"It has been our privilege and our honor, Good Dragon," Captain Barding boastfully admitted. "This will make quite a story for some years to come, I would imagine, and I am proud to say that I was here when it took place."

"Well thanks once again to all of you," Amansun said. "Best I be on my way now before it gets too late in the day, for I have no idea what awaits me and where I will be bedding down next when darkness falls."

"Best of luck to you, then, Sir Amansun the Dragon," Radibus said while choking back some tears. "You will always be welcome in our field and considered a friend by my people. Remember to be watchful when flying over the Black Woods!"

With that, Amansun walked a few paces away from the two small field mice so as to not blow them away upon his departure, and he slowly beat his immense wings together and rose into the air above the mouse king's field. He was soon flying at a height several hundred feet above the forest canopy. From this elevation he could see a few things for certain. First, the forest seemed to roll off in all directions with no end in sight. Second, the forest below him was still made up of primarily light and dark shades of green. Far off in the distance he could see that the trees appeared to be much blacker, as the top of the forest was clearly much darker. Remembering what King Radibus had warned him of just a short time ago, he made a note to himself not to fly over the center of the darkest portion of the woods as he continued east. Instead, he would choose to carefully fly at the edge of the Black Woods where the darker trees met with the light green hues of the Old Great Forest.

Amansun had a difficult time spotting the river below him, so he allowed himself to drift a bit more south as he continued flying in an easterly direction. Not seeing any signs of the river below, he decided he would have to drop down lower. After a short time, he noticed that the trees to the south seemed to be spaced out more than they had been just a few miles to the north. In time he began to see glimpses of the gray-blue river running through the woods just under the tops of the trees. "At least I have managed to find the river now," he said to himself. "Now it's just a matter of following this line until it leads me either to the lake itself or the end of the woods at the eastern end. I suppose if I run out of trees, I will know that I have flown too far, and then I will just have to retrace my steps and look a bit further north and south until I find the lake."

As Amansun continued his flight, his thoughts shifted from past to present to future and back again. It was true that he had not enjoyed a peaceful sleep, but fortunately for him he had managed to nap much of the previous day away in the king's field while he was waiting for his meeting with the elves. Still, flying non-stop can be quite tiresome and before long his mind was once again drifting in and out of consciousness. As his thoughts drifted, so did his flight path. While he was still managing to keep an easterly bearing, he gradually began drifting northwards again. After he had crossed a good deal of the forest he suddenly glanced down and realized that the trees below were almost entirely black and ominous in appearance. Glancing across his right shoulder he could see the bright green patches of forest just a few miles south from where he was currently. Suddenly feeling quite panicked, he banked to his right and began beating his wings faster than he had in some time, anxiously making for the greener section of the forest.

As Amansun flew along heading southeast, he became aware that he was talking aloud to himself for no apparent reason and with no intention of doing so. "I'm flying to the castle of men to kill or capture the king's daughter," he heard himself say. "She lives in the castle on the east side of the Silver Lake, or so I have been told." He paused. "Because I have been sent to do so," he then quietly muttered under his breath, beginning to wonder if he was dreaming again or finally cracking from the pressure of his quest.

As Amansun's mumblings continued, he began to hear or imagine a little voice inside his head asking a stream of questions to which he already knew the answers. Why was he questioning himself, he wondered? The questions continued steadily and Amansun, feeling powerless to stop them, continued to speak to himself, sometimes loudly, sometimes in just a whisper, but all the same the questions and answers kept going, regardless of how silly he thought it was or how much he wanted to stop them. "I've always lived with the colony in the Smoky Black Mountains," he heard himself say. "Yes, I am quite sure. Because I am not like the others." He was now almost yelling. "I guess I can't help but be different!"

As Amansun got nearer to the edge of the black woods where the green trees took over again, he could feel the voice in his head growing fainter and fainter. "We will meet again," he heard himself say as he finished crossing over from the black woods into the green, but he was uncertain as to whether he had wanted to say that particular statement or if he had been instructed to say it by the now missing voice he had imagined these past few minutes. Now that Amansun was once again flying directly over the green section of the forest, the voice that had troubled him had completely vanished. As his giant wings beat upward and downward over and over, he began to doubt whether he had actually had the strange experience, thinking maybe he had just been having one of his strange day dreams again. In time he convinced himself it had all been in his imagination.

As Amansun had been flying for quite some time now, the thought occurred to him that he might be getting close enough to the lake to see it from high above. With some extra effort Amansun once again started a steady climb up to a high elevation where he could see far off into the distance and yet take cover in between the passing clouds from time to time to help avoid being detected. Far off ahead lay the magnificent snow-capped Granite Mountains that were much closer than before but still a good distance away. The ring of emerald-colored trees at the base of the mountain now looked much taller and wider than he had first thought, and as he peered ahead he couldn't help but imagine the castle that Aarowen had discussed the night before.

As Amansun began to view the lands closer into his present location, he suddenly felt a wave of excitement when he realized that there appeared to be a large body of water off in the distance. As he peered ahead to be sure, he shook his head in disbelief as he realized that the end of his journey was now in sight! Not wanting to bring any unnecessary attention to himself, he flew into a thin cloud and hovered there while he surveyed the lands below. To his left and just underneath him he could see that the Black Woods ended, giving way once again to the green and yellow hues of the Old Great Forest. Up ahead the forest went on, reaching out further east until the ridge of trees gave way to a softer hue of light greens and soft browns. Amansun imagined he was seeing the edge of the forest and beyond into the plains that appeared to lie between the easternmost section of the old forest and the mountains and Emerald Forest ahead. Just in front of him, however, the forest gave way to a large body of water that did indeed appear to shimmer as if made from pure silver. To his right the green woods continued towards the south, and there he also could make out what appeared to be the edge of the forest as it gave in to the brownish plains similar to those he had flown over just two days prior.

Amansun stayed there, hovering in space as his enormous wings beat the air about him, relishing the moment. Here he was at last, within striking distance of his goal. As he squinted his eyes, he could make out what appeared to be a whitish structure clearly made by man, as it was too square and precise to be a boulder or grouping of stones sitting at the far side of the lake. "There it is," he said aloud to himself. "Now what am I supposed to do?" He surveyed the size of the lake and the distance he still needed to approach, unseen, to reach his objective. "Well, I certainly can't fly in there in broad daylight, and hovering here in this cloud is out of the question."

Amansun decided that his only option was to try and survey the lands nearby, find a suitable spot to set down until dark, and then try a scouting run to get a better idea of what challenges were ahead. One thing was clear, though; he had reached the lake and could see the castle off in the distance. He suddenly became painfully aware of two opposing feelings he was experiencing in equal measure. On the one hand, he was quite proud of and pleased with himself that he had made it this far all by himself, in spite of all the challenges he had faced these past few days. On the other hand, he quickly admitted to himself that there was no way he could go through with his quest, as it was not possible he would be able to kill this poor princess who had never harmed him in any way. This was truly a crossroads for him and one with no obvious outcome in mind.

With those opposing thoughts in mind, Amansun circled back and flew west once again, keeping his altitude in line with the lowest lying clouds as much as possible. He would drop down to the level of the treetops once again and then search the northern and southern banks of the forest for a safe place to settle down until nightfall. He flew west for a few moments until he reached a high ridgeline that would provide cover once he dropped up and over the back of it. From behind this ridge no one east of his location would be able to see him, as the top of the ridge stood high above the flat spots of the forest.

Once hidden from view behind this ridge, Amansun first flew south to see if there were any suitable places to touch down. While the trees were not grown in as thickly as they were up north, there didn't appear to be any acceptable landing spots that made him feel comfortable. He had experienced enough challenges when choosing landing sites that appeared to be safe but weren't to know better than just set down at the first clearing he found. Not seeing anything to his liking, he turned north now and flew until he was once again above the point he had originally started from. As he flew over the vastness of the forest, he noticed a sizeable clearing that was large enough to provide him with a landing spot and also hidden enough to avoid unwanted attention should something or someone else happen to be in the area. As Amansun circled over the spot a few times, surveying the area carefully, he did notice that the edge of the Black Woods was relatively close to this area, but there was enough of the green woods in between to make him feel comfortable that he would be safe settling down. Besides, he thought to himself, he was tired from having flown for quite some time now and he hadn't seen any other areas that looked any better than this one.

With very little effort, Amansun lowered himself into the middle of the clearing and looked around. Seeing nothing alarming, he decided he would walk about his chosen resting spot and make sure nothing was amiss. The clearing itself seemed quite harmless. The grasses were growing at a normal height, so he was confident no trolls had been stomping across the area. The woods that surrounded the clearing seemed normal, although they did grow together in very dense clumps in some spots that made him just a little uneasy, as he imagined there could be foes hidden deep inside them. Perhaps even an elf or two may be spying upon him right now from the darkness of the thickets. All in all, he decided this place looked all right, so he chose a soft bed of clovers as his spot to settle down and rest; not too close to the trees, yet close enough to provide some cover should someone or something happen to fly above the area.

Amansun sat in the clearing for the remainder of the day, passing the time by looking up at the clouds and seeing what creatures and other shapes he could make out. It seemed to him that he had done this sometime, long ago, yet he couldn't remember having done so. All the same, the game seemed familiar and comforting, so he sat there and imagined he could see centaurs and great black bears and other animals he had either seen or heard of. One particularly large cloud that drifted by changed shapes as the crosswinds hit it and for just a moment or two he could make out the outline of a large troll, and the thought brought back a rush of memories as he once again pictured

Gargaroth the stone troll that had almost ended his quest nearly a week ago now.

As Amansun sat there in his field, staring up at the clouds in the distance, his eyes slowly came to focus on a tiny brown spot far off in the distance. The spot seemed to be frozen in place and yet he was almost certain that it was growing larger in size, if only by a little bit, and he stared at it with great curiosity. After a moment, he was sure the brown spot was either growing in size right in front of him, or that it was getting closer to his position. Feeling more curious than fearful of the brown speck that was now the size of a small stone hanging in the air, Amansun realized that the spot was doing both, growing larger and getting nearer.

Over the course of the next moment or two he could see that the object was indeed flying in his direction, and as it grew closer and closer, he could now make out that the object was actually a very large owl, much like his friend Barnby. Caught quite off-guard by the owl's unexpected and sudden approach, Amansun didn't know what to do. The thought of taking cover under the trees crossed his mind, but he imagined it would look quite absurd to see a dragon such as he cowering in a thicket of pines to avoid a single approaching owl. *I will let this creature approach and try and determine what his intentions are*, he thought to himself. *If he seems to be a threat, it will just take one breath to dispatch of him.*

Now quite intrigued by the owl's direct approach, Amansun watched in amazement as the creature flew straight into the landing and settled not twenty paces from where Amansun was now resting. As the owl settled down, he glanced up at the dragon, waved one wing in an upward motion at him as if in greeting, and sputtered out, "Begging your pardon, your Majesty." *Cough, cough, cough.* "But I'll be needing just a moment or two." *Cough, cough.* "To catch my breath." The creature appeared to be gasping for breath and somewhat lightheaded.

"Take all the time you need," Amansun countered, "for I am just resting here and have been puzzled watching you these past few moments, as you flew directly unto my field here apparently unbothered or fearful of my size and presence."

"All will be explained." *Cough, cough.* "In just a moment, your Majesty." *Cough.* "Just another moment, please." *Cough, cough.*

Amansun sat there, looking down upon this poor creature that was obviously exhausted from his flight, and wondered to himself if this might possibly be one of Barnby's relatives from the east he had mentioned. *Is it possible?* he thought to himself. *Can they have actually found me so easily after all this time and these hundreds of miles that I have traveled since leaving Aranthus back at the hill near the black granite tower?*

"Pleased to meet you, your Majesty," the owl finally offered once he had caught his breath again. "My name is Carceren, son of Carcophus of the Lake. I am pleased to make your acquaintance."

"And I am pleased to meet you as well, Carceren," Amansun replied, still quite intrigued by this unexpected visitor. "Have you happened upon me by chance, good owl, or have you been seeking me out, as it would now seem?"

"We have been expecting you, it is true, Sir Dragon," the owl explained. "Relatives from the west flew countless miles over the past few days to alert us to your coming. We knew your goal was to reach the Silver Lake, so my relatives and I have been keeping a watchful eye out for you these past two days now. I saw you from a great distance some time ago, high off in the sky, and flew in your direction as fast as my short wings would allow." He smiled. "I had nearly reached you when you suddenly turned and flew off westward again. I have spent the better part of the past hour chasing after you, as I did not want to miss your location, having guessed that you would likely seek out a spot to rest after your long journey."

"Well, I would imagine that my friendship with Barnby of the West has led us to this unlikely encounter, then," Amansun said cheerfully. "You and your kind have been quite gracious and helpful to me since I left my home some time ago now, and I am quite pleased indeed to meet you here, as I am a stranger in these lands and have in fact no one I can turn to or confide in for counsel or advice."

"Well, I am glad that I found you this day, then," Carceren replied. "'Tis true that these lands can be quite welcoming to some, and quite inhospitable to others. I am hopeful that you were not seen by others, but only time will tell. Though you were difficult to spot once hidden in the clouds, I must admit that I was able to detect your flight quite easily even from a distance. Although I was warned of your coming, of course, and was in fact keeping an eye out for you, knowing you would be approaching from the west as you did."

"That would be unwelcome news to be sure, if I was spotted while making my first approach to the lake," Amansun muttered with a look of displeasure. "It was my hope to remain unseen if possible, for I have business here in these parts that would be better suited to anonymity. I had not expected to reach the lake this day, if truth be told, and was quite surprised when I first glanced downwards and realized I was in sight of it."

"Well, we will both hope for the best, then, Sir Dragon," the owl agreed. "These lands may appear to be quiet to the casual eye, but make no mistake, there are many eyes always keeping watch, both day and night. On the eastern edge of our great lake lies the Castle Eladrias and its scouts have perches set all about the edges of the lake on all sides. The woods themselves are quite laden with elf folk, particularly on the northern shores, although their bands can be seen tracking about the entirety of the lake if one looks carefully enough."

"And those are the two forces I should be worried over?" Amansun asked of the owl.

"Those and others to be sure," Carceren replied. "Best to not forget about the dwarves of the southern lands who come up to meet with the king of the castle from time to time. It is said they do business together. And then there is the enchantress of the Black Woods. She is the true seer of these lands and one not to be trifled with. Though she keeps to her own, it is said that her powers are great and that she can travel as far as wants be should she choose. She has power over many of the creatures of these woods, 'tis said, even the trees and streams themselves if you believe the tales of old!"

"Those are quite a large number of eyes to avoid indeed!" Amansun muttered half to himself and half to the owl. "Is it likely at all that I might have not been seen when there are so many that may have causally glanced up into the sky and noticed me approaching?"

"Best we just hope for the best, Sir Dragon. No sense worrying about the things we cannot change, as my father was wont to say."

"Well, what are your thoughts and opinions then? Have you any news for me or advice that is meant to be shared?"

"None that will be of much use to you now, Sir Dragon. The only real message passed on from messenger to messenger all these past days and countless miles was that you were approaching from the west and that we were to assist you in any fashion possible once you arrived here at the lake as you have now done."

"Well, I am quite pleased to have your counsel just the same, good owl. If not for you I would still be sitting here aimlessly staring up at the sky, as I was doing prior to our meeting, waiting for day's end so I could go out for a night flight to see what was to be seen. At least now I am aware of what lies ahead, who might be out there that needs be avoided, and that I am not completely alone in these woods."

"Well as I said at the first, Sir Dragon, I have no real message to share; but counsel, that is a different story altogether. I am but a fisherman of the lake, as was my father before me and his before him, and so on and so on. But make no mistake, I have a keen eye, and there is little that takes place or that moves about in these parts that is not seen by or known to me. When it comes to counsel and advice, I have plenty to share if one such as you is willing to listen."

"You have my attention, then, good owl," Amansun said sincerely, now stooping lower to hear the words spoken by the owl with certainty. "Please do go on!"

"Well, I am certain we are both thinking that it is quite unlikely that you were not seen," Carceren began, noting that the dragon was nodding his head in agreement. "It is likely that someone or something likely spotted you as did I, but I also believe that since you departed the area so quickly, vanishing from sight over the hills here, I doubt any know of your whereabouts now."

"That would be good news to be sure," Amansun muttered, still nodding his head in agreement with the owl. "And that is in fact why I did retreat westward once again. It was my intention to hide out of sight until cover of darkness so that I could then fly high above the lake at second dark to see what the lands look like without prying eyes to see me."

"Well, if your intention was to be hidden, then I would say you have been successful in that. Since your whereabouts are apparently unknown for now, it would be my counsel that you remain hidden away here in this field, perhaps a little closer to the cover of the trees, until after I have had an opportunity to fly out over the ridge and lake areas to see what might be taking place."

"It is not my way to impose on strangers," Amansun replied awkwardly. "Know that you are not bound to me in any fashion, and I do not intend on getting you caught up with my own personal agendas."

"I do not consider you as a stranger, Sir Dragon, even if we have only just met. Like the other members of my family you have already met, we owls take great pride in all we do, and we consider integrity, honesty and loyalty to be among the most important characteristics one can have."

"Then let me introduce myself properly, good owl," Amansun said confidently now, feeling more at ease. "I am Amansun of the Smoky Black Mountains, son of Wraith, and I am here in your lands on a special quest set forth by my colony."

"I am honored to call you friend, Sir Amansun the Dragon," Carceren replied, now bowing low once more in a gesture of humility. "It will be my task and pleasure to serve you bravely and loyally as best as I am able. Please stay here in this field. I will report back to you as soon as I am able."

"Agreed," Amansun replied. "Do not put yourself in harm's way on my account if you can help it."

"Fear not, Amansun," the owl cheerfully replied. "This is my home and there are none who will question seeing me flying about in my normal fashion. You are the stranger here, so stay hidden and do not venture from this field. If truth be told, I am somewhat uncomfortable with the closeness of the black woods to this location. Be sure to keep a wakeful and watchful eye to the woods. There are many unknown dangers that lurk inside that realm, and none of my kind will fly even close to those black trees, much less into them if we can help it."

With that, the owl took flight and disappeared over the ridge. Amansun sat in his field and glanced up at the sky, noticing that it was just now starting to darken as the day passed by. He looked westward across the field and could only see the ring of trees that encircled the field where he had chosen to rest. He couldn't see the black trees of the woods to the west, but he could almost feel the darkness and intensity that came from their direction. Putting aside his dislike for being too close to them, he moved further under the trees on the eastern side of the field as the owl had suggested, just to ensure that no others flying over might spot him.

CHAPTER 14

As Carceren approached the top of the ridge that blocked Amansun's hiding spot from the eastern side of the hills by the great lake, he was anxious beyond anything he had ever felt before in his life. While he wanted to believe that the dragon had been unseen, his better judgment thought it was certain a scout from one party or the other had to have noticed the dragon flying earlier in the day. He beat his wings relentlessly, pushing himself faster than he would have normally chosen to fly, and approached the crest of the trees on the ridge and then dropped effortlessly over the eastern side, now gliding upon the wind currents towards the lake.

From first appearance, nothing seemed out of place as he glided slowly towards the western edge of the lake. Everything here seemed as it should. Still floating on the currents, Carceren glided towards the southern side of the lake and noticed almost at once that a troop of soldiers on horseback was making its way along the old dirt road that followed along the edge of the lake to one of the furthest view towers used by the men from the castle. Slowly making a wide circle around the general area where the tower stood, some fifty feet tall, made of huge wooden beams and canvas, he could see that there was quite a bit of activity going on, as compared to usual, and he guessed that the men from the castle were building up their troop size there. Not wanting to appear obvious, or risk getting shot at by a bored watchtower guard for that matter, Carceren circled back out over the water once again and this time flew off across the lake to see what might be happening on that side.

As Carceren got near the center of the lake he noticed a small flotilla of boats and counted no less than one dozen men, all sporting long bows and crossbows, apparently scanning the skies. This was something peculiar to be sure. The owl had grown used to seeing boats from the castle out fishing on the lake, but he had never seen them bunched together like this before. He kept his distance from the boats below and, when he noticed one of the men pointing up in his direction, he sped off across the lake, heading for the northernmost edge.

As the owl approached the northern edge, he once again saw a sizeable troop of mounted soldiers riding along that road as well. They were riding in the direction of the northern watchtower, he was quite sure, and this group also had several large wagons in tow, pulled by teams of enormous oxen who appeared to be laboring quite heavily under the weight of the loads they were pulling. As it was quite apparent that something unusual was going on, Carceren decided he may just as well do a flyover of the castle grounds, as he did from time to time out of idle curiosity, and he flew the remaining distance to the eastern edge of the lake.

As he had suspected, the castle grounds were a buzz of activity. Carceren had learned years ago that it was not prudent to fly too low or close to the castle walls, as he had in the past been fired at by archers and children alike. Though he had never been hit up to now, he had encountered several close calls, and he knew today was not the day to get shot down when his new friend lay in hiding, counting on his full report. From a safe distance Carceren observed that there were many of these covered wagons lined up inside of and along the outside perimeter walls of the castle. Near each wagon there were three armed soldiers sitting in wooden chairs, talking amongst themselves, just like the men he had seen floating out in the middle of the lake. Realizing the importance of his making it back to the dragon in one piece, but also wanting to gather as much useful information as possible to share, Carceren decided it would be worth the effort to get closer to one of these wagons and see what could be learned from the men stationed alongside them.

After flying overhead and carefully selecting the most suitable spot for intelligence gathering, the owl flew past the wagons below then quickly circled back in a silent gliding fashion and came to a quick rest in a maple tree with large limbs overhanging near one of the small groups of men. Hidden in the boughs of the tree, Carceren edged closer to the group, carefully walking out over one of the larger branches, and settled in for a listen.

"These be odd times an' make no mistake," one of the men below announced to the other two present. "Can't says I recall the last time one of these beasts was within one hundred leagues of these here parts."

"So, yous think it be true that one of them flyers be seen earlier taday, then?" another voice chimed in.

"All's we knows is that the captains are on their game an' we with our marching orders to sit at these wagons an' be ready for an attack, come day or night, says he," the first voice answered.

"Well, if yous asks me, fellas, I'll believes it for meself once I see the beast's yellar eyes peering down at me from on high, that's wat I says", the last voice added with a snort. "Never believes anythings ya hear and less than half 'o wat yer sees, says me ole man, an' he was quite a clever gent, was he."

"I reckon we best be ready to get this machine up an' running quick-like jus' the same, should the time a-come," the second voice suggested. "No sense takin' any chances with a flyer about, I say, an' we don't needs to be getting the capt'n on top of us neither, now, do we?" He gave a serious glance to the other two men beside him.

"That be true indeed, boys," the first voice agreed once more. "Guess there's no sense in alla us being tired now, though, is there? I suggest we take shifts on watch, ya know, like they does up over at the towers on the lake's edge, so's everybody gets a chance at some shuteye. I reckon I'll take first nap." The first voice stated this in a tone that defied argument, and with that he made himself a soft spot under the tree to rest with some blankets and his coat, and pulled his hat over his eyes.

Well, I've heard enough and then some! thought Carceren to himself. *I best be leaving now while I can still make it back to our hideout before it's pitch black. Last thing we need is for Amansun to get worried and come flying over that ridge to see what's taken me so long!*

Just above their heads, the three men heard a slight commotion and, as they turned to see what the fuss was, they spotted a large brown owl taking flight in a sudden burst of flapping. One of them bent over to pick up a rock and hurled it at the large bird as it retreated east towards the foothills behind the castle. "Probably jest heading out for an evening meal, I guesses," the man lying down grunted. "Now the two of yous, please try an' keep the racket down for awhile so's I can get some shuteye please!" he added in an unfriendly tone.

Once Carceren had managed to put some space between him and the men of the castle, he flew directly westward over the open lake. This time he would be sure to not fly directly over its center, as he didn't want to give the archers on the floating boats another shot at him. He looked ahead and could see that the sun was already setting in the west and behind him the first shadows of nightfall crept across the eastern lands. Though he was already tired from a busy day of flying, the large owl beat his wings relentlessly, knowing that the sooner he reached the field where Amansun was hiding, the better.

* * *

As time ticked slowly by back at the field, Amansun soon became bored with the idleness of waiting for the owl to return. It seemed like ages since Carceren had flown off, and even longer since he had first laid eyes on this field after retreating once he had found the Silver Lake. Knowing he was so close to his objective was quite frustrating and he started thinking to himself, "How much trouble can I get into if I just take a short flight to the top of that ridge there and peer over the other side?" These thoughts plagued Amansun for the next hour and he had to convince himself to take the advice of the owl he had just barely met and stay put.

Staring off into the distance, Amansun tried counting the trees that surrounded his field to pass the time. Every time he got up to a large number his mind would drift, and he would have to start all over again. Now, he wasn't sure which was more frustrating and bothersome—trying to keep his mind occupied counting trees, or not counting trees and continually thinking about flying off to the top of the nearby hills to peer over and see what was happening down at the lake. As he became more and more despondent over waiting for the return of the owl, he decided to come out from beneath the pines from where he had been resting on the eastern edge of the field, and he moved instead over to the trees on the westernmost side of the field. In this way, he reasoned, he would be better able to see the owl as it approached from the east.

Having relocated across the field now, with his immense body tucked just under some large fir trees as he sat on large piles of needles, he stared off into space once more and did his best to remain positive and stay focused. As his thoughts faded in and out from where he had been, where he now was, and where he would be going, Amansun drifted off into another of his now common daytime dreams.

Amansun found himself walking up a steep slope of snow-covered woods. The immense trees towering over him were blanketed in snow as well, as it was now deep into winter. Up ahead he could clearly see several large, muscular men leading the way through the knee-deep snow. Each of them was bundled up in thick furs of gray and brown and they had heavy leather boots on their feet. Across their backs they had large bows hanging at the ready along with quivers of long, sharply barbed arrows. He could also hear voices behind him, laughing and joking about as they moved along in single file. "Won't be long now 'till we reach the hunting grounds," one of the men in the lead called back to the others in pursuit.

"Don't forget that we promised we wouldn't head back until he bags his first white wolf," another called out from behind him.

"I remember," the first voice replied, laughing. "That's one proud father to be sure, and I know he wishes he could be out here on the trail with us right now instead of planning the next meeting of the Great Council."

"Well, let's be sure not to disappoint him, then," another voice chimed in. "Our king is a gracious man, to be sure, but let's not give him any reason to doubt having selected us to be the leaders on this hunt now!"

"There you go again with your negative thinking," the first voice called out, laughing along with the others. "The beasts must be quite hungry by now, and I wouldn't be surprised if they are stalking us even now," he added with a whisper.

"The whole lot of you better keep it down now!" a new voice called out confidently from ahead. "We're almost at the clearing now, and I don't want any of you fools scaring the animals away before we even get the chance for him to get a shot off."

Amansun followed the men ahead of him as they disappeared into a thicket of trees. He had lost sight of them for a moment, but it was still easy to see their deep tracks in the snow ahead. As he passed slowly through the dense cluster of trees, he soon found himself stepping into a large clearing that appeared to extend out for several hundred yards. The still falling snow began to land softly on his cheeks and hands and as he looked ahead, he thought he saw the others crouched low just ahead of him a few paces into the few remaining short trees left between the forest itself and the open field.

As Amansun looked down at the falling snow gathering on his hands, he wondered to himself how it was that he was not seeing two large taloned claws in front of him. Was he having another vision through another creature's eyes once more? He also thought it strange that the snow did not feel cool to the touch, as he was accustomed to when traveling in the upper reaches of his own home mountain ranges. As he reached out and attempted to brush the snowflakes away, he became suddenly confused and alarmed when he realized that the snow, though white and soft, actually felt quite sticky, and it appeared as though he was unable to brush any of it away. Instead, the more he brushed at the white stuff now starting to cover his entire body, the more his hands seemed to be unable to move.

As if waking from a dream suddenly, Amansun opened his eyes and realized he was nearly covered in white, stringy, sticky strands of weblike material. As he anxiously turned his massive head from left to right, as much as he was able, he noticed that it was now night, and in the darkness that surrounded him he saw the twinkling of a thousand stars, or so it seemed. Peering more intensely into the darkness under the trees, he realized quickly that he was now surrounded by massive black spiders. These were not just large but immense spiders, measuring a full three to five feet across at their widest, and each of them had an enormous set of pinchers which, as he soon realized, were entirely too close for comfort. Each spider was also busy shooting a direct spray of abdominal fluid directly at him from every side and angle imaginable.

After a few short seconds of complete panic, Amansun blew out a tremendous blast of fiery breath, turning his head from side to side. In the brilliant flash of light he had created, he could now see that there were dozens of the large beasts swarmed all around him. As the spiders closest to him burst into flame and erupted into balls of fire, the others all squealed in terror, and as he sent another burst after the retreating beasts, he lighted up another dozen or so and watched as their spindly legs and fat, bulbous bodies ignite into flame and burst apart, sending large globules of black pus and white web fluid showering across the floor of the field. The sticky web material that had been covering his body quickly burnt away from his thick skin as he continued to fire off blast after blast of dragon's breath. The only remaining spiders were now completely engulfed in flame and off in the distance he could see others, still on fire as they fled, scrambling westward as they tried in vain to escape back to the safety of their black woods.

Having gotten over the initial fear of the spider attack now, Amansun surveyed the field that had been up until now his hiding spot. All around him trees were either burning or just catching fire. Within minutes, most of the western side of the field's edge was engulfed in flame, with sparks floating off into the sky some hundred feet or so, as more and more of the woods ignited from the heat. Amansun glanced about in disbelief as he began to imagine what the scene he was viewing from up close must look like to any and all who happened to be within a few miles of this spot. He glanced upward in an easterly direction and wondered to himself where Carceren was now and how much longer it would be before his friend the owl returned.

To say that Carceren the owl, son of Carcophus, fisherman by trade, was surprised to see Amansun's entire hiding spot engulfed in flames and glowing like a summer bonfire would not do justice to the pained and shocked look on the large brown owl's face as he crested the ridge of trees heading west and got his first glance of the chaos below. "What in the world has happened here?" he squawked out loud, still incredulous as he drifted down towards what was left of the open field, peering into the brilliance of the fire amidst the blackness of the night. "Where are you, Amansun?" the owl called out again and again as he swirled above the madness below. "Are you injured?"

"I am fine," came the booming voice from below near the center of the fire. "There was a bit of trouble while you were away."

"I believe I can see that," the owl hooted out, now nearly laughing to the point of tears at the sight below and realizing that his new friend was safe.

"Perhaps we should consider choosing a less conspicuous place to spend the night?" Amansun called out to the owl now flying close overhead, grinning and chuckling himself.

"That would seem to be a wise choice, friend, as I am not accustomed to bedding down next to open flames," the owl screeched back, laughing as well. "Get out of that inferno and follow me. I know of a few places we can go that might be a little less obvious than this wonderful field you torched!"

Amansun took one last glance at the trees all ablaze about him then lifted off into the night air. Up ahead he could see the outline of his friend, Carceren, and he thought he could still hear the owl laughing as they flew off into the darkness of the evening in a northeasterly direction.

* * *

Even though Carceren flew as fast as he possibly could, it was very difficult for Amansun to stay behind the large owl, as his wingspan dwarfed that of the small bird. As they flew in silence now, their chuckling having ended a mile or so behind them, Amansun alternated between flying ahead of the owl and then swooping back behind him again and again to not lose sight of his friend and guide. "Just a little further," the owl called out to the dragon as they came in close proximity once again. "I am taking you to a safe spot where I go when I want to get away from it all."

Amansun followed his guide up and down over hills and ridges, until at last the owl began to slowly spiral downwards to the base of a large cliff. The two settled down carefully, as it was now dark and there was very little moonlight this evening to help them see. Once on the ground, Amansun looked over his new hiding place and decided that his friend the owl was a great friend indeed. Tucked into the face of the cliff there was a large indention leading inwards, much like a cave, which was large enough for Amansun to walk into and take shelter.

Better yet, right alongside the sandy beach that they now stood upon, a generous pond flowed out into the darkness. This was a great sight to behold for Amansun, as he had not had a drink of water in some time now, and he also thought it would be reasonable to expect that the pond may have some fish that he could enjoy for breakfast!

"What a truly magnificent spot," Amansun exclaimed while still taking in his new surroundings. "If I had days to myself to fly about and find a campsite, I would have never found anything better, I am sure."

"I thought this would suit you well, Sir Amansun," the owl said with a hint of satisfaction. "And this spot is made of stone as well, so you are not likely to set it ablaze as you did with that last spot!" He laughed once more.

"That was certainly unintentional, my friend," Amansun snickered. "You never said anything about boulder-sized spiders attacking. I had to defend myself once I realized they were trying to spin me into a giant cocoon as if I was nothing more than an oversized moth!"

"Well, I am going to guess that you didn't keep your eyes looking west as I had suggested, now, did you?" the owl chided in good nature.

"I will be sure to not take your directions lightly in the future," Amansun offered sheepishly. "I am quite parched with all the flying and smoke and fire and such, Sir Carceren. Please excuse me while I take a drink from that lovely pond."

"Be my guest, good dragon," Carceren exclaimed. "Just do be sure not to fall in as I won't be able to fetch you back out again." He grinned and watched the dragon as he walked over to the edge of the pond.

"Please tell me that there are fish in this pond," Amansun stated while walking to the water.

"Big and plenty, I can assure you, Sir Amansun!" the owl called out. "I have been content to catch the smaller ones that skim the water's surface, but there are some monsters in there down deeper that I think you will be able to catch without much difficulty, judging by your size and those impressive talons you have there."

After Amansun had drank his fill, he walked back up the sandy beach to where the owl was now resting upon a large branch that was sticking out of the ground. "I still can't believe those spiders came after me like that!" Amansun said in surprise.

"Those stupid bugs will attack anything that comes within walking distance of their home," Carceren stated. "They are not the brightest of creatures, to be sure, but they are quite fearless as you can attest to now!"

"Fearless indeed," Amansun agreed. "I will be sure to mind my naps in the future if ever I come across those black woods again."

Once the large dragon had settled down, Carceren turned to face him and said, "Well, I have some good news to share and also some bad news to give you. Which would you like first?"

"I suppose I will take the bad news first, if I must," the great dragon said rather sappily.

"The bad news is that from all the activity I witnessed down at the lake and castle this afternoon, the men of Eladrias Castle already know you are here in the area. They have posted extra scouts on all sides of the lake now, and I even saw soldiers and scouts floating out on boats in the center of the lake!"

"That is terrible news," Amansun agreed, looking down at the ground and shaking his head. "So much for the element of surprise, I suppose. What is the good news?"

"The good news is that, based on the enormous fire you decided to set this evening, they would have surely guessed that something was wrong anyway," he said cheerfully. "I would imagine that every living creature within ten miles of that spot saw the blaze, and is now either running towards that field to see what the cause is or running away from it as fast as possible to escape whatever it might have been that set the blaze in the first place."

"I see your point, Master Owl," Amansun said sullenly. "I suppose this is where you are going to advise me that tomorrow will not be a good day for me to go out and do a flyaround now?"

"Right you are," Carceren agreed, nodding his head violently. "I believe you will have to hole up here in this cavern for at least a few days until things settle down. It would be madness to try and go scouting after tonight's episode, even if you traveled under cover of darkness."

"I was expecting that, I guess," the dragon muttered half to himself. "At least I won't have to go without food or drink, thanks to my new guide!" He gave a big grin.

"It is settled, then," Carceren said rather directly. "Tomorrow I will fly off to see what events are shaping up once again, and you will remain hidden right here. And try your best to stay hidden in the cavern as much as possible, if I may say so."

"It's a deal, then, friend," Amansun managed to say with disappointment. "I will stay here as you suggest and once again trust in you to find out what is happening out there. Just remember to stay out of trouble and don't get yourself hurt on my account."

"It's a deal, Sir Amansun. Let's turn in for the night and I will see you at some point tomorrow, likely well into the afternoon, as I have errands to run and family members to seek out as well. Good night, then." And with that, Carceren flew up into one of the large trees that was near the cliff face and settled in for the night.

CHAPTER 15

Amansun woke up the next morning and stretched as he looked upon his new hideout for the first time in daylight. He was still in darkness, as the cave he was sleeping in went far back, providing him shade from the sun. Peering out from where he lay, he could see the blue-green surface of the pond outside, as well as the dense trees that were just beyond the pond's edge. The thought of a nice fish convinced him it was time to step out and get a better look at his new fishing hole. Standing on the edge of the pond, he could see through the clear water that it was indeed quite deep. No doubt the cliff face behind him provided a large waterfall during rainy season, and he imagined the strength of the falling water had carved out quite a deep hole into the ground beneath it. There were some very nice-sized fish in the water that would not be difficult to grab.

As he stood there, looking over the ones that were closest to his side, he spotted one that appeared to be in easy reach, and with a sudden flash of movement he had reached in, caught the fish with his enormous talons, and pulled it out to lay at his feet. After a short burst of flame and a short walk to the shady side of the beach he was soon having his first meal of the past few days. Looking about at the dense trees surrounding the pool, he guessed that the spot was indeed quite empty, as there appeared to be no easy way to get down to the pond. On one side was the enormous cliff face. On either side of the cliff there were steep hillsides plunging down from the plateau of the forest, densely covered with trees of various shapes, sizes and colors. Only on the far side of the pond, where the other two sides channeled together to form a deep valley, did there appear any real way to walk into the area.

Feeling pretty good about this new spot, Amansun wandered back into his stone hideaway and settled down for some more rest.

The previous day had been quite long and filled with tension, so he thought the extra rest would do him good. Besides, he thought as he sat there in the semi-darkness, where was he to go? He was under orders from his new friend to stay hidden until his return, and with all the excitement he had caused the previous night he knew it would be unwise to venture out.

* * *

Off on the northern side of the Silver Lake, Carceren the owl was meeting with some of his cousins. He had awoken before first light and flown to an area of the woods where he and most of his family members resided. "I'm telling you he is quite friendly, and very intelligent besides," he was explaining to the owls gathered about him.

"Easy for you to say," one of the owls muttered, "but what do you have to say about that blazing wildfire he started last night? You could see the glow of the burning trees on the other side of the ridge even from where we now sit! That didn't seem to be very intelligent or friendly, if you ask me."

"He ran into some trouble with the great spiders of the black woods is all. Quite unexpected and unintentional, I can assure you."

"Well, he certainly seems to be the type that could get us all into quite a bit of trouble, if you ask me," another owl chimed in.

"I have him hidden away in a very secluded and safe spot for now," Carceren insisted. "We won't be seeing any more trouble like that from him again, trust me."

"Well, what is the plan now, anyway, now that this beast has actually flown in and arrived as the messengers said he would? What are we supposed to do with him, anyhow?" the first owl grumbled. "What are any of us supposed to do with a dragon? He could set this whole forest on fire if he chose to do so. What can he possibly need us for?"

"I am not exactly sure, as of yet," explained Carceren, "but remember that the story shared with us is that he is a true friend of our relatives to the distant west, and they have requested that we assist him with his journey in any way we can."

"Well, I say we can help him if needs be," the second owl agreed freely. "Just be sure and explain to him that we aren't looking for any trouble, so the less reckless he is while he remains here in our land, the better!"

"Understood!" Carceren agreed. "For now, all I am asking of you is to pay close attention to what is going on up at the castle and down at the watchtowers along the lake's edge. Let me know if you see anything unusual."

"Well, we can certainly do that," another owl stated, now jumping into the conversation. "I think this is all very exciting, actually," he said with a great grin. "How often do we even get to see a dragon like this, much less get to assist one, for goodness sake?"

"That's the spirit!" Carceren exclaimed with a smile. "This should be the most interesting thing that has happened in these parts since we were all nestlings! Now don't forget to keep your eyes open and take note of what's going on out there while I am away. Let's plan on meeting here tomorrow morning once more, same time and place."

The others agreed that this would be fine, and one spoke up and said, "Until tomorrow, then. Just be sure to keep your dragon hidden and out of trouble!" He turned and flew off into the trees.

With their meeting completed, Carceren flew off alone once more, heading south and leaving the safety of the trees as he flew out over the open water of the lake. *Think I'll take one more look at those boats floating in the middle of the lake as long as I am here*, he thought to himself. Within moments the large owl was drifting with the air currents over the water from where the bundled boats were, still floating where they had been the day before, and he slowly circled over them as he looked to see what the men on board were doing. Most of them appeared to be sitting together, talking amongst themselves once more. They didn't appear to be paying any attention to him at all.

As he continued to bank slowly over the spot, now a little closer in to where the boats were anchored, he suddenly heard a very large snapping sound and then without warning an immense bolt, probably measuring some six feet or so long, capped with a shiny point, went hurtling by him just missing him by a foot or so. As he swooped higher into the air and glanced back he could see two men standing on one of the outer boats, laughing and patting each other on the back as they pointed up in his direction. Beside them was a machine he had never seen before, a large wooden device that was pointing up at the sky in the direction he had been just a moment before. Beside it was a small pile of logs, like the bolt he had just seen flying past his head.

"Guess we know this thing actually works now," he heard one of the men shout out to the others.

"Damn near hit that owl, even from this distance," the other man standing on the outer boat added.

As Carceren started a slow circle, now much higher than before as he didn't want to get hit by one of these immense arrows, as he guessed they must be, he heard another man start shouting from the group that had been seated, "What do you fools think yer doin'? Do ye think we has an unlimited number of these bolts for use to be shooting like target practice at any bird that happens to pass by? Don't be tryin' that agin or I swears I'll bolt yer both onto that machine and shoot you off at that dragin meself if we run outta bolts on your part!"

Carceren flew off and drifted out of hearing range. *Well, I guess I know what was hidden under all those tarps yesterday*, he thought to himself. *I'm lucky they missed me, but if I had been any larger, that thing would have gone right through me. I had better warn Amansun of that new weapon as soon as I get back. Even he may have some real problems against something like that.*

* * *

Back at the hideout, Amansun's large body twitched and shook as he drifted off into sleep. He had been more exhausted than he had realized and the combination of the large fish and the coolness of the sandy-bottomed cave he was now resting in had lulled him into a deep slumber in no time. *I wonder what the owl has learned while I have been hidden here?* was the last thought that crossed the dragon's mind as his heavy eyes closed and he drifted off to sleep.

Amansun found himself walking out of a dark wood into a large clearing. The earthen road he had been following suddenly disappeared into a field of soft green grass and patches of clovers, daffodils, violets and other flowers. The field sloped down towards the center where an enormous black leafless tree appeared to have sprung up from an even larger boulder that was cracked and split in several places. Large, gnarled roots burst out of the stone on all sides, and in the front of the boulder facing him there appeared to be a dark hollow leading down and into the earth below the stone. To the right of the boulder, just fifty paces or so away, a small brook burbled along, heading off into the woods at the other end of the field.

As Amansun carefully approached the tree he thought it quite frightful looking, as there were twisted and shattered massive boughs and branches reaching out into the air like skeletal hands with bony fingers reaching out to clutch at something. He could see thin wisps of gray and white smoke curling out from a hole in the top of the rock, and the smell of burning wood permeated the air. Getting even closer to the opening now, he peered down the hollow and thought he could hear someone or something speaking in the depths. "Come in, come in," a shaky, raspy voice called out. "I've been expecting you for some time now." The voice cackled. "Don't be shy, now. No one is going to hurt you."

As Amansun eyed the small entrance before him, he knew there was no possible way he could squeeze even a small portion of his large body through that small, narrow space. "I appreciate the offer to enter," he answered back in a hushed tone, "but I don't think you quite realize with whom you are speaking to. I am actually quite large, and I will not be able to get through this small entrance leading into your home."

In a very straightforward and confident tone, the voice called out once more, "Do come in and don't tarry long…I can assure you that you may enter, for I have made it so…not all things are as they appear, as you should know." The voice cackled once more in a puzzling manner.

What can this person mean? Amansun thought to himself. *Either they are quite mad, or they truly have no idea that there is a full-sized dragon at their doorstep right now.*

As he stood there outside the hollow's entrance, deciding what to say next, the voice called out again, this time in a less-friendly manner with an obvious hint of anger starting to show, "Come in now or you will make me quite unhappy indeed."

"But how?" the dragon called out to the voice inside.

"Just put one foot in front of the other and walk," the voice boomed, then added with sarcasm, "You can walk, can't you? I am becoming impatient, dragon!"

Peering at the small path leading into the hollow, Amansun decided he would at least get in as close as he possibly could. *Maybe*

I can at least stick my head into the hole, he thought to himself as he started to edge closer and closer to the hollow's entrance. The giant beast slowly edged further and further down the path, and as he slowly inched nearer the entrance to the hollow, he noticed that the edges of the earth seemed to rise to meet him and the footpath he was now following seemed to grow deeper and wider. *This isn't possible*, he thought to himself as he found himself walking down and into the cavern below. *Either I am shrinking to be sure, or the very earth and stone are growing taller and larger as I approach.*

"Just a little further now," the shaky voice said as if speaking to him with indifference. "You are almost there."

Amansun took a few more steps, and then a few more, as he glanced above him and saw that he was now inside the hollow and that the roof ceiling was now directly over his head. Looking back over his shoulder, he glanced up the footpath he had just walked down and, to his amazement, he could see that he was now well within the cavern and the field and woods behind him were above him and out of sight. "Surely this be some sort of magic spell, or I am dreaming," Amansun said out loud.

"Well, of course it's magic, silly beast," the voice in front of him said calmly. "How else could I fit a golden dragon into a six-foot entrance?"

Peering ahead into the dimly lit chamber, Amansun started to take a visual account of the room he was now in. The floor, ceiling and walls all appeared to be made of stone and earth. There were no windows to speak of, yet light glimmered in from several cracks in the dirt and stone above. There were benches, tables and shelves of every fashion scattered about the space, all covered with an abundance of glass jars, wooden boxes, bowls and such. Several of the shelves and dressers were covered with big heavy books with leather and parchment bindings. Standing in the faint light in front of him stood an old hag, bent over an earthen fire with a bubbling cauldron hung above it, appearing be mixing in various ingredients as if making a large batch of soup.

"I am Amansun, son of Wraith, from the Smoky Black mountains far to the west," the dragon spoke aloud in the direction of the old woman standing twenty paces in front of him, cloaked in ragged clothing, with gray, twisted and bunched hair sticking out from beneath a worn red scarf.

"I expect I know who you are, Master Dragon. Or should I say who you believe you are," she said, cackling once more. "Besides, that is not of importance at this particular time."

"Why am I here, then?" Amansun asked now, quite puzzled by most of what the old woman had said.

"We are destined to meet, I am quite sure, Amansun," the old hag went on. "But that time has not come yet. For now, I just wanted to meet with you and give you a gift of sorts, a glimpse of that which you seek."

"How would you know what I seek or even who I am?" Amansun demanded in a rather harsh tone now.

"Save your anger for someone else," the hag replied. "I am no enemy of yours. You have one much greater than I, to be sure, but I believe our paths are meant to cross, though, so I will share this glimpse with you now, before you decide what your next move will be."

Confused by the old woman's words still, yet wanting to see what she might be able to show him, Amansun moved a few steps closer and said, "Let's have a look, then, old woman. What it is that you have to show me?"

With that, the old hag erupted into a fit of laughter, shaking her head right and left and shaking her opened hands in the air in front of her. "Careful what words you choose to speak, Master Dragon," she warned. "True, we are not enemies, I have shared, but don't be too quick to judge a person by outward appearances alone! Step closer now. Move here beside me and look into my cauldron."

Amansun took a few more steps until he was beside the old woman, and he looked down into the large copper bowl of swirling, smoky liquid. "I see naught but swirling broth and steam," he complained.

"Have some patience, my good boy," the hag laughed. "Look deep into the depths of my pot. Look beyond the surface and steam that is the first impression you see. Look beyond the obvious!"

Feeling quite silly, and convinced he was speaking with a crazed woman, Amansun stood there peering into the vat of steaming liquid. As he looked more and more deeply into the dark liquid, he did start to see an image that was at first quite fuzzy but seemed to get clearer and clearer as he lowered his head and peered in further. Soon the dark liquid cleared away and he found himself gazing at a stone balcony, softly lit under moonlight, with a silvery lake below. There was an opening in the stone wall at the rear of the balcony, with white cloudy drapes billowing from inside, and as he gazed at the draped entrance suddenly a beautiful young woman appeared and walked out onto the balcony.

She appeared to almost float upon the stone flooring beneath her as she made her way to the edge of the stone wall that looked out upon the lake. Dressed in a flowing white nightgown, with long blonde hair softly hanging across her perfect shoulders, she gazed out at the lake below her and cradled her head in her soft hands, as her glorious blue eyes sparkled and shined like the stars filling the night sky above. He had never seen anything more beautiful or perfect in all his life! "Princess, princess!" he called out as the image started to fade. "I must speak with you, if but for a moment!"

"I'm certainly no princess," a raspy voice answered back, coughing, "and I have no intention of speaking to a half-asleep dragon either, even if we are new friends as of yesterday. You are likely to blast me into a puff of ash if you are still daydreaming, Sir Amansun," now came the unmistakable voice of Carceren the owl.

Amansun opened his eyes, and sure enough, standing just a few feet away was the large brown owl, appearing out of breath once more from an obvious long flight that had just ended. "What on earth are you mumbling about, friend?" the puzzled owl said to the great dragon lying beside him.

"Not a bother, I am sure," the dragon replied. "Just another of a long line of strange and puzzling dreams I have suffered through since beginning my journey. What news have you?" He was now coming out of his dreamlike state.

"Good news and bad news once more, I am afraid."

"Right then, let's have the good news first this time around."

Carceren relayed the latest troubling news about the soldiers in the lake and the loglike arrows. "Well, things certainly have started rather poorly, I have to admit," he replied almost comically while looking at his friend directly in the eyes with a piercing glance. "Meeting you yesterday is the only thing that has gone right since I first saw the lake."

"Not to worry, good dragon," the owl stated confidently. "You have friends now and we will be sure to help even the tally!" Seeing that the dragon was in a talking mood for now, Carceren quickly brought back the subject of what the dragon's business in the east might be. "So, you were about to tell me why you were here at the lake?" he asked in a soft, harmless tone.

Amansun looked out at the pond in front of the cave, which had turned a different sheen now that the afternoon was passing, and then turned to the owl and asked, "What can you tell me of the enchantress of the black woods? Has anyone seen her? Do you know what she looks like?"

"It's difficult to say," the owl muttered with a quizzical look on his face. "Some tales say that she has the appearance of an old, frightening woman. Others say she is a very young and beautiful woman. The eldest in our clan believe that she can take any form she chooses, such is her power."

"And is there anything else you can share?" the dragon asked with obvious great interest. "Anything about her magical powers or abilities?"

"Just that she is said to be a very powerful spellbinder and controller of thoughts. I remember hearing long ago that she was supposedly capable of bending others' will to hers, regardless of the creature or thing. Some believe that she can control the very land itself where she lives, including the trees, streams, animals, everything. Why do you ask?" Carceren studied the face of the large dragon beside him, who appeared to be hearing everything he said and yet looked as though he was far off, lost in his own thoughts at the same time.

"Never mind why I ask," Amansun replied, now appearing to be back in the moment. "Just curious, I guess."

"Curiosity kills the cat," Carceren said with a small grin.

"Well then, it's a good thing that I am not a cat, isn't it?" the dragon said while smiling once more.

"And as for your business here?"

Amansun looked at the owl standing near him once again and appeared to be having a battle with himself on the inside. Every time he appeared as if he was about to speak, he would suddenly shake his head back and forth and grunt softly to himself. Finally, after what felt like ages, the dragon sat up straight, looked into the owl's face, and started talking. "We have only known each other for two days now, yet in this short time you have proven to be a very good and helpful friend. On top of that, I have always had great luck in friendships with your kind, starting with my great old friend Barnby the owl from where I originally come."

He paused for a moment. "Still, there is much I can't tell you, and much that is simply best you do not know. For now, let me just say that I have been sent here to complete a special task. This task involves my meeting with the princess who I have been told lives in the castle at the east end of the lake. That is probably more than I should share for now, but I feel I owe you at least that much for all the trouble I have already put you through these past two days."

The owl gazed back at his friend the dragon with a look of despair and sighed. "This presents a great challenge," he mumbled, almost as if he was talking to himself rather than the dragon. "I had a hunch that your business had something to do with the castle, or the men that live within, but I had no idea your goal was to meet with the princess!" He shook his head in disbelief.

"I realize this is going to be a difficult challenge," Amansun countered, "but then, I never said my task was an easy one either."

"Not easy!" the owl repeated. "Not easy!" He now studied the dragon's face in the hopes that he would suddenly burst into laughter and announce that the idea was just a made-up joke of some sort to distract him from the truth. "Burning the watchtowers to the ground, now that would be easy. Setting the lake on fire, that would be easy.

Meeting the king's daughter? Now that's going to be a challenge and then some, mark my words! It's said that the king values his dear daughter above all else. How are you, a dragon, and a giant one at that, supposed to meet with the daughter of the king?"

"The two of us are quite clever," Amansun said, looking at the owl with an encouraging smile. "I am sure that between the two of us we will think of a way for this meeting to take place!"

"Well, even though I must admit that I am sorry I asked the question in the first place," Carceren muttered, "at least I have a much clearer idea of what it is you hope to accomplish here. Now I can let my cousins know what we are up against! I will meet with them early tomorrow morning once more—the time and place have already been set—and I will ask them to help me keep an eye out for the princess… see what she does, where she goes, how she gets there, that sort of thing." The owl now started to look much more focused and positive. "Have no fear, Sir Amansun!" he suddenly said with gusto as one who has finally decided to take a great leap off a high cliff into a pond below. "If there is a way to make this meeting between the two of you happen, then we will find it!"

"That's the spirit!" Amansun cried out in triumph. "I too believe that together we will solve this puzzle and then I can make the first part of my task come true."

"The first part?" the owl whined now, looking over at his friend and looking deflated once again.

"Yes, the first part!" Amansun said jokingly. "Have no fear, you said, remember? Don't worry about what comes after the meeting because, truthfully, I haven't figured that part out yet myself." He grinned at the owl from ear to ear.

"On that note, I do believe I will step out to the pond and catch something to eat for dinner," the owl said in an obviously puzzled and lost tone.

"Let's do that!" Amansun agreed confidently. "I have already spent too much of this day hidden here in these rocks, and I would like to enjoy the last rays of sunlight today before darkness closes in upon us."

With that, the two friends made their way out to the edge of the pond and started looking for supper.

CHAPTER 16

Early the next morning, Carceren met with his cousins once more. There were now eleven owls present, rather than just the original six from the previous day, as word had spread that something big was afoot, literally, and they wanted in.

"You were quite right about the men being busy getting their watchtowers filled up," one of the younger owls present stated. "I flew around the entire lake yesterday, and everywhere I went, I saw archers and soldiers hidden amongst the trees and boulders, as well as their watchtowers where we are normally used to seeing them."

"Same thing goes for the castle," another replied. "I have never seen so many soldiers lined up inside and outside of the castle walls. It looks as if they are getting ready for a battle."

"They are preparing to defend the castle, not to do battle," came the voice of Melanter, an old owl that had flown in to see what all the fuss was about. "Everyone is talking about a dragon hidden in the hills to the west of us now, even the men and elves. I haven't seen this much scattering around of men since the old battle with the dwarves of the south some decades ago now. You should have seen the numbers of soldiers that were gathered for that war," he said as if picturing the war going on in his mind. "That was back before this king's time, back before the truce between men and dwarves."

"Well, we have all seen and now agree that the soldiers of the castle are out and about," a new voice jumped in. "But what, if anything, are we supposed to do about it?"

"Glad you asked," Carceren said, smiling. "I met with our dragon late yesterday and I have more details to share with you all now." He looked around at the owls gathered about. "I can't say exactly what we are to do, but I do know I need your help."

"Well, let's hear it, then," one of the owls said rather grumpily. "Why don't you get to the point and be done with it?"

"Yes, yes, of course," Carceren stated, giving the owl a wicked look now. "I was just about to before you interrupted! What I need from you all is to help survey the castle and the areas surrounding it, keeping a particularly sharp eye out for the king's daughter. Our friend the dragon has personal business with her, and he needs to know her whereabouts."

"So, it's to be a raid on the king's daughter, then?" Melanter blurted out while shaking his feathers about and stretching out his immense wings. "That would not be a good thing for any, I am afraid, and I don't think we should be helping if that is his intention."

"I didn't say anything about a kidnapping or raid, and neither did the dragon for that matter!" Carceren said quickly, now trying to lessen the impact of Melanter's unexpected comment. "He merely wants to speak with the princess, that is all. I am sure he has no intention of hurting anyone if he can help it."

"Well, I for one have no intention of getting in between the meddling of a dragon and a human king," Melanter quaffed, as he slowly raised himself up off his haunches, turning to fly off. "Have a care what you get started here this day," the old owl called back over his shoulder as he flew off into the woods.

"I'm not looking for any trouble either," one of the younger owls stated. "No one said anything about getting involved with the king or his daughter." He too turned and flew off.

"Well, if you are here to help, then settle in closer to me so we can discuss our plans," Carceren advised the group still remaining. "I am not asking any of you to do anything you are not willing to do, and there will be no disgrace in leaving if that is your choice."

There were some whispers shared between the owls remaining as they broke into smaller groups and muttered softly between them. After a few moments, four of the remaining owls stated that they had no interest in going any further with the group and they flew off together. As Carceren looked about at the remaining owls, now totaling five in number, six with himself, he summoned up his best cheerful and positive demeanor and said, "Our numbers were entirely too large for a covert operation anyway! It's for the best that we keep our group small so as to stop any word from leaking out as to our plans and ambitions."

The ploy worked, as the five remaining owls all looked about at each other, nodding their heads in agreement, as they settled closer in to where Carceren was perched. "Some of the youngsters would have just been in the way," Bathis the owl said matter-of-factly.

"And I for one am happy to see the old-timer gone as well," replied Methistus, one of the older owls present but not nearly as old as Melanter had been. "That old meddler would have been trying to boss us about, no doubt, and we would have been bored to tears listening to him tell his old war stories over and over again, as he is wont to do when given an audience." He laughed, then went on to Carceren, "Lead on with your meeting now. Those of us remaining are here to the end, and we will do what needs doing to help this beast out." He looked intently at the others.

"So it is," Carceren agreed, looking quite pleased now, as the apparent unraveling of his small band appeared to be at its end. "Let's discuss who is to go where, and what needs to be done."

* * *

While Carceren was busy laying down plans to spy on the princess, Amansun was just starting to stir back at the cliff's cave, having slept quite soundly after gorging himself on another one of the large fish that lived in the depths of the pond. As he moved his immense body out towards the cave's entrance, still hidden in shadows, he looked out and could see that though he had slept in, it was still early in the day and the trees that ringed the pond outside were still mostly covered in shadow. Peering out to make sure he was still alone, as his friend the owl had requested of him, he was surprised to see movement at the far end of the pond. As his eyes began to clear from sleepiness, he could now clearly see that there was a small group of centaurs gathered at the foot of the pond, having a drink and splashing water over their faces as if trying to freshen themselves.

Now, Amansun had encountered these creatures not long ago during his journey, and he had found those he had met to be quite hospitable and friendly; but he had no intention of making himself known to this group, here so far from where he and Arxes had met. Stepping back ever so slowly and carefully, he edged back into the cliff's face, all the while keeping a watchful eye on the group who were clearly unaware of his presence. All was going as he planned when suddenly the air filled with a large *snap* as his retreating feet stepped upon a branch that had been lying on the ground unseen to him.

Amansun glanced back to where the centaurs were standing and could see that they were now all staring right at him where he stood, still in shadow, but not yet within the cave's recesses. "Don't make a move," he heard one of them quietly say to another from across the water. "Perhaps the beast has not noticed us here!"

"I think it best we turn and run for the trees while time still remains to do so," another whispered.

"Hold your ground and keep your spears at your sides!" another, deeper and more confident voice said with authority. "His kind are not known for fearing the likes of us. And besides, it is said they are unnaturally clever and curious creatures, it is likely he will not hurt us until he has determined who and what we are."

Not knowing what else to do, and realizing that he and his hiding spot had clearly been discovered, Amansun spoke in as softly and non-threatening of a voice as he could muster, "Yes, I see you all there, and no, I don't intend on harming any of you if you can assure me of the same."

"The beast speaks our language!" one of the centaurs whispered to the others in amazement.

"As I had suspected all along," the leader's voice replied calmly, no longer bothering to whisper.

Stepping forward to the very edge of the water, ever so slowly, the largest of the group lifted his hand in greeting fashion to the dragon, saying, "We are here at the pond merely to quench our thirst, for we have been out gathering food since first light. We knew not of your presence until just now and in no way want to cause you any harm or disturb your morning."

"I am here merely resting myself," Amansun replied. "It was my intention to stay here unnoticed until ready to move on, though clearly my secret is out."

"Your secret is safe with us, I can assure you," the centaur in charge said earnestly. "We only pass through these parts on occasion, as we live some distance from here, and we have no ill-will towards you, nor would we gain anything by disclosing your whereabouts to any."

"Indeed, I would like to take you at your word, good centaur," Amansun stated while stepping out a bit further from the cliff's hollow. "For I had become quite comfortable in this spot and am unlikely to find it's equal. Yet it is difficult to trust in the word of strangers when one is in unfamiliar territory.

"So you know of our kind?" the centaur asked respectfully.

"Yes, I do," replied the dragon. "I actually have several centaur friends in the lands far west of here. An entire village, you could say." He smiled.

"We keep to ourselves for the most part," the centaur answered back. "These lands were once friendly in years past, but now it is difficult to trust in the kindness of strangers, as you yourself have stated, Sir Dragon. What may I ask are the names of your centaur friends of which you speak?"

"None that you would recognize, I am sure," Amansun said. "These friends live further than you can imagine, I would guess, back over the barren plains west of the forest you live in. Does the name Anthroughs mean anything at all to you?"

All of the centaurs in the group began to whisper amongst themselves excitedly, stamping their hoofed feat and looking over at the dragon with wide open mouths and looks of bewilderment. "Did you say Anthroughs?" the centaur in charge asked in apparent amazement.

"Yes I did, Anthroughs," he repeated. "My friends from the west told me that should I in fact run into any of their people while visiting in this land, I should mention that I am a friend of the Anthroughs clan of the west."

Clearly he had hit a nerve with the small group of centaurs across the water, as they were now huddled about in a circle, whispering among themselves, occasionally glancing back at the dragon to see what he was doing. "We too are of the Anthroughs clan!" the elder centaur said proudly now, raising his spear high in the air. "If you be a friend of the Anthroughs clan of the west, then also shall you be greeted as friend to the Anthroughs clan of the east," he announced loudly, now shaking his spear up and down while the others around him did the same. "May we approach your side of the pond and introduce ourselves, Sir Dragon?"

"Please do so," Amansun said kindly while smiling. "If you are anything like my friends from the west then surely you are honest and trustworthy yourselves."

Three of the centaurs, including the main leader, walked around the edge of the pond while the other four remained at the far side, still apparently in shock that not only did he know their language, he had also named aloud one of their most important ancestors who had been in these woods hundreds of years earlier. Once the centaur trio had made it to where Amansun was standing, now fully out of his cliff side cave, they all bowed lowly and paused there, apparently waiting for the dragon's blessing to rise once more. "Please do rise," Amansun said uncomfortably. "No need for all of that, I am sure."

The largest centaur stood and, looking squarely up at the dragon's eyes, said, "I am called Eodren and these are my sons, Eldenham and Articlese." He pointed to each of them in turn.

"I am Amansun of the West, son of Wraith and Scythe," the dragon shared in return. "I am pleased to meet you all." He laughed. "And I am pleased to see that only one of you has a name beginning with an 'A'!" The three centaurs looked at him puzzled and he went on, "Forgive me. I don't mean to imply there is anything funny about your names. It's just that the group I know in the west seem to have an entire village with names starting with 'A.'"

The three centaurs standing in front of the dragon all smiled as one and nodded their heads, now understanding what the joke was about. "It is true, indeed," said Articlese, still chuckling himself. "Even here in the east, many of my friends and cousins have names as such."

"And more proof to me that you do speak the truth, sir Amansun, as how else would you come to know such information should your words not be true!" said Eodren.

"And what of the others remaining at the far end of the pond?" Amansun asked.

"Forgive them, please," Eodren said, "for they are thrilled to see you here in these woods but are not quite ready to approach one as large and powerful as you, even from afar."

"That is fine and no harm done," the dragon said while smiling at the small group now huddled even closer together at the opposite side of the lake. "Always time for introductions later."

As the three centaurs stood there, gawking at the immensity of the beast now standing not thirty paces from them, Eodren asked, "If it is not too much to ask, good dragon, may we ask how it comes to be that one of your kind is now taking shelter in these woods after so many years have passed in between seeing one such as yourself?"

"I am sure it is a rare sight for you," Amansun replied, "but where I come from, we dragons are as numerous as the fish in the pond behind you. I am here on business of a personal matter which I cannot share, but I can tell you that I am merely passing along and will be well out of your territory soon enough."

"Begging your forgiveness for my direct question, Sir Amansun," Eodren said while bowing once more, "but it is just such a wonderment to see you standing here, in the flesh, as you are. I assure you that you are welcome to stay here at the pond and even in the entirety of these great woods, as long as you please, I am sure."

Looking down at the red-faced centaur, Amansun replied, "No offense taken, I can assure you, good centaur. I would imagine I would have been caught quite off-guard and speechless myself had the tables been turned."

Not knowing what to say next, or how to make up for having so bluntly questioned this enormous beast who had been so surprisingly hospitable, Eodren bowed once more, nodding at his sons to do the same, and said, "With your leave, then, Sir Amansun, my party and I will be leaving the area now so as to not disturb you any further." They began backing away from the dragon.

"That is fine, Eodren," Amansun replied. "And I have your word and the word of your sons and fellow travelers to keep my whereabouts unknown, then?"

"I give you my word and the word of my people, both present and within the forest throughout, that your location and presence will remain unknown as you had intended, good dragon."

"Then it's been a pleasure meeting you this fine morning, Eodren and sons Eldenham and Articlese. Keep in mind that a dragon remembers things for a lifetime, and we are not likely to forget those who cross us," he added while smiling yet seeming quite serious at the same time.

"Your meaning is well understood, Sir Amansun," Eodren said while making direct eye contact with the dragon. "Your secret is safe with us, as I have now sworn, but have a care to stay hidden well in your chamber there. Our gathering party noticed a small number of elfin scouts passing through the woods not far from this valley, and I now guess that they may have been seeking out your location, if that be at all possible?"

"Well, thank you indeed, then, for the warning, Eodren of the eastern Anthroughs clan," Amansun said graciously. "It is possible that some unexpected fireworks the other night may have given me away to some degree or another." He now looked about the area much more closely than he had before.

"I am happy to have helped you in some small way," Eodren answered back, now turning nearly forward to start making his way back around the pond's edge. "I hope our paths cross again someday," he added as the three now trotted off to the group on the other side, then disappeared into the wood.

Amansun walked up to the water's edge, drank deeply, then turned and made his way back into the relative safety of his stone hideout. He had a look of great concern, his forehead now wrinkled as he squinted his eyes while looking out at the dense trees surrounding his pond. *Guess there'll be an elf behind each and every tree now, or it will seem, I am sure, every time I step from this cave*, he thought to himself, now less than pleased at the mention of the elf scouting party. "Perhaps they are out looking for something completely different," he muttered aloud to himself, not even believing his own words as he shook his head from side to side and continued studying the trees in the distance.

* * *

As Carceren the owl glided down towards the sandy beach area just outside of the hideout, his eyes were immediately drawn to a number of tracks seemingly pointing in many directions, including heading towards and also away from the cliff's face. Now dropping a bit lower, he flew off to the far side of the pond, where an even greater number of prints seemed to point in every direction possible, some larger than others, some smaller, and many directly on top of the others, as if a great dance had taken place in that very spot since the time he had left earlier that very morning. Turning and swiftly covering the distance between the far end of the pond and the cave entrance on the opposite side in quick fashion, the large owl swooped into the mouth of the cave located there and called out his friend's name in alarm. "Amansun! Amansun, are you still here?"

"Right over here," came a bored voice from the rear of the cavern. "I've been sitting in here for some time now, not wanting to venture out since earlier this morning."

"What in heaven's name happened outside?" the owl demanded while selecting a spot to set down. "It looks as if you threw a great party outside whilst I was away!" The owl groaned. "More small problems?" he said while snickering at his friend who looked anything but happy.

"This time I really had nothing to do with it!" the dragon said grudgingly. "I was just minding my own business when I was spotted by a band of food-gathering centaurs!"

"And I suppose you were hidden away within this cavern when this all took place?"

"Well, almost," the dragon said now grinning. "You never did say that I had to stay inside the cave *all* the time."

"Oh bother!" the owl said while laughing once more, seeing that his friend was safe and not harmed. "Tell me all about it, I suppose, so we can decide what needs to be done next!"

Amansun spent some time explaining exactly what had taken place while the owl was away, and when he was done telling his story, the owl shared his morning news with the dragon. "Well, I guess it has been a very exciting and eventful day for both of us!" the owl joked once they had each finished telling the other their stories. "The centaurs are a quiet bunch, I must say, and quite hard to figure out as well, but it is said that they are loyal to a fault and once they have given their word it is as if written in stone. We shan't have to worry about Eodren and his clan. However," the owl continued, now not looking quite as pleased, "the part about elf scouts on the prowl, now that is something we should be concerned about."

"Do you suppose we will have to move, then?" Amansun asked in a rather bothered tone. "I was really starting to enjoy this place."

"This is as good a spot as any I can find," the owl said matter-of-factly. "Unless you think the elves are actually out hunting you for some reason, we may as well stay put until we hear otherwise."

"The only elves I know are over a day's flight from here. I can't imagine any of them have made it out here that fast, and besides, I can't think of any reason they would be out searching for me anyway."

"Well, if that's the case, then we will stay put as I said," Carceren assured the dragon. "No sense giving up a perfectly good hiding place just because some curious centaurs stopped by, and elves are apparently searching for you nearby. I doubt that they would think of looking for you down here, and it's likely they would have spotted you by now if they were still searching in the area. I guess things will still work out. This just means that there will only be five of us spying on the castle now instead of six," he said as if talking to no one in particular. "I will have to post a sentry in the trees outside of your hiding spot from here on out."

"Is this the part where you tell me that I have to stay hidden in this cave *all* the time now?" Amansun said knowingly.

"That's why you are such an intelligent creature." The owl laughed. "You're practically a mind reader, you are!" With that, the owl flew off once again, promising to return before dark, and Amansun settled back into a comfortable resting position, knowing he was grounded in the cave for good or at least until his personal guardian arrived.

CHAPTER 17

With the sun beating down outside, the interior of the cave warmed up a bit and soon Amansun found himself fighting to keep his eyes open. Between the boredom of being trapped inside, and the comfortable temperature of the air in his makeshift den, it was only a matter of time before the great beast nodded off to sleep.

Amansun found himself walking along a cobblestone path leading out of a dark patch of woods. Up ahead he saw a lovely clearing with a small hill in the center. Atop the hill was a charming cottage, painted solid white with blue trim on the doors, windows and eaves. The path that he was on appeared to lead up directly to the front door of the cottage, and to the left of the cottage a small brook bubbled by on its way, meandering towards the woods on the far side of the clearing.

As Amansun approached the cottage, he could see that smoke was rising out of the small rooftop chimney in curling wafts as it rose up into the sky. The front door of the cottage was ajar, and as he got even closer, he thought he heard a woman singing with a beautiful melodic voice, although he could not make out the words and the tune was unfamiliar to him. As he approached the door, he heard a smooth and subtle voice, at once disarming and inviting, say, "I have been expecting you, Amansun the Great, son of Wraith from the west. Come in now, the door is open."

Amansun looked at the small doorway in front of him and thought, *There is no way I will be able to get my enormous body through that small doorway!* Although he could not understand why, he had the feeling that something similar had happened to him long ago, in a similar but different place. "I appreciate the offer, kind woman, but I shan't be able to make it through your doorway," he replied.

"Nonsense," the voice replied sweetly. "I have made it so. Just step closer and you will see!"

Amansun was not convinced, but wanting to see who this beautiful voice belonged to, he started walking towards the door, leaning his head and shoulders down as he approached, expecting that he would likely knock the entire cottage over once he had gotten nearer. To the dragon's amazement, the closer he got to the door, the larger it appeared to him. It didn't seem possible, but now that he was just a step or two away, the top of the door and the roof above looked to be even taller than he, and he found himself walking right beneath the door and into the small cottage. "I don't know how that happened!" he said aloud, mostly to himself. "But I appear to be in now." He walked towards the center of the room.

Looking about, Amansun noticed that there were beautifully decorated wooden tables all about the room, and the walls were covered with brightly colored shelves, all covered with books and scrolls of every shape and size one could imagine. There at the opposite end of the room a woman, with her back turned to him, was standing over a desk and placing various items into a beautiful silver bowl. "Come closer," the sweet voice encouraged. "You have nothing to fear in my home."

As Amansun drew closer, he noticed that the entire room had a wonderful smell to it, like a grassy field right after a summer rainstorm has passed by. The woman, her back still to him, had long shiny blonde hair braided into a beautiful ponytail, tied off in the center with a blue bow that matched the trim on the window frames and doorway. As she suddenly turned and faced the dragon, he was overcome at her beauty and radiance. "Come and stand here by me, kind dragon," the voice pleaded. Not wanting to disappoint this beautiful woman, Amansun walked the few remaining steps and stood at the woman's side as she dropped several more items into the bowl. "You look surprised and confused, Amansun," the woman stated while smiling at him and picking up a large spoon to stir with. "Is something troubling you?"

"I can't quite say,", he replied softly, "but I feel as though we have met before, under similar circumstances, and yet nothing looks familiar to me now."

"Don't be alarmed, good dragon," the woman said. "I have brought you here to show you something…something you desire above all else, although you do not realize it yet." She gently laughed and smiled at the beast. "Look into my silver bowl as I stir," she commanded in a tone that could not be denied.

"What am I looking for?" the dragon asked.

"You will know when you see it."

Amansun leaned over the bowl and he at first saw nothing but pieces of fruit and petals of flowers as they softly swirled around the bowl in ever-tightening circles. "I don't think I see anything," he started to say.

"Shhh…" the woman insisted. "Just keep your eyes on the floating petals," she encouraged as she now stopped stirring and backed away slightly from the bowl.

As Amansun looked deeper and deeper into the bowl of liquid that was now starting to slow, causing the ripples to settle and the surface of the liquid to soften, he started to notice details he had not been able to see earlier. As the swirling became less and less, the vision in front of him began to take shape. There in the center of the bowl on the liquid's surface, Amansun could see what appeared to be a balcony made of stone set high atop a castle wall, floating above a large and silvery shimmering lake. He thought he had seen this vision before, but he could not guess how or when.

Next his eyes noticed that at the back of the balcony against the wall, there appeared to be a doorway that led into the stone wall of the castle. A soft billowing drape was blowing gently in and out of the doorway and from inside he could here two voices talking. Just as he was about to turn his head and ask who was hidden in the room, a beautiful young woman, dressed all in white with long blonde hair, walked onto the balcony and over to the edge so she could stand and gaze out at the shimmering moon dancing on the lake's reflection. "She is the most beautiful creature I have ever seen," Amansun mumbled to himself. "Who is she?"

Almost as suddenly as the image had appeared, it now vanished, as if made from wisps of smoke, and Amansun found himself looking down at the bottom of an ordinary silver bowl with pieces of flower, fruit and herbs. "That is all I can share with you for now," the woman of the cottage whispered as she walked away from the dragon and towards a lighted doorway at the opposite side of the room. "You must go now, the same way you came in," she insisted while disappearing out of view.

"But who was the girl in the vision?" Amansun pleaded.

"Go now at once!" the woman's voice demanded from the room next door. "I have shown you all that needs to be seen. And remember, not everything is always as it may seem," the voice echoed as the lit doorway across the room now closed, leaving him all alone in the room.

As Amansun turned and started to walk towards the open doorway he had entered through only a short time earlier, he suddenly felt a chill and noticed a strong wind blowing in from outside. Stepping out into the clearing that surrounded the cottage, he looked up and was surprised to see that it was now night and quite dark. A deep haze hid the moon above and the air felt cool to the touch. As he hurried off down the pathway to the woods, he felt a presence behind him and he slowly turned to look back, hoping to see the woman from the cottage standing there. Instead, as he glanced back over his shoulder, he saw a strange greenish-yellow light flickering above the cottage, floating some hundred feet or so above, and he suddenly was overcome with a feeling of fear and raced off into the woods, as scratchy branches from the trees brushed against his face.

"Wake up friend, wake up!" a familiar voice called out as Amansun brushed something away from his face. "Here you are, sleeping once again, and me doing all the hard work outside," laughed Carceren the owl as he gently touched the dragon's cheek with his talons.

"Welcome back," Amansun managed to eke out. "I suppose it was you scratching my face just now?"

"Well, I had to do something," the owl snapped back. "You were twitching and jerking about like someone who has an entire mound of ants crawling upon them."

"To tell you the truth, you did save me from a strange dream just now, I must say." Amansun was now quite happy he was awake and nowhere near the green shining light from his dream.

"You can tell me all about it another time," the owl said excitedly. "I have someone here that really wants to meet you and I have assured him that you are not normally prone to jumping about in your sleep, as was the case when the two of us flew in but a moment ago." He smiled.

"Am I still dreaming?" Amansun asked of the owl, "or are you both dripping wet at the moment?"

"Quite true, and thank you for noticing, I should say," laughed the owl. "It started raining several miles back and the two of us are quite drenched, thank you very much."

"Well, that explains why I felt so cold in my dream, at least," Amansun mumbled to himself. "The chill of the storm outside appears to be blowing right in through the mouth of the cave." In a louder voice, he asked, "And who is this?"

"May I present to you my cousin Bathis," Carceren replied. "Bathis will be your new guard, as he has agreed to stay in the trees outside as your lookout while I am away gathering information on the princess and her whereabouts."

Amansun looked at the owl perched to the right of his friend Carceren and noticed that he was a good deal smaller in stature, though obviously close to full-grown. The owl's feathers were more of a grayish shade mixed with black and white spots, especially along his chest. The owl looked quite excited, as if wanting to burst out in song, and he was nervously eyeing the dragon as if waiting to be spoken to. "'Tis a pleasure to meet you, young Bathis," the dragon began. "I am pleased that you have offered your assistance while I am here visiting in your lovely land."

"The honor is all mine," the owl blurted out rapidly, now that he had the opportunity to speak. "It will be my pleasure to stand watch over you, day and night if needs be, until you are ready to move on with your journey."

"Well, I will try not to keep you too long," the dragon promised good-naturedly.

"Not to worry, Sir Dragon," young Bathis quipped. "I am off to the trees now to select an appropriate vantage point. Just whistle should you need anything at all." He then nodded to his cousin and flew off into the still-raining sky outside.

"Once again I am indebted to you, kind owl," Amansun stated while graciously nodding to the owl. "And what are your plans now?" Carceren spent the next half an hour or so filling Amansun in on all that had been discussed at his morning meeting, including who was doing what and how. "It sounds like you have everything in order," Amansun said positively. "You will be sure to come and let me know when you think it will be fine for me to have a look at things for myself, now, won't you?"

"Of course, Sir Amansun," the owl laughed. "You are no one's prisoner here, and it's not as if anyone could stop you from leaving if you chose to do so. I do think it best that you remain hidden for at least another day or two, though, at least until things settle down a bit more."

"You haven't let me down yet, friend," the dragon said. "I am in your capable hands, or wings I should say, for now." They both had a good laugh. Amansun suddenly looked out at the darkening sky with a concerned frown and then glanced curiously at the large owl beside him. "At the risk of sounding a bit mad," the dragon said softly to the owl, "I want to share some of the visions I have had these past few days, if you wouldn't mind, that is, just to see what your thoughts might be?"

"By all means!" Carceren answered. "I have no intention of flying out into this stormy weather anyway, and it appears I will have some time to stay and hear what you have to say." With that, Amansun began to tell the owl all about the unusual dreams or visions that he had experienced over the past few days, including his apparent glimpses of the sorceress and princess. The owl sat there in the semi-darkness of the cave now, slowly turning his head from side to side, obviously going over everything he had heard from the dragon's recounting of his dreams. After several minutes of silence, he stroked his beak gently with the tip of his right wing and started speaking again.

"I am no wise elder of the council," Carceren suddenly stated, now stopping at the end of the boulder closest to the dragon, "but it would seem to me that you are seeing the enchantress as both a young woman and an old woman because that is how she chooses for you to see her." The owl paced back and forth a few more times, then once again stopped on the stone facing Aamnsun and added, "And the princess, or at least the young woman of your visions, appears in the same way each time, unchanging."

"That is correct."

"Then it would appear that the enchantress of the black woods has somehow connected with you, even here in this hidden cavern known only to us, and she is showing you a glimpse of the princess as she truly is, but for what purpose I cannot say."

"So, you think that they are not just dreams in my head then?" Amansun asked, puzzled.

"Not likely," the owl said softly. "Something is happening here, for good or evil I cannot say, but this is sure to be a sign of some kind." The owl suddenly flapped his wings excitedly. "This gives me an idea! I shall focus my attention on the west walls of the castle, in particular on the many balconies I have seen there before, all looking out upon the lake, as seen in your dreams."

"And you think you will see the princess there, on one of those balconies, then?" Amansun asked excitedly.

"Everything happens for a reason, good or bad, the elders of my people say," Carceren replied, "and I think it not an accident that your dreams seem to match with reality so closely. I am off to look over the castle now, with Methistus and young Obrides, and we will focus all of our attention on the balconies of the west wall, I should say." He seemed to be in a hurry to leave. "Stay hidden as much as possible, good dragon. I shall return as soon as I am able. Don't forget, young Bathis is just outside should you need anything at all. Goodbye." And with that, Carceren was off in a blaze of motion.

* * *

Eodren and his group of gatherers had been walking about the woods for most of the morning and afternoon when the rain began to fall. Still being quite a few miles from their home, they decided it best that they settle down for the night and avoid getting caught in the worst of the heavy rain that was likely to fall, based on the darkness of the sky and the size and shape of the clouds that rolled on endlessly. Having passed through this way many times, they knew where all the suitable resting places were, and they decided upon a dense thicket of fir trees that grew in so tightly together that virtually no rain made its way down to the ground beneath them. It was here that they settled in and took shelter, sharing some of the wild sweet potatoes, beans and nuts that they had been collecting all day.

"Can you believe the size of the beast?" Articlese asked of his brother. "I knew they were large creatures, but I never imagined how truly immense they were until today."

Nodding his head up and down in agreement, his brother Eldenham added, "It was quite a shock when we looked up and saw him standing there just across the pond, to be sure. For the first moment after spotting him I don't think I drew a single breath!" He gently laughed.

"He was pretty big, I'll admit," one of the younger centaurs said now, jumping into the conversation, "but I actually thought his talons and teeth would have been longer," he added as if he had been unimpressed.

"What are you talking about, Brethus?" Eldenham snapped while laughing and looking at the younger centaur. "You were so afraid, you couldn't even gather up the courage to walk over with us to introduce yourself." He looked at the other centaurs who were also chuckling and nudging the youngster in agreement.

"That's not the reason at all," the young centaur answered back swiftly. "I decided to stay back with the others so we could provide a line of defense if the beast had decided to charge is all." For just a moment there was complete silence among the group of resting centaurs…then at once the entire group erupted into spontaneous laughter that continued for some time with even Eodren, the eldest, smiling and chuckling to himself.

"Best we do not talk about our encounter this morning, here or anywhere on the path," the wise centaur added grimly. "These woods are filled with unknown eyes, as you should all know by now," he said in a fatherly voice. "Best we leave the storytelling for campfires when we are home among our own kind and in familiar lands."

"Agreed," they all said as one. "No more talk of the great winged serpent again until we are in our own homes!" And with that, the subject changed back to the rain that was falling.

High above the heads of the centaurs, tucked deep into the thickest part of the firs, two unseen elf scouts exchanged knowing glances at each other and whispered as faintly as the softest of winds, "We'll stay here until morning after they have moved on…then we can go and find the captain and share what we have heard this night."

CHAPTER 18

Some miles east of the pond, two elves were just now making their way back to their camp in search of Captain Eonias. "Just wait 'till the captain hears what we have to tell!" the first elf said excitedly to the other. "We're sure to get double rations and a good night's sleep with no duties, I'm sure."

"Don't be so sure the captain's going to be in such a good mood," the other said not quite as confidently. "I suppose the captain will be quite upset when he learns that the beast is so close to our campsite and none of us getting so much as a glimpse of the serpent, would be my first guess."

Now suddenly looking a little less sure of himself, the first looked over at the other and softly asked nervously, "But you still think we should tell him what we heard, right?"

"Well yes, we need to share what we heard, you fool!" the second said incredulously. "Can you imagine the pickle we would be in if he ever found out we knew something and then didn't report it? It'd be the dungeons for us to be sure!" He shook his head in disgust at the other's idiotic suggestion.

* * *

Even further east of where the two elves were walking, Eodren and his band of centaurs were just crossing over into the section of woods that they called their home. Looking over at his father, Articlese could see that he had a worried look on his face, as his forehead was crinkled tightly together and he hadn't said much over the past hour. "Something bothering you, father?" he whispered over to his dad as they walked along the forest trail.

"Just thinking about last night," his father replied. "Just wish we hadn't spoken so openly about the great serpent the way we did. I can't explain it, but my stomach tells me that somehow it was a big mistake." He paused, then shrugged his shoulders. "Not aught we can do now. Best we just forget it and move on home quicker," he said now, bringing the group to a slow run.

* * *

Back at the castle, the three owls assigned to watch its west wall were scouring for the best place to have a clear view of the balconies on that side. After surveying the wall and grounds for some time, Carceren signaled the other two to join him once again. "We will need to split the wall into sections so that we cover its entirety and don't miss a thing," he said. "I do not know how long the princess will linger on the balcony, if she comes out for a look at all. Obrides, you will take a position in the trees at the lake's edge on the northern side. Methistus, you will do the same but on the south shore. Remember, we must stay focused and awake so we don't miss anything. I have decided my best vantage point will be perched directly atop the castle wall on the western side, looking down upon the balconies from on high."

"And what are we to do should we see the princess, anyway?" young Obrides asked.

"Just stay in place until the morning unless I come and collect you." Carceren advised. "We don't intend on doing anything ourselves anyway, tonight or any other for that matter. We are merely collecting information for Sir Amansun. We will meet at our usual spot tomorrow morning as planned; until then, stay put and stay alert." With that, Carceren left the other two behind and flew off towards the castle heights to seek out a good vantage point.

As the morning wore into the afternoon, Certrex and Belfest, who had been speaking with each other after every round of the lake as they had been directed to do, were beginning to become bored. They were still quite young and easily distracted. "These rounds about the lake and watchtowers are becoming quite a bore," Certrex was complaining to Belfast. "I think I'll fly in close to one of the stations where the men are camped with their wagons and listen in to see what I may find."

"Have fun with that!" Belfest responded comically. "I for one don't plan on getting skewered by an arrow today so I will keep to the air, a safe distance, mind you, from any wandering arrows, and stick with just being a scout."

"As you wish," Certrex said in a demeaning tone of voice. "I plan on being the big hero of the day. If you want to stay safe and sound high up in the air and hiding in the trees, suit yourself, then. I'm off to get as close as I can to some of these soldiers to learn what is afoot."

The first spot where Centrex set down turned out to be a bust. After moving in as close as possible, he heard the men below complaining about having been rained on all evening the night before without proper tents or equipment for the poor weather. "Easy for them that's nice and comfy back at the castle," the soldier complained. "Let's see hows they likes it if'n they spend a night like last out here in the mud an' cold, I says!"

One of the others chimed in, "An' what's all this nonsense 'bout a flyer up in these parts, besides." He groaned unhappily. "Taint been one up these a-ways in years an' years. Probably jus' a wildfire the other night were all it be!"

No sense sitting here listening to these complainers all day, Centrex thought to himself. *Maybe I should be trying a larger group where someone in authority is likely to be posted. That way I might hear something worth sharing.* He took flight and went in search of a better spot.

After having flown about most of the road leading into the main castle gate, Certrex noticed that there was a larger post just off the main road where there were several small tents and wagons set in a tight group. "Now that looks like a likely spot to hear some good gossip," he said to himself as he swung back around and quietly glided back over the site. Seeing that there was a small tree just behind the tented area, he made his way onto one of the lower branches and tucked himself in; close enough to hear what the men were saying, yet far enough and hidden enough to go unnoticed.

Certrex had only been settled into his hiding spot a short time when he saw the group of men below suddenly stand and walk a few feet over to the roadway as they stared along its path as it bent southeast. There in the distance he could make out small figures heading this way, apparently heading towards the castle. "Told you they'd be a-comin' soon," one of the men said loudly to the others gathered about. "I heard they was headin' this way from parts all over is wat I heard!"

"Well let's jest wait an' see who this is 'fore you start getting all high and mighty on us now," another smirked. "Jes' cuz we see someone comin' doesn't make it a knight now, does it?" He snorted.

As the figures up the road got closer, it soon became apparent that there was a small group of riders on horseback with a few men marching along behind them. Now drawing even closer in, they could see that the first rider was carrying a tall pole in his arms and at the top of the pole a small banner waved in the air, flicking this way and that.

"Looks like a knight and his riding party to me!" the first voice smugly announced once more.

"Okay, okay, you were right, then. No sense in getting all gloaty on us now," the second replied, now in an even grumpier mood.

"Beside," he snapped, "what's it to the likes of us if a knight be on the way…doesn't do a thing fer any of us, now, do it?"

"Don't be mad cuz I'm right now," came the first man's retort. "It's jes' like I was a sayin' earlier 'fore you interrupted me an' all. The king's invited the knights from all about to come to the castle an help with the killin' of the beast. I even heard that he might be holding a tourney to have them challenge for his daughter, the princess!"

"Well, don't get yer skirt all up in a bunch, now," the second soldier remarked, now laughing. "Won't be you or any of us getting the princess's hand, I can guarantee you of that, I'm sure!" With that, the soldiers stepped out into the road with arms raised and challenged the approaching group. "States yer name an yer business here at the castle!" they shouted to the advancing party.

From atop the first horse, the man bearing the pole with the banner called ahead, "Berardren the Red and host, here by invitation of the king!"

"Proceed!" the sentry on the roadway announced. "Welcome to Castle Eladrias. You are expected." He bowed low as the group moved past and onwards towards the castle.

As Certrex observed the group now passing by, he counted six riders on horseback along with another dozen foot soldiers keeping step quickly behind. It was easy to spot the knight in the group as his horse was dressed in red and his suit of armor, though mostly black in sheen, had traces of red as well. On the knight's shield, a large red sun shined brilliantly as its rays spread out in every direction. The owl also noticed that the banner atop the pole of the first rider had the same red sun emblazoned upon it.

"That be the first of many, I'm sure," one of the soldiers at the roadway offered to the others.

"Well, welcome to them all, I says," said a new voice who hadn't spoken up until just now. "If they be here to help with killin' the dragon, then I says they be alright by me."

Realizing that he had just overheard something quite useful to the group, Certrex flew off from the roadway and headed off to make another pass of his designated route. He didn't really care what else happened the rest of the day, as he was quite certain that this news would be big all by itself. As he flew along the northern edge of the lake, looking for any new movement along the road that followed, he noticed that many of the small streams and creeks that fed into the lake were now flowing quite heavily. As he glanced off at the mighty mountains to the north, he guessed that the heavy rainwater that had fallen the previous night was just now making its way down the valleys and plains and finding its way to the great lake below.

* * *

Back at the cliffside cave, Amansun had been lazily daydreaming while counting clouds as they drifted by, having grown bored with looking for shapes in them some time earlier. As he lay there with his feet sticking out just slightly from his hiding spot, he was suddenly startled when something quite cold hit his foot. As he turned to look at what the cause was, he felt another cold sensation on his other foot. Next came another, and then another, and then another. As he glanced out towards the pond in front of his resting spot, he noticed that large drops of water had begun to appear falling gently in front of him as if he was standing in a shower. Soon the few drops here and there were replaced with a curtain of water falling as it plummeted from above to the waiting pond below.

Amansun, no stranger to water but not looking forward to getting drenched, stood and called out to his sentry in the trees. "Come down here at once, Bathis, or I fear I will be taking a bath of my own soon!"

"I'm afraid that's not possible, sire," the soft voice replied. "I am not allowed to leave my post."

"And whom are you in charge of guarding?" the dragon called out once more.

"Why, you, sire!" the muffled voice called back again.

"And whom do you think is in charge between us two, then?" the dragon called out.

"Begging your pardon, sire," the young owl called out while taking flight from his tree. "I see your point now." Amansun could just barely make him out, now that the waterfall was making a good deal of noise. Flying in at an angle and from the side, the owl was able to make his way into the now hidden chamber without getting his feathers wet. "And what may I do for you, sir Dragon?" the owl asked.

"It appears my home is about to become a part of the surrounding pond, or so it would seem," the dragon stated while pointing out at the curtain of water now between him and the forest outside.

"Not to worry," the young owl said while smiling confidently at the dragon. "My cousin advised me that this could happen, and said that it normally takes several days of solid rain to flood the cavern you are now resting in. The floor of the cave is still several feet above the pond below, so you should be safe and dry here unless today brings another round of storms."

Looking about at the still dry cave floor and nodding his head as if agreeing with the owl, Amansun said, "Looks like you are right, young Bathis. My apologies for taking you from your post. On your way now…I shan't bother you again unless I find myself floating away," he said while laughing and smiling at the owl.

"As you wish then, sire!" young Bathis replied, and he flew out the side of the cave once again and made for his roost up in the tree once more.

* * *

Several miles north from where Amansun and Bathis the owl were hidden, the two elf scouts, Araneth and Mythiel, were informing their captain, Eonias, of the conversation they had overheard the night before. "And you are certain the centaurs you overheard were talking about a dragon, right?" the elf captain demanded.

"Quite certain, Captain," Araneth replied. "We heard the centaurs mention a 'great beast' and they also referred to him as a 'winged serpent' as well."

"There can be no mistake, then," Captain Eonias muttered to himself while looking at the other elves gathered around. "We are very close now, friends," he announced excitedly. "This is the day we find the beast's lair!" He smiled grimly.

"In what direction do we head, then?" one of the elves asked, trying to sound unafraid.

"Araneth and Mythiel mentioned a pond in their report, did they not?" Captain Eonias replied. "There can't be more than a half-dozen ponds in the area where they were last scouting. We will break up into pairs and each take one of the ponds that are known to us. This way we can cover the most ground."

While the captain divided his squad into pairs, he eyed the two scouts who had brought in the news. "You two," the captain barked out at Araneth and Mythiel. "You seem pretty good at sneaking up on centaurs unawares. Why don't the two of you head north and follow the centaurs back to their home? Maybe you can eavesdrop some more and learn other secrets from our four-legged neighbors," he said with a smile. "It's possible the beast may be in league with them, and we should have some eyes on their home just in case it makes an appearance there."

Now staring at Mythiel with a smirk and a shake of the head, Araneth leaned over to his friend and whispered, "Double rations and a rest, hah! Told you not to get too excited until we heard what the captain had to say."

Within minutes the captain had all of the elves broken into pairs, and he was giving them their final instructions. "Now be sure to stay alert and watch for signs of other centaurs out and about," he cautioned, "and make sure the dragon doesn't see or hear you either! We are just seeking out the beast for now, so don't do anything foolish. Just locate the dragon and then meet back at the trailhead by the great old stone fortress."

With that, the elves headed out in their pairings and Araneth and Mythiel found themselves standing in the abandoned camp. "I guess we deserve a little break, don't we, after our successful scouting mission last night?" Mythiel asked.

"Don't suppose there would be any harm in it," Araneth replied. "Besides, there's no one left to see anyway, as the captain will be driving them hard the rest of the day, you can be sure."

And with that, the two scouts made themselves comfortable and helped themselves to the little bit of food that had been left behind when the others marched off in a rush. Mythiel suddenly grinned from ear to ear, and looking over at his partner with a smug grin, said softly, "Double rations and a little rest, just like I said," and the two broke into soft laughter.

* * *

When the first drops of water had begun to cascade over his cliffside retreat, Amansun had been quite nervous. However, now that his concerns had been put to rest, he quite enjoyed it. The rhythmic sounds of the water cascading down the side of the cliff face was mesmerizing and, try as he might, it slowly caused him to drift off into a light slumber.

Amansun found himself staring into the face of a large man with long dark hair cascading over his immense shoulders and leather vest. He held an immense broad sword in one hand and a large, heavy shield in the other. Though he wasn't sure why the man was attacking him and smiling at the same time, he did understand the words when the man shouted, "Defend yourself!"

With that, two mighty swords met with a loud ringing clash, and he could feel the sting in his own hands as he watched the two swords bounce off of each other and then pull away. As he looked ahead, now squinting somewhat, he realized that he didn't have a perfect view of the battle he was apparently taking part in, as there was something obstructing much of his view. Indeed, he found that he could only see things directly in front of him as everything below, above and on both sides seemed to be blackened out by something resting upon his head. As he realized that he too was holding a shield in his left hand and an immense sword in his right, he looked forward just in time to see his adversary's sword coming down hard at his shield. *Crash* went his shield as his opponent's sword rained down on him, and he felt a sudden burst of pain along his entire left arm and shoulder.

"You can do better than that!" his adversary shouted wildly. "Lift your shield to meet the blow, as I have shown you time and time again!" The man prepared to take another hit to his shield. *Crash!* His shield echoed once again as he felt the excruciating pain once more.

"Swing at him, lad!" he heard another voice coax from his side. "You'll never take the captain just standing there and taking the full force of his blows, now. Take a swing at him and give him what for now."

As the dark-haired man began to circle to his right, Amansun lifted up his sword hand and swung forward with all his might. *Crash* went his sword as it glanced off the other's painted shield, and now he felt the stinging in his right hand and arm.

"That's the stuff, son," the voice from behind called out excitedly. "Now you're taking the fight to him!"

* * *

While Amansun dozed the afternoon away, two elves approached the hidden pond from the east, tracking along the now flowing stream that had been dry just the day before. As they peered out from beneath the trees at the foot of the stream, they glanced all about the pond and the area surrounding it, looking for any signs of the great winged beast. "Nothing to see here aside from that lovely waterfall on the other side," one of the elves whispered quietly.

"No beast in sight, to be sure," the other agreed. "That beach along the edge is too narrow for anything bigger than a man to stand atop, for certain, and it's not likely the dragon is hiding among these trees either."

Up at the top of his tree lookout, Bathis watched intently to see what the two elves were going to do next. They had appeared literally out of nowhere and he had not had sufficient time to fly down and warn the dragon of the danger nearby. *With any luck at all they will move along once they see there is nothing below but a large pond with water spilling into it*, he thought to himself.

One of the elves stepped out from the treeline and peered into the deep pond below. "Some great fish in here, from the looks of it," the first called over to the other.

"Not now!" the second countered. "No time for eating now; the captain will be expecting us back at the stone fortress along with the others shortly. We'll plan on coming back another time, after all this commotion has passed by." With that, the two elves faded back into the woods and disappeared just as quickly and quietly as they had come.

Not completely certain that the elves had left the area, Bathis decided to remain in his tree, standing watch. He figured that if he flew to warn the dragon now, he might be seen. *Besides*, he thought, *all the elves likely saw was a waterfall spilling out and over the large cliff face as it tumbled into the pond below. From where they were standing, they would have been looking directly into the water, and they wouldn't have any way of knowing that there was a large cave hidden just behind the curtain of water.*

Amansun and Bathis had been quite fortunate indeed, as the heavy rains from the night before had completely washed away and removed all the tracks that had been on the edge of the pond the day before, when Amansun had encountered the centaurs. The centaurs had hiked up the valley to the great pool using the dry soft creek bed as their path, and all signs of their coming and going had washed away with the rising stream's waters, hours before the team of elves had arrived seeking out the dragon. "Maybe one of the other teams had better luck," one of the elves whispered to the other as they quickly sped off to the meeting spot.

"Certainly no dragons anywhere near here!" the other agreed as they glided along the forest path at a clip, one in front of the other.

CHAPTER 19

As the afternoon passed by and the first shadows of the approaching night began to appear, Carceren, Methistus and Obrides all peered out from their hiding spots and made note of the many balconies that protruded from varying heights along the castle's western wall. *There are at least eight places where the princess might appear*, Obrides thought to himself, *and that's just the places I can see from my side of the lake. Poor Carceren is going to have a frightful night trying to keep an eye on the entire western wall. Better him than me.*

Back on the eastern end of the castle, Certrex was sitting atop a lonely pine that stood higher than any other tree. Far below him and a good distance away, he casually watched as another procession of horses and marching soldiers came walking up the road. *And here comes another knight now!* he thought to himself. *Guess that fool down at the checkpoint was right after all.* He grinned. Below him the procession of riders and marchers halted suddenly, waved at the sentries posted along the road, and then continued on their way towards the great castle gates.

Though it seemed like an eternity to the three owls perched in waiting along the western walls of the castle, it was actually just an hour or so after second dark when the princess emerged from within the castle walls. Obrides was the first to spot her standing on one of the taller balconies, peering out across the water just as Carceren had said she would. "That's got to be her!" Obrides said to himself aloud as he sat there on his branch looking out. "Guess I had better make sure I can remember which balcony she is standing on, so I can tell them all later in case Carceren misses this." The young owl quickly made a mental note of which balcony the young woman was standing on by counting sections of the castle both upwards and across. "I've got you now," he mumbled to himself happily.

High above on the topmost wall of the castle, Carceren had not missed the appearance of the young girl either. *Simply amazing*, he thought to himself as the young woman walked from one of the hidden doorways below and effortlessly glided over to the short wall looking out over the lake. "It's as if I am living the dream," he said softly. There far below him stood the princess, long blonde hair flowing out across and over her white nightgown, just as the dragon had described in his vision. As the owl looked out over the water, he just shrugged his shoulders when he saw the sparking refection of the rising moon, sitting atop the lake like a flower on its stem, just as Amansun had described.

Amansun will be delighted, the lead owl thought to himself as he sat and watched the woman below staring off across the lake. He was quite pleased with the success of his operation and was quite relieved that they had not had to wait days to get a glimpse of the princess, as he had originally guessed they might. In time the princess walked back towards the castle wall and was gone. All three owls stayed put for the remainder of the evening as they had agreed. None of them saw the princess again that night, though they did see lots of activity below, with soldiers coming and going in shifts and the sentries posted at the various groups of wagons changing out throughout the night. At first day's light they all flew back towards their meeting site and gathered together to share their news.

As Amansun awoke to a new day in his cave he was happy to see his friend Carceren flying into his retreat. "You couldn't have done that yesterday!" the dragon said while smiling at the arriving owl. "That entrance was completely covered with a blanket of water for most of the afternoon and well into the night. Now it's nothing more than a trickle."

"I forgot to warn you about that!" the owl muttered as if in a bother. "That's not important now, though. We have spotted the princess, just as you described. It was as if I was looking at a living dream! Each and every detail was exactly as you had described to me."

"This is great news indeed," the dragon repeated back, just as excited as his friend now. "What is our next move?" he asked like a young child waiting to open his birthday gifts.

"I am afraid you will have to remain patient at least a little longer," the owl stated softly but firmly. "We have only seen the princess just this once. Now we need to see if she will reappear in the same spot once again this evening." He gave his friend a sympathetic look.

"So, you and your cousins will be watching the castle wall again tonight?" Amansun asked.

"It's already taken care of," the owl assured the dragon. "We will all be on watch once again tonight. With any luck the princess will once again make an appearance at the same location and time."

"And then what?" the dragon asked with wide eyes.

The owl stood tall, ruffled his feathers, and stared right into the immense dragon's eyes just ahead of his own. "What do you mean, and then what?" he asked the dragon, appearing quite puzzled. "I don't have all the answers! This is your quest, remember?"

"Right you are, then," Amansun muttered. "I guess I hadn't thought beyond this point. Guess I'll have to think of something between now and tomorrow." He peered out into the trees.

"Well, for now we can celebrate our good fortune!" Carceren boasted.

"Right you are!" the dragon agreed. "And thanks for a job well done, I am sure!" he added, now bowing to the owl beside him. "Part one is now complete," he announced quite happily.

Just then Bathis the owl flew in to see what all the commotion was about. "I guess there is good news, then?" the young owl asked inquisitively. "This would be a good time to tell you about our close call yesterday afternoon, then, I am guessing?" he said nervously while smiling at both the dragon and his cousin. As the young owl went ahead and retold the story of the wandering elves from the previous day, both Amansun and Carceren took turns groaning, and sighing, and showing great signs of distress.

"Well, I suppose this place was too good to last," Amansun said sadly. "It's the closest thing I have had to a home since I left my own cave weeks ago now." He was now rather sullen.

"We have no choice, Sir Amansun," Carceren said forcefully. "You can bet those elves will be back again, once they run out of places to look for you. It's just by the luckiest of chances that you were not discovered yesterday, since the waterfall conveniently hid you away!"

"Where are we off to now?" the dragon asked.

"I still have a few hiding places that may work," Carceren answered back. "Follow me and I will decide where to take you while we are in the air." And with that, the owl flew out, followed by young Bathis and then the giant winged serpent.

* * *

Just a short time later, a small band of elves appeared at the head of the stream that led off into the woods from the pond. "Is this the spot that the two of you say you checked yesterday?" Captain Eonias demanded.

"Yes, it is," came the faint answer of two elves standing just behind the leader.

"And did the two of you bother looking inside of that cave on the far side of this pond yesterday?"

"Well, it's a strange thing, Captain," one of the elves started to stammer. "You see, yesterday there was a great waterfall flowing down the face of that cliff, and that cave was nowhere to be seen."

"It can't be," the captain groaned loudly as he made his way over to the far side of the pond and stepped up and into the cave now in plain sight. There in front of him, and all about the interior of the cave, were tremendous claw marks and indentations where the great beast had lay down upon the soft earth of the cave. "This is where he was!" the captain shouted back to the others still on the opposite end of the pond. "But there's no telling where he went off to now, I suppose," he said rather angrily while staring at the two elves who had been responsible for checking out this spot the day before. "Guess there'll be extra rations for the rest of you," the captain called over, smiling, "since these two won't be eating anything the next two days!" he snapped as he made his way back over to the rest of the group.

Pointing at the two elves who were now looking quite anxious, Captain Eonias snapped, "The two of you can stay here for the next two days, just in case the beast decides to return." He headed off into the forest and motioned for the others to follow. "And don't be eating any of the fish from that pond, either!" he called back as he faded into the trees. "You two are forbidden from eating for two full days for your stupidity!" they heard as they stood looking at each other and the large fish swimming just a few feet from where they stood.

* * *

The rest of the day passed rather uneventfully, once Amansun and Bathis had settled into their new surroundings. Carceren had taken them further south this time, having guessed that the elf patrol had come from up north. Though the new spot was not as hidden or comfortable as the cliffside had been, Amansun was grateful for the change in scenery. He had been quite restless these past two days and the move had helped to brighten his spirits. Truth be told, he had been fighting to control himself from the urge to just fly over to the castle and see if he could see the princess for himself.

As he sat there in the small field, tucked under a row of pines, with Bathis on watch high above once again, he pictured the princess walking out onto her balcony the night before and felt quite strange. Thinking of her made him feel quite different but he was uncertain as to why. He chalked it up to the strange visions and dreams he had been having ever since leaving the Smoky Black Mountains some time ago. "See anything?" he called up to the owl hidden amongst the trees.

"No, sire," the owl called back down. "I suppose it not be the best for us to be yelling back and forth to each other like this," he said while trying to not sound too bossy.

"Right you are then, sir owl," Amansun replied, half as loudly this time. "Not another word unless you need me, then."

* * *

As first dark slowly faded into second, Carceren, Methistus and Obrides once again turned their attention to the castle's west wall. As if set by the sands of an immense hourglass, the princess suddenly appeared once again, on the same balcony as before. As Obrides and Carceren watched from afar, the princess walked out upon her balcony, leaned on the wall facing the lake, and remained there for some time. Then, without warning, she retreated into the castle again, just as she had the previous night. *Excellent!* Carceren the owl thought to himself as he pictured sharing the good news with his friend the dragon the next morning.

Once again, the three hidden owls kept watch over the castle while Certrex and Belfast watched over the roads leading into and away from the castle. More groups of soldiers and marching units arrived throughout the night and early morning, Certrex observed, now growing more concerned that the castle would soon be protected by quite a host of knights, as had not been the case in some decades, he was certain.

Back at Amansun's new hiding spot, the great dragon was twitching and twisting about in his sleep as he once again was experiencing one of his vivid dreams. This time he pictured himself sitting in a pine tree watching wave after wave of armed knights and soldiers riding in and marching into the great castle to the east. As he imagined the castle walls filling to capacity with heavily armored warriors, he felt certain he would be unable to fight the mighty force that was now building against him. Waking suddenly from his dream, eyes wide open and his heart still racing, he vowed he would not wait another day before taking action against the castle.

Squinting into the dead of night at the tallest of the pines above, he thought he could make out the silhouette of his guard owl, Bathis, as he sat there perched on a branch still wide awake and alert. He closed his eyes once more and tried to get back to sleep once again as the cool night air brushed over his body like water flowing over a stone.

* * *

When Amansun awoke the next morning, he was quite surprised to see not one owl beside him, or two owls, but now six! "I take it this is your entire squad, then?" Amansun asked while smiling at the group of owls perched all around him, making eye contact with his friend Carceren.

"Yes indeed," Carceren said proudly. "These are the individuals who helped me locate the balcony of the princess as well as keep an eye on the castle itself, along with all the activity taking place all around it."

"Well, please accept my thanks, then, each and every one of you, for I am quite grateful for all that you have done these past few days," the dragon said sincerely.

"It was our pleasure," they all announced in one way or another as a group. "Happy to help one such as yourself!" one of them added proudly.

"You are all free to go now," Carceren announced to the others. "All except for young Bathis, I should say. I will need a scout in the trees just a bit longer, I am afraid, while Sir Amansun and I discuss the details of the night."

"If that is the case, then you shall have five!" Methistus countered. "We will all share in the honor of staying on watch while you two discuss your plans." With that, all the owls, save for Carceren himself, flew off and took positions in the row of tall pines that lined the near edge of the field Amansun had been hiding in.

"And what news have you to share this new day?" the dragon asked aloud.

"Good and bad once again, I am afraid to say, sir Amansun," the owl replied, smiling.

"Let's have the bad first this time, then."

"Well, it appears that the king of the castle has sent for knights from near and far to help protect his kingdom, presumably from you. My scouts have overheard the soldiers on guard speaking about knights gathering here at Castle Eladrias. My cousin Certrex himself observed no less than five knights arriving these past two days, along with their entourages."

"It has never been my intention to make an all-out attack against the castle anyway," the dragon said while still smiling, "so I guess that is really not all that bad of news after all."

"I am pleased to hear that, Sir Dragon", Carceren replied while eyeing the great beast to see if his words were true.

"And the good news?"

"The good news is that the princess appeared as we had hoped from the same location and at the approximate same time as the night before!"

Amansun stood there for some time, taking in the news his friend had shared, pacing about briefly. "It would appear that the good news outweighs the bad in this particular instance," he said finally. "I too had a suspicion that the castle's strength was growing, as I had another of my visions last night. In my dream, a great host of warriors gathered within the castle walls until they were about to burst from the pressure of containing so many armed men. It is for this reason that I have decided I must take action this very night!"

"And what action do you intend to take, if I may ask?" the owl said inquisitively. "Surely you must have more of a plan than merely flying up and speaking with the princess as she stands out on her balcony?"

"That is pretty much the sum of it," he said while laughing slightly.

"Surely you cannot be serious?" Carceren now looked painfully alarmed.

"Well, my friend,",the dragon started to say, now looking quite somber and leaning closer to the owl nearby. "I never really had much of a plan to speak of anyway. As a matter of fact, I never really expected I'd even get this far, to tell you the truth!" He grinned and gave a light snort.

The large owl looked at his friend sadly, shaking his head, and said with all traces of humor now gone, "Clearly my endeavors these past few days have been in vain, then, for it appears you have chosen a suicidal path, which your plan is clearly."

"Come, come, friend," the great dragon countered, still attempting a smile. "My mission was always going to be suicidal, it would seem. My guess has always been that my colony had wished to get rid of me and so sent me on a quest that was unattainable."

"I am afraid that I can no longer assist you, then, Sir Amansun," the owl sad sadly. "It is not in my nature to stand by and watch as a friend of mine flies off into a hopeless battle. I shall pray for you this night and hope for the best, though I doubt the two of us shall ever see each other in this life again."

"Then it is farewell, my great friend and counsel!" Amansun said while bowing low. "It has been my great pleasure to have made your acquaintance."

"And mine," Carceren said, now visibly shaken and upset. "I wish you all the best and hope that you achieve what you hope for. When you seek the princess this evening, you will want to approach the middlemost balcony on the northern side of the west wall. Plan on seeing the princess there just after second dark has come on. It is there and then that you shall find her." He took one last look at his friend the dragon and then turned and flew off, calling his scouts to do the same as he flew past the trees.

"Until we meet again!" Amansun cried out as he watched the owls fly off in formation, but no reply came back.

Amansun had not been entirely alone for some time now. His guardian owl, young Bathis, had always been close by, and his good friend Carceren had visited with him several times daily as well. Having watched the six owls fly off together, he quickly realized that he was once again all alone in a strange field in a far-off land. The great dragon suddenly felt all alone, and he sulked off further into the tall pines, not wanting to be seen by any prying eyes up on high.

The rest of that day passed by quite uneventfully. There were no large spiders to attack him as he rested. No stone trolls hiding beneath rocks. Not even any sign of a passing elf scout or centaur gathering berries. The field was quite empty and, aside from the wind whistling through the tall pines above, there was no sound to speak of. As Amansun whiled the hours away, he had plenty of time to think over how his quest had turned out so far. He had flown a tremendous distance, made some friends along the way, and actually found not only the great Silver Lake, but also the castle itself, along with the princess who was hidden within somewhere. It was hard not to feel pleased with himself and the great success he had achieved so far.

None of this really seemed to matter, though, the dragon thought to himself as he sat there in that empty field all alone. The truth was that he really had no idea of what he was going to do once the sun set. He knew that he had to do something, and soon. The castle's defenses were growing stronger every day. He also knew that he would never actually be able to hurt the princess, of that he was certain. *Maybe I can just grab her and take her away somewhere safe until I have more time to think things through*, he thought quietly.

Not likely, another part of him thought. *I'm likely to hurt the poor girl if I grab her with these claws of mine. And besides, where would I go? Seems as if everywhere I turn up, there is always someone or something waiting just behind the next tree or under some large stone waiting to do harm to me.*

As Amansun sat there deep in thought, he suddenly thought back to the day when he flew off from his cave far to the west. He could clearly remember his father's warning: "Don't plan on returning without the princess, as you will not be welcome in this home again without her." This was the end of the road, the dragon thought to himself as he listened to the sound of the wind whistling above. He wasn't taking the princess home, dead or alive, so he had nowhere else to go.

"Well, I may as well get one good look at this princess while I am here," he thought. "I have already seen her in my dreams often enough…now it's time to see what she looks like up close and in person." And with that, Amansun's fears faded away along with any uncertainty he had been feeling. Tonight, he would fly to the princess's balcony, speak with her if possible, or at least make the attempt. Anything after that he would figure out later, he assured himself.

Far off in the distance, some large and ominous dark storm clouds were gathering and starting their journey across the flat wastelands to the south. Amansun peered off into the distance and watched as enormous bolts of lightning shot down from the sky and struck randomly at the ground below. He imagined the storm would be heading this way, but was not worried because he had bigger concerns this night.

CHAPTER 20

Back at Castle Eladrias, the men camped outside all began groaning and complaining once more as they stared off south and saw the approaching storm. "Looks like we're in fer another cold an' wet one, fellers," one of the sentries announced.

"Me boots are still soaked from the last bout 'o rain we had the other night," another replied.

"Well, no sense leaving everything out ta get soaked, now, is there?" the man in charge said sullenly. "Let's get this gear covered much as can be, so we don't have a huge mess to be dealin' with in the mornin.'"

All about the outside of the castle and along the roads leading to the great watchtowers, the soldiers assigned outdoors were busily tying down their gear and covering their equipment and supplies with large sheets of canvas as best they could. The wind that had been blowing from the north earlier in the day suddenly changed to a southern direction and began to blow quite hard, tossing things about. "Looks like it's gonna get nasty out here," one of the archers called out to a friend who was stationed at the next set of wagons just down the road a ways.

"Sure does!" the other replied. "Don't know' bout you fellas, but we plan on crawling inside of this here wagon tonight once it gets dark, an' we're gonna try an' stay dry this time around."

"That's sound advice, friend," the first archer replied as he looked about at his own set of friends.

"I'm all for that," one of the men closest to him agreed.

"Count me in too," said the third man from the campsite as he tied off a piece of canvas over their wagon. "Let's try an' stay dry if we can tonight, fellas. I don't feel like sittin' in the dark wet all night."

As the afternoon grew long, and the first shades of nightfall crept across the land, the winds blew ever stronger and the sky above Silver Lake darkened under the black rolling storm clouds that had now moved into the area. Soon it was pitch black as if second dark had come hours early this evening, and everywhere the encamped soldiers were taking refuge and preparing for a rain of mighty proportions.

* * *

Still hiding under his pine trees to the south, Amansun had already begun to feel the first drops of rain that had moved over to the area where he had been some time earlier. Looking up at the darkening sky, he suddenly smiled and realized that along with the storm there would be an incredibly dark night this evening. "This should work well to my advantage," the dragon muttered to himself. "I should be able to stay quite hidden while flying in over the lake tonight if these clouds stay in the area awhile."

Suddenly the dragon's face changed from quite happy to very sad as he also thought about the possibility that the princess might choose to stay indoors this evening if the rain was pelting down as it had just the other day. "I shall just have to take my chances and hope for the best," he said to himself as the raindrops grew larger and more abundant. "Perhaps she is the type that enjoys feeling a bit of cool rain on her head now and again."

Far off north from where Amansun was resting, a small band of owls were taking shelter within the hollow of an immense oak tree. Looking out through one of the large holes from within the tree, Carceren the owl was smiling as he watched the sky turning black and the first rain starting to fall. "Looks like a good night for a dragon raid," he said while laughing to the others gathered about. "Maybe our large friend will have some good luck after all."

Further west from where the owls were gathered, two elves were making their way from one side of a pond to the other, where a cave was set into an enormous cliff face. "Might as well stay dry!" one said to the other. "The captain never said anything about having to stand out in the rain now."

"I didn't hear anything about not hiding in the cave neither," the other replied as the two made their way into the large dry cave and looked out upon the gathering storm. "And what do you suppose we'll do should the dragon return whilst we are hiding in his den, then?" he added, just now realizing what they were doing for the first time.

"You know," the first elf said to the second, now smiling and looking about into the sky somewhat nervously, "I don't suppose it's really going to rain all that hard tonight. No reason getting all dirty up in this dark hole, now. What say you we just take shelter under those trees over there?" He pointed in the general direction from where they had just come.

"Sounds great to me," the other said hastily as they quickly raced out of the cavern, laughing out loud and running for the cover of the trees.

* * *

Deep within the fortified walls of the castle, the royal family was sitting down for their evening meal. Along with the king, queen and princess were other lords and ladies, all sitting around an immense wooden table draped with expensive linens and covered from one side to the other with all types of fruits, vegetables, nuts, cheeses, platters of meats, large casks of wine and great big steins of beer. In addition to the usual dinner crowd, seven knights were seated, having come from north, south, east and west at the king's beckoning.

Standing from one end of the great table, with the queen seated to his side, King Hasselfeth now raised his goblet of wine in his right hand and welcomed his guests to dinner. "Welcome to all," he said while raising his glass above his head. "We are gathered here at Castle Eladrias to join forces against a great beast that has suddenly shown himself from out of the west where creatures of his kind are still many. Ladies and lords," he uttered as he looked around the table at the collection of well-dressed noblemen seated. "I have called upon the knights of our kingdom and beyond to join us in this noble crusade, and I am sure you join me in thanking them for coming to us during our hour of need!" He took a drink.

As the crowd seated around the table raised their glasses in kind and toasted the knights present, they let out a cheer and shouted, "Hurrah! Hurrah!" now clinking their glasses against each other's in a great toast.

"It would appear that the great beast has gone into hiding, or so I am told," the king went on to say. "None of my soldiers out in the woods have been able to find his lair as of yet; and even the elfin king's scouts, who are assisting us in this search, have been unable to locate the great beast."

"Well, we shall be ready for him when he shows himself!" shouted Baerden, the king's captain of the guard, as he stood and raised his stein to the king and queen. "My men are in position around the entire lake along with here at the castle, with our new wagon-sized crossbows, and the beast will soon regret his visit," he said confidently as he took a large draught of beer.

"Not if we get to him first!" said the knight dressed in red and black armor, smiling at the guests seated around the table. "I have not traveled for days just to sit back and watch whilst others beat down this winged serpent."

"Well said, Knight Berardren," the king replied. "I look forward to seeing you and my own men joined together if and when the giant shows up at our doorstep," he continued. "But have no fear, as your journey to our great castle will not be in vain even if the beast decides to fade away back from whence he came."

"How so, good King?" the red knight asked.

As the crowd gathered around the table now quieted down and stared over at the king who was still standing, he announced, "I have arranged a great tournament for our special guests, and noblemen from our very own castle as well." He now glanced back at his wife and daughter still seated nearby and smiled. "A great test of strength, courage, skill and intelligence!" The crowd continued to cheer loudly and pat each other on the backs wildly.

"And what shall be the prize, good King?" another of the visiting knights asked quickly.

"The winner of this tournament, the champion of this series of contests and challenges, will get the best and most valuable prize my kingdom has to offer," the king said proudly, now looking over his shoulder directly at the princess. "My daughter's hand in marriage!" he roared while slamming his fist into the table below. The knights gathered around the table, along with Baerden and many of the other men from the castle, all leapt to their feet and hoisted their glasses above them in surprise and exhilaration, while the diners gathered about the table cheered and roared once more.

"A toast to the king!" Baerden cried out loudly, raising his stein upwards once more, "and also to Princess Lyleth! Let every man know that this is a prize beyond all others and surely I will capture the good king's daughter or die trying!"

"Watch what ye asks for, as it may come to pass," the blue knight said while raising his glass to the princess and smiling as he looked directly upon her.

Princess Lyleth, the only person at the table who was not excited or cheering, stood and looked at her father the king, and leaning closer to him whispered, "So this is why you have summoned all of these strangers into our castle? And why did you choose to announce me as your prize before even letting me know what was afoot?" She turned and walked out of the great hall.

Two attendants who had been standing back from the table, both young girls of the same age as the princess, followed her out of the room and down the hall back towards her sleeping chambers. As they hurried to catch up with the princess, who was walking quite swiftly, they heard the unmistakable sound of weeping coming from the young woman who was normally known for her brilliant eyes and winning smile.

* * *

Back in his field to the south, Amansun the dragon had waited as long as he was willing. Looking up at the now black sky and feeling the soft drops of rain that were still swirling about, he beat his enormous wings and began the flight that would finally take him to his quest's objective, the great Castle Eladrias, and hopefully the princess. As he flew eastward and towards the low ridge that had kept him out of view for some time now, he made a point of flying just above the treetops so as not to be seen by the watchtowers that he knew had to be just ahead of him on either side of the great lake.

As he crested the trees and was finally able to look into the valley that contained the great Silver Lake, he noticed immediately that it, along with just about everything else, was shrouded in darkness from the large storm that was still slowly passing through. He flew up just to the point where he would be hidden in the mist, and then out over the main body of the lake so as to avoid any archers who may still be on watch in the pouring rain. As he crossed over the halfway point, he glanced down and saw the cluster of boats that his friend Carceren the owl had warned him of. The winds were still gusting quite strong, and the ships below were being tossed about violently by the storm surge slamming against their bows. *I won't be needing to worry much about them now*, he thought to himself, as he saw the small boats bouncing about beneath him like puppets on a string. *Looks like I can fly straight into the castle without worry.*

Tucked safely inside her royal chambers, Princess Lyleth was locked into a discussion with her two ladies-in-waiting. They were doing their best to convince the young princess to abandon her nightly viewing of the lake from her balcony because of the thunder and lightning flashing out over the lake this stormy night. She, on the other hand, was quite convinced that this was the perfect setting for her mood, ruined this night by her father's unwanted and unwelcome announcement.

"'Tis dreadful out this evening, Princess," one of the young women said pleadingly. "You're bound to be struck by lighnting should you step out onto that balcony tonight!"

The other maiden chimed in, adding, "If the lightning doesn't get you, surely you will catch your death of the cold from that nasty wind and driving rain out there!"

"Nonsense, you two," the princess insisted. "You know I step out to look upon the great lake every night, and this will be no exception! Besides, the stormy weather outside suits my mood this evening, and I believe I will feel much more alive and welcome out there this night then tucked safely here within these castle walls that plot against me and my happiness."

Seeing that they would not be able to convince her otherwise, the two maidens took a heavy cloak out of one of the princess's dressers and wrapped it about her as she made her way towards the door leading out to her private balcony. "At least keep this on while you are out, for us," the maidens pleaded.

"Very well, as you insist," the princess offered, "but don't bother me while I am out there. I feel I need to be out there more this night than any other, for some strange reason. It's as if I am meant to be out in that storm tonight." She walked out the door and closed it behind her as she did so.

As Amansun was closing the distance between him and the west wall of the castle, he thought he saw a quick flash of light up ahead amidst the dull gray stone, as if a door or window had suddenly opened and then closed quickly once more. Not quite sure exactly where the princess's balcony was, he decided to make for this light. The storm was at its peak just then and the rain was coming down in sheets, while the wind tossed the waves about on the surface of the lake. Anyone still on watch trying to look out from their battle stations would have had a difficult time just managing to keep their eyes open.

Princess Lyleth, standing on the edge of her balcony as she always did, was somewhat protected from the storm by the castle's walls directly behind her. Though she was getting quite wet from the sweeping rain, she could still look off into the waters ahead and appreciate the enormity of the storm as it passed by. She stood there as still as a statue, hands on the stone railing of her balcony, eyes fixed straight ahead as she tried to make out the boats she had seen earlier in the week anchored out at the middle of the lake; but all she could now make out were the whitecaps from the waves tossing about on the now jet-black lake.

Amansun, having made it nearly all the way to the west wall of the castle, fought to hover in mid-air as he peered ahead at the stone walls of the great fortress ahead. The whipping winds and pouring rain made it difficult for him to make out much, but he continued to stare out into the blackness, trying to see if he was near the spot where he had seen the glimpse of light flashing just a moment earlier.

Now gazing directly out at each other, neither being able to see the other because of the intensity of the great storm, dragon and princess were nearly locked in upon the other, not knowing that once seen, neither of them would ever be able to forget the other.

Overhead there was a tremendous *crack* and *boom* as the immense storm clouds roared in anger, and then a sudden brilliant flash lit up the night as a tremendous lightning bolt raced down to the lake's surface and shattered into a thousand fingers of light. Looking directly at the large beast, appearing to be floating in the darkness just ahead, now illuminated brilliantly, the princess let out a piercing scream as her eyes met the dragon's.

Amansun, now looking directly upon the beauty and wonderment of the princess, cloaked in her white coat, blonde hair whipping about in the swirling wind, gasped in awe as he realized the thing he had traveled so long and so far for was just a few dozen feet away now.

Another brilliant flash of lightning illuminated the night and then another. Each one lit up the two unexpected strangers as they stayed motionless, each studying the other intently during each brief second of light, transfixed in their positions; the dragon hovering in place in the raging storm, the princess frozen to the railing of her stone balcony.

"Did you hear a scream?" one of the maidens asked the other excitedly.

"No, just the booming of thunder and the sound of lightning crackling outside," the other said more calmly.

"Suppose we should go out and check on the princess?" the first asked, still quite flustered from the sound she thought she had heard.

"Not tonight, dear!" the other quickly replied. "The princess is in a terrible mood tonight, now, isn't she?" She gave the other an insistent glare. "And besides," she added, "'twas her orders herself to not disturb her. You heard her yourself, did you not?"

"I guess you're right, then," the first said, still not quite convinced. "But I think I'll step just a bit closer to the door, just in case I hear it again." She moved closer to the doorway leading outside.

Outside on her balcony, Princess Lyleth was torn between fleeing for the doorway just a few steps behind her now and staying to stare out at the mighty winged beast hovering just in front of her. Even now in the darkness she could still see the dragon quite clearly, as the rain had slowed slightly and the beast seemed to move closer. Not feeling any apparent danger, she stood her ground and looked directly into the large eyes of the dragon who was clearly looking back at her as well. She was amazed by the enormity of the dragon's presence and she couldn't help but wonder what was causing the magnificent beast to be flying here, just outside her bedroom quarters.

Amansun, likewise, was overcome by the princess's beauty and fearlessness. How was it possible that she had not fled to the safety of the castle, now that she had clearly seen him here just a short distance from where she was still standing?

The two strangers stayed there, locked together unblinking, each trying to decide what to do next, when the sound of a great horn suddenly blew from off in the distance. *Toooodooooo*, the horn sounded from afar once again. *Toooodoooo*. The princess glanced over at the lake's shoreline, realizing that someone else had now spotted the dragon. Within seconds, the sounds of alarm rose from seemingly every direction. Great triangles of steel were being struck by forceful hammer blows, drums were being beaten, soldiers were yelling, and from all sides of the castle you could hear the continuing blast of the horn drifting out across the wind: *Toooodoooo*.

Amansun and the princess each glanced about and then returned their eyes to each other once more. The princess, fearing for the dragon suddenly and unexpectedly, waved her arms at it in a pushing fashion, as if to say "go away, get out of here." Amansun, not wanting to leave and unsure of what to do next, continued to hover in mid-air. It took just a few more seconds and then the first volley of arrows flew across the castle wall at the large flying beast, now that he had been spotted. "He's over here!" came a muffled cry in the still-blowing wind. "Over by the princess's quarters!" the voice called out desperately.

Suddenly realizing that the great beast before her was likely staying there because of her presence, the princess ran across the balcony and made her way back into her room once more. "Are you alright?" the maidens called out in alarm as they realized the sounds they had been hearing had been coming from outside now and not from within the castle as they had originally guessed. "Is there something out there?"

"There may have been," the princess said rather reluctantly, choosing to mask the truth for now. "I thought I saw something out beyond the castle walls, but it was so dark and stormy, it was quite difficult to see with certainty."

Out in the stormy night, Amansun was being pelted by a barrage of small, harmless arrows that hit his armored hide and bounced off only to fall into the lake below. Seeing that the princess was now clearly gone, he decided it best that he get as far away from the castle as possible, and soon. He continued to make a hasty retreat as the men below quickly scrambled to their stations to defend against the invading beast. As he sped by, he glanced down and he could see that many of the wagons that he had passed by earlier on his way in were now uncovered and soldiers were standing directly behind them as they fiddled with the large bolts his friend the owl had warned him of a few days earlier. *Best I not tarry long enough to get struck by one of those*, he thought as he picked up speed, now flying directly westward and not quite as near to the shoreline as before.

Twang went the large release mechanism as one of the large bolts streaked upward towards the fleeing dragon. *Twang* went another, and then another, as Amansun watched several large bolts flash below and above him as he closed on the farthest edge of the lake. "Just have to make it a little further," he cried out as he pushed himself as hard as he could. "There's the edge of the lake now."

Suddenly Amansun heard a volley of bolts being fired as if all at once, and he realized that there had been one last tower, hidden amongst the trees. As he closed upon the farthest edge of the lake, he looked down and saw a quiver of bolts all heading in his direction at once. There was no way he could possibly avoid being struck by all of them, he thought as he felt a sudden and severe pain strike at his left wing. Suddenly brought to a near-stop, the great winged serpent appeared to float in the air, as its enormous wings flapped about relentlessly, trying to avoid falling to the water below.

"Hurrah!" went the cheer from the men somewhere below. "We've hit the beast! Prepare another volley!" Below in the darkness and mud, the heavily clad soldiers were hurriedly twisting the cranks on the back of each of the large crossbow machines. As their muscles bulged and their hands strained, the leads from each team shouted out desperately, "Pull with everything you've got, now, you slackards! Pull as if your very life depended on it!" As the enormous bolts slowly moved back into the firing mechanisms, the sound of heavy breathing and swearing could be heard, as the men struggled to reload as quickly as possible.

Sticking out of Amansun's left wing was an enormous steel barbed bolt, at least six feet long and quite heavy he could tell as its weight was pulling that side of his body down. As he struggled to stay in the air, he promised himself, "this is not how it is going to end!" he growled. "I refuse to die here in this lake after having come this far and seeing the princess for the first time!" and with that he made a tremendous effort to put the pain out of his mind and he flew as best he could into the cover of the trees just ahead.

Glancing down in the direction from whence the bolts had come, Amansun suddenly lowered his head down and forced out tremendous bursts of flame spraying out towards the darkness below. As the soldiers below, now temporarily blinded by the sudden flashes of fire above, ducked down to take shelter from the blast, the injured dragon beat his wings as best his he could, his left wing flapping failingly like a swallow with a broken wing fluttering about on the ground, and slowly made his way forward once again, heading for the safety of the trees in the distance. "Quickly, quickly," he could hear the voices calling from behind him now. "He's almost out of sight." He felt a few harmless arrows flying by, some hitting him, others not. And with that, Amansun flew off over the tops of the trees, wings flapping wildly as he struggled to maintain his height, and he disappeared into the darkness.

Back on the eastern end of the lake at the castle, the king's men looked out over the dark waters in the direction the dragon had disappeared. As they looked into the darkness, they were amazed when a brilliant flash of fire illuminated the dark. "That was no lightning strike," one of the lords cried out. "The beast is attacking the western watchtower, or I am a fool!"

"To arms, to arms!" the captain of the guard called out to his men. "Mount up and ride with me now while there is still time to catch the beast!"

As Baerden and a large group of mounted soldiers and archers rode off along the muddy courtyard towards the castle gates, now being raised by great turning wheels, several of the knights who had arrived the previous day and night also saddled their steeds and called out to their men to follow. Within moments, a group of one hundred riders were speeding along the muddy track that followed the northern edge of the lake. "Make haste!" Baerden cried out as he rode by the men who had been stationed along the road in their wagons. "Join us now as we ride to help our brothers on the western tower!"

Still safely tucked into their warm and dry tree hollow, Carceren and his cousins glanced out and watched as the cool night air ignited into flame on the western end. "That has to be our dragon!" the owl said with a large grin. "Looks like the fool has gone and done it." He stepped out onto one of the great tree's branches and peered off west. "Let's go out for a bit and have a look to see what the men of the castle are up to," he requested as he prepared to fly off. Suddenly looking back at the other owls who were walking out of the hollow behind him, he cautioned, "Have a care where you are flying, cousins, for there are likely to be many trigger-happy archers out and about this evening!" and off he flew.

Back at the castle, King Hasselfeth and a group of armed guards had made their way up to the princess's quarters. Knocking loudly upon the door to her chambers, the king called out, "Are you alright in there, my dear?"

The large wooden door opened slowly and out stepped the princess. "We are quite fine," the princess announced. "And what is all this fuss about outside? You haven't started your tournament in this horrendous storm, now, have you, Father?" She grinned.

"The beast has been sighted just outside the castle walls, Lyleth!" the king replied. "Stay in your room and do not go out on your balcony until I say it is safe to do so." He turned and walked off briskly down the hall as his personal guard followed close behind. "Collect my sword and shield at once!" he commanded while looking at one of his personal attendants. "I'll meet you at the stable as soon as I have donned my armor." He stormed off in the direction of his own chambers.

CHAPTER 21

Struggling to stay above the treetops, Amansun was doing his best to keep flying further into the woods. He knew he would be pursued by the king's men soon so the further he was able to fly, the better chance he would have of getting away. *I suppose I shouldn't have sent out those blasts of flame*, he thought to himself as he tried to concentrate on anything other than the terrible pain he was feeling in his left wing, *I practically announced to everyone about the lake where my exact location was*, he mused, now smiling through the pain.

As the dragon continued to struggle and flutter his way over the trees, he peered down below for a suitable spot to touch down. "First thing I shall have to do is get rid of this cursed bolt in my wing," he said aloud to himself as he glanced ahead. "Don't think I'll be able to go much further…"

Amansun made it a half-mile further into the woods and then spotted a small clearing in the trees, just big enough for him to set down, and he came in for a wobbly landing. Easing his gigantic body down as slowly as possible, his wing tips lightly brushed against the branches of the trees on the edge of the clearing, and then he fell the remaining few feet with a loud *thud*. Amansun sat there in darkness, listening for the sounds of pursuit, but heard nothing other than the rattling of tree branches from the gusts of wind that were still blowing from the storm which was now passing onwards to the north.

Guess I'm safe for the moment, he thought to himself as he glanced at the large piece of wood sticking out from his wing. Staring at the bolt through squinting eyes as he continued to feel waves of pain rush through his body, he decided his only option would be to bite the wooden bolt in half. Lowering his head to the left while he gingerly tried to lift his wing up, still weighted down by the protruding bolt, the great beast began to bite down on the wood with his saber-like teeth. With little effort the piece of wood was soon bitten in half and lying on the ground below. He lifted his wing slowly and gently to test it and found that although he was still in considerable pain, he felt he might be able to go a little further if he had to.

Looking into the darkness of the trees around him once more, he steadied his breath and listened carefully once again. At first, he only heard the sound of the wind blowing through the trees, but then off in the distance, still soft but growing slowly louder, he could hear the baying of hounds and he pictured a hunting party of soldiers, being led by a group of howling dogs, plunging into the darkness of the trees and making their way to his hiding spot. *Staying here is certainly out of the question*, he thought. *I'm going to have to risk tearing my wing further and fly at least back over the ridge once more, or I am sure to be found before this night is over.*

Having made up his mind that there was no other choice, he readied himself for the inevitable pain he would soon be feeling, and he flew upward and out once more over the treetops, heading west as best as he could manage. His progress was quite slow, and not without considerable pain, but as the minutes passed by he put more and more distance between himself and the lake.

Flying a little further west than where he had originally been hiding, he was suddenly stuck by an unbearable pain as his left wing tore nearly from top to bottom, and he plummeted toward the ground in an awkward spiral as he fought to stay in control. Landing with an even louder *thud*, he looked over at his torn wing and realized that he had flown as far as he would be able for now.

Doubled over in pain, and looking about at the trees that surrounded his landing spot, even in the blackness of second dark he could see that he had flown too far and too straight into the woods. The trees ahead and around him were blacker than any he had seen before, at least from the ground, and it became apparent to him that he had inadvertently flown right into the black woods he had been so often warned of avoiding.

* * *

Unseen by the many men racing through the trees below, a small group of owls made their way up and over the ridge line separating the main forest from the easternmost edge where the great Silver Lake lay. Peering ahead into the dark night, Carceren saw his friend flapping and fluttering just above the treetops ahead, and then suddenly he was gone. The group of owls circled in the air once, calling out to each other, then spiraled down one after the other and came to rest in the branches of a great pine. "There's naught we can do for him now, Carceren," Methistus said sadly to his friend and leader. "He's crossed over the barrier now and lies somewhere up ahead in her black woods."

"He speaks the truth, cousin," young Obrides agreed. "Was it not you yourself that said we were never to enter past the first row of blackened trees no matter what the circumstances?"

"These things I have said, it is true," the owl admitted reluctantly, "and yet he has only just crossed into the denser part of the wood. Perhaps we can reach him still and warn him of his peril?" He turned to look at each of the owls gathered about him.

"It is against all teachings that we have had since we were but nestlings, including those teachings we received directly from you," Methistus disagreed. "I shall not enter past this line of trees, and neither should any of you, I am afraid. You are letting your feelings for the great beast cloud your better judgement, friend."

"Perhaps you are right, cousin," Carceren said softly while turning once more to look out over the trees ahead, "but I can't help but feel that I must at least try to help him. I will fly in and out as quickly as possible, just long enough to tell the beast where he is now resting, and then join you back here."

"I will go with you," young Bathis said quite suddenly and expectedly. "Aside from you, he knows me best as I was his personal guard for several days. I too feel I must try and warn him of his error in taking shelter in the black woods."

Looking at the young owl with a new sense of respect, Carceren advised the others that they were to wait for them in the pine until they returned shortly. "If we are not back in a reasonable time, fly home at once and leave us be, for our fates will surely be sealed by then," Carceren called out as he and Bathis took to the air. As the two owls nervously approached the spot where the large dragon had fell from the sky, they were both gripped with fear as they thought of all the old tales and stories they had ever heard of the black woods.

* * *

"It cannot be!" Amansun called out as he saw the two owls gliding in from above. "How is this possible that you have found me here in this blackness?"

"We were following you the last few miles as you struggled along, Sir Amansun," the large owl spoke while looking closely at his friend. "You are in grave danger and the three of us must make haste to fly back east out of these black trees at once." He nervously looked all about.

"That is not possible," the dragon replied knowingly. "I realize I have ventured into the black woods you warned me of, but alas, my wing is damaged beyond repair, I am afraid, and I shall not be flying anywhere anytime soon."

Walking slowly over to the dragon's side, Carceren looked upon the dragon's torn wing, grimacing, and said aloud, "It's a miracle you made it as far as you have, Sir Amansun. I can only imagine what pain you must have suffered these past few miles as you flew."

"That explains how we were able to catch up to you now," young Bathis said, now also looking over at the greatly damaged wing.

"The two of you are quite brave indeed, and foolish I might add," the dragon said as he smiled at his two small friends. "Did I not tell you both not to put yourself in harm's way on my account?"

Carceren looked at the darkness of the trees surrounding the group and felt a shudder run up along his back. "This is clearly the last place we would have hoped to find you, Sir Amansun," he started whispering now, "and yet I suppose it is as good a place as any in your condition, what with not being able to fly." Looking about once more as if expecting something dreadful to happen at any moment, he went on. "A great hunting party has set into the woods from the west end of the lake, as you may have seen, and I am quite sure they will continue to pursue you through the night and into the next day if I am not mistaken."

"So, being here, injured and unable to fly, in these cursed woods is a good thing, then?" the dragon asked, now puzzled by the words of the owl.

"In this case it is, friend," the owl muttered softly. "I can assure you that none of the king's men, not even the bravest among his warriors and knights, will venture into these woods in darkness. If you were to have to choose a place to take refuge until that wing of yours heals itself, this is likely the only spot you could have chosen to ensure your pursuers would not follow."

"Be that as it may, good friend, I must insist that you and young Bathis depart at once and leave me to these woods right away," the dragon said firmly.

Peering about again, Carceren looked up at his friend and with a half-smirk on his face said calmly, "You don't have to ask twice, friend!" while looking at the younger owl only a few feet away. "It took all the courage I had within me just to fly into these woods for a moment, and even now I can feel the flesh on my bones crawling with fear and apprehension. We will depart at once and wish you luck, Sir Amansun."

"My thanks to you both once more, then, friends. Now go!" the dragon insisted. With that, Bathis and Carceren quickly took flight and made for the large pine where their cousins were still hidden away.

Surrounded by hundred-foot-tall trees black as midnight, Amansun now lay down in agony, trying to move his injured wing as little as possible, as he lay there unmoving, not wanting to make a sound. Glancing up to the sky he could see that the clouds were clearing up and giving way to a blanket of stars. Though he could not see the moon, he guessed it was out and shining, judging by the glow he could see on the edges of some of the remaining clouds. *At least I won't have to worry about the soldiers chasing me into these woods*, he thought, remembering the words his friend the owl had shared not long ago. *I'll just sit here lodged in these trees and pass the night away, and with any luck nothing big and nasty like those sticky spiders will turn up.* He glanced from side to side and listened as intently as he could for any signs of noise or movement in the surrounding trees.

* * *

Far back and over the ridge, the men from the lake were still making their way into the blackness of the woods, torches in one hand and swords in the other. "This be madness, friend!" one of the soldiers whispered to those nearby as they dodged tree branches and tried not to fall into the small ravines. "What do they think we are to do, even if we do corner the beast?"

To the man's left another man, panting loudly and clearly out of breath, added, "Pray we don't find the beast is what I says. He'll likely turn us into a grand bonfire should we happen to find him lying in wait in the darkness ahead."

From some distance ahead from where they were, the grumbling men heard the unmistakable voice of their captain shouting out orders. "Archers to the front, spearman next, and keep your eyes open, men. The beast was hit and is likely grounded, now waiting in some black hole or thicket of trees just waiting to flash us into cinders!"

"At least the captain and his archers are out in front, says I," the same grumbling voice whispered once more. "Watch for a bright flash of light up ahead, and if you do see one, be sure to turn and head the other way." He quietly laughed.

"Not much good them archers will be anyhows," the second added, wheezing for another breath. "I saw them arrows bouncing off the beast's scales as if they were no more than drops of rain!"

* * *

Back at the castle, Princess Lyleth had sent her maidens off to bed for the night and she was resting in her room alone now. She sat on a large, quilted chair with a serious look on her face, as if she was deeply troubled and trying to make sense of something that made none. *How is it that I felt so little fear when the great winged serpent was there in front of me, staring into my eyes so steadfastly, almost as if he was trying to speak?* she thought to herself. *Every instinct inside of me should have been telling me to run, to save myself, to take shelter, and yet I stood on that balcony, unafraid, unmoving, feeling no sense of fear or dread at all.* As she sat there lost in thought, she closed her eyes and pictured the great beast's penetrating eyes once more, remembering how they looked into hers, how they seemed to be reaching out to her, and she felt great confusion and wonder.

* * *

Back once again in their tree, Carceren, Bathis and some of the other owls gathered together one last time before retiring for the night. "Well, you certainly did all you could have," Belfest said, trying to cheer up his cousin.

"More than the rest of us were willing or able to do, to be sure!" Obrides agreed.

"I know," Carceren said hesitatingly, "and yet I can't help but feel that we let the dragon down, leaving him lying there injured in the blackness of those evil woods, all alone." He sighed.

"Well, you did manage to give him some hope at least," Bathis remarked, "if that is what you were trying to accomplish. That was brilliant, trying to make something good out of his being hopelessly trapped in those black woods by saying he would be safe from the men of the castle."

"All I said was the truth," Carceren said softly. "No one will likely follow him into those woods, especially now that he has flown so far into them. All we can do is hope for the best now, and hope he makes it at least to see the light of a new day."

* * *

That night was one of the worst and longest nights the great dragon had ever endured in his entire life. Laying there in pain, fading in and out of a restless sleep, the only thing that kept his spirits up was thinking repeatedly about the princess he had finally seen for himself, even if only at a distance. All that long night he pictured her beautiful face, her enchanting eyes, her billowing hair flying about her shoulders. That is what Amansun focused on through that long and painful night, and that vision gave him the strength to endure the pain from his wing and the courage to lie there, deep in those enchanted woods, all alone in the blackness.

CHAPTER 22

Far out to the east the sun had already risen, but its glorious rays had not yet begun to penetrate the dark woods where Amansun still lay. Slowly opening his weary eyes and trying to make sense of where he was, why it was so dark, and why he hurt so bad, the first remembrances of the previous night started to settle into the dragon's waking thoughts. Rising too quickly, his torn wing shot flashes of pain into his head, and he quickly stopped moving, remembering that he was going to have to take things very easily and slowly from here on in.

Looking about, he saw he was still bundled up in between a patch of very tall and incredibly black trees that appeared to be all round him, leaving very little room for him to move. As the sunlight above started to lessen the darkness, he was surprised to see that just to his right the trees seemed to be less dense and dark. There almost seemed to be a touch of light coming from just beyond the first row of trees ahead. *That's odd*, the great dragon thought as he tried lifting himself once more, this time moving much more slowly and remembering not to use the left side of his body. *It seems as though I fell right into a dense patch of trees last night, and yet there appears to be some sort of opening just there.*

As he gingerly raised his immense body to a standing position, he glanced ahead towards the dim light to his right, and he started to slowly walk in that direction. To his great surprise and delight, just a few paces ahead of where he had spent the past night, there was a well-worn dirt path, large enough for even the great beast to walk along. It went in two opposite directions, one appearing to lead east, the other towards the west. Stepping out onto the path, Amansun was quite happy as he realized that he would not be forced to squeeze himself through a never-ending thicket of dense trees and branches. He had in fact spent a good portion of his time last night wondering how he was going to move his large body through the tightly packed trees. *Well, one problem is solved*, he thought happily to himself.

Now standing squarely on the dirt path and staring up at the towering trees that went on endlessly on each side of it, he had to decide which way he should go. Looking to his left, and then turning and glancing to his right, he could see that the path seemed to be about the same in either direction. Both were covered with a light sprinkling of grass and bare earth, and it was impossible to tell which direction was used more than the other. Remembering that he had been flying west and directly into the black woods, he quickly reasoned that his best bet was to take the path that led off to the east so that he could avoid walking into the middle of the woods. Even if the soldiers of the king were in that direction, he surmised they posed less of a risk to him than the sorceress of the woods who was said to live at the very center. Amansun began walking along the path, the sky above continuing to brighten, and he thought things were actually looking better than he could have hoped for.

As Amansun marched along, trying to maintain a steady pace, even though his wing was ringing with pain every step, he continually glanced up at the sky above and tried to determine where the sun was. From the depths of the forest all he could really make out was a pale blue sky with no real indication of direction whatsoever. Still, he felt confident that he had chosen the right direction to walk based on his flight the night before, so he continued to press on and cover as much ground as possible, eager to find the edge of the black woods as soon as possible.

As Amansun walked along that path, which at first had appeared to be quite straight in its course, he noticed that it seemed to be bending. Feeling like he had to stop for a moment to try and get his bearings once more, he turned to look back at the way he had just come, and was in disbelief when the path directly behind him split off into two separate directions. *This is madness!* the dragon thought as he stared back in wonderment. "How can this be? There has been one path and only one path this entire time," he said loudly to himself, beginning to feel a bit panicked. "Best I make haste in my present direction," he assured himself, now wanting to get out of the woods even more than before.

Staring straight ahead, Amansun now wobbled visibly from side to side and leaned over on his right wingtip to prevent himself from falling over. There, directly in front of him, in the direction he had been traveling this past hour or so, the path that had been one was now three. As Amansun half-stood and half-kneeled there in the middle of the dirt pathway, he looked ahead at the three separate paths: one leading to the left, one to the right, and one right down the middle. "This cannot be," he spoke aloud once more, "or surely I have found myself in a dream." He looked at his damaged wing, gave it a little shake, and immediately felt a rush of pain rushing through his body. "Well, that still hurts, so I must not be dreaming. I don't believe one feels pain when in a dream."

Looking ahead at his three possible choices, he suddenly felt that moving forward might be a poor choice. "I have no idea what direction I am now going in, and I certainly don't know which of these three paths is likely to lead me in the direction I want to go," he convinced himself. Turning once again into the direction he had just come from, he reasoned his best bet would be to follow one of these paths back to the spot where he had spent the night, so that he could get his bearings once again and then decide what his next move should be. *Since I thought I was traveling east all this time, then walking back in this direction must be west?* he thought to himself. "So now all I have to do is choose which of these paths I should take," he said confidently.

Looking along the earthen pathways, he searched to see if his tracks remained. To his dismay, he saw tracks that might have been his own coming from both paths. "Clearly some sort of magic is afoot, or I have merely lost my mind," he reasoned. "I cannot have walked down both paths simultaneously, so one of these must be the correct choice." While both paths led back in the direction he had come from, they were split by an ever-widening section of the tall black trees so that there was clearly a left path and a right path.

"If I am to head back and west once again," he tried to reason, now talking the problem out to himself aloud, "then the path to the right must lead northward and directly into the heart of the woods. Clearly I must take the path on the left, as eventually it should lead southwards and away from the wood's center. I shall walk down this path to the left until I find the spot where I came out from the woods, and then I am certain to see some solution to this puzzle." He tried to sound convincing to himself but failed.

Amansun started walking down the path on the left, being sure to pay close attention to the left side of the path, as he really wanted to find the spot where he had rested the previous night. He was making good progress and feeling good about his decision when he made his way around a bend and found to his surprise that the pathway up ahead went up and over a small stone bridge that crossed over a narrow stream. "Magic at work once again or I'm a fool," he said angrily. "There was no stream anywhere in sight when I first left my nook in the trees, and I haven't seen any water until just now."

As the dragon approached the stream, he argued with himself on whether he should take a drink, as he was quite thirsty by this time. "You are walking inside of a magical wood," one side argued, "so clearly this must be a magical stream, and drinking from it would be quite foolish." "Still," the other side countered back, "you are already seeing things and following paths that spring up from nowhere, so what can be the harm?" In the end he decided he may as well parch his thirst. He dropped to his knees at the stream's edge and lowered his head to the water below.

As he started taking large gulps of the cool water, he began to have the uncomfortable feeling that someone was watching him. He lifted his head up quickly and glanced all about but saw nothing. As he lowered his head once again to continue drinking, he heard a soft voice giggling close by. He looked all about at the trees on either side of the pathway as well as towards the other side of the bridge. Seeing nothing there, he lowered his head once more then jumped back, nearly falling over himself suddenly. There just a few feet ahead of him and directly in the surface of the water was a small child's face, with long dark hair floating about in the current of the stream. The young girl smiled at the dragon playfully as her head slowly raised up and out of the water.

"Is this another one of my visions or have I completely lost my mind?" he said aloud, now staring at the young girl who had risen out of the water high enough for him to see her shoulders.

"No need to fear me, silly beast!" the young water spirit said while smiling and giggling. "I thought you might be thirsty so I brought the stream to you, as I could see you weren't going to find it by yourself." She shook the water out of her hair.

"Then you are real…and this stream that I see is real…and the water I am drinking is real too?" the dragon asked.

"Of course it's all real, silly," the girl said. "No need to drink too much, as there are many streams to be found in the Lady of the Woods' domain." She grabbed a flower that had been floating down the current and placed it in her hair. "Don't try so hard to decide which paths to take. All roads lead to her." And then she giggled and disappeared into the depths of the clear water.

After his drink, Amansun continued along his chosen path, walking over the bridge and moving forward at a reasonable pace. It didn't take long for the path to start curving well to the right and, as he moved along, he became aware that he was likely walking directly into the middle of the woods once again. "If only this wing wasn't torn, I could at least fly above these trees to see which way I am heading," he said, now quite frustrated.

The sky above appeared to be lighter as he continued, and the path he was on began to rise and fall. The never-ending trees went on and on with no apparent breaks in them, and in time a small wall of hand-placed stones appeared and lined both sides of the path. *I'm not quite sure if that is a good sign or a bad one*, he thought to himself, now looking at the stone wall bordering his path. "At least I know someone was here once to build this wall," he said as he imagined whom or what it might have been that had carefully placed all these stones on top of one another long ago.

After another march along the wall-lined path, Amansun came to a point where the path ahead dropped down at a severe angle, as if leading into an even lower and darker section of the woods. Looking down the hill before him, he guessed the change in elevation had to be at least a good hundred feet or so. *This can't be right*, Amansun thought to himself. *I think the last thing I want to do now is walk deeper and deeper into these woods. Guess it's time to turn around and see where the other path will take me.* He slowly turned around, being careful to not move his damaged wing too much, and found much to his dismay that he was now looking directly at a wide stream that blocked his way. On the far bank there was nothing but tall black trees as far as he could see. "This really is getting quite silly!" he announced loudly, as if someone nearby might hear his complaint. "Now I see why Carceren was so insistent I not come in these dreadful woods!" Amansun carefully made his way down the meandering path as it twisted about one way and then the other, rising up in some places and back down again in others.

In time, the dragon found himself approaching what appeared to be an opening in the trees ahead, the first he had seen since he had started walking earlier in the day. Approaching the last few feet up to the clearing ahead, Amansun suddenly stopped, unsure of whether he wanted to move any further forward, as he tried to investigate the clearing now directly in front of him. As he stood there on the dirt and grass pathway, a thought suddenly occurred to him. He was overcome now by the thought that he really had no other choice but to move forward. "I'm sure if I turn around and look now, I am bound to see something strange and completely different than what I would expect to see there," he whispered to himself. "May as well keep going, as this path seems to take me only where it chooses anyway." He suddenly realized the absurdity of his situation. "Guess I just can't help myself but to at least turn around and have one look," he said aloud to himself.

Still standing in place, but now turning to look back from whence he had just come, Amansun suddenly broke into a fit of laughter as his eyes stared backwards. There, directly behind him and not twenty paces back, an immense stone wall, at least thirty feet tall and going from one side to the other as far as he could see, was completely blocking his exit, should he had decided to try and go back again. Amansun smiled at the great wall, as if surrendering to it and the odd path he had stumbled onto, here in this magical place, and he turned and began walking towards the clearing. Moving forward, he was almost certain he could hear the sound of many faint voices laughing behind him, but he didn't see the point in turning around to look and see where they might be coming from.

* * *

Miles away and far off to the east, King Hasselfeth was sitting on his throne and watching intently as a small group of armor-clad soldiers were walking his way. Looking down upon the group as they halted a good twenty paces back from the first of the stone steps that led up towards his royal throne, Captain Baerden bowed low and presented himself to the king. "What word have you from the field, good Captain?" the king inquired.

The captain explained that the great beast had disappeared into the cover of the great forest and was for the moment still unseen. "We have reason to believe that we wounded the beast gravely," the captain said, "yet he managed to escape our men, flying west in a manner of speaking. Although from the accounts I have been given, he was clearly in distress and flying quite awkwardly."

"And what are your thoughts as to his intentions now, my captain?" the king asked.

"We believe, your Highness, that the great beast has taken shelter in the Black Woods of the west. Clearly his judgment was clouded by his injury or perhaps he is not aware of the legends of the enchantress who lives there."

"Then it is your belief that we have possibly seen the last of the serpent, then?" King Hasselfeth guessed.

"It is, your majesty," Captain Baerden concurred. "Most who enter that deep, dark place are never seen or heard from again. If his injuries do not kill him, the Lady of the Woods is likely to do so."

"Very well,", the king replied. "Our thanks to you all, and let us pray that the beast is indeed either dead or dying. In the meantime, double the guards on all the towers, especially our tower on the western shore, and keep two squads of our finest archers stationed just outside the woods in case the beast manages to find his way out."

"As you command!" Baerden replied quickly while bowing low once again and then retreating with his men out of the grand chamber.

As he and his soldiers closed upon the great doorway leading out of the chamber, they noticed three lovely ladies standing off to one side, the princess being among them. "And how may I assist thee, my Princess?" Captain Baerden said sweetly.

"Pray, tell me what news you have of the flying beast, good Captain?" the princess asked.

"I have only now just informed your father that we injured him during last night's battle and we believe he has taken to hiding in the Black Woods," the Captain informed her.

"Well done, then, Captain," the princess replied, although inside she was quite displeased to learn that the beast had been wounded. "Please thank your men for their courage."

"You grace us with your kind words!" the captain replied, stopping long enough to bow lowly before the princess.

Princess Lyleth turned to walk out as well and, seeing her two handmaidens softly giggling and smiling nervously at the passing men, felt quite uneasy about the news, although she could not imagine why.

* * *

Back at the clearing in the woods, Amansun was now standing just a few paces from where the last ring of trees were growing. Up ahead he saw a plain and mostly level field that stood out as quite a contrast from the heavily treed woods he had been walking beside all day long. Near the center of the field there was a plain-looking cottage, mostly white in color, though it had several brightly colored windows and there were lovely flower beds planted all along the pathway leading up to the front door. Over to the right side of the cottage a slowly moving stream curved in a great "S" shape as it made its way from one end of the field to the other. All about he could see small animals moving, most eating the taller patches of grass and clover that covered much of the field's surface. *That is a good sign*, the dragon thought to himself, as these were the first living things he had seen since he had entered these woods. *At least something is still alive in here.*

As Amansun left the woods behind him and made for the cottage, he couldn't help but think back to the visions he had seen in his dreams. The cottage, though somewhat different than he had remembered it, was still quite familiar, as were the stream, the field, and the smoke rising slowly out of the chimney on the cottage's rooftop. *Clearly I am in the enchantress's field now and we will be meeting, in person this time, unless I be quite mistaken.* Even before Amansun reached the doorway leading into the small cottage, he imagined the voice that would soon be calling out to him and asking him to enter, as it had in his previous encounters with the sorceress. He studied the small doorway just ahead of him now and guessed that by some sort of magic, he would soon be walking into it, even though he could clearly see once again that it was entirely too small for him to squeeze through.

Amansun walked the few remaining feet to the doorway and, as he suspected, a soft voice from inside called out to him, saying, "Come on in, Amansun of the West. I have been expecting you."

Amansun sized up the door and started to bend lower to start entering. He tried to guess which sorceress he would be seeing this time, old and haggardly or young and beautiful. *No matter, I suppose,* the dragon thought to himself, *as they are both one and the same. Clearly, I will see the enchantress as she wants me to see her this time.* He now started to pass through the doorway as it expanded to fit him in, as had happened in his prior visions.

Once inside the cottage, Amansun glanced around the room and was not surprised to see that it too was very much like the one he had seen in his earlier vision. Small ledges built into the walls held stacks of books of all shapes and sizes. There was a large wooden table at one end of the room. The wooden floor had brightly colored rugs placed here and there, and he also noticed that there were lots of pots scattered about, some with lids and others without. Standing at one end of the room, an attractive middle-aged woman with black hair pulled up above her head was glancing back at him. "So, we meet in person at last!" the woman said in a very friendly manner. "I have foreseen this day for a very long time, but I could not say when it would actually take place or how it would be that you would be coming into my woods. You are quite impressive, I must say, though that which I now see will not be lasting much longer." She gave a hint of a smile.

Amansun was quite alarmed that he was actually now standing in front of this ever-changing enchantress. Bowing to the floor, he lowered his head and said as politely as he could, "It is my pleasure to meet you as well, good lady, though I am quite certain I am in a place and position that are not to be to my advantage. Will you be eating me then, or just keeping me here as your prisoner until you tire of my presence?"

The dark-haired woman laughed heartily and, still smiling, said to the dragon, "I have no intentions of harming you, silly boy." She walked closer and looked the beast up and down. As she stopped just a few feet short from where Amansun stood, she shook her head approvingly and muttered to herself, just loudly enough for Amansun to also hear, "Very impressive, I must say." She slowly walked around the great beast now. "Very impressive indeed. Clearly this was a very powerful spell and one that would last indefinitely, had you not eventually found your way to me, boy." She gazed deeply into his eyes with such intensity that he was quite alarmed and had to look away.

"What type of spell do you mean?" Amansun asked, now quite puzzled. "Do you mean the spell that has allowed me to fit inside this small cottage?"

Once again the woman laughed, and smiling at the dragon said, "You have much to learn, I am afraid, and we have much to do." She took a few steps backwards. "He really is quite clever, you know," she stated as if to herself, "and I am quite certain he will be very unhappy with me for helping you." She smiled again but in a much more threatening and uncomfortable manner. "Yes," she almost hissed as the *sssss* rolled out of her mouth like a hissing serpent. "He will not be pleased and there will be great trouble when all is said and undone."

Looking quite confused, Amansun said, "Excuse me?" in a rather high-pitched voice for someone of his size and stature.

"Don't worry," the woman said softly. "This is what is meant to happen, my visions have always said so. We will take care of your problem, and then you will have many decisions to make." The woman turned and walked over to the far side of the room, motioning with her right arm for the dragon to follow. "This way, this way," she called to the dragon. "I keep my really strong potions over here. I will need some time to gather the proper ingredients now that I have had a chance to see you up close." Stopping at a large counter covered with all sorts of bowls, jars, pots, and dried things that Amansun could not even begin to guess at what they were, she turned and, looking into his eyes, asked, "And what was it that caused you to finally come and seek me out, my boy, after all this time has passed?"

"I am afraid there has been a misunderstanding, good lady," Amansun said quite carefully, trying not to say the wrong thing now. "I have not sought you out. As a matter of fact, I was warned again and again by several individuals to stay clear of your woods at all costs." He tried to smile as politely as possible as he noticed the woman's face turn from a smile to a look of bewilderment. "I was chased here by the men from the castle last night, with an injured wing as you can see." He turned his left side to the woman so she could see what he was speaking of. "I happened to fall into your woods, so to speak."

Nodding her head up and down now, the woman suddenly reverted into the haggardly old woman he had seen during his first vision, and she seemed to be whispering to herself as she listened to what the dragon was saying. "That explains why I had to lead you here to my home," the old woman said as she grinned to herself, as if thinking of something quite funny just then. "I had to twist and turn you about quite a bit to get you here this afternoon, didn't I?" she said while winking at the dragon.

"If by that you mean changing the path I was on again and again and making me see things where they could not have been, then yes, I didn't come easily," Amansun replied.

"You could have saved us both quite a bit of time and trouble, silly boy," she cackled as she reached into one of the jars in front of her on the shelf. "Don't you know all roads lead to my home?"

"You mean to say all paths in your woods lead directly to your cottage, then?" the dragon asked politely.

"Yes," the hag said now, looking rather distracted with their conversation. "That is to say, all roads and none of them! Once you enter my domain, I decide what you shall and shall not find. I choose who makes it into the center of my woods and who wanders about in circles, lost for days, or weeks, or even years if I so choose. That is why the creatures of the old great forest, and the elves and men as well, stay clear of my woods. Once you enter here, it is up to me to decide what shall happen with you, and it is well-known that I do not like to be bothered." She now reached for a small box and placed some of the powder from it into a very large cauldron of steaming water that was just to her left. "So you really have no idea why you are here, then, do you, boy?" she said as if it was quite amusing.

"I am afraid that I do not!" Amansun said once again, though he felt as though she thought him quite foolish for not knowing. "And may I ask, please, why you keep calling me boy?"

"This is truly rich!" the old hag cackled, now turning around to look at the dragon face-to-face once more. "Even with all the clues, the visions, the memories you have seen in your dreams, the way you feel when you see or think about the princess, you still have no idea?"

"I have no idea of what you speak, Madame," Amansun said, now feeling quite frustrated as he watched the hag turn and place a few more items into the great pot, now stirring it gently with a large wooden paddle.

"Come forward, child," she motioned to the dragon once again as she stood there with her back to him. "Come here beside me and all will be explained." Amansun edged up to where the hag stood and shuffled beside her, using great care to not accidentally step on her small feet with his. "Look into the cauldron, my boy," the woman hissed softly. "Deep into the swirling waters there."

Amansun lowered his head a bit and peered down into the liquid that gently swirled within. *No surprises here*, he thought to himself as he looked at his own reflection looking back at him from the large pot. Then he looked more deeply into the liquid as it started to swirl less, and the surface became quite still. *What is this?* he thought. "More magic and visions?" he asked aloud of the hag as he now stared at the face of a young man with long brown hair falling over his broad shoulders, with fair skin and jet-black eyes, peering back at him. "Who is this young man and why are you showing him to me?" he demanded, feeling quite confused as he had expected he would be gazing at the princess once again. "Is this the face of the man destined to marry the princess of the castle?"

"That is for you to decide, I would imagine, young Prince!" the hag said, now staring at the dragon standing beside her and laughing once more. "Why don't you ask yourself?" She added a pinch of a white powder to the brew.

Amansun stepped back from the cauldron and stared down at the small, hunched woman. Nothing she was saying seemed to make any sense at all and he was starting to get quite annoyed. "Why are you toying with me?" he asked in a rather pitiful-sounding voice. "Is it not enough that I am wounded, trapped here in your woods, and confused beyond belief?"

"Calm down, son,", the hag said softly, now transforming again into the beautiful young blonde woman from his second vision of the enchantress. "I am sure you are quite puzzled by all of this, as I believe anyone would be." She smiled sweetly as she spoke. "But as I said, all will be explained." Motioning to the cauldron in front of them once more, she asked, "Did you see the young man in the water's reflection just now?"

"It was hard to miss, Madame," he said enthusiastically but much more politely, now that he was speaking to the enchantress in her less alarming form. "Who is he and why have you shown him to me?"

"That reflection you just saw now, looking up at you from the cauldron, is how you truly appear!" she said while looking into the dragon's eyes to see if he comprehended her words.

"Are you saying the young man in the reflection is me?" the dragon asked, now thoroughly confused. "But how is that possible? What does this mean?" He took another step back, looking rather faint.

"You are no dragon, Sir Amansun from the West, son of Wraith and Scythe," the woman said calmly. "That is only what you have been led to believe all these years."

Amansun suddenly sat down on the wooden floor with a *thump* and shook his head as he tried to grasp the meaning of the enchantress's words. He looked at the beautiful woman now moving beside him and asked, "So I have been a man all this time, then, hidden in the guise of a great winged beast? Is that what you would ask me to believe?"

"That is precisely what I mean to say," the woman replied. "The face you saw in your reflection was that of your own, of how you truly appear, free from the spell of the Underlord who enchanted you years ago when you were but a young boy."

"But why?" the dragon asked, still looking lost. "Why did this person place me under a spell and make me into a dragon? For what purpose?"

"You are a true prince, Amansun, from the land of men, though Amansun is not your true name as you may have guessed by now," the enchantress said softly, trying not to confuse the beast any more than he already was.

"My…my name? My name is not Amansun?" the dragon stuttered.

"It is not," the woman said, smiling quite widely just now, "but it certainly was quite a clever one to give you, wouldn't you agree?"

"How do you mean?"

"Amansun," she replied once again, still smiling, "A-man-son! Get it?"

"I don't think I follow," the dragon said awkwardly.

"A-man-son!" she said once again, now more slowly than at first. "You are a son of man, hence Amansun." She seemed quite pleased with herself. "The Underlord was quite clever coming up with that name, I must say."

"And why did this person, this Underlord as you say, want to turn me into a dragon, then?"

"I can't say with certainty, I am afraid," the woman answered, "but I am sure it had something to do with your father, the king. Your father must have done something that greatly upset the Underlord, and I am guessing he turned you into a dragon as a way of getting revenge."

Now taking a moment to look down upon his large dragon body, covered with scales as it was, great talons and immense wings still at his side, Amansun looked over at the enchantress and asked, "If I am but a man, then why do I still see myself as a beast? Have you not changed me back into what I was originally now?"

"It is not that simple," the woman replied. "The potion I just created merely allowed you to see yourself for what you truly are. I will need more time to make a potion that changes you back into the man that you are meant to be. You will stay here with me in these woods while I learn the secret of the spell. Only then will I be able to transform you back into flesh once more."

As the words of the enchantress started to settle in, Amansun thought of his family back in the Smoky Black Mountains. Looking at the enchantress with puzzled eyes, he asked of her, "And what of my dragon parents back home? How is it that they came to treat me as their own all this time?"

"Only the Underlord and the dragons you thought of as your parents know the answer to that riddle," she answered. "The Underlord is a very powerful being, perhaps the most powerful sorcerer in the land, I am sad to say, and it is likely that they owed him some favor for some kindness or blessing he bestowed upon them."

Amansun looked over at the enchantress once more and asked in a calm and soft voice, "What is my name, then, if not Amansun?"

"I do not know as of yet," she replied. "I have been able to gain much from your thoughts and memories, which I have been able to view ever since you first crossed over my black woods some days ago, though much is still hidden, perhaps by the very spell that changed you into a dragon, and only time will tell, I would imagine. I am certain you are a prince because all your memories indicate to me that the king from your visions and memories is your true father. I don't recall his face, but I believe you are from the lands far to the east of my home, judging by the armor the soldiers in your visions wear and the scenery I have been able to see."

Amansun sat there on the floor, trying to make sense of everything he had heard, and he thought to himself, *Perhaps this is all just a dream, another of my visions.* Looking over at the young woman who was once again leaning over the table and paging through one of the large books he had seen on a shelf earlier, he asked, "Would it be very rude of me to ask if I may lay here and close my eyes for a bit? I have had very little rest since the day before last and now feel quite faint with all that you have shared."

"You are my guest now, for as long as this takes, Prince," the enchantress said happily. "Rest as long as you care to and when you awake, we can discuss our plans once more in greater detail."

Amansun, now quite tired, sore, confused and bewildered, happily closed his eyes and imagined that when he awoke, he would be either asleep in the dense thicket of trees he had crashed into after fleeing from the castle, or out wandering in circles along the ever-changing dirt pathway. Either of those he felt would be more welcome than where he was. "Till we meet again," he whispered over to the young woman reading from the book up ahead, then he closed his eyes tightly and prayed for sleep to take him away.

CHAPTER 23

Exhausted as he was due to his lack of sleep the previous night, as well as his significant injury, Amansun slept for the remainder of the day, only opening his eyes just as the sun was going down and the sky outside began to darken. Slowly opening his eyes, he first noticed that there was a wood beam ceiling over him. Next, he became aware of the sound of humming, as if someone nearby was singing softly. Lastly, he glanced across the room and saw the enchantress, still in her youthful and attractive form, sitting at the table he had seen earlier, books of every shape and size scattered all about her.

"Begging your pardon, Madame," Amansun's dry and parched throat scratched out, "but is this a dream I am now in, or are you sitting there at that table reading books, as it would appear?"

"Oh, I am quite real, boy," the enchantress replied. "As real as you, anyway, and soon you will be even more real than you are presently!"

"Then I am to understand you are still working on the potion to change me back into the prince you spoke of earlier?"

"Yes I am, as a matter of fact. The answer was buried deep in one of my oldest books, a scroll, actually, I should say. It has been long since I had to counteract a charm of transformation, especially one as strong as this, but I am sure I have nearly everything I will be needing to change you back into your true form now."

Now standing and making his way over to where the woman was seated, Amansun shuffled his immense feet sleepily and asked, "Will you be changing me back right now, then?"

"I am afraid we will have to wait until tomorrow, boy," she said as if disappointed. "I have nearly everything I will need aside from one plant that only grows outside of my woods. There is a waterfall off to the north and beside it there is a particular plant, Wysterium it is called, and I will need a few leaves of it to add to my brew."

Looking over at the young woman, Amansun seemed concerned that this trip to the falls may delay his time here by a good amount. "How will you be getting to the falls where the plant grows, then?" he asked the woman. "Are you able to fly or use some other magic spell?"

"You'll be taking me there, of course," the young woman giggled while smiling at the beast. "We may as well take advantage of your dragon form while we can now, shant we?"

"Begging your pardon once more, Madame," Amansun said, now feeling quite helpless and useless. "I injured my wing gravely the other night when the men of the castle shot a great bolt of wood at me, and I am afraid I will be no use to you until the wound heals."

"Broken wing, you say?" the enchantress asked while motioning her hands over her head in small circles and then chanting a few words and pointing at the dragon's wing suddenly. As Amansun stood there, eyes staring directly at his wing, he watched as the tear sealed itself together and then healed completely in mere seconds. "And what injured wing would you be speaking of?" the woman asked while smiling and looking up at the beast.

"I guess it's no bother at all," the dragon muttered still staring at his mended wing incredulously. "I shall be happy to fly you wherever you desire," he said. "Shall I be carrying you with my hands and feet, then?"

"That would be quite tiring for you, I am sure," the woman replied, "and probably not very comfortable for me besides. I have just the thing for our trip tomorrow, my boy, don't you worry yourself one bit."

Noticing that the windows were now looking out at a dark evening, Amansun realized he would have to wait all the way until the new day for this trip to begin. "I am afraid that I have only just now woken, good lady," he said hesitatingly, "and yet we still have the entire night to make it through. I think I shall not be able to sleep a wink now, with all the rest I just had and now with the anticipation of our adventure in the morning."

"Not to worry, my boy," the woman said sweetly. "I have a simple charm that will put you fast asleep and allow you to rest more deeply than I am sure you have rested in quite some time. Walk back over to the clearing in the middle of the floor there and lie down once more."

Amansun glanced over at the enchantress who was now standing at the table facing him as he sat down upon the floor. The young woman appeared to be moving her hands in a weaving motion in front of her chest while muttering phrases that he could not make out. When she stopped speaking and lowered her hands to her sides, he saw her smiling at him pleasantly and then he suddenly had the overwhelming feeling that he must close his eyes and set down his head right away.

* * *

Back at the Castle Eladrias, young Princess Lyleth was quite upset with the recent turn of events that began when the knights of the surrounding countryside and nearby lands had started arriving. She had known that her father the king had sent for help, but she had always imagined they were coming merely to assist in protecting the castle and their kingdom from the dragon. It had never occurred to her that the king had intentions of marrying her off, though now that she was nineteen, the thought was not improbable.

Princess Lyleth had seen all the knights, or suitors as they now appeared to be, over the past two to three days; and while some of them were in fact handsome and fit, she didn't consider any of them to be the man of her dreams, or a person she would like to spend the rest of her life with. "Why has my father placed me into this terrible position?" she asked herself while fighting back tears of desperation. "I must go ask my mother what can be done, if anything, to put a stop to this travesty."

The princess made her way through the various great halls and corridors of the castle, passing posted soldiers as she crossed more and more deeply into the main stronghold of the castle where the king and queen's personal resting quarters were located. As she passed each sentinel, they bowed low and offered a greeting to the princess. When she came to the main hall leading up to her parents' chamber, two posted guards greeted the princess, bowed their heads, then stood aside to allow her entry.

The princess knocked upon her mother's heavy wooden door using the ornate knocker that was placed at chest height. A small metal latch slid open at eye level and a young chambermaid peered out and asked what was needed. "I am here to speak with the queen," Princess Lyleth replied. "She is not expecting me, but I would like a few moments of her time." The metal latch closed once more, and after a few moments the princess could hear the large dead bolts being opened one at a time and then the thick wooden door swung inward, allowing her entry.

Sitting at a magnificent desk beside a large open window looking out upon the lake, her mother the queen was busy trying on jewelry, preparing for another night's festivities. "Which do you like more?" she asked, looking at Princess Lyleth's reflection in the large mirror before her. "Red rubies or the blue sapphires?" She held two dazzling necklaces against her neck.

"That all depends on what you are wearing, I would imagine," the princess replied.

"How silly of me," the queen said while standing to walk over to a large carved armoire. She sorted through a large collection of evening gowns, finally stopping at a silver and gray dress and saying, "I suppose this will do."

"In that case, I suppose either will do, since they both will match that gown quite well," Princess Lyleth replied. "Besides, you will look quite elegant in either, I am sure."

Now holding up the gown to herself and looking at a large paneled mirror that was built into the opened armoire door, taking turns to hold each of the necklaces up one at a time, the queen asked, "And what brings you to my chamber at this hour of the day, sweet Lyleth? Shouldn't you be getting dressed for dinner as well?"

Looking at the queen through sad eyes, Lyleth replied, "I am afraid I am in no mood for dinner, or company for that matter. Besides, I have no appetite for the moment, and would feel terribly awkward sitting at the table and not eating while everyone is enjoying their meals."

Finally looking up from her reflection in the mirror and saying that the sapphires would be her choice for the night, the queen looked at the princess and only now realized she seemed quite upset. "Why the long face, my dear?" she questioned. "There is a room full of suitors down in the main hall, all hoping to get another good luck at you. Any young woman should be quite pleased to be in such a position."

"I would imagine most women would feel that way," Princess Lyleth began, "but I am not just any woman. And besides, I would prefer choosing my own mate rather than letting the luck of a tournament dictate who wins me in the end."

"Your father has already made the announcement, as you know," the queen said sharply, "and we are not to question his judgment nor his decision. Remember to keep your place, child!"

"I am not questioning anything!" the princess said emphatically. "I just want to know if there is a way out of this mess. Is there anything that can be done at all?"

Looking at the princess with a stern glare and looking not at all pleased, the queen replied, "The announcement has been made, and that is final. Best you should go and cheer on the man you most like at this point, as that may give the lad the impetus to fight even harder in the tournament for the right to your hand! Now be on your way, whether it be to prepare for dinner or to retire to your chamber, but don't bother me with this foolishness anymore. You are a grown woman now, and it is about time you start behaving like one." With that, Princess Lyleth found herself being escorted out of the queen's chamber, and she heard the sound of the deadbolts being locked into place once more as the guards again bowed low as she slipped by.

Well, I suppose I am safe, at least until the tournament commences, the princess thought to herself as she walked down the halls leading back towards her own chamber. *I'll just have to hope for some miracle to save me from this nonsense. Maybe the great dragon will return to my balcony and fly off with me to some exciting land.* She smiled from ear to ear at the thought of a dramatic rescue from her plight.

* * *

Farther below, in one of the training rooms located adjacent to the castle's armory, two leather-suited men were trading blows with each other using mighty broadswords and large shields. Both had long hair falling to their shoulders, though one of the men had traces of gray in his, showing that he was clearly the elder. *Clang* went the swords as they bounced off each other's shields, each man spinning and stabbing with intensity as if locked into a real life-and-death struggle.

"You have improved much, Captain," the older man, who was still quite muscular and chiseled in appearance, said to the other as he struck a mighty blow upon the younger man's sword in a slicing motion.

"Glad am I to hear it!" the younger man replied, now countering his opponent's move with a spinning backward thrust at the other as he grinned widely. "I will need to be at my best should I hope to have any chance at all at the princess's hand."

"Do not fret, Captain Baerden," the older warrior replied as he casually blocked the younger man's thrust with his shield and swung down hard with a circling blow. "I have seen the knights gathered here at the castle, and by appearance none should pose that great of a challenge to you, though we can't know what their strengths be in battle until the tournament begins."

"Easy for you to say, my good friend Hrothgar," the younger man countered as he raised his shield to block the elder's parry. "You are not challenging for the princess and have no concern as to the outcome of the king's tourney."

Now quickly stepping aside and preparing for a straightforward thrust, the elder said as if hurt by the other's comment, "Quite untrue ye be, good Captain." He now stepped in with a stabbing motion. "It is my wish and hope that you will arise as the victor in the end, thus winning lovely Princess Lyleth for yourself!"

"Kind you are to your young, friend then," the captain said, smiling still yet narrowly avoiding the elder man's sword point. "I didn't realize I had a fan to cheer me on in my quest."

Suddenly stopping where he stood and lowering both his sword and shield, the elder looked into the captain's eyes earnestly and said, "'Tis the least I can do for you who has done so much for me over these past years. You and the king welcomed me into your land as if I were one of your own, after my own king was lost and our kingdom fallen into chaos and disrepair without a royal family member to take the throne." He shook his head as if troubled greatly by a sad memory.

"Those days are long since passed, good friend, and there be no need for thanks, as you have done more than repay us with your years of faithful service," the captain said, now also lowering his weapons.

"Best you be off to prepare for the evening meal now, Captain!" the elder man said with urgency. "You do not want to appear to be rude or disinterested in the gatherings of the king, make no mistake!"

Now looking quite panicked and placing his weapons back onto their racks, the younger man raced towards the doorway, then turned suddenly just before disappearing from the chamber. "Can we practice again later this evening, Hrothgar?" he said, almost sounding like a child half his age.

"Of course we shall continue!" the elder said, now laughing and less somber once more. "Eat lightly, I warn ye, for we will try the staff after dinner, and I won't be showing you any quarter, either!"

"And no quarter shall you receive either, then, friend," the captain shouted back before turning and running out of the chamber and out towards the main soldiers' quarters.

The elder man walked over to the rack of weapons and carefully put his sword and shield away, taking time to straighten up the captain's items that had been put away in haste. He had a far-off expression on his face once more, and he seemed to be lost in thought as his face tightened and his lips trembled slightly, as if wincing in some unseen pain.

* * *

That night at the king's table, all the regulars were seated and in attendance, along with the many knights who had been visiting over the past few days. The princess's chair sat empty, to the disappointment of most of the men present, but none made a great deal of her absence, as she was after all the princess and able to skip a meal here and there as she so chose. King Hasselfeth got up from his seat to address the group of diners gathered about the table as large platters of food were being set, and announced that the tournament of champions would begin in three days' time. "In this way I can be more comfortably assured that the dragon will not be making another appearance," he explained. "The last thing we need is for the great serpent to appear in our skies right when we are all distracted, watching these brave men battling each other for the prize."

Sitting among many of the knights who would be challenging for the princess's hand in the tourney, Captain Baerden made sure to eat lightly during the meal and to avoid drinking any ale or wine. Sitting there glancing upon the others who were enjoying the meal immensely and drinking more than necessary, he grinned suddenly as he thought to himself about the thrashing he would surely be getting soon, as his practice partner, Hrothgar, was quite capable with an oak staff.

* * *

Back in the Black Woods, Amansun was still slumbering away. Outside of the cottage an eerie green and yellow light flickered and faded, sometimes appearing quite bright and strong and at other times quite pale and fragile. Standing just below the glowing light, which was hovering in place no more than ten feet above the field's surface, an old haggardly woman was bent over and gesturing with her arms in the direction of the light. Many of the small animals that had been feeding near the cottage during the day were now hiding in their burrows and dens, some peering out anxiously as the odd light dimmed and grew. Off in the distance, a thin sliver of light was just starting to appear where the mountains' highest ridges and tops kissed the sky. Day was coming.

Waking from a particularly restful sleep, Amansun lifted his head just in time to see what appeared to be a soft glowing yellowish light outside of the cottage. Lifting his head higher and cocking it at an angle to see what he might be able to hear, all he could discern was a hoarse cackling sound. *Surely that is the enchantress now in hag's form*, he thought, and then the light vanished and there was silence. A sudden *crack* from behind caused him to throw his head back quickly in the other direction, and there in the doorway to the cottage, just for a fleeting moment, he saw the figure of the hag walking in. As she crossed over the threshold of the door she quickly changed back into the younger woman's form, and she smiled as she entered the room, saying softly, "Early to rise, I see." As she drew nearer the beast she once again said, "Good morning, my young prince. And how did you sleep?" she added, already knowing the answer.

"Good morning, Madame," he replied. "You were quite right indeed about that rest, as I feel as though I am new again and completely rested!"

"That is good to hear," she replied. "Do you still feel you will be up to a flight north to the great falls today?"

"Thanks to your mending spell, good Lady," he added politely, "I shall be able to fly you wherever you desire." Looking at the young woman who was still smiling and looking at him, he asked, "Were you just speaking with someone outside, perhaps? I thought I saw a lantern outside just now, before you appeared in the doorway."

The enchantress looked back at the dragon and, while still appearing to be in a good mood, pointed a finger at the beast and said, "Not to worry, young Prince. Just having a chat with a passing acquaintance of mine, 'tis no concern of yours. Keep in mind that you are my guest in this house, young prince, and leave the questions to me."

"I meant no harm," the dragon quickly replied, not wanting to offend the enchantress. Now looking away from the woman's eyes, he quickly changed the subject and asked, "Will we be flying off soon, then?"

"Best we wait till there is more sun showing," she said while making her way over to the boiling pot and reaching for the wooden paddle to give it a stir. "There are some creatures still out and about in this darkness between night and day that best be avoided."

"As you wish, Madame," he answered politely. "Is there something particular I should call you, Madame?" he added, as he realized that he still did not know the enchantress by name.

"Madame will be just fine, young Prince," she laughed. "My name is quite long and so unknown that I seldom if ever hear it used myself. Some names have power in themselves, and it is often best to keep them to yourself."

"As you wish, Madame," the dragon muttered, once more eager to keep the enchantress in a pleasant mood. "I shall be ready whenever you determine we need to go. I will leave you to your books now if that pleases you." And with that, he walked away to sit at the furthest part of the large room.

"Feel free to walk about in the field if you desire," she called over to the beast as he walked away. "I am sure a nice drink from the stream will do you good."

"An excellent suggestion, my good lady," he replied, now changing his course to head out the small doorway to his left.

As the great beast walked out into the light of the new day and opened his immense wings once again, still quite amazed that there was no pain at all in the wing that had been severely torn, he had to chuckle to himself as he glanced out into the field. The stream that had been gently flowing to the right of the cottage just the day before now wound itself along on the left side of the cottage instead. *Truly there can be no more magical place!* he thought as he walked over to take a drink.

As the sun's rays began to cover the entire field, many of the small animals he had seen the other day started to come out from their resting spots. Mice, squirrels, rabbits, skunks, and even an old fox appeared as if out of thin air, and all were soon going about their daily ritual of gathering food, grooming themselves, and drinking from the stream. *It must get quite confusing, never knowing where the stream will be from one day to the next*, he thought to himself. *I suppose they really don't care, as long as the stream is somewhere and there is water to drink.*

Amansun sat there in the field for some time, staring off into the trees as if searching for signs of movement. He was quite startled when the enchantress suddenly spoke from directly behind him. "All ready to go, then?"

Although Amansun had nearly jumped out of his own skin by the unexpected voice, he wanted to appear to be just fine, so he settled his nerves and voice, saying, "Ready when you are."

Before he had time to stand up, the enchantress directed him to stay seated another moment while she approached him. In her hands, she carried a beautifully stitched and decorated leather saddle, similar to ones he had seen on horses over the years. "Stay still while I slip this on you," she said while smiling at the beast. "It has been quite some time since I had use for this. There was a time when I flew on the backs of dragons like yourself quite frequently, believe it or not."

The young woman pulled on the saddle's straps and adjusted it for a tight but comfortable fit. Looking directly into the beast's eyes now as she stood just beside him, she cautioned, "Now be sure to stay still until I am on and sitting peacefully." With that, the enchantress climbed up onto the dragon's back, using his wings like a handle to pull herself up, and then she sat upon the saddle and flung her hair to the right and over her shoulder, saying, "Off we go now. Be sure to follow my directions, for you may be flying but only I know in which direction we head." Pointing ahead towards some mountains far off in the distance, she said, "Go in that direction until I say otherwise, my boy."

Amansun nodded his head, picked up his speed a bit, and then made for the mountains as instructed, being very careful to take note of everything he saw, as he wanted to be sure he knew where they were going and how to get back to the same spot. Tapping the dragon softly on the shoulder and lowering herself so the beast could hear her words over the sound of the wind swiftly blowing past them, she said with a grin, "Don't bother trying to remember where my field was, as I change its location within the woods each time I leave and return."

"You mean the field isn't directly in the center of your woods?" Amansun asked as if surprised.

"To you and others it may appear so," the woman laughed, "but it actually exists only where I want it to be, and sometimes it cannot be found at all if that is what I choose."

Glancing behind and below him now, the dragon saw that the entire field had completely vanished and all that remained to be seen was an endless canopy of black and dark green trees.

CHAPTER 24

Amansun and the enchantress flew for some time, both enjoying the wonderful views of endless forest and the mountains becoming ever nearer in the north, as well as the massive mountain ranges off to the far distant east. Eventually as they flew further and further north, the trees began to thin out a bit, and for the first time Amansun could see patches of grass and dirt paths that wove in and out of the trees below. The forest gave way to a landside of soft rolling hills and open fields. Just ahead, the foot of the mountain lay, sloped much less steeply than higher up, and he could see several large streams flowing down through deep valleys, some cascading down layer upon layer of sparkling waterfalls. Pointing at one of the larger fissures in the land below, the enchantress pointed and said, "That's the one we want over there. Glide down into that valley and set down on the beach of the pond you will find there."

Amansun carefully flew into the narrow gorge and, seeing a crystal-clear pond below with a massive waterfall pouring into it, made for the sandy beach at the southern edge of the water, away from the swirling mists that were rising on the opposite side. The sides of the gorge were very steep, covered with beautiful green ferns, bushes with brightly colored flowers of red, orange and white, and patches of midnight-black rock. Once they had landed on the soft pebbles of the bank of the pond, the enchantress climbed down off the dragon's back and looked towards a patch of trees that sat along the edge of the stream that led off from the pond as it flowed to the south. She appeared to be searching for someone, as if she had expected someone or something to come out of the shadows. Looking into the dragon's eyes soothingly, she whispered, "It's all right, young prince. I am expecting some old acquaintances of mine to meet us here. You may even see someone you recognize, unless I am mistaken!"

Looking quite puzzled and a little bothered, Amansun replied in a less-than-pleased manner, "I thought we were here to collect leaves from the Wysterium plant for your potion, kind Lady?" He was growing more and more uncomfortable at the idea of having to meet someone new.

Sensing the beast's uneasiness, she stroked the dragon's side softly and whispered once more, "No need to be alarmed, my boy. No harm will befall you while you are with me, of that I can assure you."

As the two stood in place, now both staring ahead at the patch of trees just in front of them, Amansun thought he saw movement from within. Appearing suddenly as if from the shadows themselves, a small band of elves silently walked out, bows drawn and arrows at the ready, as they closed the distance between the treeline and the winged serpent. "Put those silly bows down," the woman ordered sarcastically. "What good do you suppose they would do you anyway?"

"No need to be curt," an elderly yet noble voice countered from within the shadows. "It's not every day that my people walk out openly into the full view of a golden dragon without at least arming themselves." There was a brief pause, and then the same voice called out, "Lower your bows and stand at the ready." Then a second group of elves made their way out of the tree line.

Amansun looked at the group approaching and saw that these elves looked very much like the ones he had met only days earlier back at the mouse king's field. They had similar outfits on, though the shading was somewhat darker, and these cloaks were more of a soft black color, tied off rather than being pinned, as had been the case with Captain Eoren and his band. An elderly elf stood at the center of the group, tall and proud, as he looked the beast up and down. Glancing over to his right at a hooded figure, he asked aloud, "And this is the beast you were speaking of earlier, then, the one that you met while visiting with King Eorethroughs?"

"This is the beast, my King," a soft voice replied as the stranger reached up with two hands to remove the hood that covered her face. Standing there was an attractive young elfin woman with shoulder-length jet-black hair, smiling at the dragon as if looking upon someone known to her.

"Mythra!" Amansun said loudly, having been caught quite by surprise. "Eoren's cousin from the east!" The group of armed elves all sighed in disbelief that this giant winged serpent not only recognized one amongst their own group, but also uttered her name loud enough for all to hear. Now staring once again at the elder elf standing at the center of the others, Amansun squinted his eyes as if in deep thought and then said, "And you must be King Eadamantus, I would suppose?" Once again, a loud sigh went up from among the elves gathered there, as they looked at each other with wide eyes and mouths wide open as if in disbelief.

The enchantress started to laugh softly, patting the dragon's side once more. Looking at the elf king, she said aloud, "I told you he was quite clever, good King!"

"And he obviously possesses a great memory, I am sure from the sounds of it," he replied, now looking much more at ease and smiling for the first time since Amansun had seen him. "We have never met before and yet the great beast already guesses correctly at my name!"

"And I am impressed as well, Sir Amansun the Dragon," said Mythra as she also approached, "for I hardly remember mentioning the king's name myself as it is."

"You spoke of him just briefly while we met in council that night on King Radibus's field," the dragon replied. "I am quite happy to see you once again, although I had no idea our paths would be crossing once again this soon."

"And who is this king I have never heard of, this King Radibus?" King Eadamantus demanded.

"No one to trouble yourself over, good King," Amansun said lightheartedly. "He is but a king of a group of field mice in a small field far, far away from where we now stand."

"Let's not concern ourselves over kings of mice for now," the enchantress said impatiently, "for I have other matters to discuss with the elf king." Looking at the dragon, she said, "Why don't you spend some time catching up with young Mythra while the king and I have a private conversation?"

"As you wish, Madame," the dragon said reluctantly, as he had hoped to listen in to what the enchantress and elf King had to say. "Please join me, Mythra, and we can discuss what each has been up to since we last met."

With that, the members of the group gathered there on the pond's bank separated and went their own ways. The enchantress and the king walked off along the northern shore of the pond towards a cluster of large rocks. Amansun and Mythra stayed where they were and began speaking with each other softly. The other elves moved back towards the safety of the trees, and they stood there, eyes wide open, watching in amazement as their young friend met in council with this enormous beast, seemingly unafraid and completely at ease. "It appears her stories were true, then," one of the elves whispered to the others standing nearby.

"I shall not doubt her ever again, regardless of what comes out of her mouth," another replied, as the others nodded their heads in agreement and continued to watch the great beast and the small elf chatting together in the distance.

Now sitting on a large flat rock that sat at the water's edge, the elfin king asked of the enchantress, "So you believe he is the one mentioned in the song of old, then, the dragon king who leads the battle against the Underlord?" He glanced in dismay over at the incredible beast at the other side of the pond.

"I know not with certainty, good King," the enchantress said in a hushed whisper, as if afraid the very rock they sat on would overhear their conversation. "Yet I believe this creature, who may be more than he appears, is somehow tied to the great prophecy of old, perhaps even he who is said will lead a great army into battle someday."

"But he is no king, I sense?" the elf king asked. "I did not know dragons even had kings, for that matter."

"He is no king, you are right," the enchantress whispered while leaning towards the king once more. "Yet do not trust all you see before you, as I have warned you in the past. Not everything is always as it would appear, and the beast you see now may be quite different in the future, though that is all I care to say at this time, even to you, my old friend."

Glancing back at the dragon again, the elf king shook his head, knowing all too well that it would be no use trying to get any further information from the enchantress once she has said all she means to say. He looked back at the young woman and said, "Well, I thank you for allowing me to meet this creature nevertheless. I do not yet know how my future twines together with this golden beast, yet I too feel in my heart that I will be seeing him again, of that I am certain."

"Then our council here is at an end for now, good King," the enchantress said. "Leave us now, for I still have business in this place and do not wish to be disturbed."

"As you wish, Aramantheum, enchantress of the Black Woods. May our paths always cross in friendship." He stood and bowed low to the woman as he backed away.

Now staring back at the king as he retreated, she cautioned sternly, "Have a care mentioning my name, good King, for there are those who would try and use its power against me if they were able, and there are more ears listening in these lands than you could ever imagine."

"As you wish, Lady of the Wood. Forgive me and know that I will refrain from calling you by name again." Suddenly the king froze in place and, looking at the enchantress directly, bowed low once more and added quite politely for a king, "Please try to not send your communications to me using the glowing beings if possible. They are an eerie and frightful sight, I must say, and even I have great trepidation when they pass by to share word on occasion."

The enchantress smiled at the king with a look of understanding and said softly, "I understand, my old friend. I am sorry to have caused you such distress, but I had very little time to communicate and no other way of asking you to meet with me here this morning. In the future I will avoid sending them to your door."

Amansun and the enchantress watched as the band of elves disappeared into the shadows of the trees once again. Young Mythra glanced back one last time, then waved before following the others into the woods. "Is everything alright then?" he asked her.

"Everything is just fine, my boy," the woman replied. "The king and I have not spoken together in some time, and I just wanted to ask him some questions is all. Sorry to have been so secretive."

"It is not my place to question you, kind Madame, as you have already pointed out," the dragon said while smiling, "but I was quite surprised when you announced that we would be meeting others here in this remote spot. Truth be told, I would have been quite suspicious of the elves had they not had Mythra with them, who I had obviously already met earlier, as the elves of these eastern woods have been seeking me out, or so I have been led to believe."

"It is true that some of Eadamantus's elves have been scouting for you these past several days, the king admitted that to me just now", the enchantress shared, "yet he and his people meant you no harm. They were just keeping an eye out for you at the request of the king of the castle of men, as they have had a truce for many years now."

Looking at the trees as if expecting to see an elf's face still staring back, the dragon asked if they would be searching for the plant that had brought them here originally now. "No need to search!" the enchantress said happily. "This small green plant growing here at the water's edge is what we seek." Looking down at the woman, Amansun watched as she plucked off several leaves of a small green plant that had white berries growing out in clusters from its stems. She carefully wrapped the leaves into a red piece of material and then placed it inside one of her pockets while humming a tune to herself. "Be sure never to eat the white berries from this plant if ever you should see it growing wild again," she cautioned, "as just a few of these will either cause you to lose all memory of your past, or could possibly make you go quite mad as well. One never knows which reaction the plant will cause on an individual."

"Ready to fly back to your cottage, then?" Amansun asked of the woman.

"Just as soon as we take a moment to take a drink from this pond, I should say," she replied as if quite happy. "I think you will find that the water from this fall is among the purest and freshest one is likely to taste. It would be a shame to not at least have a small drink while we are here."

The dragon bent down low and took a sip of the water and his face suddenly lit up as if he had received some great treasure. Now looking over at the woman, and gulping down great quantities of the sweet, cool water, the enchantress had to laugh and caution him, "Have a care how much you drink, young prince, lest you suffer on our flight back home!"

The beast laughed a bit and choked as he continued to guzzle down as much water as he could, then stood up with a refreshed look on his face and he said quite merrily, "I shall have to make plans to stop by here again, at least once, for that is truly the most remarkable water I have ever tasted!"

The two smiled at each other as the enchantress once again climbed atop the beast's back and settled into her saddle. "Off we go," she exclaimed. "Head due south until you see the black trees of my woods once more. Once we are close, I shall direct you back to my field, as it is likely you will be unable to see it."

* * *

As the dragon and enchantress flew overhead heading south, they passed high above a squad of elves marching unseen in the trees below. King Eadamantus was now walking alongside Mythra and the two were sharing a quiet conversation together. "So you say he was quite friendly and open when you met him last as well?" the king asked suspiciously.

"Yes, my King," Mythra replied. "He appeared to be quite comfortable with us and the mouse King Radibus as well, even though we had all just met. He said he was flying to the east on some sort of quest."

Looking at the young elf, the king made a funny face, as if trying to solve some puzzle in his mind, then said to her, "Clearly his quest has to do with Castle Eladrias or someone who lives there, as he was spotted flying just outside its walls just a few nights ago."

"Whatever his mission may be, I don't think he has any ill feelings towards us or our people," the elf maiden replied.

"True, that may seem," the king agreed, "yet any who threaten King Hasselfeth in a sense also threaten us, as we have a pact of mutual peace between our people, as you well know. If the king felt we were taking the side of the dragon, it would not bode well for our peace, and I for one do not wish to have any more enemies to have to keep an eye out for. Those dreadful dwarves from the south seem to visit our lands more and more frequently, always seeking tribute for their lord, the sorcerer. I would not be surprised if we were forced into battle with them in the not-too-distant future, judging by the way they try and lay claim to more and more of the lands here in the north and east these past few years."

"If that is the case, then perhaps a mighty Dragon may not be a bad ally to have on our side, my King," Mythra replied. "Besides, the dragon told us that where he comes from in the west, dragons were as common as wolves are here in our woods. Imagine a whole sky of dragons flying with us into battle like the old stories tell. Wouldn't that be something to behold!"

Looking up to the sky and watching the giant serpent flying off high above them as they marched on, the king sighed and whispered to Mythra, "It doesn't hurt that the dragon appears to be in the good graces of the Lady of the Woods either, my child! If ever we are forced into war once again, I would certainly like to have the enchantress and her magic on our side."

* * *

After flying back in sight of the Black Woods once more, Amansun's passenger leaned over and whispered instructions on where to fly next. The dragon looked below him when he approached the area she had described but saw nothing but treetops. At her insistence, he started to lower himself towards the trees below, very slowly and carefully, as he did not wish to get entangled into the branches he was now just a few feet over. Just as he made himself ready to feel his wings beating against the tops of the trees, the field below became quite visible and he found that he was actually setting down just a few feet from where the cottage was, still sitting in the middle of the field where it had been when they left earlier that day. "Truly you are a master of deception," the beast said to the woman upon his back as they touched down gently on the ground.

She just smiled back at the dragon and said, "Now it's time for me to get to work once more. Stay out here and enjoy the day until I call for you. It may take some time." She disappeared into the cottage.

Amansun glanced at the small stream that was now running along the right side of the cottage and decided it was time for a drink after their long flight. Stooping low to take a sip, he immediately felt disappointment once he had taken down a gulp or two. While the stream was quite cool, clear and fresh, it was in no way nearly as good as the water he had tasted up in the pond to the north.

After drinking his fill, Amansun walked over to the old fox he had seen earlier in the morning, as he was laying out in a soft patch of grass enjoying the afternoon sun. "Greetings," he called out as he approached the small creature.

"Good afternoon to you as well, Sir Dragon," the fox replied with a smile. "I see you have decided to stay here among us for a spell now. That means either you chose to stay here at the field, or the Lady of the Woods has chosen for you to stay.",

"I believe it is a little of both for now," the dragon replied, now smiling as well. "Do you make it a habit to stay here in this enchanted field?"

"The Lady of the Woods decides who stays and who goes, of that you can be certain," the fox said rather bluntly. "I am actually one of her scouts in these woods, and I am called Sophelus." He now sat up on his hind legs to see the dragon better.

"I am pleased to make your acquaintance, Sophelus," the dragon offered. "You can call me Amansun, for now anyway." He rolled his eyes quizzically.

The fox looked at him strangely and asked, "For now? Do you have plans of changing your name sometime soon?"

"Not that I am aware," the dragon muttered. "Forget I said that. I am called Amansun and that is what you should call me." He said this quite rapidly and almost incoherently, as if quite confused as to his own identity.

"Amansun it is, then," the fox said while looking at the large dragon with a questioning look. "At least for now!" He laughed and smiled at the dragon as if he was quite amusing. "And why are you here?"

Amansun looked down at the fox and, realizing that this creature seemed to be quite clever, thought the less said the better. "I am here to visit the Lady of the Woods, as we had business to discuss. I am an old acquaintance of hers."

"Funny that you should be standing out here in the field, then," the fox mused, "while she is clearly inside the cottage now." He grinned mischievously at the beast. "We don't see many of your kind in our woods, I can tell you truthfully, friend."

The dragon was starting to feel awkward at the fox's prying and said, "Well, I won't be staying long, as you shall see. In fact, I think I had better go off to get some rest myself, as you never know when I will be flying off again. It's been a pleasure speaking with you." He walked back in the direction of the cottage, looking for a suitable spot to sit and relax.

"It was a pleasure meeting you as well, Amansun For Now," the fox said coyly as he watched the dragon walk off. "Have a care how close to that stream you settle down, for it has a habit of changing course quite unexpectedly." He snickered. "I should be going as well, for I have slept away most of the day. Goodbye for now." The fox then stood up on his hind legs as two large wings grew out from his shoulders. Amansun watched in wonder as the creature transformed right before his eyes from an old fox into a large eagle. As he looked into the large bird's eyes, he thought he could still sense the fox's smugness, and then the eagle flew off and disappeared over the treetops to the east.

Feeling quite distracted by his short conversation with the fox and his unexpected transformation, Amansun decided a true nap would be a good idea, even if he had made the idea up just to get away from the fox's prying questions. He laid down and quickly drifted into slumber.

Looking ahead from where he sat upon a majestic white stallion, as he raced across an immense open field charging towards an enormous company of dwarves covering the far side of the plain as far as the eye could see, Amansun could see that he was surrounded by other riders, some suited in full armor, others wearing leather vests as they all rode together towards the mass of approaching enemies. Behind him he sensed that a great horde of beasts was trailing them, and as he looked back and then up he was startled to see an enormous gathering of dragons, all flying just a hundred feet above the group of warriors, heading in the same direction as they belched out great blasts of flame and smoke into the air as they flew onward.

Off in the distance he saw what appeared to be small gray hills moving towards them, mixed in with the madly running dwarves, and he realized that these were enormous stone trolls, much larger than the one he had killed that night all alone in the field, and they were hurling massive boulders in their direction as they marched along. Looking to his left, he saw a longhaired man, gray tresses flowing in the breeze as he stared off towards the enemy, and he somehow knew this was the old captain Hrothgar whom he had known as a child. The man looked over at him as he rode on and smiled widely as he let out a blood-curdling war cry.

Looking over to his right, he saw a well armored group of knights, all surrounding one who was suited all in black, and the group was also cheering and yelling wildly as they urged their steeds faster and faster. As the great winged beasts above started to move ahead of the stream of riders, still shooting out blasts of flame, he thought he recognized several of the dragons as they peered down at him briefly, then flew on even faster than before.

Looking over at the black suited knight to his right and then the gray-haired soldier riding to his left, he suddenly felt himself rising up and above the horse he was riding upon. As he lifted further and further from the ground the men all around him started calling out a name loudly, screaming as if they were mad, and they shook their swords and spears in the air as they cried out the name again and again.

Now looking down at the riders who had been beside him just a moment before, he could clearly see one white steed, riderless, with an empty saddle still fitted to its back as it raced along with the other horses, and he realized that he was now flying up among the dragons in the sky and they looked at him, nodding their heads as if welcoming him to the pack. The dragons started calling out one name repeatedly, the same name he had heard coming from the riders below, and he realized that they were all chanting his name, over and over again, as they flew together into the battle ahead.

Amansun spread his enormous wings out as far as they would reach, and he soon found himself moving up to the front of the group as the others darted to the left and right to make room for him. Now leading all the others, in the air and on the ground below, he called out his own battle cry and flew towards the rapidly approaching line of dwarves, trolls and other creatures ahead, and let out an enormous spray of fire that projected itself outwards a hundred feet or more, as all those behind and around him erupted into a cheer.

"Wake now, young prince. The time for dreaming has passed," a soft distant voice called out. "Come back to me now for I have much to share, and we have already used up two days preparing for your return." Opening his eyes and looking upwards, Amansun saw the Lady of the Woods, now in her middle-aged form once more, leaning over him and urging him to awaken. Now tugging at the beast's wings, the woman encouraged him to rise as quickly as possible and follow her into the small cottage. "We have much to do and much to discuss, my young prince," she said excitedly, "and I want to get you properly prepared for your return while there is still time for you." Seeing the look of confusion in the dragon's eyes, the enchantress said quite insistently, "Hurry into the cottage, my boy, and I will explain everything. I believe you need to set out much sooner than I had anticipated, as I have received news that will interest you greatly, I am quite sure."

CHAPTER 25

Amansun struggled to rise as quickly as he was capable, and still being somewhat sleepy, he half-walked and half-shuffled along as he headed for the small doorway that led into the cottage. "I'm coming, I'm coming," he insisted as he smacked his enormous head into the top of the doorway while the enchantress disappeared into the cottage. "So what's this rush all about?"

The woman stood at her pot while stirring its contents without saying a word but motioning for the dragon to move closer beside her. Amansun watched as she took the same red piece of material out of her pocket that he had seen her wrap the leaves of the Wysterium plant in, and then she crumbled the leaves in her hands and dropped the pieces into the steaming brew. "This won't take long now," the enchantress said while appearing to be lost in thought. "Once these leaves have been absorbed into the brew, then we will be able to start your transformation back into your true form once more."

"But what about the sudden rush?" the dragon asked. "What was the big hurry to get me in here now, after I have been lying around these past few days?"

Now turning to look at the beast standing beside her, the woman looked up into the dragon's eyes and said, "I had a visitor while you were napping outside in the field today. He is one of my scouts that patrols outside of my woods, always listening and searching for any information and news that might be good to know."

Now looking awake for the first time with eyes wide open, the dragon asked, "And what is this news that you have heard, good Lady?"

Now smiling back at the dragon, the enchantress suddenly changed back into her younger maiden form and said, "The princess you searched out, the one from the castle, will soon be given away in marriage by the king!" She watched for the dragon's reaction.

"Given away? In marriage? What do you mean?" Amansun asked, upset and confused. "How does one give a person away?"

"The king has announced that he will be holding a grand tournament at the castle, and many knights and noblemen will be entering for the privilege to marry the king's own daughter." She studied the dragon's facial expressions.

"What does this have to do with me?"

"Don't you see, my young fool? This is your chance to go and take the princess for your very own. That is why you came for her, is it not?"

Amansun looked back at the young woman and said honestly, "I am not sure what I had expected to do with her, my Lady. I was sent to kill the princess, which was my task as set forth by the elders of my colony. I knew I would not be able to harm her, but I never really gave the rest much thought. I knew I wanted to see her, that much is true."

Now shaking her head, the enchantress asked the dragon, "Well, now that you have seen her and realized how much you want to see her again, don't you suppose you would like to be with the young woman?"

"I believe you are right," Amansun said. "I have only learned that I am a prince in the guise of a dragon from you, and that was just the other day. Am I to believe that I would have a chance at winning the princess myself?"

"That is why we must hurry, my boy. I must complete your transformation and prepare you to go to the castle at once so you can enter the tournament yourself, if that is your desire."

Standing there and thinking back to the beauty of the princess he had seen both in his visions and in his short flight to the castle, Amansun realized that his quest did have a larger purpose than what he had originally been given. He knew some time ago that he would never be able to return home, as he would never be able to harm the princess. He also knew that the princess was the most beautiful creature he had ever laid his eyes on, and the thought of being able to be with her was almost more than he could bear. "Carry on, then, my good Lady!" he cried out excitedly. "Let's get this over with as quickly as can be."

"Now you are making sense!" the enchantress said excitedly. "You are a prince, after all, don't forget. It is fate that has brought you to me now, just in time to change back before the young princess is to be given away by the king. Clearly the fates are at work here, make no mistake."

Standing there beside the enchantress and feeling quite helpless, Amansun looked over at the woman and asked, "And what am I to do to make this transformation happen? Is there something I should be doing?"

Glancing over at the dragon with a serious look upon her face, the woman replied, "There is naught for you to do but stand there and be silent! Once I have the potion ready, you will have to drink a bit. Mind you, this will taste quite dreadful, but that is the extent of your involvement. I, on the other hand, will need to recite several charms and incantations, so once we begin it is imperative that you remain still and silent, understand?"

"Still and silent! Yes, my Lady. I believe I can do that." And with that, the dragon went silent and decided he would not utter another sound unless directed to do so.

As the young woman continued to work over the steaming kettle, she began to speak to the dragon with short bursts of information.

These statements seemed to come out randomly and in no apparent order, but the beast listened intently, nodding his head up and down for yes and sideways for no, keeping his vow of silence in play. "This transformation will likely hurt, but you must try and remain standing at attention until I have told you it is alright to move again, yes?" Amansun quickly nodded his head up and down. "It is likely that your mind will be flooded with images, both from your past life and your present one, so you must try not to panic and lose control of your thoughts. Stay focused on where you are, alright?" Again the great beast's head moved up and down in the affirmative. "You are likely to become quite fatigued once the transformation is complete, so it is alright for you to lay down and sleep until you feel recovered. Don't try to get up and ask me a thousand questions at once, alright?" The dragon's head bobbed up and down. Suddenly looking at the great beast beside her, the woman broke into laughter and leaned over as she smiled and said, "It's all right for you to speak for now, my young prince. I will tell you when it is time for you to be silent, alright?"

The dragon found himself nodding his great head up and down once again, then smiled foolishly and apologized, saying "Sorry, my good Lady, I guess the intensity of the moment scared me into silence."

"That is alright, my dear boy," she said calmly. "There is still more we must discuss before I start the transformation. We will begin very soon, young prince, but before we do there are a few more things I feel I should tell you now before we proceed any further. There are always risks involved when dealing with magic, especially when one is dealing with very old and strong magic as we are in this case. The sorcerer who placed this enchantment upon you all those years ago, he is perhaps the most powerful sorcerer of our time, I am afraid to say. It is very likely he will sense his spell has been broken once the transformation is complete, and that will be a problem, I believe."

Now looking at the enchantress much more intently and feeling concerned for the first time, Amansun asked, "And what type of problem are you speaking of, good Lady?"

Looking up at the dragon, the enchantress explained, "When someone places an enchantment upon another, such as the one made upon you, it is generally meant to last forever. The Underlord of the South, as he is known in these parts, will likely be very displeased with me when he senses I have set you free. It is very likely he will come to seek revenge on me for interfering with his concerns. There are few who have the knowledge and power to break a spell such as this, so it is very likely he will deduce I was involved, and he will likely send his troops up or perhaps even travel here on his own."

Sensing that the Lady of the Woods herself was feeling threatened by the impact his transformation was likely to have, he looked at her in disbelief and asked, "Why then would you risk this harm to yourself for another you have just met?"

Looking up and nodding her head in understanding, the woman said, "There is little choice in matters such as this, my young Prince. There are simply things one must do when faced with them. I have always foreseen that you would be coming to me at some point in time, as my visions have seen this for many years now. When fate steps in and shows you what is to come, it is not fortuitous to hide from it to protect one's own interests, you see. If I were to choose to not help you for my own benefit, it is likely that even worse things would happen in our world. Fear not, for I choose to help you with this transformation of my own free will. That is the only way magic like this can happen."

Now looking upon the enchantress with a completely different feeling of who and what she was, Amansun said, "Clearly I will be indebted to you, then, for helping me with this change, as it would appear that I will be placing you in great peril on my behalf."

The young woman smiled broadly and, looking back at the dragon, said, "I sense that you are not grasping completely what it is that I am trying to say to you now."

"What do you mean, my Lady? What am I missing?"

Reaching out to touch the dragon's immense hand just in front of her, she wrapped her hands around a portion of his large clawed hands and said while smiling, "I am not the only one who will be in peril here. The sorcerer will be searching for the two of us is what you are missing. Once you have taken the shape of a man once again, it will be the sorcerer's intention to either change you back once more, or more likely than not simply kill you."

"I see," Amansun said, now comprehending the position he would likely be placed into if moving forward with the transformation. "If I remain as I am now, I am likely to live in peace and stay out of the sorcerer's path, then, is what you are telling me?"

"That is precisely what I mean to say," the enchantress replied. "Stay as you are now, safe and of no concern to the Underlord, or change back into the prince and place yourself into peril."

Standing there in the cottage and thinking back to those fleeting moments when he and the princess had made eye contact, seeming to bond with each other on some level, the choice was an easy one to make. "Proceed with the transformation, then, my good Lady," the beast declared. "If you be willing to risk everything for me then I am also willing to move forward, sorcerer or no sorcerer!"

"That is a wise choice, young prince, and one the hands of fate will likely reward, I am certain," the enchantress declared happily. "Now that you have made your decision, as have I, there is some good news to share as well! Magic has a mind of its own, I have learned, and when things are changed, for the good or the bad, they can never truly be placed back as they were in the beginning."

"Then I am not to be the same prince?" Amansun asked in a puzzled voice.

"You will be the same prince as before, only different," the woman replied. "Once you take the form of another creature, some of its abilities will always remain with you from that point on, whether you wish them to be or not."

"And how is this meant to be good news to me?"

"You will be blessed in ways you cannot have imagined. Because you have been a dragon for some time now, once you are changed back into a man, it is very likely that many of the best attributes of the beast will remain within you."

Now looking quite interested and not quite sure of what she meant, Amansun asked, "Such as?"

"Such as the ability to speak to all the creatures of the land. Dragons are some of the most clever creatures that have ever lived, and they have the ability to speak with and understand the languages of most animals they encounter. It is likely you will retain this ability, though I can't say that with certainty."

Realizing what a great ability this had been, even though he had taken this for granted all these years while living as a dragon, he smiled, as he understood the power this would give him in his new life. Now quite excited, he asked, "And are their other powers that I will have?"

Seeing that the dragon was comprehending the impact this ability would have on him, she smiled and said, "There are other powers that will likely remain as well, although you and I will not know for certain until after the transformation has taken place. I am confident you will be left with supernatural strength as well, though. You will be in the form of a man once more, it is true, but I expect you will have the strength of ten men within you, unless I am mistaken."

"That will certainly come in handy if I am to enter into the tournament of the king," he said happily. "It would seem quite likely that any adversary I face will not have a chance to match me in battle if you are correct."

Shaking her head in agreement yet looking somewhat concerned, the enchantress suddenly cautioned the beast, "I sense your notion is a correct one, young prince, yet you must be careful in how you use this new power you are likely to have. It will not go well for you if you are to abuse your talents, as those who see you may learn to fear you and your abilities, and there are those who would try and destroy you out of fear."

"That is good counsel and a warning that I will take to heart, my Lady," Amansun replied. "Are there any others you can think of?"

"The last that I can think of for now is that you will be wise beyond your years. Should you ever become a leader of men, you will have great counsel and advice to share based on your natural instincts and ability."

With that, Amansun and the enchantress began the transformation process, beginning with his drinking some of the still-steaming brew. He bowed low and drank as the woman held the bowl to his enormous mouth. Once he had drained the vessel, she stepped back, saying, "Now is the time for you to remain silent and still. Don't try to say or do anything until you see me saying that it is alright for you to do so."

Amansun's face puckered as the horrendous taste of the brew settled in. He had never tasted anything quite so vile, and he coughed up a bit of the remnants as he realized that he would not have been able to speak just now even if he had chosen to. At first nothing appeared to be happening and he thought that this might have been a big mistake. *Maybe she has been wrong this whole time and I am actually a dragon through and through?* he thought to himself as the pangs of pain grew stronger and stronger.

As the enchantress stood and watched, the dragon folded over in pain, as his entire body started to twitch and convulse with the strength of the magic now working deep within. "Remember to try and stay calm and do not move from where you stand!" the enchantress commanded.

And where would I move to? Amansun thought as he bent over further, his entire body now racked in pain. *As if I could move anywhere like this anyway.*

At first all the beast experienced was pain, deep and constant, rolling through his entire body, causing his muscles to expand and contract uncontrollably. After a few moments, though, he became aware of a great many thoughts and images filling his head unconsciously; and as he tried to control his thoughts, he saw images passing, some he had seen in his earlier dreams and visions, others he had no recollection of, though as they passed by, he guessed that these had been seen and felt by him at some point earlier in his life. The images continued to ebb and flow, as did the pain that rolled through his enormous body, like the relentless waves rushing up and crashing on some distant shore. As the images became stronger and clearer, and the pain more intense, Amansun struggled to maintain his composure and not lose himself into panic and fear.

The dragon settled down upon his knees after a time, and as he remained there, head hanging low, eyes closed up tightly while his teeth gnashed upon each other, he became aware of a sense of shrinking, as if the very skin and bones of his body were now collapsing into themselves. The feeling grew stronger and stronger and all the while he felt more and more like fainting and giving in to the pain. Just as the strange senses were starting to be more than he thought he could bear, he fell to the floor, collapsing into a ball, and he felt the room go dark.

CHAPTER 26

Back on the eastern edge of Silver Lake, the afternoon was waning, and the sentries posted on the main roadway leading to Castle Eladrias were taking turns nodding off from the boredom of guarding the road. It was very rare that any travelers would be arriving this late in the day, as most preferred to move about during the hours of daylight. With the shadows of the trees starting to spread out towards the east, most of the guards were already thinking about their relief arriving so that they could head over to the castle for some food and ale.

"Won't be much longer now 'till we see those poor bastards coming up for the evening stretch," one of the still-standing guards said to the other who was also posted right on the road.

"Seems to me they shoulda been here by now, says I," the other grunted unhappily. "Seems like our shift always gets the long watch by my reckoning!" He spit onto the roadway disgustedly.

"Right you are, Ezera," the first guard countered, "but jest be glad it's not us out here in the dark, don't you think? I'd hate to sit out here staring down that black road all night, trying to make out if anything's coming this way."

The other man grunted again, looked back to the castle and, seeing no one approaching yet, said, "I guess you're right, Aderas, but it just don't seem fair that we seems to always get the long shift no matter."

"Keep it down over there, you two!" another man grumbled from underneath the canopy of a brown tent. "Some of us are still hard at work here, trying to sleep!" He laughed aloud as the others around him joined in.

"Don't pay him no heed, Ezera," Aderas said softly. "Ole Barder there is just sore 'cause he's still stuck on sentry duty after all these years. Serves him right, though, seein' as how he never tries to better himself out here anyways. I'm surprised he's even awake right now."

Looking down at his foot as he dragged his heel across the dirt beneath him, Ezera snorted and spat again, then acknowledged his friend and added, "Guess it wouldn't be so bad it if weren't so damn boring out here all the time. 'Cept for that flyer passing through the other day, we ain't seen no action in weeks. It's enough to drive ya mad, says I."

"Be careful what you asks for, is what my ole man always used to say," replied Aderas. "I kinda like it when there's nothing goin' on an no one passing through. Never been a hero and I don' reckon I wants to start anytime soon, neither!"

Looking back at the castle once more, Ezera saw that a small group of armed men were marching up the road very slowly, clearly in no hurry to get to their station. "'Bout time you good-fer-nothing louts decided to show!" he said sarcastically. "You forget again that you're supposed ta be here before sundown?"

"Keep your cryin' to yerself," said a voice from one of the approaching guards. "It's not our problem you want to run for the safety of the castle before it gets dark, you scaredy cat!" The men about him roared their approval.

"Why don't you draw that sword of yours, then, mister big talker, an' we'll all see who the scared one is," said Ezera brashly as he took a few steps in the direction the relief men were approaching from.

Seeing there might be trouble brewing, Ole Barder jumped up from the cot he had been resting on and made for the roadway, aiming to get in between his man and the approaching guard who had already pulled his sword out of its sheath. "No time for any of that!" he said forcefully. "I reckon my watch is over now, and I won't be staying out here on this damn road another moment, just 'cause you two hotheads want to slice each other up." The men from both sides laughed loudly.

"Better not get in between Ole Barder's drinking time, now, fellers, or you'll really see a raving lunatic!" one of the older men joked as he walked up and slapped Barder on the shoulder.

As the two groups of soldiers moved about preparing for the changing of the guard, one of the younger men just coming on duty looked down along the roadway and suddenly asked, "An' who in the heck do ya suppose that is coming up the road at this hour of the day?" The other guards thought the youngster was speaking in jest, but as they each turned around, they could plainly see that a group of figures was indeed approaching, a very large group for that matter.

"Seems to me they're all on foot, as far as I can tell," Ole Barder said while staring down the road.

"Must be crawling on their knees, then," another muttered while snickering, "as from here it looks like they can't be more than a few feet tall, I reckon!"

Taking a few steps further down the road, Aderas noted that the approaching host was quite large and said, "I suppose we should sound the alarm. There must be over a hundred of them, whoever they are."

"Just my darn luck!" Ole Barder said in a fit of rage. "An' here I was, just fixin' to march on back to the castle for a nice draft!" Looking over at the younger sentry, he nodded his head in agreement and said, "Sound the horn, then, lad. Give it a few good blasts, now. We don't want anyone saying we didn't warn the castle proper, now with this many strangers approaching, specially at this time o' day."

Aderas lifted up a large, polished horn to his lips and began to sound the alarm. Blowing three times into the horn, a loud *tooooot, tooooot, tooooot* filled the air.

"One of you run back to the castle now and let them know there's a large group of people coming up the road," Ole Barder commanded, finally looking like the leader he was supposed to be. "I reckon they'll be here just as the sun is setting, so be sure to ask for more troops than usual, since we may not be able to see well out here for much longer. Guess the ale will just have to wait until later, boys."

As the youngest sentry from the relief group that had just arrived ran back towards the castle, a large group of mounted soldiers raced by upon horseback towards the main roadway gate. There were at least twenty men in the first group that passed by, and as he got nearer the castle, another wave of thirty or so armored men went galloping by. Now standing in the center of the castle's main courtyard, Baerden was just putting his helmet on and preparing to mount his steed as a group of armored soldiers waited on horseback for their captain. The young sentry ran in the main gates, huffing and puffing from his sprint up the roadway, and he stopped in front of the captain and his men. "Seems to be a right large group of people coming up the road, Captain!" the young sentry managed to get out in between his gasps for air.

Now getting atop his horse and looking down upon the young lad, the captain asked, "Any idea who they might be?"

"Not that I can say, Captain, though one of the guards mentioned they didn't appear to be very tall."

"Dwarves it is, then! Wonder what they want this time? Suppose they're looking for more treasure for that wicked lord of theirs. Let's ride!" he called out as they rode off in a sudden burst of speed, leaving the young sentry choking in a cloud of dust that swirled about the courtyard.

In the main dining hall, servants of the king were already busily setting the table with glassware, silverware, and centerpieces of freshly cut flowers for the evening meal. The princess had come down early to check on what the main dishes would be for the night, as she was once again not feeling very hungry and had hoped to just grab a few small things to take back to her room. The king passed through the room quickly as he strode off towards the main courtyard and he saw her as he passed by.

"What was the alarm for, Father?" Princess Lyleth asked excitedly before the king made his way across the room. "Has the winged beast shown itself once more?"

Slowing his pace just enough to answer the one question, the king said with a frown, "I am not quite sure yet, but I believe there are visitors approaching on the roadway from the sounds of it. Not sure who would be approaching at this hour of the day, but they are certainly not expected and probably not welcome either."

"Well, call me if you need me, then," the princess called out to him, "for I don't feel well and shall be taking dinner in my chambers once again this evening."

Stopping for a moment, the king spun around on his heels, looking at his daughter and saying, "Very well, then, if you must. But you can't hide up in your silly room forever!" Then he turned once more and was gone.

Back at the roadway gate, Captain Baerden, the sentries who had been gathered there, and over one hundred mounted soldiers blocked any further progress up the road leading to the castle.

"Dwarves it is, as I had suspected," the captain said loudly. "These are most likely more of the same as has been coming around these past few months, seeking tribute for their lord down south." As he looked about him to see the size of his forces, he added, "Not likely they're here to cause any trouble, but send for six dozen of our best archers to fill the woods on either side of the road anyway, and quickly, so they can be hidden and in position by the time the host reaches us!"

Two of the soldiers on horseback broke from the group gathered there and swiftly rode off towards the castle to pass along the command. Within a matter of moments a large group of archers marched up to the blockade and fanned out into the woods on both sides of the roadway. "Have your arrows at the ready, but none shall fire save for my command!" the captain instructed as the archers quickly blended into the darkness of the trees.

As the sun faded further toward the horizon, the shadows of night began to approach in earnest and the host of marching dwarves came within a few hundred feet of the well-guarded gate on the road. The host stopped when it was just two hundred feet away and a group of three heavily armored dwarves proceeded to move forward toward the gate. The dwarves on the outside each carried a thick, barbed spear, shining as if tipped with silver and gold, while the dwarf in the middle was carrying an enormous double-sided hammer, much like the type one would pound stakes into the earth with, though it too shone with glints of metal and precious jewels, as even in this low light the dazzling gems could be seen as the hammer swung about.

At fifty paces Captain Baerden called out, "State your names and business at once before you approach any nearer!"

"Hail, Cap'n Baerden!" said the dwarf standing in the center as he took a few more paces closer. "It is I, Kairadus, lead scout o' the northern edge of our lord's plains. We's have met before, yet our welcomes was much friendlier when last I passed this ways."

"You may approach, Kairadus, for I recognize you now that I have heard your voice," Baerden replied. "In this dim light it is difficult to see you from a distance. We have had some unexpected excitement in our lands these past few days, so forgive our lack of hospitality this day. You should know that none are given free entrance to the castle's main roadway after dark without being challenged."

"Trues you are," the dwarf replied as he started walking towards the group gathered at the gate, seeing that the captain was heading in his direction. The captain of the Guard and the dwarf scout continued walking towards each other until they were just a few paces apart.

"What is it that brings you to our lands, especially at this hour?" the captain questioned.

Now resting his massive hammer on the ground, one hand still wrapped around its handle, the dwarf answered, "We been a-marchin' fer days without rest to reach'n your castle and had not planned on riving at dusk, good cap'n. Word reached me through me scouts thats a drag'n was seens here'n a few days back and we cames up at once ta see if we could lends yous assistance."

Not being particularly fond or trusting of the dwarves, Captain Baerden had no intention of letting this patrol approach any nearer to the castle; yet for relations' sake, he knew he would have to be as diplomatic as possible to avoid any sort of awkward incident. The king did not want to upset the Underlord, the captain was quite aware, and the last thing he wanted to do was upset or embarrass one of his emissaries. "It is quite thoughtful of you and your troops to have come so far to see if we were in need," the captain began. "The dragon was here two days ago, but we shot the beast down and he dropped from the sky. It would seem as though your trip was not needed, though we certainly appreciate your concern."

"Killed the beast, you says?" the dwarf repeated aloud as if in disbelief. "Quite a feat, I would think, since nones of his kind what been seen here in years, and yous and your men just happen to shoots the beastie down as'n he was some o'overgrown bird."

Taking a step forward so as to tower over the solid but short-statured dwarf, the captain repeated the comment once more but in a less friendly manner than the first time. "That is what I said, scout. Killed the beast dead, just…like…that."

Still standing in front of the captain, Kairadus reached up with his free hand and pulled the heavy metal helmet from his head and set it atop the handle of the hammer now standing at rest in front of him. Running his fingers through his long, wavy dark hair repeatedly as he looked at the captain sternly, he glanced over his troops behind him then looked back at the captain and asked, "Well, seeings as hows we are already here, and seeings as hows my troops haven't had any rest in two days and nights, mights we impose upons ya to settle down for the nights?"

The captain looked at the large group of dwarves, still in the distance and now shrouded in darkness, and said, "You are welcome to set camp here on the road where your troops now stand, but I can't allow you any closer. It is night, after all, and our king has rules about receiving visitors after sundown for safety sake. I'm sure you can understand."

"Very wells, then!" the dwarf said disgustedly. "We will makes camp here on the hard dirts road, but knows thats I will report this lack of hospitality to my lord whence I returns to his castle."

"Rules are rules," the captain said, still smiling and making the pretense of being courteous. "I am sure your lord, being the wise man he is, will understand the king's position on this matter."

As the dwarf scout donned his helmet once again and took up his hammer, he suddenly looked up at the captain once more before walking off and asked, "And how many mens did ye lose in the battle with the beastie?"

"None," the captain replied matter-of-factly. "We shot the beast down while he was in flight and none were killed, nor injured for that matter."

"That's quites a tale yous have to tell," the dwarf muttered as he turned to walk back to his troops. "We should be gone by mid-days tomorrow if'n that bes alright with ya, Cap'n?"

"That should be just fine, Kairadus. I shall give the king your greetings and let him know that no tributes are called for this visit, then?" Captain Baerden retorted.

"Thats is correct," the dwarf said disgustedly. "No gifs needs be this times around…but we'll be backs again, I can assures ya." He laughed then marched back down the road towards his troops.

Captain Baerden walked back to his troops that were still at full alert back at the gate and let them know of the arrangement. "I want two full squads out here on the road until they pack up and leave tomorrow, is that understood? And leave the archers where they are as well. I have seen this scout before, this Kairadus as he calls himself, but I'll be damned if I trust him. Stay alert and at your posts!" He mounted his horse and rode off to tell the king of his conversation.

Kairadus took the few steps back to where the other two dwarves had been standing while he met with the captain of the castle. Both dwarves were eying him carefully, along with the large man who appeared to be walking back to his own company further down the road. "And what's the words, then, Kairadus?" one of the dwarves snarled as he rubbed his long beard in his right hand, now holding his spear with the left. "What dids that fool have ta says about the winged beastie?"

Looking nervously at the dwarf captain who had been impatiently waiting the past few moments while he met with the captain of the Guard, Kairadus replied carefully, "Thar cap'n had little to says other thans that the dragon was here two days agos as we hurd. He says hes and his men shot the beastie rights out the sky. Says they killed it too!"

The two dwarves standing with their spears laughed cruelly as they looked upon the scout with disdain, and Balden, the senior of the two, said sharply, "You be a greater fool than I's imagined if you believed that cursed man's dribble."

"More than likely the men of the castle hid in its walls in fear at the sights of the winged beast, says I," Kildren the lieutenant said while staring at the scout as he drew nearer.

"Did the man say anything about the beast other than that they killed it?" Balden demanded.

"Just that the beastie was deads and that none of his men were killed or hurts," the scout said sheepishly.

The two dwarves looked at each other with serious glances and Kildren suddenly whispered to his captain, "This beast did no harms to any of the mens, the sames as whens he attacked us back at the bridge, Cap'n. Surely this must be the same beast, the one our Lord sent us in searches of?"

Now looking back at the younger dwarf standing beside him, Barden growled back in a low whisper that only the two of them could hear, "That be enough said, lieutenant, or I shall be forced to clap you in irons. Forget not that we are on a secret mission fores the Underlord and none are to knows what we are about!"

"My 'pologies, Cap'n," the younger dwarf said while bowing his head slightly. "I will mind my tongue in the future."

As the three dwarves walked back to their main group, Balden advised the other two not to say anything about the dragon or what had become of it. "'Tis certain that the man was either a fool or a liar, as it's not likely they were able to or lucky enough to have killed the beast. Best not says anything to the men other than that the beast was spotted up in these parts some time ago. Say no more or you will have to answer to my sword!"

Kairadus and Kildren nodded their heads in agreement, and each muttered that it would be so. The three dwarves walked back to their troop and gave the orders to make camp for the night. Once the dwarves were busy unpacking their tents and setting up cooking stations along the edge of the road, Balden asked his lieutenant to join him for a private council further up the road where none would be able to hear what they were discussing. "Lot of good Kairadus did us this evening!" he snorted once they were alone. "I knew it would be a waste of times sending him to meet with the castle's captain."

Nodding his head in agreement, Kildren replied, "We really had no other choice, as he was the only one in our group that knew the men from the castle well enough to have a talk with them at this times of day. We would likely been turned flats away had he not been recognized by their captain."

Balden shook his head up and down while staring at his companion. "Still leaves us no better off than we were before. Looks like I'll have to request a meet with that Captain Baerden tomorrow 'fore we pull out. He didn't seem any too pleased to see us, but it's possible he may be able to share some bit of information, even if he lets it slip by accident. We need to at least find out what color the beast was. If the serpent wasn't a goldie then this is all for naught anyway." He rubbed the hair on his chin, as was his custom.

"If anyone can fool the bugger into leaking some information, it be you, my cap'n!" Kildren quipped, trying to make his captain feel a little better about how the day had gone. "Just acts nice an' friendly and he's likely to let something spill, I'd 'magine."

Looking up the dark roadway toward the guarded gate, Balden exhaled loudly before turning to look at his companion again and added, "Best we get some kind of useful information for the Lord or there'll be no good reason for us to return again. I don't think he would be too pleased at all if we went back with nothing to report other than that the men from the castle said they killed the beast without so much as a fight. That'd likely get us both turned into toads or something worse, I'd imagine."

Kildren shuddered, as the thought of becoming some misshapen small creature by a spell from the Underlord in a fit of rage seemed all too real. "Best you gets something, Cap'n, as I don't wants to go round hoppin' on four legs for the rest of my days," he said half-jokingly, but knowing their chances of being punished were great if his captain failed to get something useful. "You going to report back to his Lordship tonights, then?"

"Not a chance, fool!" the captain snapped back. "He's likely to blast us even from this distance if we report back with no news. Better to wait until after my meeting tomorrow. Least that ways we have some chance of giving him something."

The two dwarves looked at each other while shaking their heads and grinning, as if to say *how did we get ourselves into this mess*, and then turned and walked back to their troops.

CHAPTER 27

Far south of where Balden and his dwarves were now getting their campsite in order, and where Captain Baerden and King Hasselfeth were discussing the unwelcome visitors out on the main road, the Great Master (or Underlord as others called him) had been sitting alone in a dimly lit room of a great stone tower while he gazed upon tattered scrolls filled with spells and incantations of dark magic. Suddenly he stood up as if he had heard a loud noise and looked about the room. Closing his eyes and lifting his arms into the air in front of him, he went into a trance and brought his hands together so that the points of all ten fingers touched each other—thumb to thumb, index finger to index finger, and so on.

The old wizard slowly lifted his chin until his face was pointing towards the ceiling and the back of his head was resting on his back and shoulders. His heavily browed eyes opened suddenly, peering upwards as if looking out and beyond the stone ceiling high above, and he called out to one of his disciples outside the room, "Amansun has been transformed back to a man once again. I have felt his enchantment spell undone just now. Prepare the seeing bowl for me. I need to speak with Captain Balden at once!"

Outside the chamber, a short balding man dressed in black robes and leather sandals hurried over to a large wooden cabinet set against one of the massive stone walls, taking out an ancient stone bowl and carrying it over to a large wooden table that sat towards the middle of the room. Next the old man walked over to a smaller table set against the wall and retrieved a silver pitcher, carrying it over and setting it beside the stone bowl he had just set out. Just as he started to pour the water from the pitcher into the stone bowl, the large door leading into the chamber the wizard had been standing in swung open with a *crack* as it slapped against the stone wall of the inner room.

"The bowl is nearly prepared, Master!" the old man stated. "I just need to fetch a pinch of dragon dust from the cabinet."

"Hurry, old one, for time is of the essence," the tall cloaked figure said in a hoarse voice. "I believe the captain's task has just changed unexpectedly, and I have information he will need to know immediately."

The Underlord was quite tall compared to the older man now heading back to the wooden cabinet at the other end of the room. Even after all these years, he still stood very straight and looked quite intimidating. His gray and silver cloak and undergarments covered all but his hands and face, so it was not possible to see how muscular and strong the old sorcerer had remained over the past centuries. His deep-set eyes on his chiseled face along with his long bony fingers on his hands were the only real visual clues that pointed to his age.

"Call for Brothemus as soon as you have set the dragon dust down, Cantalus, and have him prepare one of the hgarlads for a journey," the wizard commanded. "I need to send the prince up to Castle Eladrias at once to assist Captain Balden."

Placing the small bag of ground dragon dust on the table next to the bowl and pitcher, the old man hurried out of the room as quickly as he could manage, saying, "I will fetch the dwarf prince at once, master. I will tell him he needs to prepare for a flight right away and then send him on to you."

"Be quick about it, then, old man," the wizard snapped as he opened the small leather pouch by the stone bowl and proceeded to take a pinch of the black ash between his thumb and fingers. "And tell the prince not to keep me waiting!"

Cantalus hurried down the stone steps leading down from the tower he and the Underlord had been in, yelling all the way as he tried to get the attention of the guards down at the bottom. "Call for Prince

Brothemus at once, you fools!" he yelled out in an eerie panicked tone. "Call for the prince right away or the master will have your heads!"

Two large dwarves who had been posted to guard the tower's entrance, Grenth and Baltis, rolled their eyes as they stared at each other in disgust. "What's the ole fool yellin' bouts now?" Grenth inquired. "Seems ta be in a bits of a panic from the sounds of it."

"Losing our heads is all I could makes out, ta tell yer the truth," Baltis grumbled in return. "Best you go and fetch the cap'n an' tells him to ask the prince if he can come an' see the master right quick, 'fore the ole fool reaches us here at the bottom an' sees we ain't done naught to respond to his cries!"

"Rights you are," Grenth grunted as he turned and sped off down one of the stone hallways. "Wen you sees the ole man, be sures to tells him I ran off quick as can be once we hurd him callin' for the prince now!" And with that, he was off.

The stocky dwarf ran surprisingly quickly, considering the amount of armor he had on, along with the heavy shield and spear he was carrying. He ran down the narrow stone corridor and down several flights of stairs, passing small groups of dwarves here and there, all the while yelling out that he needed the captain right away.

"Cap'ns down at the armory checking on some new swords, last I heard," a lone dwarf called out from a small side room as he watched the larger dwarf making his way down the corridor. "Best you calms yerself down 'fores you speaks with him, or he's likely to run you through," he warned as Grenth rushed by.

* * *

Back at the enchantress's cottage, Amansun was just starting to recover from the transformation. As he slowly raised himself into a sitting position, he became aware of several unusual sights and feelings all at once. For one, he looked down upon himself and realized that he had in fact changed into the body of a man. He was sitting on the floor of the cottage, completely naked, and he stared in wonder as he reached each arm up, one at a time, and looked at his hands and fingers for the first time in how many years he could not guess. His long dark hair fell over his shoulders and back and hung across his face, so that he had to pull it back in order to look over and see the enchantress who was still standing just a few feet away as she had been before.

"Your new body will feel quite strange to the touch for the first few hours, I am afraid," the woman said as she smiled at the young man seated before her. "You are still used to your old dragon's body, so this new shape will take some getting used to." As he sat there opening and closing his hands and fingers, he still could not believe that the woman had been right and that he was in fact a man once again. Amansun attempted to raise himself off the floor, but his new legs wobbled from the effort and he quickly sat down once more. "Best to just sit and try and become accustomed to the feel of your new body," the enchantress suggested. "You were a man once before, if only a boy at that time, but your memories and ability to use this new form should come back quickly now that the transformation is complete."

Shaking his head in agreement at the woman's wise advice, Amansun sat and continued to move his arms, hands and fingers as he got use to the feel of moving his tiny limbs about. "I suppose it shall take some time to get used to seeing things from this height," he said while smiling. "I had become quite used to looking down at everyone and everything over the years, I suppose."

The enchantress smiled once again and said, "I believe you will find that everything has changed, young prince, but do not be afraid, as this is the true shape you were originally born into. In time you will feel much more comfortable as a man once again than you ever could have been as a dragon."

Just then the prince realized he was sitting in front of the enchantress without clothing, and for the first time since he could remember he recognized that he felt awkward being naked. He had never given this type of thing any thought as a dragon, of course. Noticing that the prince was flushed in the face and not looking her in the eye anymore, the enchantress suddenly laughed and said, "I see you have just noticed that you are without clothes now. I shall be back in just a moment. I had expected this, of course, and have some men's clothing set aside in the other room, though I can't say if they will be to your fit or liking." She left the room.

As he looked down upon his chest, Amansun could see the large, raised scar marks that covered his chest from the wolf attack he had suffered as a child. "I remember getting these," he announced out loud, though no one else was in the room now. "That vision I had was a true memory!" He now realized that many of the dreams and visions he had been experiencing these past weeks were actually real. As the enchantress walked back into the room with a handful of clothing, he looked over at her and asked, "How will I know which of my visions and dreams I have experienced since leaving the dragon colony are real?"

Now walking across the room and handing the garments to the prince, the enchantress looked him in the eyes and said, "Only you will know for certain. In time you should be able to remember which thoughts and visions are memory and which may be visions of things yet to come. I have seen many of your mind's images while studying you these past few days, but only you can know for certain what has happened to you in the past."

Still sitting, Amansun started to dress himself, the first time in many years, starting with a shirt as he noticed the enchantress was holding one hand up to her head now. "Is everything alright?" he asked.

"Strong spells like the one that held you in dragon's form are very difficult to break and require a good deal of energy to counteract, young prince," the enchantress replied. "I am afraid that is all the time I can spare with you for now, as I must go and rest before I fall over myself, I am afraid." She turned once more to walk to the small room he had not been into yet. "Get some rest now and we can talk more in the new day. I should have recovered by then." She walked out of the room and left Amansun alone to continue putting his clothes on.

* * *

The Underlord didn't summon Prince Brothemus very often, and certainly not after nightfall normally, so he had been quite surprised when his captain had rushed up to his chambers and announced that his presence was required up in the wizard's main tower at once. "Best you hurry," the captain had said in between gasps for breath. "The old servant was quite flustered when he founds me and warned that his Lordship did not wish to be kept a-waitin.'"

Slipping a beautifully crafted silver chest plate over his head, Prince Brothemus looked over at the captain who was clearly anxious to see him leave for the tower at once, and asked quizzically, "And you say the wizard wants you to get a hgarlad saddled and ready for flight right now?"

"That's what was the servant's orders, my Prince," the dwarf said emphatically. "Send the prince up to the Underlord's towers at once, and get a hgarlad ready for flying is whats he said, I am sures!"

Fitting his sword into its sheath at his waist and putting on his gloves, the prince eyed the dwarf captain warily and said, "I hope this is no wild goose chase, my captain, as I was nearly preparing for sleep and I shan't be pleased should I find this is all a ruse of some kind."

Holding the prince's chamber doors open, the dwarf eagerly waved him onward and replied, "This is no story o' mine, I can assures you, my Prince, and I does remembers his Lordship's servant warning that heads would be lost if'n we didn't have you up there quickly, though I am sure he was not referring to your head." He bowed low to the prince as he headed out the doorway.

When Prince Brothemus entered the Underlord's tower, he observed that the wizard was already standing at the table in the center of the room looking into the stone bowl he had seen the wizard use so many times before. Standing off to one side of the room, Cantalus, one of the Underlord's servant priests, appeared to be quite afraid, and was hunched over with his arms collected neatly into his chest. "And of what service may I be to you, my Lord?" the prince asked as he entered the room.

Not bothering to look up and seeming quite focused, the wizard commanded, "Come and stand here at my side, young prince. I am just now reaching out for your Captain Balden who is still up north outside the castle of King Hasselfeth."

"You had him sent there to meet with our scout Kairadus to seek out truth to the rumors of a dragon in that area, did you not, my Lord?"

Now glancing up at the prince, the wizard nodded his head in the affirmative and said, "I believe there has been a great change in the balance of powers this very night, young prince, and I will need you to fly up to their position at once." He looked back into the liquid that filled the stone bowl once more.

"I will do as you request without question, my Lord," the captain offered quickly so as to not anger the wizard, "but what is it that I am to do?"

Still studying the bowl's contents, the wizard went on to say, "I had sent the captain and his lieutenant to seek out a dragon in the north, it is true, but the object they now seek has changed, I am certain, and they will need your assistance, I am quite sure." He added some powder into the already smoking bowl. "Be still now and say no more! I am reaching out to the captain now."

As the prince and the wizard stood there, peering down into the steaming liquid, the surface of the water began to change, and what at first appeared to be nothing more than gray swirls gave way to an image of the captain and lieutenant sitting side by side next to a campfire in the dark of night. The two appeared to be speaking with each other, as the prince could clearly see their mouths moving, their heads nodding up and down and from side to side in turn. Suddenly the captain's image looked down at his right hand and, as he lifted it, the prince could see the large blue stone ring he wore was now glowing a bright bluish color.

Up to the north, Captain Balden nodded towards his companion and said, "Looks like'n we'll be checking in tonights after all," as he showed his glowing ring off to the lieutenant sitting beside him. "Guess I had better go and sees what this is about right away!" He stood and walked off towards a tent a few paces from where the fire had been set. Once inside, he unpacked a small silver bowl from within a leather bag that had been set near his pack. He placed it upon the earthen floor of the tent, poured some water from a pouch into it, then twisted the now brilliantly glowing ring off from his finger and dropped it in. Within seconds the water began to steam and swirl, and as the captain glanced into the clearing water he could see the image of the Underlord and Prince Brothemus staring back at him from the water's surface. "How may I serve thee, my Lord?" the dwarf captain asked while bowing to the images in the bowl.

"Your mission has changed, Captain," the wizard's voice replied. "There has been an unexpected change and you will no longer need to seek for the dragon, it appears."

Looking quite puzzled but not wanting to make any comment that would possibly anger the wizard, Captain Balden merely replied, "And what or who would you have me search for now, my Lord?"

"The thing you now seek is a man, most likely young in appearance, perhaps no more than twenty years of age, I should say," the wizard began. "He will likely have dark eyes and dark hair, though his complexion will be fair. He may already be there at the castle, I would imagine, but it is not likely. You and your troops will need to keep your eyes out for this man, as I am sure he will be in the area or not far away."

The dwarf captain asked of the wizard, "My Lord, there are hundreds of men here at the king's castle, I am afraid. How shall I know which of these is the one you wish to find?"

"The man you seek will likely be traveling alone, perhaps with a single female companion," the wizard replied. "You must watch for a stranger who is not known to the king and his people, a wanderer perhaps."

"We will begin searching for him at first light, my Lord," the captain assured the wizard. "Are there any other markings or clues you can give us, my Lord?" He thought to himself how difficult it would be, searching for one man amongst so many.

The image of the wizard appeared closer and larger in the bowl suddenly, as the Underlord leaned lower towards the bowl on his table and then said, "Look for the man who bears great scars across his chest. They will be gouged into him like the markings of a great wolf."

"Very well, my Lord, it shall be done!" the dwarf captain agreed, bowing once more.

"I am sending Prince Brothemus up to assist you, Captain Balden," the wizard added, now speaking in a normal tone once again.

"Look for him at first light tomorrow. He will meet you at the clearing south of your position by the old watchtower. Don't fail me!"

As Captain Balden continued to look into his silver bowl, the glow of the ring faded and the images in the water faded away into nothing more than clear water once again. Wiping the sweat off his forehead as he began to mumble to himself, he called out to the lieutenant sitting just outside, "Get in here, Kildren. New orders from the Lord Himself!"

"What news from down south?" Kildren asked, having missed the entire conversation from where he had been waiting outside of the tent.

"We are searching for a man now, it appears. This should prove to be quite challenging, given that King Hasselfeth must have hundreds of men under his command. Oh, and the best part I neglected to share. Prince Brothemus will be joining us here tomorrow morning. Imagine that!" He chuckled.

Now looking quite ill, the lieutenant turned to his captain and asked, "And how will the prince make it from the Underlord's castle to our position heres by tomorrow mornin'?"

Now standing and emptying the silver bowl out carefully, the captain glanced over at the lieutenant with a sly grin and remarked, "He'll be flying out, of course," and he proceeded to re-pack the bowl into the leather bag he had taken it out of only a short time earlier.

"You mean…on a hgarlad…don't you, Captain?" Kildren asked uncomfortably.

"Well, of course on a hgarlad, you fool!" the captain snapped. "What do you suppose he would be flying up here on?"

The lieutenant shook visibly where he stood and then shared that he was never comfortable around these strange creatures. "They are an abomination created by the Underlord. Not for anything would I get on one." He shook his head and studied the captain's face for his reaction.

"Well, I don't supposes you will be needin' to worry about that, old friend," the captain replied. "I'll be meeting the prince a few miles back down the road at that old broken-down watchtower we passed hours ago. Suppose the Underlord doesn't want any spies seeing the prince getting off the beast. You will stay here and keeps an eye on the troops until I return."

Now looking much happier, Kildren grinned at the captain and said, "You can counts on me, Captain. Everything will be fine until your return. We'll save you some breakfast rations in case you misses your chance to eats tomorrow mornin'."

Smiling at the younger dwarf, Captain Balden suddenly looked himself once more as he patted the lieutenant on the back and said, "Knew you would be happy not having to see the beast in person. I'll be sure to tell you all about it when I get back. In the meantime, make sure the troops are looking good when I return. It's not every day the prince comes out and spends time with us out in the field." He started to pack up some of his items for his trip. "I'll be taking a dozen of our finest with me so's to make a good impression on Prince Brothemus. Don't make me look foolish when I get back or I'll slice you open where you stand!"

Back at the Underlord's castle, Prince Brothemus was back in his room, packing up some of his items with the help of two of his personal aides. "Not sure what I will be needing on this trip, so be sure to pack up my battle gear along with some of the finer garments as well," he instructed. "Make sure it's all packed up tight, as I'll be flying out on the back of one of those hideous creatures, and I don't want anything falling out on the way."

CHAPTER 28

In the cool morning air of the new day, hidden inside a small thicket of trees just across from an old worn and beaten-down tower of rock and mortar, Captain Balden and his small patrol waited for the arrival of Prince Brothemus.

"Won't be long now," the captain said loud enough for his group to hear. "Make sures none of you do anything that might startle the flying beast when he arrives now. I've heard that even though the Underlord has created these beasts to suit his purpose, they still have minds of their own when threatened, and they are likely to attack anyone they see as threatening."

The dwarves gathered around their captain all nodded their heads, indicating they understood, until one of the braver souls present said softly, "None of us has any intention on gettin' anywhar nearers the beastie than what's necessary, you can be right sure now, Cap'n!"

Just as the sun started to show its first rays from the tops of the Granite Mountains far off in the distance, the group noticed an object approaching, flying high in the air but getting closer and lower to the ground as it neared. "Thar's the creature nows!" one of the dwarves announced, pointing up at the spot in the sky and watching with fascination. "We don't get much chance to see them beasts up in these eastern ranges. Not sure any of us has ever been this close to one, as fars as I can tells."

Now standing and preparing to move out into the open, the captain looked at his small group and said, "You all be sure to stay hidden in these here trees until the beast has flown off, then. We don't want to spook it now, 'specially with the prince sitting on its back."

On a soft patch of grass just a short distance from where the dwarves were hiding, the hgarlad set down with a gentle landing on all four hoofed feet as his dragon-like wings slowly came to rest. Its long bear-like snout sniffed the air in both directions and then the animal stared ahead towards the trees where the dwarves were hidden, as it began to snarl lowly and it showed its massive fangs and teeth. Balden stepped out of the darkness of the trees slowly, with his arms lowered at his side and his face staring mostly towards the ground, so as to not look the beast directly in the eyes. Approaching as softly and carefully as possible, the dwarf softly called over to the prince who he knew was still sitting atop the flying bear-like creature. "Welcome, my Prince," he said. "We are pleased to have you join us here."

The Prince stepped off of the horse-like body of the hgarlad and motioned for the captain to approach closer, using his hands to point at the bags that had been tied to the sides of the animal. "We'll need to remove those quickly before the beast decides it's time to fly back, Captain," he called out. "Where are the others?"

"Hiding in the trees across the road," the captain said softly, hoping that he had not upset the prince. "I thought it best to come out alone so as to not startle the beast."

"Clever thinking," the prince replied. "I'm not quite used to these beasts myself. It's hard to say what these animals are thinking, you know. Can't tell if it wants to wait for me to untie my things before it leaves or if it plans on taking a bite out of me." He carefully removed his packages, being sure to not get too near to the animal's head and mouth.

Captain Balden and the prince got the gear untied quickly and stepped away just as the beast raised itself on its two hind legs, reared for a moment as it snarled and continued to look at the trees where he sensed the presence of others, then galloped off down the path a few yards and leaped into the air, as its enormous wings opened up and once again began beating rhythmically as it lifted into the air. By the time the captain and the prince had exchanged a few short words, the beast was off in the distance, flying south once more.

As Balden's troops filed out of the thicket of trees the captain announced, "Right this way ,Prince Brothemus. My men will gather your things. We have a short walk of a few miles to reach the castle where the rest of our patrol is at camp." And with that, the small group started off along the roadway heading back to Castle Eladrias.

* * *

Amansun managed to stand up some time after the enchantress had left him for the evening. As he practiced walking across the small room of the cottage, he quickly found his balance once again, and within a short time he found himself able to bend, twist and turn in ways he could never have imagined as a dragon. "I know I should listen to the enchantress's advice," he whispered to himself, "but how can she possibly expect me to just lie here and go to sleep after all of this?" He held up his arms once again, still looking at them with disbelief. The young prince spent the better part of that evening working on his balance and other physical feats while the enchantress slept in the other room, until at last his weariness overcame him and he lay down with a wrap he found in one of the cabinets of the cottage.

He was still sound asleep when he felt someone touching his face. Glancing up, he saw the enchantress, back in her middle-aged form, looking down at him and smiling. "This is a good look for you," she said while smiling and encouraging him to get up. "We still have lots to do to get you ready for the king's tournament that starts tomorrow. Best get up so we can start preparing you. Did you have any unusual dreams last night?"

Slowly lifting himself up into a sitting position once more and wiping the hair from in front of his eyes, Amansun looked at the woman with a blank expression then said, quite surprised, "Then it wasn't a dream after all," as he looked once again at the feet sticking out from the bottom of the pants he was now wearing. "I could have sworn I had imagined the whole thing until I just saw you standing there over me." He laughed.

"This is the new you now, so you had better get used to it quickly," the woman said pleasantly. "Just rest over there at the table and I will get a real breakfast together for us. I would imagine it's been some time since you actually had a real meal." She walked off to the side of the cottage where the still-glowing coals of the fire were burning from the previous night's events.

"I had a dream last night, more like a vision really, in which I was seated with the king and queen of a great castle," Amansun started to say. "The king wore a suit of armor made completely in white and on its crest there was an image of a large lion, standing on its hind legs roaring, and behind it a large sun with flames reaching out in all directions. The woman had a beautiful crown of jewels upon her head, and she was dressed in a silver and white gown."

"That was your mother and father, I am quite sure," the enchantress called out from across the room. "There are many castles still scattered across these lands, though the Underlord has taken over many in the past few years, I am afraid. In time your memories will come more clearly to you, and then you will truly know who you are and from whence you came."

Now standing and walking across to the table near the enchantress, Amansun added with frustration, "It would be nice to at least know my true name."

"In time…in time, my prince. Have a little patience. You have been a man for less than a full day now." The woman cracked some eggs over a flat black pan resting over the fire. "Perhaps after we have eaten you will start to feel more like yourself again. You will have to use a knife and fork at my table, so you'd best start practicing with those on the counter!"

* * *

Back at the castle, Captain Baerden had already been up for some time. He and his close friend Hrothgar were seated at a small wooden table in the main courtyard, discussing the group of dwarves camped out on the main road, as they shared some crusty bread with jam and a few pieces of salted ham. "Seems like it was a quiet night down on the road after all," the older man said while reaching for a piece of ham on the platter set between the two. "Suppose they will be off and on their way now, as they said yesterday?"

Setting down a pewter goblet of water and wiping his chin off with his sleeve, Baerden looked over at his friend and said, "We can only hope, friend. It's not like I can run them off without creating a big problem for the king with that damned devil of a wizard down south."

Now reaching for his own goblet of water, Hrothgar shook his head in agreement as he tanked the last of the liquid in the container. "Right you are, Captain. Guess it's their move now. I suppose they won't be giving us any trouble, leastwise, what with our outnumbering them ten to one and all."

"They aren't here for a fight, that's for certain," the younger man agreed, "but I sure don't trust them anyways. Seems like his dwarves are always up to no good whenever they appear in our lands. Wouldn't be surprised if they were here to spy on us and take a count of our strength and numbers." He tore off another chunk of the loaf of bread they had been sharing.

Looking over at a group of men who were busy setting up tables and hanging banners up around the courtyard, Hrothgar looked at the captain again while shaking his head with a strange smirk on his face, "You think the king's still going to move forward with this tournament of his, then?"

"Seems that way," the captain replied as he too looked about at all the activity taking place in the normally quiet courtyard of the main castle. "From the looks of it, they plan on getting everything set up by end of day."

"If it were up to me, I would put it off, least till those dwarves have moved on," Hrothgar said as he offered the last piece of ham to his friend.

"Don't think the king wants to keep these knights and princes waiting, would be my guess," the captain replied while declining the ham. "Best I eat light today, just in case the tournament does start tomorrow," he laughed. "Don't want to be too full in the stomach, you know." He patted his flat stomach with his right palm.

Standing up from the wooden chair he had been sitting on, Baerden placed his cape back on, as well as his headpiece, and looking down at Hrothgar said, "Time to head down to the road gate, old friend. Best we see what those little monsters have been up to since we last saw them. I suppose I'll be needing to meet with that Kairadus at least once more before they head off."

Standing up from his chair and reaching his arms up to the heavens as he stretched his back out, Hrothgar nodded his head in approval and muttered, "Best that scout keep his manners today, or I imagine he may find himself getting hisself chased down that road a bit." He gave a loud laugh and smile as he reached for his sword and slashed it about in front of himself for a moment. "Let's be on our way, then. Looks like a nice morning for a ride, anyways."

* * *

Kildren had been keeping a watchful eye out for the return of his captain while the other dwarves busied themselves breaking camp and getting their supplies packed up and ready for travel once more. The roadway that had been covered with tents and fire pits and leather packs all strewn about now looked quite clean and organized. "Snap to it!" the lieutenant shouted as he saw the small band of dwarves marching up the roadway. "Here they are now!"

Coming down the dirt road in two lines, the dozen dwarves along with their captain and Prince Brothemus were closing the last half-mile between them and the campsite. Captain Baerden and the prince were out in front, speaking with each other as they walked along.

"Seems quite talls ain't he?" one of the dwarves near Kildren commented.

"That he is!" the lieutenant replied. "He's at least a full head higher than most of us, I'd say, and quite capable in battle, or so I have heard. Best not to stare at him, though, as I hear this one has quite a temper!"

"Beggin' your pardon, sir", the younger dwarf said earnestly. "I meant nothing by it. Please don't mention anythings to the cap'n nor prince, please." He quickly scampered off to put some distance between himself and the approaching party.

As the party drew nearer, Captain Balden called out to his lieutenant, "Stop the packing for now! Orders are, we stays put whilst the prince meets with the king of the castle!" Kildren in turn turned and yelled out to the dwarves who were just finishing the last packing of their things that they would be staying put.

"Here we goes agin!" one of the larger dwarves groaned out loud to those standing about him. "No sooner does the prince shows up than we's got new orders! This will be a long day to be sure, you can counts on that, friends!"

Now walking up to the group on the road, Captain Balden explained to his lieutenant that the prince would be requesting a meeting with King Hasselfeth prior to their departure. "Send

Kairadus up to the gate right quick!" Balden snapped. "Tell him he's to get a meeting with the king set up today for Prince Brothemus, and tell him don't take no fer an answer or he'll be heading down to see the Underlord right quick!" He shook his head and smiled in a threatening manner.

"As you wish!" the lieutenant said quickly as he turned and excused himself from the prince. "I will send Kairadus out at once!" And with that, he ran down the line of troops, searching for the scout.

By the time Kairadus had suited up in his leathers and armor and walked up towards the still heavily guarded gate, Captain Baerden and Hrothgar had been there for some time, speaking with the men on watch. "Looks like the same one's back fer another meet!" one of the guards on the gate announced as he spotted the dwarf scout approaching alone. "This be the same one as yesterday, I reckon, as he has that same mean-looking double hammer in his hands."

"Send out a rider to meet him halfway and see what the poor dolt wants," commanded the captain. "Don't let him approach any closer than one hundred paces, though, as I don't trust any of these dwarves now. Likely that ill wizard who commands them is looking right at us through his scout's eyes, it is." He squinted in the direction from where the scout was approaching.

From the fortified gateway the captain and his men were standing behind, they observed as their rider met the lone dwarf on the roadway as instructed. As the two conversed, the black stallion the rider was on paced back and forth and chomped on his bit, as the smell of the dwarf made the beast uncomfortable. After a few moments of apparent conversation and gesturing, the rider turned and sped back towards the gate.

"Their scout is tellin' us that a Prince Brothemus from the Southern Barrens has been sent to meets with the king, my Captain," the rider announced upon his return. "They wishes to arrange a meet

Amansun the Dragon Prince

later today and their scout Kairadus waits for a reply. They also wanted me to say that the Great Master, their wizard leader, has requested this meeting between the prince and King Hasselfeth, and that he will be greatly displeased should the request not be granted."

After giving the request some thought for a moment, Captain Baerden instructed his rider to return to the dwarf who still remained out in the middle of the roadway. "Tell him to return when the sun is directly overhead and we will have his answer. The king is tending to his duties for now and cannot be disturbed."

No sooner than when the words from the captain's lips were uttered, the rider sped off to share the reply with Kairadus, who looked less than pleased in not getting a direct reply. "I will return at high noon for yer king's reply," he said, "but prays it not be the wrong one, or I fears things will go poorly, rider." He turned and marched off towards his camp.

After sharing the dwarf's reply with the captain, the rider dismounted from his steed and walked back to the circle of men he had been chatting with earlier. "Don't think the cap'n's too pleased with their scout's words," he shared with the other soldiers back over at the tent. "They made a threat of sorts, seems to me, making like our king had to do as they say or else! You shoulda seen the look on the cap'ns face when I told him the reply. Thought he were goin' to ride out there an' lop off that scout's head then and there, I did!"

As the captain and Hrothgar slowly rode back to the castle, the two friends discussed the scout's message and regarded the way the new day was starting to turn. "Looks like the day has gone all to hell already," Hrothgar muttered as he spat into the dirt from atop his horse. "Threatening us and our king in one swoop, it sounded to me!"

"Best we leave this up to the king," the captain replied. "He'll know better how to handle this sort of situation now…being the king and all, you know…I'm sure he'll be able to turn this thing around so we still look strong and in control without offending the Underlord, just watch and see." He stared off ahead to the great castle walls looming ahead.

As the two riders approached the castle, they looked up and down the outside of the castle walls and saw that the same activity they had witnessed earlier in the courtyard was also taking place outside. Everywhere one looked, men and women were busy setting up tents and tables, tying great banners to stakes pounded into the ground and even around the tree trunks that surrounded the castle along both roadways leading off towards the great lake. Riding up to one of the booths being set up along the road leading to the north of the castle, Hrothgar brought his steed to a halt as he read the wording painted across the heavy cloth banner:

tournament of champions

As the two rode along a bit further, they came up to several booths made up of long wooden poles with heavy tarps tied upon them to make walls and ceilings. Many of these had large wooden boards hand-painted in various colors, announcing what items could be purchased there.

The first booth announced the following:

Pickled Trout: 3 pence
Roasted Boar: 5 pence
Bard's Wheat Ale: 2 pence

The next booth in line stated:

Fresh Baked Meat Pies: 4 pence
Grilled Chicken and Onions: 4 pence
Savory Partridge Stew: 3 pence
Ruby Red Mead: 2 pence

Another booth set on the opposite side of the roadway had a white tarp rather than a wooden sign like the first two, and on it was neatly printed:

Oven Baked Custards: 2 pence
Sweet Bread with Gooseberry Jam: 2 pence
Maple Bark Biscuits: 3 pence
Juniper Berry Wine: 2 pence

"Looks like the crowd will be eating and drinking well, at least," Hrothgar said with a loud laugh. "Can't remember the last time I got drunk on juniper wine."

Captain Baerden glanced over at his friend while shaking his head and grinning, and cautioned, "None of us needs to be getting drunk now, old friend, of that I am quite certain. 'Specially not with those darned dwarves right at our doorstep!"

Now looking much more serious and nodding his head in agreement, the older rider acknowledged the captain, saying, "Best we tell the King's Guard that no man will be permitted to drink over the course of the tournament, then, though that will not likely be taken very well."

Now bringing his steed to a halt and pointing a single finger directly at his friend, the captain looked directly into the older man's eyes, saying quite clearly, "The job of keeping the men alert will be on your shoulders, old friend. Best not forget that I myself will be taking part in the tournament and fighting for the princess's hand along with the others."

"Quite true…quite true," sighed Hrothgar, who had only now remembered that he would likely be left to keep the troops on their best behavior since the captain of the guard would be busy. "Suddenly it seems not as quite a good idea after all, your participating," he said with a smile.

"Too late for that now, old friend," Baerden replied with a laugh. "You'll just have to be the bad guy this time around. You can always threaten the men on my behalf, of course. That ways they won't hold a grudge down the road when you want to drink some ale with them in the Guard's quarters. Now it's best we get back to the castle proper so I can share this message with the king." He suddenly realized they had become entirely too distracted by the activity taking place all about them.

Once inside the courtyard, the two men stepped down from their rides and prepared to go separate ways. "I'm off to see the King now, Hrothgar," the captain said, "but save some time for me later this afternoon. I still need to get some practice in before the tourney begins."

"Fret not, Captain," the other replied. "We should have ample time to train later today, provided the king finds a way to make the Underlord's troops happy, that is. Seems to me your swordplay and jousting is fine. Best we spend some time down at the archery range and spear field, I would say."

"Sounds great," the captain said as he turned and started for the entrance to the corridors leading to the king's quarters. "I'll catch up with you once the king has decided what he wants to do." He vanished into the castle interior.

As Hrothgar walked off towards the armory, he muttered to himself unhappily, "Damn those cursed dwarves, and the wizard too! Whoever heard of a tourney where you can't drink any ale? It's damn barbaric is what it is!"

CHAPTER 29

Back in the large tree where Carceren and the other owls often gathered to chat, several of the younger owls were busy telling their leader what was happening up at the castle. Carceren, who had become quite depressed since his friend Amansun had disappeared into the Black Woods several days earlier, had been holed up in his tree and hadn't bothered venturing out in quite some time.

"I'm telling you, the whole castle is alive with activity!" Bathis eagerly blurted out. "They are setting up tents and the like all up and down the roadways and just outside of the castle's walls, the likes of which I have never seen."

"He's right, he is," Methistus chimed in. "There's going to be a big tourney, from what I gather...or so I have heard the soldiers mentioning, anyways."

Certrex slowly walked along the branch he had been perched upon, edging closer to the group, then added, "There's a large host of dwarves camped out on the east road leading to the main gates as well. They've been sitting tight there these past two days now, though it appears as though they might be moving on, as they seem to be packing things up today."

Carceren took all of this in patiently and looked at the owls gathered about him for some time before making a reply. "Quite curious indeed!" the leader of the owls finally mumbled, as if lost in thought. "It's as if the men of the castle have lost all fear of the dragon that they were so carefully guarding against just four days ago now."

"My guess is they think the Lady of the Woods has done him in, just as we were thinking," young Obrides said out loud without thinking first.

All the other owls gave the youngster an evil glare and Bathis quickly jumped in, saying, "None of us think that Amansun is dead, Carceren. He's just been taken up by the enchantress is all. Maybe they are getting along grandly?" he said nervously as he nodded his head to the others to chime in.

"That's right, Carceren," Certrex echoed. "It's not so likely that the enchantress would have any need to get rid of such a noble beast as Amansun!"

Carceren looked off into the distant trees across the lake and softly said with a heavy sigh, "We all know it's likely that Amansun is done for by now. Even King Hasselfeth and the men from the castle seem to think so, from the looks of it. There's no way the king would hold this tourney if he thought his lands and people were still in peril."

"Just the same, there still is a lot of excitement going on right now, and this is a bad time to be hiding out in your tree," Methistus said politely.

Now looking back at the others, Carceren nodded his head in agreement and agreed to take a look about to see all the action taking place. "I'll take a short trip over to the castle later today, I suppose. Guess no good can come from just sitting in this tree day after day."

"It has been some time since the dwarves were last here," Carceren said suddenly. "It's never a good sign when they show up. Think I'll start by seeing what those mischievous tunnel dwellers are up to. Has anyone seen any elves in the area lately?" The owls looked at each other for a moment before seeming to agree that none had been spotted. "Best a few of you scout out the woods today, then," he continued. "If the dwarves are about, it's likely King Eadamantus knows about it and has his scouts out keeping an eye on things as well."

* * *

After Amansun and the enchantress had finished their meal, the two walked out into the field so that Amansun, now in human form once again, could start training for the upcoming tournament. "I can't say what contests you will likely be thrown into," the enchantress began, "but there are many that have been used for centuries when proving one's mettle in events such as this. At the very least we will need you to be ready and able to defend yourself with a sword and shield, throw a spear, shoot a bow, run at speed, swim, joust, and use a crossbow."

Amansun looked at the woman with eyes wide open and blurted out, "Surely you can't expect me to learn all that in one day?"

"No need to panic, Amansun!" the woman replied while laughing. "From the visions and dreams I have read in your mind, I am quite certain you have had experience with most of these skills, even if it was years ago, before the Underlord turned you into a dragon."

Running his fingers through his long hair as he pulled it out of his eyes and back over his head, Amansun shook his head in agreement, as he too remembered that he had been taught many of these during his time with the soldiers of his own castle long ago. "You are right once more, my Lady," Amansun replied. "I may have lost my touch since then, but at one time I was able to swing a sword and handle a shield with grace, though I can't say how long it's been. I seem to recall hunting with a bow and crossbow as well, and I can't imagine throwing a spear can be all that difficult, either."

"That's the spirit!" the enchantress said exuberantly. "We may not have much time, but with your unusual dragon-like strength you should be able to do quite well tomorrow in spite of your newness to your new form."

Looking about the field, Amansun noticed that there was already a rack of weapons standing off to one side where the field was particularly flat and open. At the far end of the field, he could see various round targets, made out of hay with rings painted in circles upon them, standing on tripods at varying distances. "Well, it appears I will have no problem getting practice in with my shooting and throwing," he began, "but what am I to do when it is time to practice my swordsmanship and jousting?"

"Don't have a care about that, Amansun," the enchantress said coyly. "When the time comes, I will supply you with an excellent partner to practice with. Just be sure to keep your guard up, as this individual takes these types of things quite seriously, and he likely won't stop from giving you a good thrashing if he senses you are not trying your best." She gave a wicked smile.

With that, Amansun walked over to the weapons carrier and selected a handsomely polished bow made of oak, as well as a quiver of long arrows, and marched off to the place where the targets had been set up earlier. "Start with the closest targets first and work your way out as you get comfortable," the woman recommended. "Once you get the hang of the bow, we will move on to the crossbow and then the spear."

Amansun fitted an arrow into his bow and slowly pulled back on the string. He was quite surprised to see how easy it was for him to pull the string back all the way into a proper firing position. As he closed his left eye, purely by instinct and perhaps by memory as well, he spoke out of one side of his mouth towards the enchantress, saying, "It seems to me that it was never this easy to pull back on the bow string, particularly with a bow of this size," and then he let the arrow fly.

*Sssshhhhhh…*went the arrow as it raced towards the target. With a loud *tthhhffttt* the arrow pierced the hay target directly in the centermost circle for a perfect bullseye on the first attempt.

"Hurray!!" the enchantress called out from the sidelines as she saw the excitement race across Amansun's face. "I knew this would be easy for you! You will need to empty all the quivers on the rack before we move on to the next weapon," she shouted over to Amansun, who was looking at his second arrow which had also hit the direct center of the target.

* * *

Back at the castle, King Hasselfeth was looking out one of the stone windows cut into his library room, as he surveyed the activity taking place outside the castle. He turned and paced back to where his captain of the Guard was standing and looking into the man's eyes, replied, "There is certainly no harm in meeting with this dwarf prince, even if the request was made with a hint of demand. It is still my choice to determine if I would like to meet with this dwarf, after all, so there is no dishonor in agreeing to meet."

Nodding his head in the affirmative, Captain Baerden bowed to his king and then restated, "So your message is to tell the prince that he can meet with you later today, then, my King?"

"Yes, yes it is, Captain," the king replied. "I don't see the harm in meeting with this prince. And besides, how much trouble can one dwarf be, anyway?" He glanced over towards the window once more, then looked back at the captain.

"I will let them know your reply at once, my King," the captain replied, and then he bowed low once more and turned to leave the room.

"Captain," the king called out before Baerden had made it out of the room.

"Yes, my King?"

"Is it your intention to participate in the tournament, then, as I have heard?"

"It is, my King," the captain replied as he lowered his head. "With your permission, of course, my Lord."

The king moved closer to the captain, studying his face more closely as he approached. "It has been my intention to marry my daughter off to a prince, if truth be told," the king said as the captain's smile fell and his shoulders stooped suddenly. "But this tournament is open to men such as yourself," the king went on, smiling at the man once more as he reached out and touched him on the shoulder. "And I will be happy to see how you do in the competition. May the best man win."

* * *

Down at the main field where the knights had been spending their days, a large grandstand had been built up so that a crowd would be able to sit and view the games in comfort. Towards the center of the stand, a spacious covered booth had been created for the king, queen and princess to sit, along with additional room for their guests of honor and the various noblemen of the area. Sitting in the newly finished booth with her handmaidens, Princess Lyleth was observing the men as they practiced hacking at each other with broad swords and staffs. The dirt areas of the arena had been layered with hay to help settle the dust that would naturally rise up during the battles, causing irritation to the crowd's eyes and noses.

"The Blue Knight looks like quite a catch," one of the maidens said as she longingly stared at the muscular man as he knocked over one opponent after the other with a thick oaken staff.

Shaking her head vigorously, the princess countered, "He looks great from this distance to be sure, but he's much older than you would imagine up close, and not nearly as attractive as you think."

"What about Berardren the Red?" the other maiden asked of the princess. "I have seen him at your side during dinner and he seems to be a man of nice face?"

The princess stared over at the knight who was presently beating down on his adversary's shield with a series of powerful sword thrusts. "He's nice, I would admit...but I am looking for more than that," the princess said while continuing to look over the arena at the other competitors. "There are some here who would make fine husbands, I am sure, but I haven't seen any yet who appeal to me in a way that would make me want to spend the rest of my days with them."

The two maidens nodded their heads as if agreeing with the princess, but in truth they were quite jealous, as either one of them would have been thrilled to have any of the suitors below challenging for their honor.

Looking quite forlorn, the princess sighed deeply as she realized that there were none in contention she felt any feelings for at all. *I suppose I shall have to hope for a miracle*, she thought to herself.

* * *

Having found Hrothgar and filled him in as to the king's wishes, Captain Baerden had made quick time over to the road gate where the guards were now watching the lone dwarf scout who had appeared some time ago, and waited patiently in the center of the road some two hundred paces away. "Greetings, my Captain!" Ole Barder called out as the two riders approached. "What message should I give to our rider for the dwarf scout waiting yonder?"

Waving his right hand from atop the horse in a gentle downward motion, as if they should stay where they are, the captain announced that he would be riding out to share the message personally. "This message is straight from the king," he announced assertively, "and I shall pass it on to the dwarf myself."

Walking closer to where the captain's horse now stood, Barder and some of the others gathered about and asked if they should prepare for battle. "Shall I alert the archers, Captain?" he asked tensely.

"No need for any of that," the captain said calmly. "The king has chosen to honor the dwarf prince with a short meet this afternoon, so there should be no concern."

Kairadus stood tall and lifted his massive hammer into the air, as it had been resting on its head on the road up until the time he saw a rider approaching. "The captain himself is delivering the message, I see," the dwarf said sarcastically. "And what be your king's response, then?"

Stepping down off his horse and casually walking up to where the dwarf stood, the captain looked down upon the dwarf and stared him in the eyes. "Our king has decided that he will allow your prince to come by for a short visit," he said in a very short tone. "Tell him that he needs to be at our gate just before sunset and that the king will meet with him briefly before he prepares for dinner."

The dwarf looked up at the tall man with obvious dislike and muttered, "I was hoping you were heres to say the request had been denied. I woulda enjoyed sharing that message withs our prince much better!"

"Don't be late or the meet will be forfeit!" Baerden called out as the dwarf raised one hand in the air, waving it about without bothering to look back again. When he arrived back to his own men, he said, "Be sure to call for me when you see their prince approaching. Hrothgar and I will be down at the field working on some drills for the tourney tomorrow."

"Our money is on you, Cap'n!" Ole Barder said enthusiastically to the shouts of the other guards nearby. "We've been scoutin' the other knights these past three days an' we don't see anyone that can touch ye, Cap'n."

Captain Baerden smiled and thanked the men for their kind words. "I will give it my best and make no mistake!" he said loudly. "There's no better prize in the kingdom, and any who wish to claim the princess over me will have to best me in every step of the tourney or kill me in the process!" The men gave him three cheers.

"Best we get goin', then, Captain," Hrothgar suggested softly. "Not much daylight left, seeing as how you have to be back here to escort our noble visitors at sundown." This last he said with an obvious sign of sarcasm.

"Right you are, friend," the captain agreed. "Be sure to try and not throttle me today, now, as I do plan on being whole when I start this tourney tomorrow, agreed?"

"I'll try to go a little easy on you today," Hrothgar chided, "but best ye don't let your guard down any, or I might whoop you accidental-like." They both laughed as they rode off towards the castle one more.

* * *

Having completed his first tasks of target practice with the bow and crossbow, the enchantress had pressed Amansun into spear throwing next. As the young prince sized up the collection of spears leaning against the wooden rack, he selected three particularly large and heavy spears to start with. "Remember that spear throwing is all about touch and feel," the enchantress coached from the same stump she had been sitting at for some time. "You will need to gauge the distance between yourself and the targets much more so than with the bow. The spear will drop much more quickly in flight, whereas the arrow and bolt move forward at a great speed for quite a distance."

Walking over to a spot approximately fifty paces from the first target, Amansun lifted the first spear into position and, while eyeing the center of the target, shuffled a few paces forward. Then, twisting his body with great concentration, let the spear fly. As the two watched in anticipation, the spear—even though it had been one of the larger and heavier ones to choose from—sailed off into the distance, missing its mark by no less than a full fifty paces. "Guess that is what you meant when you said I may have unnatural powers," Amansun joked as he turned and smiled at the woman.

"No need to show off, my Prince," the woman cackled in agreement. "Remember that the goal is to hit the target, not throw the spear clear over. Try it again, but this time think about how hard you are throwing it. Sometimes a gentle touch is all that is required, much like when you and the princess are together, I would imagine."

The young prince blushed and replied only with, "Soft touch," as he once again raised a spear over his shoulder and focused intensely on the same target. This time he took just two short steps before letting the spear fly, and he only twisted his torso a quarter-turn instead of the full turn he had done on the first attempt. As he anxiously watched the spear in flight, he was pleasantly surprised when it hit the target fully, though not in the exact center as had been the case with the bow and crossbow earlier.

"Here is something that needs some fine-tuning, obviously," the enchantress stated as she stood up and started walking off towards the cottage. "I'll be back with some biscuits and jam, along with ham slices and cheese. It's well past lunchtime now, and you will be needing your strength for the next batch of skills, I am quite sure."

Wiping the sweat from his forehead, Amansun looked over at the woman as she wandered off and called out, "Is it alright if I stop a moment to get a drink from the stream?"

The enchantress looked back at the young man while nodding her head up and down and replied, "Just be sure to keep an eye out for the water spirit that lives in its waters. She has taken a fancy to you, I have heard, and she is likely to pull you in if you're not careful."

*　*　*

When Kairadus approached his party after his meeting with the men on the road, it was clear the king had agreed to meet with Prince Brothemus. Even though he had taunted Captain Baerden earlier, he was now grinning from ear to ear, and even through his heavy beard Balden and Kildren could tell that he was happy. "That no-good king of theirs has agreed to meets with you, my Prince!" he announced eagerly. "They are requesting that you meets their captain ats the roadside gate just befores sunset."

Shaking his head up and down slightly, Balden grasped the hairs of his chin gently, and while stroking his beard he looked over at his lieutenant and announced that the troops should start making camp once more. "Looks like we'll be staying at least one more night from the looks of it," he said to Kildren with a grin. "Tell the men to unpack once more and prepare to bed down for the night here on the road again."

Kildren nodded obediently and walked off to share the orders with the rest of the troop without waiting to hear what the Prince might have to say.

"Looks like you have yer meeting, my Prince," Captain Balden said proudly as he turned and faced the tall dwarf beside him. "What are you and the king s'posed to talks about, anyways?"

Looking directly into the captain's eyes, the prince smiled strangely and replied quietly so that other couldn't hear, "I actually don't have much to say to their king, to be honest. I'm here to scout out a special man who should be in the castle or nearby. Meeting the king is just a ruse to get me closer so I can try and find him. Be sure not to mention a word of that now, Captain, or I'll be forced to report you to his Lordship upon our return. When the time comes, you and I shall venture to the castle to meet with the king, but our true intention is to spot a man, someone who sticks out as different or new to the area, someone who seems apart from the others who call this area home."

Now looking up at the taller dwarf once more, Captain Balden assured him that he would do his very best to help with the search. "Sounds a bit difficult, my Prince, but rest assured that I will keeps both these eyes wide open, day or night."

"This will be quite a task, I am sure," the prince agreed. "Best we do not fail, however, or the Underlord will likely send us both down to the mines to dig for the remainder of our days!"

Down the road a bit where most of the dwarves had been waiting for word, Kildren walked by briskly as he shouted out the orders to make camp and bed down for another night. Once again the large dwarf who had complained earlier spoke up, though just loud enough for the dwarves standing nearby to hear and not the lieutenant, "Sees…I tole you alls this would happen, now, did'n' I!" He looked about with a smug expression on his square face. "Never fails ever… once a prince or sum such noble comes along…wham…you start moving backwards fer everything you had already done…this won't be the last of it, niethers, I can betcha!"

CHAPTER 30

Up in their private quarters, King Hasselfeth and the queen were sharing a quiet lunch out on their terrace as they stared out upon the magnificent silver lake below. "You're quite sure this is the right thing to do now, my husband?" the queen asked suddenly. "You know Lyleth is beside herself with worry right now. She's afraid that the winner of your tournament will likely be the man she is the least attracted to, I am afraid."

Spreading some pickled trout over a large piece of crusty bread and then setting it down upon a small plate sitting on the table just in front of him, the king glanced over at his wife calmly and replied, "The girl is already past eighteen now, my dear, and you well know that one of the knights from nearby is likely to win the tournament. It's not entirely important who wins now. What matters is that her union will strengthen our land and add an entire castle and army of soldiers to our own." He lifted his glass of mead up to his lips and took a sip.

"And you will be quite alright regardless of who wins her hand?" the queen asked inquisitively.

Now reaching for his bread and nodding his head in the affirmative, the king replied very confidently, "The tournament is only open to princes and noblemen, my Queen. Surely our daughter should be fine with either."

"And what of the captain of the Guard, young Baerden?" she asked aloud, not seeming at all comfortable with the entire plan.

"I've made an exception for him, of course, my Queen, as he is among our most trusted and loyal servants," the king said while trying to swallow a particularly large chunk of bread, causing him to cough unexpectedly. "Now leave me alone so I may enjoy the rest of the meal without injuring myself!" He gave her a big grin.

The queen reached for her own goblet of mead and, after taking a sip, added, "I am sure you have the whole thing worked out in your head, my King. I shall pray for the man our daughter likes the best to win."

* * *

The afternoon was moving along steadily now, and Amansun had completed his spear throwing along with some sprints, long jumps back and forth over the stream, and throwing of round fist-sized stones at various targets the enchantress had set up. "Looks like it's time to start on your swordsmanship and staff play, young man," the enchantress said as Amansun walked over to the stump she was once again resting on.

"And who shall be my opponent?" Amansun asked respectfully. "Will you be tutoring me this day?"

Shaking her head and grinning widely, the woman chuckled and said, "I am sure you would find me quite challenging indeed, my young Prince, but I have another who will be better suited for the job." With that, the enchantress whistled quite loudly, in an impressive high tone that caught Amansun off-guard as he rushed to cover his ears with his hands, and together they watched as an old fox came trotting out of the woods from across the clearing.

"Ready for me, My Lady?" the coy fox asked with his trademark grin.

"That we are, Master Sophelus!" the woman replied. "Time for you to show this young man a thing or two about how to handle a staff and sword, if you are up to the task."

The fox stood up on his hind legs as Amansun had seen him do before; and this time, instead of transforming into the eagle as had been the case the first time Amansun witnessed this creature change, the furry animal began to grow in height and size, and before the young prince had time to wipe his eyes in disbelief, the fox had changed into a tall and muscular man with massive arms, legs and shoulders.

"Best we get some clothes for you, Master Sophelus," the woman said suddenly. "I don't believe our young prince wishes to engage you in combat in your present condition."

Glancing down upon himself, the large man shook his head in agreement and, turning to the enchantress, said, "With your permission, my Lady, I will retreat into your cottage and gather some appropriate garments."

"Best you go and select an appropriate sword and shield now, young Prince," she advised Amansun. "Sophelus is an expert swordsman, and he is no sloth with the staff either! Best you prepare yourself for a vicious encounter now, as he truly enjoys giving a good beating to others whence he has the chance!"

Shaking his head in disbelief as he once again walked over to the now half-empty weapons rack, Amansun looked over at the enchantress and said aloud, "Now I am to be schooled by a fox who is sometimes an eagle and apparently also a man when needs be." He laughed as he took a moment to study the various swords that were resting on the armory.

In just a moment Sophelus appeared once again, this time wearing a full set of leathers, a metal vest with armored sleeves, and a fine helmet with slits over the spot where his eyes looked out. "Ready for a good thrashing?" the large man asked happily.

"It would appear that way," Amansun said nervously. Now looking over at the heavily armored man approaching, the prince looked over at the enchantress who appeared to be thoroughly enjoying the day's events, and he asked out loud without meaning to, "And am I to face this giant suited in only this cloth shirt and pants?"

Looking at the two combatants, the enchantress suddenly noticed her error and held her hand up towards Amansun, saying, "A mere trifle, young man." She waved her hands in the air, muttered some unintelligible verse, and just like that Amansun found himself dressed in a snug but well-fitting suit of armor, from his feet all the way up to the highly polished metal helmet upon his head.

Looking out at the advancing foe nervously, Amansun swung his sword about a few times and checked the balance of the shield on his left arm. "Here goes nothing, as they say!" Amansun called out, and then he marched towards the approaching fox turned man and thrust his sword forward, wanting to be the first to take the offensive. The enchantress cheered loudly as the two men took turns beating each other down with violent sword thrusts and parries.

* * *

Perched high on the topmost of the castle's walls, two owls sat side by side, unnoticed by all, as they looked down upon the excitement taking place. "You certainly weren't exaggerating when you described the size of the tournament they are preparing for," Carceren said to the owl seated to his right. "Clearly King Hasselfeth plans on putting on a grand tournament from the looks of it. I haven't seen this kind of action since the year Kings Eadamantus and Hasselfeth brought the elves and men together in a weeklong celebration, after they agreed to the truce that has lasted all these years since."

Looking over at the older, wiser owl, young Bathis curiously asked his companion, "So do you suppose the two sides would still join each other in battle should the need ever arise?"

Carceren thought over the question for a moment before answering. "I believe the men and elves have grown apart over these past ten years or so. But should they have an enemy in common, then yes, I do believe they would fight side-by-side once more, as was done so many decades ago when this area was last in peril."

* * *

For the remainder of that afternoon, all the participants who planned on trying for the princess's hand practiced as much as their bodies would allow. Amansun and Sophelus took to their staffs once the enchantress felt satisfied with the young prince's swordplay. Hrothgar and Baerden worked on archery skills and target practice with the crossbow and bolt on the castle field. The knights took turns using the various sections laid out for the tournament as best they could—some working on swordsmanship in the main arena, others jousting in the long lanes set aside for the horsemanship skills, and others trying their speed at running and swimming. It was a full day of hard work and great effort on everyone's part, and all too soon the slowly setting sun indicated to all that the time for practice was nearly at an end.

"Best we head back down to the gate soon, my Captain," Hrothgar suggested as he noticed how far the sun had set. "That dwarf prince should be marching down the road shortly."

"Right you are," the captain agreed. "I suppose that will have to do. Let's go see what this dwarf prince looks like." He winked at his companion. The two walked over to the main courtyard, climbed up on their horses, and sped off towards the main gate.

"Looks like they're headin' up this way just now, Cap'n!" Barder said, seeing the captain riding up. "Only two appear ta be coming from what I can sees."

Looking down at the guard who was well-known for sleeping through most of the day, Baerden smiled and asked, "An' whaddya doing still on duty, my good man? Seems I saw you here in this very spot earlier this morning."

"That's jus' my way, Cap'n," the old sentry replied. "Just tryin' ta do me duty an' all that, I saspose. Been here keeping watch all day now." This caused a loud roar of laughter to rise from the rest of the men who were also posted at the gate.

"Well, good work, then, Barder," the captain said while winking at the others gathered about and softly chuckling.

Hrothgar and the captain rode out to meet the two dwarves walking down the road and, as they drew nearer, they were both quite surprised by what they saw. Instead of Kairadus the scout, there were two new dwarves approaching, though one was clearly much taller than the other. Both had the characteristic beards hanging a half-foot below their chins and both had broad stocky shoulders, but that is where the similarity ended. "The tall fellow…he looks to be a dwarf…but he's the damned tallest one I've ever seen!" Hrothgar blurted out as they got even closer. "And why is he all dressed up like that, do you suppose?"

Baerden was a little caught off-guard as well, but he tried to remain calm so as to not let the approaching dwarves see his concern. Turning his head slightly so that he could whisper over to his friend, the captain replied, "The tall one's got to be the prince. It would appear he really wants to make an impression on our king! Those are some really colorful clothes he has himself wrapped up in."

Now having met the dwarves head-on, the two men stepped down from their horses to properly introduce themselves. They were, after all, meeting a prince, or so they were told, even if this prince was a dwarf from the southern kingdom. "I am Baerden, captain of the King's Guard," Baerden began, "and this is Hrothgar, my loyal guard and second in command." Neither of the men bowed, though it was generally expected when being introduced to royalty.

Taking one step forward, Balden went next, saying, "I am Balden, captain of the Underlord's troops in the eastern regions of the Barren Plains, and this is Prince Brothemus, son of our deceased King Bergrath the Great, and right hand to the Great Master."

"Pleased to meet you, I am sure," Captain Baerden replied with little fanfare. "Please follow us and we will take you to see King Hasselfeth as arranged earlier."

Not wanting to appear rude, the two men remained on foot and walked along with the dwarves, though there was very little said by any in the group. Upon reaching the outer wall, Barder and his men raised the heavy gate that blocked access any further past that point normally, and he and the others made an effort at bowing and nodding as the colorfully dressed prince and the heavily armored second dwarf passed by. "Welcome to Castle Eladrias. You are expected," the senior sentry said in usual fashion to the guests as they moved past.

Once the group had moved out of hearing range all the sentries and guards on duty immediately started commenting on the prince and his attire. "Who does he think he is, coming in dressed like that?" Barder said aloud before anyone else could do so. "Looks like he's dressed to be anointed the new king in that get-up."

"You sure he's a dwarf, there, Ole Barder?" another man asked. "Damned tallest dwarf I ever done see!"

"Don't let his height fool you," the senior sentry said. "If he looks like a dwarf, and he smells like a dwarf, he's a dwarf. Even if he is a prince!"

The four silent marchers moved along the roadway until the castle came clearly into view, and even from this distance it was apparent that something unusual was taking place. Everywhere one looked, one could see brightly painted banners, signs and tents, and draped booths scattered all about the outer areas of the castle. Hrothgar leaned a bit closer towards the captain, whispering softly, "Damn all these foolish signs…even a half-wit would notice that something was happening here."

The captain nodded his head in agreement but chose not to say anything out loud, as the dwarves were now quite near the men as they walked along, and he did not wish to give anything away unnecessarily.

"Looks as though you are preparing to have a tournament here tomorrow?" Prince Brothemus questioned as he and Balden took note of all the banners and signs flapping in the breeze.

"The king likes to keep his soldiers inspired," Baerden started to say. "Just a little something to keep everyone's spirits up, really."

Now walking into the main castle courtyard, a full squad of armed soldiers and archers lined the road as the small group pressed on. With a wave of his hand and a nod, two guards rushed over and took the leads from the captain and Hrothgar's horses and quickly led them back towards the main stables. Both dwarves suddenly stood up a little straighter as they saw that there were no less than two hundred armed soldiers lining the courtyard, with another fifty posted along the walls of the castle, particularly above the heavy main gate that had been raised into an open position at a sign from Captain Baerden as they had approached. "Quite a welcome for two dwarves," Captain Balden said somewhat sarcastically.

"Be prepared, or so they say," Baerden replied in turn, with every bit of sarcasm to match. "Now follow me and I will lead you to one of the meeting chambers where our king is waiting."

"Yes, please lead on, good Captain. I am anxious to meet this king whom I have heard so much about," Prince Brothemus said as he glanced over at Captain Balden and smiled.

* * *

Amansun and Sophelus had been raining down blows upon one another with swords at first, followed by heavy wooden staffs. Both were covered in sweat and reeling from the exertion of their battle. "I believe he is ready to fend for himself adequately, my Lady," Sophelus stated as he dodged a heavy blow and took several paces backwards. Amansun, sensing that this round was over, bent over suddenly, using this opportunity to catch his breath while surveying his swollen hands and fingers to see how much damage he had suffered.

"Right you are, my good man," the enchantress replied enthusiastically, standing and clapping her hands. "Well done, Amansun. I am certain you will vanquish all who stand up to you tomorrow. You matched Sophelus' blows again and again."

Looking up at the darkening sky, the fox turned man walked over to the man he had been trying to squash for the better part of the afternoon and, patting him on the back, said, "Thanks for the match, Amansun. I shall try to make myself available again once more if ever you should need my services." And with that, he walked over to the enchantress and bowed low, asking her permission to leave.

"Yes, and thanks for your efforts," the woman replied. "Run along now to your family, and give my best to that wife of yours and the new pups! Be sure to pop in tomorrow after sunrise in case I think of other matters that might need tending to."

"As you wish, my Lady," the large man replied, then he turned and started to walk in the direction of the woods. After a few paces he started changing shape and in no time at all he was once again a walking fox on two legs, then simply a fox running along on all four as he sped off into the darkness of the trees.

"Quite a handy fellow!" Amansun said respectfully to the enchantress. "Which of the three did he start off as?"

The enchantress looked into Amansun's eyes deeply as if recalling a fond memory, then said, "He was but a fox when I first found him, with his front foot caught in a hunter's steel trap…though that was years ago. When I pulled him from the trap, he was so grateful he pledged his unending service to me, and we have been dear friends ever since. And how do you feel, Amansun, now that you have had all of one day to train for the king's tourney?"

Setting his helmet down upon the ground, and shaking his hair about so as to enjoy the cool breeze, Amansun smiled and said, "As good as one could expect, I suppose…for having trained for one day, that is." He gave a radiant smile. "But what of my jousting training?" he asked, suddenly realizing that they had never reached that segment of his training.

"Don't give it a second thought," the woman said playfully. "You know how to ride a horse, I know. And you are stronger than any other as well. Just sit atop the saddle and knock over anyone that rides in your direction."

"Right then…sit straight and knock them down…seems easy enough to remember," he replied with a laugh. "I don't suppose it might be time for dinner, would it?"

"Come, young prince. Let's go inside and decide what we are having for dinner," the enchantress offered, and the two walked back around the cottage and disappeared inside.

* * *

King Hasselfeth was seated in an enormous, ornately carved wooden chair that sat alongside a long window looking out upon Silver Lake when Captain Hrothgar and the king's invited guests arrived. Bowing low and removing his helmet, Hrothgar announced their arrival. The king stood and walked over to where the four men were standing, followed closely by two very large men armed with swords and spears. "Forgive my royal guard for their lack of trust, good Prince," he said, "but they are merely doing their jobs, of course." With that, the king approached closer and raised his hand out, palm facing down as was custom, so that the prince could kiss the back of his hand.

"No need for all that, good King," Prince Brothemus said in unexpected fashion. "There is only one true master I bow to, and he is in his mighty fortress many days' ride from here." He smiled oddly at the king and his guards who were still standing close by.

"Well, then, what is your purpose here?" King Hasselfeth demanded, no longer willing to tolerate the rude dwarf prince's presence much longer.

"The Underlord has sent me to investigate the presence of a great winged serpent in the area, good King. A dragon, if you will."

Waving his hands at the prince as if completely uninterested, the king said rather plainly, "That is quite old news. My men disposed of the foul creature many days ago. If that is what you seek then your time here is wasted, and you should run along now back to whence you came." He turned to walk back to his chair once more.

Now looking quite put out and red in the face, Prince Brothemus composed himself and, after glancing over at the other dwarf in the room with a hateful gaze, looked at the retreating king, saying, "That may be the case, good King, but my orders are to scout the area and see with my own eyes whether the beast be here or not."

Turning just halfway so as to be able to look into the prince's eyes, King Hasselfeth shook his head as if in disgust and uttered, "You may have one day to look about if you must, but just the two of you, that is all. The remainder of your party will remain camped out on the road where they are presently. Those are my conditions."

Prince Brothemus was less than pleased by the king's response, but he nodded his head and then thanked the king for his offer. "My captain and I will remain until tomorrow evening, then, as agreed, and then we shall leave your lands, good King."

The king nodded his head in agreement, and then glancing back at the dwarf once more, noticed the beautiful blue stone ring that jutted out from his right ring finger. "That is a very impressive ring you have there, Prince Brothemus," the king said.

Turning to glance at Captain Balden for an instant, the prince turned back to the king and replied, "Why, yes. I am quite fond of it. It was a gift from a very close friend." And with that, the two dwarves nodded once more, then watched as the king retired back to his chair. Spinning on his heel unexpectedly, Prince Brothemus called over to the king one last time. "What is the nature of your tournament, King Hasselfeth?"

Without thinking his response through, the king replied, "I am holding a tournament for my daughter's hand in matrimony. She has come of age now." Back at the other side of the room, Hrothgar and Captain Baerden both winced noticeably, as if struck, and they glanced sideways at each other and shook their heads.

Leaning closely to his captain, Prince Brothemus whispered softly, "That is news the Underlord will certainly find most interesting, I am sure." He smiled and continued walking out of the room, following behind the two men who were also discussing something in private.

As the group of four made their way across the courtyard once more, the dwarves glanced over at one of the brightly painted banners that hung across one of the castle walls:

**Grand tournament Starts Tomorrow
Come One Come All!**

Prince Brothemus smiled as he read the banner, then glanced over at the captain of the Guard who appeared to be in an even worse mood than when the two had first met. "Guess I'll be sure to make some time to stop by to see that," he said while staring at the captain unpleasantly.

Back at the roadside gate, Hrothgar and Baerden watched as the two dwarves made their way back down the road towards their camp. The sun had set by now and it was just starting to get dark. Looking at the sentries posted on the road, the captain snapped loudly, "Those two have the king's permission to come and go until this time tomorrow night. Be sure to have them escorted by at least four men wherever they go, though, and notify me at once whenever they pass this gate!"

CHAPTER 31

That night over their dinner together, the enchantress spent hours teaching Amansun all the things he would need to know in order to appear normal to the men and ladies of the castle. She showed him how to bow, how to eat, how to drink, even how to take a lady's hand in his and kiss the top of it gently while looking up into her eyes. Amansun was an excellent student and he paid attention to everything the enchantress had to say. "And you are sure I will be allowed to enter this tournament, my Lady?" he asked nervously.

"Why, of course you will be allowed," she said matter-of-factly. "You are a prince, after all, are you not?"

Amansun smiled at first, then looked over at the enchantress as if puzzled, and asked, "But how will they know I am a prince, my Lady? I don't even recall my own name yet."

The woman stared back at the young man blankly for a moment, eyes blinking as if lost in thought, then replied enthusiastically, "Well, we'll just have to make one up for you, I suppose." She began to smile once more. "There are many kingdoms several days' ride from here, and some that were abandoned years ago as well. We'll just announce you as being from one of these, possibly from up north. Not many travel up there anymore, not with all the giants and fairies and barguests that live in those parts now."

"What's a barguest?"

"Those are shape shifters. Bears mostly. They take the shape of immense hairy men when they want, but normally they appear as normal woodland bears, though quite large and fierce they are."

"And are they friendly or mean?" the prince asked, thinking back to his old friend Gruawth whom he hadn't seen in weeks now.

The enchantress looked over at Amansun smiling and said, "That depends on what you are up to when you come across one, I'd say. They are terribly territorial, and they don't like any that move into their lands, especially those that start clearing out trees and settling down homesteads. They will normally leave you be and move along if you are just passing through quietly and not causing any trouble."

"Well, I suppose I shall be a prince from the north, then," Amansun said smiling. "Once I remember my true name, I can share it with the princess, as with any luck she will be with me by then anyway." Sitting at the table looking puzzled once more, he looked over at the enchantress and asked, "And how shall I be getting to the castle now, my Lady? I obviously can't fly myself there anymore."

Reaching over and patting the young man softly on the top of his hand that was resting atop the wooden table, the woman said, "Don't you worry about getting there, young man. I have everything planned out. You'll see." And with that, she instructed her student that it was time to retire for the evening.

* * *

Back at the dwarves' campsite, Captain Balden and Prince Brothemus sat together in a large tent dimly lit inside from a small candle that flickered gently. "Ready to summons his Lordship?" Balden questioned Prince Brothemus.

"Yes, it's time. Let's see what the Great Master has to say about this tournament of the king's," Prince Brothemus replied with an evil grin.

"Your ring or mine?"

"Mine, of course. It is me who answers directly to our Lord whenever I am present and best you do not forget that!"

"Begging your pardon, my Prince. I meant no offense," the captain replied while hunching lower into his seat. "Shall I fetch my silver bowl and water?"

Now seeming more at ease, the prince slipped the ring from his finger while directing the captain to get the bowl and water. "Be quick about it, Captain!" the prince commanded. "I am sure the Great Master is expecting us."

Prince Brothemus and the Captain spent the next few moments sharing everything they had seen and heard with the Underlord. Rubbing his hands together, as if quite intrigued by the news he had just received, he nodded his head up and down and then instructed his servant, Cantalus, to go and fetch several powders and dried plants to create a new potion. "You will be entering the king's competition tomorrow, young Prince," the wizard said unexpectedly. "Though I am quite sure King Hasselfeth will be assuredly against the idea."

"If the king will not allow it, then how am I to do so, my Lord?" Prince Brothemus questioned.

"Silence, impudent fool!" the wizard snapped. "Do not dare to question me nor my intentions again, or you will feel my wrath upon your return!"

Falling to his knees suddenly, Prince Brothemus began begging for forgiveness and assuring the Underlord that he had not meant to question or doubt his desires. "I shall do all that you command, My Lord," he said enthusiastically.

Grabbing the items that old Cantalus was now gently setting down upon the wooden table where the wizard stood, he looked up from the bowl in front of him for a moment and explained, "The king shall have no choice but to allow you to compete my dawdling fool. He has made it clear that princes and other noblemen may try for the princess's hand, correct?"

"Yes, that is what we were told at the castle today," Prince Brothemus stammered.

"Well, then," the Underlord said slowly and deliberately. "You are a prince and therefore you must be allowed to enter. Be sure to make this point when the king objects to your request…and he will." He smiled to himself as he measured off a small portion of white powder and then reached for the next bag of ingredients. "Leave me now, prince, for I have much to do this night. When I finish with this potion there will be none who are able to defeat you in tomorrow's contest. Leave your ring in the silver bowl covered fully with water this night, and when you next slip it on in the morning it will contain all the power you need to be the victor tomorrow."

Once they had left, the prince said directly to Captain Balden, "Best we stay entirely out of that tent this evening. Go fetch us another tent for this evening at once." Captain Balden bowed low to the prince and disappeared down the camp, calling out for his lieutenant as he ran.

* * *

That night there was much feasting and celebrating inside and outside of the castle. Men, women and children from all around enjoyed music of all sorts, along with food and drink served up in healthy portions at the many food booths that were now open for business. Down along the lakeside of the castle, a great display of fireworks of all shapes, sizes and colors were being shot out over the water, creating thousands of colorful reflections atop the lake's surface. High up on the castle's west wall, Princess Lyleth and her handmaidens clapped and giggled together as they watched each new explosion of fire send plumes of glittering ash and sparks cascading down from on high.

Down on the castle's main level, Captain Baerden and Hrothgar were mounted up and riding about for one last time to ensure that the castle was protected and that all of the guards were still in place and doing their duties, rather than sneaking off to enjoy the festivities of the evening. Now riding up to the main gateway in the darkness, the captain checked in with the sentries standing on duty. "No sign of the two dwarves you asked to keep watch out fer, Cap'n," a sentry announced without needing to be asked. "No movement at all to speak of, so fars anyway."

Leaning back and stretching out his tired shoulders as he surveyed the darkness of the road, the captain breathed heavily then said, "Be sure to wake me should they show up…regardless of the hour!" then he and Hrothgar turned and rode back to the castle to retire for the night. "Best you get a good night's rest too, old friend," he said while smiling at the elder man. "Don't forget that it is you who will be responsible for the running of the king's security tomorrow whilst I attempt to win Princess Lyleth's hand!"

"Right you are, my Captain," Hrothgar replied. "Now off to bed with you. I'll do one more pass of the outside grounds and then turn in myself."

* * *

Amansun had needed no enticement to crawl off to bed this night. His muscles ached more this evening then at any other time he could remember. Within a few moments of having lay down to rest, the young prince was fast asleep, muscles twitching as he let out a soft snore.

From where Amansun was standing, he had a clear view of the immense stone city and fortress that rose upwards into magnificent towers, spires and cathedrals, reaching up towards the bright blue sky. The fortress was massive and its layers, stacked up one upon the other, seemed to reach up endlessly from the low field he now found himself marching on. Further beyond the castle's walls and towers, an incredibly beautiful set of mountains rose even higher, standing tall and majestic as their tops disappeared into the very clouds themselves. Following the ridges downwards as his eyes slowly stared off into the distance, he was amazed by not only the scale of the mountains themselves but also by their beauty, as well as that of the emerald green trees that circled the base of these majestic towers of rock.

"One never gets used to seeing their beauty, even from this distance," a voice from behind him said pleasantly. "The builders of our own castle here tried to mimic their shape and color when this old fortress was built centuries ago."

Looking up once more at some of the taller spires that rose up above the fortress's walls, Amansun nodded his head in agreement as he suddenly could see the similarities between the towers and the mountain peaks rising directly up behind them. "I never really noticed much before…not until just now when you pointed them out, Father," the small boy said as he turned and looked back at the tall man standing just behind him, draped in magnificent cloaks of white and silver, long hair blowing lightly in the stiff morning breeze.

"Someday, Halldor my son, you will be the ruler of this mighty fortress," the cloaked man said with a proud smile, "along with all the lands that surround us."

Amansun twitched slightly in his sleep, as if some type of revelation had just been revealed to him, and then he rolled over onto his side, still breathing heavily and snoring even louder than before.

CHAPTER 32

The new day started just the same as any other. The sun's rays slowly shown out from above the peaks of the distant Granite Mountains, chasing the darkness from the valleys and woods below. Birds began to sing in the trees and fields while rabbits, squirrels and field mice hurried about, searching for tender morsels to eat before the first ravens and hawks came out to feed.

Out on the roadway, tired sentries rubbed their eyes as they peered down the dirt path, searching for any signs of movement from the troop of dwarves that they knew were camped there, just beyond their field of vision.

Out in front of the castle walls, women were carrying their laundry down to the lake's edge to begin their washing duties, as had been done since years long forgotten. Their children, laughing and cheering, splashed about in the chilly water, sang songs and chased one another about, while others jumped into the water feet-first, causing great splashes that sent the birds along the shoreline scattering about in all directions.

Down in the castle's main stables, groomsmen and their apprentices were busy at work dressing the knights' horses, tying brightly colored bows onto their manes and tails, while the younger men busied themselves with polishing the riders' suits of armor and weapons to a high shine.

Deep in the vaults of the castle's main guard quarters, Captain Baerden was already up and getting into his leathers while he played the events of the day in his head over and over again. "Thrust and block, thrust and parry," he muttered to himself, imagining each and every movement he was planning on using against his adversaries this day, much like a master chessman thinks through his every move before the first piece is ever played.

Wafts of smoke rose from behind the canvassed food stations, as cooks and maidens began to ready the first of the morning food items that crowds would soon be clamoring for, as they jockeyed for the best viewing seats in the various roped-off sections of the tournament grounds.

Back hidden away in the Black Woods, Amansun had woken early, and he was just getting dressed when the enchantress entered the room. "I know my name!" Amansun said. "It is Halldor. It came to me in a dream last night. I saw my father and he spoke it aloud."

"Halldor," the enchantress repeated. "That is a fine name. Strong. Clear. Simple. Seems to me I have heard that name long ago." Placing several logs onto the dimly lit fire and reaching for a kettle of water to place over it, the enchantress said the name aloud repeatedly a few more times. "Did your father say anything else in your dream?"

"Not that I recall," Amansun answered. "We spoke very little, but he did mention that I would be the ruler of an immense fortress that sat at the foot of an enormous mountain range."

Now adding some dried leaves into the kettle, the enchantress walked over towards the young man, looking quite interested, and asked, "Did you see the fortress at all? What did it look like?" Amansun closed his eyes for a moment, thinking back to the visions he had seen, then he described as best he could what he had seen the night before. "Most intriguing," the woman replied as she walked over to one of the small windows that opened out into the field outside. She released a small latch then pushed the window open and looked off into the distance. "Describe the mountain peaks once more," she asked of the prince.

"Their base was covered in pure green pines and firs, taller than any I have seen before," he began. "They rose up into the very heavens above, with tops that could not be seen, as they disappeared into the clouds themselves."

Turning away from the small window and walking back over to Amansun, the enchantress, who had been in her middle-aged form up to this point, suddenly transformed back into her young woman's shape, and she smiled at the man standing before her. "It is very obvious to me now, Amansun," she shared as if suddenly seeing the answer to a difficult question for the first time. "You are from the great castle fortress of Argonathe in the east!"

Looking at the young woman before him, Amansun nodded his head up and down slowly as he muttered to himself, "Yes…yes…that is it…I remember now…the fortress of Argonathe…of course…and my father…the king…his name is Hanthris the Bold…and my mother…Queen Osselathe." He felt as if he were waking from a long, cloudy dream.

"You have come home, young Prince Halldor!" the enchantress exclaimed. "Your father's kingdom is but two weeks' ride from here, east of the Castle Eladrias, though I have not passed that way in quite some time."

Amansun, who had been smiling up to this point, thrilled that the mystery of his beginnings was finally unraveling and becoming clear to him, became puzzled when he glanced over at the young woman and saw that she had a very sorrowful look upon her face now. "What is the matter, my Lady?" he asked.

Looking down upon her hands for a moment as she decided how best to give the prince before her the bad news, she looked up suddenly, taking a deep breath and exhaling slowly, then said, "I am afraid I have some ill news to share with you, Amansun." She reached out and took the man's large hands into her own. "Your mother and father, the king and queen, they are no more."

"No more? No more? What do you mean no more?" Amansun demanded, pulling his hands from the woman's and taking a step back as if trying to dodge a blow.

"They disappeared years ago, I am afraid," she replied. "Both of your parents went missing years ago is what I have heard…though I have never ventured to your father's lands to see for myself. I am afraid your father's castle lies abandoned now, taken over by a host of goblins if the stories be true…sent to your father's fortress by the Underlord himself, as I have heard."

Amansun walked a few paces over to the wooden table where he and the enchantress shared their meals and collapsed into one of the chairs there. Looking over at the woman, he announced, "I must leave at once for Argonathe, then, to see what has become of them."

The enchantress walked over to the prince and sat in a chair beside him. "There is nothing there to see, Amansun, and no good will come from this move should you make it. Best to move forward with the king's tournament for now as you have planned. If you still want to go to Argonathe after that, I shall offer what assistance I can." She patted the young man on the shoulders softly.

Shaking his head in disbelief and sorrow, Amansun looked up into the eyes of the enchantress to see if she spoke the truth, and it was clear to him that she was not lying. He placed his head into his left hand as he rested his arm on the tabletop, still looking bewildered and in disbelief. "I finally remember who I am and from whence I come… only to learn that my parents are both missing…perhaps dead…and my father's kingdom overrun by dark creatures of the Underlords," he muttered softly.

"You have been absent for many years, I am afraid, young Prince," she responded. "These lands are still quite wild, and the Underlord has spent the last century swallowing up all he can to increase his strength in these northern reaches. He is not content with being the master of all the lands to the south."

"I will do as you suggest, my Lady," Amansun replied. "But once I have won the princess's hand, the Underlord and I have unfinished business, I can assure you."

Now standing and walking over to the fireplace to remove the steaming kettle, the enchantress said while pouring two mugs of hot tea, "You shan't have to seek out the Underlord, I am afraid. I believe his intentions will be to track you down soon enough, mark my words. Even now he is likely searching for you."

* * *

Back at Castle Eladrias, crowds of people were beginning to gather outside among the food booths and tents. The seating areas besides the main tournament venues were already filled, and everywhere you looked, more and more people were searching about for good vantage points.

"Best we check down at the gate one more time," Hrothgar said to the captain as he walked into the captain of the Guard's personal quarters. "The tourney won't be starting until mid-morning is what I have been told, but those good-for-nothing dwarves are bound to be out and about anytime now."

As the captain finished pulling his boots on and reaching for his sword and sheath, he nodded in agreement and made for the doorway where his friend was waiting. "I am ready to go, old friend," he said anxiously. "I have a knot in my stomach the size of a pumpkin, I am afraid to say, and the sooner the contests begin, the better."

Laughing at his companion and slapping him on the back squarely, Hrothgar shook his head knowingly then advised his friend, "Once the first sword thrust rains down upon your shield, you will feel much better, Captain. Just be sure to keep your eye on the prize! That should motivate you enough to get through your queasiness."

"Easy for you to say," the captain replied as they made their way out of the room and along the corridor leading out to the castle's main courtyard. "Just be sure to keep your eye on that Prince Brothemus for me, alright? I have a hunch those two will be up to no good just as soon as the distraction of the tournament begins."

"I will keep both eyes on them myself," the elder man replied assuredly. "Likely I will miss your entire tournament performance while I babysit the wandering dwarves." He laughed and kept close behind the captain, who was now walking speedily out to the stables.

Out in the courtyard, several groups of knights and their men were gathered into tight bunches as they finalized their preparations for the day. Each group had their own colors, and they were easily recognizable by the standards they held atop long poles reaching ten to twelve feet into the air. "Looks to be about nine competitors for you to dispatch," Hrothgar said calmly. "I think you should blow right through most of these, though the Black Knight looks to be quite formidable."

"Thanks for the vote of confidence," Captain Baerden muttered. "I'll be sure to remember to save the Black Knight for last, then." He smiled and looked off towards the group of bulky soldiers who were tending to the Black Knight's weapons and steed.

Hrothgar looked at his companion once more oddly, seeing that he was still dressed in just his leathers and asked, "What about your armor, my Captain?"

"It's too early for all that," the captain replied. "Let's see what the dwarves are up to first. I'll ride back and get suited up before the king's opening speeches."

"As you wish, Captain," Hrothgar said while nodding. "Off to the gate, then." Together they rode off towards the eastern roadway.

When Hrothgar and the captain reached the roadway gate, they were surprised to see that a small group of dwarves were making their way up the road. "Here they come now!" Hrothgar announced, though all the men at the gate could easily see the group of eight dwarves as they drew nearer.

"Guess the prince is hard of hearing as well as being quite rude!" the captain announced. "King Hasselfeth clearly stated that only the prince and his captain would be allowed inside the kingdom, as I recall."

Shaking his head vigorously in agreement, Hrothgar said loudly, "That is what I heard as well, my Captain. I shall take great pleasure in informing the dwarf prince that his other guests are not welcome!"

The captain, Hrothgar, and the other men on duty waited impatiently as the small band of dwarves continued to approach. "Stop where you are!" Hrothgar shouted out as he moved from behind the lowered gate and rode up towards the dwarves. "Only the prince and his captain may proceed any further, or have you forgotten what the king agreed to just yesterday?"

Stepping several paces forward from the rest of the group, Captain Balden looked up at the man on horseback and said loudly and clearly so all those gathered about could hear, "The prince is no longer coming as justs an invited guests of the king to survey your lands. Prince Brothemus now approaches as a suitor of the princess, said to be given aways at the conclusion of the tournament abouts to begins this very morning, and his attendants shall be given free passage as wells."

There was a sudden deep silence as Hrothgar, the captain, and all the sentries, soldiers and archers hidden away in the woods on either side of the road took in what this stocky dwarf had just said. Then, as if timed by signal somehow, the entire group from all sides of the roadway broke into riotous laughter, some hooting loudly while others seemed nearly to fall over as they guffawed and snorted.

Captain Balden, standing upright and staring up at the large man on the horse before him, still wiping tears from his eyes as he tried in vain to keep a straight face, said coldly and plainly, "Has someone said somethings humorous? Surely nones of you are having a laugh at the expense of my prince, sent heres by orders of the Underlord of the Southern Barrens, Great Master Wizard and ruler of all kingdoms and lands south of the Archain mountain ranges?"

Now calming himself and sitting squarely on his saddle once more, Hrothgar watched as his captain rode up on his horse, making his way towards the band of dwarves that stood there together, swords unsheathed, axes and spears raised as if awaiting the order to charge. "Clearly there has been some mistake!" the captain exclaimed as he covered the final distance between he and the dwarves. "This tournament is not open to the likes of Prince Brothemus, be he royalty or no!"

Captain Balden changed his gaze over to the younger rider now and, staring him down with equal disdain as he had with the elder rider, calmly replied, "If there has been a mistake, young captain, than it has been mades by your own king. The word we were given is that King Hasselfeth has arranged a grand tournament opens to all princes and noblemen of the surrounding lands, with the prize being that of his own daughter's hand in matrimony."

Hrothgar looked over at his captain and stated aloud without thinking, "Clearly this be madness, my Captain?"

Now stepping forward from the rest of the group for the first time, Prince Brothemus approached the two riders and, also glancing up at them with a look of pure hatred, responded to Hrothgar's comment, saying, "The only madness will be if you and your king choose to deny me my right to enter this contest, Captain Baerden. My lord has instructed me to enter this tournament without hesitation or question, and I can assure you that should you choose to disallow this, the Great Master's retribution will be swift, unwavering and complete!"

Sitting atop his horse with a look of confusion and disbelief in equal parts, Captain Baerden looked over at his second in command and said in a voice loud enough so that the dwarves present could hear, "Lead the prince and his attendants to the preparation tent at the tourney field and wait there. I shall go and seek counsel from the king." And with that, the captain turned his steed about and made haste up the roadway, waving to the sentries on the way back to raise the gate.

"Right this way, Prince Brothemus," Hrothgar said unhappily as he fought back the urge to pull his blade and settle the matter right there and then. "I will be happy to show you the way to the waiting tent."

* * *

Outside the castle near one of the tents that offered pan-fried trout with eggs as well as roast boar with juniper berries, a large, muscular man, dressed very simply in a pair of loose-fitting trousers and a sack-type shirt, was inquiring as to when the tournament would be starting. "Any idea as to when the tourney b'gins, friend?" the man asked one of the patrons who was already in line to buy some breakfast.

Looking back at the man as if he had been interrupted, the patron glanced over his shoulder and with a glare said, "Sign over there posted on that stick says 'mid-morning,' friend," and he turned back to watch the kitchen attendants as they pulled a large piece of roast from the fire as a heavenly aroma wafted about the tent.

Turning without taking the time to thank the patron, the man walked off towards a patch of trees and quickly disappeared out of sight.

Just a moment later, several young children screamed out in delight as they pointed at a large eagle that had just lifted off from behind some nearby trees, as their parents stared in wonder, quite surprised to see such a large bird taking flight from so close by.

* * *

"I don't wish to question your plan, my Lady, but shouldn't we be concerned about missing the start of the king's tourney?" Amansun asked meekly.

Helping herself to a second piece of bread with orange-blossom honey, the enchantress assured Amansun that everything would be fine. "I am just waiting on news from Sophelus who went out on a fact-finding mission earlier this morning," she said.

Amansun was quite anxious with everything that had taken place and that he had learned over the past few days, so he excused himself and stepped out of the cottage for some fresh air. Just as he made his way to a small tree stump to rest on, the eagle came into view high off in the distance. "My Lady," he called out, "it looks as though Sophelus is just returning now."

Walking out of the cottage doorway, bread still in one hand while the other reached up and shaded her eyes so she could look into the sky without being blinded, the enchantress said, "See? Nothing to worry about. I am sure we will find that we are in great shape. One must remember that the tournament can't begin without the royal family present, and they aren't likely to be fed, dressed and ready to make their grand entrance this early in the morning!" Amansun nodded his head as he thought through the enchantress' logic.

Within a few steps after landing, the eagle transformed once again into a man. The enchantress reached down and picked up some garments she had set outside the door earlier that day, and tossed these towards the approaching man. Once dressed, Sophelus explained that the king would be announcing the tournament's start later in the morning. Amansun still wondered to himself how they were going to cover the distance from the home of the enchantress to the castle in such a short time.

"It's really quite spectacular," Sophelus stated excitedly. "There are tents and booths and fields with bleachers set up all about the castle grounds…and people…people as far as the eye can see!"

"Just as I had expected," the enchantress said as she glanced over at Amansun.

"Shall we be riding out on horseback soon, then?" Amansun questioned.

"No time for horses," the enchantress responded. "I have something much faster in mind. Now follow me back into the cottage. I have a nice surprise for you." She winked at the prince. Once inside the cottage, the enchantress motioned for Amansun to follow her into the room adjacent to the main portion of the small cottage, the only section he had not been into up to this point.

As the prince passed through the doorway leading into the enchantress's private quarters, he was quite shocked to see that the room appeared to be at least several times larger than the section he had been residing in. It spread out in all directions and there appeared to be other walls indicating that the cottage went on and on, even though from outside it looked little more than a small peasant's home. "How is this possible?" he gasped, mouth wide open, as he looked about the enormous room which was filled with everything from beautifully carved wooden furniture to statues of mythical creatures and men and women, along with a large collection of stunningly crafted suits of armor all lined up against one of the far walls.

"Remember, young Prince," the enchantress said, smiling as she grabbed the young man's hand and led him off towards the far wall where the armor suits stood. "Not everything is as it appears, as I have told you since we met." Making a sweeping gesture toward the countless suits of armor lining the wall, she said, "Take your pick, Amansun. Choose any set you like."

Bowing to the young woman standing beside him, the prince raised his head and smiled at the woman, saying, "You are full of surprises, aren't you, my Lady?"

"You have no idea, young Prince," the enchantress laughed. "No idea at all."

* * *

Back at Eladrias Castle, King Hasselfeth and Captain Baerden were locked into a loud conversation along with several trusted noblemen from the kingdom. "This is absurd!" the king shouted again and again. "How can the Underlord think for even one moment that I would allow my daughter to marry one of their kind? It's an abomination, it is, and make no mistake. Never would I allow this to happen!" He smashed his fist down onto the large wooden table that the group had been standing around.

"That is precisely the point, my King," one of the noblemen said.

"That is exactly why the Underlord has instructed Prince Brothemus to enter your tournament, don't you see!" exclaimed Lord Mallthus.

Standing a few feet back from where the king and his nobleman stood, Captain Baerden struggled to understand the gentleman's meaning. "What do you mean when you say it's just what the Underlord expects? Doesn't he want the dwarf prince to enter and win the tournament so he can take Princess Lyleth and claim these lands as his own when the king is no more?"

"Not at all," Lord Mallthus continued. "Don't you see? The wizard knows that our king will refuse to have Prince Brothemus marry his daughter. He's counting on it. Then when the king refuses to allow him to enter the tournament, the Underlord can say that we have dishonored the prince along with himself, and he will declare war on us along with all the kingdoms represented here today. It's actually quite clever," he added with an odd smile.

"You are quite right, Lord Mallthus," the King said begrudgingly. "When I state that the prince is barred from entry, the Underlord will certainly use this opportunity to end the fragile truce we have held onto these past few years. But what can we do?"

"There is no choice to make, my King," Lord Mallthus said. "You must let Prince Brothemus enter, as there can be no other way."

"Very well," the king stated. "We must hope that any but the dwarf win the tournament. But is this wise? Can we be sure that Prince Brothemus will not win?"

Lord Mallthus and the others gathered about shook their heads as one and all agreed, saying with certainty, "No dwarf, prince or not, will defeat our finest warriors from across these lands. It is not possible that all should fail."

"I too am entered into the tournament," the captain reminded the group suddenly. "I shall find a way of dispensing of the dwarf if needs be, or die trying."

"Then it is settled," said the king. "Send word to Prince Brothemus that he may enter my tournament, but also advise him that he will be given no measure of safety in these games. It is possible that he may come to harm during the matches that take place over these next two days, and he and the Underlord are not to hold us liable should the prince be injured, perhaps even killed by the hands of fate."

Bowing to the group once more, Captain Baerden said that he would give the message to Prince Brothemus personally, and departed swiftly. King Hasselfeth glanced over at the noblemen gathered about him, seeming quite pale suddenly, and then stated in a concerned voice, "Just wait until the queen realizes there is a dwarf prince contesting for her daughter's hand. She is likely to kill me long before I need worry about the Underlord!"

* * *

After looking over the various suits of armor, Amansun decided upon the white suit, saying, "I seem to remember my father wearing something similar, or at least that is what my dreams and visions have shown." He reached out and ran his fingers over the smooth metal.

"An excellent choice," the enchantress said warmly. "White has always been the color of purity, and it shows a glimpse into your soul that of all the suits to choose from you have selected this one."

Now looking quite princely in his well-fitting suit, Amansun followed the enchantress into the next room, and there to his amazement was an armory filled with swords, shields, daggers, and all the other weapons any good knight would need at his side when going into battle. "Truly this is a house of surprises, as well as gifts of unexpected treasures," the prince said happily. He quickly stepped into the smaller room and began handling the various swords, looking to find one with just the right hand fit and balance.

"Take your time, young Prince," the woman encouraged. "I have something that needs tending to outside. I shall return in just a moment."

Amansun was very careful to select just the right pieces of weaponry, as he knew that these items would likely save his life in the future. The enchantress came walking back into the room and encouraged him to finish up as the time to depart was quickly approaching. Lifting a perfectly balanced sword along with its matching sheath and belt, as well as a sturdy round shield and an attractive jewel-encrusted dagger, he indicated that he was now ready.

Once outside, Amansun found himself looking at an odd collection of animals along with his new friend Sophelus. There, lined up as if they were soldiers being inspected in a line-up, stood two field mice, a rather plump rabbit, and an older-looking squirrel whose gray whiskers made one think that he was probably well into his years by now. The Lady of the Woods, seeing the look of bewilderment on Amansun's face, grinned as she walked up to Sophelus. "Thanks for rounding them up so quickly, old friend," she said. "These should do just fine." The enchantress cautioned Amansun to stay where he was and not utter a sound until she had completed working her spell.

Watching the enchantress intently, Amansun observed while she uttered seemingly unrecognizable words and sounds as she moved about the four small animals standing in front of her. With a flash of her hands, and a sudden crack as one would expect a thunder cloud to make, the animals were suddenly transformed into four gigantic flying beasts the likes of which the prince had never seen before. With wings like those of a great eagle, bodies shaped like a horse, and the heads, shoulders and torsos of a man, the large creatures flapped their wings about briefly as they looked about and waited for orders from the enchantress.

"Very impressive indeed," Amansun said while clapping his hands together and smiling. "Now I see how we are to make it to the castle grounds on time!" Looking at the four winged beasts, champing in place and looking quite restless, he realized that there were only three riders and asked, "Who is the fourth creature for, my Lady?"

"One for each of us and one for your weapons, of course, my Prince," she said while instructing the two men to strap Amansun's equipment onto the beast on the end.

"Of course!" Amansun repeated while laughing. "I should know by now that for everything you do there is a purpose."

Stepping up and onto one of the three remaining winged creatures, the enchantress suddenly commanded the two men to do the same. "Best we be off now, for the sun has risen higher than I would have liked already," she said while looking up into the sky.

Amansun and Sophelus each jumped onto one of the remaining beasts, and within moments the three were flying high in the sky, the enchantress leading the way, followed by Amansun, Sophelus, and then the lone beast packing the weapons. "Stay close to me,, she called out to the riders behind her. "We shall have to land far enough away from the castle to ensure not being seen, but we don't want to arrive too late or you may miss your chance to compete."

Amansun peered down at the ground, now quite some distance below, and found himself lowering his chest towards the beast's back and grabbing on with both hands tightly. Seeing the prince's reaction from where he was sitting further back in the line of flying beasts, Sophelus laughed loudly and called out to Amansun, "It looks and feels much differently when you are up at this height without wings of your own, doesn't it, my friend?"

CHAPTER 33

After meeting with Prince Brothemus, Captain Baerden went back to his quarters where he changed into his own armor. Though slightly dented in some areas from past battles, and lacking the highly polished sheen of the other knights present, the captain looked quite handsome and even a bit noble as he walked out of his room proudly, head held high, as he imagined himself kneeling in front of the king at the end of the tournament and accepting his award.

"Can't believe the king's agreed to let that wretch enter the contest!" Hrothgar said with disgust as he walked along the corridor beside his friend.

The captain reached out and patted the man on his shoulder and informed him that the king really had no choice in the matter. "It's a long story and a little difficult to explain just now," the captain said. "Just trust that the king has made the best decision possible for our kingdom, and now it's my job to ensure that the dwarf does not win!"

"That's the spirit, Cap'n!" Hrothgar roared. "Just keep picturing yerself winning the tournament and before you know it, she will be yours."

* * *

Up at the main grandstand, a loud roar went up from the crowd seated in the stands, along with those who were standing outside of the fenced-off area, as the royal family made their way to their box seats. A troop of heavily clad soldiers marched in front of, behind, and on both sides of the king, queen and princess as they made their way up the road and onto the path leading to the first set of steps leading up to their seats. As their procession arrived at the first step, a long line of trumpeters sounded off, and everyone who had been seated stood as one as they cheered the name of the king over and over again. Once the royal family was seated, the rest of the noblemen and upper class of the kingdom followed, and in no time the main section of the grandstand was filled, aside from one area where twenty seats were still vacant.

Another roar came from the crowd, followed by another series of trumpet blasts, this time announcing the arrival of King Eadamantus and his own entourage. King Hasselfeth had thought this a great opportunity to re-strengthen the bond between the elves and men, so he had invited the elf king and his guests to come and enjoy the tournament as spectators.

Leaning over to her mother the queen, Princess Lyleth whispered softly, "I didn't know the elves were going to be attending."

The queen looked back at her, saying, "This is a very important day for you…and also for your father. Having King Eadamantus here just makes it that much grander." Now smiling at her daughter who finally appeared to be in a talkative mood, the queen leaned closer and asked, "Have you had time to pick the man you want most to win yet, my child?"

The princess frowned one more, shaking her head, then said sadly, "I still don't like the idea of being 'given away.' There are none here I would choose to spend all my days with. If I had to make a choice from those I have seen, I suppose it would have to be Captain Baerden. He has always been kind to me, and he at least is close in age to my own."

"Very well, then," the queen replied while smiling at her young daughter. "I shall cheer for the captain the loudest and pray for his win!"

As the knights and tournament entrants lined up in a long-fenced chute, waiting their turn to be announced, King Hasselfeth moved onto an elevated section of the platform stand where he and the other dignitaries were seated, to address the crowd. "Ladies and gentleman, we are gathered here today to watch the finest men from our lands do battle against one another in contests of skill, strength, agility and reasoning, all in the hopes of winning the hand of my daughter, Princess Lyleth, in matrimony." This was much to the satisfaction of the enormous crowd, who were all standing and cheering as loudly as one could ever imagine a crowd could cheer.

"For the next two days we will watch these warriors as they test their mettle, will, resourcefulness, and ability against each other," he continued to the roars of the masses present. "By sundown tomorrow a winner will be announced, and it will be my great pleasure to shake the hand of the man who will become my son-in-law."

At a signal from the king, the trumpeters began sounding their horns once more, and the king motioned for the gates to be opened so the contestants could begin riding into the main arena, one after the other, as their attendants carried their banners and led them in. A brightly costumed man, the master of ceremonies for the tournament, announced each combatant by name, along with what part of the kingdom they were representing. "Berardren the Red," he announced first, shouting out loudly to rise over the din of the cheering crowd. "Representing the Lands of Equinocke to the east." The first knight and his attendants made their way into the arena.

In a small field sitting a half-mile north from where the king's tournament was beginning, four large winged beasts settled down in the waist-high grasses, sending all the animals who had been gathered in the area scattering for the cover of the surrounding trees. "Dismount quickly!" the enchantress commanded, "and unload the beast bearing the weapons." She looked about for any who may have seen their arrival.

Amansun and Sophelus quickly untied the weapons, and once that was accomplished they looked back at the woman, who was busy lining up the flying creatures. "Stand back now," she warned once more. "We still need to make a proper impression when we arrive at the tournament, and I have plans for these four."

Standing directly in front of the four winged beasts now, the enchantress closed her eyes, raised her hands out in front of her, then whispered several words that Amansun could not quite understand, as she was speaking in a foreign tongue. First there was a bright flash and a loud boom, then the animals started to move and shake. As Amansun looked on, the wings of all four animals began to retreat back into their bodies. Next, three of the beasts who had appeared as men from the chest up transformed into beautiful horses, all with gleaming coats of matching brown, standing tall as they stamped at the ground with their hoofs. The fourth beast, which had been the bearer of Amansun's weapons, transformed into a thin, tall man with silver hair and broad shoulders.

"Just one more thing to do," the enchantress said out loud as she prepared another spell.
As quickly as the beasts had been transformed into three horses and a man, they were all suddenly dressed in perfect attire, each horse saddled and covered with matching bolts of white and silver cloth, tails tied perfectly and manes combed out, with their magnificent black hair hanging over their right sides. The man, who had been standing nude up to that moment, was now dressed in attendant clothing, with polished boots and pants, vest, cap and jacket all matching the colors of the bolts on each horse. In the man's hands, a large wooden pole rose high into the air with a banner blowing in the breeze. "Now we are ready," the enchantress said.

Amansun smiled, as he normally did when he had been taken by surprise again by the enchantresses abilities, and then he said, "Please lead on, my Lady. It sounds as though the tournament is already beginning." The sounds of blaring trumpets drifted across the breeze from not far off.

Tilting her head and hearing the trumpets as well, the young woman walked over to the lead horse and prepared to step up. "Silly fool!" she scoffed as she looked down upon herself suddenly. "I don't suppose I would fit in much looking like this now, would I?" She looked over at Amansun and Sophelus who were mounting their own animals, then muttered another chant to herself. With a flash, the attractive young woman who had been standing before them was now a tall handsome man, dressed in heavily matted soldier's clothing, with long brown hair falling over his shoulders and shiny black boots. In his hands he carried a round shield, as well as a large lance with a barbed metal tip. "One more surprise, Prince," the enchantress called out while pressing her fingers towards each other and whispering to herself.

Looking about at the enchantress, Sophelus sitting on his steed, and the attendant now standing at the front of the group waiting to march onward, Amansun pursed his lips as he tried to guess what other changes had transpired. "I'm not sure I see what your latest enchantment was," he said questioningly as he looked back at the enchantress, who now appeared as the soldier seated on the third horse.

The enchantress smiled back at Amansun and said happily, "You will have to turn your shield about to see what I have done, young prince."

Amansun turned his shield around so that the front was facing him, then his eyes widened and his smile stretched from ear to ear as he looked with wonderment at the design on his shield. Looking back at him was the image he had seen several times before in his dreams and visions—a radiant sun with flames reaching out in all directions, with a large white lion standing on its hind legs, front legs raised into the air, a golden mane flowing down its head and back. "How is this possible?" Amansun demanded. "It is the very image I saw in my visions, right down to the last detail."

The enchantress looked over from the back of the horse she was sitting on and smiled broadly as she spun her own shield towards Amansun, revealing that it too had the same image. "It was quite easy," the enchantress-turned-soldier replied while chuckling. "I too saw the image from your vision, so I have placed it now upon all our weaponry and garments."

Overwhelmed, Amansun looked back at the enchantress and said, "I shall never be able to repay you for your kindness, my Lady!" He suddenly glanced up at the standard the attendant was carrying and laughed as he realized that the banner, still blowing in the breeze, was also adorned with the image.

"Let us go now whilst there is still time," the enchantress commanded. Looking at the attendant who was standing at the lead of the group, she shouted, "Double-time at once, my good man. We haven't a moment to spare!" The group sped off into the trees in the direction from where the trumpet blasts had originated.

Back in the main arena, the master of ceremonies was announcing Prince Antilus from the Northern Mountains. As the knight and his attendants made their way into the center of the arena, Captain Baerden readied himself, as he was the next challenger in line. "And here from our very own castle, representing the lands of the Silver Lake, may I present Captain Baerden, Commander of the King's Guard," the announcer said proudly as the captain made his way in, led by four of the soldiers from the king's guard. Up in the stands, the queen and Princess Lyleth stood momentarily as they clapped and waved at the young captain making his way in. Captain Baerden glanced up at the royal family's box and nearly fell over when he realized that the princess and queen had both stood when his name was announced, and he was filled with pride.

Next in line, Prince Brothemus and his attendants made their way in, marching on foot as they had not brought any horses along with them. As the announcer called out the prince's name and origin, the crowd went deathly silent at first, followed by gasps of bewilderment and whisperings amongst the gathered crowd. "Prince Brothemus from the Southern Barrens?" the queen and princess said in unison, repeating what they had just heard the announcer say. "Is that the dwarf prince you have been dealing with?" the queen demanded of her husband.

"Have a care," the king warned the two ladies sitting beside him. "Do not appear to question me here in front of our guests."

The queen leaned closer to the king, whispering something that only the king could hear, then she sat back in her chair as she watched the king's face turn crimson red, as if he had stopped breathing for a moment. "All will be explained in time," the king said to the women, who were now quite distraught. "Trust that I have everything in order." He motioned for the two ladies to remain seated and settle down.

Down in the chute, only three knights remained, still waiting their turn to enter the arena. The field was mostly filled with knights, attendants, horses, banners, and of course the small band of dwarves that looked quite out of place. "This is it," the enchantress announced as she saw the chute with the small line of knights patiently waiting for their names to be announced. "We will simply get into line and walk in as if we have been expected the entire time. Once they start asking questions, and they surely will, let me do the talking. And remember!" She pointed a finger back at Amansun and Sophelus. "Not a word until I give you the nod that it's alright for you to speak!"

As the cheers from the onlookers ebbed and flowed, the announcer continued onward until the last knight who had been originally entered into the tournament rode into the arena, leaving Amansun and his three attendants alone at the edge of the field. Amansun, Sophelus, the enchantress and the banner carrier looked at the faces of the crowd that had been hugging the chute as the knights and their entourages had waited in turn to enter. Now that Amansun and his team were the only group still waiting to be announced, all eyes turned to them.

Having reached the end of the scroll that he had held tightly in his hands, the announcer was visibly confused when he glanced over at the gate leading into the arena and saw another knight, dressed in white, sitting atop his steed as he waited his turn. Looking at the group of men who oversaw the tournament, he shrugged his shoulders and gestured in the direction of the unknown entrant. A curious calm settled over the crowd as they began to realize that something unplanned was now taking place before their eyes. The announcer had clearly seen this last knight and his small group, yet no name had been given, and the "white knight," as people began to refer to him, had been left outside the arena, still waiting to be invited in.

A small group of armed soldiers walked over to where the unknown knight was waiting, and the crowd watched as a conversation obviously took place between the white knight's group and the men from the tournament committee. After a few awkward moments, one of the men from the tourney ran across the arena field and started up the stairs to where the king was still seated. From the reaction of the king, something was clearly amiss, as he and his private guard suddenly stood up and began making their way down to the chute entrance. The king waved at his captain, already on the field, to follow.

Reaching the unexpected party, Lord Mallthus was the first to address Amansun's lead attendant, who had taken charge of the conversation. "Who are you and what is your business here?" he demanded.

"Prince Halldor, son of King Hanthris the Bold, and heir to Fortress Argonathe of the Granite Mountains, here to challenge for His Majesty's daughter in this tournament of champions," the enchantress said clearly, as she lifted one hand upwards in the direction of Amansun with a sweeping motion and bowed lowly towards the king and his party. Several people in the group gasped aloud and exchanged glances as they peered from the attendant to the prince and back towards the king.

"This is not possible," Captain Baerden said firmly, loud enough for all around to hear. "Though you clearly bear the symbol of Argonathe, the king's one and only son was lost in battle some ten years past!"

"This is Prince Halldor and make no mistake!" the enchantress repeated once more, this time even more firmly. "He has returned to these lands to reclaim that which is his, and he now chooses to battle for Princess Lyleth as is his right!"

The king and his noblemen who had wandered down to see what the commotion was about all shook their heads with puzzled looks as they chattered amongst themselves, some pointing at Amansun, others looking at the lion flapping on the attendant's pole banner. Captain Baerden moved his horse closer in towards the unwelcome group and said while looking directly at the man wearing the white suit of armor, "You may or may not be who you claim to be, sir knight, but there is one here among us who can be the judge of that with certainty." He looked at the king and asked permission to proceed.

"By all means," King Hasselfeth replied as he looked at his captain nodding his head up and down, as if understanding what was about to take place. "Call for him at once!"

"Best to make some type of announcement, my Lord," Lord Mallthus suggested. "The crowd and other contestants are growing restless."

The king motioned for the announcer to move closer, then instructed him to say something to appease the waiting crowd as they tried to determine if this white rider was indeed who he said he was.

As the master of ceremonies addressed the crowd, he said, "We appear to have one last entrant who has just arrived, so please be patient."

Captain Baerden gave orders to his men to ride off and find Hrothgar at once. "Hrothgar will be able to prove or disprove this claim," he said as he warily eyed Amansun who sat still and seemed quite sure of himself. "Bring him here at once and be quick about it."

Yes...bring Hrothgar here at once... Amansun thought to himself as a slight curl began to appear on his lips. *Let's see if our old captain can still recognize me after all these years.*

When the captain's men finally located Hrothgar, he was standing at one of the food booths, sampling a piece of pickled trout. "Captain Baerden and the king need you at once," the rider said breathlessly. "Something about having to prove if the white rider that just showed up is Prince Halldor, they said."

Hrothgar looked up at the rider with wild eyes as he spit out the bread and fish that he had been chewing on a second earlier, gasping and choking from the effort. "Prince Halldor, you said?" Hrothgar asked as he attempted to control the bursts of coughing and choking he was experiencing, "You said Prince Halldor?"

"That is what the captain said, sir, word for word. I suggest we hurry," the rider replied as he watched the older man leap onto his horse as if he was still but a young man filled with energy.

"Ride!" Hrothgar yelled out as he sped off down the dirt roadway, leaving the captain's messenger in a cloud of dust. It took some time for him to maneuver his horse through the ever-growing crowd that was now bunching up around Amansun and his entourage, as many were trying to determine just what was going on. "Out of my way!" he called out as he forced his steed between the masses, "Out of my way or you shall answer to the king!" He was now quite beside himself, as the thought of seeing his beloved king's son was overwhelming him with emotion.

Hrothgar finally broke free of the crowds and rode into the center of the arena field as he made his way over to the area where the king, Captain Baerden and the others were still gathered. As he drew nearer to Amansun, his eyes started to water when he recognized the standard on the carrier's pole that was billowing in the cool morning breeze. *It cannot be!* he thought to himself as he made his way over to his captain.

"Make some room people, please!" Captain Baerden commanded as he saw Hrothgar approaching. "Now we will get to the bottom of this." It was bad enough that he was going to have to deal with the dwarf prince whom his king had been forced to allow to compete in this tournament. Now it appeared that a ghost from the past, a prince no less, was also crashing in on the event.

"What is the meaning of this?" Hrothgar demanded as he rode alongside Amansun, carefully studying every facet of the man—his weapons, his suit of armor, and in particular the standard that was painted on the man's weapons and armor. "King Hanthris is dead! I watched him die ten years ago!" he said as he struggled to keep his emotions in check. "His son was with us that day, and he was not among the few of us that escaped with our lives," he choked out, nearly overcome with grief he had kept bottled inside all these long years.

"It is truly you, my captain and friend," the white rider spoke as he reached up to remove his helmet that had been partially blocking his face up until now. "Though your silver hair is something new," he added with a soft laugh.

"It cannot be," the older man said as he rode his horse once around the man with the white armor. "The prince was but a small boy when last I saw him, and at that time he was surrounded by flying beasts controlled by the Underlord himself!"

King Hasselfeth stepped in a little closer, his guards close at hand, and he looked up at Hrothgar and asked finally, "Well? Is it he? Can this really be the son of King Hanthris, here now? After all this time?"

Hrothgar moved his horse right up to the white rider's once again, this time bringing him to a halt, and he studied the face of the stranger not three feet away now. As the older man struggled with the thought that this may indeed be the king's son, he leaned his body this way and that as he studied every detail of the young man's face. "It's difficult to say, my King," he finally managed to say. "It's been so many years now…and he was but a child when last I saw the prince. This could be the king's son…but I can't tell just by merely looking at his face, I am afraid, my King."

King Hasselfeth looked up at the stranger seated on the horse but ten feet away and said while shaking his head, "I am afraid that it will not be possible to allow you to enter the tournament, stranger, not without clear proof that you are who you say you are."

Hrothgar stared into the black eyes of the rider beside him now, noticing that while his facial features were strikingly similar, his black eyes were no match at all to the dark blue eyes that the true prince had when last he saw him. Then he suddenly turned back to the king and said, "There is one way to be sure, my King. When the prince was a child, he was injured by a beast, which left him with scars across his chest."

Handing his shield and helmet to Sophelus who was at his side, Amansun began to unfasten his chest plate and, lifting the polished metal piece over his head carefully, he looked back at his old captain, now smiling even more than before, and said loudly and clearly, "Here is your proof, old friend. Will you believe me now?" And with that, he pulled off his undershirt and exposed his badly scarred chest to all who could see.

There were gasps of surprise and wonder from all who stood close enough to see. Still on his horse, Hrothgar wept openly, then stepped down from his steed and stood at Amansun's side. Looking up at the young man with the piercing black eyes, the older man wiped the tears from his face and, taking Amansun's hand in his own, begged the prince for his forgiveness. "We thought you were dead, my Prince, I swear it is the truth," he struggled to say with his failing voice. "You were surrounded by dragons when we saw your father fall, and then the air around you turned black with ash and red with flame. How could we have known that you survived?"

"There is nothing to forgive," Amansun said calmly. "It was not by luck alone that I survived that day. The Underlord himself had other intentions for me at the time, and any who had followed to attempt my rescue would have fallen that day like my father the king." He leaned from his horse and placed his hand under the older man's chin, forcing him to look up and into his eyes once more.

Turning to look back at the king and captain, Hrothgar shook his head, saying, "This is he…this is the prince…I would stake my life on it!" He turned to face Amansun once more.

"And you are sure of this, loyal servant?" the king asked of the older man who had been in his personal guard these past nine years since. "There can be no mistake?"

Shaking his head up and down, and laughing and smiling amidst his sobs, Hrothgar turned to the king once more, saying, "This is he, my Lord…I would recognize those scars anywhere…I helped tend to the injured prince myself all those years ago…there is no mistake."

Now turning to look at the captain, lords and others gathered around, King Hasselfeth looked into the eyes of Amansun, saying, "You may enter the tournament after all, young prince. I knew your father, and any son of his is welcome here in my lands!" A cheer went up from the crowd that stood within hearing range.

"Best we move along with announcing the prince, then," Lord Mallthus suggested. "This crowd is getting restless, and we are already behind schedule as it is."

"Right you are," the king agreed. "Announce the prince at once!" he shouted over to the master of ceremonies. "Let the tournament begin!" As Prince Halldor was announced, the dwarf prince and captain looked at each other suddenly and laughed as they watched Amansun moving across the field.

"It would appear that we will no longer need to search for the prince after all," Prince Brothemus said with an evil grin.

"I fancy you may even have the chance to kill him in this tournament?" Captain Balden suggested as he too wore a wicked smile. "Imagine how pleased the Underlord would be should you tell him you eliminated the prince all on your own!"

The dwarf prince nodded his head in agreement as he looked Amansun up and down, sizing up his new opponent. "That would be quite a feat indeed," he replied as he looked down at the glowing blue stone on the ring he wore, suddenly feeling a surge of power running through the veins within his muscular body.

Up in the stands, Princess Lyleth looked over at her mother, saying, "I did not know Prince Halldor would be competing here today. Isn't he the young boy who disappeared all those years ago?"

The queen looked at her with a surprised look as well, saying, "It appears your father's tournament is full of surprises, doesn't it?" She smiled as she tried to get a better glimpse of the white knight who was once again wearing his helmet so that his face was impossible to see.

At last, someone interesting! the princess thought to herself. *I hope he is a handsome prince.* She stepped up to the grandstand rail to see if she could get a better look at this new contestant.

CHAPTER 34

As Amansun sat there on his horse, looking at the cheering crowds that circled the entire arena and field where the contestants had been placed, he realized that this was the most people he had been around since he was a child back in his own kingdom. The thunder of the crowd's cheers and the sight of so many people brought back a flood of memories that made him realize how much he had missed his old life and how much the Underlord had taken from him. Gazing up into the grandstand, he saw Princess Lyleth leaning against the railing, and he suddenly remembered why he was here and what he had to do.

About halfway down the row, Amansun was quite startled when he saw what appeared to be a small band of dwarves standing amongst the other competitors. He nudged the enchantress, still in soldier's form, who was seated just to his right, and motioned for her to look down the row. The enchantress glanced over, also saw the dwarves there, and then shook her head at the prince with a puzzled look as well. "We'll just have to wait and see why those dwarves are here," she said. "This is some kind of mischievous work of the Underlord, no doubt." She eyed the tall dwarf dressed in armor.

Still looking about at the various sections of the grandstand, Amansun spotted the area where the elves were seated, and just for a moment he thought about waving up to King Eadamantus and Mythra whom he recognized right away. Looking up into the stands in the direction that Amansun was staring, the enchantress quickly reached out and tapped the prince on his shoulder to get his attention. "Don't show that you know any of the elves," she cautioned as she leaned over and whispered in his ear. "Remember that they know you only as Amansun the Dragon, not as Prince Halldor, son of the king from Argonathe!"

Amansun's smile faded quickly as he at once realized the truth of the statement. Then a frown spread across his face as he also realized once more that even the princess really had no idea who he was. *I shall have to win her heart over now in this form*, he thought to himself. *Best you focus on the tournament at hand and worry about the princess later, silly fool!* He straightened his posture and once again focused on what the announcer was saying. As he looked back at the man speaking to the crowd, he realized he was announcing the events that were to take place over the next two days.

"Finally, this afternoon we will be holding the long-distance run around our own Silver Lake, followed by the swim out to the center and back…" the announcer droned on. "Once those competitions are completed, day one will be over and the evening's festivities will begin." Then he began reading out all the events and entertainment that would be available.

The enchantress looked over at Amansun with a smile and said, "Looks like you won't have to worry about the joust event until day two." She winked. "Just remember, once the events start, try to not make it too obvious that you are able to beat these other contestants without much effort. You are still getting used to your new form, it is true, but with your unusual strength, you should best everyone here without much difficulty."

At the conclusion of the starting announcements, the trumpeters sounded their horns again, and then the combatants were led off the field so that the first competition's materials could be set into place. "What shall we be starting with?" Amansun asked as he admitted that he had not been paying attention for part of the speech.

"Archery!" Sophelus offered as they rode out of the arena and back to the waiting tents where the contestants were to gather. "They also said that you should remove all of your armor for the first day, as you won't be engaging in any contests that require it until day two."

"Fine, fine," Amansun repeated with a smile. "Starting off with the easy ones first to get everyone warmed up, I suppose."

"Now don't go and get all cocky, now," the enchantress warned. "You may have superior strength, it is true, and cunning for that matter, but don't forget that the other contestants gathered about you are also experienced warriors. And they, unlike you, have been wearing their own bodies all of their lives."

"Yes, my Lady," Amansun replied apologetically. "I will focus on performing at my very best, no matter the event."

"And do keep an eye on the dwarf prince," the enchantress cautioned. "There is something about that one that causes me concern. He is here at the direction of the Underlord, I am sure of that, and there's no telling what enchantments the Great Master may have cast upon him."

After a short wait in the contestants' staging tent, a soldier walked into the center of the space and announced that the field was ready for the archery contest to begin. "You may bring one attendant out to the field with you only," the man directed as he asked the competitors to head out to the site.

Amansun nodded at the enchantress and the two followed the others as they exited the tent and walked along the marked path towards the main arena once again. Walking past row upon row of spectators, Amansun was pleased to see that he had already started to win a following, as many were chanting his name aloud when he came into view. Looking out over the field, he could see that eleven targets had been set out at the far end, looking very much like the one he had been training on just the day before. On the side closest to them, there were eleven wooden stands set into the ground, each with a large bow along with a quiver of long arrows.

"Choose a stand and we will begin, once everyone has had a chance to prepare for their first shot," the announcer advised. "For the first stage, each competitor will be allowed to fire three arrows at their target. The top six will move on to a second round, followed by the top three, then finally the top two."

Amansun chose a spot just two lanes down from the dwarf, as he wanted to be able to keep an eye on this unlikely adversary. As he tested the pull on his bow, he looked at the unusually tall dwarf and was caught off-guard when the dwarf suddenly glanced in his direction and stared at him with a look of pure hatred. "Seems as though that one already has a score to settle with you", the enchantress whispered to him as she too noticed the evil look from the dwarf. "Best we try and avoid him when we are able, as I am sure he is up to no good."

"Prepare to fire," cried the voice of the announcer, followed by the single clear command, "Fire!" Eleven arrows went searing through the air with a *hisssss* as they sought their marks on the targets. Eleven soldiers walked over to the circular straw bales, and as they studied the arrows' resting places, they each held up a stick with a color corresponding to the area on the target that had been hit. Four black flags were held in the air, representing the bullseye of the target; five yellow flags were raised, indicating a shot to the next ring out; and finally two white flags were raised, indicating the outermost circles closest to the outer edge of each bale.

Looking two lanes over, Amansun noted that the dwarf's lane had a black flag held high. *So this dwarf can aim, it would appear*, he thought to himself as he reached for his second arrow.

"Fire," the announcer's voice called out once more, and again eleven arrows sped down their lanes, ending with loud *thump*s as they hit. Once more the flags were raised, and once more each contestant looked about, seeing how they had measured up to the archers around them.

Once the third volley had been fired, an official, dressed in flowing robes of bright colors, walked over to the targets and selected the top six contestants based on the colored flags held by each soldier standing beside the targets. "Prince Halldor, Sir Berardren, Captain Baerden and Prince Brothemus, all black," the official called out. "Prince Antilus and Sir Farimus, two black and one yellow. All others are out!" A cheer rang out from the crowd as the five men who had been eliminated walked back to the edge of the field to watch as the winners of the first round moved on.

"Archers ready," the announcer called out once more, followed by "fire!" Again the contestants went through the process of firing their three arrows, followed by their shots being judged by the official.

"Prince Halldor and Prince Brothemus, all black!" the voice called out, followed by, "Captain Baerden, two black, one yellow. All others out!" Again a small group of contestants marched off the main field, leaving just the three top archers to compete.

Looking down the field and seeing all three contestants standing ready once more, the announcer yelled "fire." Down the field, three black flags rose.

"Fire," the voice called out again. Again, three black flags were lifted high.

"Fire," came the call of the announcer. In the distance, two black flags were raised, blowing slightly in the breeze, along with one single yellow flag.

"Prince Halldor and Prince Brothemus, all black!" the official cried out. "Captain Baerden is out!"

Taking a moment to look at each other, the two remaining competitors notched their arrows, then looked down their lanes at the targets once more. "Fire," came the familiar voice, followed by two black flags coming into view.

"Fire," the voice called out again, and two more black flags rose.

"Fire!" the voice screamed, and as all eyes looked down the field, once again two black flags were waving in the morning air.

The announcer walked in towards the main seating area of the grandstand and called out, "We have a draw! We will move the targets back fifty feet and fire one final arrow to determine the winner."

Once the targets had been moved into place, and the challengers asked if they were ready, the announcer gave the order to fire once more. Way down the field, at a distance that was far enough to be difficult to see for many of the viewers in attendance, two black flags raised into the air once more.

"Draw!" the official yelled out to the crowd. "Prince Halldor and Prince Brothemus are even after the first event."

On the far side of the field, directly across from the main grandstand, a large wooden signboard had been constructed and raised some fifteen feet into the air. Several men moved up the stairs that led to the sign board and began placing the names of the contestants into finely cut slots that allowed name placards to be slid into place, with the highest placing competitors' names being set at the top. Amansun looked behind him and was pleased when he saw his name being placed in the uppermost slots, although it did share the position with the dwarf prince's name. "Off to a good start," he said to the enchantress standing beside him.

"We still have nine events to go, Amansun," the enchantress replied.

"Understood," Amansun said sheepishly.

The master of ceremonies walked out to the center of the arena once more, as a large group of workers began moving things about, and called out, "Spear throw next, once the field has been prepared."

The enchantress continued to look at the names listed on the far side of the field as she squinted her eyes and rubbed her chin. "This does not bode well, I am sure," she said mysteriously, appearing to be lost in thought. "Best you throw that spear as far you are able. Something smells foul already, I fear, and I shall not be surprised to see that dwarf's name near the top throughout this competition."

The spear throwing competition started out much like the archery contest had. The object here was to throw the spear with accuracy at three targets at varying distances. After each round of throws, the competitors were judged once again on who had come as close to the center of the target as possible, if their spears had reached the targets at all. While most of the competitors fared well, some had difficulty hitting the targets furthest out.

After three rounds had been completed, the dwarf prince and Amansun were tied once again for first place. Sensing that a draw was eminent, the official in charge of the games decided that the two remaining competitors would throw for distance rather than accuracy as before. In this way he felt there would have to be an outright winner.

Walking up to the two remaining competitors, the robed man asked who would like to throw first. "It matters not to me," said the dwarf prince somewhat rudely.

"Let the dwarf go first, then," said Amansun.

Prince Brothemus walked over to the remaining stand of spears and selected a finely polished spear made of oak with a silver tip at the end, and walked to the throwing line. "Let's see you match this, white knight," he said as he took several steps back then raced towards the throwing line and heaved the spear upwards. The spectators watched in awe as the dwarf's spear floated in the air and flew some fifty feet further down the field than where the furthest target had been set. Walking back to where Amansun was standing, the dwarf raised his head at the prince and laughed as he walked past, bumping into Amansun's shoulder as he passed by.

Amansun shook his head calmly and, looking back at the dwarf, said softly so no one else could hear, "Where I come from, even our women can throw further than that!" Then he selected a spear and walked to a spot some ten paces back from the line that marked the spot where the spear had to be released. Moving the spear in the air back and forth a few times as he imagined his throw, he looked down the field at where the dwarf's spear was sticking into the ground, then judged how hard he would have to throw his spear to pass that spot. With a final look back at the dwarf who was standing well behind him with arms crossed and a pouty look upon his face, he ran towards the release line then, leaning back as far as possible, rotated his chest and shoulders as his right arm rose up and released the spear, his body twisting dramatically to the left.

Once again, the crowd went silent as all eyes followed the flight of the spear, floating through the air as if carried by some unfelt breeze. Then wild cheers and applause erupted as Amansun's spear landed some twenty feet beyond the dwarf's. Pointing at him with his right arm and hand, the master of ceremonies cried out, "Winner, Prince Halldor!" The crowd began chanting his name, even more so than previously.

Walking back towards the dwarf, Amansun looked over at him and smiled, then turned his head back to the robed man and asked casually, "What's next?"

Across the field, the men at the board lowered all the names one notch as they placed Prince Brothemus's name one spot from the top, so that Prince Halldor's name was all alone at the highest position. "Well done, young Prince," the enchantress said as Amansun walked back to the waiting tent. "That should put the dwarf in his place for the time being."

Captain Balden and Prince Brothemus looked quite surprised as they walked along with the other competitors, as if they were puzzled as to how the dwarf prince could have lost. Looking down at the blue ring on Prince Brothemus's hand, the captain said, "Perhaps it's the intent of the Underlord to not makes you win every event, my Prince?"

Shaking his head, and with a particularly nasty look on his red face, Prince Brothemus glanced back at the captain and said, "The pitiful fool has had his one win for the day…I am sure that will be the last," and he stormed off towards the tent, pushing people from the crowd out of his way as he walked along.

As the tournament combatants rested in the tent outside from the main arena, the master of ceremonies made his way out once more to the center of the field to announce the next contest. "Next up will be the hammer throw," he shouted above the voices of the crowd, who were already starting to guess and speculate on who the eventual winner was likely to be. With a wave of his hands, the soldiers walked down the chute towards the holding tent to fetch the entrants once more.

Captain Baerden glanced up at the names board as he walked into the field and noted that his was now down in fourth position. "Not the start I was hoping for," he mumbled to himself as he glanced at the others walking along beside him. "I suppose there's still plenty of time to catch up, though."

Being a test of brute strength, the hammer throw was much like the spear contest had been earlier. Rather than skill or ability to aim with precision, the event called for simply picking up the hammer, swirling it about along with oneself at great speed, and then releasing the hammer with as much force as possible so that it would fly as far down the field as possible. While many of the contestants appeared to be larger and better built than Amansun, after three rounds of throwing he was among the three finalists. After announcing Prince Halldor, Prince Brothemus and Sir Glandin, an immensely built giant of a man from an area southeast of Castle Eladrias, the official once again asked in what order the remaining competitors would like to go.

"The white knight had the honor of going last in the spear throw, so I believe it is my turn to be the last," the dwarf said with a stern voice.

"As you wish, Prince Brothemus. That seems a fair request, wouldn't you agree?" the official asked as he looked over at the other two contestants.

"Fine with me. It makes no matter who throws first," the giant man said with disgust. "I am the champion in this event in my homeland and none here shall best me."

Amansun, though his face betrayed him, said, "That is quite fair, I would agree. Let the dwarf throw last." He walked away to the waiting area while Sir Glandin made his way over to the throwing ring.

The giant man, standing nearly six foot ten, grabbed the five-foot hammer with his enormous hands, then stepped into the ring and looked off into the direction down the field where he intended it to land. Spinning gracefully and with perfectly trained precision, he released the hammer and watched it as it flew down the field, hitting once and then bouncing several times before coming to rest. "Two hundred seventy four feet," the men at the other end of the field called out once their measurement had been confirmed and checked twice.

"Well done, Sir Glandin," the robed man said as he motioned for Prince Halldor to take his position in the ring. "You may throw when ready," he stated as he stepped away into a safe area.

As Amansun had never trained in this particular event, as the enchantress and Sophelus had not had time to do so, he was actually quite pleased that he had made it into the finals. Steeping into the ring, both hands grasped tightly about the hammer's shaft, he slowly started twisting the hammer over his head and then started to swing his entire body in ever-tightening circles, as he picked up more and more speed and momentum. At the apex of his spin and just before he lost control, he released the hammer and bounced on his feet, being careful to not step over the line that marked the release boundary, and watched as his hammer flew another few feet further than the mark of the giant mans.

"Prepare to see your name fall," the dwarf said to the prince who was standing twenty paces back from the ring, and then he began swirling the hammer over his head and spinning eight times with great speed before releasing the hammer. To the dwarf prince's great relief, and the true bewilderment of his own, Amansun watched as the dwarf's hammer flew just a few feet past his own mark.

"Two hundred eighty nine feet," came the voice from the other end of the field to the jeers of most of the crowd who were now yelling their discontent at the dwarf prince, who had lifted his hands over his head in triumph.

Pointing now to the dwarf prince, the master of ceremonies announced loudly, "The win goes to Prince Brothemus of the Southern Barrens!" and then he walked away quickly, wanting to distance himself from the dwarf who was clearly agitating the mob standing around the field.

As he walked off the field towards the chute once more, Amansun leaned towards the enchantress and said softly, "I suppose I was bound to lose that event, seeing as today is the first time I have tried it," as he looked at the enchantress for a response.

"I fear your lack of training had nothing to do with the outcome of that match, young Prince," the enchantress replied. "I doubt any others were able to see it, but as the dwarf prince was taking his turn there was a very visible blue aura that surrounded his entire body...I believe the Underlord has enchanted him with some sort of unnatural power. Perhaps one even greater than your abilities will be able to match."

Looking over at the name board as he watched the men move Prince Brothemus's name back to the top notch besides his own once more, Amansun frowned unhappily and asked, "Then how am I to defeat this prince from the south if the Underlord's magic is at work?"

"Give me some time, Amansun," the enchantress replied as the brows on her forehead bunched together as if she was in great concentration. "Just give me some time and I will discover the secret to this spell...on that you can be sure."

CHAPTER 35

As the remaining contestants cleared the field, and a wave of children crashed out into the large grassy area, each pretending to be competing as they had just seen the knights and lords do, the announcer informed the crowd that the tournament would pause for lunch and then begin again once the sun had passed its zenith.

"Tied for first, I see," Sophelus said with a huge grin as he looked up at the name board. "Now you just have to find a way to get that cursed dwarf's name down a notch or two."

"I am working on that," the enchantress said in a rather unpleasant tone. "The Great Master's spells are in play, I am afraid, and this tournament could turn out to be more challenging than any of us could have imagined a day ago."

Back up in the grandstands, the spectators were clearing out to head towards the food booths that were now jammed with hungry patrons. Up in the royal family's section, a tall, handsome elf was patiently explaining to some of the King's Guard that he had a message for King Hasselfeth. "We'll pass yer message along," the guard in charge said as he looked suspiciously at the elf who seemed to not be willing to take no for an answer.

"I am afraid that will not be acceptable," the elf said firmly. "King Eadamantus has requested that I give this message to the king, and only the king."

"Stand here and watch him," the guard said as he turned and walked over to where the noblemen were seated as they waited for their meal to be served to them.

Pointing out the elf at the ropes of the king's seating area, the guard passed along the elf's request to speak briefly, and Lord Mallthus instructed him to send him along. When the elf approached, Mallthus introduced himself, shaking the elf's hand, and asked him to follow. Reaching the king, Mallthus bowed once then introduced the elf to his king. "This is Prince Erathrin, sent by King Eadamantus himself, to pass along a message," he said as he gestured towards the elf that stepped a foot closer.

"Welcome, then, Prince," the king said. "And what is it that your king would say?" Bowing his head once before speaking, as was customary, the elf responded by saying that his lord was requesting a moment of the king's time during the lunch break so that the two could converse briefly. "I would be delighted to speak with King Eadamantus," King Hasselfeth replied with a warm smile. "Please tell your king that I shall be expecting him in my private tent just behind the grandstand there." He pointed to a roped-off tent in the back of the stand, surrounded by guards bearing spears and crossbows.

"With a thousand thanks!" the elf prince replied, and then he bowed once more, excusing himself, turning and walking back to the elves' seating area.

While the king's servants busied themselves carrying in great platters covered with breads, meats, fruits and cheeses to the king's seating section, King Hasselfeth and his guards, along with King Eadamantus and his elves, made their way down the private back stairwell heading to the king's tent. Once outside the tent, King Hasselfeth motioned for the elf king to join him, and together they went into the private tent to enjoy their meal while they conversed. Over lunch, the elf king voiced his concerns with the dwarf prince competing in the tournament.

Holding one hand up with its palm facing forward slightly, King Hasselfeth allowed the questionable tone of the elf to pass, then said in his defense, "There is more going on here than meets the eye, old friend." And with that, the king went on to explain in great detail the events that led up to his agreeing to let the dwarf compete.

"I see," the elf king replied as he thought over all that he had heard. "And you are certain that this Prince Brothemus can be defeated? He appears to be doing quite well up to this point."

"Our other challengers will soon pull away," the king said, trying to sound convinced himself. "These first challenges are but child's play compared to those that follow on day two." He raised himself from the table and indicated that their lunch was at an end.

Looking across the wooden table, King Eadamantus said earnestly, "I hope that you are correct, old friend, for the consequences of a loss to this servant of the Underlord would be great to all of us, as you surely must know!"

"Just watch and see," the king said again, sounding surer than he had moments before. "There are many knights likely to win this tournament and our unexpected challenger, young Prince Halldor from the east, has the blood of a champion flowing through his veins, I can sense it." He gestured towards the opening in the tent and encouraged the elf to leave.

After the lunch break ended, the spectators made their way back to the stands, bunching around the edges of the arena field as they had done earlier that day. Once the king and other important guests had been seated as well, the master of ceremonies stepped into the afternoon sun and made further announcements. "Three events remain on this first day of competition, though this shall be the last event held here in the main arena field. Once the crossbow competition has been completed, we will move over to the east side of the castle for the lake run and lake swim."

Walking out onto the field once more, the contestants quickly realized that the field had been set up very similarly to the way it had been for the archery competition earlier in the day. The only real difference was that the targets this time around were much smaller and set back quite a bit further. Looking up at the name board, the enchantress looked at the top position once more, shaking her head as she exhaled loudly, being quite concerned that Prince Brothemus's name shared top honors with Amansun up to this point. "Three contests down and seven to go, and the two of you are all even," she reminded him. "Best you keep your mind and body focused now, and try to finish day one with a lead if you can!"

Looking up at the board, Amansun was also concerned and feeling the pressure. "I'll do my best, my Lady," he responded.

Three rounds of firing took place and, in the end, Amansun, Prince Brothemus and Sir Blackstone, a gifted marksman from the Northlands beyond the Old Forest, were all tied for first place. Captain Baerden had done well but was no match for the other three in the lead. Stepping out onto the field, the announcer gave the signal to move the targets back another fifty feet. Once this had been done, he turned to face the stands where the royal family were seated and called out, "We will be placing a small round circle on the targets now, no larger than an apple, and each contestant will be given three bolts to hit it with. The contestant who hits this target, or hits it the most often, will be the winner."

As the three contestants made their way to the firing line, each loading a bolt into the firing mechanisms as they walked along, the crowd grew silent with anticipation. Standing upright, with crossbows tightly tucked into their shoulders, eyes staring down the sights, they slowed their breathing to almost a dead stop as they waited for the signal to fire.

"Fire!" a voice cried out suddenly, and three bolts whizzed down the field, each hitting the newly added targets. There was a quick check from the men downfield, and then three black flags raised into the air.

"All even after one shot," the announcer called out to the applause of the crowd. The announcer waited a moment while the two men and lone dwarf loaded their weapons once more, then, seeing that they were ready, called out for the second volley. "Fire!" Again the three bolts flew down the field, hitting the hay bales simultaneously, as the crowds waited breathlessly for the score. In the distance, only two black flags rose this time, one in the dwarf's lane and the other in the lane belonging to Amansun. Sir Blackstone's shot had missed by less than a fingernail's length, high and to the right.

Having already seen these two combatants in head-to-head competition earlier in the day, the announcer realized that these two could probably stand here and match each other, shot after shot, for much of the afternoon, so he raised his hands and quieted the crowd once more. "Move the targets another fifty feet back," he yelled out to the men down at the other end of the field.

The spectators looked on with wide-open mouths and eyes as they watched the targets being carried even further down the field. "I can barely sees the bales themselves from this distance," one man called out as he laughed nervously.

"If they moves them any further away, they'll be sitting in the woods," another man added, bringing cheers and laughs from many of the onlookers.

Amansun slowed his breathing once more, carefully lining up the miniscule target at the opposite end of the field and trying his best to not let the sweat that was dripping down his face bother him, as he focused with all his might on the target. Beside him, Prince Brothemus was locked into firing position, hands steady as if made of rock, and his gaze also focused with intensity.

From some forty paces away, the enchantress watched helplessly as she saw the blue aura surround the dwarf again as it had done in the hammer throw event. This time the blue glow was even stronger, though she alone was able to see this enchantment at work. *I must think of something, or the dwarf is bound to win!* she thought quietly to herself as she waited for the announcer's call.

"Fire," came the announcer's command. All eyes turned downfield once more. Not a sound could be heard as two men off in the distance approached the targets, too far for the others to be able to see with certainty from this far away, and then a single black flag rose. "Winner," the announcer called as he pointed at the dwarf prince once more. "Prince Brothemus takes the win with the crossbow," he said loudly as groans of shock and concern rumbled from the lips of the spectators who had expected Prince Halldor to win easily.

"This bodes ill, my Lord," Lord Mallthus whispered to the king with a look of great concern upon his face. King Hasselfeth waved him off, trying not to worry the queen and princess who were seated just a few feet further away on his other side.

Amansun looked back at the enchantress standing some distance behind him and shrugged his shoulders. The enchantress lifted her arms and moved her hands gently in front of herself, swaying them slightly back and forth as if to say, "Calm down, it's not over yet."

"Please follow the roadway over to the north end of the lake," the announcer called out as people began to move towards the steps. "The lake run will be starting next, once our competitors have had the chance to walk over and get lined up."

As Amansun and the enchantress walked across the field to exit the arena, they both looked up and watched as the men on the stairs moved Amansun's name down one notch, leaving the dwarf's name all alone in first place. "How are you at running and swimming?" the enchantress asked as they walked along side by side.

"I suppose we will find out soon," the prince replied, and the two shared a good laugh together, even though both were quite alarmed as to how the tournament was progressing.

Up in the grandstands, Princess Lyleth was beside herself as she stared in horror at the dwarf's name at the top of the board. "I hope you know what you are doing, Father!" she said carefully, making sure that no others could hear.

"The dwarf appears to be skilled with his aim, that is all," he said to his wife and daughter, trying not to sound alarmed. "He will quickly fall once the real tests of skill and strength begin, wait and see." He sped his pace and walked ahead with his main guards to catch up with Lord Mallthus, who had departed the stands earlier.

Down in the competitor's tent, Prince Brothemus was being congratulated by his troops. "Well done, Prince," they chanted together as they made their way out of the tent and onto the roadway leading up past the castle. Captain Balden, who was standing immediately to the dwarf prince's right, leaned close and asked very quietly, "I am sure you can run just fine, my Prince, but what are your plans regarding the swim?" He knew that no dwarf willingly gets into water of any sort.

"I haven't quite figured that out myself," the prince answered back as he gave his captain a scornful look. "Perhaps I shall have you accompany me in the water?" he said in jest, knowing this would not be allowed but wanting to see the horrified look on the captain's face.

As the horde of spectators made their way down the roadway, many became distracted once they reached the area where the food tents had been staged. As the scents of grilling boar, searing trout, and freshly baked breads permeated the air, more than a few decided it was a good time to have another meal or at least stop for a pint of ale.

As the king and his guests and family settled into their new seats, the announcer made his way over to a wooden platform standing some five feet in the air so that he could be easily seen. "One lap around the main roadway, beginning and ending on the white painted line just in front of us here," he announced. "We have spotters all along the course, so there's no need to worry about any of the runners getting off-course or not completing the entirety of the lap." Many of those gathered nodded their heads up and down, seeing the value of this precaution.

The announcer requested one of the trumpeters to join him on the platform, and then he looked down upon the runners, saying, "Once all are ready and have given me their signal by raising your left arms in the air, I will give the signal for the race to begin." The crowd watched as, one by one, the hands of the competitors rose above their heads. When the last man lifted his arm, indicating he too was ready, the ceremony master lowered his right arm, signaling the trumpeter, and a single loud and steady note signaled the start.

While most of the competitors sped off quickly, wishing to take a lead from the very start, a few of the runners chose to start slow and steady, as they appeared to have in mind a sort of race where they paced themselves and saved their strength for the final push at the end. With wild cheering and screams all around, the ten men and lone dwarf made their way along the first stage of the race along the northernmost edge of the monstrous lake.

Hidden up in some trees, a large gathering of owls had been disturbed by the latest trumpet blast. They ended their meeting and took positions along the uppermost branches of the great oak tree they had been meeting in, and looked down upon the commotion taking place on the roadway below. "Looks like a foot race," Carceren announced with a smile.

"Well, then, the king's tournament is finally underway," young Bathis chimed in. "Sure wish Sir Amansun was here to see this. I am sure he would get quite a laugh out of this."

"I do as well," said Carceren, looking somewhat somber. "For such a terrifying beast, he sure did have a great sense of humor." The other owls gathered about nodded their heads in agreement as they watched the runners making their way along the dirt road.

By the time the lead runners hit the north watchtower, it was clear who would not be winning the foot race. Lagging far behind in last place was Sir Glandin, the enormous man who had put on a great performance in the hammer throw. His massive frame simply couldn't keep up with the smaller, swifter runners, even if his strides were much longer than the rest of the group. Sitting in the middle of the pack were Farimus, Blackstone and Antilus. These three seemed content with running a smooth, evenly paced race, and though they were falling further behind as the race went on, they seemed to be capable of making a comeback when the time came based on their smooth and even strides.

Up in front, the usual suspects were once again establishing their dominance. Leading the way, Captain Baerden had taken a quick lead, and he appeared to be leaving everyone else in his dust. Further back Amansun, Sir Berardren and the dwarf were all pretty evenly matched. While the dwarf prince had shorter legs, resulting in strides much smaller than the other runners, his pace was quite furious, and it appeared he would be able to keep up with the other two, providing his endurance made it through the entire race. As the short dwarf sped by, neck-and-neck with the two men, the soldiers who were standing near the tower on watch were shocked to see how quickly the short man could move. "Looks like his feets ain't even touchin' the groun'!" one of the soldiers called out to his friend who was on the topmost level of the tower.

"They's only made it one quarter of the way now," the man up top called down. "Let's wait an' sees how he finishes her up at the end!" He playfully spat at the man some thirty feet below, missing him by just a few feet.

"Let's have none o' that now!" the man on the ground yelled back up. "One a' these times yer goin' to hit me with that nastiness, then I'se gonna have to come up there an' put a hurt on you." He shook his fist in a threatening manner, causing the man on the tower to laugh even harder.

"Can you tell who is in the lead from here?" King Hasselfeth asked as he peered across the large lake, looking towards its western shore.

"Not with certainty, my Lord," Lord Mallthus replied, "but I don't think it's the dwarf."

"Let's hope you are right," the king replied nervously as he peered over his shoulder and saw the queen and princess staring back at him coldly.

As Captain Baerden made his way across the stone bridge that rose over the beginning of the western side of the Steel River, he glanced back and saw that there were now only two runners trying to keep up with him. Berardren had apparently lost his edge and he was now dropping back almost to where three other runners could be seen, still trying to hang in there.

Amansun looked over at the dwarf running alongside him and wondered at how this short man was managing to maintain his place, even though he was clearly exerting considerably more effort than he. *More of that damned wizard's spells*, he thought to himself as he pushed on. *I'll just have to make sure this fool doesn't beat me…it looks as though Captain Baerden has this thing in the bag from here.*

As time passed by, ten of the runners continued around the lake's perimeter, trying their best to keep moving as they started to huff and puff for breath from the effort. Sir Glandin, so far behind he was now out of sight from the other runners, had decided to walk the rest of the way, seeing that he had no chance of winning. Up ahead, moving with great speed still, Captain Baerden was some three hundred feet ahead of the next two runners as he approached the southern watchtower, marking the final leg of the race. As the captain flashed by, a soldier who had been posted there earlier let out a blast from his horn, indicating that a runner was closing in on the end of the race.

Even as the dwarf and Amansun started to close in on the captain's lead, they both could see that they had allowed him to get too far ahead, and they would have no chance of catching up with the swift runner. They both exchanged glances back and forth with each other, still looking as if they would prefer they stop running and have it out right there, and together they pushed on, red in the face but still running.

When the horn had sounded, all the spectators back at the starting point stood and peered down the dirt roadway, trying to get a glimpse of who was in the lead. "It's Captain Baerden in the front," the announcer yelled to the cheers of the waiting crowd, "with Prince Halldor and the dwarf not far behind!"

The king and queen exchanged a quick glance, and the king said softly, "At least it won't be the dwarf winning this event!" in a very relieved tone, then he glanced back to watch the approaching captain.

Captain Baerden came running across the painted white line a few short moments later, to the thunderous applause of the crowd standing there, and then a few moments later the dwarf and prince followed, Amansun just edging out the dwarf by a foot at the very end when he leaned forward as the two sprinted for the finish.

Throwing his hands up in the air to get the crowd's attention first, then pointing over to the three runners who were bent over and struggling for breath, the announcer cried out, "Captain Baerden with the win…Prince Halldor in second and Prince Brothemus third!" Lagging just a few moments behind, Farimus, Blackstone, and Antilus came running across the finish line, followed by Berardren, who had managed to lose his lead to the other three runners who had been pacing themselves the entire way.

Lifting his head so that he could look over at the prince he had just narrowly lost to, the dwarf shook his head in disgust and said quite abrasively, "You can thank your stupid long legs for that win!" Amansun smiled back at the dwarf, and realizing there was no point in saying anything at all, simply turned and walked over to where the enchantress was standing.

Walking up to Amansun, the enchantress patted him on the back gently, noticing that he was still catching his breath from the long run, and she congratulated him on beating the dwarf. "I don't know how you managed to beat the dwarf, especially with the enchantments he clearly has on his side, but I am very happy that you did, young prince," she said with the voice of the male soldier she was now residing in.

"It took everything I had to beat him in the final steps," Amansun said. "I don't think he anticipated my final lean at the end…I was very fortunate! Still, I managed to lose to the captain of the castle. That man can really run!"

"Don't worry about not coming in first," the enchantress said calmly. "The main thing is that you beat Prince Brothemus again. He was one up on you after the crossbow event, but now I believe the two of you are all even." She gave a big grin. "Just the swim event left for day one, so be sure to go out there and swim your heart out."

Looking at the enchantress, peering into her eyes to try and see deep down, Amansun took a deep breath and then exhaled, saying, "I don't have much hope of winning the next event, unfortunately. I can't recall the last time I was actually in the water, much less swimming in it."

"Don't worry about winning the event," the enchantress said as she stared directly into Amansun's gaze. "All you need to do is finish ahead of the dwarf. Just keep that thought in your head as you race out to that float and back!"

"Beat the dwarf! Got it!" Amansun responded. "I'm pretty sure I can remember that." He headed off towards the edge of the lake where the other competitors were starting to bunch up.

As the crowd jockeyed for the best vantage points along the edge of the lake, Amansun's attention shifted over to a small clump of people, Prince Brothemus being among them, who appeared to be having some sort of disagreement. He walked a bit closer so he could hear what was going on, as it was obvious the swim was going to be delayed at least until this problem had been solved.

"The rules of the tournament are that every contestant must enter all ten of the events being held," the master of ceremonies was saying very firmly. "If a contestant refuses to attempt any of the ten challenges, then he forfeits the entire tournament. That is that."

An even louder and agitated voice argued next, saying, "Nobody said anything at the start that I would have to participate in this damned foolish swim! I am not going to get in that water, and you can't make me!" Prince Brothemus clenched his fists as if preparing to start throwing blows.

"What is the meaning of all this?" demanded Lord Mallthus as he walked over to see what all the commotion was about.

"Prince Brothemus here is saying that he refuses to participate in the swim, my Lord. You know what that means!" the ceremonies master said quite rudely as he looked back at the dwarf.

Lord Mallthus knew of course exactly what this meant; it meant there might be a way to end this foolishness of having this dwarf participating in this tournament after all…and in a manner that would allow the king to remove him without any fear of retribution from the Underlord. "Let me consult with the king briefly," Lord Mallthus replied as he turned quickly away from the dwarf and his small band so that they would not see the large smile erupting onto his face even now.

"Yes!" the dwarf prince demanded as the lord walked off towards the king's seating area. "You do that, and be quick about it!"

As Lord Mallthus began filling in the king as to what was taking place over at the water's edge, King Hasselfeth's face brightened for the first time since the morning's event when the dwarf had unexpectedly won the hammer throw event. The two men made a good show of pretending to discuss possible options on how to get around the issue when in fact they were both just joking about how fortuitous it was that the Underlord's servant was about to disqualify himself of his own accord.

Walking back over to the dwarf and ceremony master, Lord Mallthus clasped his hands together in front of himself, doing his best to look sympathetic to the dwarf prince's concerns, then he said simply and plainly, "I am afraid there is nothing that can be done, good prince. Should you choose to not enter the swim portion of the tournament, you will be forfeit in its entirety."

Now seething with rage, Prince Brothemus threw his hands up in the air, obviously very upset, and said in a tone just short of screaming, "Fine! I will enter your silly swimming event, but that does not mean I have to complete it. According to your own rules, all I needs do is enter. Once I am in your smelly lake, I will have entered the race and therefore cannot be disqualified from the tournament!"

Seeming quite surprised by the prince's new tactic, Lord Mallthus and the ceremony master looked at each other briefly, rolling their eyes and looking about at the surrounding crowd as if imploring for some kind of help, then at last the master said in a half-questioning way, "Well, I don't believe there is any rule that says he can't do that.

Unless someone here knows of a reason the prince cannot enter the race in this manner, we will need to move on and get this race started."

"Then the matter is resolved," Lord Mallthus said happily, though he was deeply disappointed on the inside. "Let the race begin." As the lord walked back to explain to the king what had transpired, the announcer called the contestants back to the water's edge and lined them up for the start.

Captain Balden told the dwarves to stay put where they were until he returned, saying, "I have to see Prince Brothemus's face when he hits that water." He said this with a smirk so pleased that he looked as though he was a little child once more. The other dwarves smiled understandingly but said little else, knowing full well that the prince would likely have them beheaded if he learned that they had shared a laugh at his expense.

"Contestants must enter the water in any fashion they choose, swim out and around the red float out towards the center of the lake, then swim back to this same spot as quickly as they can," the announcer said loudly so the crowd could hear the rules. "First man... er, contestant out of the water wins." He glanced over at the dwarf, who was still fuming. "Swimmers ready...and start!"

With a sudden flurry of motion, all the men dove headfirst or jumped into the lake, causing a frantic display of splashing and scrambling as the crowd looked on. Still standing at the lake's edge, the lone dwarf, with great care and effort, raised his right hand to his face, pinched his nose as tightly as possible, then jumped into the waist-high water, sinking completely out of sight for just a moment. When he reappeared above the surface, splashing and floundering like a young child, all eyes focused on him and tremendous waves of laughter ensued. Swearing at the top of his lungs in several languages as he made his way out of the water, the crowd went completely silent as they realized just how upset the dwarf prince really was.

Captain Balden walked over to the prince, doing a very impressive job of not laughing, at least on the outside, and offered him a dry coat. Snatching the coat out of the captain's hands, the dwarf prince sent a piercing glance over at the announcer, saying, "There...I entered your swim!" and he stomped off back towards the contestants' staging tent, knowing full well that the events for the day had concluded. "Stay behind and see what else needs be done to complete this pitiful day!" he snapped as he walked right past his captain who was staring at him blankly.

"As you wish, my Prince," Captain Balden replied, then he turned to walk away just in time as a fit of laughter overtook the stocky dwarf's body.

Glancing back towards the shore which was now a few hundred feet behind him, Amansun saw that the dwarf had indeed jumped in and then got out of the water as quickly as he had been able. Realizing that he no longer had to win the event, he slowed his strokes down to a casual pace and decided to enjoy the experience, along with the coolness of the lake's clear waters. *Let someone else win this event*, he thought to himself as he settled into a reasonable pace, and thought to himself how funny it must have been watching the dwarf prince floundering at the lake's edge.

"I came in towards the middle of the pack," he told the enchantress as he dried himself off. "Just didn't see the need to push myself, since the dwarf wasn't even really in the race."

The enchantress stood there, nodding her head in agreement. "There was no sense in tiring yourself needlessly," she agreed. "And this way you appear to be more normal as well. It would have looked odd if you had won virtually every event, especially after appearing suddenly out of nowhere the way you did."

Over on the announcer's platform, the master of ceremonies was reading off his scroll once more as he reminded the crowds what was being offered that evening. Along with the food booths and fireworks, there would be entertainers of all sorts, a show, and of course the king was holding a very special "by invitation only" dinner event back at the castle. In closing, the master reviewed the tallies for the day, then read out clearly, "At the end of day one, we have Prince Halldor in first place, followed by Prince Brothemus in second, then Captain Baerden in third."

A big cheer rose from the crowd as they realized that their very own captain was in close contention for the win. As the group broke into fragments and melted away, Amansun and the enchantress made their way back to the tent to check on Sophelus and the attendant who had been left behind to keep an eye on Amansun's equipment. "I suppose you will be attending the king's dinner, then?" the enchantress asked with a grin.

"I suppose," Amansun replied back, also smiling with a hint of red blush in his cheeks. "That is, unless you think it would be a mistake, my Lady?"

"Nonsense," the enchantress blurted out quickly. "Go and have your fun. See the princess once more if you can. Just have a care what you say…to anyone. No one here knows you or your story, just remember that. And for goodness sakes, don't drink anything," she added with a loud laugh. "Just be sure to return early enough to get some rest for tomorrow's events!" She turned to go and have a look at one of the food booths, as she was actually feeling a bit hungry now.

CHAPTER 36

Amansun met with Sophelus briefly and was pleased to see that the enchantress had brought along some formal clothing for him to wear, as she had guessed that he would need it. As he walked across the tent to a small area that had been set aside for changing, his old captain Hrothgar appeared, still looking quite distraught. "I didn't see you much today," Amansun said pleasantly at the older man, who appeared to have been tearing up again.

"Begging your pardon, Prince Halldor," the man replied. "I am the second in command of the King's Guard now under Captain Baerden. With the captain entered into the tournament, the security of the king, the castle and the tournament has fallen to me now."

Looking the man up and down as he began to have a rush of memories from his childhood before the Underlord had transformed him, Amansun asked, "And how is it that you came to be here at this castle with King Hasselfeth?"

"After the dragon attack out west near the Smoky Black Mountains, the few of us that survived made our way back to Argonathe," the man began. "When we arrived, we were devastated to learn that the Underlord had sent a horde of goblins from down south to take the fortress while we were away. With so few to guard the stronghold, the goblins were able to take control of the fortress, and I am afraid to say that your mother was lost there." He hung his head and stared at his hands as if trying to find something in them. "We realized then that we were too few to try and take the fortress back, so we had to leave the city behind."

Amansun looked at the man standing before him, clearly in turmoil even after all these years, then reached out and grasped his shoulders tightly, saying, "There is nothing you could have done, I am sure, old friend. There is nothing to regret."

"Once I realized I no longer had a home, I spent the next year roaming these lands, living day to day, hunting for food as best I could and scavenging when I had to," the older man said as he looked shamefully at Amansun. "Eventually my path led me here to Silver Lake and Castle Eladrias. The captain of the Guard took me in like one of his own, and over time I decided I would just stay. I never dreamed that you had been spared by the Underlord. If I had known I would have spent these last ten years searching for you, no matter where the search would have led me."

"I know you would have, my dear friend," Amansun said in an assuring tone. "You already saved me once before, remember?" He pointed towards his chest. "In a way you have saved me again, dear Captain."

Looking confused, the man asked of the prince, "And how have I saved you this time, my Prince?"

Amansun said, "Why, you have given me my name back, old friend. Without you as my witness, no one here would have believed who I was."

Smiling, Hrothgar thanked the prince, bowed lowly, then said, "By your leave, my Prince, I must go and make my rounds now, as the captain is preparing for the king's event." Then he turned and walked off. Turning around suddenly, he approached Amansun once again and asked, "Where have you been these past ten years, my prince? Why have you returned only now after all this time?"

Amansun looked at his troubled old friend, and knowing he would not be able to share or explain anything in a way that would make any sense, he merely replied, "Like you, I was lost for some time after my father's death. I was held captive for years and only recently escaped. I was on my way to Argonathe when I learned of the tournament, so stopped here along the way home."

"Sorry am I to have been the one to tell you of your mother's passing," Hrothgar said sadly. "Should you want me to accompany you on your way home, all you need do is ask." He then turned and walked away. Noticing that it was later than he had realized, Amansun made haste to the changing room, spurred on by his desire to get a seat somewhere near the princess with any luck.

* * *

Outside the castle, Prince Brothemus and his small band of dwarves spent a few moments snooping about and investigating the various food booths that were scattered about. "Nothing here we'll be eatin'," Captain Balden said roughly as he stared at the foods being offered. "Suppose a few pints of ale wouldn't hurt none, though."

"Drink if you must, but be quick about it!" Prince Brothemus snapped. "I need to report back to his Lordship soon, and if he feels we took too long getting back to him, I shall be happy to pass the blame onto you!" He gave a wicked smile.

"Damn the ale!" The captain called out to his dwarves who were just starting to move up in the long line. "We needs to double time it back to camp…and I means now!" he shouted in a voice threatening enough to send all the dwarves scampering ahead of him.

* * *

As Amansun walked up the corridor leading to the main dining hall, he glanced about at the lovely tapestries that hung from the stone walls, and admired the many statues and paintings that adorned the path. *Not as fancy as Argonathe by a long shot*, he thought to himself, *but still nicer than anything I have seen since I left.* As he made his way closer to the immense wooden doors that led into the dining hall, it was obvious that he had taken too long, as the greeting chamber was already packed full of ladies and noblemen, all dressed in their finest gowns and robes, as they waited to be allowed entrance into the hall.

Standing there for a moment as he considered just turning around and forgetting the whole idea, he suddenly heard a young attendant calling out his name and clearing a path as he made his way towards him. "Clear a path, clear a path," the young man repeated over and over again. "The leader of the tournament has arrived." He reached out to the prince and asked him to follow. "The king has been expecting you. You have a seat of honor this evening in light of your high ranking in the events today. We have a seat saved for you at the princess's side. You will be the envy of all the other competitors this night!" He pushed people this way and that as they made it to the main hall entrance doors at last.

Once they had made it through the tight squeeze of guests outside the hall and into the main chamber, Amansun knew he had arrived. There in front of him were several tables, some round, some square and some oval, and in the center of the room was one massive rectangular table with the king and queen along with their daughter, Princess Lyleth, seated at one end, along with Lord Mallthus and his wife. There to the left of the queen sat the princess, looking lovely in a soft blue and white gown, her neck draped with beautiful necklaces of gold and silver. Atop her head was a radiant tiara covered with precious stones, causing it to sparkle as if made from cool stream waters on a sunlit day, when a thousand sparkles are reflecting off the quick moving water.

"There is your seat, Prince Halldor," the attendant said as he motioned the young man to continue along towards the main table. "You will need to be introduced first, of course."

Suddenly standing from where he and his wife were seated, Lord Mallthus walked over to the prince and took his hand. "Here is our guest of honor now, ladies and gentlemen, king and queen, and of course Princess Lyleth," he said quite dramatically, as he glanced about the room to ensure everyone was now looking and listening to the introduction, "May I present to you Prince Halldor, son of the late King Hanthris, heir to Fortress Argonathe of the Granite Mountains and leader in the king's tournament of champions after the first day of competition!" All about the room, people stood and cheered, leaning this way and that to get a better glimpse of this mysterious prince who had almost magically appeared on the castle's doorstep just moments before the tournament was to begin. "The king has arranged a seat of honor at the side of his daughter, Princess Lyleth, as reward for coming in the top position after today's events," Lord Mallthus cried out.

Standing up from his massive wooden chair, King Hasselfeth raised his glass of mead, nodding his head for others to do so, then added, "A toast to Prince Halldor, who has appeared just in our hour of need, so it would appear, as he is the only man to best the dwarf prince Brothemus up to this point, who also entered the contest unexpectedly. I ask that you all keep him in your heads and hearts tomorrow as he fights once more for the hand of my daughter, along with our other brave contestants seated about you." With that, the king sat once again, and with a wave of his hand at the head of the service team gave the signal to commence with the serving of dinner.

Red in the face from all the fuss over him, Amansun moved down the outside of the table until he was at the chair that had been reserved for him. Looking down upon the princess, his tongue almost swollen into silence from his nerves, he bowed his head once and begged permission to take his seat. "By your grace, I request to take my chair at your side," he managed to choke out before losing his ability to speak.

"You have won the rights to that chair, young Prince, and there is no need to ask for it now," the princess said coyly as she got her first good look at Amansun who had competed so mightily this day. *He is much better looking than I could have ever imagined*, she thought to herself as she watched the young man fumbling with his chair as he attempted to settle into place. *Now to see if he has the wit to match his brawn and good looks.*

Amansun, feeling more uncomfortable than he could ever imagine, reached for his goblet of water to try and get some moisture back into his mouth, which now felt as though he had spent the day marching across a barren wasteland broiling in the heat of summer. His trembling hand knocked the glass over on its side, sending a wave of water splashing over the table. His face suddenly a bright crimson, he looked nervously over at the princess while saying, "A thousand pardons for my clumsiness. I shall be more careful with the rest of the meal, I assure you!"

With a good-natured laugh, the princess motioned to the server assigned to their section of the table and signaled for another glass of water for the prince. "It's nice to see you are human after all, young Prince," she said while smiling at the flustered young man, "After your performances out on the field today, some were beginning to suggest that you had supernatural powers, with the way you were walking over the other competitors!"

Amansun laughed nervously once more, quite taken aback by just how much the princess's words had rung true, and he bowed once more, saying, "You are too kind, princess. I merely wanted the prize more than any other out there, is all." He looked into her blue eyes with his own.

"Such flattery from a warrior such as yourself," she said while giggling at the prince. "I see you have the skill to disarm the ladies as well as those you meet out on the field of battle!"

As the dinner went on, Princess Lyleth and Amansun spoke as if they were seated in the Grand Hall all by themselves. They soon found that they were both very similar in their ways of thinking, enjoyed many of the same things, and shared a love of adventure.

Looking into Amansun's deep dark eyes, the princess suddenly said without meaning to, "I feel as though I know you somehow…as if we have met once before…looked into each other's eyes…it's madness, I know." She now blushed with a pale red color that just made her look all the more beautiful to Amansun.

"There is no madness in your eyes, I can assure you, Princess," he said as he stared right back at her, his shyness falling away. "And if we have met before, then it was in a dream and surely the best possible dream I could ever hope for."

Before either of them could have ever imagined, the meal was over, and it was time for the guests to start departing, as the king had addressed the crowd while the two had been lost in conversation. Looking about at the standing guests, the princess turned to Amansun and said, "It appears we have missed our opportunity to eat." She laughed and smiled at the young man. "Everyone is starting to depart already."

"No meal could have matched the night I have shared with you this evening," Amansun said softly as he took the princess's hand in his own for just a fleeting moment. "I shall watch for you during tomorrow's tournament." He kissed the young woman's hand.

"And I shall cheer for you, Prince Halldor of Argonathe!" she said as she withdrew her hand and looked to see if anyone had seen. There, a few seats down from where the king was standing, the queen was looking over at her daughter with a peculiarly happy look upon her face, as she nodded her head encouragingly then turned away to reply to Lord Mallthus's wife, who had apparently been trying to carry on a conversation with her.

"By your leave, then, my Lady," Amansun said as the two stood and prepared to leave the table. "Know that I battle for thee!" He looked into her eyes once more, then he walked off towards the hall's exit, anxious to share his wonderful evening's events with the Lady of the Woods.

* * *

Down on the darkened section of road that led east and away from the bright lights of the castle and the many events taking place there, Prince Brothemus and Captain Balden were having an unpleasant conversation of their own, although it was the Underlord that they were locked into words with.

"I am very displeased in you, young Prince," the Underlord said as he learned of the day's events and the outcome of the first day's tournament results. "Even with the ring I have enchanted for you, you still failed to beat this young fool of a prince I mistakenly allowed to live all those years ago." He looked into the bowl resting on the table before him. "I feel there is a crossroads approaching with the new day, Prince Brothemus, and one that bodes ill for the two of us! Should the dragon prince be allowed to win the king's tournament, it will likely set in motion a series of events that will lead to a great battle that I have foreseen for countless years now, though never before was I so sure that an adversary was likely to rise up and challenges my forces. You must smote this dragon prince tomorrow!" He raised his two hands into the air and clenched his fists tightly, staring all the while at the two dwarves' images that shown upon the reflection of the water in his bowl of seeing. "Vanquish the dragon prince now while there is still time, or I shall have to do the job myself! And you and your captain there will be very unhappy if I should have to take matters into my own hands, of that I can promise."

* * *

While Prince Halldor slept in one tent outside the castle, his main adversary, Prince Brothemus, lay in another, over at his campsite surrounded by his troops. Up in the castle's main quarters, Princess Lyleth was having difficulty sleeping, so she decided to step out onto her balcony to see the moon's reflection on Silver Lake as she had done so many times before. Standing on the polished stone in her bare feet as a cool breeze blew off the water, the princess's long blonde hair drifted about like the leaves of a tree. As she stared out into the darkness, thinking back to the unusual dinner she had shared with the prince from Argonathe, she couldn't help but picture the large flying serpent, hanging in the air just ahead of her, as she saw its magnificent black eyes staring at her from across the distance. Standing up from the railing she had been leaning against until then, she suddenly realized why she had felt she had met this prince before…they both had the same penetrating stare and matching black eyes. "It's uncanny!" she said to herself, as she stood there in the darkness alone, thinking of how similar she had felt when looking into their deep, dark eyes.

That night the revelers partied well into the morning hours along with some of the contestants, who had realized by now that they had no chance of winning the king's tournament. *May as well stay up and have a good time*, Sir Glandin thought to himself as he looked at the bevy of young maidens who were eyeing him with passion from across the music hall, where he had been listening to groups of troubadours singing songs of old.

CHAPTER 37

When dawn broke the next day, Amansun and many of the competitors, at least those who had decided to go to sleep at a reasonable hour, began to awaken and start preparing for the second day of the contest. There at the foot of his cot, the soldier who was the Lady of the Woods in disguise was standing tall and looking down upon him. "Did you have lovely dreams of the princess?" the enchantress said quietly with a chuckle.

Looking up at the soldier with a sleepy grin like that of a child, Amansun replied back, "Why yes, as a matter of fact, I did!" and the two exchanged happy glances.

"Well, best you have a light breakfast now, while the others are still sleeping, so you have an empty stomach when today's matches begin," the enchantress advised. "Today you will be wearing your full armor for the first time in true battle conditions, so you best be in the best shape as can be."

Amansun realized just then that he was in fact quite hungry, having had no more than a bite or two the night before as he and the princess talked the night away. "Breakfast sounds like a great idea!" he replied as he sat up. "What say we take a walk down to the food booths to see what they have cooking this morning?"

"Just what I had in mind," the enchantress replied. "This will give us some time to talk as well. There are still a few things I need to share with you before you go into the next round of events. Let's be sure to bring something back for Sophelus and the attendant today, as I don't believe they took time out to eat much yesterday either."

Once Amansun and the enchantress had purchased some bread and jam along with a few pieces of smoked and cured ham, they sat on a large rock down at the water's edge where no one else would be able to overhear their conversation. Breaking off a chunk of the still-warm bread and slathering some jam over it, Amansun took a large bite and, after swallowing carefully, looked over at the enchantress seated next to him and asked, "So what are these 'things' that you have left to share with me, my Lady?"

Nibbling on a thin piece of the ham, the enchantress looked to the left and right once, to ensure no one was nearby, then wiped her mouth on her sleeve delicately and leaned closer to Amansun. "Remember the night I told you that once you have been transformed to some other creature, a part of that creature will always remain with you?"

"Yes, I remember that clearly. That is why I can now hear and understand what the creatures are saying to each other," he said as he pointed over to two small squirrels that were busy picking up roasted nuts that had been dropped by one of the many spectators the day before.

"Precisely!" the enchantress said with a nod. "But that is only part of what I meant to tell you, Amansun. There is more to it than that. Particularly in your case, I am afraid."

Looking at the enchantress once more, Amansun asked, "What more could there be? What have you decided to leave out until just now?"

"No need to take offense," the enchantress warned. "You were not ready to hear that which I am about to say three days ago!"

"I meant no harm by my comment, truly!" he said as he looked forward with an ever-increasing look of doubt. "Is there some terrible thing that will befall me now that I have been transformed into a man once again?"

"The problem is that something could trigger you into changing back into the dragon's form once more…that is to say, back into yourself as you were as Amansun the dragon."

"So, you are telling me that at any time I could suddenly transform back into the dragon again?"

"Not at any time. Just under certain circumstances, like when you are under stress, or perhaps when you are in grave danger!"

"And why have you decided to tell me only now, just hours before the second day of the king's tournament begins again?" he asked.

"You see," she began, "yesterday you were in no events that I felt would be particularly stressful to you or that would put you into harm's way. But today…today will be different. Yesterday all you were doing was shooting at things, running around, swimming. Today is much different. Today you will be battling with swords, staffs, even jousting from atop swift steeds. Today you will truly be in danger."

Starting to grasp the meaning of what the enchantress was trying to tell him, Amansun put it into his own words, asking the enchantress, "So what you are saying is that since I am going to be engaging in contests where my own life is on the line…because of that stress, I could change over?"

"Precisely!" the enchantress replied.

"So there is nothing that I can do to prevent this from happening?"

Shaking her head, the enchantress answered, "This is where the good news lays, Amansun. It is entirely up to you on whether or not the transformation will occur."

Even more confused than ever, Amansun repeated, "The choice is mine?"

"Yes it is, Amansun. The choice is yours. All you need to do to prevent the transformation from occurring is to maintain your composure and focus. If you are able to do that, there will be nothing to worry about at all."

"And if I can't? If I cannot maintain my cool during these times of stress?" Amansun asked, already knowing the answer to his own question.

"Then the dragon reappears. It's as simple as that. Oh, except for one thing. Should someone you love or care deeply about be in great peril, then the transformation is also likely to occur. That's about it."

Looking a bit queasy, Amansun took a few moments to review everything he had heard, and then said out loud, though he was just thinking the thought to himself, "And will I be able to return to this form again, I wonder?"

Reaching out and placing her hand on Amansun's shoulder, the enchantress explained in an even tone, "The answer is yes and no, I am afraid. That is to say, I believe I will be able to break the spell again, at least once and maybe twice, but should you change back and forth more than that—say, three times or more—then it is anyone's guess, to tell you the truth. It's just hard to say."

"It just keeps getting better now, doesn't it!" he replied with a huff. "Oh well, no sense getting sick about something that may or may not happen, I suppose. Let's head back to the tent now. All this talk of transforming from one thing to another has taken my mind off of the tournament, and that can't be a good thing!"

"Right you are, my boy!" the enchantress agreed, standing up. "Let's not forget to stop and get a few things for Sophelus and the attendant now. I suppose we'll need to get some kind of vegetables or fruit," she added as she remembered that the attendant was but an animal and therefore not likely to be interested in anything else that the people of the castle might have for sale.

The rest of the morning sped along at an astounding pace, and before you knew it, it was time for the second round of events to start. As the crowds filled the arena seating once more, and the royal family and guests took their positions, the trumpeters announced with several blasts that day two was about to start. "He is really quite handsome," the queen said softly as she looked over at her daughter, who was obviously looking down in the direction of the rider in white on the field.

"Yes, I know that, Mother," she said playfully. "He's actually very interesting to speak with as well."

Looking at her only child, the queen laughed and said, "I wouldn't have been able to tell…seeing how the two of you spent the entire night conversing with each other and completely ignoring the rest of us at the table."

Down on the field, the contestants had been lined up once more, this time dressed in full battle gear. The master of ceremonies approached the center of the field as he had done the day before, though this time the scroll in his hands was much shorter. "Day two of the king's tournament of champions will begin with the quarterstaff," he announced. "The contestants will be set into matches of two, with winners from each match moving on. We will continue paring down the group with these matches until only two remain. The winner of that final match will win the event!" He then started to announce which competitors would be facing who.

"Time to put those practice rounds with Sophelus to the test," the enchantress said to Amansun as she looked through the slits in his helmet. "You are not likely to draw the dwarf at the start because the two of you were at the top of yesterday's competition. However, when you do, be sure to guard your legs. Prince Brothemus may be tall for a dwarf, but he's still much shorter than you, so he will likely try to sweep your legs!"

Amansun reached for his hawthorne staff, nearly eight feet long and sturdy as if made from steel, and walked over where his opponent, Sir Antilus, was already waiting. "Thanks for the tip," he said as he walked away, and then he looked up at the board, seeing his name at the top, though followed closely by the dwarf's.

At a signal from the announcer, the trumpeters blew a single brief note and then the matches began with the sounds of wood beating down upon wood. As the competitors blocked and parried, thrust and swiped at each other, the crowd cheered wildly, some calling out the names of their favorite competitors. Amansun was too focused to hear that his name was being chanted quite loudly by many of the spectators, but this was not missed by the princess who sat at the edge of her seat, paying close attention to how the prince in white was doing.

Match after match went by as competitors were slowly eliminated for most of the morning, and in the end, the four remaining contestants were Amansun, Prince Brothemus, Sir Berardren and Sir Glandin. Captain Baerden had fought a tough match but Sir Glandin, a giant of a man who had an enormous ten-foot staff made out of a thick branch of dense oak from his homeland, eventually did him in. He had used his size and the weight of his weapon to beat the captain down again and again until at last he was unable to stand, though he had not given up.

Walking over to his captain, Hrothgar congratulated him on a well-fought match and acknowledged that he had likely drawn one of the toughest competitors in this event. "I suppose I shall have to cheer for the white rider at this point," the captain said with a defeated look, as he struggled to get his breath back and listened to the names in the final matches. "It's not likely I shall be able to catch up over the next events."

"Nonsense!" Hrothgar said as he offered his friend a drink of water. "Three events are left and you have a very good chance of winning all three, I would have to say, even if I am on your side."

Now standing tall once again, having gotten his strength back, the captain looked at his right hand man and said, "Let's go and have a look at these remaining matches, then. I should like to see if any can best this giant who smote me."

As the announcer called out the next set of matches, the crowd cheered again as they realized that the dwarf prince and Prince Halldor would not likely be meeting until the final match…that is, if they each survived this next match. "Prince Halldor will face Sir Glandin and Sir Berardren will meet Prince Brothemus," the voice called out.

As Amansun entered the section where Sir Glandin was waiting for him, Princess Lyleth, high up in the stands, looked over at her mother fearfully and asked, "Do you suppose the prince has a chance against such a large opponent, Mother?"

The queen smiled at her daughter, shaking her head up and down and saying, "This is where we find out how much the young prince truly wants you, my dear. Judging by the way young Prince Halldor was staring at you last night, I would say it's the giant who has to be careful." They both laughed uneasily.

Looking over at the monstrous man he had been paired with, Amansun quickly realized that it would be very unlikely he would be able to knock this opponent over with sheer power alone. *I suppose I shall just have to sweep his very legs out from underneath him*, he thought to himself as he visualized the strike he had in mind.

At the first sound of the trumpet, Amansun stepped forward quickly, as if he intended on taking on the giant head in a match of strikes; then when he saw that his adversary had firmly planted both feet into a defensive posture, he lowered himself to the ground at the same time, spinning viciously to his right as he swung his staff out in front of him with both hands gripped tightly onto the end closest to him. Before the giant had time to realize what was taking place, Amansun's staff struck his legs just above his ankles, and the sweeping motion took out both of Sir Glandin's legs. As Amansun's spin returned him to his original position facing his opponent, he slowly raised himself again into a standing position as he watched the frame of the giant man floating into the air and falling down square on his back.

"Winner!" cried the announcer as he pointed at Prince Halldor.

"I do believe your prince just smote that giant of a man with one fell strike!" the queen said as she looked over at her daughter, who was now out of her seat and jumping wildly into the air as she cheered for the prince who took a moment to look up her way and raise his fist in victory.

Standing to one side, Captain Baerden looked over at Hrothgar, who was also staring at the large man still flat on his back, and said calmly, "I suppose that is what I should have done as well," and together the two burst into laughter.

While the match between the dwarf and Sir Berardren lasted much longer than Amansun's had, the outcome was quite predictable after the first few moments had passed. Sir Berardren was a powerful man and quite skilled with the staff, but it soon became apparent that the dwarf prince, with a lower center of gravity, was simply immovable. In the end, the dwarf simply outlasted the knight who failed to meet his attacks with the same level of intensity. Finally falling to one knee, the Red Knight was eliminated.

After announcing the final match, the ceremony master advised the spectators that for this final fight, an hourglass would be used, as it had become expected that their match would end in a draw. There was no sense in prolonging the tournament and wasting the day away, watching these two fight each other to a standstill. Holding the hourglass high in the air, the announcer explained loudly, "When the sands of this hourglass have run out, if there is no declared victor at that time, the match will be called a draw and we will move on to the next event."

At the sound of the trumpet, Prince Brothemus and Amansun wasted no time in moving forward and attacking. Before the sound of the trumpets had faded away, each had struck the other no less than three times, and the *clack clack*ing of their staffs filled the air like some strange drumbeat from a far-off land. Strike after strike fell as the two fought to dominate the other, but to no avail. When one struck high, the other countered with a perfect block, when one swung around low, the other anticipated the move and lowered their staff to defend, and so the battle went. There were none there to cheer for the dwarf prince as even his small group of attendants and his captain were stunned at the spectacle that was unfolding before their eyes. Amansun, on the other hand, had begun to build up quite a loyal following, and once again this growing group of spectators busied themselves with chanting his name in unison and waving their hands up in the air wildly after every great strike or block Amansun put forth. As predicted, the sands of the hourglass ran out long before either had done enough damage or struck the other sufficiently enough to warrant a clear victory. Throwing in a red cloth between the two combatants to indicate the duel was at an end, the announcer cried out loudly, "Draw!" and the match ended just like that.

Glaring over at each other, the two now familiar foes both seemed upset that they had not been able to defeat the other. With some final parting words, the two turned and walked over to their attendants to hand over their staffs and prepare for the next event. Looking up at the board, Amansun saw that neither his name nor the dwarf's was moving, so he knew right away that he still remained one up on the dwarf. Walking over to his two aides, he leaned over to the enchantress and whispered, "Have you figured out the secret to his power yet, my Lady?"

The enchantress shook her head as if frustrated, yet feeling confident that the answer would be revealed shortly. She said, "I cannot quite put my finger on it yet, but I know the answer is likely in plain view if only I could see it. Fear not, for I believe the next event will give me a better chance to determine how the dwarf is managing to meet your power. I can still see the blue aura about him, yet it was not as bright in this past event, so likely he did not need its assistance as much as in the other events."

"Begging you pardon, my Lady," Amansun said quite meekly, "but there are only the three events left. It would be grand if you could find the Underlord's secret before we come to the end!"

"Next will be the battle of spiked flails!" the announcer cried out as most of the contestants looked at each other with groans of anguish.

"I dislike the spiked flails more so than any other," Sir Blackstone said to Sir Farimus loudly enough so that Amansun had been able to hear.

"Pity the man who draws the giant!" Sir Farimus replied as they looked at the tall man walking back to the tent, face red with anger from his last defeat that had come so suddenly and unexpectedly.

Looking over at the enchantress, Sophelus, who had joined the other members of his group, shook his head somewhat dejectedly, saying, "Pity, really. We hadn't counted on that one. Amansun has had no time to train for this next event. Straight ahead and into the fire, as they say, I guess." He looked over at Amansun who was obviously not aware of what his latest challenge involved.

"What exactly are the spiked flails?" Amansun said quite innocently.

"Nothing to get overly concerned about," the enchantress said, attempting a smile. "They really aren't much worse than the swords you will be fighting with later today. These just take a little getting used to is all." She looked over at Sophelus and waved a finger, as if to say *stop scaring the prince*.

Back in the combatants' staging tent, Amansun looked ahead with interest as Sophelus returned carrying a very unusual weapon in his hands. He had gotten permission to bring one of the flails to the tent so that Amansun might have a few moments to look at the weapon and get a feel for it before heading out for full contact with the device. Lifting the heavy object with his right hand, Sophelus began to describe the weapon in detail first so that the prince would have some idea of what it was he would be fighting with. "The spiked flail is made by first taking a solid ball of steel and adding spikes all about it, these here on this particular flail being about two inches high. Next the ball is attached to a heavy steel chain. Finally, the chain is affixed to a metal spike, which is then placed into a hollowed-out piece of oak so the user has a better grip. As you can see, when it's all done what you have left is a spiked steel ball hanging on the end of a two-foot chain attached to this handle. This allows you to swing the ball with great force at your opponent's head, body or shield."

"Not the friendliest looking thing, is it?" Amansun said as he reached out and took the flail in his right hand. As he tested the device out with a few swings here and there, he managed to hit himself in the chest with an errant swing, and the heavy spiked ball made quite an impression in his otherwise still unblemished armor. "I don't suppose I'll be mastering the use of this in the next few moments now, will I?" he said in jest as he looked over at Sophelus, who was looking quite amused.

"Not likely," Sophelus replied, still chuckling at Amansun and shaking his head.

"Just swing the ball around and try not to hit yourself with it," the enchantress said sharply. "We can't have guessed every little event they were going to throw at us." She said this quite angrily, although she was feeling guilty, as she had not had time to prepare Amansun for the tournament and she knew it.

"Just like the joust, I am sure," Amansun said good-naturedly. "Just stand there and knock anyone down that comes at me, right?"

"That's the spirit!" the enchantress said excitedly. "And try to keep the dwarf busy if you get to him in this next round, so I can have a closer look at him." She looked at the heavy spiked ball whipping through the air as Amansun continued to practice.

While Amansun made it through his first few matches alright, even managing to defeat several of the other competitors, he had the misfortune of being matched up against Sir Glandin in the semifinal match, who was in fact quite happy to have the opportunity to meet the prince in battle, so soon after having been humiliated in the quarterstaff competition. "No hard feelings, right?" Amansun said to the giant man as the trumpet sounded, announcing the start of their match.

"Oh no…none at all!" the towering man laughed as he moved towards the prince. "I'm just going to smash your head in with this steel ball is all!" He began to swing his flail about over his head.

Amansun hung in there for quite some time, to the surprise of Sophelus and the enchantress, who had been unable to watch the match as she was sure Amansun was going to get killed. As the two opponents traded blows, each doing major damage to the other's shield, Amansun started to improve. *I think I'm actually starting to get the hang of this now!* he thought to himself as he tried not to smile. And then, suddenly and without any indication, Sir Glandin swung his flail over his head and downwards so powerfully and cruelly that the ball knocked Amansun's shield out of the way, striking the prince directly on the head as it sped towards the ground. All the spectators gasped in shock as Amansun fell to the ground with a thud, failing to even try and slow his fall as he had obviously been knocked senseless by the knight's mighty blow.

The announcer looked over at the prince lying motionless on the ground, then called out, "Winner!" as he pointed to the giant who looked quite proud of himself now.

Over on the opposite side of the field, Prince Brothemus was just finishing off Captain Baerden, who had fought valiantly but had also been injured when a particularly forceful blow had broken the captain's shield and fractured his left arm at the same time. In his weakened condition, it was only a matter of time before the captain had to concede to the dwarf, who looked as if he was willing to fight to the death.

"Winner!" the announcer called out once more as the dwarf prince stood over his defeated foe with an evil grin. "Shame I won't be able to do the same to that cursed Prince Halldor," the dwarf complained as he watched his name being moved up equal to his biggest rivals once more.

When Amansun awoke next, he was lying in the staging tent with the enchantress, Sophelus and the attendant, who was sitting down and gnawing on one of the fresh carrots they had purchased for him earlier in the day. "Would you like the good news or the bad news first?" the enchantress asked of the groggy prince.

Trying to sit up briefly, a sudden rush of pain swept through his head, and then Amansun lay down once more, looking up at his friends, and said, "I suppose I shall have the bad first."

Sophelus stepped in a bit closer and then said, "The bad news is that the giant you were fighting snuck in a high crushing blow and knocked you unconscious. This means that you and the dwarf prince are tied in first place once more."

"That is bad news," Amansun muttered softly as the ache in his head throbbed more and more. "And the good?" he asked.

Stepping forward, the enchantress smiled proudly and excitedly and said, "I have found the secret to the dwarf's power."

Sitting up excitedly, choosing to ignore the pain in light of this latest announcement from the enchantress, Amansun smiled and said, "And what have you learned, my Lady?"

"The secret is in the dwarf's blue ring that he wears on his hand. It was there right in front of me the whole time, but I didn't realize it until I saw him battling in his last match. While the blue aura I have been describing seems to cover the entire dwarf in a cloak of invincibility, the ring on his finger appears to glow the brightest and the most often."

"And this is good news because?" Amansun said, now feeling less excited and lying back down on his cot again.

"This is good news because now we know how to defeat the Underlord's spell, of course," the enchantress said excitedly. "Don't you see? Now you have a target…a means of defeating the dwarf prince once and for all."

Still looking and feeling somewhat fuzzy, Amansun looked up at the enchantress with apologetic eyes and said, "I am truly sorry that I am not following you, but I will need you to spell this out for me clearly. How does this help?"

Shaking her head in disbelief, the enchantress said with a sarcastic tone, "I guess that blow to your head really did scramble your thoughts All you need to do is smash the dwarf's ring while you are battling him in the sword event coming up shortly. Once the ring has been damaged, the wizard's spell will be broken as well. Then you can fight the dwarf on a fair playing field and you are certain to defeat him."

"Oh!" Amansun said while nodding his head very slowly due to the pain. "Smash his ring, I get it now." He closed his eyes again. "And do you have anything you can give me for my head?" he asked in a shaky voice.

"Yes, of course," the enchantress replied, handing him some leaves she had taken from one of her many pockets. "Chew on these leaves for a few moments. You should feel as good as new in no time."

Out on the field, to everyone's great surprise, Prince Brothemus ended up defeating Sir Glandin in the final match of the flails contest. As the competitors began marching back into the staging tent where Amansun was resting, they were surprised to see that the prince was now sitting up and conversing with his attendants. "Thought the white rider was done for!" one of the knights said as he passed by the prince's cot.

"Just resting is all," Sophelus replied as he watched the man walk by. "And who won the last match?"

"The blasted dwarf did, can you believe it?" he asked with incredulity in his voice. "That bastard dwarf is tied in first place with your man now. Hope you can get him up and back on his feet by the time they call us for the next event. There's none of us wants to see that dwarf win. Not a one." He walked off.

Feeling much better within moments as the enchantress had promised, Amansun got up from his cot and grabbed for a flask of water so that he could splash some on his head which still throbbed a bit. "Don't you worry," he said as he looked around at his three helpers. "I'm up and ready for the next challenge."

Just then a finely dressed steward approached from the tent's entrance and walked over to where Amansun was standing. "Begging your pardon, good sirs, but the princess has sent me to see what has become of the prince, though it would appear that you are alive and well, I suppose?" he asked.

"Tell the princess that I am just fine," Amansun said. "Tell her also that it will take much more than a little bump on the head to keep me from my prize!" he added with a smile as he winked at the enchantress to his side.

As the young steward made his way out of the tent, the ceremonies master walked in and, after making his way into the middle, announced that the final two competitions would take place after the lunch break. "Happy to see you up on your feet!" the announcer said as he walked by Amansun. "The crowd is still counting on you to win the tournament! Especially now that the captain has had his arm banged up and all," he said sadly as he faded out of the tent.

As Amansun and the enchantress started walking towards the front of the tent to go and secure lunch, a group of the king's personal guard walked in and made their way directly over to the prince. "The king wishes a moment of your time, Prince Halldor," the soldier in charge said rather demandingly. "He is just outside the tent if you are able."

"Certainly!" Amansun replied, nodding at the enchantress to go on without him. "I'll catch up with you at the booths," he muttered. Following the soldiers out of the tent and off to a clearing away from any prying ears, Amansun soon found himself standing alone with King Hasselfeth, who had a very alarmed look on his face.

"You really gave me quite a fright, young Prince!" the king said with a pained expression. "It would appear you are the only competitor here able to defeat this cursed dwarf prince. When you were knocked out in the last event, I thought the queen and the princess were going to come after me with daggers!"

"And what is it that I may do for you, King Hasselfeth?" Amansun asked.

Looking at the young man standing before him, the king leaned in closer and said quite simply, "Win, that is all I ask of you. Just win. I'll declare war against the Underlord himself, if necessary, before marrying my daughter off to that cursed dwarf, but it would be much better if you were able to defeat him in the tournament. Then there can be no retribution, no reason for war and bloodshed."

"I will do my best!" Amansun replied honestly. "I failed in the last event, it is true, but make no mistake, I mean to win your daughter's hand in marriage and no dwarf, prince or no, will stand in my way."

"Glad to hear it, my boy," the king said with a hopeful look upon his face. "Go out there and destroy him!" He and his guards sped off to the main grandstand to join the others for lunch.

Stepping out from behind one of the nearby tents, the enchantress, still in soldier's form, walked over with a giant grin, saying, "Personal councils with the king himself now. You are moving up quickly, Amansun!"

Amansun turned bright red as he smiled back at the enchantress, then said, "Let's go get something to eat!" and the two walked off down the roadway in search of lunch.

CHAPTER 38

Far down in the Southern Barrens, a great army of dwarves, goblins, giants and other foul creatures was on the move. This massive group had started marching days earlier when the Underlord had first begun to hear rumors of the flying serpent up in the area of the Old Great Forest. Over five thousand strong, and led by Prince Karazed, a dark dwarf prince from the southern mountain ranges of the Erathis region near the Cartithian Sea, he had been called for by the powerful wizard who lacked faith that Prince Brothemus would be able to do the job he had been given.

Looking into his seeing bowl, the Underlord and his servant, Cantalus, watched as the enormous army marched northwards, now moving past the Archain mountains along a vast dry valley of dusty plains intermingled with grass-covered fields and hills. "Your army is making quick progress over the barren plains of the south, oh Lord," the old man said softly as he watched the countless lines of wagons and warriors moving along.

"I have commanded Prince Karazed to arrive at the castle along Silver Lake in three more days' time!" the Underlord replied with a harsh voice. "He knows what will befall him should he fail to do so."

"But what of Prince Brothemus's task, my Lord? Do you not plan on having him marry the king's daughter once he wins the tournament?" the servant asked.

The ancient wizard looked back upon the scene of quickly moving dwarves and goblins marching along in the liquid's surface once again, then, laughing softly, said, "I never gave that fool much of a chance against the dragon prince, old man. It matters not whether he wins or loses. By the time the tournament has ended my army will be just two days' march from King Hasselfeth's castle. Prince Karazed and his troops will crush that foolish king and any there who choose to stand beside him!"

"Then you mean to take the castle at Silver Lake for your own?" Cantalus asked.

Looking quite upset at the old man's bothersome questions, the Underlord raised his right hand upward, palm facing forward as if to say "stop," and he said quite sarcastically and cruelly, "Of course I intend on taking the castle, old fool! Those men of the lake have been living in that region for far too long, and the pittance they send me each year is far too little to allow them to stay there and prosper. Soon Prince Karazed will be sitting on the throne in that castle by the water with his troops of dwarves and goblins. Once that is taken care of, I will start building a new empire to the north with Castle Eladrias and the Fortress at Argonathe as my places of power. With both towers at my command, it will be easy to sweep across the lands of the north and east, and my reign will go unchallenged for a thousand years!" A look of pure hatred welled up in his eyes.

* * *

Over at one of the food booths, Amansun and the enchantress were sitting under the shade of a giant oak tree, nibbling on their lunch of braised rabbit with turnips, elderberry cakes, and freshly baked rosemary bread with butter and blackberry jam. "Best not eat too much," the enchantress cautioned as she watched Amansun wolfing down his rabbit. "You'll need quick feet and your wits about you in this next round." She reached over and pulled the bread and jam away from where Amansun was seated.

Nodding his head in agreement as he washed the meal down with large gulps of fresh stream water, Amansun said, "This morning's events were tougher than I had imagined, and I have worked up quite an appetite. But I am sure you are right once again." He looked at the elderberry cake resting beside him, then took it and handed it over to the enchantress.

"Well done," the enchantress said with a smile. "There'll be plenty of time for sweet cakes and ale after the tournament." She wrapped the cake in a piece of cloth and tucked it into a brown satchel hanging at her side. Looking over her shoulder and from side to side now, the enchantress looked at Amansun with a very serious look and said quite softly, "Now don't forget your goal in the sword event coming up, young prince. It is imperative that you find a way to damage that ring, or you will likely lose the tournament."

"Fear not, my Lady," Amansun responded as he drank yet more water. "I shall smash that ring if it is the only part of the dwarf my sword hits the entire match. Let's just hope I don't take another hit to the head, as my ears are still ringing from the last one."

Seeing others starting to make their way back towards the main tournament site, the enchantress tapped Amansun on the shoulder lightly, saying, "Time to get going," and the two made their way into the crowd that had filled the dirt road as they plodded back to the arena. As the last groups of spectators pushed forward and fought for the few remaining good seats, the master of ceremonies made his way once again to the center of the field and began announcing the rules of the sword event along with the list that broke the competitors into pairs.

"Captain Baerden's injuries in the last event will prevent him from moving further along in the tournament," the announcer cried out, "so we are down to ten competitors now, with Prince Halldor and Prince Brothemus still tied in first position with two events remaining."

The crowds began chanting Prince Halldor's name loudly as he took his place in the center of the field. Waving his right hand into the air and nodding up in the direction of the royal family, Amansun turned and looked down the line of competitors until his gaze met the hands of the dwarf prince. There atop his hand sat the sparkling blue ring, the object he would be doing his best to hit, and he started planning his sword fight with the dwarf in his head as he imagined ways he might want to swing at his foe's hand so best to smash the ring into shards.

As Amansun's attention began to return to what the announcer was saying, he realized that he would be meeting Sir Farimus in the first match, while the dwarf would be fighting against Sir Armaris from the south. *Looks like the dwarf has pulled an easy mark for the first match*, Amansun said to himself as he glanced over at the blue knight, who so far in the tournament had not had much success. *Not likely the dwarf will be in any danger from this opponent*, he thought again as he looked over at his adversary, Prince Farimus, who was a very competent competitor and appeared to be quite handy with a blade.

Once the competitors had been split into areas marked off with individual circles marked with white chalk, the announcer waved at the trumpeter to prepare to sound off the start of the match. "Remember," the announcer cried out loudly. "Any competitor driven out of his own circle, or who steps out on their own to avoid being struck, will be disqualified and the win shall go to his opponent. Competitors may also take a knee if they should wish to forfeit." With that being said, the announcer lowered his hand quickly and the trumpeter played three quick blasts from his horn.

Most of the combatants took their time sizing up their adversaries before moving forward to engage in battle. Circling to the left or to the right, each opponent held their sword in one hand firmly and their shield in the other, as they peered out from the slits in their helmets and watched for any sign of weakness or fear from the other.

Prince Brothemus was not like the other competitors. He knew his enchanted ring protected him and this gave him superior confidence in all the events the tournament had to offer, save for the swimming event, which obviously proved to be too daunting of a challenge for the dwarf. Stepping in boldly as soon as the trumpets had sounded, the dwarf took the battle directly to his adversary, who had wanted to spend some time posturing and feigning movements for some time before engaging. With a series of hard overhand slices followed by powerful thrusts and swings with his shield to the tall man before him, Prince Brothemus quickly took the advantage and before long had his opponent hopelessly blocking the seemingly endless blows raining down upon him. Not wishing to suffer a fatal blow, the younger Blue Knight saw that he was completely outmatched, and he took several steps backwards, thus removing himself from the ring.

"Winner!" the announcer called out as he raised his hand towards the dwarf, who appeared to have not even begun to breathe heavily at this point.

Sir Glandin was next to finish off his opponent. Striking relentlessly at the smaller man's shield, Sir Antilus soon found that his shield arm was beaten and battered from the powerful blows of the giant man from the southeast. He too wisely decided to end his match before he was injured too greatly, wishing to have a go at the joust in the final matches of the tourney. Stepping two steps back once there was an opportunity, the knight took a knee and lowered his weapon to the ground in a show of forfeit.

The announcer called out the winner then moved along. This time he came to rest a few paces from where Sir Farimus and Prince Halldor were locked in battle. Sir Farimus was a very skilled swordsman, and he was able to anticipate most of the moves the younger man was attempting. Blow for blow and thrust for thrust, each seemed to be the other's equal as they circled first one way, then the other, the sounds of clanging steel and the ringing of swords hitting shields continuing to roll across their section of the main field. Up above the contestants, the crowds in the seats cheered loudly for both competitors, as even Sir Farimus had a loyal following by day two of the tournament. He had been a great warrior up to this point, and there were many who would have liked to see this older, friendlier knight win the event.

Amansun continued to match his opponent's strikes well, and his guard was impassable as he swung his shield effortlessly back and forth, meeting every blow with ease as if the shield was part of his own arm. Looking at the eyes of his opponent through the narrow slits in his helmet, Amansun looked for any signs of weakness or fatigue and, seeing none, decided he would have to end the match before he had spent too much of his energy. Stepping back and allowing the other man to take the lead in the fight for a moment, he waited until the knight had committed to a thrust then raised up his sword hand high above his head and drove it down upon his opponent's shield with as much force as he could muster. As soon as the sword hit the shield, it buckled from the force of the blow, bending inward and onto the left arm of the knight. Even from where the announcer was standing, the sound of Sir Farimus's arm breaking could be heard as the knight suddenly fell to one knee and cried out in pain.

"I yield!" Sir Farimus called out as he looked upon the badly damaged shield still firmly attached to his shattered arm. He glanced up at Amansun who was standing down now and said, "Well done, young Prince. That was as solid a blow as I have ever felt in all my years."

The ceremonies master signaled that Prince Halldor had won the match, then he walked over to where the two remaining groups were still locked in battle. In the final two matches, Sir Berardren defeated Sir Watersford and Sir Blackstone forced Sir Camaris into a forfeit, when he caught the aggressive knight's helmet with a smashing blow from his sword's handle, knocking the man unconscious.

As the crowd waited to see how the remaining five competitors would be matched up for the second match, Sir Blackstone could be seen down on the field as he fumbled with his sword and seemed to be having difficulty trying to swing his blade to and fro. Time and time again the knight dropped his sword from his hand as he shook his head in obvious frustration. Seeing the knight's awkward gestures, the ceremony master walked over to the knight who had once again dropped his sword to the ground. "What ails you, Sir Blackstone?" he asked quite plainly.

Looking at his right hand in disgust, the knight announced that he had apparently broken his hand while he was doing in his previous opponent. The knight stood there and tried to open and close his fist but appeared to be unable to do so.

"It would appear that you will be unable to move forward in the tournament, Sir Blackstone?" the announcer half-asked, half-stated, as he watched the man struggling.

"Aye. It appears that will be it for me, I am afraid," the man said with great frustration. "My hand has failed me, to be sure. I fear I will not be able to grasp my weapon even to raise it up to my chest."

Looking over at Sir Camaris who was still seated on the ground with his aides tending to his head, the ceremony master asked, "With Sir Blackstone's departure from the contest, a door has been opened once again for you, Sir Camaris. What say you?"

Shaking his head slowly from side to side, the knight on the ground looked up towards the direction of the announcer's voice and said softly, "Not today, I am afraid. I am seeing three of you even now from the blow I received. You will have to move on without me, I am sad to say." He lay his head down upon the ground once more as his aides placed cool linens atop his head to soothe the aching.

Walking up to the center of the field to address the crowd, the announcer called out, "We have lost two competitors to injury, leaving us with just four for the second round of swordplay. Therefore, the next round of battle will be Prince Brothemus against Sir Glandin and Prince Halldor against Sir Berardren." The crowds erupted in laughter and jubilation as they learned that the dwarf prince, the shortest of all the competitors, would now be matched against the tallest man in the tournament, Sir Glandin. High in the stands, King Hasselfeth glanced over at Lord Mallthus with a look of relief, and the two men nodded at each other while smiling, each believing that the dwarf prince's run would be coming to an end shortly.

Down on the field, the two pairs entered the centermost rings so that the crowds would have the best view possible of this next-to-last match. With a wave of a hand and the sound of a trumpet blowing, the combatants went at each other once more. Looking quite anxious and fearful, Princess Lyleth leaned over to her mother and said, "This is the worst possible outcome, I fear!"

"How so?" the queen asked as she patted her daughter on the shoulder and tried to put her at ease.

"The giant knight is facing the dwarf in this round, Mother!" the princess said anxiously. "That means if the dwarf loses, and I am sure he will, and then Prince Halldor wins his match, then the prince will have to face the giant in the final match!" She sobbed as tears began to flow from her eyes.

"There, there," the queen said as she smiled at the princess. "Prince Halldor has done quite well for himself so far, hasn't he? Let's just wait and see how this round goes before we give up hope, alright?"

Still sobbing lightly but nodding her head up and down as if agreeing with her mother's logic, the princess sat there and wiped the tears from her eyes with a beautiful lace kerchief while she looked down at the action taking place on the field. To say that the two pairs of combatants were battling it out would be an understatement. What was now taking place on the tournament field was nothing less than war. All four remaining competitors were proving themselves to be skilled swordsmen; and the ferocity of their strikes, matched with the speed and intensity of their movements, was testament to this.

While many eyes were watching the match taking place between Prince Halldor and the Red Knight, most of the spectators actually had their eyes glued on the battle taking place between the two grossly mismatched opponents. While Sir Glandin clearly had the height and reach advantage, the dwarf prince moved with a grace and speed as till now unseen before in any of the previous matches or events. No sooner would the giant man swing his sword at the small dwarf than the dwarf would bob and dodge or bend and twist so that the larger man's blows missed him completely, or just managed to glance across his well-grasped shield. The dwarf prince, on the other hand, missed no opportunity to thrust and strike out at the taller foe, and in no time the legs of Sir Glandin were covered with bruises and cuts from the dwarf's merciless slicing and stabbing.

Running out of breath and apparently in quite a bit of pain from the way he was trying to defend his legs and lower body, the giant known as Sir Glandin stunned the crowd suddenly when he strode quickly out of his marked-off circle to get away from the still-swinging dwarf who seemed unfazed by the larger man's size and strength. "Winner!" came the voice of the announcer as he pointed to the dwarf, still standing in the very center of his ring as if not wanting the match to have ended so quickly, and then all eyes turned to the battle still in progress.

Sir Berardren had been one of the top competitors up until this point, so it was no surprise when he and Amansun battled each other to a standstill, each seeming to be able to last as long as the other. In the end it was the weaponry that failed the Red Knight. After an incredibly long and even match, Amansun managed to strike a brutal blow upon his adversary, and with the sound of a thunderclap from the heavens the Red Knight's sword broke in two. As the Red Knight stood there, looking down at what was left of his shattered sword sticking up from the handle he still had tightly grasped in his hand, he looked over at the ceremony master as if to say, "What now?"

Looking at the two out-of-breath warriors as they took an unexpected break, now that the Red Knight had no satisfactory weapon with which to defend himself, the announcer held up a scroll that he had been carrying in his hands throughout the competition and read from it. "In the event that a competitor's sword is broken while battling, said combatant will have to either forfeit the match or choose to go on fighting with the remnants of his weapon if he so chooses."

"Surely I am no match for you with this stump of a sword," the Red Knight admitted to Amansun who was still standing at the ready. "I am afraid I must forfeit." He bowed low to the prince, then turned to look up towards the royal family and also bowed in their direction.

Moving to the center of the field, the master of ceremonies announced that Sir Berardren had forfeited his match due to a failed weapon. "This means that the two princes will be meeting each other in the final match of sword fighting," he called out "We shall begin once these two challengers have had a moment to gather their wits and breath."

Looking across the field some thirty paces away, Amansun saw the enchantress standing there, still in soldier form. As he nodded his head, she slowly lifted one hand up then, using the other, pointed towards a finger. Amansun nodded again, realizing the motion was meant to be a reminder to try and destroy the ring on the dwarf's hand as quickly as possible once their match had begun. He gave a thumbs-up to the enchantress.

To the roars and cheers of the crowd, the ceremony master took the field and signaled to start the match. As the two competitors stared each other down, Amansun realized it was going to be quite difficult to get at the dwarf's ring, as the gloves he wore hid it. *I must strike at his hands and knock his gloves off somehow*, he thought to himself as the pair started to circle each other.

When the blows started raining down on each other, it became apparent that each of these princes would be able to last as long as the other, and that with regards to skill they were also equally matched. Looking at the taller man across from him, Prince Brothemus said to the other, "You may as well forfeit, young Prince, for I have the strength and the stamina to stand here all day if it becomes necessary!"

"You won't have to," Amansun said in a humorous tone as he looked back at the circling dwarf, "for I will finish you off long before that time comes."

As the crowd cheered and hissed, booed and applauded, the two foes met each other's strikes time and time again. Thinking back to his original goal, Amansun realized he would have to change his swordplay if he was to succeed in breaking the dwarf's ring. *I am going to have to take some chances*, he thought to himself as the dwarf met his every thrust and parry with ease. Stepping back from the dwarf suddenly, he began to leave his sides exposed as he held his shield higher in the air than was necessary, hoping to entice the dwarf into thrusting in at his ribs, leaving his hands exposed. As the two moved back and forth, each trying to outmaneuver the other, the dwarf prince started to take the bait and step in with forceful thrusts whenever he saw the man's side exposed. Prince Brothemus bade his time, then when he felt he had a clear shot at the man's ribcage, he thrust his sword arm forward. His eyes winced in pain as the sudden *clang* rang out from where Amansun's sword's blade struck upon his wrist.

So, he is out to break my wrist? the dwarf thought to himself with a smile. *No bother. I shall allow him to swing at my wrist, then…and when he is not expecting it, I shall pull my hand away and swing up at his neck, if that is how he plans on fighting me.*

Time and time again the two met each other towards the center of the ring, Amansun daring the dwarf to stab at his side and the dwarf watching for his opportunity to swing up and take the white rider's head off with one clean swipe. So went the battle for longer than one could imagine until finally, lured by the openness of his unprotected side, the dwarf lunged inwards a bit too far. In that instant, Amansun swung his sword down mightily and with a great smile of success watched as the dwarf's glove flew from his sword hand and landed some five paces beyond the outermost edge of their circle.

Glancing down at his hand to check for bleeding, the dwarf prince laughed when he realized he was uninjured. "Congratulations!" the dwarf yelled out to his opponent. "You have managed to kill my glove!" He laughed hysterically, then bore down on the prince once more with even greater force and speed.

Smiling within his own steel helmet, eyes focused on the blue stone that glittered and sparkled as the dwarf's sword swung this way and that, Amansun took his time setting up his next strike. Even as the dwarf's sword battered against his head and helmet repeatedly as he lay in wait for just the right angle, Amansun waited patiently. With one overly anxious thrust meant to cut into the man's belly, the dwarf prince left his uncovered hand exposed for just a second too long, and Amansun swung down with all his might and watched as the edge of his steel blade struck directly on the blue gem resting upon the dwarf's hand.

With a tremendous popping sound and a brilliant burst of blue light, the exposed stone shattered into several shards, and blue pieces of stone went flying all about the circle of battle. With a stunned look of disbelief, Prince Brothemus stood still for just a moment, as he looked down upon the shattered ring stone that had been resting upon his hand. As he stood there unmoving, Amansun rained down upon his head with the blunt side of his sword, and the stunned dwarf blinked his eyes open and closed once. Then all went dark as he passed out and fell face-first into the dusty field, chalk scattering in all directions.

"Winner!" the announcer cried out wildly to the cheers and joy of the crowd, now jumping up and down and hugging one another.

Up in the stands, the entire royal family—king, queen and princess—all rose as one and shouted with joy as they looked down at the field and saw the dwarf prince still lying face-down, as the announcer called out Prince Halldor as the winner. As they looked across the field and watched Prince Brothemus's name being lowered one spot so that Prince Halldor's name was once again all alone in the first position, King Hasselfeth said with a smile, "I knew the whole time he would do it," and the queen and princess stuck out their tongues at him as they grasped each other's hands and swung around in circles.

"Just one event left now," the enchantress said as she walked over to where Amansun was standing, still looking down at the small pieces of blue stone that were sparkling from down on the ground.

"Does this mean the spell is broken, then?" he asked cautiously, not wanting to get excited too soon.

"The ring has been destroyed, my Prince," the enchantress answered back. "Whatever special powers the Underlord passed on to the dwarf prince shattered along with that ring." She gave Amansun a hug. "Well done, young man…now let's finish this joust event so you can go and claim your prize!"

CHAPTER 39

Standing in the center of the battlefield now, the ceremonies master cleared his throat then announced that there would be a break in the action before the joust portion of the tournament began. "We will see you over at the joust field once the royal family and their special guests have made it over to their seats," he cried out as the enormous crowd began to stir and make its way over the fields to fight for the limited seating available at the smaller venue.

"I'm still not too comfortable with the whole joust thing," Amansun admitted to the enchantress walking along beside him

"Just remember what I told you before," the enchantress advised.

"I know, I know," Amansun jumped in before she could finish. "Knock over anyone who rides in my direction." He laughed.

"That's all you need to do," she repeated while smiling at the young man. "And remember, you are in first place all by yourself now. In order for the dwarf prince to win, you would have to lose early on in the rounds and he would need to win the event outright. I am sure that without the power of his enchanted ring he will fall before ever he meets you."

Making his way over to the jousting field surrounded by his troop of elves, King Eadamantus said softly, "It looks as though King Hasselfeth may have had some good fortune after all. There was a time there when I thought the dwarf prince might actually pull an upset." The other elves nodded their heads in agreement and peered back, as they watched the now somewhat staggered dwarf slowly making his way behind most of the other competitors who still looked ready for the next event.

Once the royal family had been seated, and the other guests and spectators began filling up the benches in the main seating area, the remainder of the crowd filled in as best they could—some moving to the far end of the lists, others crowding the spaces on either end of the long and narrow lanes. Others, who knew they had little chance of seeing more than a glimpse of the action, started to climb up and into the trees that surrounded the field where the joust arena had been set up. As Amansun made his way over to the tents to the side of the jousting field where the horses were kept, he looked over at the seating areas, checking to make sure the princess was there.

"Don't worry, my Prince," Sopehlus said with a grin as he walked alongside the prince and enchantress. "She has been watching your every move these past two days, and she was beside herself with joy during the last event when you defeated the dwarf!"

Amansun blushed, realizing just how obvious his thoughts had been, and he coughed into his hand a bit, trying to cover his red face, mumbling something about just wanting to see if the royal family had been seated so that the tournament could continue.

"Best you spend less time thinking of Princess Lyleth and more time choosing a proper jousting lance, Amansun!" the enchantress offered. "As you can see, there is a large selection to choose from, and you need to find a lance that suits you quickly."

Staring at the long row of lances that had been provided by the king's armory, Amansun was at a loss, having never competed in this event before. There ahead of him were at least fifty lances of all lengths and colors, starting with shorter lances of nine feet and going all the way up to the longest lances measuring a full fourteen feet. Seeing that Amansun was confused as to which lance to select based on the empty look on his face, Sophelus suggested that he try something right in the middle, one not too long or too short. "I've always felt a twelve-footer worked best in my hands, Amansun," he said helpfully. "The weight and balance seem to be just right at that length."

"Be sure to get one with a proper vamplate on it as well," the enchantress added. "Last thing you want in the final event is to get your hand smashed."

"What's a vamplate?" Amansun asked innocently.

Pointing over at one of the closer lances with a conical shield attached to it where one's hand would grasp, Sophelus said, "That's a vamplate! The cone shields the holder's hand and arm from the tip of the opposing lance so that a blow to that area is deflected."

"There…there is the perfect lance," the enchantress said as she walked halfway down the row and pointed at a jet-black lance with a silver vamplate. The highly polished ash wood had been painted to a high sheen and the weapon looked quite majestic. "Best you grab that one before someone else beats you to it!"

Sophelus walked over and grabbed the lengthy weapon just as the other competitors started filing into the tent to select their own weapons. "Yes, my Lady…this one should do just fine," he commented as he picked up the twelve foot lance and looked down its length at the coronal on the end, which had been adorned with four blunted metal prongs, each painted in silver to match the vamplate on the opposite end. "This lance should suit you fine, and it's a real looker as well," he said in a very pleased voice. "I shall go and fetch one of our steeds now." And with that, he disappeared out of the tent.

* * *

As the contestants gathered in their recess, checking their armor, weapons and horses over to make sure all was in order, the crowds outside listened to the master of ceremonies as he gave the invocation. On each side of the lists, wooden walls had been constructed, standing eight feet tall and helping to create the barriers that fenced in the jousting site. On these wooden walls, a tree of shields had been arranged on each side, so that all spectators could clearly see which competitors would be jousting this day. Missing of course were the shields of Sir Farimus, Sir Blackstone and Captain Baerden, who had all been eliminated earlier due to injuries.

"I shall miss seeing you in the joust competition," Hrothgar said to the dejected captain who was sitting at his side. "I think you would have done quite well in this event…even against Prince Halldor," he added, trying to cheer up the king's champion.

Looking even more disappointed than ever, Captain Baerden looked over at his friend and, shoving him in the ribs with his good arm, said, "It would seem your old prince is likely to take it all, my friend; the joust, the tournament, and the princess."

"Well at least Prince Brothemus seems to be on the outs," Hrothgar said with an upbeat tone. "There would have been hell to pay if that abnormally tall dwarf had somehow managed to win the tourney, and that's for sure!"

Looking over at his second in command, Captain Baerden looked into the older man's eyes sorrowfully and asked, "Do you suppose Prince Halldor will take her back to his own lands? Back to the fortress at Argonathe?"

Hrothgar simply nodded in the affirmative and gave his captain an empathetic look. "It's as I suspected, you know," he said as he glanced back over his shoulder to where the royal family sat. "I always knew that if he should win the princess, they would be leaving us." Placing his hand on his friend's shoulder, he continued, "She will not be leaving right away, old friend. The prince still needs to take back that which is his by birthright. But don't forget the fortress has been overrun with goblins and dwarves these ten years past. It will take a great battle and considerable time and effort before Prince Halldor chances taking his newly-won bride back to the lands of the Granite Mountains and the Emerald Forest."

"And what of you old friend? What will you say if the prince asks you to join him on his quest to reclaim his father's palace?" the captain asked, already guessing at the answer.

"You and the king have been very good to me these past years, of that I am plainly aware, my Captain," the elder man said as his eyes began to moisten. "Yet in the end, I have been and always shall be loyal first to my own king, though he died many years ago. As long as his son still breathes, I shall have to pledge my allegiance to him till the end."

Patting his friend on the shoulder as he smiled, the captain replied, "I wouldn't have expected any less from you, my friend. You are a man of honor to the end, and that is just how it must be!"

* * *

When Sophelus returned with the horse Amansun would be riding, Amansun could not believe his eyes. There before him stood a magnificent steed, dressed in white from head to tail, with his own crest displayed brilliantly on both sides of his chest. Atop his head was a polished steel helmet that fit perfectly so that only the horse's nostrils could be seen. The beast's eyes, ears and nose were all covered to prevent injury, should the opposing rider's lance strike the horse by accident. His long mane had been combed over and braided so that the entire animal had a look of grace and dignity but also looked powerful and quite intimidating.

"Your horse," Sophelus stated proudly as he walked the steed over to Amansun. "May he lead you to victory!"

Looking over at the enchantress beside him who had a large grin, Amansun bowed low, right arm tucked into his chest, and said, "A thousand thanks once again, my Lady! Is there nothing that escapes you? No detail too small to be missed?"

"When you have been around as long as I, Amansun, one knows what is necessary and essential in every circumstance," the enchantress said. "I just want to make sure the princess sees you at your best!"

As Amansun prepared to mount his steed, Sophelus walked over once more with a heavy steel plate that bore the same crest of Argonathe upon it. "Not till I fasten your chestplate on, my Prince," the muscular man said as he positioned the chest piece over the prince's left side and began to fasten the many leather bindings that held the piece in place. "You won't last very long out there without this,, he said with a kind-hearted chuckle. "Remember, when you are out there on the field, this is the target you need to be aiming for. Should you happen to strike your opponent anywhere else, no point will be scored, unless of course you knock the other rider clear off his steed."

Amansun asked Sophelus, "Are there any other tips you can give me, my wise and knowledgeable mentor?"

"Hit the other rider first…and don't fall off your horse, ever," he said quite plainly. "If you can manage those two simple things, the rest shall take care of itself."

Amansun mounted his steed and started to head out of the tent as Sophelus and the enchantress followed him out, each carrying an additional lance. Looking in front of and behind him, the prince noticed that the other riders also had their attendants carrying additional lances, and he quickly looked over at Sophelus who was walking on his right. Seeing the puzzled look in his eyes, Sophelus answered the prince's question before he even had to ask, saying, "These are back-ups, Amansun, just in case your primary weapon gives way during battle. It happens quite often, as you will see, and you need to have a spare ready and in your hands within moments for your next pass, or you can be eliminated from a match by forfeit."

"There really is much to learn about this wonderful event, isn't there?" he said jokingly as he looked at the enchantress and Sophelus in turn. "Shame I shall be doing most of my learning whilst my competitors are trying to knock me on my arse, now, isn't it?" All three shared a good laugh.

As the eight competitors rode into the main field, the announcer read out their names as they passed by. Each time a rider passed by the crowd would yell and cheer, sometimes more, sometimes less, depending on the rider. When Prince Brothemus rode in, the crowd was silent at first, but then erupted into loud boos and hisses as the arrogant dwarf held his head even higher and scoffed at them while prancing in. Sir Berardren rode in next and the crowd made a good deal of noise, as he had been a favorite right up until the time that the white rider had shown up unexpectedly. After Sir Watersford rode in to a mixed welcome, Amansun made his way in, sitting nobly on top of his magnificent ride. The wooden stands rattled and groaned under the weight of the cheering crowd, and some of the king's guards got quite nervous, fearing that the entire seating area might crumble under the exuberance of the crowd. Outside of the many field and seating areas, the many tall trees that ringed the area shook suddenly, as the many spectators sitting inside them joined in with loud yells and hoots, shaking the very branches they were sitting on.

Looking down at the white knight as he made his way to the center of the lists, Princess Lyleth felt suddenly faint. "He appears as one from a dream!" she whispered to her mother, who was again seated at her side.

"He certainly appears to be the catch of the tournament, my dear," she replied with a smile and a wink. "It appears that your father's idea is not so to your dislike now?"

The princess scowled at her mother briefly, trying her best to pout as if still quite angry, but then she broke into a smile once more and, looking down upon the prince, said softly, "I guess it's not so bad." The two giggled together as the remaining riders made their way in.

Once all eight riders had been announced and the rules of engagement had been explained in detail, the master of ceremonies walked over to a wooden stand that had been placed towards the center of the field, grabbed the eight flags that had been placed there in his arms, and walked over to the side closest to the main seating area. Requesting that Lord Mallthus join him on the field, he explained that the nobleman was to close his eyes and draw two flags at a time until all eight had been paired into groups of two. In this way the order of the jousts would be selected so there could be no complaints of favoritism. After each grasping of the flags, the crowd reacted wildly as they saw which competitors would be matched up against one another.

Setting the pairings of flags onto the wooden wall so all could see, the announcer called off the first round of matches: "Prince Halldor against Sir Armaris. Prince Brothemus against Sir Antilus. Sir Berardren against Sir Watersford. And Sir Camaris against Sir Glandin. Competitors, please ride to the recess provided at the north end of the field. I will call you when it is your turn." The riders began making their way to the safe haven that had been set up, where no fighting was allowed.

Looking over at the enchantress, Sophelus bit his lip and asked, "How do you suppose our prince will do?"

Looking at the flag bearing the crest of Sir Armaris, the enchantress nodded her head up and down positively, saying, "It could be worse. At least he has not drawn the giant or the dwarf first time around. I think he should hold his own in this match. Let's hope he gets the hang of it quickly, as he may not be as lucky in the next."

Over in the recess, Sir Camaris glanced nervously over at the giant he would soon be jousting against as he cursed his bad luck. "Give me the dwarf prince…even the white knight…just not this cursed giant of a man!" he muttered angrily as he lowered his helmet visor hoping to hide the fear in his eyes.

On the other side of the recess, Captain Balden looked up at the dwarf prince, who looked even more formidable now that he was seated upon a large horse dressed in armor, and said, "Sir Antilus is no match for you, my Prince. He will go down easy, I am sure."

"Silence, you fool!" the dwarf prince snapped back. "Of course this knight is no match for me. None of them shall be. Mark my words, I will win this tournament yet, or die trying. Now go and fetch me some water."

The ceremony master walked in front of the main grandstand to call out the first match. "Sir Armaris rides against prince Halldor," he called out loudly as the crowds stamped their feet and clapped their hands. "Riders please approach!"

Still feeling a bit awkward but knowing he had no other choice but to proceed, Amansun made his way over to the jousting lanes and waited to be assigned an end. Once that had been done, the enchantress and Sophelus walked over to their end, each carrying a lance, and set these down on the wooden rack provided. Looking up at Amanusn as he moved his horse into position at the top of the lane, Sophelus nodded his head once more, saying, "Remember, aim for the chestplate and try not to fall off if you are struck."

The two riders stared down the lanes at each other and closed their visors as they held their lances up in the air. With a blast of the trumpet, both riders started their horses down the two lanes, separated by the wooden-railed tilt, lowering their lances as they tucked the handles of their weapons under their armpits and grasped the lances firmly under the vamplates that each had.

As Sir Armaris began to close the distance between them, Amansun narrowed his eyes and tried to look directly at the small chestplate upon his adversary as he started to lean into his left side, dropping his right shoulder in anticipation of the blow he was expecting to feel at any minute. As both lances found their mark, both riders were driven backwards in their saddles, and the crowd erupted into cheers as the flagmen indicated a point for each man.

The two riders turned their steeds around and brought themselves back into position for the second pass. Over at the opposite end of where Amansun now found himself, Sophelus glanced at the enchantress beside him and said softly with a bit of concern, "Well, at least he managed to hit the target without getting himself knocked off."

Once again the trumpet sounded and the two riders were off, charging down the lanes as they tried to find some way to get the advantage on the other. This time Amansun leaned in a bit further and extended his shoulder forward, hoping to make his lance strike the other rider first. As the two met in the middle, Amansun's lance struck the other rider first and he was sent sprawling backwards before his lance could find its mark. At the ends of the field, only one flagman raised his flag this time, leaving the prince one point up after two passes.

As Amansun brought his horse around once more, this time on the side he had started from originally, his attendants moved in closer and congratulated him on his success so far. "Just one more point and you move on to the next round, Prince," Sophelus said excitedly.

The enchantress looked more worried than before, and she walked up to Amansun's horse and steadied the beast as she motioned for Amansun to lean closer. "Sir Armaris is one point down now, Amansun. He will be the aggressor on this pass, to be sure, as he knows he must win this time to stay in the match. When you are just about to meet in the center this time, lean over to your right side a bit and his lance should miss your chestplate. He may strike you in the shoulder or left side, but he will miss your plate and no score will be given."

"As you wish," Amansun said without question, knowing that the Lady of the Woods had never been wrong up until this point. As he sat up in his saddle once more, waiting for the sound of the trumpet, he realized that leaning to the right as the enchantress had suggested would leave his side exposed to the opponent's blow. *I guess I should prepare for a nasty knock to my ribs*, he thought to himself as he glanced down the lane and heard the trumpeter sounding.

Again the riders made their way down their lanes, each sizing up their opponent's speed and position. Just as the enchantress had guessed, Sir Armaris leaned far forward and at at the last moment his lance struck the prince hard in the side then glanced off his armor. Amansun's lance, meanwhile, glanced off his opponent's shoulder, as he had been leaning so far to the right that he could not get the tip into position for a clean strike. As the two riders brought their horses to a trot and glanced back at the lanes once more, neither flagman raised their flag.

"The win goes to Prince Halldor," the announcer cried out to the delight of the crowd, "with two points to one."

The next series of matches went as one may have expected. Sir Glandin easily won his match against the smaller Sir Camaris, who was knocked completely off his steed on the second pass. Sir Berardren bested Sir Watersford two points to none, as he was clearly the more experienced rider of the two. Prince Brothemus proved to be a worthy rider as he beat out Sir Antilus by a margin of two points to one. As the ceremony master invited Lord Mallthus down to the field once again, there were four remaining contestants left—Amansun, Prince Brothemus, Sir Berardren and Sir Glandin.

Closing his eyes tightly and turning his head to look in the opposite direction of the flags before him, Lord Mallthus reached out once more and set two flags to one side and the remaining two to the other. Opening his eyes once more and turning to see the outcome of his selections, he saw that Prince Halldor was now matched up against Sir Berardren and the dwarf prince was set against the giant, Sir Glandin. *Excellent*, the Lord thought to himself as he imagined the larger man easily winning his match against the dwarf, who by comparison was quite tiny.

Over in the recess, Amansun was receiving advice on how best to proceed against the skilled and more experienced Red Knight whom he would be meeting in battle next. "He's likely the best rider out here," Sophelus admitted as he looked at the other two. "You're not likely to outmatch him with skill alone."

The enchantress shook her head in agreement as she looked over at the Red Knight. "Sophelus is correct," she said frankly. "Now is the time to use your superior strength, I would say."

"And how would you suggest I do that, my lady?" Amansun asked nervously.

"You are just going to have to out-muscle him," she said unblinkingly. "Sit down tight in your saddle on every pass, hold on, and force your way through his strikes. It is the only way you can win against this veteran knight."

Looking very uncertain of this new suggestion, Amansun asked, "Aren't you afraid he will beat me on points alone, My Lady?"

"He may," she said honestly, "but I don't believe he will be expecting you to meet him head-on at every pass. He will be anticipating some unexpected move, so that is where your strength will be. He will anticipate some odd move or strike after the first two passes. On the third pass, when he is looking for something out of the ordinary, you must simply plow him over with your lance and try to unseat him."

"Sounds a bit risky to me, but then again, this is my first tournament," Amansun said sullenly. "It's worth a try at the least."

A moment later the familiar voice of the announcer called the first two competitors to the lanes. "First up will be Prince Halldor against Sir Berardren," he belted out as the two riders and their attendants began making their way over to the jousting lanes. At the sound of the trumpet, Amansun started his steed down his lane, picking up speed quickly and leaning forward as he prepared for what was likely to be a solid strike. As the two riders met in the center, both lances rang out as each took a tremendous hit to their armor. The Red Knight's lance found its mark easily, while Amansun's missed yet delivered a staggering blow to the other knight's armor.

Up on one end of the lanes, a flag was raised, indicating that Sir Berardren had earned one point while none had been given to Amansun. As they made their way to the starting points at the end of each lane, Amansun focused once more on trying to sit down in his saddle and hold on tightly. On the other end, though not visible to the crowd of spectators and flagmen, Sir Berardren was gasping for breath as he tried to recover from the blow to the ribs he had received during the first pass. Looking down the lane at his opponent, he tried to maintain his composure and focus in on his target once more.

At the sound of the trumpet, both riders bolted down the lanes, lances at the ready, as they quickly closed the distance between them. Once again there was an enormous *crash* as the two riders struck each other with severe force, each rising backwards as they struggled to remain seated. This time no flags rose. Neither rider had been given a point on this pass. Amansun had managed to miss the Red Knight's chestplate completely once again, though his lance had crushed in his opponent's armor even further. Fearing a mighty blow as the two riders had approached, the Red Knight had flinched at the last moment, and as a result his lance tip struck high and off his mark as he braced for the impact he knew would be coming.

As Sir Berardren approached his attendants at his own end of the lanes once again, he motioned for one of them to approach and see if his armor was still in place properly. "He hits like a rolling boulder," the Red Knight complained as he attempted to take in a large breath. "I think he has crushed my ribs!"

On the opposite side, the enchantress and Sophelus congratulated Amansun on managing to not only hang on but also to avoid being scored against this time around.

"Down by one point after two passes is very admirable against this foe," Sophelus said excitedly as he held Amansun's lance for a moment so he could rest his arm.

"I think you may have injured him from the way he held himself on that last pass," the enchantress said as she looked down the length of the field at the opposing knight. "Buckle down once more and just try to hit him square in the chest. Don't worry about hitting his chestplate, just try and drive your lance tip right into his center."

As the crowd looked on with nervous anticipation, each rider prepared for the final pass. At the sound of the trumpet, they started their horses down the dusty lanes once more, lances lowered, each leaning forward as they prepared to hit hard one last time. As the distance separating the two closed, Amansun squeezed his thighs together tightly and leaned in as far as he could, lance aimed straight down the center at his foe. Sir Berardren, on the other hand, having a difficult time not only breathing but even holding onto his lance this time, lost concentration. Instead of focusing on the small chestplate that should have been his target, he looked up at his opponent's helmet, trying to see any signs of fear or letdown in his charge. Seeing none, the Red Knight braced for impact rather than aiming his lance properly, and as the two met, the Red Knight's lance skipped off Amansun's shoulder harmlessly, while Amansun's lance found its mark dead-center in the Red Knight's chest.

At first Amansun's lance started to bow up in the middle, as the force built between his own arm and body that gripped the lance and the lance point that was now driving itself into the Red Knight's armor. In a flash of splinters and the crackling of wood breaking away and splintering off into a thousand smaller pieces, Amansun's lance exploded as the Red Knight flew off the end of his horse, floating through the air for a moment, then landing squarely on the dirt lane flat on his back with a thud.

"Winner!" the announcer shouted out as he pointed at the only rider still seated. Back on the other end of the lane, two men—one a well-suited soldier, the other a large muscular attendant bearing the prince's crest—danced about merrily as they hugged each other and skipped about like two young girls.

Turning to look down at the knight still lying flat on his back as his attendants made their way to him, Amansun suddenly realized that his lance had disintegrated and he thought to himself, *I suppose it's time to go and pick out a new one.* He smiled and rode to where his companions were, still jumping in the air and waving as he rode towards them.

Once Sir Berardren and what was left of Amansun's lance had been removed from the jousting lanes, the ceremonies master announced the next pair facing off. "In match two we have Prince Brothemus riding against Sir Glandin!" he shouted as the two competitors made their way to the starting points of their lanes. After the excitement and suspense of the previous match, the joust between the giant and the dwarf was quite ho-hum. While Prince Brothemus managed to hang in there against the giant knight for the first pass, on the second he was knocked clean off his horse in an even more forceful manner than the Red Knight had been just moments earlier. Flying high into the air and spinning once, head over heels, the dwarf ended up landing flat on his face. As he lifted his head and looked up, the crowd erupted into laughter as they saw that he was entirely caked in dirt and dust.

"Winner!" the announcer shouted as he pointed to the enormous man who seemed to be too big even to sit upon a horse. "It shall be Prince Halldor meeting Sir Glandin the giant in the final match!" The spectators applauded loudly and made their way to the stands selling ale to quench their thirsts before the final jousts began.

Up in the stands, Princess Lyleth glanced at her father the king with an alarmed look upon her face, saying, "Do you suppose Prince Halldor has any chance of defeating the giant, father?"

"It matters not," the king replied while displaying a very happy grin. "The prince entered the final event in the lead, and he has outlasted the dwarf in the joust competition, so even if he should lose the match now, in the end he shall still be declared the champion of my tournament!" He looked over with relief at the queen and Lord Mallthus, who also appeared to be quite relieved.

Further down towards the lower level of the stand, Captain Baerden looked over at his friend and said, "Well, that is that, I suppose. It would seem the king has his champion now."

"It would appear that way," Hrothgar replied, seeming much happier than the captain at this moment. "I suppose it's all just a formality at this point." He pointed a finger out towards the jousting field where the two remaining competitors were preparing themselves.

After Prince Brothemus had been given time to gather himself and move off the jousting field with the help of his captain and attendants, the announcer signaled for the final match to begin. The dwarf, still steaming mad now that he had caught his breath again, stood to the edge of the lists just a few feet from the stands and watched eagerly, as he desperately wanted to see Amansun tossed from his steed as well.

At the sound of the trumpet, and with a new carefully selected fourteen-foot lance, the longest they had available, Amansun started his horse down his lane. Approaching from the opposite side, looking more like a moving wall dressed in armor than an actual knight, Sir Glandin came barreling down as well, or at least as quickly as his poor horse could manage. At the mid-point of the lane, when all eyes were directly focused on the two riders, most expecting to see the smaller man knocked clean from his horse, there was a sudden gasp when Amansun's lance actually made contact with the giant's chestplate first, followed by the larger man's lance skipping of the prince's shoulder. One white flag rose into the air, signifying a point for Amansun.

"Imagine that," Captain Bearden said to the elder man at his side with obvious surprise. "This white rider may just take the joust after all."

On the second pass, the young prince's longer lance proved too much for the larger man once again, and a second white flag rose in the distance as the giant shook his head in frustration and disbelief. "It would appear your suitor wants to ensure there is no chance of his failing in winning your hand," the queen whispered to her daughter as the two clenched their hands together tightly.

"I can barely stand to watch!" Princess Lyleth replied. "I do hope the prince manages the third pass without injury."

At the sound of the trumpet, both riders started their last trip down the lanes, each wanting to dethrone the other. When the two met at last near the center of the lane, Amansun lowered himself as close to his saddle as his armor would allow, fully realizing that his opponent would be making his best effort to throw him from his horse. Though Sir Glandin's lance hit the prince squarely, his tip missed its mark a third time, and Amansun breezed by without ever caring to see if his own lance struck well or not.

"Winner!" the announcer called out to the crowd as he pointed to Amansun who was bringing his horse to a stop. "By a score of two to nothing, Prince Halldor is the winner of our jousting event. As a result, he has also won the king's tournament outright. Please join us in cheering our new champion!" he yelled with what was left of his voice after two days of screaming and cheering.

While all around the stands and field spectators rose and cheered the name of the prince repeatedly, there was one who did not feel he was deserving of the win. Mounting his steed once more and riding over to the Tree of Shields with a fighting lance held high in his hand, not one of the tournament lances that were topped with rounded prongs, Prince Brothemus banged the lance handle against his shield and yelled out to the crowd to be silent. "I challenge!" the dwarf cried out so loudly that most of the spectators turned to see what the commotion was about. Pointing to the shield bearing Amansun's crest and banging his lance tip against it firmly, the dwarf called out once more, "I challenge the white rider to a duel!"

Having been so caught up in the moment with Amansun's win and the announcement of the tournament champion, everyone from the master of ceremonies to the king to the enchantress herself were caught quite off-guard by the dwarf prince's unusual and unexpected actions. "The tournament has ended!" the ceremony master yelled out to the dwarf as he sat on his steed, staring at Prince Halldor with an evil glare. "The champion has been declared and there is no going back now!"

"I seek not the tournament win," the dwarf shouted out in a hostile voice, "Nor do I seek the hand of the king's own daughter. I seek to challenge the white rider to a duel, here and now, to truly decide who the best man is."

Walking over to where Amansun was sitting on his steed, looking quite puzzled as were most who surrounded the jousting field, the enchantress said softly so those around could not hear, "You have nothing left to prove, Amansun, and no one shall fault or question you should you choose to ignore this impudent dwarf's challenge." She looked upon the young man's face, trying to guess what his answer would be.

Looking over at Sophelus, who the prince had come to respect a great deal, Amansun nodded his head and asked fearlessly, "What say you, my friend and tutor?"

Sophelus shook his head from side to side, breathing deeply, then said, "Not accepting the challenge would be the prudent choice, my Prince, but it may be better when all is said and done to accept this fool's challenge and end this here and now, rather than casting doubts upon yourself." He frowned as if quite unhappy with his own answer, though it was the one he meant to give.

Making his way down the many flights of wooden steps, King Hasselfeth, surrounded by his personal guard, motioned for Prince Halldor to ride closer. Once he was in hearing distance without the need for yelling, the king called over to him and repeated what the announcer had stated only moments earlier. "You are our chosen champion now, Prince Halldor, and none shall question you should you choose to ignore this unwarranted challenge. However, if you choose to accept, keep in mind that duels of this sort are usually done to the death."

Now appearing to be not quite as certain and, glancing up at the princess who was standing at the edge of her sections railing, he surprised himself when the words jumped out of his mouth without apparent hesitation: "I accept!" He turned to return to his attendants to seek counsel on how to proceed.

"So be it!" said the king loudly as he addressed the crowd, who by now had bunched in even tighter than before, "But be it known that this is a personal duel only, and the outcome shall have no bearing upon the winner or placement of the tournament, which has already officially ended."

"Very well," Prince Brothemus shouted eagerly. "I shall grant you time to go and fetch a true lance of your own choosing, and then we shall meet to settle this. Choose your side and advise me when you are ready!" He rode off towards his small band of followers.

"Brilliant, my Prince!" Captain Balden cried out as he looked at the dwarf prince with a new sense of respect. "You may have lost the tourney but you can still defeats the man-prince. The Great Master will be quite pleased should you slay this foe."

"Exactly," the dwarf prince replied. "One way or the other, I shall return south with honor!"

CHAPTER 40

As Amansun spoke with the enchantress, Sophelus excused himself to go and get a lance for the joust. Being so new to jousting, the prince had asked the more experienced man to select for him. "Be sure to pick a winner!" Amansun joked as he watched the man walking away.

"You know I will do my best, young Prince," he called back. "I shall also return with your sword and dagger, as you may very well need them before this duel is over."

Looking at the enchantress who still wore a grim look upon her face, Amansun asked why he would need his sword if the duel were to be settled by jousting. "In a jousting duel, a true duel, one rider is usually knocked off their horse before three passes have been made," the enchantress explained. "Once a rider has been knocked off his steed, it is customary for the rider still seated to get down from his horse, and then the duel moves forward with swords until one combatant either is killed or yields."

"It would appear I have gotten myself into quite a predicament, wouldn't it?" Amansun stated as the words of the enchantress sunk in. "I must either kill or be killed from the sounds of it."

Looking at the young man before her, the enchantress sighed and agreed. "That is why challenges are never to be taken lightly, Amansun. Before this day is over you will have learned a valuable lesson. I only hope that you live long enough to learn from it!" She glanced across the field to where the dwarf was preparing himself.

Trying to stay positive and make the most of a bad situation, Amansun looked at the enchantress once more and asked, "Do you have any new advice for me, now that we are not vying for mere points?"

"Just make sure you hit the dwarf well! This is not the time to miss. And watch out for treachery, young prince. I feel this dwarf has more evil tricks yet to play, even though his ring of power was destroyed earlier today." She squinted her eyes and studied the dwarf's movements carefully.

After Sophelus had returned and Amansun had his sword and dagger in place, he waved his hand in the air over to the dwarf and announced that he was ready. As he rode over to the end of the jousting lane closest to where he had been waiting, he accepted his new lance, a solid black fourteen-foot one with an incredibly sharp steel point at the end, and prepared himself for the biggest challenge yet of his new life as a man once again.

The large crowd, which had grown since the dwarf's challenge if that were possible, waited in silence as the master of ceremonies and Lord Mallthus walked out to the center of the lists. "This will be a personal duel between Prince Brothemus the dwarf from the Southern Barrens against Prince Halldor, heir to the Fortress of Argonathe and champion of the king's tournament completed just earlier today," he called out. Lord Mallthus then stepped forward and repeated what the king had said earlier, making sure that all present, including the small band of dwarves gathered about their prince, understood that the result of this duel had no bearing on the king's tournament, which had already ended.

As Lord Mallthus looked over at each rider in turn, making sure each was ready for their first pass, he turned to look up at the king, waiting to be given the signal that he could start the duel. With a nod from King Hasselfeth, Lord Mallthus waved at the trumpeter and, at the sound of the blaring horn, the two riders started their horses down the lanes as they raced at each other.

Unnoticed until just that moment, the enchantress realized that Prince Brothemus had changed shields, and the one he now carried seemed to glint and sparkle as he rode down the lane. As she began to realize what he was up to, it became obvious to her that it was too late now. Nothing could be done to warn Amansun.

"He means to blind him!" Sophelus yelled out as he too now noticed that the dwarf's shield was reflecting the sun's rays onto Amansun's armor. "Once he gets the angle just right, Amansun won't be able to see a thing!"

Loud boos and screams rang out as more and more of the onlookers, including the king himself, saw that the dwarf was using his shield to try and blind his opponent with the sun's reflection, a wide beam of brilliant light now shooting directly at him. Amansun, lost in the moment and completely focused on the approaching rider now, couldn't hear a thing as the flagmen and crowd yelled out their desperate cries of warning. The two riders closed upon each other and, just as Amansun started to raise his lance to point it in the proper direction, a brilliant and blinding flash of light hit his eyes, causing him to shut them for just a moment. Then he felt the dwarf's lance impacting on his chestplate, knocking him over to one side as he fought to remain on his horse, his lance torn from his grip.

The gathered crowd groaned and gasped in horror as they watched the horrific impact of the two riders' lances upon each other. Prince Halldor was bent back over to one side, and it was clearly a miracle, or a testament to the young man's will and strength, that he had not been thrown from his horse. Prince Brothemus, however, had fared less well, perhaps by some grace of the gods as punishment for his cheating, and he floated through the air backwards for a distance of ten feet, landing flat on his back with a terrible thud.

As Amansun turned his horse around and trotted back to where his opponent was struggling to get to his knees, gasping for breath as he had clearly had the wind knocked out of him from the impact of hitting the ground, he was stunned to see that the first three feet of his lance had pierced through the dwarf's armor at the shoulder and the tip was now protruding a good half a foot out from his back, while on his front side, another two feet of the black wooden lance was sticking out right up to the point where it had shattered when it struck the dwarf solidly.

Unaware that he had managed to bring this terrible injury upon himself, the dwarf's trickery of blinding his adversary had actually worked to Prince Halldor's advantage. In the final seconds before the two opponents met, Prince Halldor had been trying to point his lance tip directly at the dwarf's chest. However, when the dwarf's shield blinded him, he had flinched unexpectedly, and this caused him to raise his arm up and out a bit, causing the tip to find the point between the top and bottom layers of the dwarf's armor, resulting in the lance driving right through the dwarf's left shoulder. When Amansun had felt his lance being torn from his grip, it was because the dwarf had been pinned perfectly by its tip, his entire weight lifted up and off his horse until enough pressure had built up, causing the lance to snap off three feet from its end. The force of the blow had still been enough to send the dwarf flying to the dusty spot where he was now trying to stand.

Bringing his horse to a gentle walk as he closed the remaining distance between he and the dwarf, who was now standing and desperately trying to pull the massive piece of wood out of his shoulder, Amansun looked down at the dwarf who was quite unaware of his presence and asked graciously, "Do you yield, Prince Brothemus?"

Looking up at Amansun as he continued to try and pull the lance from his body, the dwarf laughed loudly and said, "And why would I do that, young Prince? You should know by now that I hold my sword with my right hand. I won't be needing this arm." He nodded down at his left shoulder and the black piece of wood protruding from it.

"Surely you can't expect me to fight you with that lance piece stuck in your shoulder?" the prince asked honestly.

"If you feel so strongly about it," the dwarf said as he tugged on the wood a few more times, "then climb down here and help me remove this!"

Amansun stepped off his horse and walked over to the stubborn dwarf, grasping the long end of the wooden lance piece with both hands and preparing to yank as hard as he could. The dwarf, meanwhile, placed both his hands on the man's chest and prepared to push himself away at the same moment that he pulled. "On three!" Amansun said aloud as the crowd of spectators watched with great fascination. As he counted off each number, slowly starting with one, the spectators in the crowd found themselves mouthing the numbers at the same time until at last he called out "Three!" and the two men pushed and pulled at the same moment.

The lance piece came out of the dwarf's shoulder and armor easily with the effort of the two combatants working together, as the dwarf prince winced in pain and the crowd cheered, stunned by the unexpected events of the match and the surprising teamwork of the two rivals. Just as they were starting to think the duel might be at an end, and while Prince Halldor was distracted as he looked to the side for a place to discard the piece of wood he now had in his hands, the dwarf reached down to his waist faster than anyone could imagine and pulled out a small dagger, its blade ridged with teeth like a saw, plunging it into the prince's left shoulder, piercing his armor and burying the blade several inches into his flesh.

As Sophelus and several of the king's guards who had been standing close by rushed toward the two combatants, Amansun suddenly raised his good hand into the air, motioning for the men to stop. "This dwarf is a cheat and a liar and no good, it be true," he said as he pulled the dwarf's blade from his armor as blood poured down his arm and chest, "but this fight is still between the two of us."

He turned to face the dwarf and drew his sword from its sheath. "You shall pay for your trickery, loathsome dwarf!" he said as he swung his sword left and right, cutting through the air.

"Just trying to even things up, young Prince," the dwarf said with a hard laugh as he reached for his own blade. "Now you won't have any problem fighting me, eh?"

Neither opponent had time to reach for their shields, due to the highly unusual start of their fight on the ground, so they circled each other slowly, measuring one another carefully, before they stepped in to commence swinging away at each other. Once the two began slicing and stabbing at each other, it became obvious that neither man would have been able to hold their heavy shields in place had they been given time to retrieve them. Each fighter stood with sword lifted high in the air from their right hands as their left arms swung limply at their sides as if dead. Again and again the two smashed their swords down upon one another, yet neither seemed able to crack the other's defense.

As the two continued to hack away at each other and circle to the left and then the right, Amansun suddenly remembered that he still had a dagger tucked in its sheath at his waist. And this was no ordinary dagger but a sword-breaking one, given to him by Sophelus, who had spotted it back at the main armory tent the first day they had arrived and had said it might come in handy if the prince got into a particularly difficult battle. Unlike a traditional dagger with a smooth edge, this dagger had deep channels cut into it that, if held at the proper angle, could be used to catch a sword's edge and, with a flick of the wrist, snap the sword's blade in two.

The two men continued to battle on for some time, and when Amansun suspected the dwarf was beginning to tire, he used what little energy he had left, fighting through the pain, and reached down for his dagger. Timing it so that he raised the dagger suddenly just as the dwarf was bringing down his sword in an overhead slicing motion, the prince caught the blade in the teeth of his dagger. Turning his body swiftly, the great piece of steel snapped in the unsuspecting dwarf's hand and he was left with little more than its handle and a stump of steel sticking from it.

Stepping in as he raised his own sword up to his opponent's neck quickly, he stopped just as its edge came to rest on the dwarf's tough skin and then demanded that his adversary yield. Standing there with a sharp blade fixed against his neck and blood pouring out of his shoulder wound, with no weapon left to defend himself or fight back with, Prince Brothemus finally lowered his head and said, "I yield to you, Prince Halldor, though your dagger trick was ungentlemanly." He spat on the ground near the man prince's feet.

"The black kettle should not call the pot black, or so I have heard said," Amansun replied as he slowly stepped back from the dwarf, whom he now realized could not be given any opportunity. He waited there, sword jutting in front of him, as he waited for Hrothgar and his men to escort the wounded dwarf and his band back to their roadside encampment.

As he passed by, Captain Balden, who was glaring at Amansun cruelly, said coldly, "Better if you had killed him, young Prince. One can only guesses what hardships the prince will face when he returns to the Underlord in defeat!" He walked off with the others who were helping carry their wounded prince away.

With this unexpected match finally at an end, King Hasselfeth, Lord Mallthus, Sophelus, the enchantress and many others rushed over to the wounded Amansun to see what could be done. Further back in the crowd, a very distressed Princess Lyleth called out to the men at the prince's side, asking, "Will he be alright? He's not going to die, is he?" She sobbed into her sleeve.

"Not to worry, Princess," came the voice of Amansun above the roar of the crowd. "'Tis but a flesh wound is all. I shall be quite alright."

"Quite a tough young man we have here!" King Hasselfeth said as he reached out and shook the prince's good hand, which was now free as Sophelus had relieved him of his sword. "I can see why he was the winner of my tournament," he added jubilantly as the realization that the dwarf prince was now out of the picture began to sink in.

Looking over at Sophelus who was now stepping in to grasp his shoulder and help him back to the tents, Amansun smiled and thanked him for the dagger. "Your instincts were quite right, my good man," he said as he started to feel a bit woozy from the loss of blood he had suffered. "If not for that dagger, I care not to guess how this day may have ended."

"Best we get you back to the tent so our Lady can have a look at that wound," was all the man said and he set his arm around the prince's waist, with the enchantress on the opposite side. Together the three made their way off the field for the last time.

As the crowd began to break up and the royal family and their guests watched Amansun being escorted away, Lord Mallthus turned to the king and said, "I believe we shall have to move the crowning of the tournament champion and the celebration feast till tomorrow, my King."

"Quite right you are, old friend," the king replied as he smiled at his daughter, who looked happier today than she had in quite some time. "Please send out our messengers at once to announce that everything will be moved back one day in order to accommodate our wounded prince." He took the queen in his hands and they marched off in the direction of the castle with the princess following, though she looked back several times to watch Amansun's progress as he and his attendants made their way to the large tent where the contestants had been holed up.

Once they had arrived back in the tent, the enchantress pulled closed the curtains that surrounded the prince's resting cot so the three could have some privacy. Transforming back into her young woman form, she helped the prince remove his armor, then cleaned his wound with a pitcher of water that was kept at the cot. "This doesn't look too bad," she said happily as she reached into one of her pockets and pulled out a piece of cloth with some dried leaves in it. Rubbing the leaves together so that the tented-off area was suddenly filled with a very pleasant aroma, like the smell of fresh apples and mint, she applied some of the liquid that had escaped from the leaves onto the wound and informed Amansun that he would be as good as new in a day or two.

"That will be the last time you let your guard down with an enemy close by," Sophelus said rather playfully, as he gave Amansun a look that implied how foolish he had been to turn his back on the dwarf while engaged in battle.

Looking up at the man from the cot he was now laying on, Amansun smiled weakly and said softly, "Just one of many lessons from a very long and interesting day, I am sure," and he closed his eyes and drifted off to sleep.

Glancing over at the enchantress who had a troubled look on her face, now that Amansun was out, Sophelus asked suspiciously, "What is the matter, my Lady? Is the prince's wound more serious than you led him to believe?"

"It's not that, my loyal servant," the Lady of the Woods said as she stared deeply into the eyes of the man beside her. "There has been a strange feeling that has been bothering me all day now…a feeling of foreboding…as if something evil was lurking nearby…or approaching from afar, perhaps." She finished bandaging Amansun's arm. "I need you to do something for me," she said suddenly, standing and grabbing Sophelus by the shoulders.

"All you need is but to ask," the fox-turned-man said eagerly.

"I need you to go out on a mission while I stay here and tend to our wounded friend," she said. "Leave us at once and when you have reached the woods, out of sight from any who may follow, I need you to fly high into the sky and see what might be about. Whatever it is I am feeling, it is not quite here yet, I sense. You must fly south, further than you would normally feel safe doing so, and see what there is to be seen."

Bowing his head low and taking a step back, Sophelus said, "I shall leave at once, my Lady! Look for my return at first light tomorrow." He vanished out of the tent and disappeared down the roadway, making for the thickest patch of trees outside the castle walls. Moments later, a large eagle could be seen as it flew high into the sky, disappearing into the clouds, as it made its way south.

* * *

As word got out that the planned celebrations for the evening had been set back a day, few moped about it, as they realized that this just meant the fun and festivities would be extended another day. This was good news for most and, as the lines at the food stations and ale tents grew longer and longer, minstrels walked about the crowd, already singing songs celebrating Amansun's victory and his glory in battle with the wicked dwarf prince.

Down at the main gateway, Hrothgar gave instructions to double the guard for the night and walked over into the trees on both sides of the roadway to inspect the archers and ensure they were alert and ready. "Double the archers on each side of the road also!" he commanded. "I do not trust this dwarf prince nor his captain. He has already shown himself to be a cheat and a coward. Don't let your guard down for one moment, and call me at once should you notice anything suspicious." He made his way back to the castle to see if Captain Baerden needed any assistance.

That night as the crowd celebrated outside the castle walls late into the evening, the royal family and some of their closest friends and allies shared a victory dinner of their own in one of the smaller, more private dining chambers. Princess Lyleth was too excited to have much of an appetite, but she sat at the table just the same this evening, as she truly felt like celebrating for the first time in weeks. "A toast to our king and his new son-in-law," Lord Mallthus cheered as he stood up from the table and lifted his goblet high into the air.

"To King Hasselfeth," the group roared as they too stood up, glasses raised, and drank heartily, followed by a toast to Prince Halldor who was still being tended to down at the tent.

King Hasselfeth stood after the others had seated themselves once again and thanked those around him for their support and assistance with the running of the tournament. As he looked over at his daughter with a happy and proud smile, he said, "I look forward to making the engagement of my daughter Princess Lyleth to Prince Halldor tomorrow night at a grand feast in the main hall. And I hope you will all be there to join us as we celebrate this momentous occasion."

Another round of cheers resonated from the room, and then the sounds of glasses clanking and plates jostling about could be heard as the small crowd set in to enjoy their meal.

* * *

Down at the tent where Amansun was resting, with the Lady of the Woods sitting at his side, many hours passed before the injured man opened his eyes again to look for some water as he was feeling quite parched. "No need to reach," the enchantress said softly. "Let me grab that for you." She poured a small glass of water and held it up to Amansun's mouth as he sat up a bit and drank.

"Nice to see you in your true form once again," Amansun said with a grin as he lowered himself back onto the cot. "I must admit it has been somewhat awkward talking with you while in that soldier's form these past few days."

"My true form?" the enchantress said with a mischievous smile. "And what would that form be, my Prince? I have so many forms, sometimes I am fooled even by myself. I suppose what you mean to say is that you are happy to be gazing at a young, attractive woman once again." She smiled at the prince who was lazily nodding his head up and down.

"My arm is feeling much better," Amansun shared as he squeezed his hand open and closed repeatedly. "Do you suppose we could give some of that leaf to the others who were also injured during the tourney? Especially that Captain Baerden. He was quite nice to me." He closed his eyes to rest again.

Patting Amansun on his good shoulder, the enchantress said, "I will see what I can do, young Prince. We must be careful to not give ourselves away, though, so I will only be able to give them something that soothes them and eases their pain. If they suddenly wake up with their wounds healed and good as new, the king and his people will likely accuse me of being a witch!"

Opening his eyes just enough to look at the attractive woman sitting at his side, Amansun shook his head in agreement, saying, "Right again, as usual, I am afraid. Best I keep resting and leave the thinking to you, my Lady!"

CHAPTER 41

Dawn came and with it the sounds of people waking up and starting their busy days once more. Since the crowning ceremony and feast for the tournament winner had been set back a day, the castle and its surrounding areas were still packed with hungry visitors, guests and townspeople, all out and about looking for a proper breakfast.

Over at the main gate on the dirt road leading in from the east, the sentries on duty rubbed their sleepy eyes as they stared down the road, hoping to see some glimpse of the waking dwarf company. "Something looks different!" one of the guards shouted over his shoulder to the tent where Ole Barder was fast asleep. "Looks ta me likes they moved on out las' night, I reckon."

Stepping out of his tent as he pulled his trousers up and tucked in his shirt, Ole Barder walked out onto the main road and peered down, shading his hand from the rising sun, and struggled to make out any sign of the dwarves who had been camped out on the road the past several days. "Send a rider to advise Captain Baerden and Hrothgar that the dwarves may have snuck off during the night!" he barked as a nervous grimace spread out across his face. "Didn't any of you fools see or hear anything las' night?" he yelled as he looked at the sentries who were still on guard. "It's gonna be yer asses an' not mine if the captain gets all bent outta shape now!" He motioned to two guards near the horses tied off near the tents. "You two ride on down there and see if they be truly gone. An' be on yer guard. Those dwarves is tricky, now, you heard Hrothgar saying so yerselves just las' night!" The two riders sped off down the roadway.

By the time Captain Baerden and Hrothgar had made their way down to the main gate, the two riders Barder had dispatched had been down to the other end of the road and back again. "It's true," they had said upon returning. "No sign of any of them dwarves down that a-ways now. Nothing but tracks leading off down the road an' a big ole mess from where they had their tents and cookin' stations set up."

Looking down at the senior sentry from atop his horse, a fearsome scowl on his face and his arm tied up in a sling, Baerden reprimanded his troops for not noticing that the dwarves had set out earlier. "There's going to be trouble for those of you who had last watch, and make no mistake!" the captain barked as he instructed the men to raise the gate so he and Hrothgar could ride down and have a look for themselves. "I want the name of every man who had third watch last night by the time I finish my breakfast!" He turned and sped off down the roadway with Hrothgar in hot pursuit.

"Damned all of you good-fer-nothings!" Ole Barder ranted as he spat and leaned over at the man closest to him, as if he were going to strike the shaking fellow. "There goes any chance of me getting that promotion back to the castle now," he added miserably as he walked off to get a drink from the pot hanging over the still-glowing fire.

After seeing that the dwarves had in fact moved on, and riding a mile down the roadway to make sure the tracks didn't double back or head to one side or the other, the two men brought their horses to a halt and discussed their next move. "I suppose them leaving last night is no better or worse than them leaving in the light of day today while we are watching," Hrothgar said, trying to sound positive once again.

"True, it makes no difference, I suppose," the captain said angrily. "It sure does bother me that none of our sentries heard or saw a thing, though."

"Those dwarves can be very silent when they want to be," Hrothgar said as he watched his captain gently rubbing his wounded arm with his good one. "Let's just be glad they are gone and we are done with them."

"Suppose I'll go and let the king know about this, then," Baerden said with an unsure look. "Send a squad of riders out to follow the tracks another ten miles or so, just to make sure there's no funny business going on, will you?"

"Consider it done, Captain," Hrothgar said energetically as he veered his horse over towards the main gatepost while the other rider continued to the castle.

* * *

Some miles down the eastern road, beyond the bend where it turned and started heading south, Prince Brothemus, Captain Balden, and their squad of dwarves were making their way to the spot that had been mentioned the previous night when they had checked in with the Underlord using the captain's ring, since the prince's had been destroyed during the king's tournament. "I've never seen the Great Master so upset before," Captain Balden said nervously as he looked over at the prince who was marching alongside him. "I am sorry that you have been relieved of your duties my Prince," he added as he looked at the prince's face for any signs of what he might be thinking.

"What was it that the wizard said to you last night after he sent me out of the tent?" the prince demanded as he looked over at the captain suspiciously.

"Nothing at all, really," Captain Balden lied, looking forward so as to not meet the prince's gaze directly. "He just wanted to ensures that we mades our way quickly to the spot wheres we are to wait for Prince Karazed and his army is all."

Glancing over at the captain once more uneasily, Prince Brothemus leaned a bit closer and whispered, "I don't believe it would be wise for me to continue any further south with you, old friend. We both know what awaits me once I return to our lord's fortress."

Suddenly calling the dwarves to a halt, Captain Balden raised his right arm towards the prince and ordered four dwarves standing by to bind and gag him. When the dwarves looked at their captain as if he had lost his mind, he shouted out, "Quickly now, you fools, do as I say or you will answer to the Underlord himself!" Before Prince Brothemus could react, he found himself locked in a vise-like grip as others bound his hands behind his back and another shoved a piece of clothing into his mouth then tied it in place with a linen cloth. "I am sorry, my Prince," Captain Balden said with a smirk as he watched the prince being secured. "The Underlord warned me that you might think of escaping, and he said that if anything happened to you before we reached Prince Karazed then I would take your place for your failing to beat the prince in the tournament. Better you than me, old friend." He shook his head, feeling pity for this dwarf who was facing certain torture, then motioned for the squad to move out again.

Still walking along beside him, Prince Brothemus struggled in vain to speak with the captain, who was marching along with a rather smug look upon his face. "No use trying to speak, Prince," the captain said as he looked over for a moment. "There is nothing you haves to say or offers me that would entice me to lets you goes at this point." He turned forward once more and began humming an old marching chant to himself.

*　*　*

With the coming of first light, the enchantress had once again transformed herself into the form of the soldier that had been accompanying Prince Halldor the past few days. Drawing the curtains back so the attendants could bring in breakfast for the tournament winner, she gently shook Amansun's foot and said, "Breakfast is being served."

As the attendants set down trays of baked muffins and rolls, fresh fruits and cheeses, and a platter of sliced smoked meats, they each bowed in turn, then walked backwards as they left the prince's resting area. "Compliments of King Hasselfeth," one of them said as they made their way out.

"Looks like we won't have to seek out our meal this morning," Amansun said as he raised himself up and looked at the great spread before him. "I'm actually feeling quite famished this morning."

"Enjoy your meal," the enchantress said as she stood and reached down to grab a roll and some meat and cheese. "I must go and find Sophelus who had to leave a short time ago. I will return soon."

The Lady of the Woods had begun to worry, now that the sun was up yet there was still no sign of her servant. *Perhaps I was mistaken in sending him out alone*, the enchantress thought to herself as she began walking up the roadway. Just as she was closing in on the lead edge of the trees, Sophelus appeared, stepping from the greenery of the trees, raising one hand into the air and waving. Standing off to one side of the roadway so no others could hear their conversation, he pulled the enchantress closer. "It is as you feared, I am afraid," he said, "perhaps even worse!"

Shaking her head as if she had expected the worst, the enchantress leaned in and demanded, "Tell me what you saw, then. Leave nothing out!" Sophelus took his time carefully explaining all that he had seen the previous night and earlier that very morning. He spoke of an immense army making its way northward. "How long do we have?" was all the enchantress said as she patted the man on the shoulders and thanked him for his help.

"Two days at the most, I am afraid!" the man said with a serious look. "They are coming at great speed, some marching but many others riding on the backs of horses, boars and wolves, and some on great wagons and trailers."

Looking back at the man through unblinking eyes, the enchantress replied, "There is no time to spare, then. I will need to tell

Amansun right away. He will need to convince the king and the others to ride out and meet this foe before they reach the castle. If they get this far, I fear for the worst!"

* * *

Up at the castle, Captain Baerden and Hrothgar had been sitting outside in the courtyard near the stables when to their great surprise they saw Prince Halldor, dressed in his leathers and wearing his sword at his side, walking towards them. Standing to greet the young prince, both men bowed low and said good morning in turn, commenting on how happy they were to see him up and on his feet once again so soon. "Thanks to you both for concern," Amansun said quickly as if in a hurry. "I have urgent news for the king that he needs to hear at once."

"If it's about the dwarf prince and his troop leaving last night, we have already shared that with him," Captain Baerden said as he eyed the prince and saw no sign of a sling or bandages on his injured shoulder.

Seeing that the captain and Hrothgar were clearly distracted as they looked upon his body looking for signs of his injury, Amansun said unexpectedly, "It was but a flesh wound, if you are wondering," and then bade them again to lead him as quickly as possible to the king.

"I believe he is still taking breakfast with his family," the captain said, motioning for the prince to sit and join them for a moment.

Looking quite anxious, Amansun waved his hand to decline the offer to sit and said once again, though this time with much more conviction, "I am afraid you do not understand, good Captain. The king and all of his countrymen, and everyone gathered here at Castle Eladrias for that matter, are in grave danger. I must see his Highness at once!"

"Very well, then," the captain replied. "Let's go at once and see if he has time to meet."

Once reaching the royal chambers, he bowed lowly to the king, removing his helmet and saying, "Begging your pardon. Prince Halldor is here to see your Majesty and share what he is calling urgent news."

"Rise! Rise!" the king said happily as he made his way over to the door and reached out to shake the prince's hand. "We had not expected to see you up and about so early on this new day, young Prince."

Lifting his head slowly, Amansun glanced forward and realized that along with the king, the queen, princess, and Lord Mallthus were all standing close by and looking at him with surprise. "Good morning to you all!" he said as he bowed low once more. "I am afraid that I bring unwelcome news for His Highness. Perhaps it would be best if we stepped out on the balcony for a moment, my Lord?"

"Very well then, Prince Halldor, if that is what you suggest," the king responded. "I shall request that Captain Baerden and Lord Mallthus accompany us, however, if that is alright by you."

"Quite alright, good King," Amansun said as he waited for the others to lead the way. Once the men had made their way onto the grand balcony and shut the door behind them, he began to explain the dire emergency that was facing the king and his kingdom. As he finished explaining the size of the approaching army, along with the anticipated time they would arrive, King Hasselfeth and the other two men stood there with mouths gaped wide open as they studied the prince's face to see if this was some sort of ill joke. "I assure you, your Highness, this is no farce," Amansun said sincerely. "We have two days at the most, then the Underlord's army will be upon us."

Lord Mallthus shook his head in disbelief as he stood there looking at the prince, who he had just met for the first time a few days prior. "How are we to believe these things that you say, Prince?" he asked with doubt in his voice. "The tournament just ended yesterday afternoon! How is it possible that the Underlord could have sent his troops so quickly after he learned that his own dwarf prince failed to win the tournament?"

"A fair question, Lord Mallthus, and one that I can only try to guess at," Amansun replied. "I believe the dwarf's entry into the contest was but a ruse, a way of taking our eyes off the normal day-to-day dealings of running your kingdom."

Captain Baerden also questioned the prince, saying, "You have been engaged in battle these past two days alongside me and the others, my good Prince. How is that you come to know of this approaching army of the Underlord's?"

Looking at the three men staring at him, Amansun replied, "My sources are my own and I cannot share how I know of these things, I am sad to say, your Majesty! Rest assured, however, that the news I have shared with you is the truth, and unless we act swiftly and boldly, we are certain to fail!"

The three men stood there in silence, staring at each other in turn, then back over at the prince again. "There is no way of knowing if these things the prince claim are true, my Lord," Captain Baerden said after a moment of silence. "Yet if they are, and we do nothing to prepare ourselves, then we are certain to be destroyed once this army makes its way to our lands."

Shaking his head in agreement, Lord Mallthus looked at the king and added, "There may be one way we can learn more, my King."

"How so, Lord Mallthus? What would you suggest?"

"The answer lies with King Eadamantus and the elves, my King," Lord Mallthus said as he glanced about at the other men present. "It is said the elves can speak with some of the beasts and creatures of the forest, is it not? Perhaps we can ask King Eadamantus to send an owl or an eagle to fly south and learn what might be approaching."

Grasping the man's shoulder with his right hand, the king said, "An excellent idea, old friend. Captain, go and send for the elf king at once. Tell him that I seek his audience downstairs right away. Tell him that this matter concerns his people and his lands. That should get his attention."

"As you command!" Captain Baerden replied. Then, bowing low, he excused himself from the group and, grabbing Hrothgar on the way out, the two sped down the corridor.

Looking over at the king once more, Amansun nodded his head as if understanding what the king and Lord were up to, and said, "I understand your desire to verify my story, good King, but I beg you, do not wait for the elf king's reply before alerting your soldiers to this danger. Even if the king agrees and can do as you have asked, we will lose at least half a day of preparing for battle."

King Hasselfeth looked over at Lord Mallthus with a look of concern on his face and asked, "And what say you, my long-time friend and counselor? Shall we proceed with preparing our troops at once, as the prince suggests?"

Shaking his head from side to side as he prepared to speak while he considered the options in his head, Lord Mallthus finally answered, saying, "It would be a grave mistake not to act swiftly with the time we still have available."

"Agreed," King Hasselfeth replied. "We must move now if we hope to have any chance of preparing for battle while we can."

A short time later, King Eadamantus and a few of his elves met with King Hasselfeth, Lord Mallthus, Captain Baerden, Hrothgar and

Amansun. "So, Prince Halldor says an army shall arrive in your lands in two days' time?" he asked with no hint of disbelief. "I am a fool for not acting upon my instincts sooner!"

"What do you mean by that?" King Hasselfeth asked anxiously. "Is the young prince's story true?"

The elf king went on to explain that he had felt a strange and evil force growing outside their lands for the past few days. "I have allowed myself to become too involved with your tournament, I am sad to say, likely due to your incredible hospitality, good King Hasselfeth. I cannot say if the prince's claims be true, but I am quite certain that a dark presence is out there just beyond our borders, and it is entirely likely it is the army of which the prince speaks!"

"This is terrible news!" Lord Mallthus exclaimed as he looked about at the others. "What are we to do?"

"It is not my place to tell you how to run your kingdom, old friend," King Eadamantus replied. "Yet I should think your best move would be to gather your troops and weapons and prepare for a march as soon as you feel capable." He turned to one of his elves and ordered them to send out an eagle to scout the lands south of the Great Forest. "We will know with certainty soon enough. For all our sakes I hope the young prince is wrong, but let it not be said in years to come that we had knowledge of an approaching enemy and stood by and did naught. We shall seek you out with the news, be it good or bad, as soon as we have it." He turned and left the room, closely followed by his band of elves.

"And your orders for me, my King?" Captain Baerden asked.

"Start gathering your troops together now. Tell them we must be prepared to ride out to battle and that there is not a moment to spare!"

Bowing crisply, then backing himself out of the room, the captain and Hrothgar sped down the corridors, making for the soldier's quarters and the armory, swearing and cursing as they went.

Out in the castle's main courtyard, four elves mounted their sleek horses and sped off, first heading along the northern roadway that led along Silver Lake, then turning up and into the dense trees and vanishing into the greenery. Riding swiftly along trails no wider than a deer trail, bending low and dodging tree branches as they raced along, the four made quick time as they rushed to the main camp where a group of some hundred elves had been waiting while their king visited with the men from the castle.

CHAPTER 42

High up in her own private chambers, Princess Lyleth was busying herself with brushing her long blonde hair and trying to decide which gown to wear for the magical evening that would be taking place. As her attendants washed her feet and rubbed oils on her skin, they joked about how lucky she was for having such a handsome suitor. "He's like one of the gods, right out of a dream," one said as she smiled at the princess.

"He is a powerful warrior," the other said as she hinted at the young man's virility. "Surely the two of you will be blessed with many children," she added while giggling.

"That's enough now, you two!" the princess demanded, though she too was laughing and giggling. "You must be sure to not speak like that when we are out of this chamber. I would die of embarrassment if the prince should hear you." She looked through her dresser, searching for just the right dress.

Helping hold two of the princess's favorite gown selections, the first attendant asked politely, "So the king will be making your engagement official this evening?"

"Yes," the princess said excitedly. "Once dinner is over, he plans on awarding Prince Halldor with the tournament of champions crown, then he will call me up and the two of us will stand together, hand in hand, as he makes the official announcement."

Lowering her head suddenly, with a look of despair, the first attendant looked at the princess with sorrowful eyes and asked, "You will take us with you, won't you? When the prince takes you back to his own lands?"

"Of course the two of you will be coming with me," the princess exclaimed. "How could I manage without you?" The two maidens erupted into laughter and clapped their hands together merrily.

* * *

The crowds outside moved about as they had for the past three days, enjoying food and treats from the many booths, swimming along the shore of the lake, and watching puppet shows and listening to the minstrels as they moved along, completely oblivious to the fact that an army of cruel and beastly foes were bearing down upon them all the while.

Captain Baerden and Hrothgar were busy getting the king's troops together. "Do you think the king should be telling everyone about the army that could be heading this way?" Hrothgar asked aloud.

"I think not," the captain replied. "That would likely lead to a panic, and that's the last thing we need right now. Besides, these people will likely catch on sooner or later once they see our troops rushing around to get all of our weapons and supplies packed up."

"I suppose we must hope that the prince in wrong, then, shan't we?" the captain offered as he moved closer to give some instruction to the men doing the loading. "Spread out the weight evenly!" he barked out. "We don't want these wagons tipping over!"

One of the men, lifting a particularly heavy box, groaned loudly and asked, "Why do we's have ta load these here wagons fer anyhow's, Cap'n? Ain't no one goin' anywhere anyway what wit' the big dinner tonight an' all."

"Don't you worry about questioning the captain now," Hrothgar warned as he spoke with a clearly detectable growl in his voice. "Just do as your told and the sooner you lads finish, the sooner you'll be back over at those ale tents, right?"

As Captain Baerden looked down the roadway, a cloud of dust caught his attention. "That must be the elf riders returning!" he said excitedly. "Go and fetch Prince Halldor quickly."

Reaching the castle gates at about the same time, the captain and the four riders walked into the castle's main entrance and then parted ways as the captain went to find King Hasselfeth and the elf riders went to find King Eadamantus.

Moments later, the two parties, men and elves, walked down into the main hall, followed shortly by Hrothgar and Amansun, greeting each other with nervous smiles and tense looks. Motioning to the others to follow him, Lord Mallthus led the way down one of the lesser-used corridors, saying, "Follow me. We will use one of our hidden chambers so we can have some privacy." Once the group was safely inside the small and musty interior room, they shut the door and sat around a small wooden table that appeared as though it had not been used in quite some time.

"What news have you?" King Hasselfeth said without hesitation, choosing to skip the normal formal introductions and greetings that were generally followed. "Is it as we feared or has the prince sent you out on a wild goose chase?"

Looking very grim as he spoke, King Eadamantus replied, "If only it were but a dream or a fanciful imagination, King Hasselfeth. The truth is that everything the young prince shared with you this morning has proven to be true! Our scouts have returned, two eagles we have long trusted and had alliances with some fifty years now, and they have seen the advancing army."

"Then the army is real!" Captain Baerden said aloud and somewhat out of turn.

"Yes, the army is quite real, I am afraid. And even larger and more alarming than the prince would have had you believe! The eagles, clever as they are and quite wise too, had no names for some of the beasts they saw approaching with the endless lines of dwarves and goblins, but from their descriptions it would appear that we have some very deadly adversaries marching our way."

"What about the time?" Lord Mallthus said in a panicked voice. "Did they say when they would be arriving in our lands?"

"Less than two days is what we have," King Eadamantus said grimly.

King Hasselfeth rose from his chair slowly then pulled out a scroll which had a well-drawn map of the nearby lands, including Silver Lake, Castle Eladrias, the Old Great Forest, and much of the lands north, south, east and west from the spot where they were now gathered. Pointing first at the castle and then moving his finger slightly northwest, he said, "We may be the first to suffer the Underlord's wrath, but you can be sure your beloved forest and woods will soon follow should we fall." He slapped his open palm onto the table to make his point. "When the time comes, will you stand with us, King Eadamantus?"

"Yes, old friend, we will stand with you,", the elf king replied. "We have but little time to prepare, but I pledge that by the time you and your men are ready to ride out, we will have six hundred armed elves ready and waiting to accompany you."

Lord Mallthus turned to Captain Baerden and asked, "And how many soldiers will we be able to send out, Captain?"

"If we mean to send out all of our troops, leaving none to defend the castle in our absence, then I shall have twelve hundred armed men ready by morning," the captain said with a nod. "It would, of course, be my recommendation to leave at least three hundred men behind just in case the castle should fall under siege whilst we are away."

Nodding his head in agreement, the king said, "You shall leave your three hundred behind, good captain, for we are all aware of what happened to King Hanthris when he left his fortress at Argonathe poorly defended ten years ago, as Hrothgar can attest."

Looking down at the map laid flat on the table, Amansun added, "What we need to do now is to plan our advance on the approaching foe so that we do not have to fight this battle here in our own backyard." He sighed. "Fifteen hundred against some five thousand plus, is it now? It appears we will need to trust in fate, as strength is clearly against us. Is that all we can muster?"

"I am afraid that is the best we can do on such short notice," Captain Baerden replied.

"We are outnumbered at least three to one by the counts given to us by our scouts, possibly even more," King Eadamantus said as he stared at this young prince.

"And that is not taking into account the giants and other beasts that have been seen traveling with the dwarves and goblins!" Captain Baerden added. "When you add those creatures into the tally, we will be hard put to the test."

Looking at the map intently and tracing a line from the forest to the castle, Amansun mumbled to himself, then cleared his throat and offered, "I think I may know how we can get the odds more in line."

"How so, Prince Halldor? Do you have other troops available that we might count on from your father's kingdom?" Lord Mallthus asked.

Shaking his head and jumping in, Hrothgar assured the others that there were none from the north that would be able to help. "The king's old army is scattered to the winds, I am sad to say. I tried to round them up when I first returned near ten years ago, with no success!"

"The help I speak of is much closer than Argonathe," Amansun said with a sly grin on his face. He placed his finger back on the map and pointed at a section of the Great Forest that was a few miles north of the lake's edge, and then said, "Here is where we may find our help!"

Looking at where the prince's finger had come to rest, King Eadamantus stared up at the young man with a look of interest, then said, "Surely you are not speaking of the centaurs, young prince? Though we share the woods with those creatures, it be true, we have virtually no contact with them, and they are a very peaceful and secretive bunch."

"Aye, King Eadamantus, it is the centaurs of which I speak. I know some of them personally, as a matter of fact, and I may be able to get them to join us in this battle. Their lands are in the same peril as ours, are they not?" Amansun said, much to the surprise of those around the table. King Hasselfeth and King Eadamantus looked upon Prince Halldor with a whole new look of disbelief and awe. *Could it be possible that what this prince is saying could be true?* they both thought to themselves as they looked into the young man's fierce eyes.

"If you are able to increase the size of our army, then by all means do so," King Hasselfeth said. "Just remember that we need to ride out as soon as possible if we wish to meet the invaders outside of our own lands!"

Standing back from the table, Amansun asked for permission to leave, then on the way out said, "Gather your armies together as quickly as you are able…I shall journey to the heart of the forest to ask the centaurs' leader for help and return by first light." With that, the prince bolted out of the room and headed down the corridor before anyone else could get another word in.

"We shall take this opportunity to depart as well, good King," said the lead elf. "Look for our troops at first light!" The elves made their way out as well.

Standing alone in the room now, the men looked at each other while studying the map intently, then agreed it best that they start spreading the word of what was taking place as soon as possible. "There will be much panic, I am afraid," Captain Baerden said to the others, "but we have no time and no other choice. Hrothgar and I shall go and alert our messengers so that the word can be spread throughout the land quickly." The two men walked out of the room, matching each other stride for stride as they discussed their strategy.

CHAPTER 43

Amansun found the enchantress and Sophelus sitting outside finishing up their lunch when he exited the castle's courtyard. "It took some doing, and they had to see for themselves that I was correct, but now the king has agreed to march off to meet the Underlord's army before they arrive here at the castle," he shared. "With any luck we will have our own army marching out at first light tomorrow."

Standing up and patting the prince on the shoulder, the enchantress said with a kind smile, "I guess the princess shall just have to wait until this battle is over before she can claim you."

"I suppose," Amansun said rather sadly as the trio started marching off to the tent. "It would have been nice to at least have had the king make our engagement official before we departed."

"I'm sure everything will be quite all right," Sophelus chimed in as he also gave the prince a pat on the back.

Glancing over at the enchantress, Amansun smiled with a mischievous grin and said, "I may be needing your assistance, my Lady." He proceeded to tell her his plan for recruiting the centaurs.

"That may be rather difficult," the enchantress said. "The centaurs are a peaceful bunch, and they are not very trusting of others. Particularly when someone is asking them to leave their precious woods!"

"Exactly why I need your help, my Lady!" Amansun explained. "I had the pleasure of meeting a few of them while hiding at the waterfall cave, as you know, and I am hopeful I can convince them that it is in their best interest to help us fight the Underlord's troops, so that they don't have to fight him off later on their own."

Nodding her head in agreement, the enchantress said, "I can see your point, young Prince, but it may be hard for you to convince them."

"Not if I have the Lady of the Woods at my side confirming that what I say is true!" Amansun exclaimed happily.

"Alright, Amansun. It's worth a try," the enchantress responded, "but you will most certainly owe me a favor, to say the least, if I manage to have them agree to help you!"

Sticking his hand out towards the enchantress as they drew near the tent's entrance, he shook her hand and said "Agreed!"

* * *

Back up in the queen's chambers, King Hasselfeth was just finishing explaining the details of the approaching army, the need to march off to battle at first light, and the fact that he would once again have to postpone the dinner where they would be formalizing the engagement between Prince Halldor and their daughter, Princess Lyleth. "I am staying out of this one!" the queen said emphatically as she put her hand up in front of the king. "Our daughter is already up in her room trying to decide on what to wear this evening, and I don't plan on being there when you tell her you are moving the event back again."

King Hasselfeth smiled at his wife at first, then his face turned grim as he replied, "There may be no dinner to celebrate, should we not defeat the Underlord's army."

"You make a very good point, my King," the queen said suddenly, as she only just now realized the seriousness of the situation. "You go and prepare for your march, my husband. I shall go and tend to our daughter, though I fear it will not make it any easier on you in the long run."

Leaning forward and kissing the queen gently on her forehead, the king thanked his wife and walked out of the room to meet up with Lord Mallthus and his other noblemen to determine what they needed to accomplish prior to the new day.

* * *

As word spread of the approaching army and the need for the king's troops to march off to battle the next morning, the feeling around the castle and Silver Lake changed from one of joy and excitement to fear and dread. Though the Underlord's dwarves had visited every year to collect tribute from the king, they had never posed any real threat, and the townspeople had become comfortable and felt they were quite safe in the area. Talk of dwarf soldiers and goblins, mixed in with rumors of giants and other foul creatures, had every woman and child, and even more than a few of the men, cowering with fright and wondering if the king's army would be able to defeat the Underlord.

"Ain't no good come from marching 'gainst the wizard an' his armies," one soldier said to another as they loaded more bolts onto one of the crossbow carriages. "I hurd the last army that faced his goblins and dwarves got all tore up something bad an' none ever heard from those mens again!"

Looking over at the older man who had been speaking, a younger soldier, fit and anxious for the battle, responded, "You can always stay an' hides here wit' the womans and childrens, old fool, least till we's get back from winning or the dwarves shows up from us a-losin'!"

"We'll see whose a-laughin' when those dwarf riders on wild boars come roarin' across the fields o' battle," the older soldier said as he eyed the youngster. "It's easy to be brave when there's no one standin' b'fore ya!" He walked around the wagon to pick up another bolt.

As Captain Baerden and Horthgar surveyed their men while they emptied out the armory and handed out weapons and armor to the hundreds of men and soldiers that had been lined up outside the castle's walls in a long line that snaked its way into and out of the main courtyard, Captain Baerden looked over at the other and said, "Sure would be a nightmare if the elves and centaurs decided not to show tomorrow! Nine hundred against five thousand seems like a cruel joke."

"I can't say about the elves and King Eadamantus," Hrothgar said as he looked at his captain with a rather sour expression, "but I know Prince Halldor will show tomorrow morning, centaurs or no!" He walked back into the armory to see how their stock of weapons was holding up.

"I didn't mean anything by it," the captain called out to his friend who was storming off, obviously upset about the comment.

* * *

It took nearly two hours of riding to reach the dense part of the forest where the centaurs had their main village, but with some guidance from Sophelus who had scouted these areas many times before, the three riders found themselves approaching a heavily wooded valley with hoofprints covering the damp earth in all directions. "We'll be at their main village in just another half mile or so," Sophelus whispered as he peered about the woods in search of sentries. "I'm surprised we made it this far without being challenged."

Suddenly from out of the deep thicket of trees ahead, a large group of armed centaurs walked out onto the dirt path the riders had been following, raising their shields and spears into the air and demanding the riders stop where they were. Stepping out from behind several of the largest centaurs at the front, a very old and wise looking centaur made his way towards the trio slowly, looking them up and down carefully. "Though I see but three men riding before me, I sense the presence of the Lady of the Woods," the elder said with a soft knowing smile.

Riding up ahead of the others, the enchantress moved her horse up a few paces so that she was looking eye-to-eye with this centaur elder. "You are as wise as you appear," the enchantress said as she suddenly transformed into her middle-aged woman's shape. "Long has it been since your kind has ventured into my own black woods, though there is no ill will between us."

Looking at the woman with a nod of his head, the elder centaur raised his right arm in friendship and responded, "It is long since we have seen you out of your woods, great Lady, and we have respected your wishes to not be disturbed all these long years. What is it that brings you now to our own lands?"

"Trouble, my good centaur," the enchantress said with a serious look. "It is trouble that brings me and my friends here to your valley. We wish to speak with the elders and our need is urgent." She bowed her head once, much to the surprise of Amansun.

Bowing in turn to the enchantress, the elder centaur replied pleasantly, "Our scouts have been watching your progress as you approached, so we knew you were seeking us out for some reason. Follow me and I will take you to the great gathering field where our council is already expecting your arrival."

Moving closer together, the three riders found themselves being directed to a narrow pathway that meandered along a steep trail, falling off on one side to a rocky stream far below, as a group of some fifty centaurs hemmed them in on the front and the back.

* * *

That evening, as women and children broke down the food booths and tents that had been set up days prior for the king's tournament, very little was said as they went about the business of gathering anything useful that needed to be moved within the castle walls. It was important that as little as possible be left remaining outside, as the dwarves and goblins could use these pieces of wood and tarp and such later if they happened to make it up to the castle in the days ahead.

Looking over at the sturdy bleachers and seating areas that had been constructed for the tournament, Captain Baerden realized there was no time to break these well-built structures down. "You will have to set these on fire should we fail," he told one of his soldiers, who would be among the group staying back to defend the castle. "If the battle goes poorly, I will send out a messenger to give you as much time as possible to prepare for the approaching army, and you must remember to burn those bleachers to the ground or the dwarves will us them to build ladders to scale our castle's walls."

"You will be victorious, my Captain!" the soldier said as confidently as he could. "It will be you and your troops we see coming down the roadway once the battle is done."

* * *

Up in the castle heights, Princess Lyleth was locked in her room, crying face-down on her bed as she wept at the thought that her soon-to-be fiancée would be marching off to war. "I won't even be able to say goodbye or wish him luck," she blubbered as one of her attendants ran a comb through her hair, trying to console her. "He's off in the Great Forest searching for more troops to fight in the great battle," she complained, though she knew the more help the prince could get, the better his chances of survival would be.

"Of all the men who march off to battle tomorrow, my Lady, yours will be the most likely to return," the maiden said as she continued to comb the princess's long hair.

* * *

As darkness spread over the land, animals scattered this way and that at the sound of the approaching army as it marched across the barren fields and meadows that lay across much of the area south of the Old Great Forest. Prince Karazed pushed his troops mercilessly as he sat atop a giant wooden platform being carried by two dozen of his strongest soldiers. "Keep them moving!" he commanded as he looked out upon the mass of bodies that was marching ahead, behind, and on both sides of his personal guard. "The Great Master has commanded that we arrive at the lake of silver by the day after tomorrow, and I do not plan on disappointing him!" He reached for his whip and cracked it high into the air, sending those closest to him scurrying all the faster.

Coming from behind, the booming rhythmic sound of beating drums could be heard as a line of fifty drummers beat on their heavy leather skinned drums, setting the pace for the marching army. Up in the lead, packs of dwarves and goblins riding on the backs of wild boars kept close to the heels of four enormous giants as they moved along with their great strides, clubs swinging from side to side in their hands as they scoured the distance for any signs of foes. Back towards the end of the quick-moving army, eight monstrous wagons rolled along, each being pulled by a team of massive bulls with horns spanning six feet across, and dwarves standing on top of the large wooden containers that sat upon each wagon as the cargo inside wailed and groaned in eerie unison as they called out to each other.

High above in the sky to the north, a greenish yellow light flickered as it appeared to float up near the clouds. "One of the watchers is out," a silver bearded dwarf said to Prince Karazed as he looked off into the sky.

"It means not to us," the prince responded with disregard. "They lost their powers long ago, the Great Master took care of that. Let them watch and be witness if they like. There is little else they can do!" He leaned over the side of his floating chariot and called out for the carriers to move faster. "Stay in pace with the beating drums or I swear there will be casualties long before we reach the battle!"

* * *

Long after second dark had come, Captain Baerden and Hrothgar made their final rounds before heading in to get some rest. As they stopped at the various sentry posts along the northern roadway along the lake and at the main castle gates, the captain reminded the men that they were expecting allies to arrive by first light. "Have a care who you go shooting this night!" the captain warned. "There should be at the very least a large group of elves approaching by first light if King Eadamantus is true to his word. Look also for the return of Prince Halldor who has set out to gain assistance from the centaurs that live north of our home." This caused quite a stir among the men who knew these creatures existed but rarely saw them, if ever, because of their reclusive nature.

"Right you are, Captain," the lead sentry said as the two men walked into the courtyard and headed into the guards' main quarters.

"Not sure I likes the idea of goin' ta war with those horse people," one of the gate sentries whispered.

Looking at the man with raised eyebrows, another replied, "Better fighting alongside them than against them!" Turning to the others standing atop the main gateway, he shook his head once, then said slowly and softly, "Besides, every one of them centaur folk that rides along with us makes one more target for them goblin archers to shoot at instead of us!" The others grinned and shook their heads as they realized how smart and practical their lead was.

As the captain and Hrothgar disappeared into the building, the elder suddenly reached out to stop the captain and said as he reached into his pocket, "I nearly forgot to give this to you, Captain. A gift from one of the prince's attendants who stopped by earlier in the day." He handed the captain a small pouch.

"What is it, old friend?" the captain asked as he eyed the leather pouch suspiciously.

Looking at the captain with a shrug of his shoulders, Hrothgar admitted, "I am not sure exactly…the man said it was something the prince uses when he is injured. I believe it is meant to help you heal?"

"I suppose it is worth trying, then," the captain said as he opened the pouch and saw some dried leaves inside the bag. A small handwritten note that was also enclosed said, "Add this to some water and drink to soothe your arm." Looking over at the older man who was ready to bid goodnight, the captain smiled and said, "If I don't wake tomorrow morning, you will know the reason." He showed the man the note, then walked off towards his private quarters.

CHAPTER 44

That dark night was filled with everything from restful slumber to restless tossing and turning, depending on whom you spoke to. Half of the townsfolk and soldiers felt like the night would never end as they tossed in their cots and beds, staring off into the darkness as they struggled to close their eyes and get some rest to no avail. The other half closed their eyes and found themselves opening them up just a moment later only to find that the night had passed already, and that even though they were tired it was now time to get up and face the new day.

Up at the north watchtower, the two sentries posted at the top whistled twice softly, then again in quick fashion, to alert those below that something was on the move at the perimeter of the woods. As the archers on the ground fitted their arrows to their bows and stared out into the blackness searching for a target, they were suddenly taken aback when to their amazement an entire legion of elves appeared out of the morning mist with no more noise than the sound made when leaves flutter in a soft afternoon breeze. The lead sentry on duty called out to the others to stand down, and they all watched in awe as a seemingly endless procession of elves marched by. "Looks like every elf in the woods has come outs to fight with our king!" he said softly to his men.

Turning to look at the man who had been standing some twenty paces from where the elves were marching by, one of the elves standing just a bit out from the others who gave the impression of being higher in rank somehow called over in a whisper, "Just six hundred of us, my good fellow." He smiled. "Don't worry, now, as the woods are still quite protected by our bothers should we fail to return." Then he faced forward once more and continued moving along with the others.

Up at the castle, an out-of-breath messenger kneeled alongside the cot of Captain Baerden and said, "The elves are approaching, Captain…it looks like all of them, too!"

Sitting up quickly, then standing and reaching for his sword and leathers, the captain waved the messenger off, saying, "Go and wake Hrothgar as well, then return to your post." The man vanished as quickly as he had come.

As Hrothgar entered the captain's room a few moments later, he looked at the captain as he finished tying his leathers in place and then asked, "Any word of the prince, Captain?"

"Nothing yet," came the captain's reply, "though I am sure he will be here by first light or shortly thereafter if he is able,", he quickly added, not wanting to offend his friend again like he had just the night before.

"Unless the centaurs capture him and hold him prisoner, the prince will return," Hrothgar said with a steady voice and a confident look. "Shall we have something to eat while it is still dark out?"

Nodding his head and slipping a dagger into his boot, Captain Baerden led the way out of the room and down the corridor, saying, "I made arrangements for a simple breakfast to be ready for all of our troops, and our visitors as well now that they have shown up." He pointed out to the main courtyard that was now lined with large wooden tables covered with platters of fruits, meats, cheeses, breads, jams, jellies, spreads and the like. "We may as well share one more good meal together, especially since this may be our last!"

The two men walked over to the main gateway, which had been raised into the open position, and watched as the countless rows of elves began appearing up the road in the dim light. At the lead of the marching elves, King Eadamantus and Mythra were engaged in conversation as they smiled and joked, giving no indication that they were preparing to march into battle against a deadly foe in the very near future.

"There's the king himself!" Hrothgar said to Captain Baerden as they walked outside the courtyard and onto the roadway facing west.

Taking his sword from its sheath and raising it high into the air, Captain Baerden suddenly called out loudly, "Three cheers for King Eadamantus and his warriors!" to which all the guards and soldiers nearby roared the name of King Eadamantus three times as they cheered, hollered, and swung their swords and spears into the air.

The king and his elves came to a halt just outside the castle gate, and then greeted the captain and Hrothgar with a handshake. "Please come in and have a bit of breakfast," Captain Baerden offered as he bowed and then pointed towards the heavily laden tables of food. "Your presence is most appreciated, my Lord."

Explaining that he and his troops had already eaten much earlier, the elf king looked about at all the wagons and carriages lined up outside the castle and asked, as if quite anxious to get moving, "And when will you and your men be ready to set out?"

Turning around and looking northeast, the captain replied, "When the new day's sun rises over the top of the Granite Mountains, we will depart. We are still waiting to see if Prince Halldor has had any luck with getting the centaurs to join us, as you are the first to arrive."

"Very well, then," King Eadamantus replied as he gave the order for his elves to spread out and wait for his signal. "This will certainly be a monumental occasion, win or lose, if the prince is able to return with the centaurs as he hoped. It has been long since the three of our kind gathered to face a common foe."

Turning to his friend, Captain Baerden told Hrothgar that he needed to go and inform the king that the elves had arrived. "I am sure the king and queen must have figured that out by now, with all the noise your cheers created," the older man said with a grin.

"Nevertheless," the captain continued, "I must give an official announcement, as you are well aware." He gave a dry smile.

Patting the captain on the back as he turned to walk over to the nearest food table, Hrothgar said, "Be sure to hurry back or you may miss your chance for a nice meal," and walked off as the captain made his way across the courtyard heading into the castle. Suddenly stopping in place and spinning on his heel, the older man stared at his captain's arm and grinned, as he realized that the man seemed to be using it as he had before it was injured in the tournament. "I see you were brave and put that gift to a test last night, my Captain?" Hrothgar muttered.

Swinging his arm back and forth and up and down, the captain smiled back and said, "Seems as good as new! Perhaps there is more to the prince than meets the eye."

As the dark of night gave way to the breaking day, more and more troops found their way to the courtyard and helped themselves to the breakfast feast. Coming out from what was the competitor's tent, most of the knights, already dressed in full battle gear with their attendants at their sides, emerged and made their way over to the stables, stopping to collect some food along the way. "I take it you all plan on joining us on the march against the Underlord's army?" Hrothgar asked as he welcomed the knights to the breakfast tables.

"Wouldn't miss it for the world," said the Red Knight as he grabbed some cheese and rolls. "Besides, should your army fail, the Underlord will likely move on to my own lands."

Walking up to Hrothgar, Sir Glandin laughed as well, saying, "There are few giants left where I come from. I have always fancied testing myself in battle against one of these creatures, and this looks to be my chance!"

Following the others, and looking less confident, Sir Blackstone approached and said, "Not sure how much use I will be with but one good hand, but I won't be known as the coward who remained behind while all others risked their lives." He shook Hrothgar's hand and moved on to the food tables as well.

"Don't you worry about that hand," Hrothgar said mysteriously, as he watched the knight walking by. "My captain has something that might just take care of that for you."

Once the king had been dressed and escorted down to the courtyard where the army was gathering, a loud cheer rose from the troops who all stood and waved their swords and spears high into the air. Even King Eadamantus and his elves stood at the sight of King Hasselfeth, who was now adorned in his own regal suit of armor. Turning to the captain who had left his quarters some time earlier, he asked if the young prince had returned with the centaurs yet. "There has been no sign of them," the captain responded sadly.

"Well, I am afraid we won't be able to wait for the prince," the king said earnestly as he gazed out at the large number of troops that now filled the courtyard, the roadway, and the fields just outside the castle walls. "If the prince intends on joining us in battle, he will just have to catch up with us on the road." He signaled for Lord Mallthus to approach. "I believe we are ready to move," he told his lead counsel, who did not appear to be dressed for battle or travel. "You will remain behind with the queen and princess and keep watch over Castle Eladrias while we are away. Pray we are successful, or you may have the worst of it."

"We will do our best to defend your fortress whilst you are away," the Lord said as he bowed lowly to the king. "May the heavens be with you!"

Captain Baerden lifted his hands to signal the trumpeters, and with the sounding of the horns, the king's army started the first steps of its journey to meet the Underlord's own troops. As the harnessed horses leaned forward to get their wagons and carts rolling, and troops began to settle into the pace of the march, those remaining behind at the castle wept and cheered as they waved at their friends and loved ones while the long procession moved along.

High atop the castle's walls, the queen and princess stood on one of the great stone balconies and waved their linen kerchiefs as they struggled to hold back their own tears. "I don't see any sign of the prince or the centaurs," Princess Lyleth managed to say in between sobs.

Placing her arm over her daughter's shoulder and squeezing her tightly, the queen said, "I am sure the prince is just fine, my dear. He probably means to catch up with the army further up the road."

As the army's pace began to quicken, the sounds of rolling wheels, marching boots, clomping horses and mumbling men filled the air. The growing noise of the moving mass grew louder and louder until the voices of those staying behind and cheering was drowned out altogether. Riding out front at the lead of the army, King Hasselfeth, King Eadamantus, and their captains and chiefs were busy chatting amongst themselves as they discussed their battle plans and commented on the size and strength of the troops they had gathered together.

As the lead of the procession passed by the main gateway where Ole Barder and his sentries were standing, a loud noise from behind caught the army's attention. Sounding faint and far off at first, and then rising to a loud and strong note, a beautifully sounding horn was being blown powerfully from somewhere back near the castle and lake. As the two kings and their leads swung their horses around to face back down the roadway leading to the castle, a lone rider raced up the dirt track, hand waving high in the air frantically as he tried to get their attention, a cloud of dust trailing behind his steed. Peering down the roadway, Hrothgar turned to his captain and said, "I do believe he is signaling us to stop, my Captain."

"I do believe you are right," Captain Baerden said as he glanced over at the king for his permission to stop the armies' advance. Nodding his head as he too leaned forward in his saddle to try and hear what the young rider was shouting as he drew nearer, King Hasselfeth gave the captain permission to bring the long line to a halt.

"The prince has returned!" the rider called out as he drew even closer. "The centaurs are here! The centaurs are here!"

Looking over at King Eadamantus and the others, King Hasselfeth raised his clenched fist into the air and shook it back and forth as he smiled triumphantly and said, "Truly the gods are with us, my friends. That young prince seems to have appeared in our very hour of need once again, as if sent from the heavens."

Looking at the front of the thick pack of moving beasts, Baerden and Hrothgar could easily make out the forms of the prince and his two attendants, as they were quite distinguishable sitting upon their horses, dressed in leathers and soldier's attire, unlike the centaurs whose chests were bare, aside from a small number who had heavy leather vests on. Riding down the road, the two men brought their steeds to a halt when they were within a few hundred yards of the approaching pack. Raising his sword into the air in a sign of greeting, Captain Baerden called out to the group and greeted them on behalf of the king.

Bringing his horse to a canter and walking the last few paces slowly, Amansun grinned from ear to ear and pointed over to the centaurs riding alongside him as he started the introductions. "This is Eodren, king of the centaurs, along with his sons Eldenham and Articlese," the prince said calmly as he drew his horse closer and shook hands with the captain and Hrothgar.

Looking at the prince with great pride, Hrothgar slapped the young man on the shoulder and stated loudly, "We knew you would return with help, young Prince, but never did we imagine your numbers would be so great!"

"'Tis true, good Prince," the captain added as he looked down the long line of centaurs all standing in place and looking forward at the group in the lead. "How many of you are there?" he asked excitedly.

"We are four hundred in number," King Eodren said proudly as he stepped forward and lifted his spear high into the air. "It is not our way to fight so far from our beloved home, but the good prince and the Lady of the Woods have explained the great danger approaching, so we will now join with you in battle against this common enemy." He looked down the line of centaurs and waved his heavy wooden shield and spear into the air once more. Up and down the roadway from front to back, all four hundred centaurs raised their weapons in kind and stamped their hoofs on the dirt loudly as they cheered and shouted out.

"We are glad to see you, Prince Halldor, and your timing is great, as we had just now started marching out to meet the Underlord," Captain Baerden said as he eyed the large gathering of hoofed men. "We should be on our way at once, as King Hasselfeth and King Eadamantus are at the front of the column. Even now, they must be wondering what is happening back here at the rear."

"We shall be ready to ride soon enough, good captain," Amansun replied, "but first I must stop at the great tent to gather my other weapons and suit of armor."

Noticing for the first time that the prince was dressed only in his leathers, Captain Baerden shook his head in agreement and then said, "Gather your things as quickly as you can and let us know when you are ready to depart, Prince. I shall go and inform the king of your presence as well as the centaurs you have brought along. Is it possible for King Eodren and his sons to ride along with me so that I may introduce them to our two kings at the front?"

"By all means," Amansun responded. "Please do the introductions for me while my attendants and I prepare for the journey. We shall catch up with you at the front of the procession shortly." He and his two riders made their way up the road towards the castle.

Turning to look at the king of the centaurs once more, Captain Baerden said, "Please follow me and I shall take you to our king at once." He then bowed and turned his horse to follow the road east.

Once inside the great tent where the knights of the tournament had been camped, the enchantress turned herself back into the form of the young woman she felt the prince was the most comfortable with. Reaching out and taking Amansun by the hand, she said, "Sit with me for a moment," and led him to the cot where the prince had rested before.

"Is something the matter?" Amansun asked, as he could clearly see that something was bothering the enchantress.

Looking directly into Amansun's gaze, the Lady of the Woods said unexpectedly, "This is as far as we will be able to go for now, young Prince," as she glanced over at Sophelus and the other attendant who had been waiting at the tent for their return. "We will not be riding on with you to meet the Underlord's army."

Looking stunned and in disbelief, Amansun shook his head and fought to overcome his emotions, as he began to feel panicked for the first time in many days. "What's the matter, my Lady?" he managed to stammer. "Have I done something to upset you?"

"It is nothing you have done…and I should have told you sooner," the enchantress replied with a sigh. "You see, I am one with my woods and they are one with me. I must remain near them, or my power weakens."

"You are one with the woods?"

"Yes, my young prince," she responded. "The woods and I are joined together, you might say. We each draw power from the other, and without one another we would perish."

"So, you are saying you get your power from the woods themselves? And if you leave them behind your power will be lost?" he asked once again as he looked at her with pleading eyes.

Nodding her head up and down, the woman answered, "That is the way it is, I am afraid. Should I ride off with you today, my powers would rapidly diminish. By the time we were one day's ride away from the Black Woods, my power would be but a shadow of what they are here. I wouldn't even be able to maintain the image of the young soldier the king's people have grown so used to seeing accompanying you."

"Then I shall be riding off to battle the Underlord's armies by myself? Is that what is meant to be?" Amansun asked in desperation.

"Not alone," the enchantress replied with a smile. "You are surrounded by new friends and allies, my Prince. Even now they wait for you to ride out and join them."

Shaking his head in disbelief, Amansun looked back over at Sophelus and then the enchantress and asked, "And what will become of you? What shall you do while I am away? Return to your home in the woods?"

"Of course not," the enchantress said as she leaned forward to comfort Amansun who was obviously quite shaken. "We shall remain here at the castle to keep an eye on the princess for you while you are away. Should you fail in your quest, we will do everything within our power to protect the princess and save her if we are able."

"Very well, then," Amansun mumbled as he stood up and prepared to load his armor onto the horse standing a few paces away. "I shall load up my things and be on my way," he added as he held back the tears that were starting to form.

"Not with that horse," the enchantress said jokingly. "Unless you want to find yourself riding atop a rabbit in a day's time."

"A fine sight that would be indeed," joked the prince, now starting to get his confidence back once more.

"I shall go and fetch you a proper steed from the castle's stable," Sophelus said as he walked towards the front of the tent. "Get your things packed up and I will be back in but a moment."

Now standing alone again, the enchantress took Amansun's hand in her own once more and, looking deep into his eyes, said slowly, "Remember, Amansun, you must control your emotions on the battlefield. If you should lose your wits, you are likely to lose more than just the battle."

"I will do my best, my Lady," Amansun responded. "But I truly would have felt much better riding into battle with you and Sophelus at my side!"

"Perhaps another time," was all the enchantress said.

Once Sophelus had returned with a true horse, the three quickly packed up the prince's items and then walked together towards the roadway where the large army was still standing at the ready. As Amansun mounted his horse, his attendants waved at him cheerfully and wished him great success in the battle.

"I will see you again soon," Amansun called out as he rode off towards the main gate. "Tell the princess that I will be back for her hand in marriage as soon as I am able!" his voice called out as he quickly faded down the roadway.

CHAPTER 45

Joining the others at the head of the column, Amansun and the others exchanged their morning pleasantries along with comments of thanks for succeeding in getting the centaurs to join the battle. Once all that needed to be said had been said, the king motioned for the army to proceed again, and with the blast of the trumpeter the great line of combatants started down the road once more. "How far off do we think the enemy is?" King Eodren asked Prince Halldor as they marched along.

"It's difficult to say," King Eadamantus said, breaking into the conversation. "Our allies the eagles spotted their position early yesterday and reported them as being at least two days' out at the time."

Looking up at the bright blue sky, Captain Baerden said, "It's been fair weather the past few days…likely they are within but a day's ride by now." The others nodded their heads in agreement. "I should expect we shall encounter them sometime tomorrow."

"And have we a plan for then?" King Eodren asked as he studied the faces of the strangers around him.

"I suppose we shall have to decide that when we take camp this evening," King Hasselfeth said honestly. "Truth is, we did not know what our total strength would be until just this past hour when you rode up to join us. Now that we are certain of what our troop size is and what it is made of, we should be better able to determine our best battle strategy."

"Very well, then," the centaur said happily. "I suppose we will just enjoy the scenery as we march along with you. It is very seldom that we leave the safety and shelter of our own woods. This shall be the journey of a lifetime, I am sure." He glanced over at his two sons and smiled.

* * *

One day's ride south from where King Hasselfeth, King Eadamantus and Amansun were, a small group of dwarves sat waiting along the banks of a stream where a small stone bridge crossed over the water. "Looks like the Underlord's army approaching," said Kairadus who had been on sentry duty, posted atop a small rock formation he had climbed upon earlier. "I see four very large moving giants at the front followed by a sea of marching ants."

Looking over at the prince who looked very uncomfortable sitting there tied up like a fly in a spider's web, Captain Balden sighed heavily as he imagined what it would feel like to be in the other dwarf's place. "Can't feel terribly happy with the southern prince approaching, I would imagine," he said as he watched the tied dwarf twisting his wrists, testing his bonds for the hundredth time in the past day.

"At least it will bring an end to my waiting, I suppose," Prince Brothemus said, trying to sound brave, though inside he was terrified of what the Underlord would do to him for failing his quest so miserably.

"Brave words from one who will be in the Underlord's dungeons facing certain torture soon enough," Kildren said as he eyed the bound dwarf. "What say you, Captain?"

"I say none here wants to be in the prince's shoes right now is what I says!" the captain snarled. "Once that army reaches us, you'll see this prince begging for death, or so I would guess." Now standing and walking over to the edge of the stone bridge, he looked out across the massive valley that separated the enormous army approaching from the south from their position here on the northern bank of the stream.

"What makes you think you are safe waiting here, anyway?" asked the tethered prince. "Seems to me that the giants are leading the army's march, right? You know as well as I how difficult it is to control those behemoths once they have spotted something they consider a danger…or worse yet, that looks like a meal," he said as he laughed loudly and watched the small band of dwarves looking at one another with fearful gazes.

"He may be tryin' to save 'is own ass, it be true," Kairadus the scout said aloud as if speaking on behalf of the others, "but seems to me what he says is true! Who says this new prince from down south even needs us? Our small patrol seems quite useless compared to what he's got coming now, right?" He turned to look at the captain.

"Kairadus is right, Cap'n!" another dwarf said as he stood and wrung his hands together nervously. "They don't needs our patrol no mores with the size of army they have gathered together. Likely they plan on killing all of us jest for being involved with the prince's failure!"

Walking over to the group of dwarves who had suddenly become vocal, Captain Balden drew his sword from its sheath slowly, then placing a finger on its edge and testing its sharpness, turned to look at the dwarf who had just been talking. He barked out, "Now what's all this fuss about there, Master Kairadus? Have you decided you'd like to take commands of my troop now?"

Dropping his head low and bending his shoulders over towards the ground a bit, like a dog trying to show its humility to a much larger animal, the stunned dwarf cowered and said politely, "No harm meant, I am sure, Cap'n. I was jest tryin' to says that there's no certainty we ain't all dead mens by now, what with the prince failing to finish off that man prince and all."

Stepping even closer to the frightened dwarf, Captain Balden held his blade out to the shaking man and said, "If it's death you are fearing from the approaching army, I can fix that for you right here and now!"

Back over at the water's edge, Prince Brothemus, still bound and seated, laughed loudly once more and said, "My bet is five to one that the giants pound all of you into jelly right where you are standing once they reach us."

"That be enough out of you, Prince!" Captain Balden snapped. "No need to waits for the Underlord to finish you off when I can saves him the trouble and slice you open right heres and right nows."

Shaking his head and staring directly into the approaching dwarf's eyes, the prince snickered and dared him to harm him. "You don't have the guts to finish me off!" he shouted, making sure all the other dwarves could hear. "You know as well as I that the Great Master will be furious if you cheat him from his fun with me. Go ahead, stab me if you think you can."

Seeing their captain hesitating as he eyed the bound prince just feet from where he stood, the dwarves began to doubt his ability to save them from the advancing giants who could now be easily seen making their way across the barren fields. "Not much time left, fellas," the bound prince called out. "Free me now and I promise you I will get you to safety far away from the reaches of the Underlord."

"Seems like a reasonable offer ta me," Kairadus barked out as he suddenly drew his own weapon out and stared at the captain, who still seemed caught off-guard by the prince's sudden antics. Looking over at the captain's lieutenant, he called over, "Which side you gonna be on, Lieutenant? You staying with the cap'n here or are you joining with us an' the prince an' running for it?"

Kildren took a few steps forward, drawing his own sword out and moving closer to where his captain stood, then said defiantly, "You'll have to take the two of us if you means to free the prince." He looked around at the dwarves who were now closing in upon the pair.

Turning to face the dwarf scout again, Captain Balden took a few steps towards the instigator and said, "Stop yer mouthin' off right now or I'll run you through right here, so help me!"

Before the captain reached his adversary, a large net flew over his head, and he suddenly found himself being grabbed at and held in place by several of the larger dwarves in the outfit. Just to his side, the same fate was befalling his lieutenant who had obviously made the wrong choice and was now looking at the same fate as his captain. "Sorry, Cap'n," one of the older dwarves said apologetically, "but seems to me the prince has a better offer. No sense sitting here and waiting for those giants to march ups and smash us now." He began tying the captain's hands together.

Thrashing about and trying his best to break free from the grasp of his abductors, the captain begged to be set free once more, saying, "Yer falling right into his trap, you ignorant fools! Can't you sees he is just trying to saves his own arse right now? Let us both free now and we won'ts mention any of this to the Great Master. I swears it!"

"Don't matter much if'n he's tryin' to save his ass or ours now, Cap'n," Kairadus answered in an even tone. "If none of us is here when those beasts cross them fields then there's not much they can do's to us, now, is there?"

As several of the dwarves made their way over to the tied-up prince and began cutting away at his ropes, they looked into his eyes nervously and said, "You gonna be a man of yer word, now, right, Prince? If we thinks you are out ta fools us we'll just gut you an' leave you behind for the goblins."

"Have no fear," the prince assured them. "None of us has a chance against those dimwitted mountains making their way towards us right now. The southern prince is likely planning on just letting them beat us down into a pulp for fun as they cross this here bridge."

"Right, then," Kairadus said as they finished securing the captain and his lieutenant. "What's the plan?"

"Quickly," the prince shouted as he squeezed his hands together repeatedly to get the feeling back in his fingers after having been bound for so long. "We need to get into the water and race along this stream to the east as quickly as we can. Be sure to keep low so none of their scouts sees us running along." The entire group raced off along the bank of the stream, leaving the poor captain and lieutenant tied up and all alone at the foot of the bridge.

"It's hard to runs in this blasted water," one of the dwarves complained as the group struggled to move along quickly.

Turning to look back at the dwarf while giving him an evil glare, the prince shouted back, "It won't do us any good to move faster if we leave our tracks all over this stream bank, now, will it?"

"What abouts them?" one of the dwarves said nervously as they raced away. "They's likely to tell them which direction we ran off in, ain't they?"

"Don't worry about them," the prince said confidently. "They'll be dead long before anyone who feels like talking to them shows up, that's a promise." He laughed at the captain who now knew how helpless he had felt the past two days. "See you in the next life," he called out to Captain Balden as the group faded out of earshot.

Lying on his side with his hands and feet bound firmly, Kildren called over to his captain, "It's not true what the prince says, is it? They're not going to kill us, are they?"

Laying flat on his back as he stared up at the sky, soft clouds blowing across like silent sentinels, Captain Balden said nothing in response.

CHAPTER 46

The Army of the Three Kings, or so it would be called years later, marched along at a quick pace for most of the day. As they passed by worn-down rock walls, abandoned dwellings, and overgrown fields where men and women had once grown crops of fruits and vegetables, the three different groups of warriors gathered together began to converse with each other. Up towards the front of the column were the king's men along with the many knights who had competed in the king's tournament. Following them were the bulk of the elf king's six hundred warriors. Though each elf was burdened with the weight of a heavy bow, full quiver of arrows, a heavy shield, a sword, and a steel-tipped spear, they still managed to move along swiftly and effortlessly, making little to no noise compared to the king's soldiers, whose heavy boots and rattling armor made quite a racket. Next came the long lines of wagons, carts and carriages filled with goods, water and ale, weapons, and the heavy crossbows carefully built into the massive shooting carts. At the rear of the procession, the four hundred centaurs fanned out as their hooves clicked and clacked upon the alternating dirt and cobblestone that made up the surface of most of the roadway leading south.

The further south the army marched, the less dense the forests and woods became, until eventually there was naught but empty plains and fields of grass, green in some places and dry and yellowish in others. As the long line moved upwards along the slowly rising roadway, they eventually came to a point where they reached the summit. Looking forward and down, the road snaked slowly back and forth along the falling hillside as it dropped in elevation several hundred feet. Running east and west, a long and somewhat deteriorated stone wall formed a boundary and offered protection with its thick impenetrable stone sides and height of some four to six feet, depending on which area you happened to be standing.

"This is it!" Amansun announced as they came upon the bluff and looked down at the massive plains below them. "Even if we searched for days, we shall not likely find a more suitable area to defend. See how the road twists and turns here as it winds up this enormous hillside? Our enemy will not be able to march in a straight line at us as they climb this hill, and we can shoot at them from up on high, taking shelter behind this old stone wall!"

"He is quite right," King Eadamantus said as he surveyed the lands from atop his own horse. "If it were up to me, we would have waited in ambush in the woods some miles ago. But if we need to face our enemies out in the open, this site seems as if it was made for such an event!"

Sitting up in his saddle and stretching his long legs, fatigued from the long ride, King Hasselfeth said, "I like this spot too. It seems very defensible. What say you, Captain?"

"The prince clearly has a keen eye for battle," Captain Baerden said as he also looked east and west at the stonewall that seemed to go on endlessly. "This is the best spot I have seen in our travels up to this point, and I would prefer we have time to settle in and prepare our troops while there is still time, rather than marching on into the darkness that will be approaching all too soon."

Raising his hand at the trumpeter, King Hasselfeth called over and instructed him to sound the horn twice to signal that the army was to dismount and set up camp. "Set up our war tent over there where the field lays flat," he said to his captain. "Once that is up, we will meet to discuss our battle plans and strategic placement of our forces."

"As you command!" Captain Baerden replied as he and Hrothgar bowed low and rode back to give their soldiers their orders. The two walked over to the stone wall at the crest of the hill as their soldiers began to set up the war tent as the king had requested. Stepping up and onto the stonewall, the two surveyed the long and wide plain below, scanning the horizon for any signs of movement from the Underlord's army that had to be approaching from the other end.

"There is something that has been troubling me since earlier this morning, though I am not sure I want to share it with you," Captain Baerden stated as he looked off into the distance.

Turning to look at the younger man, Hrothgar said, "You and I are old friends now, my Captain. Surely you do not mean to go into battle while there are unspoken secrets between us?"

"It is true, old friend," the captain said. "I do not want us to have secrets, but there is something I wish to discuss that may make you angry, as it involves the prince and I know how loyal you feel to him."

"Speak your mind, Captain," Hrothgar urged. "It is true that I am close to the prince, since I have known him since he was but a child and I fought alongside and served his father for most of my life, but I still owe an allegiance to you and consider you a loyal friend as well."

Turning to look the older soldier in the eyes, the captain shook his head in agreement and then said, "Very well, then, Hrothgar, but please do not take offense or hold my words against me. It is merely because of my desire to protect our kingdom and the king that I even mention this to you now."

"Agreed!" Hrothgar said suddenly, starting to get a little annoyed with the captain's restraint. "Out with it, then. What has you so concerned?"

"Do you remember this morning when we first rode up to meet the centaurs?"

Shaking his head in the affirmative and looking at the captain blankly, Hrothgar said, "Of course I remember, it happened just today, did it not?"

"Did anything that King Eodren said strike you as peculiar?"

Tightening his lips and shaking his head as if understanding where the captain was going with his questioning, the older soldier said uneasily, "You mean the part when he mentioned that the prince and the Lady of the Woods had convinced the centaurs they should ride off into battle, don't you?"

"Precisely!" Captain Baerden snapped. "Didn't you think it odd that King Eodren mentioned Prince Halldor and the Lady of the Woods at the same time, as if the two of them had been meeting with the centaurs together?"

"Yes. Yes, I did think it peculiar, though I did not want to mention it myself either," Hrothgar admitted while he stared intensely at the captain once more. "What do you think it means?"

Turning to look out over the plain far below once more, the captain shook his head as if confused, then replied, "Perhaps nothing at all. Or maybe it is something quite important. I haven't been able to decide for myself either. One thing is for certain, though, our young prince and the Lady of the Woods are connected somehow…and hopefully not for the detriment of us all."

"Your arm!" Hrothgar said softly, as he pointed at the captain's arm that appeared to be as if he had never injured it.

"Yes, I know," Captain Baerden said as he raised his arm high in the air and squeezed his fist shut tightly. "There is the healing of my arm as well. Didn't you say it was one of the prince's attendants that left the parcel for me the other night?"

Nodding his head uncomfortably, Hrothgar breathed in deeply, and then said, "Yes. It was one of his attendants. Strange that he has chosen to ride out here without them, now that I think of it."

"I hadn't given it much thought, to tell you the truth," the captain replied. "It is said that the enchantress of the woods seldom if ever journeys far from her own lands, isn't it?" The two men stared at each other, growing more curious with each moment.

"What are we to do, then?" Hrothgar asked with a puzzled expression on his face.

Captain Baerden said, "I suppose we shall just have to bring it up during our council this evening. If the prince has nothing to hide, then he won't be upset at our asking."

"Agreed," Hrothgar said as he watched the captain step down from atop the wall and start walking back to where the soldiers were now hammering great stakes into the ground to tie the tent ropes off. "I will follow your lead and let you do the talking." He too jumped down from the stone wall and followed in the direction of the captain. As the two men walked off together, he turned to his captain and asked, "Do you have any more of that healing material the attendant gave you? I sort of told Sir Blackstone that I could get him something that would help heal his hand before we went off to battle."

"Sure," Captain Baerden said as he laughed to himself. "Why not? I have the rest in my pocket right here. Be sure to get some to Sir Farimus as well while you are at it. Just don't tell them what it is or where we got it from!"

Grabbing the small packet from the captain, Hrothgar thanked him and headed off towards the area where he had last seen the knights gathered. "I'm sure they'll both be of much greater use to us tomorrow in the battle with two good hands," he said as he walked along.

Once the war tent had been set up and the leaders of the army had been gathered, the planning of the following day's battle finally began in earnest. Representing the men were King Hasselfeth, Captain Baerden, Hrothgar, Prince Halldor, and all the knights who had decided to accompany him on this quest to battle the Underlord's army. For the elves there was King Eadamantus, Mythra, Captain Eonias and Prince Erathrin. In attendance for the centaurs were King Eodren and his two sons Eldenham and Articlese, along with Chief Feradren, one of the senior centaurs, who up until now had wanted to keep his presence secret, as he did not fully trust the men of the castle whom he had avoided for so many years.

As it had been impractical to bring chairs and such along on this arduous trek, the guests were seated atop blankets that had been brought along by King Hasselfeth, knowing they would be needed at some point. As the large group sat there in a circle facing each other, introductions were given so that all were familiar with those seated about them. The centaurs, being used to resting on their four legs, settled onto the earthen floor of the tent and graciously declined the blankets that were offered to them.

Standing up and taking the lead of the great council meeting, King Hasselfeth took a moment to thank King Eadamantus and the elves, along with King Eodren and the centaurs, for joining with them in this historic battle. "Long has it been since the songs of old spoke of the three armies joining together as one to fight against the Underlord and his evil army," he said to the applause of those gathered around. "We know we face a grave enemy sometime tomorrow, but for now let us rejoice in each other's company and discuss how we can best meet this evil foe that rapidly approaches from the south."

Several attendants that had been standing in the tent but to its back edges now emerged carrying trays of metal chalices filled with a superior red wine, and the king encouraged everyone to take one so a toast could be made. Raising his own chalice up into the air and looking around at those in the circle, he said, "A toast and a blessing to all those who are now joined as one to fight the Underlord and those that fight under his lead. May we be victorious in battle and may those who meet their ends tomorrow be celebrated in this life and in the next!"

Now rising to his own feet, King Eadamantus raised his chalice as well, saying, "Though we may be outnumbered greatly, woe be the enemy who takes us for granted, for those gathered here have much to fight for and we will gladly lay down our lives to ensure the safety of our lands and loved ones back home!" There was thunderous applause from all present.

Raising himself up onto all four hoofed legs, King Eodren also raised his chalice and added, "My people are very private and prefer to stay unto themselves, it is true, but let it not be said that we make our neighbors fight our battles for us. Come tomorrow you will see just how brave and fearless our kind can be when put to the test." Once again there was thunderous applause and cheers around the circle.

Now waving his hands at the attendants to signal that they should leave the tent, King Hasselfeth sat down once more and suggested that the planning for the battle begin. Once the planning finally started, many if not all of those present shared their thoughts, beliefs, ideas and proposals one at a time, though many of the speakers found themselves being interrupted on more than one occasion. After much discussion and a good deal of heated argument, all parties agreed to three main objectives.

First, everyone agreed that the main threat facing them in the coming battle would be the numerous giants that had been spotted by the eagles the day before. Being such large and dangerous creatures, it was decided that the crossbow wagons would be positioned along the wall strategically, so that all crossbows could be focused on these moving mountains as they approached. Captain Eonias had pointed out quite simply, "Nothing else matters if the giants reach our defensive line. Once they are on top of us, our troops will scatter and chaos will reign."

Second, it made great sense that as many of the enemy as possible be killed at a distance, so as to lessen the amount of hand-to-hand combat that would eventually result once the dwarves and goblins, who were both known as fierce and fearless fighters, reached the stone wall where the defenders would be taking cover. Prince Erathrin had agreed to post his six hundred elves at the front so they could take down as many of the closing enemy as possible, seeing as they were all skillful archers who rarely missed a shot.

Third, those who had horses would stand at the ready at the gap where the stone wall broke so to let the roadway pass through. As this area would provide the least amount of defense, it was likely the enemy would make a run at this spot as soon as they had climbed the hill. With the mounted soldiers standing at the front, and the four hundred centaurs following right behind them, there would be no less than seven hundred souls protecting this exposed area.

Other than that, the battle would have to be taken as it came to them, with troops shifting from one side to the other as was called for.

"These plans make much sense," Hrothgar said as he stood and took a turn speaking. "However, there is still much that can be done in the remaining light of this day, as well as into the evening hours."

Looking over at the man, King Eodren of the centaurs asked, "And what would you suggest we do?"

"For one," Hrothgar started to say, "we can create a fence of spears stuck into the ground right at the edge of our archers' range. That way when the enemy reaches the kill point, they will be forced to slow down to avoid the spears, and our archers can pick them off in droves!"

"An excellent suggestion!" King Hasselfeth said as he nodded his head in agreement and gave the elder soldier a smile. "What other ideas have you all?"

"I think we should dig a trench into the roadway several hundred feet from our position," Sir Berardren said as he stood to explain himself. "If the enemy's army has any wagons or rolling weaponry, which they are sure to have, the trench will force them to go off the road and onto the uneven plains. That will give us more time to hold them off."

"Another great idea, and one we will implement as soon as this council ends," King Hasselfeth exclaimed.

Slowly rising from the far side of the circle from where the two kings were seated, Sir Antilus now rose and cleared his throat as if he had something to add. "Some may question my intentions of wasting perfectly good carts, but I know of a trick we might want to use tomorrow also," he said as he looked about the tent. "I noticed many good-sized stones laying about on both sides of the stone wall. We can load some of these onto three of the carts that are not needed once their supplies have been removed, then we can use these carts to block off the section where the wall opens up to let the road pass through."

Looking over at the knight who was red in the face and clearly shaken from his efforts to explain himself, Captain Baerden questioned, "Won't that block us in on this side of the wall, though? Won't we want our horsemen to be able to ride out into the battle when the time calls for it?"

"Yes, good Captain," the red-faced knight said as he once again took the floor. "We won't leave the carts blocking the road the entire battle, just until we see the enemy advancing up the hill. Once they have cleared the trench obstacle and returned back onto the roadway, we will set fire to the three heavily laden carts, and we will send these rolling down upon the enemy as they burst with flames!"

Nodding his head in agreement now that he understood the whole concept, Captain Baerden raised his fist in the air as a sign of support and replied, "An excellent idea, Sir Antilus, and one the enemy will certainly not be expecting, I am sure."

"Are there any other ideas?" King Hasselfeth asked as he looked at the faces around the circle.

"I have a request," Prince Erathrin said as he took his turn standing up. "I would ask that we have poles set into the ground with flags attached to their tips at varying distances from the stone wall—fifty paces, one hundred paces, and one hundred and fifty paces. These will allow my archers to better judge the distance of the approaching enemies. In this way we can ensure that our arrows are not wasted with shots that are too high or beyond our reach as the enemy closes in on us."

Pointing his finger at the young elf prince, King Hasselfeth replied, "It shall be done as you request, good Prince, and thank you. Are there any others?"

Raising his hand slowly while looking over at his father, young Articlese said, "I may have an idea you can use."

"By all means my son, please share it then and the king can be the judge of its merit!" Eodren said proudly.

Rising to his feet and wringing his hands together, the young centaur explained his idea. "I noticed that the grasses and bushes on the other side of the stone wall are dried out and yellow and brown in color, as if they are dead or dying."

"I noticed that as well," King Hasselfeth said as he encouraged the young centaur to continue.

"My idea is that we can rake the dead grass and bushes up into great piles on the slope of the hill, and then when the enemy approaches our archers can shoot flaming arrows into them, creating a field of fire the dwarves and goblins will have to fight through!"

"An excellent idea, and one that we will certainly want to use!" the king said enthusiastically. "I would ask that you see to it that your plan is carried out from start to finish!"

"It will be my honor to do so," the young centaur replied, sitting down quickly and smiling at his father who was beaming with pride.

Looking about the tent and seeing no other hands going up or individuals standing to take the floor, King Hasselfeth stood once more to end the counsel. "Now that we all know what our plans are and what we must accomplish before the enemy arrives, let us all go out and spread the word with our troops and get as much done today as possible, in case the Underlord's troops should surprise us and arrive in the evening or early morning hours. If everyone does their share, we can accomplish much this day!"

All those gathered within the tent now stood and shook hands, wishing each other success in the hours ahead. King Eadamantus and the elves walked out of the tent to start working on their range distance posts and to scout the walls for the best shooting points. Chief Feradren, King Eodren and the other centaurs walked out to help start digging the trench across the roadway and to help build the piles of dead grass on the hillside. King Hasselfeth started walking out towards the opening in the tent, but before he could get out, Captain Baerden and Hrothgar stopped him and asked Prince Halldor to remain for a few moments as well. "There is much to do and little time to do it all," said Amansun, who was anxious to get outside and start preparing for the battle.

Motioning to Amansun and King Hasselfeth to sit back down on the blankets that were now scattered about the tent, Captain Baerden smiled and said, "This will take but a moment of your time, my King and Prince."

"What is it, then?" asked the king, who also wanted to get outside and help supervise the troops. "Is this not something that can wait until another time?"

Captain Baerden said, "There is a concern we need to share with the prince is really all we need to discuss. I am sure it is nothing at all…but still…I feel we should address it now rather than waiting any longer."

Looking over at the captain with a look of puzzlement, Amansun said in a mystified tone, "A concern with me? Now? On the eve of our great battle? What is this concern that would cause you to rob precious time when we have so little to spare?"

"Yes…what is this all about?" the king echoed as he too looked at his captain of the Guard curiously.

Turning to face the prince once more, Captain Baerden asked, "Do you remember earlier today when Hrothgar and I first met up with you and the centaurs on the road by the lake?"

"Why, yes, of course I remember it," Amansun answered. "What of it?"

"King Eodren mentioned at that time that 'you and the Lady of the Woods' had convinced the centaurs to join us in this worthy cause to fight against the army of the Underlord…is that not correct?"

Looking over at the king somewhat nervously, Amansun admitted, "Yes…I believe those were his words…or something to that effect."

"Then you openly admit that you are or were in league with the enchantress of the Black Woods? The Lady of the Woods, as she is also called by many?"

Looking over at the king and seeing that his face was suddenly flush and his mouth was ajar, Amansun realized that this seemingly harmless statement by the centaur may have placed him into a regrettable position. "The Lady of the Woods was present at our meeting," Amansun blurted out, deciding it would be best to tell the truth at least partially, since there was no way of knowing what else the centaurs might say later. "She met with us at the centaur's village and she was able to convince them it was in their best interest to fight alongside us."

The king rose up from his blanket, the three others following his actions, and as he stared over at the young prince, he said with a troubled voice, "It is quite strange indeed that the Lady of the Woods should 'happen' to stop by at the centaur's village on the one day when you are racing there to find assistance for our battle. Would you care to explain yourself or shed some light on how the enchantress happened to be there?"

Looking over at the king, then the captain, then lastly his old friend Hrothgar, Amansun said, "I have neither the time to give nor the words of explanation that would set your troubled minds at ease. Let me just say that the Lady of the Woods is known to me, as were the centaurs that are now here to help us in our war with the Great Wizard. Is that not enough for you?"

"The enchantress of the woods is a powerful and mysterious being, and one we have avoided all these years," King Hasselfeth said with concern. "It is said that she has supernatural powers and that she enchants those who fall into her realm, young Prince. The fact that you know her and happened to meet with her just yesterday, all facts that you have neglected to share with us until just now when you were questioned, all make me very uncomfortable with you, to say the least."

Shaking his head with a soft nod, Amansun sighed once then replied, "Well, you will just have to be uncomfortable with me for the time being. We have a battle to prepare for and there is nothing I can or care to say that will make you feel any the better." He glanced over to the captain and gave him an angry glare.

"This does not bode well for your intentions to marry my daughter," King Hasselfeth said. "It is true that you won her hand fair and square in my own tournament of champions, but know now that I will be watching you closely from here on. If I see or sense anything suspicious or unusual about you from now 'till the time we return to Castle Eladrias, should we be victorious tomorrow, then I shall have to call the marriage off! I cannot and will not put my one precious daughter in harm's way with someone barely known to me who is in league with the enchantress. Surely you can understand my concern."

Bowing to the king and asking his permission to leave, Amansun said in a hurried and obviously bothered tone, "I am sure there will be nothing further you see or hear that will alarm you, good King. I am off to make my rounds and see that all our plans are being put into action." He turned away and walked out of the tent, leaving Hrothgar, Captain Baerden and the king looking at each other with puzzled faces.

Watching the prince as he left the tent, King Hasselfeth turned to Hrothgar who was standing there with a blank expression, like one who has just been slapped for no apparent reason and is trying to understand what they had done to deserve the strike, and he said, "I know the prince is an old acquaintance of yours, and the son of your old king who you held in high esteem, but you should know now that I am very perplexed by this new revelation and I fear there may be more to this prince than we were aware. You and Captain Baerden must always keep your eyes on young Prince Halldor from here on in and report back to me with anything that seems unusual."

Coming out of his trancelike stare, Hrothgar acknowledged the king and replied, "I will not leave the prince's side, my Lord. If he says or does anything I think might cause you alarm, I will report it at once as you have requested."

"I too will keep a close eye on the prince," Captain Baerden chimed in. "This prince who popped out as if from nowhere just a few short days ago seems to be quite an enigma. If there is more to be learned about the man, Hrothgar and I will find it."

The two soldiers bowed to the king, then walked out of the tent to see where the prince had gone and to check on the progress of their men who were working on several projects at once. "Well, I suppose that went as well as could be expected," Hrothgar said as he turned to look at the captain walking to his left.

"Can't blame the king for being concerned for the safety of his only daughter," the captain answered back. "After all, it's not every day someone claims to personally know the enchantress of the woods, who has struck fear into every living person within our realm for the past five centuries!"

"At least he appears to be on our side," Hrothgar said with a mischievous grin. "He did go and get the centaurs to join us in battle, after all."

Nodding his head up and down in agreement as the two men walked along, the captain muttered, "Quite true, old friend. I suppose if he meant to do us harm, he wouldn't have bothered finding us another four hundred warriors, now, would he? Look, there he is now." He pointed over at the wall where a group of soldiers were putting a crossbow carriage into place. "Be careful what you say to him now, as he is likely to get quite defensive after our conversation."

For the remainder of that day and well into the evening, the elves, centaurs and men worked side by side, completing as much work as possible. By the time the sun had dipped down in the west and the first dark of night had fallen, most of the work required to prepare their defenses had been completed. Seeing that the moon would be close to full, Captain Baerden gave orders that no fires were to be lit. "No sense letting the Underlord's army know exactly where we are," he said to the three kings who agreed right away.

"We generally travel without any fire anyway," said King Eadamantus who had walked over with King Hasselfeth to see how the defenses were coming along. "No better way to give away your location to an enemy than to start a roaring fire!"

"That's fine by us too," said the centaur king who had been walking along with the other kings for much of the afternoon. "It will be easier for our scouts to spot any advancing enemies in the dark without the distraction of light here in our own campsite."

Only the soldiers from the castle complained about the lack of a fire to keep warm and prepare their evening meal, which was going to be very disappointing as it was, compared with the feasting they had just enjoyed during the past several days of the tournament. "Cold taters and dried meat is alls we get tonight, I reckon," one such soldier standing post by his crossbow said to his partner.

"Least we gets a meal," the other said as he reached over and grabbed one of the cold potatoes that had been delivered earlier by one of the men on meal duty.

Tearing a chunk of the tough meat with his teeth and beginning to chew, the first mumbled, "You'd think they'd a-given us a better meal, seein' as how this may be our last."

"Speaks fer yerself," the second man replied. "I plan on makin' it outta this here battle tomorrow jest fine. Once I sees the eyes of one of them there giants—*bam*—I'm gonna shoot it out with this here bolt an' make no mistake!"

"Not if this meal kills ya first," the first said with a grin, and then both fell into soft laughter as they divided the food that had been delivered between them.

Eventually all but the scouts and sentries who were taking their turns on watch went to sleep, though many spent much of the night tossing and turning on the lumpy ground while thoughts of charging dwarves and goblins filled their heads. Up in one of the small tents that had been set up for the leaders of the army, Amansun lay inside his tent as he thought about the unfortunate statement Eodren the centaur king had said earlier in the day. *If only he hadn't mentioned the enchantress*, he thought to himself as he stared out the foot of the tent at the stars that shone brilliantly in the night sky. *How am I going to be able to convince the king I am no threat to his daughter now? I guess I will just have to save the day somehow in tomorrow's battle… that should win the king's good graces back.* He closed his eyes and tried to get some sleep.

CHAPTER 47

Further down south, the enemy's army was still on the move, though its pace had slowed considerably once the sun had set. As the four giants leading the way came up to the small stream, they were able to step across the narrow gap of water easily with their tremendous strides. The goblins riding their wild boars, however, did not enjoy getting wet unnecessarily, so they made for the stone bridge that crossed the stream along the main roadway the army had been following the past few days. The first group of goblin riders sped up and over the bridge quickly, not wanting to get separated from the giants they were responsible for driving in the proper direction. As others started to arrive, though, they traveled at a much slower pace, allowing them a better opportunity to scour their surroundings and hunt for tidbits of food they may find along the way.

Slowly walking his boar over the bridge, one goblin rider suddenly pulled up hard on his beast's lead and edged him closer to the edge on the east side of the small bridge. "Me smells meats, me does!" he exclaimed as he jumped down off the boar and peered over the edge into the darkness below.

"Whats is its?" another rider said as he too pulled his boar over to the side and leaned over to see what the other was looking at.

"Looks like some nasty dwarves, it does…all tied up an' helpless, they is," the first rider said as he licked his lips and took a deep breath through his nose. "They ain't spoiled yet neither." He climbed up and over the edge of the bridge. As a small crowd of goblin riders pulled up, all wanting to see what was so interesting on the bridge, the first goblin that had arrived poked at the bound dwarves with his spear, gently at first and then a little harder when they showed no signs of movement.

"Better not hurt them dwarves," one of the goblins called out from above as he peered down into the darkness. "They may belong to the Underlord, though why they be so far ahead of us I can't guess."

Poking at the smaller of the two dwarves with his spear tip again, the goblin called up, "It's okay if we eats them if they's dead already, aint's it?"

"Better waits until one of the chiefs comes up and checks on this," the captain replied. "If'n Prince Karazed finds you ate up one of his lost men, you'll be done for fer sure, an' I'm sure the Underlord's dungeons will be happy to sees ya!"

Suddenly realizing that he was being poked at by some unknown person, Captain Balden—who had fallen asleep some time ago, along with the lieutenant, as they were both thirsty, hungry and weak—shouted out with as much force as he could muster, "Untie me, you fools! Do you know who I am? I am Captain Balden, dwarf captain of the Underlord himself! Release me now or you will feel the pain of the Underlord's vengeance!"

"He is the captain!" Lieutenant Kildren yelled suddenly, having just woken himself and realized that they were in some sort of danger.

The goblin that had first spotted the two dwarves quickly scampered back up the side of the bridge and, jumping back onto his boar, sped off into the night in the direction the giants had gone without so much as a sound, wishing to put as much distance between he and this shouting dwarf captain as possible. "Better untie 'em and holds 'em here at the bridge tills the dwarves march up," the captain who had been taking control of the situation advised. "Don't let them slips away, now, as we don't yet knows fer sure if they be a-lying or speaking the truth." He then got back on his own boar and rode off as well.

Several of the goblins crawled over the side of the bridge and untied the two dwarves then led them over to the southern side of the stream and waited there, surrounding the two with knives and spears at the ready in case the two had any thoughts of escaping. "Don't thinks we wants to be here when that dwarf prince comes along," one of the goblins said to the others gathered around. "Never can tell what them nasty dwarves is going to do."

"We'll jest holds 'em here until the first dwarves come along, then we can throw them on them an' takes off quick-like", another suggested to the agreement of all, who wanted nothing to do with these unexpected captives.

* * *

Back up at the stone wall near Prince Halldor's tent, Captain Baerden and Hrothgar were looking out into the darkness of the plains beneath them as they discussed the upcoming battle. "It's been years since any of us was off to a proper war," Captain Baerden sighed as he took a bite of dried meat and chewed tensely.

"Except for small countryside skirmishes and dealing with some rogue wood elves, I haven't seen much action since the great battle when I lost my king," admitted Hrothgar as he looked over at his friend. "What do you think our chances are tomorrow?"

Finally swallowing the tough piece of meat he had been working on, the captain looked behind him before he spoke, then glanced back at the older soldier and said with a dry mouth, "I'm thinking our chances aren't so good, old friend. If all we had to deal with were the dwarves and goblins, I'd say we had some hope…but add in those giants and whatever other foul creatures the wizard has sent our way and our luck will be pretty much out." He reached for a leather bag of water he had set down on the rocks beside him.

"I'm thinking the same thing," Hrothgar replied coldly and without any emotion. "We'll be outnumbered over three to one as it is, and who knows how well our crossbows will do against those giants. I think it will take a miracle or some stroke of fate for us to win the day."

"Well, there's no sense both of us fighting tomorrow without at least some sleep," the captain said. "I'll take first watch keeping an eye on the prince's tent while you get some sleep. I'll wake you when my eyes get tired. Run off now while there is still time."

"Be sure and wake me, now!" Hrothgar said as he eyed his friend suspiciously. "No sense being a hero and taking the whole watch. I'll be mad at you if I wake up and it's already morning!"

* * *

High up in her bedroom chamber, Princess Lyleth was having a restless sleep as she tossed and turned in her oversized bed, pillows tossed about and blankets pulled to one side. As her nose twitched and her breathing sped up, she was lost in the great depths of a worrisome dream.

Looking out over the water of Silver Lake on a moon-filled night, she was standing once again on her large stone balcony as she looked at the magnificent serpent that hovered in the air just fifty paces from where she stood at the railing. As she focused on the beast's face, her eyes met the dragon's, coal black and unblinking, then the creature's mouth opened and a soft voice spoke, saying, "I will return for you my princess. Wait for me…" and the image in her mind faded away.

Sitting up in her bed abruptly, flushed in the face and still breathing heavily, the princess gasped and said to herself in a panic, "It cannot be!" then stepped from her bed and walked out onto the cold stone balcony in her bare feet and light nightgown, the chilly night air waking her. "Those eyes…I have seen those eyes before," she said to herself as she stared out across the lake, glimmering with the sparkles of a thousand stars up above. "It cannot be! The great winged serpent and the young prince have the same black eyes, dark as midnight. How is it that I didn't realize this sooner? And the voice in my dream…I am sure it was Prince Halldor's." Her forehead crinkled with confusion.

Hearing noises coming from next door, one of the princess's chambermaids came out onto the balcony and called out to the young woman, "Is everything alright?"

"Yes. I am quite all right," Princess Lyleth answered back. "Just getting some fresh air is all. Go back to sleep now, and I'll see you in the morning."

"Very well," the chambermaid replied, "but don't stay out too long. You're likely to catch a chill!" Then she disappeared into the main chamber and walked back to her own room.

There is more to my prince than meets the eye, the princess thought to herself. "I pray they do well in tomorrow's battle," she said aloud, and then she peered at the lake once more and turned to go back to bed.

* * *

Back in his own small tent, having finally managed to fall asleep as he tried to put the centaur's words out of his thoughts, Amansun was having his own dream, though his was more like a nightmare.

Staring out over the hillside, now black to the eye as thousands of armed and screaming dwarves and goblins charged up it from every which way, Amansun looked upon two enormous giants, each waving a monstrous wooden club in front of them as scores of the king's men and centaurs flew through the air with each thrust of the club. Looking back at the stone wall a hundred paces behind him, he could see the elf king's warriors doing their best to fend off the endless stream of enemies spilling up and over it. Up in the air, screaming creatures the likes of which the prince had never seen circled high above the battlefield, as dwarf archers sitting on the beasts rained steel-tipped arrows down upon the men, trying in vain to shoot them down from the ground. All around him, scores of dead men and centaurs lay, some still moving and screaming out in pain, though most simply lay there, motionless and silent.

Feeling an intense rage building inside of him, Amansun tried desperately to keep his emotions in check, but the sight of so many of his allies lying dead and being struck down all around him was more than he could handle. As he struck his steed in the sides with his armored feet, he rode towards the nearest giant, yelling out a battle cry as he went, and suddenly he felt a familiar pain running through his body as he felt his arms and legs stretching and twisting. Before he knew it, he had grown wings that were expanding outwards and he found himself lifting above the battlefield as his arms and legs transformed into large scale-covered limbs with sharp talons at the end, slicing through the air as he flew.

Sitting up in his tent, beads of perspiration falling from his brow, Amansun looked about and realized he was still laying in the safety of his own tent, and outside it was still pitch-black. The new day had not arrived yet. "Just another dream," Amansun said to himself as he lay back down once more and tried to calm his heavy breathing. His thoughts drifted off to the princess back at the castle, and as he remembered her beautiful eyes and smile, he allowed himself to drift off to sleep once more, this time with a slight grin resting upon his lips as he twitched and twisted a bit.

* * *

Down on the roadway, a group of Prince Karazed's dwarves were marching up towards the small stream that ran across their path. Looking ahead at a small group of goblins that were standing in a circle, Captain Kelden shouted out angrily, "You there! What are you fools doing? Why are you not up with the giants?"

Stepping out from the small band of goblins, Drakxmier, one of the larger of those left behind to guard the captives, bowed low and clumsily as he tried to speak. "We's was ordered ta stays an' keeps these here dwarves safe until one of you cap'ns came alongs," he said as he pointed at the two dwarves hidden in the center of the group.

"Who be you and why are you here at the front?" the dwarf captain demanded, as he waved the goblins off and told them to run along. "State your names and business here or I'll have you run through where you stand!"

Stepping forward with his chest puffed out and head held high, the captain shouted, "Captain Balden and Lieutenant Kildren from the Western Barrens, abandoned here and left to die by Prince Brothemus, traitor to the Underlord and leader of a rogue band of dwarves that have run to the east, hoping to escape from the coming army of Prince Karazed."

"I've heard of you twos," Captain Kelden replied. "Come with me and I shall hands you over to our prince, though I don't knows what he will do's with the two of you, ta be truthful."

"We have been hoping to meet with the prince," Captain Balden said as he walked forward. "My lieutenant and I may have useful information for him, as we were with Prince Brothemus while he was competing with King Hasselfeth's knights up at the tournament by Silver Lake."

Looking at the two unarmed dwarves suspiciously, Captain Kelden barked out at his men, "Keep a close eye on these two. I don't trust either of thems, but if it be true that they were up at the castle, then theys may be worth a good deal to the prince."

As the small group of dwarves marched back down the roadway, Captain Balden and his lieutenant were awestruck as they saw the size and scope of the Underlord's army that was on the move. "Must be some four or five thousand strong," the captain said as he peered over at Kildren.

"No talking!" one of Captain Kelden's soldiers said as he slapped Captain Balden smartly on the back of his head. "Another word out of yous without the cap'n's say-so and I'll bury my dagger in yer back!"

As the night drew long, sentries and lookouts exchanged turns, and all was quiet at the campsite of the Army of the Three Kings. Rumblings of snoring men and the chirping of small birds hidden amongst the small bushes scattered about the field was all that could be heard as the black of second dark slowly gave way to the lighting of a new day gently rolling in.

CHAPTER 48

Before the sun rose in the east, the sentries who had been unlucky enough to pull the last watch went about and roused the sleeping men, much to their dissatisfaction. Already standing in place and wide-awake, Prince Erathrin and his elves were at their posts, standing as silently as trees in a windless field. Back towards the rear of the encampment, Chief Feradren and his lead centaurs were engaged in a discussion of how they saw the battle going. As they huddled closely in the cool morning air, each of those present was allowed to speak their turn regarding how and when they should charge on the enemy to best inflict casualties while minimizing their own losses.

Shaking the captain gently, Hrothgar whispered to his friend who had only had a short time to rest, "The sun will be rising soon, Captain. Time to get up and prepare for the battle."

"Any sign of the approaching army yet?" the captain said as he bolted into a sitting position and rubbed at his weary eyes.

"No sign of movement yet," the older soldier assured the startled captain, who was clearly surprised that morning had already arrived, seeing as how he felt as if he had just closed his eyes a moment before.

Stepping out from his tent and looking over at the prince's quarters, Captain Baerden asked, "Anything unusual from our prince?"

"Nothing but a few groans and some rustling is all I heard," Hrothgar answered back. "It's my guess the prince didn't have a restful sleep last night either."

"Very well, then," the captain replied. "Let's wake the prince and get dressed. Then we can all head over to meet with the king and finalize our plans."

When the three men made their way over to the area where King Hasselfeth, King Eadamantus and King Eodren were standing, along with some of the knights who had already woken, the sun was starting to rise higher in the east and the first rays of sunshine were starting to light up the land. "We have a good wind today," said Chief Feradren, who sniffed the cool morning breeze that had started to pick up just as the sun rose. "It's blowing out of the south, so we will be able to smell the enemy before they can smell us."

"We still see no signs of the Underlord's army," said Prince Erathrin who was making his way over to the group, after just having left the stone wall where his troops were still standing on watch.

Suggesting that they all walk over to the crest of the hill, King Hasselfeth said, "Let's use what time we have left to finish the projects we started yesterday. From what I saw, nearly everything was in place, but there is always more that can be done."

"Agreed," said the elf king. "My people have already been in place for hours, just waiting for the light of day to make sure there was no enemy lurking out there before we moved beyond the wall to complete the job."

"The grass stacks are piled and ready," said young Articlese who had walked over with his brother to join the council, "but I believe we can do more digging to complete the trench."

As the group surveyed the sloping hillside before them, King Hasselfeth shook his head approvingly, then said, "We appear to be in good shape, friends. Let's dig the trench deeper as our young friend suggests, and the rest of us can make sure the wall is as fortified as possible and loaded with every weapon we have available, since we appear to have some time still."

"We shall take care of the trench," said Chief Feradren. "Do not worry over that task." He motioned to King Eodren and his sons to join him as he walked off towards the section of the encampment where most of the centaurs were waiting for word.

"Our men can take care of loading the remaining weapons alongside the stone wall," Captain Baerden said as he waved at Hrothgar to join him. "We shall make sure every station is prepared and staged for battle." He turned and walked off after bowing to the two kings present.

Seeing that the centaurs and men had already volunteered to complete the small bit of work that was left to be completed, Prince Erathrin said, "I will send two scouts ahead to see what can be seen while the rest stay here on guard at the wall. Perhaps we may get a glimpse of the army as it approaches from beyond the plain." He too bowed lowly then departed.

"It seems everything is in order," said King Hasselfeth as he turned and looked over at Prince Halldor who was still standing with the kings. "Thanks to your early notice, we are better prepared than even I thought possible. I am sure the Underlord's army will be quite surprised when they climb the hill and find us waiting here, more than half a day's ride from where they are expecting to find us!"

"And it is we who now have the element of surprise!" King Eadamantus said with a grin as he patted Amansun on the shoulder. "Regardless of how the battle goes today, at least we were given enough warning to ride out and meet the enemy away from our own lands. Should we fail here, at least we will have given our friends and loved ones back home time to prepare for a final assault against an army that has been weakened by our efforts."

Just then, two horses came running up the roadway and headed out past the stone wall and then down the grassy fields heading south. "Looks like young Mythra if I am not mistaken, though I couldn't make out the other rider," King Eadamantus said as he watched the two scouts riding off. "She is an excellent scout and one of our fastest runners as well. Should anything happen to their rides, she should still be able to return in time to tell us what they have seen."

Bowing to the two kings, Amansun said, "To victory this day, my Lords! I suppose I should go and help with checking our fortifications now." He turned and walked away.

King Hasselfeth, looking over several hundred feet from where Prince Halldor was now walking, smiled as he saw Hrothgar walking directly toward the prince, waving at the king and acknowledging that he would be keeping an eye on him. Looking up at the clear blue sky, which was by now completely illuminated, he said to the elf king standing at his side, "It's a glorious day for battle, my friend."

Shaking his head in agreement, the elf king replied, "It certainly is. All that is missing is a thick wood between the enemy and us. My people are much better suited for fighting in the trees!" He smiled at the king and patted him on the back.

* * *

As the Underlord's army continued marching north, its dwarves and goblins fatigued from marching days on end without rest, Prince Karazed finally took the time to meet with the two dwarves who had been captured the night before. "So, you say Prince Brothemus has turned traitor now and has fled from battle?" he asked the two captives.

"Yes, my Prince. He turned our men against us and had us bound and left on the roadway in hopes your approaching army would kill us not knowing who we were before we had a chance to speak," Captain Balden explained.

Looking at the two unarmed dwarves, shabby-looking and covered with dirt from their ordeal, the prince laughed and said, "And what would you have me do? Spare you for your incompetence? Prince Brothemus should have saved me the trouble and just killed you yesterday rather than leaving me the job."

"We can help you, though, my Prince," Captain Balden pleaded as he and the lieutenant struggled to keep up with the pace of the marching army. "We have been to the castle at Silver Lake and knows of their troop size and weaponry!"

Turning to look at the dwarves once more, the prince said confidently, "It makes no matter what their troop size or weaponry is. I have brought an army along that will crush and extinguish any and all that dare to stand and fight. Still, I suppose there is no harm in leaving you two alive…for now. Tell me everything you have seen and heard while you were with Prince Brothemus's troops, quickly, and I may spare your pitiful lives for a time."

As they marched along, Captain Balden told the prince everything he had seen, speaking to the size of the king's army, the size of the castle fortress at the lake, and of the visiting knights who still might be in the area. "Seems as though we will be faced with no more than a thousand or more men," Prince Karazed said with a silly grin. "Hardly seems worth the effort of moving my army up there! Me thinks I'll just let the goblins handle the whole mess and save my own men for the cleanup." He laughed and listened to the cheers of the men carrying the weight of his princely throne.

* * *

Standing at the far end of the plain beside their horses, looking down the roadway as far as their eyes could see before the road bent to the right and disappeared behind some low-lying hills, Mythra and the other scout heard the approaching army long before they were actually able to see anything. Booming in rhythm, the prince's drummers continued to beat their drums over and over again, sounding the cadence for the marching army. "They must be just behind those hills," Mythra said to the other scout as she motioned over to the horses, indicating they should be on their way. "Be sure to stay well off the road!" she shouted over to the other rider. "We don't want to leave any fresh tracks behind that they will be able to spot easily." The two sped off along the drier patches of dead grass.

Up on the hill above the immense plain, Prince Erathrin and the others on watch all saw the riders speeding in their direction, and they called out to the men, elves and centaurs nearby, "Scouts are returning…get ready for battle!"

"Our scouts approach!" an elf messenger said quickly as he bowed to the kings and then exited the tent.

Standing up from their blankets, leaving the remnants of their meal sitting half-eaten, the kings made their way out of the tent and started the short walk over to the stone wall, King Eadamantus saying, "Let's see what Mythra has to share."

Once the two riders had crossed over to the northern side of the wall, the carriages were propped back into place, sealing the roadway entrance, and they quickly dismounted and made their way over to where the kings, knights and prince were standing. "We haven't seen them yet, my Lord, but they are very close now," Mythra explained. "We heard the beating of many drums coming from behind those hills there, and they should be coming into view very soon." She pointed across the plain to the small hills lying southwest of their position.

"This is it, then," King Hasselfeth said in a flat tone, showing neither fear nor excitement. "Ride down the line and make sure everyone knows the time is near and they should be ready and in place by the time the head of the army comes into view." Looking over at Prince Halldor who was heading for his horse tied off just a few feet away, he added, "Tell everyone to stay low until we are sure they have seen us. No sense giving our position away until we have to."

Amansun nodded his head in agreement, then jumped onto his horse and sped off towards the east side of the wall. "I will ride along with the prince and stay at his side," Hrothgar said as he rushed off to get his own horse, forgetting to bow to the kings as he left in a hurry.

"Tell the men to cover the wagons with tarps for now," Captain Baerden called out to the retreating soldier running for his horse. "That way they will blend in with the stone wall more until the enemy has reached us."

Waving his hand in the air as he rode off to indicate that he had heard the captain's request, Hrothgar sped after the prince, all the while yelling, "They're almost here, get ready!"

As the distant sound of beating drums started to carry across the plain below, Eodren took a deep breath and said calmly to those standing nearby, "They are here…I can smell them!" Just then, the first of the goblin riders on their giant wild boars came riding into view at the very far end of the plain.

"No one is to fire until I give the command!" Prince Erathrin called out to his archers kneeling alongside the wall. "We won't give away our position until it's absolutely necessary!"

"That goes for you too, archers and bolt men!" Captain Baerden called out down the line. "Save your bolts for the large enemies! Don't waste them on goblins and dwarves!"

Amansun motioned for Hrothgar to follow him back to his tent so he could change into his armor. He hadn't wanted to put it on until the army was seen, as it was quite heavy to wear and awkward to walk around in unless the added protection was really called for. As the older soldier helped Amansun out of his leathers and into his armor, he leaned over and whispered to the prince, "The king is quite worried about you knowing the Lady of the Woods, Prince. He has asked the captain and I to keep an eye on you to ensure that you don't have any other hidden secrets he should know about. He fears for the safety of the princess."

"And why are you telling me this now, old friend? Aren't you worried that you would get in trouble if I say something about this to the king?" Amansun asked as he studied the older man's face.

"I know you better than that, my Prince," Hrothgar replied with a smile. "I pledged my life to protect you and your father long ago, and I don't intend on breaking that promise, even if it has been ten years since we last saw each other. Whatever business you may have with the enchantress of the Black Woods is yours and yours alone. You will always be the son of King Hanthris to me!"

Reaching for his helmet and gloves, Amansun patted his old captain on the shoulders, and said while smiling, "You are a good man, Hrothgar, and I should not want to do anything that would cause you any harm. Know that my intentions to the king and his daughter are of the highest purity. Should something happen to change the king's opinion of me, today or any other, it will not be because I am acting in a manner that would threaten either of them or put them in harm's way." He stepped over to mount his horse.

"Honor and victory, my Prince!" Hrothgar said as he watched the prince get atop his steed.

"Ride with me, old friend," Amansun replied back. "We shall meet these enemies together as you did with my father so many years ago!" The two rode up towards the stone wall, staying just far enough back so they could not be seen by the approaching army's scouts.

A short time after the first goblin riders had been seen, the first of the four giants came into view. Standing some twenty feet in the air, the beast carried an enormous club in one hand, and as he walked along the goblins running at his feet dodged about to avoid being stepped on. Soon a second, then a third, then a fourth giant came around the bend, and as they started to cross the field, they spread out so that each was about two hundred paces from the other.

Looking at the giants from their position where they had crouched down behind the wall, King Hasselfeth and King Eadamantus exchanged nervous glances. "Those will be hard to bring down, no doubt," the elf king said as he looked back at the immense moving monstrosities. "It is said their skin is tougher than leather and almost impossible to pierce with an arrow."

Staring at the giant that had rounded the bend first and was closest to their hillside, King Hasselfeth said confidently, "They are big, yes, but clumsy-looking too, and I am sure our crossbolts should be able to bring them down."

"Let us hope that you are right, my friend. Should those behemoths make it up to this wall, it will take more than just courage to face them," replied the elf king.

Following behind the giants, a sea of fast-moving goblins—some atop boars, some riding on the backs of large gray wolves, others running along on foot—covered the grassy plain to the point where the whole field seemed to turn black. Sitting atop his horse with just the very tip of his head showing above the rocks of the wall, Amansun looked on in wonder as he saw his dream from the night before coming to life. *It's exactly as I had pictured it*, he thought to himself. "Once they reach us, the visions from my dream are sure to come true," he whispered to himself as he clenched his fists tightly with apprehension.

The plain below was now covered halfway back to the small hills from where the first riders had appeared and still no dwarves could be seen. "Where are the dwarves your eagles mentioned?" Captain Baerden called over to Prince Erathrin. "I see naught but giants and goblins so far!"

Squinting with his superior vision, the elf prince turned to the captain, who was some fifty paces away from where he was kneeling on the ground, and said, "Look again, good captain. There are your dwarves, and more than we need." The first rows of marching dwarves, all heavily clad and armed with weaponry, began coming into view.

As wave after wave of dwarves appeared around the corner, the plain below was becoming filled to capacity. The dwarf prince's chariot had not even rounded the bend when the first of the goblin riders started the climb up the hillside leading up to the hiding place of the Army of the Three Kings. "Steady now, archers…hold and stay steady until I give the command," Prince Erathrin reminded his troops. "Wait until they come up past the stacks of dead grass, now!"

As the speeding goblin riders approached even nearer, the men and elves behind the wall could finally see just how large these charging boars and wolves were. Standing nearly as tall as a horse, the beasts moved at great speed and their long tusks stood out like daggers from each side of their jowls.

"Hold…hold…now!"

CHAPTER 49

A volley of arrows flew to their targets and fifty goblins fell from their rides, hitting the hard earth with thuds as their arms and legs flailed helplessly. Many of the boars and wolves also fell or stumbled as they were struck while others, now riderless, continued to charge at the stone wall, or turned to the left and right, looking for a means to avoid the barricade in front of them. "Keep behind the wall!" Amansun shouted to the troops as he watched the first wave of riders falling. "Those in the back will not realize what has happened yet and keep approaching!"

As more riders got within range of the elf's archers, volley after volley of arrows flew, most finding their targets, some missing their original mark but hitting other riders in their arms and legs. The large row of spears that had been planted just the day before helped slow the approaching enemy; but as they came upon it, some goblins went to pulling at the spears or breaking them in two so that those coming from behind could avoid the hazard.

As Prince Karazed's marching chariot finally came around the bend, the prince was able to look over the large plain in front of him and see that something was happening atop the hillside on the other end. "Looks likes the goblins have mets with some resistance," Captain Kelden called up to the prince. "Maybe a small troop of defenders posted at a watchtower?" He looked and saw what appeared to be goblin riders falling from their rides at the very top of the hill.

Looking over at the two dwarves still plodding along beside his floating chariot, Prince Karazed asked, "Did you two pass any watchtowers or guarded defenses on your way down the road when you first came by?"

"No, my Lord!" Captain Balden replied quickly, as his lieutenant wagged his head up and down in agreement. "We saw no one when we cames by this way."

"Likely just a small scouting party caught off-guard by our approach," Prince Karazed called over to the captain. "Signal the drummers to stop at once and we will wait here on the field while the goblins take care of these nuisances." As the drummers stopped beating their rhythmic cadence, the army of marching dwarves came to a stop and the bands of goblins and four giants closed upon the far hill as the prince's dwarf troops stood still and watched from a distance.

"The dwarves have stopped moving!" King Hasselfeth called out excitedly. "They must think they are facing a small resistance, so they have let the goblins come forward to do their work. This may be to our advantage. We must strike at the goblins now while their army is divided."

Looking at the king and nodding his head in agreement, Captain Baerden shouted back, "Once the first giants have come into our range, we can make our move, my King. Let's wait until we see how well our crossbows do."

"Agreed," King Hasselfeth responded as he watched the first of the great giants making his way up the hill, taking tremendous strides as he went and covering the ground as swiftly as one riding a fresh steed.

Raising himself just above the level of the stonewall, Captain Baerden called out to his crossbow teams, "Prepare to fire on the giant coming up on the left!" as a flurry of goblin arrows flew over the top of his head. "Fire!" he called out when he thought the creature had come within range of his weapons. *Twang! Twang! Twang!* went the carriages firing the large bolts as their teams released the first wave at the approaching giant. *Twang! Twang! Twang!* went the second volley immediately after.

Down the slope of the hill, the heavy bolts whizzed by the twenty-foot monster, most missing their mark and burying themselves into the hard ground, while others struck goblins squarely in the chest, flinging them back through the air some fifty feet from the force of the impact. Raising himself up again to see how they had fared, Captain Baerden gave a shout as he looked upon the giant who was now down on one knee, pulling at a bolt that had pierced him in the thigh, as another protruded out from his shoulder where it had buried itself halfway through the tough skinned beast. "Two hits!" he shouted as a flurry of arrows once again flew over his head, some hitting the men who were in hiding behind him. "Reload and fire at will! Try to finish the creature off while he is down!"

Peering over the wall himself, Hrothgar was surprised to see that many of the approaching goblins were making it through the barrage of arrows being fired by the elves and were in fact almost upon their position. "Prepare for hand-to-hand!" the elder soldier called out. "They are nearly upon us!" He drew his sword and turned to see if Prince Halldor was ready to defend himself.

Looking up the hill from halfway across the plain, Darak 'Ur, the chieftain of the goblins, could see that something was very wrong. Too many of his warriors were being shot down and repelled at the great stone wall. "Not right!" the large chieftain called out. "Much trouble up ahead!"

Speeding back down the hill from the main battle area upon a wolf of incredible size, one of the goblin captains rode up to the chieftain with a look of hatred as he held out an arrow in his right hand. "Elves!" was all the captain said as he handed the arrow to his chieftain and spun around to return to the battle.

"Elves out in grass?" the chieftain said with disgust as his face winced tightly and he spat out on the ground. "Skinny tree elves!" he snarled as he turned his own wolf around and sped off towards the dwarves some half-mile behind. "Trap!" he said to no one in particular as he grabbed onto the fur of the creature he was riding and sped off.

As the top portion of the hill turned black with the thick hordes of approaching goblins, Articlese looked over at his father anxiously and asked, "Now, Father?"

Looking out over the wall and seeing nothing but bands of approaching goblins on foot and riding beasts, Eodren looked back at his son and yelled, "Yes! Quickly now!"

Running on his four swift legs, Articlese carried a torch and sped past several archers who had been waiting for the signal, and lighting their arrows said, "Light the grass! Now!" A new volley of arrows flew out from behind the stone wall, this time flaming as they sped towards the dozens of tall stacks of piled grasses and brush. As the first piles started to roar to life, the goblins nearby scattered in panic as they realized they were now climbing a hillside ablaze.

Far across the plain, as he sat atop his cushioned chair and stared in disbelief while dots of flame began to erupt all over the far hillside, Prince Karazed recognized the goblin chieftain approaching upon his wolf. "Why are you not fighting with your troops?" the prince demanded as he watched the rider drawing closer.

"Elves, your majesty!" Darak 'Ur called out in a panic. "A trap it is! My warriors is dying an yer dwarves sit here all safes!"

Taking the arrow from one of the dwarves below as he handed it up to him, Prince Karazed growled in anger as he stared down at the two dwarves standing below. "Lot of good you two have been to me!" he cried out as he shook his fists into the air. "They must have known we were coming somehow! They have ridden ahead to meet us here, far from their own lands! Signal the drummers! Send the first wave ahead!" he called out to Captain Kelden, who was still nearby. "Time to kill that nasty king and all those fighting with him!" He looked again at the elf-made arrow in his hands and, placing it over his knee, snapped it in half. "Send those two up to the front lines!" he said as he pointed over to Captain Balden and Lieutenant Kildren. "And don't give them any weapons neither!" he added with a laugh. "Let's see how they like going into battle unprepared! Damn fools didn't say anything about any elves fighting with the king!"

Up at the stone wall, the hand-to-hand fighting had begun in earnest, as mobs of running goblins had made it to the top of the hill and were now climbing and jumping over the wall, curved swords in some hands, others carrying sharp spears with nasty blades made with jagged edges that held in place and tore at the flesh like a saw when they were pulled out of their opponents. "Set the wagons on fire!" Captain Baerden called out over the sounds of battle. "Quickly now, while there is still time to roll them down the hill!"

A group of men gathered near the wagons grabbed stakes of wood that had been wrapped in a tar-like liquid and, using flints and stone to send showers of sparks down upon them, set them ablaze as they ran over to the heavily weighted wagons. Once on fire, dozens of soldiers pushed at the carts until they gradually moved over the edge of the hill and started rolling down on their own, picking up speed as they went.

Seeing that the wall was now becoming overrun with goblins, King Hasselfeth gave the signal to sound the horns and send the riders out into the field to help keep the coming goblins away from the already overwhelmed elves, who stood and continued to fire their arrows at the oncoming goblins even as they were being attacked from within their perimeter. *Tooodooo* went the horns as they sounded across the land, sending hundreds of soldiers on horseback and hundreds more centaurs riding out through the narrow channel where the ends of the wall met at the roadway. *Toooodooooo.*

As the flaming carts banged and rattled down the roadway, sending goblins and beasts scrambling to get out of the way, the army of men and centaurs took the field and began hacking away at and spearing those goblins that suddenly found themselves being shot at from one direction and attacked from the other.

"Watch out for the giant!" King Eodren shouted as the second of the towering creatures made its way into range. *Twang! Twang! Twang! Twang!* went a volley of bolts racing at the approaching beast as the carriages set their sights on the new target. *Twang! Twang! Twang!* Reaching up to its head with both hands, its wooden club dropped to the earth as it realized it had been mortally struck, the enormous creature pulled futilely at the heavy wooden bolt which had pierced it in the head.

"Told you I'd hits it in its damned eyes!" laughed a soldier at one of the carriage stations as he glared over at one of his partners.

"Damned if you didn't!" the other man replied as he laughed as well, then looked down only to see that a goblin arrow had just pierced his own chest as he stood there holding the next bolt meant to be loaded.

Looking over at his friend who was now lying on the ground dead, the first looked over at a group of soldiers battling alongside the wall and yelled out, "I need a loader over here!"

As his band of dwarves made quick time across the plain, Prince Karazed could see that an enormous army had rode out to meet his goblins on the grassy slope in front of the stone wall. He quickly realized, seeing centaurs and men spreading out thickly everywhere, that he was facing much more than a thousand men, and he gave the command to release some of his other weapons. "Release the minotaurs!" he commanded as he waved furiously at his captain below. "Send them up the road at once!"

From further back in the rows of dwarves, several guards bearing special keys approached a single line of massive beasts that had been chained together at their hands and feet. Standing some eight feet tall at the shoulder, these beasts stood atop two hoofed feet, much like a man would, but they were covered in hair and at their neck they had massive bull heads, with enormous horns extending from either side. With bulging muscles covering their bodies, and arms and legs thick and muscular beyond belief, they champed with their feet and blew air out their ringed nostrils as they waited for their handlers to release and arm them.

From a wooden cart just behind the hairy beasts, a small group of dwarves handed large two-sided axes over to the waiting minotaurs, some fifty all told; and holding these in their hands, they ran off in the direction from where the sounds of battle were coming, dressed in heavily matted leather vests with leathers hanging down towards their knees, as they looked from side to side for signs of their enemy.

"What abouts the cyclops?" Captain Kelden shouted. "Shall we release him now too?"

Standing atop his cart and turning to look back at the rear of his army, Prince Karazed fixed his gaze on the enormous one-eyed giant, standing some fifty feet tall at the very rear of the army, and he nodded his head up and down. "Yes!" he said as he reached into his front pocket and produced a small silver whistle some half a foot in length. "Release the beast from his chains once I have played the magic flute the Underlord provided." He placed the whistle upon his lips and prepared to blow.

All about the enormous creature, bands of dwarves ran to get out of its direct path, knowing full well that once the giant was released it would pay little attention to who it killed or stepped on as it moved forward to do the prince's bidding. Sending out a series of high-pitched sounds as he played a short melody, the beast looked alertly towards the prince and nodded his head, as if understanding what each note had meant. As great steel shackles and chains were released from the monster's ankles, it started to walk forwards towards the prince's chariot, then nodding his head up and down once, the beast strode up along the road and towards the far hillside as dwarves darted to the left and right to avoid the giant's enormous feet as it stomped along, the ground literally shaking from its enormous weight as it passed by.

"What is that?" King Hasselfeth said in awe as he saw the towering giant making its way across the plain, clearly visible from even this distance.

Turning to see what the king was looking at, as he had been absorbed watching the battle taking place close by, King Eadamantus groaned and said unhappily, "They have brought a cyclops along, my friend! I have not seen nor even heard of one of them in two hundred years!"

Calling out to Prince Halldor who was at the great wall battling against goblins with Hrothgar at his side, King Hasselfeth cried out, "I need you here, Prince Halldor! You must gather the knights at once and prepare to take on this new adversary!"

Fighting his way over to where the two kings stood, surrounded by a thick band of soldiers and elves protecting them, Amansun looked off across the plain and set his eyes on the frightful cyclops making his way across the battlefield. "Even your bolts will have little chance against that moving mountain!" Amansun said out loud, not meaning to.

"You and the knights must find some way to bring down that monster," King Hasselfeth said as he looked into the young prince's eyes with a look of fear for the first time.

"We will do what we can," Amansun answered back without question, realizing that he and the knights had no chance against this new enemy. "Focus on the battle at hand and we will ride out to challenge this beast before it reaches our camp," he said bravely as he and Hrothgar glanced once more at the towering giant that was quickly making its way across the plain, taking strides the length of five wagons end to end, as it crushed anyone or anything in its way. Turning to face his companion, he told him, "Go and round up the knights, all of them! Meet me back here as soon as you can! Together, we will ride out to meet this monster!"

Nodding his head and trying to not look too fearful, Hrothgar turned and sped off, saying only, "It will be but a moment, my Prince."

As the men on horseback and the centaurs out on the field began to have success slowing the rush of goblins coming up the hillside, the two remaining giants made their way up the slope, each coming from a different side of the hill. "Fire upon the giants," Captain Baerden cried as he hacked at goblins that had made their way onto the north side of the wall. Hearing no shots being fired, the captain called out the command once more, then still hearing nothing, turned at the nearest row of carriages to see what the matter was.

Up and down both sides of the wall, elves and men stood side by side and back to back as they fought the fierce-toothed and heavily armed goblins that had made it over the wall before their forces had ridden out to stop the flow. The carriage men, who should have been manning their crossbows, were now locked in battle with the goblins who fought as if possessed by demons, as they clawed, stabbed, kicked and bit at the king's troops.

Standing near the entrance to the main field where the stone wall parted, Amansun watched as Hrothgar and the knights, accompanied by their attendants and own soldiers, rode up, Hrothgar's hand holding the lead to the prince's own steed. Pointing down the slope to the enormous one-eyed giant making its way across the plain, he shouted out so all could hear, "That is our target, brave knights. The king has asked that we find a way to stop the creature before he reaches our wall of defense!" He turned his horse and, with a kick of his booted heels, sped out of the kings' camp and rode into the open field where the enemy's forces were locked in battle with their own.

"To the prince!" cried Sir Berardren, as he too dug in on his ride and raced off to follow the prince into battle.

Looking down at the towering cyclops making his way closer, Sir Glandin, the largest of the men in the Army of Three Kings, smiled widely and said, "At last, an opponent worthy of a challenge!" and he followed the Red Knight as he raced out from the safety of the northern field.

As Amansun and the other knights made their way through the battling masses, he could see that the two remaining giants were doing incredible damage to his side's forces. Just as they had in his vision the night before, each giant was wielding their club with tremendous force as scores of centaurs and men were flung from side to side with each sweeping pass of the heavy wooden clubs.

Seeing the look in the prince's face, Hrothgar, who had managed to make his way up to the Amansun's side by now, grabbed the young man by the arm and said, "We can't worry about them right now, my Prince. The great giant is still coming and the king has demanded that we take care of him first!"

Turning to look at the older soldier as if waking from a dream, Amansun answered back, "You are right, old friend. Ride with me now." Again he began to make his way down the hillside, hacking at goblins and wolves from atop his horse as he made his way.

Far down the plain, taking shelter behind one of the burning carts that had managed to roll itself all the way down to the bottom of the hill and then some, Captain Balden and his lieutenant were watching the battle taking place as they tried to decide if they should try to find a weapon and join in, or use the chaos of the moment to try and flee to the east as Prince Brothemus had done just one day earlier. "We should have listened to the prince," Lieutenant Kildren said as he watched the steady stream of goblins, men and centaurs falling in battle.

"Now is not the time to argue over that," Captain Balden snapped back as he suddenly felt the very ground beneath him starting to shake.

"What on earth is that?" Lieutenant Kildren said as he turned around, a look of sheer terror suddenly coming over his face.

Captain Balden turned in the direction his friend was looking, and with a gasp of surprise and shock glanced up just in time to see the foot of the enormous cyclops bearing down upon the two of them. *Splat! Splat!* was the sound that came from beneath the immense creature's foot as it lifted up onto its heel again, having crushed the two dwarves flat where they hid, the creature continuing forward, having not even noticed that it had just now killed two soldiers from its own side.

Peering up in the direction where the minotaurs were now slicing and hacking at their opponents, Prince Karazed smiled and said, "They won't hold out much longer against our two remaining giants, the cyclops and the minotaurs, now that we have sent them into battle. Even now the enemy seems to be struggling, and our first wave of dwarves haven't even made it to the hill yet. Nothing shall keep me from victory this day unless they have some other ally that has not shown its face yet."

Suddenly a glint shining on the far hillside caught the dwarf prince's attention. As he squinted his eyes and held one hand over his brow to shade his eyes from the sun, he spotted a group of knights making their way down the hill, seeming to be heading towards the cyclops as it made its way to the bottom of the hill on the far side. "The white rider!" he exclaimed as he slowly stood and peered across the plain as if seeing something he had been hoping to find for many years. "There is the white knight now! He whom we have been sent to destroy by our own master!" Waving and yelling to get his captain's attention, he shouted as loudly as he could, "Time to release the flying beasts, Captain! Go and get your flyers together and fly out to meet the white knight now!"

A sudden look of concern spread over the captain's face, and he looked up at his prince once more to be certain he had heard correctly. "You wish for me to mount the hgarlads now, my Prince?"

"Yes!" the dwarf prince repeated with the same excitement and urgency. "Fly out at once and take down that white knight. If you succeed, I will make you my general when we return home!"

Making his way back to the row of wagons carrying the large wooden crates that made up the end of the army's caravan, Captain Kelden gave the command to open the large wooden boxes up and prepare to mount the eight winged creatures that were contained inside. As the company of dwarves that oversaw this special part of the army began to unfasten the chains and bolts that held the crates in place, seven lightly clad dwarves marched over, each carrying a large bow and an oversized quiver containing no less than thirty steel-tipped arrows of unusual thickness and length. The dwarf leading the small band of archers held in his hands a second set apart from his own which he handed off to the dwarf captain once he was within arm's reach.

"Time to ride!" Captain Kelden said as he placed the arrow quiver over his back and set the bow across his shoulder. "We go for the white knight at the far end of the plain." He walked over to one of the winged beasts that was now flapping its wings and sniffing at the fresh air, happy to be out of the confines of the box it had been secured in.

As each rider stepped onto the wooden wagon where his own hgarlad was still tethered down, they carefully approached the beasts from the side or the rear of the dangerous creatures. One dwarf flyer, not paying attention as he climbed upon the cart before him, the anxiety of mounting this intimidating beast distracting him, made the mistake of climbing up from the front of the cart. As he stepped up and onto the wagon, he suddenly found himself face-to-face with the creature, still quite agitated from having been kept confined in the small box for so many days. The creature's wolf-like head lunged forward, biting the dwarf's head off with one clean snap of his razor-like teeth.

Looking over at the slumped over, headless body some three wagons from where he now sat on his own beast, Captain Kelden pointed over to a dwarf who had been standing on the ground at the edge of the wagon, preparing to untie the creature's legs when the signal was given. "You there!" the captain said as he singled out the dwarf who looked deathfully afraid. "Yes, you there. Climb on up and take that rider's place at once."

Looking over at the other dwarves standing nearby, the frightened dwarf stood frozen solid, eyes unblinking, as the realization that he would have to get on top of one of these monstrosities set in.

Now pointing to the dwarf standing closest to the first who was still unmoving, the captain said loudly, "Tell your friend there to get up on that beast or I will have you drive your spear through his chest by the time I count to three. One…"

Immediately, the dwarf who had been paralyzed with fear found the courage to climb up the wagon, from the rear unlike his unfortunate companion, grabbing onto the winged beast's saddle and pulling himself up, realizing mounting the beast and risking death was much better than standing there and being killed without question.

"Wise decision," the captain called over to the newest flyer on the squad. "Now someone hand him his quiver of arrows and bow, as he seems to have forgotten them in his excitement to climb aboard his beast." With some effort, the dwarves standing along the cart managed to remove the large bow and arrow quiver from the body of the dead dwarf who was still lying atop the cart, and once passed up to the new rider, the group prepared to fly off.

"Release the beasts!" the captain called out; and as one, the dwarves holding the tethers that had prevented the beasts from flying off released their bindings, and all eight hgarlads took to the air, wings beating forcefully as they rose higher and higher into the sky above the dwarf prince's army.

Waving his fist into the air high above his head, Prince Karazed called out to the flyers as they passed by overhead, "Take down the white knight or don't return at all!"

Back on the other side of the plain, Amansun and his small band of knights had made their way over to where the cyclops was now starting up the slope of the great hill. As he looked at the towering giant, the thought occurred to him that he really had no idea or plan on how they were going to slow or kill this formidable creature. As some of the riders had brought spears with them, he encouraged them to throw them at the cyclops in the hopes they might be able to put out his one massive eye. As one rider after the other rode up as close as they dared, giving their spears the best throw they could, he soon realized that the beast was just too tall for that to work. "Did any of you bring your bows with you?" he called out, as he realized he had left his own back at the stone wall.

Coming from behind his own position, a familiar voice shouted, "I have my own, young Prince. Move aside and I will try to shoot at the beast." The prince turned around and to his great surprise saw Mythra sitting atop one of the king's horses, heavy bow in hand, an arrow notched and ready. "You didn't think I was going to stay behind and let you have all the fun?" the elf said as she tossed her hair back behind her and took aim at the tall, moving target.

Ssssshhhhhh went the arrow as it whizzed through the air, coming to rest inside the creature's immense eye. The cyclops stood still for a moment, reaching up with one hand as it tried to remove the splinter that had penetrated its eye. Looking down to see where the object had come from, he saw the small group of riders huddled together just in front of where he now stood. As the cyclops lunged forward again, trying to step on the knights assembled in front of his path, another *sssssssshhhhh* filled the air, and then another, and another.

"Great shots!" Amansun shouted out as he watched the elf's arrows finding their mark in the creature's eye again and again. "Keep it up while we see what we can do about taking down the beast!" he called out, then motioned for some of the knights to ride closer along with him while the giant was busy trying to ease the pain coming from his eye.

Taking the lead from the prince, Sir Glandin and Sir Antilus rode up to the cyclops fearlessly and started hacking at the creature's legs with their long swords. *Clang! Clang!* went the swords as they bounced off the creature's tough skin repeatedly, "It's no use," Sir Glandin shouted out as he swung his sword repeatedly. "Its skin is like stone!"

Looking down the hill a bit further, Hrothgar suddenly realized they had an even bigger problem coming their way. Shouting over to the prince, the elder soldier yelled out, "The dwarves are nearly upon us, my Prince. We must turn and retreat to the stone wall once more." Amansun and the knights looked down and saw some one thousand or more heavily armed dwarves marching up in their direction.

"We shall have to find another way to kill the one-eyed beast!" Amansun yelled, as he too realized they were far too outnumbered to stay behind and fight. "Make your way back to the kings!" He turned his horse and started back up the hill.

After having traveled just a short time, Amansun was stunned when he saw two knights riding just ahead of him fall from their horses, large arrows sticking out from their suits of armor. "What is this devilry?" he said to himself as he looked back to see which archers had managed to take these lucky shots. Hanging some fifty feet above the battlefield, hovering like giant bees, a small group of winged creatures seeming to be eagles at first glance caught Amansun's eye, as he realized the arrows were coming from dwarves riding atop these strange beasts, with heads like wolves and bodies like that of a horse. *It's the creatures from my dream!* Amansun thought to himself as he cursed at their misfortune. Turning to tell his companions to flee, several arrows whizzed by his head and body, striking the ground with vicious impact as they buried themselves a foot into the hard earth.

Looking up the hill, seeing the king's soldiers being cut down by the enormous axes being brandished by the band of minotaurs, and still higher, bodies of centaurs and men piled up near the two giants that still were battling their way up the hill, Amansun finally came to realize that they were losing the battle. There was no way they would be able to win, given the foes they had to face and the number of warriors they had left to battle with. Looking over at the soldier who had served him as a child, and who was now doing everything once more to shield the prince from the goblins and other beasts nearby, Amansun opened his mouth and shouted to his friend, "Forgive me, my friend, for what I am about to do. It seems I have no other choice!" He turned his horse around and started back towards the still unmoving cyclops, all while arrows continued to rain down at him from the riders above.

Sitting up in his saddle, channeling all of his hatred, fear and emotions into his conscious mind, Amansun gave in to the feeling emanating from deep inside his chest. Just like in his dream the night before, he felt a sudden pain, starting in his chest and then spreading out over his entire body, arms and legs shaking from under the armor that was still protecting him from the arrows being shot at him from above. Whether by some enchantment of the Lady of the Woods, or because of the quality of the craftsmanship of the suit he had selected, the dwarf captain's arrows, and those of his other flyers, continued to bounce and skip off Amansun's armor again and again.

A rush of memories and images, some imagined and others quite real, flashed through Amansun's mind, as back on his horse his muscles and nerves twitched and twisted while the transformation began to take hold. Falling suddenly from his horse, landing flat on his back, eyes staring up at the sky but seeing nothing but the flashing images, the prince's body began to stretch and grow, the exact opposite of what had taken place when the Lady of the Woods had undone the Underlord's spell.

As Hrothgar looked on in horror from a distance, the army of dwarves continued marching closer, now just some two hundred paces from where he could see the prince lying on the ground. "He is dead!" the other knights yelled as the soldier tried to turn his horse around to ride to the prince. "Leave him be or you will surely be laying beside him in a moment," they urged as they attempted to grab his horse's reins and pull him along. "He would not want you to die in vain!"

Sitting atop his winged beast, pulling another arrow from his quiver and taking aim at Amansun lying below as his body and armor shook unnaturally, Captain Kelden suddenly had a feeling in the pit of his stomach that something very unusual was taking place below. "This isn't right," he said to himself as he took aim at Amansun and let another arrow fly. "We haven't even struck him yet and still he lies there on the ground, shaking as one who has been mortally wounded."

Looking up the hill as they converged on the helpless downed knight, relishing in the thought of an easy kill, the dwarves of Prince Karazed's first wave began to charge at the fallen foe. Picking up speed as they drew closer, their eyes suddenly opened wide, most in disbelief, others in complete shock and horror, as right before their very eyes Amansun's armor began to split apart and bulge as the man inside started to swell to incomprehensible proportions. As the marching dwarves came to a halt, and the flyers above looked down in wonder, the man's arms and legs began to grow and change, even as two tremendous wings seemed to sprout from the knight's body as if by magic. Shaking its enormous armored head back and forth, scanning its surroundings as it tried to make sense of where it was, and who all these beings were that were standing so close, the winged serpent stood upon its taloned feet. Spreading its wings out as far as it could, it suddenly took to the air, fire shooting from its huge mouth, as it made for the small winged beasts flying nearby that seemed to be endangering it by their very presence.

Looking down the hill in silence, as men and beasts alike turned to marvel at the immense flying serpent that had appeared from out of nowhere, Hrothgar and the remaining knights who hadn't perished looked on in shock and awe as the man they knew as Prince Halldor took the shape of the enormous golden dragon that was now attacking the very beasts that had just moments before killed two of their own. "What can it mean?" Sir Berardren called out as he watched the dragon burning one flying beast out of the sky after another.

Shocked into speechlessness, Hrothgar could only mumble to himself as he watched in horror and excitement while the winged serpent began chasing after the army of dwarves who were now dropping their weapons where they stood and, screaming and yelling, ran back across the barren plain as the beast shot blast after blast of red and yellow flames down upon them, killing scores with every breath.

From high up the hill, many of the goblins and the band of minotaurs stood frozen in place as they looked back at the flying serpent and realized it was not on their side of the battle. Suddenly turning and attempting to flee back down the hill, the elves and men who still had arrows left picked off the fleeing enemy one by one with ease, as there was finally no one fighting them at close quarters. Even the two giants who had up until now done so much damage seemed dazed and confused by the chaos around them. As the two beasts stood there, staring at each other from across the distance, the king's men, finally having time to reload their carriages and take aim, fired bolt after bolt at the pair, striking each multiple times as the beasts fell to their knees and then to their chests.

Not sure of what was happening or why, but seeing that their enemy was now scattering to the winds, the men, elves and centaurs who had made it through the battle raised their hands up in triumph, screaming at the top of their lungs, crying with tears of joy as they hugged each other and danced about. Off in the distance, watching his army coming apart before his very eyes, Prince Karazed gave the order for the horn of retreat to be sounded, even as he stood atop his chariot and gazed with wonder at the giant flying beast that was turning his first wave of soldiers into balls of moving fire. "Run as fast as you can!" the prince shouted down to the dwarves who still held his floating chariot in the air. "Make for the hills before the beast makes his way over to us!" He reached for a whip at his feet and began to whip the dwarves below.

"I don't think I know what just happened," King Eadamantus said as he stood and walked closer to the wall they had been protecting.

Shaking his head in bewilderment, King Hasselfeth replied back, "Neither do I, but I suppose we will learn everything once Prince Halldor and the knights return from the field. It appears they were right on top of the area from where the dragon appeared." He wiped the sweat from his brow and placed his sword back into its sheath. Looking down the hill, and seeing that the cyclops was still standing there, hands up to its face as it tried to pluck a string of arrows from its eye, he shouted over to his teams who were once again at their carriage stations, "Take down that last giant now before he comes to his senses and decides to charge us!" A few moments later, the *twang! Twang! Twang!* of the crossbows sounded again as shot after shot was fired at the towering beast, standing all alone now as the other creatures and soldiers of the Underlord had long since scampered down the hill, fleeing from the dragon.

Captain Baerden gathered those who were not wounded and, along with the elves and centaurs, they began searching through the bodies strewn about the battlefield on both sides of the wall, searching for survivors and separating their dead from those of the Underlord's, whom they threw into large piles so that they could be set ablaze as there were far too many to be buried. "What of our own dead?" one of the soldiers asked as he walked through the piles of bodies nearby.

"We will take them back with us and bury them with honor," the captain said somberly. "Just as soon as we make certain the Underlord's army has retreated for good and we find out where that blasted dragon came from." He looked off at the horizon and saw blasts of fire erupting on the plain far below, as the beast continued to seek out and destroy any creatures that were still moving or trying to flee south.

From the moment the transformation had been complete, Amansun realized that he was once again in his dragon's form, even though his thoughts and awareness were as if he was still the prince. Seeing the flying beasts above him, and the army of dwarves beyond them at the foot of the hill, he knew at once that his main purpose now would be to wipe out the Underlord's army, creature by creature if necessary, to ensure that his love, Princess Lyleth, would be spared from these horrible beasts. As he flew and began breathing flames out at the retreating flying beasts, two thoughts went through his mind simultaneously. First, that even though he had never relished the thought of killing anything before, he clearly knew that killing every living enemy of the Army of the Three King had to be done, and he knew he was the one to do it. Second, he realized that by now most if not all the friends and allies he had were quite aware that the prince and friend they had known was now an enormous winged serpent, flying through the air and burning the Underlord's army to the ground.

There goes the wedding! he thought as he showered group after group of retreating dwarves with flame, who in their blind panic and terror scattered over the plains without any thought of trying to fight back or face the enormous flying beast chasing after them. *I don't suppose it will matter much to the king that I won the battle almost singlehandedly*, he thought as wave after wave of fleeing dwarves crumpled to the ground, looking more like coals from a fire rather than living, breathing creatures. Once the first waves of dwarves had been incinerated, the great serpent looked off towards the far hillside and grinned as he saw the remainder of the enemy's forces fleeing down the roadway as fast as their wagons and feet could carry them. *I suppose I should fly back and make sure that giant one-eyed creature is not doing any harm*, he thought to himself as he changed his course and flew north.

"The dragon is returning!" several sentries called out as they saw the shape of the beast heading their way, its enormous body casting a black shadow that moved across the plain over the hundreds of corpses scattered below.

"Shall we try and shoot the beast down?" Captain Baerden called out to the three kings who had turned to look at the approaching beast.

Waving his hand in a fashion to indicate they shouldn't, King Hasselfeth replied, "Have your crossbows loaded and ready but do not fire! This beast seems to only be concerned with killing our enemies for some reason, and he therefore should be considered a friend to us, even if the beast is a dragon!"

"Well said," King Eadamantus replied as he looked over at the king. "I know not why the beast suddenly came and rescued us, but it is certain we would have fallen in defeat had the serpent not shown up."

Flying high overhead and seeing that the cyclops had been brought down by the bolts of his army, as the giant lay there with no less than a dozen bolts sticking out of his chest and head, the prince decided he would fly back south once more to ensure the dwarves were still retreating away from the battleground. As he dipped his wing and started a great, slow turn to the south, a round of cheers and shouts sprang up from those below, and he realized his sacrifice had meant everything to those he had helped defend, even though his secret was now out and he had likely lost any chance to marry the woman of his dreams. Flying south towards the low-lying hills, the dragon's head sunk low, as if in great despair, and he scoured the lands below, anxious to kill any who had made him make this terrible decision.

"What are our losses?" King Hasselfeth asked as he watched his captain approaching on horseback.

"I don't have a count yet, my Lord," he replied grimly, "but I would put it at roughly half of our force."

Approaching from another direction, Prince Erathrin, holding a wounded arm and covered in the blood of the enemy, shouted over, "And we have lost a third of our soldiers, my King," as he gingerly stepped over some of the bodies of their own side that had not been carried off yet.

"We have won the day, but our losses were great!" King Hasselfeth said as he glanced around at the bodies scattered about. "Thanks be to the heavens for sending us the winged beast in our hour of need! Where is the prince?" He looked sadly at the faces of the knights who had made it back. "Fallen on the field of battle?"

"Nay," said Sir Berardren as he rode closer. "Though I still don't believe it though I saw it with my very own eyes, the prince fell to the ground as the white rider but arose as the tremendous dragon you saw killing off our enemies!"

"What did you say?" King Hasselfeth and King Eadamantus said almost at the same time as their mouths dropped open and their eyes grew wide.

"'Tis true, my Lords!" Hrothgar said as he stared at the two kings with a blank face. "The young prince transformed into that flying serpent you saw, though how he did it I know not."

Shaking his head as if greatly displeased, even though his army was now safe and free from the battle that was clearly being won, King Hasselfeth said ominously, "He was in league with the enchantress this whole time, as I suspected since the other day." He turned and looked directly at the others gathered about one at a time. "The prince was enchanted by the Lady of the Woods. It is a blessing I learned of it before handing over my precious daughter to the beast!"

"The prince did manage to save us all," Hrothgar said rather humbly as he looked over at his captain, who was also looking a bit pale from learning the truth.

"That does not excuse the fact that this man-beast, this freak of nature or magic, it matters not which, meant to fool us all and marry the princess while we were unaware of his true self!" King Hasselfeth said as if the very words left a bad taste in his mouth.

As the flying serpent disappeared into the distance, Captain Baerden called out to those who still had their health, "Round up the dead and wounded. We shall depart for home as soon as we are able. Best we do not stay here out in the open another night, even if it does appear that the Underlord's army has fled."

CHAPTER 50

As the remnants of the Army of Three Kings began packing up their comrades, the group of men, elves and centaurs gathered into small groups of two or three and all began to discuss the incredible scene that had unfolded this day. Though most agreed some sort of devilment might have been in play, most could agree that the coming of the dragon had marked the beginning of the end of the Underlord's troops, and all were glad they had been spared by this creature.

"I says the prince is a saint, says I," one of the older soldiers whispered to his companions as they loaded the dead onto a cart.

"The beast didn't kills us," another said with a confused grin, "an' that makes him one 'o us if'n you ask'd me." He grunted as he strained to lift the dead man above his head and onto the pile.

After seeing that the Underlord's army, or what was left of it anyway, was making its way south, still moving at a fast pace, Amansun started to think about what his next move would be. "I suppose I need to fly back to the castle to see if I can find the Lady of the Woods," he said to himself as he flew back north in a path that would keep him out of sight of King Hasselfeth's army. "She changed me back once before, after all! Don't think the guards at the gate will likely welcome in a dragon, though." As the large winged serpent sped northward, a memory flashed by in his mind and suddenly the answer came to him, *The owls*, he thought as the smile returned to the large beast's mouth. *The owls can help me search for the enchantress*. He began to beat his wings even faster, suddenly feeling like there just might be a way out of this mess.

Long before the Army of Three Kings was ready to start its march back to the castle at the lake, Amansun flew in from the south and, circling high in the sky behind the cover of some slowly drifting clouds, decided he should approach the lake from its westernmost end, hopefully catching the attention of the owls before he was spotted by the king's sentries.

High up in a tree, Obrides, one of the youngest owls in Carceren's group, gasped as he looked up into the sky and saw the silhouette of a dragon high off in the distance. "I think I just saw the dragon!" he chirped as he took several steps forward on the branch he had been resting on. "I think Amansun has returned!"

The other owls flapped their wings and turned to see what this youngster was taking about. "What have you seen now?" Carceren said sarcastically, as the young owl was known for making things up to stir up trouble in the group.

"A dragon!" the young owl responded quickly, appearing to be quite serious. "Right up there behind those clouds." He lifted a wing and pointed it out towards the southwest side of the lake.

"Let me see…" Carceren said as he and the others made their way towards the southern side of the tree. "What clouds are you taking about?" He peered up into the clouds, hoping beyond hope that his friend the dragon had really returned once more. As the clouds shifted just a bit, thinning in places while growing thicker in others, a dark shape did seem to be peeking in and out of view. To the wonderment of all the owls gathered, all staring at the same spot up above, a majestic golden dragon suddenly came into view, beating its wings and clearly heading west as it drew nearer towards the far end of the lake. "It is he!" the owl said excitedly as he leapt into the air and started flying at once in the direction the great beast was headed. "He's finally found his way out of the enchantress's woods, and he is seeking us out, I would imagine." He beat his wings faster and encouraged the others to follow.

A small group of sentries posted on the northern tower along the lake looked up with surprise as they saw a large flock of owls all flying swiftly over the water and heading west. The dragon, which was now hidden from view behind the clouds once again, could not be seen, so they had no idea the enormous beast was once again nearby. "I never seen them owls flying all togethers like that b'fore," a sentry at the top of the tower said as he watched the owls fading across the lake.

Shaking his head in agreement, another guard, this one standing on the roadway and looking west, replied, "Ain't normal to be sure! Must be something spooked them outta their tree." Chewing on a piece of grass sticking out from between his teeth, he turned to look northwards where the owls had first sprung into view.

Looking over his shoulder, Amansun saw the owls flying in his direction, and as he smiled and thanked his good fortune, he decided it would be best to continue flying up and over the western ridge of the woods, as he had done before, so that he and the owls would be out of view when they had their reunion.

"He's making for the ridge!" young Bathis squawked to those around him. "Probably spotted us and now he's heading for a safe spot to meet, I'll guess."

"Follow me!" Carceren squealed as he continued to lead the group onward, still in front of the others who had no chance of catching their now giddy leader.

* * *

Much farther south, making their way over a second plain that led towards the Archain Mountains, Prince Karazed was still trying to figure out how his army had been so quickly dispatched; and even more, where this terrifying dragon had come from. "Twas the White Rider, my Lord," one of the dwarfs who had survived the dragon's brutal attack said with urgency, trying his best to convince the prince that the impossible had happened. "One minute he was the white rider, lying on the ground…the next he was that giant serpent, raising from the ground on enormous wings and breathing out fire at all of us as we ran for our lives!"

Turning to his captain who was now marching along just beside his floating chariot, the prince said softly, "No wonder the Great Master wanted this prince killed. He is an enchanted being, apparently…and quite dangerous at that!" He rubbed his beard and replayed all he had seen and heard in his mind.

"I can't sees how the Underlord can blames you for losing, what with the dragon and all," Captain Kelden half-asked and half-stated as he marched along. "Seems we were sents in ill-prepared when you considers what we were up aga'n'?"

Nodding his head in agreement but saying nothing, Prince Karazed thought over the captain's words and, mixed along with his own, started planning what exactly he would be saying when he met with the wizard and tried to explain how he had not only failed in his quest, but managed to lose the better part of his whole army.

* * *

Seeing a clearing ahead, Amansun gently glided down in a slow spiral and landed right in the center of the grassy field. *No need to hide*, he thought to himself as he realized that the king's army, along with the elves, were all down south picking up the pieces from their battle with the Underlord. He also no longer had to fear the Lady of the Woods, as the two had become close friends.

Within a few moments, the owls landed all about the dragon, with Carceren and Bathis landing the closest, as they knew the beast the most. "It has been much too long since you came by to see us!" Carceren called out to his friend as he ruffled his feathers and spun his head in excitement. "I see you escaped from the clutches of the enchantress."

"You could say that, old friend," Amansun responded as he smiled at the little creatures staring at him in wonder. "Turns out she is not as bad as the stories say."

Walking a bit closer to the immense beast, Carceren looked up at the creature's eyes and said, "We have missed you much, friend. Come now and tell us everything that has happened since the night we left you lying in the Black Woods."

"Another time, perhaps," Amansun replied. "Much has happened to me since we last spoke, my good friend, and most of it you would not believe anyway. I do need to ask you and your friends for some help now, though." He looked at his enormous claws again, remembering how different it felt to be in this body once more.

Nodding his head repeatedly up and down, Carceren muttered, "Sure…sure…we can do that," even though inside he was dying to know what the dragon was talking about. "All you need is ask and it shall be done."

"I need your help finding a certain soldier that is camped over at the castle grounds." After describing who needed to be found, several of the owls flew off immediately, headed straight for the castle.

Looking up at his friend, Carceren suddenly smiled, realizing the dragon would not be going anywhere for some time, and said to the others still present, "I believe I will stay here with Sir Amansun until you return, so that he is not all alone."

As the remaining band of owls flew off heading east, Carceren settled down on a stone near to where the dragon was resting and said, "Looks like we have plenty of time for your tale now, my friend.

Why don't you start with what happened the morning after we left you in the Black Woods with your wounded wing!"

* * *

Down at the site of the great battle, it was quickly becoming evident that it would not be possible to take all the bodies of those lost in battle back to the castle in one trip, or even two or perhaps three. Meeting together in the war tent that had not been taken down yet, King Hasselfeth, King Eadamantus and King Eodren agreed that each would leave behind fifty of their warriors to guard the dead while the others made their way back home.

"The Underlord's army has clearly fled to the south from whence it came," the elf king said confidently. "All that remains to do here now is protect those who fell from the wild dogs, wolves and other beasts that roam the wilds at night."

"Agreed," the centaur king said as he stamped his feet on the hard earthen floor of the tent. "While my people are anxious to get back to their woods, we too shall share in the task of guarding the dead until all of our brave troops have been taken back for a proper burial."

Thanking the two for agreeing to stay and help, King Hasselfeth said gravely, "I shall dedicate a section of my grounds where my tournament was held just days ago, and there all of our honored warriors can be laid to rest, joined together as one, the same as they died."

As the three divisions of the Army of Three Kings chose those who would be left behind to stay and guard the battlefield, the men, elves and centaurs continued to load those who were wounded and couldn't walk, along with the dead that they had room for, on the remaining carts. "Leave five of the crossbow carriages behind," Captain Baerden ordered, as his troops began to arrange the various wagons, carts and carriages into a line for the trip home, "just in case some lingering beast happens to come upon our troops while we are away."

* * *

Sitting out on one of the wooden tables that had been left outside in the rush of gathering the troops together and marching off to battle, the enchantress, still in soldier's form, along with Sophelus and the attendant, were enjoying a simple afternoon meal of bread and cheese when they were suddenly confronted by a whirling frenzy of flying owls. "Are you looking for me?" the enchantress asked. "What brings you to me now?"

Stepping quite close to the enchantress still in the form of a man, the owl leaned forward and, trying his best to speak softly, said, "There is another who wishes to speak with you now. Not a man, but a large creature that says you and he are old friends."

"What does this creature look like?"

Leaning back a bit and taking a short breath, the owl said with a laugh, "Well, this friend is quite a bit larger. And he has great big wings, golden skin, and occasionally shoots flame from his mouth."

"The dragon has returned?" the enchantress excitedly asked as she stood from the table suddenly, startling the owls somewhat.

"Yes…that would be him," the owl said, sensing that this was indeed a man known to their friend waiting back on the other side of the ridge. "He wants to speak with you at once…says it's urgent. I can take you to him if you wish."

Looking over at the muscular man standing beside him, the enchantress said, "That won't be necessary, my good owl. Just tell me where he is and we will go to him at once."

"It may take you a while to get there," the owl said with a concerned voice. "It's a good way off from where we are now."

"Don't worry about me," the enchantress said. "I have my own ways to travel quickly when the need calls for it. Just point me in the right direction and I shall take care of the rest."

As Bathis and the other owls watched in surprise, the three men quickly disappeared down the roadway towards the woods, then, appearing as if out of nowhere, a giant eagle took flight from behind the same group of trees, appearing to have a man clinging to its neck as he held something in his hands. "That can't be the soldier now, riding on the back of that eagle, can it?" Certrex asked as he and the others watched the majestic bird flying west over the woods just north of the lake.

"Well, they are certainly going in the right direction if it is," Bathis shouted as he jumped from the table. Starting to rise into the sky himself, the others quickly followed his lead, trailing behind.

"I was afraid this might happen," the enchantress said as she leaned forward and spoke with Sophelus who had transformed into an eagle once again. "I wonder how the battle with the Underlord has gone?"

Turning its head only slightly, still beating its large wings at great speed as it flew west, the eagle answered back, "Well, there have been no messengers to say the battle was lost, so it would seem the wizard's army was defeated, would it not?"

"True," the enchantress agreed as she thought over the possibilities. "That may be the very reason that the prince has changed back into the dragon's form once more. Fly as fast as you can now!" She crouched low, carrying the small animal that had been the attendant just moments before in her hands carefully as the three sped along.

***

At about the same time the eagle flew into view of the open field where the dragon was waiting near Silver Lake, down south King Hasselfeth signaled his trumpeter to sound the army forward. With one long and steady blast, what was left of the Army of the Three Kings began the long trip back to the castle at Silver Lake. "Shame to be leaving behind our fallen warriors," King Eadamantus said as he looked back at those staying behind to guard the area.

"Our troops will return soon enough to collect the rest," King Hasselfeth said as he looked at the elf king and tried to console him. "They will be safe with our troops standing guard until our return."

Captain Baerden, bringing up the rear, mounted on his horse once again, waved back at those remaining and yelled out his promise to return as soon as they were able. "Look for us tomorrow when the sun is at its crest," he shouted, then rode up to the front of the column again to sit at the side of his king as they rode north. "Do you think we shall ever see Prince Halldor again?" he asked the king.

"It matters not!" King Hasselfeth said as he looked over at his captain of the Guard. "Whether he returns or not, he shall never have the princess's hand in marriage. The white rider is not who or what he claimed to be, and I will not risk my only child, my precious daughter, with one who has the stain of the enchantress on himself. Even if he did save us and win the battle, I cannot bear the thought of my daughter marrying such a freak of nature. Besides, he defeated the Underlord's army, did he not? Surely the Underlord will spend all his days trying to get even. I cannot bless this union knowing that the princess will be in harm's way for all her days while they are together."

***

As the enchantress stepped down from the great eagle, glancing all the while at the enormous winged serpent sitting out in plain sight on the grassy meadow, she thought to herself how much had taken place since last she looked upon the prince in this condition.

"I see you were not able to heed my warnings and advice," the enchantress said as she approached the dragon and noticed the small owl perched not far away. "A friend of yours, I suppose?" she asked.

"A great friend!" Amansun answered with a smile, "and one I trust a great deal."

Coming to a stop just a few feet from the beast, the enchantress turned back toward the large eagle that was now settled on the ground. With a wave of her hand, the eagle turned into a large, muscled man standing nude before them, and she threw a small pile of clothes his way. "Hold this little one while I speak with our friend," the enchantress said as she set the animal she had been carrying down on the field, where it immediately scampered away in the direction of some nice green clover. Sophelus picked up the pants and shirt from the ground where his clothes had landed, dressed himself, and then walked over to sit beside the rabbit that was now happily nibbling on the delicate clover leaves.

Carceren, taken aback by the sudden transformation of the eagle, looked at the soldier with unblinking eyes, then muttered as if he was speaking to himself, "I suppose that would be the enchantress, then?" as his eyes never left the soldier standing not ten paces away. "I hadn't really believed your story until just now."

"I am afraid so," the enchantress laughed as she suddenly transformed into a young woman and turned back to face the dragon. "The battle went poorly, I take it?"

Nodding his immense head, Amansun waited a moment, and then replied with a half-smile, "We were losing terribly, to be true. The Underlord sent many foul creatures to confront us, many of which I had never heard of nor seen before. At the point where I could see all hope was lost, the pain overtook me, and I became the dragon once more, I am afraid to say."

"I am not surprised," the enchantress said as she smiled at the beast and walked closer to touch its scaly skin. "I had imagined this would be the outcome from the beginning, though I wasn't sure if it was a true vision or merely one of many possible outcomes that might occur once you left for battle. You have fulfilled the prophecy of old, whether you aware of it or not."

"What do we do now?" Amansun asked helplessly as he looked at the woman for comfort and an answer.

"We go back to my woods is what we do," the enchantress replied. "I will need to start all over again, it would seem. It shouldn't be too difficult…this time! But we have much to discuss, and I am sure you are anxious to go and see that princess of yours, right?" She gave him a devilish grin.

Nodding his head and smiling even more greatly than before, Amansun said happily, "That is why you are the Lady of the Woods… you are truly a mind reader!"

As the three were chatting amongst themselves, the rabbit that had been eating clover over by Sophelus had managed to wander off some fifty paces or so to a clump of nasturtium. As he busily munched away, a small fox, not much bigger than a pup, snuck up from behind and gave chase suddenly with a yelp as it bared down upon the furry creature. Sophelus, seeing that their friend was in danger, shouted over at the enchantress to get her attention, and pointed to the small rabbit bounding away, running for its life from this young predator. With a grin and a wave of her hands, the enchantress changed the rabbit into the form of the attendant once more, and the young fox, who had been closing in on its prey, suddenly found itself staring at a man, resting down on the ground on all fours, some ten times its size, chomping his teeth together as a rabbit would do, and staring back!

All four of those gathered in the field laughed heartily as they watched the young fox turn tail and flee for the safety of the woods, its tail tucked firmly between its legs as it scrambled off.

"That may be the last time that fox tries to catch a rabbit, I am afraid," the enchantress said with a giggle as she waved her hands once more and changed the man back into a rabbit. "Serves him right for interrupting us."

It was some time before Bathis and the other owls made it to the field where the dragon was, so Carceren, Sophelus, the enchantress and Amansun had some time alone to chat, laugh and share stories while they waited. Even though the prince was happy to be back among friends, his mind wandered frequently back to the princess and the realization that by changing back into a dragon once more, he may have ended his chances of ever marrying her.

* * *

The march back to Eladrias Castle took most of the day, so by the time the first riders made their way up the roadway towards the main gate, the sun was already setting in the west. As Ole Barder and his sentries looked down the road and saw the banners of their king approaching, a great cheer rang out and the old guard ordered a sentry to ride off to the castle right away to inform the queen that their army was approaching. As the rider sped towards the castle, he shouted out that their troops had been victorious to all that he passed, and women cried and children squealed, as all waited breathlessly for the return of their soldiers.

Up at the castle, the queen, princess and Lord Mallthus stepped out onto one of the large stone balconies to watch as their army rode back in. It didn't take long for them to notice that the line of soldiers making its way back was considerably shorter than it had been when they had rode out earlier. "It would seem that we won the battle but paid a high price," Lord Mallthus said softly as he watched King Hasselfeth approaching.

Scanning the riders making their way in, Princess Lyleth looked all about, desperately trying to spot Amansun, but was unable to make out his familiar white armor. As she stood there with tears streaming down her face, the queen took her in her arms and, embracing her, said, "Perhaps he is at the rear of the army, daughter! Do not lose hope before we have had a chance to speak with your father and hear all he has to share."

Turning to run to the doorway leading back into the castle, the princess said hurriedly, "I am heading down to the courtyard to see what Father can tell me of the prince." Moments later the princess appeared running across the courtyard and out past the main gate as she ran down the road towards the king.

Looking down from above, Lord Mallthus said sadly, "I fear the princess may not hear the words she is hoping for. I see the other knights returning there with the king and Amansun is not among them."

"Our army looks quite small now," the queen replied as she continued to look out upon the soldiers making their way up the road. "Even the elves and centaurs seem to have lost a good deal of their troops."

"If the prince was lost in the battle, the princess will not be the only one crying this night," Lord Mallthus said grimly as he looked at the queen and suggested they begin making their way down to the courtyard so they could greet the king.

The process of unloading the wounded and dead took hours and ran well into the night. Even though the king's army had returned in victory, so great was the loss of men that it hardly seemed so. King Eadamantus and the elves, along with King Eodren, decided to stay and help with the work, and also to participate in retrieving the rest of the fallen warriors from the battlefield over the next few days. They sent out messengers to their lands to inform their loved ones that the battle had been won and many would be returning home soon.

King Hasselfeth had not wanted to tell Princess Lyleth the truth of what had happened that day out on the battlefield. It seemed enough that the man she had fallen in love with would not be returning. Still, Captain Baerden and some of the others had convinced him that eventually word would get out—soldiers would talk—so in the end he had taken his wife and daughter into one of the castle's private rooms and shared the truth about what had taken place that day, even though he knew it sounded like a fairytale more than fact.

Princess Lyleth took the news about as well as would be expected. At first, she tried to imagine the whole story was made up, a fabrication created by her father who for some reason had suddenly decided that the prince was not good enough for her. Then, after remembering her vision from the night before, and the midnight black eyes of the dragon that so closely matched those of the prince, she knew in her heart that the story had to be true.

"He did save us all," King Hasselfeth had said as he tried to comfort his sobbing daughter. "If not for the appearance of the dragon, we surely would all have perished out on that field."

Not quite ready to take comfort in the fact that Prince Halldor had managed to save the day, the princess excused herself as politely as she was able, trying to keep her composure until she had retreated to the safety of her own quarters, then she tossed herself onto her bed face-down and cried well into the night until at last fatigue set in and allowed her to drift off into a restless, dream-filled sleep.

* * *

Having left the owls back at the field some time earlier, Sophelus, the enchantress and Amansun had flown back to the cottage at the center of the Black Woods. After thanking Sophelus for all of his help over the past few days and setting the rabbit loose on the field outside her home, the enchantress waved to the fox as it happily and anxiously trotted over the field to head home to its own family. "Don't forget we shall still have to return to the castle to collect our other friends," she called out to it before it had disappeared into the woods.

Turning and lifting one paw into the air, Sophelus replied back, "I shall return mid-morning tomorrow, my Lady! Good luck with transforming the prince." He then turned and disappeared into the darkness of the trees.

"Shall we?" the enchantress asked as she stared up at the large dragon and laughed, as she recalled how challenging it had been to get the great beast into her cottage the first time around. Looking just as unsure as he had the first time, the dragon slowly walked towards the doorway of the tiny cottage, staring as the frame of the door seemed to expand of its own will. He forced himself to walk towards the cottage, ducking as low as his immense frame would allow.

Sitting inside the main room of the cottage now, looking about once more at the familiar sights of books and chairs and pots lying about, Amansun looked over at the enchantress and asked, "So what are these 'things' that we need to discuss?"

As the enchantress continued to work over the steaming kettle at the other end of the room, she occasionally looked over at the dragon and explained another of the mysteries of magic that might come into play with the prince's situation. "You see, my young prince, the Underlord started off an unnatural chain of events when he turned you into Amansun the dragon. And I have added to this chain of events by turning you back into your original form of the prince."

"And?" Amansun asked as his impatience started to get the better of him.

"And…now you have continued this chain by once again reverting back to the shape of a dragon. The cycle has repeated itself!" She said this excitedly, as if the prince should be able to draw some conclusion from all of this.

Looking back at the woman with puzzled eyes, Amansun asked as politely as he could under the circumstances, "So what is it you are saying, my Lady? Am I now stuck in the dragon's form for good? Is that it?"

"Not at all, my young fool!" the woman laughed as she reached out and patted the beast. "I will be able to return you to the prince's form once more…this time…but be warned that there is no certainty how many times this cycle can be repeated before it comes to an end, and you become trapped in one of the two forms."

"I see," Amansun muttered as he stared over at the now steaming kettle at the far end of the room. "What you are saying, then, is that I can change back and forth from prince to dragon again and again, but at some point I will become trapped, and in which form and at what time that happens you cannot say."

Nodding her head and smiling at the great beast, the young woman said, "That is precisely it, my prince. I will change you back now, just as soon as the potion is ready. But always remember that there is no telling when you may become trapped in one of your two forms. It might be the next time you change over again, or you may be able to change back and forth dozens of times. There is just no knowing!"

"Very well, then," Amansun replied. "I can see I will have to be very careful about changing back into the beast in the future…that is, if I don't want to remain a dragon for all my days, I suppose."

Walking back over towards the kettle, the enchantress gave the contents another stir, and then looking back over to the dragon said, "It's ready!"

* * *

Over the next three days, Amansun, back in the form of a young man once again, rested at the home of the enchantress and recovered from the transformations he had recently undergone. Switching back and forth from one body to another was quite tiring, especially when one of the bodies is an enormous dragon and the other is that of a normal-sized man. Even though he had been quite anxious to rush out and see the princess, he had taken the advice of the enchantress and allowed some time to pass, so that it would not seem so startling when he did eventually reappear back at the castle in the form of the prince once again.

Over this same time, The Army of the Three Kings completed the task of retrieving their fallen warriors, and a large burial ground was erected where the main field of the tournament had stood. "Let this place always be treated as sacred ground," King Hasselfeth said once all those lost had been laid to rest. "The lives given by those buried here was our freedom from the Underlord secured, and let no one ever forget them."

With so many lives touched by the loss of their friends and loved ones, life at and around the castle seemed quiet and mournful for some time. Only when the king decided it was time for a celebratory feast to acknowledge their victory against the enemy did any signs of happiness fill the air. "Our friends and loved ones would not want us to mope about in gloom and sadness for the rest of our days," the king said as he addressed the crowds gathered to hear his speech. "Instead, they would want us to celebrate their victory, so that they knew we shared in their glory and celebrated their sacrifice!"

And so it was that on the fourth day since the great battle, Amansun and his two attendants rode into the castle's courtyard once again, seeking an audience with the king to see about the arrangements for marriage between the young prince and princess, as the people of the kingdom ran about preparing for the great feast. "I swear it is he!" Hrothgar said, wildly out of breath from running swiftly to find his captain once he had seen with his own eyes that Prince Halldor had returned. "It is he in the flesh, looking the same as last we saw him, though he is dressed differently now and wears a suit of black armor."

Standing from the table where he had been seated, eyes open wide and taking in a huge breath of air as he ran his hands across his face as if trying to wipe a bad dream off it, Captain Baerden replied without losing his composure, "I thought this might happen, old friend. It would seem the prince is bewitched, and now he has returned to claim the princess for himself once again, now that he has once again taken the form of a man. I must go and tell the king!" He rushed out of the room, leaving poor Hrothgar standing there blinking his eyes and looking quite lost.

By the time King Hasselfeth and Lord Mallthus arrived at the courtyard, a crowd of several hundred had already gathered, as word of the prince's return traveled swiftly. Walking over to where Amansun stood, his attendants at his side, King Hasselfeth said, "There is nothing more left for you here, 'Prince Halldor' or whatever you are. You saved all of us in battle, 'tis true, and we are and will always be grateful for that. Yet now that we have seen you in the beast's form, there is no way I can allow you to marry the princess."

Amansun, bowing to the king, said, "Surely an honorable man such as yourself has no intentions on backing out from the marriage I have earned by winning your tournament?"

As the queen and princess came into view on the steps leading out to the courtyard, Princess Lyleth raced up towards the prince just in time to hear her father say, "You shall never lay a hand on my precious daughter! We have all seen your true form and know of your ability to change into the great winged serpent! I cannot allow the princess to marry one who has been tarnished by magic and sorcery such as you."

"Father!" Princess Lyleth called out as she closed the distance from where the king and Prince Halldor were standing, both seeming as if they were about to lock into battle any moment. "How can you say that about the man I love? The man I plan on marrying? Did you not yourself say days ago that it was the prince in dragon's form that saved you and all your soldiers? None of us would have been spared if not for Prince Halldor!"

She sobbed as she tried to run to the prince. Stepping forward and catching her before she could, Captain Baerden clutched the young woman tenderly, saying, "'Tis true, Princess. Prince Halldor is but a serpent in man's appearance. Never could you marry one such as he."

"I shall marry whom I choose!" the princess yelled out as she struggled to break the soldier's grasp. "I will not be kept from the one man among all others I choose to be with forever."

Looking at the captain of the Guard with vengeful eyes, Amansun cautioned, "Have a care how you handle my wife-to-be, soldier, or I shall be forced to slice you in two where you stand!"

"Enough!" the enchantress standing to the prince's left shouted loudly. "Enough with these threats and words of hate. The prince has come to demand the hand of Princess Lyleth as was promised him at the conclusion of the king's own tournament of champions, no more and no less. Are you prepared to grant the prince his request now or no?"

"No!" said the king as he looked at the prince and his two attendants callously. "I shall not agree to hand over my daughter to this 'Prince of Dragons,' not now and not ever! She will be forever barred from entering into this unholy matrimony."

Stepping forward and looking into the princess's tearing eyes, Amansun forced himself to smile, and with tears running down his own face said, "One day I shall return for you, my princess! Our love cannot be denied forever. I will go and claim my family's land once more, and then watch for me as I shall return for you! Only as a king this time, equal to your father, with a kingdom and army of my own!" Then he stepped back and watched as the captain and queen led the crying young princess back towards the castle's main doorway.

Stepping forward once more, the king uttered sternly, "Never shall you have my daughter, Dragon Prince! Not as long as I am able to protect her, regardless of how she feels for you."

"You judge me wrongly!" Amansun said. "I stand for good, and always will. Maybe you will think of me differently once I have reclaimed my father's kingdom and return here as a king. Our love can wait, of that I am certain. Now, if you are as anxious to see me leave as I would guess you are, simply give me a worthy steed and I will be on my way."

Turning to the group of soldiers now surrounding the group, half of them tearing up themselves at the way their king was treating this man who had saved all their lives just days earlier, the king demanded that one of his finest horses be brought out at once. "And be sure it has a proper saddle," he yelled as two of the men raced off to the stables.

"He will be needing two horses!" an elderly soldier shouted as the men turned abruptly to see who was speaking. "I shall be going with the prince," Hrothgar said as he walked over to where Amansun was standing.

Walking back over to the group, having helped the queen get the princess back into the castle, Captain Baerden smiled and said, "I had guessed as much, old friend. I shall miss you greatly!" As Hrothgar stepped forward, tears in his eyes as he struggled for words, the captain threw his arms around the man and said honestly, "No need to explain yourself, my friend. I would have done the same myself had I been in your place. Long life and happiness!" He grasped Hrothgar's shoulders and gave them a shake, then turned and said to Amansun, "Take care of this man, young Prince! He is a noble friend and warrior, and know that you ride with one of our best!"

Nodding his head in agreement and smiling now at the captain, Amansun said, "I already knew that, Captain. And you watch over the princess closely while I am away. If something should befall her while I am gone, there will be hell to pay, I assure you!"

"She will be safe here with us!" the captain replied as he stepped over to the king's side. "Now go, and know that my men and I thank you for saving us at the great battle. You shall not be forgotten!"

Stepping up and mounting the two horses that had been led over from the stable, Amansun and Hrothgar waved at the crowd gathered around them. Amansun looked down at the enchantress and the man standing beside her and said, "Thanks to both of you. For everything. I will see you again!"

The enchantress smiled deeply and then said, "Till we meet again, my young Prince! Good luck taking back your father's lands at Argonathe!"

"They shall be given safe passage wherever they wish to go!" King Hasselfeth said as he looked up at the prince and motioned at the two attendants he was leaving behind. "We are indebted to you for your service, as Captain Baerden has already stated, but know that you will no longer be welcome in these lands. Take your magic and your dragon's form and be off with you now!"

"Farewell!" Amansun shouted to those gathered about as he and his old captain turned their steeds to ride out along the roadway leading east. "Tell the princess I shall return for her when I take back Argonathe and become king!" The two spurred their steeds and rode off along the dirt road, waving at Ole Barder and his sentries as they flew past, slowly disappearing from view.

AMANSUN THE DRAGON PRINCE
CAST OF MAIN CHARACTERS

DRAGONS
Scythe
Wraith
Amansun
Darken
Flame
Sarforth
Arkxin
Greyden
Thrax
Graulding

OWLS
Barnby
Barthus
Aranthus
Arthan
Carceren
Carcophus
Melanter
Bathis
Methistus
Obrides
Certrex
Belfest

CENTAURS
Arxes
Artec
Altus
Anthrus
Eodren
Eldenham
Articlese
Brethus

DWARVES
Burgling
Balden
Halfred
Goren
Bulgurth
Bergrath
Halford
Bairdus
Kildren
Kairadus
Brothemus
Grenth
Baltis

ELVES
Ilfden
Eorden
Eoren
Eonus
Hyaclis
Aarowen
Mythra
Eorethrus
Eonias
Araneth
Mythiel
Eadamantus
Erathrin

MEN
Bartle
Hrothgar
Berardren
Hasselfeth
Baerden

Lyleth
Ezera
Aderas
Ole Barder
Halldor
Cantalus
Hanthris
Osselathe
Mallthus
Antilus
Farimus
Glandin
Blackstone

MICE
Radibus
Radington
Barrington
Barding
Harting
Feridus

OTHERS
Carack the eagle
Digger the badger
Gargaroth the stone troll
Aramantheum the Enchantress
Sophelus the fox/eagle/man
Gruawth the great bear

CPSIA information can be obtained
at www.ICGtesting.com
Printed in the USA
BVHW050714090323
659868BV00028B/503/J